Praise

'Tim Powers is a brilliant writer'   William Gibson

'Powers is a tremendous writer'   Cory Doctorow

'Tim Powers is one of our best writers'   Raymond E. Feist

'Powers writes action and adventure that Indiana Jones could only dream of'   *Washington Post*

'Influenced by SF master Philip K. Dick, Powers taps into Dick's surrealistic style to great success'   *Library Journal*

withdrawn

Also by Tim Powers

Novels

The Skies Discrowned (1976)
Epitaph in Rust (1976)
The Drawing of the Dark (1979)
The Anubis Gates (1983)
Dinner at Deviant's Palace (1985)
On Stranger Tides (1987)
The Stress of Her Regard (1989)
Last Call (1992)
Expiration Date (1995)
Earthquake Weather (1997)
Declare (2000)
Three Days to Never (2006)
Hide Me Among the Graves (2012)

Short Story Collections

Night Moves and Other Stories (2000)
Strange Itineraries (2004)
The Bible Repairman and Other Stories (2011)

EARTHQUAKE WEATHER

TIM POWERS

This edition first published in Great Britain in 2015 by
Gollancz
An imprint of the Orion Publishing Group
Carmelite House, 50 Victoria Embankment, London EC4Y 0DZ
An Hachette UK Company

1 3 5 7 9 10 8 6 4 2

A CIP catalogue record for this book is available
from the British Library

ISBN 978 1 473 21205 3

Typeset by Input Data Services Ltd, Bridgwater, Somerset

Printed and bound by CPI Group (UK) Ltd, Croydon, CR0 4YY

The Orion Publishing Group's policy is to use papers
that are natural, renewable and recyclable products and
made from wood grown in sustainable forests. The logging
and manufacturing processes are expected to conform to
the environmental regulations of the country of origin.

www.orionbooks.co.uk
www.gollancz.co.uk

For Serena
again, and still, and always

And with thanks to Chris Arena, Bonnie Badenoch, John Bierer, Jim Blaylock, Russ Galen, Tom Gilchrist, Doug Goulet, Ann James, Delphine Josephe, Dorothea Kenny, Jim Crooks, Phil Mays, David Masesan, Kitty Myshkin, David Perry, Celene Pierce, Brendan and Regina Powers, Richard Powers, Serena Powers, Fred Ramer, Randal Robb, Jacques Sadoul, Marv Torrez, Rex Torrez, and Greg Wade.

Her wanton spirits look out
At every joint and motive of her body.
O, these encounterers, so glib of tongue,
That give a coasting welcome ere it comes,
And wide unclasp the table of their thoughts
To every ticklish reader, set them down
For sluttish spoils of opportunity
And daughters of the game.

—William Shakespeare, *Troilus and Cressida*

My brain I'll prove the female to my soul,
My soul the father, and these two beget
A generation of still-breeding thoughts;
And these same thoughts people this little world,
In humors like the people of this world ...
Thus play I in one person many people,
And none contented ...

—William Shakespeare, *Richard II*

So long as you do not die and rise again,
You are a stranger to the dark earth.

—Goethe

Introduction

Tim Powers is a magician.

An honest-to-goodness not-merely-a-figure-of-speech magician. His novels are so powerfully compelling I sometimes wonder if he hasn't taken a sabbatical into the dustiest corners of the collective subconscious, to live like Jane Goodall among the nightly phantoms of our dream lives. Perhaps he has. For, like any magician worth his salt, he's a bit of a mad genius, too.

And not in the vein of a snake-oil huckster, either; he's the Real Deal. When Powers opens the door and beckons us into his mad laboratory – always with a showman's wink, of course – we expect to find wires, mirrors, and trapdoors, yet find instead an empty room devoid of artifice. Why empty? Because what we've seen is neither deception nor illusion. It's true magic.

I've heard it asserted that if magic were real, it would work according to the logic of a Tim Powers novel. I agree. More than that: I've seen it first-hand. So when I tell you that Tim Powers is a master magician revealing the true but forgotten rules of our world, I speak from experience. But more on that in a moment.

To read a Powers novel is to glimpse a para-reality that exists half a heartbeat out of phase with our own. Powers' greatest talent may be the overwhelming sense of narrative authority he etches into the magical underpinnings of his tales.

Powers' evocation of magic feels real because it is real. And we readers sense that. We know it. Not consciously, perhaps, but in the subconscious residue of our australopithecine past. It resonates with us because it evokes a time when we told our stories on cave walls and huddled against the darkness of a world governed by unknowable, implacable rules. Powers reminds us how the world works. How it really works. And when he presents us with these reminders, they suddenly become self-evident.

Of course I shouldn't play cards on a houseboat. *Of course* ghosts are attracted to palindromes and loose change. *Of course* earthquakes are caused by the Fisher King.

The magic of Tim Powers' fictional worlds is neither arbitrary nor ad hoc. It's measured and structurally unassailable – the craftsmanship of a master architect. No matter the era, no matter the locale, no matter the characters and their travails, the magical rules of the world always adhere to an unstated yet undeniable logic. Each novel affords us a different perspective on the same underlying truth. Nowhere is this more evident than in the expert synthesis of *Earthquake Weather* (1997).

The soul-stealing gamblers of *Last Call* (1992) and the ruthless ghost-eaters of *Expiration Date* (1995) populate what appear to be their own unique supernatural settings. But when Scott Crane and Koot Hoomie Parganas join forces here, in the culmination of the Fault Lines trilogy, we see they're navigating the very same magical space. Not coincidentally so, but necessarily so. Their magical world is our magical world – the world where you are reading these very words at this very moment.

I say all this as somebody who once found himself snared in a ghost trap ripped straight from the pages of *Expiration Date*. May I lose my soul in a game of Assumption, may my personality be shattered, may ghosts inhabit my body if I'm lying.

Traveling through Australia some years ago, I found myself waiting for a tram in a leafy suburb of Adelaide. Sitting on the bench at the tram stop, I looked up and took note of the suburb name: Glenelg. As it happened, I'd read *Expiration Date* just prior to this trip, using a copy borrowed from my traveling companion. We'd discussed the book at length earlier in our travels, so it wasn't a wrenching *non sequitur* when I pointed out the palindrome on the sign.

"Good thing we're not ghosts," we joked. Ha, ha.

Not a minute later, I noticed a handful of coins scattered on the bench between us.

"Hey," I said, "I think you've got a hole in your pocket."

So, of course, I tried to gather them up. And tried. And tried. Until I realized they were glued to the bench.

First the palindrome. Then the coins. And then, as they say, the penny dropped: This is a Tim Powers ghost trap *and it's working on me*.

It was one of only two moments in my life so utterly disorienting that the gears of my mind seized up. For a split second I honestly did not know what was real. Was I dreaming? Had I fallen into a Powers novel? Was I a refugee from a Powers novel? Or had I always been a fictional character who merely dreamed he was real?

Strange things happen when you read Powers; you become susceptible to the magical undercurrents of the world. And the world sends you signs and portents, rewards and warnings and encouragements. I first read *Earthquake Weather* as a battered second-hand mass market paperback. The kind of used book from which forgotten things sometimes fall: a grocery list, a photograph, a receipt, a Christmas card. In this particular case, just as the focus of the story shifted to San Francisco, a scrap of paper fluttered from between the pages: an old but un-punched transfer slip for the famous San Francisco cable cars.

I still have it. It's not every day a magical artefact falls into your lap.

I can't claim that *Earthquake Weather* will reward you with a talisman. But it will convince you – or, perhaps, remind you – that ours is a magical world.

Ian Tregillis
Santa Fe, New Mexico
May 2015

PROLOGUE

The Dolorous Stroke

LAS VEGAS – A small earthquake rattled Boulder City on New Year's morning, and workers at the nearby Hoover Dam reported feeling the shock.

—Associated Press, January 2, 1995

CHAPTER ONE

PANDARUS: ... she came and puts me her white hand to his cloven
        chin—
CRESSIDA: Juno have mercy; how came it cloven?
                        —William Shakespeare, *Troilus and Cressida*

A pay telephone was ringing in the corridor by the rest rooms, but the young woman who had started to get up out of the padded orange-vinyl booth just blinked around in evident puzzlement and sat down again, tugging her denim jacket more tightly around her narrow shoulders.

From over by the pickup counter her waiter glanced at her curiously. She was sitting against the eastern windows, but though the sky was already a chilly deep blue outside, the yellow glow of the interior overhead lighting was still relatively bright enough to highlight the planes of her face under the disordered straw-blond hair. The waiter thought she looked nervous, and he wondered why she had reflexively assumed that a pay-phone call might be for her.

The counter seats were empty where the half-dozen customers who lived in town usually sat chugging coffee at this hour – but the locals could sleep in on this New Year's Day, and they'd be right back here tomorrow at dawn. This morning the customers were mostly grumpy families who wanted to sit in the booths – holiday-season vacationers, drawn in off of the San Diego Freeway lanes by the spotlit billboards beyond the Batiquitos Lagoon to the north or the San Elijo Lagoon to the south.

The woman sitting in the dawn-side booth was almost certainly a waitress somewhere – when he had taken her order she had spoken quickly, specified all the side-order options without being asked, and she had sat where she wouldn't be able to see into the kitchen. And she was hungry, too – she had ordered scrambled eggs and poached eggs, along with bacon and cottage fries, and coffee and orange juice and V-8.

... And now she had set something on fire at her table.

The waiter clanked her plates back down on the counter and hurried across the carpet toward her booth, but he quickly saw that the smoking paperback book on the table was just smoldering and not actually flaming, and even before he got to the table the woman had flipped open the book

3

and splashed water from her water glass onto the ... *cigarette butt!* ... that had ignited the pages.

The pay telephone was still ringing, but the overhead lights had gone dim for a moment, and a waitress back by the electronic cash register was cussing under her breath and slapping the side of the machine, and nobody else had happened to notice the briefly burning book; and the blond woman, who was now folding the soggy thing closed again, had gone red in the face and was smiling up at him in embarrassed apology – she couldn't be thirty years old yet – and so he just smiled cautiously back at her.

'Yesterday you'd have been legal,' he said sympathetically; then, seeing that she was confused, he added, 'Seven hours ago there'd have been ashtrays on the table, you wouldn't have had to hide it.'

She nodded, pushing the book away across the tabletop and frowning as though she'd never seen the object until it had started smoldering in front of her. 'That's right,' she said to him sternly. 'No smoking in restaurants at all in California now, as of midnight last night.' She looked past him now, with a forgiving, we'll-say-no-more-about-it air. 'Where are your public telephones?'

'Uh ...' He waved in the direction of the ringing telephone. 'Where you hear. But your breakfast is coming right up, if you want to wait.'

She was hitching awkwardly forward out of the booth and levering herself up onto her feet. 'All I ordered was coffee.' The waiter watched as she walked away toward the telephone. Her left leg swung stiff, not bending, and he was uneasily sure that the dark, wet spot on the thigh of her jeans must be fresh blood.

She picked up the telephone receiver in mid-ring.

'Hello?' Again the restaurant's lights dimmed for a moment, and the woman's face hardened. In a harsher, flatter voice than she'd used before, she said, 'Do I know you, Susan? Sure, I'll tell him. Now, I don't mean to be abrupt, but I've got a call to make here, don't I?'

She hung up and dug a handful of litter out of a jacket pocket and dumped it onto the shelf below the telephone; from among these matchbooks and drywall screws and slips of paper and bits of broken green stucco she selected a quarter, thumbed it into the slot, and then punched in a local number.

After ten seconds of standing with the receiver to her ear, 'Hi,' she said, still speaking in her rough new voice. 'Is this the Flying Nun?' She laughed. 'Gotcha, huh? Listen, Susan says to tell you she still loves you. Oh, and what I called about – I'm going to assume the Flamingo, you know what I mean?' She listened patiently, and with her free hand picked up one of the fragments

4

of green-painted stucco. 'Potent pieces of it ... persist in percolating in the ... what, pasture? Can you spell alliteration? What I'm trying to say, sonny boy, is that even though they did tear it down, I've got a chunk of it, and your ass is grass. Don't waste time chasing the long stories on the front page this morning – skip right to the funny papers.'

After hanging up, she smacked her lips and frowned as if she'd eaten something rancid, then stepped across to the ladies' room door and pushed it open.

She dug a little bottle of Listerine out of another jacket pocket as she crossed the tile floor to the sink, and by the time she was standing in front of the mirror she had opened the bottle and taken a swig; she swished it around in her mouth, looking down at the chrome faucets rather than into the mirror, and she spat out the mouthwash with a grimace.

She re-capped the bottle and hurried back to her table.

Already the sky had brightened enough outside the window to cast dim shadows from the steaming plates and glasses that now sat on her table, and as she slid carefully into the booth she frowned at the elaborate breakfast. From her open purse she lifted a waitress's order pad and another, larger bottle of the mouthwash, and for the next half hour, as she ate, she flipped through the pages of the pad, frowning over the inked notes that filled nearly every leaf, and paused frequently to swallow a mouthful of Listerine. She held her fork in her left hand to eat the scrambled eggs, but switched it to her right to eat the poached eggs. The cash register on the other side of the room kept on spontaneously going into its cash-out cycle, to the frustration of the cashier.

When the first ray of sunlight from over the distant Vallecito Mountains touched a pastel painting on the far wall of the restaurant, the blond woman lifted her right hand and made a fist in the new daylight; then she packed up her order pad and mouthwash bottle, got up out of the booth, and tossed a twenty-dollar bill onto the table next to the soggy, blackened old paperback copy of Ian Fleming's *On Her Majesty's Secret Service.*

The waiter was Catholic, so he caught what she was muttering as she hurried past him: 'In the name of the Father, the Son, the Holy Ghost.' Then she had pushed open the glass front door and stepped out into the chilly morning sunlight.

Through the glass he watched her hobble out to a little white Toyota in the dawn-streaked parking lot; then he sighed and told a busboy to bring along a towel and a spray bottle of bleach to that booth, because there was probably blood on the seat. 'The booth where Miss Chock Full o' Nuts was sitting,' he told the busboy.

*

5

She drove west on Leucadia Boulevard, past old bungalows set back under pines and fig trees away from the new, high pavement, and then crossed a set of railroad tracks; the street descended sharply, and she made a right turn onto a wide street with big old eucalyptus trees separating the north and south bound lanes; after driving past a few blocks of dark surfboard shops and vintage clothing stores she turned left, up into one of the narrow lanes that climbed the bluff beyond which lay the sea. Fences and closed garage doors batted back the rattle of her car's engine.

A long fieldstone wall with pepper trees overhanging it hid a property on the seaward side of Neptune Avenue. At the entrance of the private driveway, by a burly pine tree that was strung with flowering orange black-eyed Susans, the woman pulled over onto the gravel shoulder and switched off the engine. The dawn street was empty except for a couple of dew-frosted cars parked tilted alongside the road, and silent – no birds sang, and the surf beyond the bluff was just a slow subsonic pulse.

Her face was set in a hard grin as she got out of the car, and when she had straightened up on the gravel she began unbuckling the belt on her jeans; and she kept whispering, 'Just in the leg, that's all, settle down, girl! Just in the leg as a *warning*, and anyway he stabbed himself in the leg already one time, just to have something to talk to some lady about – and he shot himself in the foot before that, with this here very spear. No big deal to him, I swear.' She unzipped her jeans and pulled and tugged them down to her ankles, exposing white panties with SUNDAY embroidered in red on the front, and exposing also a two-foot-long green-painted trident that was duct-taped to her knee and thigh.

It was a short aluminum speargun spear, with three barbless tips at the trident end and three diagonal grooves notched into the pencil-diameter shaft. The tan skin of her thigh was smeared red around several shallow cuts where the points were pressed against her, and it was with a harsh exhalation of relief that she peeled off the tape and lifted the spear away. Gripping it with her elbow against her ribs, she wrapped one length of the tape back around her thigh, covering the cuts, and then she pulled her pants back up and re-buckled her belt.

She stuck the spear upright through the gravel into the loam underneath, and then leaned into the car and hoisted out of the back seat a Makita power screwdriver and a yard-square piece of white-painted plywood with black plastic letters glued onto it. She fished two screws out of her pocket and, with an abrupt shrill blasting of the Makita's motor, screwed the sign to the trunk of the pine tree.

The sign read:

REST IN PEACE
'THE LITTLE LAME MONARCH'
LATE OF LEUCADIA;
PREVIOUSLY OF SAN DIEGO, SONOMA, LAS VEGAS
AND REMOTER PARTS.

For a moment she just stood there on the dew-damp gravel, with the Makita in her hand still harshly stitching the dawn air with its shrill buzz, and she stared at the sign with a look of blank incomprehension. Then her fingers relaxed and the machine crunched to the gravel, quiet at last.

She plodded over to the upright spear, plucked it free, and strode around the pine tree and down the unpaved private driveway, away from the street.

Fifteen minutes later and two hundred and fifty miles to the northeast, an earthquake shook the deep-rooted expanse of Hoover Dam, forty-five million pounds of reinforcing steel and four million cubic yards of concrete that stood braced across Black Canyon against the south end of Lake Mead as it had stood for sixty years; morning-shift engineers in the powerhouse wings below the dam thought that some vast vehicle was traversing the highway at the top, or that one of the gigantic turbines had broken under the weight of water surging down through the penstocks buried inside the Arizona-side mountain. Vacationers aboard houseboats on the lake were shaken awake in their bunks, and in the nearby city of Boulder more than two hundred people called the police in a panic.

Dawn-patrol prostitutes and crack dealers on Hollywood Boulevard reeled and grabbed for walls or parking meters as the sidewalk pavement, already sagging lower than normal because of shoddy tunneling being done for the Metro Rail line, abruptly dropped another inch and a half.

Just across the highway from Colma, the gray little cemetery town on the San Mateo Peninsula to which all the evicted burial plots of neighboring San Francisco had been relocated, a pregnant woman wrapped in a bedsheet and screaming nonsense verses in French ran out into the lanes of the 280 Highway.

Along Ocean Beach on the west coast of San Francisco a sudden offshore gale was chopping up the surf, blowing the swells at chaotic angles and wrecking the long clean lines of the waves. The couple of surfers out past the surf line who had been riding the terrifying winter waves gave up and began struggling to paddle back in to shore, and the ill-at-ease men who had been clustering around the vans and pickup trucks in the Sloat Boulevard parking lot cheered up and assured each other that they had stayed out of the water just because it had been obvious that the weather was going to change this way.

Similar abrupt gales split and uprooted trees as far north as Eureka and as far south as San Diego, all on that same morning.

And in a bedroom in a run-down old apartment building in Long Beach, south of Los Angeles, a fourteen-year-old boy was jolted awake – out of a dream of a woman running madly through rows of grapevines and clutching in her hand an ivy-wrapped staff that somehow had a bloody pinecone stuck on the end of it.

Koot Hoomie Sullivan had sat up in bed at the shock of the vision, and now he swung his bare feet out from under the blankets onto the wooden floor. His heart was still pounding, and his left hand had gone numb though his watchband was comfortably loose.

He glanced out the window, past the lantana branches that pressed against the glass; the carob trees and the parachute-draped van outside were casting long shadows across the broken concrete, and he could hear wild parrots shouting in the tree branches. It could hardly be seven o'clock yet – he was certainly the first person awake in the apartment – but the warm interior air was heavy with the smell of burning coffee.

'Call me Fishmeal,' he whispered, and shivered. He had not smeared mud on the foot of his bed at all this winter, and he had eaten several slices of rare London broil for dinner last night – he had even been allowed to drink a glass of champagne at the stroke of midnight! – but nevertheless he was again, clearly, experiencing the sense of being nearly able to *see* the whole American West Coast in some off-the-visible-spectrum frequency, as if with eyes underground as well as in the sky, and almost *hear* heartbeats and whimpers and furtive trysts and betrayals as if through the minute vibrations of freeway-shoulder palm trees and mountain sage and urban-lot weeds. And below the conscious level of his mind, faintly as if from distances remote beyond any capacity of natural space, he thought he could hear shouts and sobs and laughter from entities that were not any part of himself. When he had felt this sense of expanded awareness before, it had generally been in breathless dreams, or at most in the hypnagogic state between sleep and waking, but he was wide awake right now.

He stood up and got dressed, quickly but thoughtfully – Reeboks, and comfortable jeans, and a loose flannel shirt over the bandage taped onto his ribs; and he made sure the end of his belt was rotated into a Möbius twist before he buckled it.

He blinked as he let his gaze drift over the things in his room – the tasco

300-power reflector telescope in the corner, the framed black-and-white photograph of Thomas Edison on the wall, the coin-collection folders, the desk with clothes and a pair of in-line skates piled carelessly on it.

He jumped in surprise, and an instant later a woman's voice mournfully exclaimed '*Oh hell!*' somewhere in the parking lot outside the window.

'It's bar-time showtime, folks,' Kootie whispered self-consciously, and he opened the bedroom door and stepped out into the hallway that led to the open kitchen and the living room.

He could hear someone moving around in his adopted-parents' bedroom, but he wanted to have something specific to say before he talked to them – so he hurried to the front door and unhooked the feather-fringed chain and unbolted the door.

The woman who was the property owner was just walking around the corner of the building from the parking lot as Kootie shuffled across the threshold and pulled the front door closed behind him; and her brown face was streaked with tears. 'Oh, Kootie,' she said, 'all the beasties are dead!'

They were already dead, Kootie thought – but he knew what the woman must mean. The morning air was sharply chilly in his curly, sweat-damp hair, but the breeze was still scented with the night's jasmine, and he felt ready to deal with this particular crisis. 'Show me, Johanna,' he said gently.

'Over by the trash cans and Mr. Pete's van.' She was plodding heavily back the way she had come, her bathrobe flapping around the legs of her burst spandex tights. Over her shoulder she said, 'I gave them some new gravel last night – could that have poisoned them?'

Kootie remembered his dreamed vision of the woman in the vineyard with the bloody, ivy-wrapped staff, and as he followed Johanna around the corner into the slantingly sunlit parking lot, he said, 'What killed them was nothing that happened around here.'

He trudged after her across the broken checkerboard of asphalt and concrete, and when he had stepped around the back end of the parachute-shrouded van he stopped beside her.

The beasties were *obviously* dead now. Three of them were sprawled on the pavement and in the ice plant here, their gnarled old hands poking limply out of the thrift-store shirt cuffs, their mouths gaping among the patchy gray post-mortem whiskers, their eyes flat and sheenless behind the scavenged spectacles.

Kootie shook his head and clumsily ran the still-numb fingers of his left hand through his curly black hair. 'Terrific,' he said. 'What are we going to *do* with them?'

Johanna sniffed. 'We should give them a burial.'

'These people died a long time ago, Johanna,' Kootie said, 'and these aren't their bodies. These aren't *anyone's* bodies. The coroner would go nuts if he got hold of these. I doubt if they've got any more internal organs than a seaslug's got … and I always thought their skeletons must be arranged pretty freehand, from the way they walk. Walked. I doubt they've even got fingerprints.'

Johanna sighed. 'I'm glad I got them the Mikasa glass candies at Christmas.'

'They did like those,' Kootie agreed absently. Her late common-law husband had got into the habit of feeding the shambling derelicts, and for the last three Christmases Johanna had bought decorative glass treats for the things, in his memory. They couldn't eat organic stuff because it would just rot inside their token bellies, but they had still liked to gobble down things that *looked* like food.

'Good God,' came a man's voice from behind Kootie; and then a woman said, softly, 'What would *they* die *of*?'

Kootie turned to his adopted parents with a rueful smile. 'Top of the morning. I was hoping I'd be able to get a tarp over 'em before you guys got up, so I could break it to you over coffee.'

His adopted mother glanced at him, and then stared at his side. 'Kootie,' she said, her contralto voice suddenly sharp with alarm, 'you're bleeding. Worse than usual, I mean.'

Kootie had already felt the hot wetness over his ribs. 'I know, Angelica,' he said to her. To his adopted father he said, 'Pete, let's get these necrotic dudes stashed in your van for now. Then I think we'd better go to Johanna's office to … *confer*. I believe this is going to be a busy day. A busy year.'

He nearly always just called them 'Mom' and 'Dad' – this use of their first names put a stop to further discussion out here, and they both nodded. Angelica said, 'I'll get coffee cooking,' and strode back toward the building. Pete Sullivan rubbed his chin and said, 'Let's use a blanket from inside the van to lift them in. I don't want to have to touch their "skin."'

Angelica Sullivan's maiden name had been Elizalde, and she had the lean face and high cheekbones of a figure in an El Greco painting; her long, straight hair was as black as Kootie's unruly mane, but after she put four coffee cups of water into the microwave in Johanna's kitchen, and got the restaurant-surplus coffee urn loaded and turned on, she tied her hair back in a hasty pony tail and hurried into the manager's office.

A television set was humming on the cluttered desk, but its screen was black, and the only light in the long room was the yellow glow that filtered in through the dusty, vine-blocked windows high in one wall. A worn couch sat against the opposite wall, and she stepped lithely up onto it to reach the bookshelves above it.

She selected several volumes from the shelves, dropping them onto the couch cushions by her feet, and took down too a nicotine-darkened stuffed toy pig; then she hopped down, sniffed the air sharply, and hurried back into the little kitchen – but the coffee was not burning.

A sudden hard knock at the door made her jump, and when she whirled toward the door she saw Kootie's face peering in at her through the screened door-window; and then the boy opened the door and stepped in, followed by Johanna and Pete.

'You're not on bar-time, Mom,' said Kootie, panting. 'You jumped *after* I knocked on the door; and Dad jumped *after* I flicked cold hose-water on his neck.'

Pete's graying hair was wet, and he nodded. 'Not *much* after.'

Johanna was staring at Kootie without comprehension, so he told her, 'Bar-time is when you react to things an instant *before* they actually happen, like you're vibrating in the *now* notch and hanging over the sides a little. It's … "sympathetically induced resonation," it means somebody's paying psychic attention to you, watching you magically.' He looked at Pete and Angelica. 'I've been on bar-time since I woke up. When Johanna found the beasties, I jumped a second before she yelled, and when we went back to the apartment to wash our hands just now, I reached for the phone an instant before it started ringing.'

Kootie led the three of them out of the kitchen into Pete's long dim office.

'It was one of your clients on the phone,' Pete told Angelica, 'Mrs. Perez. She says her grandparents' ghosts are gone from the iron pots you put them in; the pots aren't even magnetic anymore, she says. Oh, and I noticed that your voodoo whosis is gone from the cabinet by *our* front door – the little cement guy with cowrie shells for his eyes and mouth.'

'The Eleggua figure?' said Angelica, collapsing onto the couch. 'He's – what, he's the Lord of the Crossroads, what can it mean that he's *gone*? He must have weighed thirty pounds! Solid concrete! I didn't forget to *propiti-ate* him last week – did I, Kootie?'

Kootie shook his head somberly. 'You spit rum all over him, and I put the beef jerky and the Pez dispenser in his cabinet myself.'

Pete was sniffing the stale office air. 'Why does everywhere smell like burning coffee this morning?'

'*Kootie*,' said Angelica, '*what's going on here today?*'

Kootie had hiked himself up to sit on the desk next to the buzzing black-screened television set, and he pulled his shirt up out of his pants – the bandage taped to his side was blotted with red, and even as they looked at it a line of blood trickled down to his belt. 'And my left hand's numb,' he said, flexing his fingers, 'and I had to rest twice, carrying the dead beasties, because I've got no strength in my legs.'

He looked up at his adopted mother. 'We're in the middle of winter,' he went on, in a tense but flat voice. 'This is the season when I sometimes dream that I can … sense the American West Coast. This morning—' He paused to cock his head: '—*still*, in fact – I've got that sense while I'm awake. What I *dreamed* of was a crazy woman running through a vineyard, waving a bloody wand with ivy vines wrapped around it and a pinecone stuck on the end of it.' He pulled his shirt back down and tucked it in messily. 'Some balance of power has shifted drastically somewhere – and somebody is *paying attention* to me; somebody's going to be coming here. And I don't think the Solville foxing measures are going to fool this person.'

'Nobody can see through them!' said Johanna loyally. Her late husband, Solomon 'Sol' Shadroe, had bought the apartment building in 1974 because its architecture confused psychic tracking, and he had spent nearly twenty years adding rooms and wings onto the structure, and re-routing the water and electrical systems, and putting up dozens of extraneous old TV antennas with carob seed-pods and false teeth and old radio parts hung from them, to intensify the effect; the result was an eccentric stack and scatter of buildings and sheds and garages and conduit, and even now, more than two years after the old man's death, the tenants still called the rambling old compound Solville.

Pete Sullivan was the manager and handyman for the place now, and he had dutifully kept up the idiosyncratic construction and maintenance programs; now his lean, tanned face was twisted in a squinting smile of apprehension. 'So what is it that you sense, son?'

'There's a—' Kootie said uncertainly, his unfocused gaze moving across the ceiling. 'I can almost see it – a chariot – or a … a gold cup? Maybe it's a tarot card from the Cups suit, paired with the Chariot card from the Major Arcana? – coming here.' He gave Johanna a mirthless smile. 'I think *it* could find me, even here, and *somebody* might be riding in *it*, or carrying *it*.'

Angelica was nodding angrily. 'This is the *thing*, isn't it, Kootie, that was all along going to happen? The reason why we never moved away from here?'

'Why we stopped running,' ventured Pete. 'Why we've been … standing our little ground.'

'Why Kootie is an *iyawo*,' said Johanna, sighing and nodding in the kitchen doorway. 'Why this place was first built, from the earthquake wreck of that ghost house. And the—'

'Kootie is not an *iyawo*,' Angelica interrupted, pronouncing the feminine Yoruba noun as if it were an obscenity. 'He hasn't undergone the *kariocha* initiation. Tell her, Pete.'

Kootie looked at his adopted father and smiled. 'Yeah,' he said softly, 'tell her, Dad.'

Pete Sullivan pulled a pack of Marlboros out of his shirt pocket and cleared his throat. 'Uh, "it's not a river in Egypt,"' he told his wife, quoting a bit of pop-psychology jargon that he knew she hated.

She laughed, though with obvious reluctance. 'I know it's not. *The Nile, denial* – I know the difference. How is this denial, what I'm saying? *Kariocha* is a very specific ritual – shave the head, cut the scalp, get three specially initiated drummers to play the consecrated *bata* drums! – and it just *has not been done* with Kootie.'

'Not to the letter of the law,' said Pete, shaking out a cigarette and flipping it over the backs of his fingers; 'but in the ... spirit?' He snapped a wooden match and inhaled smoke, then squeezed the lit match in his fist, which was empty when he opened it again. 'Come on, Angie! All the formalities aside, basically a *kariocha* initiation is putting a thing like an alive-and-kicking ghost inside of somebody's head, right? Call it a "ghost" or call it an "orisha." It makes the person who hosts it ... what, *different.* So – well, *you* tell *me* what state Kootie was in when we found him two years ago. I suppose he's not still an *omo*, since the orisha left his head, voluntarily ... but it did happen to the boy.'

'I saw him when he was *montado*,' agreed Johanna, 'possessed, in this very kitchen, with that *yerba buena y tequila* telephone. He had great *ashe*, the boy's orisha did, great luck and power, to make a telephone out of mint and tequila and a pencil sharpener, and then call up dead people on it.' She looked across at the boy and smiled sadly: 'You're not a virgin in the head anymore, are you, Kootie?'

'More truth than poetry in that, Johanna,' Kootie agreed, hopping down from the desk. 'Yeah, Mom, this does feel like *it*.' His voice was unsteady, but he managed to look confident as he waved his blood-spotted hand in a gesture that took in the whole building and grounds. 'It's why we're here, why I'm what I am.' He smiled wanly and added, 'It's why your Mexican wizard made you give a nasty name to this witchery shop you run here. And this *is* the best place for us to be standing when it meets us. Solville can't *hide* us, but it's a fortified position. We can ... receive them, whoever they might be, give them an audience.'

Angelica was sitting on the couch, flipping through the pages of her battered copy of Kardec's *Selected Prayers.* Among the other books she had tossed onto the couch were Reichenbach's *Letters on Od and Magnetism*, and a spiral-bound notebook with a version of Shakespeare's *Troilus and Cressida* hand-copied into it, and a paperback copy of Guillermo Ceniza-Bendiga's *Cunjuro del Tobaco.*

'How far away are they?' she snapped, without looking up. 'Like, are they coming from Los Angeles? New York? Tibet? Mars?'

'The ... thing is ... on the coast,' said Kootie with a visible shiver. 'Sssouth? Yes, south of here, and coming north, like up the 5 Freeway or Pacific Coast Highway.'

CHAPTER TWO

Our doctors say this is no month to bleed.
—William Shakespeare, *Richard II*

The caged clock high on the green-painted wall indicated exactly eleven, and most of the patients were already filing out the door to the yard for their fifteen-minute smoking break, following the nurse who carried the Bic lighter, and Dr. Armentrout was glad to leave the television lounge in the care of the weekend charge nurse. The big, sunny room, with its institutional couches and wall-mounted TV sets, looked as though it should smell of floor wax and furniture polish, but in fact the air was always redolent with low-rent cooking smells; today he could still detect the garlic-and-oil reek of last night's lasagna.

The common telephone was ringing behind him as he puffed down the hall-way to his office; each of the patients apparently assumed that any call must be for someone else, and so no one ever seemed to answer the damned thing. Armentrout certainly wasn't going to answer it; he was cautiously elated that he hadn't got his usual terrible dawn wake-up call at home today – the phone had rung at his bedside as always, but for once there had been, blessedly, only vacuous silence at the other end – and for damn sure he wasn't going to pick up any ringing telephones that he didn't *have* to answer. Resolutely ignoring the diminishing noise, Armentrout peeked through the wire-reinforced glass of the narrow window in his office door before turning the key in the first of the two locks, though it was nearly impossible that a patient could have sneaked inside; and he saw no one, and of course when he had turned the key in the second lock and the red light in the lockplate came on and he pulled the door open, the little room was empty. On the weekends the intern with whom he shared the office didn't come in, and Armentrout saw patients alone.

He preferred that.

He lowered his substantial bulk into his desk chair and picked up the file of admission notes on the newest patient, with whom he had an appointment in less than a quarter of an hour. She was an obese teenager with a dismal Global Assessment Score of 20, diagnosed as having Bipolar Disorder, Manic. Today he would give her a glass of water with four milligrams of yellow benzodiazepine powder dissolved into it; instantly soluble and completely tasteless, the drug would not only calm her down and make her suggestible but also block the neurotransmissions that permitted memorization – she would remember nothing of today's session.

A teenager! he thought as he absently kneaded the crotch of his baggy slacks. Obese! Manic! Well, she'll be going home in a few days, totally cured and with no manic episodes in her future; and I will have had a good time and added some depth-of-field and at least a few minutes to my lifespan. Everybody will be better off.

With his free hand he brushed some patient's frightful crayon drawings away from the rank of instant-dial buttons alongside the telephone. When the girl arrived he would lift the receiver and punch the button to ring the telephone in the conference room, where he had left good old reliable Long John Beach jiggling and mumbling in a chair by the phone – though it was possible that Armentrout wouldn't *need* Long John Beach's help anymore, if this morning's reprieve from the hideous wake-up call was a sign of the times, a magical gift of this new year.

The ringing of *this* telephone, the one on his desk, snapped him out of his optimistic reverie; and under his spray-stiffened white hair his forehead was suddenly chilly with a dew of sweat. Slowly, his lips silently forming the words *no, please, no*, he reached out and lifted the receiver.

'Dr. Armentrout,' he said slowly, hardly expelling any breath.

'Doc,' came a tinny voice out of the earpiece, 'this is Taylor Hamilton? Desk sergeant at the San Marcos County Sheriff's branch? I'm calling from a pay phone in the back hall.'

Armentrout's chin sagged into his jowls with relief, and then he was smiling with fresh excitement as he picked up a pen. For the past several years he had been alerting police officers and paramedics and psych techs all over southern California to watch for certain kinds of 51-50, which was police code for involuntary-seventy-two-hour-hold psychiatric cases.

'Taylor Hamilton,' noted Armentrout, consciously keeping the eagerness out of his voice as he wrote down the man's name on a Post-it slip. 'Got it. You've got a good one?'

'This lady seems like just what the doctor ordered,' said Hamilton with a nervous laugh. 'I bet you anything that she turns out to have gone AWOL from your place yesterday.'

Armentrout had already pulled down an escape-report form from the shelf over the desk, and he now wrote *12/31/94* in the date box.

'I'll bet you,' Hamilton went on, '*one thousand dollars* that she's a runaway of yours.'

Armentrout lifted the pen from the paper. 'That's a lot of money,' he said dubiously. A thousand dollars! And he hated it when his informants made the arrangement sound so nakedly mercenary. 'What makes you think she's … one of mine?'

'Well, she called nine-one-one saying that she'd just half an hour earlier killed a guy in a field above the beach in Leucadia this morning, like right at dawn, stabbed him with a *speargun spear*, if you can believe that – but when the officers had her take them to where it supposedly happened and show them, there was no body or blood at all, and no spear; in fact they reported that the field was full of blooming flowers and grapevines and it was obvious nobody had walked across it for at least the last twenty-four hours. She told them it was a *king* that she killed there, a *king* called *the Flying Nun* – that's solid ding talk, isn't it? The officers are convinced that her story is pure hallucination. She hasn't stopped crying since she called nine-one-one, and her nose won't stop bleeding, and she says some guy rearranged her teeth, though she doesn't show any bruises or cuts. And listen, when they first tried to drive her back here, for questioning? – the black-and-white wouldn't start, they needed a jump; and when we've been talking to her in here the lights keep dimming and my hearing aid doesn't work.'

Armentrout was frowning thoughtfully. The electromagnetic disturbances indicated one of the dissociative disorders – psychogenic amnesia, fugue states, depersonalization. These were the tastiest maladies he could cure ... short of curing somebody of their very *life*, of course, which was ethically problematic and in any case contributed too heavily to the—

He shied away from the memory of the morning telephone calls.

But *a thousand dollars!* This Hamilton fellow was a greedy pig. This wasn't really supposed to be about *money*.

'I don't,' Armentrout began—

But she did go crazy on *this morning*, he thought. She might very well have been reacting to the same thing, whatever it might be, that saved me from my intolerable wake-up call. These poor suffering psychos are often psychic, and a dissociative, having distanced herself from the ground state of her core personality, might be able to sense a wider spectrum of magical effects. By examining her I might be able to figure out what the hell *has* happened. I should call around, in fact, and tell all my sentries to watch especially for a psychosis that was triggered *this morning*.

'—see any reason not to pay you a thousand dollars for her,' he, finished, nevertheless still frowning at the price. 'Can I safely fax you the AWOL report?'

'Do it in ... exactly ten minutes, okay? I can make sure nobody else is near the machine, and then as soon as your fax has cooled off I'll smudge the date and pretend to find it on yesterday's spike.'

Armentrout glanced at his watch and then bent over the police-report form again. 'Name and description?'

'Janis Cordelia Plumtree,' said Hamilton. 'She has a valid driver's license, and I Xeroxed it. Ready? DOB 9/20/67 ...'

Armentrout began neatly filling in the boxes on the escape-report form. This morning a manic teenager on benzodiazepine, and, soon, a dissociative who was strong enough to interfere with both AC and DC ... and who might also provide a clue to why Armentrout had been, at least for this morning, freed from the attention of all the resentful ghosts and ghost fragments!

This was already shaping, up to be a fine year, though it was only eleven hours old.

When he finally hung up the telephone he looked at his watch again. He had five minutes before he should send the fax or expect the bipolar girl to be brought in.

He got his feet firmly under the chair and stood up with a grunt, then crossed to the long couch that couldn't be seen through the door window, and lifted off of the cushions a stack of files and a box of plastic Lego bricks. Clearing the field, he thought with some anticipation, for the cultivation of the bipolar girl's cure. The plowing and seeding of her recovery. And it *would* be a real cure, as decisive as surgery – not the dreary, needlessly guilt-raising patchwork of psychotherapy. Armentrout saw no value in anyone dredging up old guilts and resentments, ever.

Finally he unlocked the top drawer of the filing cabinet and rolled it partway out. Inside were only two things, two purple velvet boxes.

One box contained a battered but polished .45-caliber derringer for which he had paid a hundred thousand dollars a year and a half ago, its two stubby barrels chambered to take .410 shot shells as well as Colt .45 rounds; some spiritualist medium had found the blocky little gun on Ninth Street in downtown Las Vegas in 1948, and there was documentation to suggest that the gun had been used to castrate a powerful French occultist there; and Armentrout knew that a woman had killed herself with it in Delaware in October of 1992, shortly before he had acquired it. Probably it had inflicted injuries on other people at other times. The tiny gun was alleged, with some authority, to be able to shoot straight through magical protections that would deflect a bullet shot from a mundane gun: the French occultist had been heavily warded, but the person who had shot him had been his wife and the mother of his children, and so she had been inside his guard and able to wound him – and the gun had thus definitively shared in her privileged position, and was now reputedly capable of shooting the equivalent of supernatural-Teflon rounds.

Armentrout had never fired it, and certainly he wouldn't be needing it for the bipolar teenager.

The other velvet box he lifted out of the file drawer.

He carried it to the low coffee table carefully. Inside the box were twenty cards from a tarot deck that had been painted in Marseilles in 1933. Armentrout had paid a San Francisco bookseller *four hundred thousand* dollars for the cards in 1990. Twenty cards was less than a third of the complete tarot deck, and the powerful Death and The Tower cards were not among this partial set – but these twenty cards were from one of the fabulously rare Lombardy Zeroth decks, painted by a now-disbanded secret guild of damagingly initiated artists, and the images on the cards were almost intolerably evocative of the raw Jungian archetypes.

Armentrout had used the contents of *this* box on *many* occasions – he had awakened catatonics simply by holding the Judgment card in front of their glassy eyes, realigned the minds of undifferentiated schizophrenics with a searing exposure of The Moon, settled the most conflicted border lines with the briefest palmed flash of The Hanged Man; and on a couple of occasions he had *induced* real, disorganized schizophrenia by showing a merely neurotic patient the Fool card.

For the bipolar girl today he would try first the Temperance card, the winged maiden pouring water from one jug to another.

And he would avoid looking squarely at any of the cards himself. When he had first got the deck he had forced himself to scrutinize the picture on each card – enduring the sea-bottom explosions they seemed to set off in his mind, clenching his fists as alien images arrowed up to his conscious levels like deep-water monsters bursting up into the air.

The experience had, if anything, only diminished his personal identity, and so he had not been in danger of attracting the notice of his ... of any *Midwest ghost* ... but locally he had been a maelstrom in the psychic water table, and for the next three days his phone had rung at *all* hours with southern California ghosts clamoring on the line, and after a few weeks he had noticed that his hair was growing out completely white.

And like a lock of unruly hair, he thought now as he picked up the escape-report form and turned his chair toward the fax machine, this teenage girl's mania will be drawn out tight by the urgent attraction of the image on the card, and I will snip that bit off of her—

—and swallow it into myself.

She was at the door; he took the telephone receiver off the cradle, pushed the instant-dial button, and then stood up ponderously to let her in.

In the Long Beach apartment building known as Solville, Angelica Sullivan had been having a busy morning; she wanted to hover protectively over Kootie, but she had found that there were other demands on her time.

Over the rental-office door that faced the alley, she had last year hung up – reluctantly, for the business name had not been of her choosing – a sign that read TESTICULOS DEL LEON – BOTANICA Y CONSULTORIO. And it seemed that every client who had ever consulted her here had come blundering up to that rental-office door today, or at least called on the telephone; they were mostly Hispanic and black, dishwashers and motel maids and gardeners, on their lunch breaks or off work or out of work, and nearly all of them were jabbering with gratitude at having been abruptly relieved, at about dawn, of the various afflictions that had led them to seek out Angelica's help in the first place. Most mentioned having been awakened by an earthquake, though the radio news station that Angelica had turned on hadn't yet mentioned one.

Many of her people had felt that this deliverance needed to be formalized with ritual thanks, and so, with help from Kootie and Pete and Johanna, Angelica had hurriedly tried to comply. In her role as a *curandera* she had got pots of mint tea brewing, and served it in every vessel in the place that would do for a cup, and Johanna had even dug out some of her late husband's old coffee cups, still red-stained from the cinnamon tea that Sol Shadroe had favored; as a *maja*, Angelica had lit all the *veladores*, the candles in the glass tumblers with decals of saints stuck to the outsides; as a *huesera* she had got sweaty massaging newly painless backs and shoulder joints; and out in the parking lot, to perform a ritual *limpia* cleansing, six men in their under-shorts were now crowded into a child's inflatable pool that Kootie had filled with honey and bananas and water from the hose.

Cures of impotence, constipation, drug craving, and every other malady appeared to have been bestowed wholesale as the sun had come up, and in spite of Angelica's repeated protests that she had done nothing to accomplish any of it, the desk in Pete's office was now heaped with coins; whatever amount the pile of money added up to, it would be divisible by forty-nine, for forty-nine cents was the only price Angelica was permitted by the spirit world to charge for her magical services.

A few of her clients, like the one who had called Pete first thing in the morning, were unhappy to find that the spirits of their dead relatives were gone from the iron containers – truck brake drums, hibachis, Dutch ovens – in which they had dwelt since Angelica had corralled and confined them, one by laborious one over the last two and a half years; the candies left out for these spirits last night had apparently not been touched, and the rooster-blood-painted wind chimes that hung from the containers had rung no morning greeting today. Angelica could only tell these people that their relatives had finally become comfortable with the notion of moving on to Heaven. That explanation went down well enough.

Others with the same kind of problem were not *so* easily mollified. Frantic *santeros* from as far away as Albuquerque had telephoned to ask if Angelica, too, had found that her orisha stones had lost all their *ashe*, all their vitality – she could only confirm it bewilderedly, and tell them in addition about the total disappearance of the cement Eleggua figure that she had kept by her front door; and as the sunlight-shadows in the kitchen had touched their farthest reach across the worn yellow linoleum and begun to ebb back, Angelica began to get the first news of gang warfare in the alleys of Los

Angeles and Santa Ana, skirmishes ignited by the absence today of the *palo gangas* that served as supernatural bodyguards to the heroin and crack cocaine dealers.

'Were those ghosts too?' asked Pete as he carried a stockpot full of small change into the kitchen and heard Angelica acknowledging the latest such bulletin.

'The *gangas*?' said Angelica as she hung up the phone for the hundredth time and brushed back stray strands of her sweaty black hair. 'Sure. The *paleros* get some human remains into a cauldron, and it's their slave as long as it stays under their control. That thing that was hassling us in '92 was one, that thing that laughed all the time and talked in rhyming Spanish.'

'The canvas bag full of hair,' said Pete, nodding, 'with the Raiders cap stapled on the top.' He grunted as he hoisted the pot up and dumped the coins in a glittering waterfall into the oil drum he'd dragged in an hour ago, which was now already a third full of coins. 'I call it a good day, when things like that are banished.'

The kitchen, and the office and even the parking lot now, smelled of mint and beer and sweat and burning candle-wicks, but under it all was still the aroma of burning coffee. Angelica sniffed and shook her head doubtfully; she opened her mouth to say something, but a white-haired old grandmother bustled into the kitchen just then, reverently holding out a quarter and two dimes and four pennies in the palm of her hand.

'*Gracias, Señora Soollivan*,' the old woman said, pushing the coins toward Angelica.

Angelica couldn't remember now what service this old woman was grateful for – some haunting ended, some bowel disorder relieved, some recurrent nightmare blessedly forgotten.

'*No*,' said Angelica, 'I haven't—'

But now a man in a mechanic's uniform blundered into the kitchen behind the old woman. 'Mrs. Sullivan,' he said breathlessly, 'your *amuletos* finally worked – my daughter sees no devils in the house now. I got the *cundida* at work this week, so I can give you two hundred dollars—'

Angelica was nodding and waving her hands defensively in front of herself. She knew about *cundidas* – a group of people at a workplace would contribute some amount of each paycheck to the 'good quantity' fund, and each week a different one of them got the whole pool; among the new-immigrant Hispanic community, to whom bank accounts were an alien concept, the *cundidas* were the easiest way to save money.

'I didn't *do* anything,' she said loudly. 'Don't pay *me* for your blessings – somebody else has paid the price of it.'

And who on earth can that have been? she wondered.

'But I need to pay,' the man said quietly.

Angelica let her shoulders droop. '*Okay,*' she said, exhaling. 'If I run into your benefactor, I'll pass it on. But you can only give me forty-nine cents.'

During Christmas week in 1993, Angelica had – finally, at the age of thirty-five – flown alone to Mexico City and then driven a rented car more than a hundred miles southeast to a little town called Ciudad Mendoza. Members of her grandfather's family were still living in the poor end of the town, known as Colonia Liberacion, and after identifying herself to the oldest citizens and staying with some of her distant relatives until after Christmas, she had got directions to the house of an old man called Esteban Sandoval, whom she was assured was the most powerful *mago* south of Matamoros. In exchange for the rental car and the cut-out hologram bird from one of her credit cards, Sandoval had agreed to complete and formalize and sanction her qualifications for the career she had fallen into a year earlier.

For three months Sandoval had instructed her in the practices of the ancient folk magics that are preserved as *santeria* and *brujería* and *curanderismo*; and on the night before he put her on the bus that would take her on the first leg of her long journey back to her new American family, he had summoned several orishas, invisible entities somewhat more than ghosts and less than gods, and had relayed to her from them her *ita*, the rules that would henceforth circumscribe her personal conduct of magic. Among those dictates had been the distasteful name that she was to give to her business, and the requirement that she charge only forty-nine cents for each service.

Pete Sullivan accepted the exact change from the two people and walked over to toss it too into the barrel of coins.

Kootie was at the open kitchen door now, silhouetted against the spectacle of Angelica's colorfully dressed clients dancing under the sun-dappled palm trunks outside, and his eyes were wide and the hand he was pressing to his side was spotted with fresh blood.

'Mom – Dad—' he said. 'They're here, nearly – block or two away.'

Pete pushed the old woman and the mechanic out of the kitchen, into the crowded office room, and when he turned back to Kootie and Angelica he lifted the front of his untucked shirt to show the black Pachmayr grip of the .45 automatic tucked into his belt.

It was, Angelica knew, loaded with 230-grain hollow-point Eldorado Star fire rounds that she had dipped in an *omiero* of mint and oleander tea; and Pete had carefully etched L.A. CIGAR – TOO TRAGICAL in tiny letters onto the muzzle ring of the stainless-steel slide.

'Take it, Angelica,' he said tensely. 'I could hardly even pick it up this morning. My Houdini hands are on extra solid today.'

Angelica stepped forward and pulled the gun out of Pete's pants, making sure the safety catch was up and engaged. She tucked it into her own jeans and pulled her blouse out to cover it.

Kootie nodded. 'We'll receive them courteously but carefully,' he said.

Through the open kitchen door, from the street, Angelica could now hear an approaching discordant rumble, like bad counterpoint tempo beaten out on a set of *bata* drums that the orishas would surely reject for being perilously tuned; and when she stepped outside, striding resolutely across the sunlit walk and onto the driveway, she saw a big, boxy red truck turn in from the street and then slowly, boomingly, labor up the gentle slope toward where she stood. Peripherally she noticed that Kootie was now standing at her left and Pete at her right, and she reached out and clasped their hands.

The red truck rocked and clattered to a halt a couple of yards in front of them. It was streaked and powdered with dust, but its red color shone through lividly; and she noticed that an aura like heat waves shimmered around it for a distance of about a foot, and that the leaves of the carob trees on the far side of the driveway looked gray where she viewed them through the aura.

The truck's driver's-side door clanked and squeaked open, and a rangy man of about Pete's age stepped down to the pavement; his worn boots and jeans seemed only deceptively mundane to Angelica, and his lean, tanned face, behind a ragged mustache the color of tobacco and ashes, was tense with care.

'What *seeems* to be the problem?' he drawled, and there was at least some exhausted humor in his voice and his squinting brown eyes.

The passenger-side door was levered open now, and a pregnant woman in a wrinkled white linen sundress stepped down onto the driveway-side grass. She too looked exhausted, and her blond hair was pulled back, like Angelica's black hair, into a hasty, utilitarian ponytail – but Angelica thought she was nevertheless the most radiantly beautiful woman she had ever seen.

'Any problem here,' said Pete levelly, 'is one you've brought with you. Who are you?'

'Good point,' said the man with the mustache, nodding judiciously. 'About us bringing it with us. Sorry – my name's Archimedes Mavranos, and this lady is Diana Crane.' He looked past Angelica's shoulder and raised an eyebrow. 'And we sure do apologize to be interrupting your party.'

Angelica glanced behind her, and realized how odd the crowd in the parking lot must look – the kneeling old women giving thanks, the men and women appearing to pantomime swimming and goose-stepping and traffic-directing as they flexed various freshly pain-free limbs, and the six apparently naked men crowded into the Little Mermaid inflatable pool.

'We're humbly looking,' Mavranos went on seriously, 'for a man with a wound in his side that won't quit bleeding.'

After a moment, Kootie let go of Angelica's hand; he held up his blood-reddened palm, and then, as slowly as a surrendering man showing a gun to a policeman, lifted his shirttail to show the bloody bandage.

'A kid!' said Mavranos with an accusing glance toward Pete. He peered more closely at Kootie, then stepped forward. Angelica let her right hand brush the hem of her blouse over the .45, but the man had only knelt before Kootie and taken the boy's left wrist in his gnarled brown hand. 'You've Möbiused your watchband?' he said gently. 'That won't work anymore, son. *Now* when you do that you're just insulating yourself from your own *self.*' He had been unbuckling the watch strap as he spoke, and now he tucked the watch into Kootie's shirt pocket. 'If you follow me. Oh, and the same with your belt, hey? *That* I'll let *you* fix. Lord, boy,' he said, shaking his head as he lithely straightened up again, 'both legs and your left hand! You must have been weak as a kitten all day.'

Kootie seemed embarrassed, as though he'd blundered into a girls' rest room by mistake. The boy quickly unbuckled his belt, straightened out the twist, and re-buckled it; then he pointed at the truck and asked gruffly, 'Why is your truck the color of blood?'

The pregnant woman by the truck closed her eyes, and Mavranos crossed his arms and nodded several times. 'The hard way, of course. You take the low road and I'll crawl in the goddamned dirt, right? That's the spirit. Oh, that was the wrong *question*, boy!'

He turned and walked back to the still-open driver's-side door, and for a moment Angelica hoped these two people, and whatever they might have brought with them in the truck, would now just go away; but Mavranos only leaned in to hook out a can of Coors beer, which, from the way it swung in his hand as he trudged back to where he had been standing, was already half-emptied.

He took a sip from it before speaking. 'But since you ask. This lady and a friend painted it red on Ash Wednesday of 1990, in Las Vegas, to elude detection by the police – like the blood of the lamb over the doorposts in Egypt, right? – and ever since then the truck spon-*tene*-eously turns red every year during Holy Week. Ordinarily it's blue.'

'This isn't Holy Week,' ventured Pete. 'This is New Year's Day.'

'Oh, the error of it hadn't eluded me, honest,' Mavranos said. He looked again at Kootie, and frowned. 'You were a street beggar in L.A. a couple of years ago, weren't you? With an old black guy and a dog? Didn't I give you five bucks?'

Kootie's eyes widened, and then narrowed in a slow, shy smile. 'Yeah, you did. And it *was* a blue truck.'

'Sure,' Mavranos said. 'I remember now I saw room for the crown on your head even then. I should have figured it would be you we'd find today.' After crouching to put his beer can down on the pavement, he straightened and spat in the palm of one hand and then struck it with his other fist; the spit flew toward the kitchen, and he looked up at the crazy old building for the first time.

He was staring at the sign over the door. 'I *met* Leon,' he said softly; 'though he had lost his *testiculos* years before.'

On top of her anxious tension, Angelica was now embarrassed too. 'It means Testicles of the *Lion*,' she said. 'All *consultorios* have animal valor names – Courage of the Bull, Heart of the Leopard, things like that. It's ... a custom.'

Mavranos looked down at her, and his eyes were bright until he blinked and resumed his protective squint. 'We're in the choppy rapids of custom every which way you look, ma'am. Now, the random ... *trajectory* of my spit has indicated your building will you give permission for my party to come inside?'

Party? Angelica was suddenly certain that there was a third person in the old red truck – a person, *the* person, central, to all this – sick or injured or even dead; and suddenly she very strongly didn't want any of these strangers inside the buildings of Solville. Apparently permission would have to be given for that to happen – and she opened her mouth to deny it—

But Kootie spoke first. 'I am the master of this house,' the boy said. 'And you have my permission to bring your party inside.'

Angelica wheeled on Kootie, and she could feel her face reddening. '*Kootie, what are you—*' Then she stopped, and just exhaled the rest of her breath in helpless frustration.

Under the tangled curls of his black hair, Kootie's face looked leaner, older now; but the apologetic smile he gave her was warm with filial affection, and sad with a boy's sadness.

Mavranos's grin was flinty. 'Just what you were about to say yourself, ma'am, I know,' he growled. 'Oh well – now that the boy's got the strength in his limbs back, maybe he could help me and this other gentleman with the carrying.' He picked up his beer can and drained it, then tossed it onto the grass. Perhaps to himself, he said, softly, 'But why couldn't the boy have asked me *whose truck it was*?'

Again Angelica opened her mouth to say something, but Mavranos waved her to silence. 'Moot point and rhetorical question,' he said. 'It always happens this way, I guess,'

'At least give me forty-nine cents!' Angelica said. If these people pay me and thus become clients of mine, she thought, if I'm following my *ita* in my dealings with them, we can be protected by the orishas; if there are any orishas left out there, if my *ita* still counts for anything, after whatever it is that has happened today.

Mavranos grinned sleepily and dug a handful of change out of his jeans pocket. 'Look at that,' he said. 'Exact.' He dropped the quarter and two dimes and four pennies into her shaky, outstretched palm. He looked past her at Kootie and Pete, and called, 'You fellas want to give me a hand? Let me get the back of the truck open.'

He plodded back toward the truck, his hand rattling keys in the pocket of his old denim jacket, and Kootie and Pete exchanged a nervous glance and then stepped forward to follow him.

BOOK ONE

To the Boats

The likeness passed away, say, like a breath along the surface of the gaunt pier-glass behind her, on the frame of which, a hospital procession of negro cupids, several headless and all cripples, were offering black baskets of Dead Sea fruit to black divinities of the feminine gender ...

—Charles Dickens, *A Tale of Two Cities*

TROILUS: Fear me not, my lord;
        I will not be myself, nor have cognition
        Of what I feel.

—William Shakespeare, *Troilus and Cressida*

CHAPTER THREE

'In short,' said Sydney, 'this is a desperate time, when desperate games
are played for desperate stakes. Let the Doctor play the winning game;
I will play the losing one ...'

—Charles Dickens, *A Tale of Two Cities*

Where Janis Cordelia Plumtree finally wound up was in a chair in the TV
lounge.

She had visited people in hospitals where the lines on the linoleum floors
led you somewhere – 'Follow the yellow line to OB' or something – but the
black lines in the gray floors of Rosecrans Medical Center just led around in
a big dented loop, with frustrating gaps where hallways crossed. Maybe the
point was that you were free to pick your own destination ... the TV lounge,
or the meds station, or your 'room' with two unmade beds in it and no bath
or shower and a door that couldn't lock.

There were wire-reinforced windows in the halls and the lounge, but the
views were only of fenced-in courtyards, shadowy in the late-afternoon sunlight and empty except for picnic tables and dome-topped swing-door trash
cans; and you generally couldn't get out there anyway.

The pictures on the walls – vapid reproductions of watercolor flowers –
had rectangles of Plexiglas over them in the frames, rather than real breaka-
ble glass. She couldn't remember how she knew this, she didn't recall having
touched one in the ... *nine* days she'd been living here.

'I think he's like you,' Dr. Armentrout went on. The rotund white-haired
psychiatrist had dragged up a chair next to the one she'd collapsed into after
finally stepping off the floor-line circuit and wobbling into the TV lounge.
He had been talking to her for a minute or two now, but she was looking
past him.

On the TV, hung behind a clear Plexiglas shield up above head-height on
the wall beyond Armentrout, Humphrey Bogart was showing his teeth, talking mean and ruthless as he told the fat man, 'We've got to have a fall guy.'
There were no colors – all the figures, the Fat Man and Bogart and Joel Cairo
and 'the gunsel,' were in black-and-white, like a memory for someone else.

Plumtree shifted on the vinyl chair and tucked her denim skirt more
tightly around her knees but didn't take her eyes off the screen. Murder had
been done, apparently, and a scapegoat would have to be ... *turned over.*

'What a flop,' she said; then added, absently, 'Who's like me?'

'This man Cochran, who's being transferred here from Metro in Norwalk,' said Armentrout. 'His wife was killed Sunday before last, New Year's Day, at dawn – dressed herself up in a bedsheet and tied ivy vines in her hair and ran out into traffic on the 280, up in San Mateo County.' Plumtree didn't look at the doctor or speak, and after a few seconds he went on, 'She was pregnant, and the fetus died too, do you suppose that's important? Last week he flew her ashes back to her family estate, in France. He appears to have had a delusional episode there, and another when he got off the plane at LAX, in Los Angeles.'

'Rah rah rah,' said Plumtree.

'What happened on that Sunday morning?' he asked, as casually as if he hadn't been asking her that question every day.

'This guy's wife was run over by a bus,' Plumtree said impatiently, 'according to you. Cockface.'

The doctor's voice was tight: 'What did you call me, Janis?'

'Him, not you. Wasn't that what you said his name was?'

'Cochran.'

The vinyl seat of Armentrout's chair croaked as he shifted, and Plumtree grinned, still watching the movie.

'Cochran,' Armentrout repeated loudly 'Why do you say it was a bus? I didn't even say she was hit by a vehicle. Why should it have been a bus?'

The TV screen went dark, and then flared back on again.

It was a Humphrey Bogart movie; apparently *The Maltese Falcon*, since Plumtree saw that Elisha Cook and Mary Astor and Sidney Greenstreet were in it too. She was surprised to see that it was in color, but quickly reminded herself that they were colorizing all those old movies now. She couldn't remember how long she might have been sitting here watching it, and was startled when she glanced to the side and saw. Dr. Armentrout sitting in a chair right next to her. She unfolded her legs and stretched them out, with the heels of her sneakers on the floor and the toes pointed upward.

'So what do you say, Doctor?' Plumtree said brightly. Partly to delay further talk, she dug a little plastic bottle of Listerine out of her shirt pocket, twisted off the cap, and took a sip of it.

On the screen on the wail, Bogart had agreed to Peter Lorre's proposal that the Mary Astor character be turned over to the police. 'After all,' Bogart said, 'she *is* the one who killed him.' He mumbled something about miles, and an archer. Had the murdered person been killed from a distance, with an arrow? Hadn't it been up close with a spear?

But Plumtree had seen this movie before, and this was not how this scene went; they were supposed to pick the Elisha Cook character to 'take the fall.' Perhaps this was an alternate version, a director's cut or something.

Plumtree looked around for something to spit in, then reluctantly swallowed the mouthwash. 'I'm sorry if I haven't been paying attention,' she said to Armentrout. She glanced again up at the screen, and added, 'I love Bogart movies, don't you?'

Armentrout was frowning in apparent puzzlement 'Why should it have been a bus?' he said.

'Why ask why?' said Plumtree merrily, quoting last year's Budweiser ad slogan.

All the characters in the movie were startled now by a knock at the door. Plumtree recalled that the story took place, in San Francisco – a knock at the door could be anything. She held up one finger for quiet, and watched the screen.

The colorized Bogart got up and opened the door – and it was Mary Astor standing in the hallway, apparently playing a twin of herself. Clearly this was some peculiar alternate version of the movie. Perhaps it was well known, perhaps there were alternate versions of all sorts of movies. The Mary Astor twin in the open doorway was wearing a captain's cap and a peacoat spotted with dried blood, and her face was stiff and white – she was obviously supposed to be dead; but she opened her mouth and spoke, in a sexless monotone: 'Forgive me. Madame has forgotten that we agreed to play in partnership this evening.'

Bogart stood frozen for only a moment, then turned and lifted up in both hands the newspaper-wrapped bundle that had lain on the altar-like table; Greenstreet and Lorre didn't say anything as Bogart handed it to the dead Mary Astor – *they* certainly didn't want it, the severed head of a murdered king. The live Mary Astor was just sitting on the couch, staring wide-eyed at her dead double in the doorway.

Plumtree's new wristwatch beeped three times. She didn't even glance at it.

Armentrout chuckled. 'Are you being paged, Janis?'

Plumtree turned to him with a smile. 'That's my *zeitgeber*,' she said. 'Dr. Muir gave it to me. *Zeitgeber* means "time-giver" in German. Dr. Muir suspects that—'

'He's not a doctor, he's just an intern. And he's not your primary, I am.' Dr. Armentrout leaned forward abruptly, staring at Plumtree's legs. 'Is Muir also the one who strapped a *mirror* to your knee, Janis?' His good cheer was gone. 'Is that so he can look up your skirt?'

Plumtree paused, and the TV picture flickered; but a moment later she gave him a reproachful smile. 'Of course not, silly!' She reached down to unbuckle the plastic band that held the two-inch metal disk to her bare knee. 'I had a *dozen* of these on this morning, I must have forgotten to take this one off. It's for the—' She paused, and then recited proudly, 'the Infrared Motion Analysis System. Dr. Muir has me sit at a computer and take a test, and while I'm doing that the computer measures how much I ... move around. I move fifty millimeters a second sometimes! Doct – Mr. Muir suspects that my *circadian rhythms* are out of whack. The *zeitgeber* watch is set to beep every fifteen minutes; it's to keep me aware of the ... the time. When's *now*.'

Armentrout leaned back in his chair. 'When's now,' he repeated. After a moment he waved at the television. 'You're missing your Bogart movie, talking.'

'That was the end,' she said.

He opened his mouth, then apparently changed his mind about what he was going to say. 'But you've had these zeitgebers all along, Janis. I've noticed that you bring the front page of the newspaper to bed with you, so you'll know in the morning what day it is; and you hardly answer a "howdy do" without looking around for a clock, or sneaking a look at that waitress pad you keep in your purse.'

Her watch beeped again, and the television set went dark.

Plumtree sat stiffly; somehow her *watch* was ... making a noise; she could feel the vibration on her wrist. She didn't touch the watch, or look at it. Maybe it was *supposed* to be making a noise. She would watch for cues.

Dr. Armentrout was sitting beside her, looking at her speculatively. 'So,' he said, 'do you feel that you've been making progress, now that you've been a patient here for two years?'

Her stomach went cold, but a deep breath and a fast blink kept tears from flooding her eyes. It's okay, she told herself. It's like Aunt Kate's funeral again, that's all. 'I reckon I have,' she said stolidly.

'I was lying, Janis,' Armentrout said then. 'You've been here only nine days. You believed me, though, didn't you?'

'I thought you said ... "with your fears,"' she whispered. Her watch was still beeping. The doctor wasn't remarking on it. Maybe all the patients had been given these stupid noisy watches today, as part of some bird-brain new therapy. *What* a flop!

At last Armentrout was looking away from her, past her, over her shoulder. 'Here's our Mr. Cochran now,' he said, getting laboriously to his feet and smoothing the skirt of his long white coat. 'Just in time for the self-esteem group. Maybe he'll have some funny stories about his visit to France.' Without looking down, he said, 'Have you ever been to France, Janis?'

She shrugged. 'I wouldn't be surprised.'

She shifted around in her chair and squinted at the man standing with Dr. Muir by the nursing station. The new patient looked a bit like Bogart, it seemed to her; a hassled Bogart, tall but stooped, and gangly and worried-looking, with his dark hair combed carelessly back so that it stood up in spikes where it was parted.

She smiled, and the television came back on, and she wondered who the stranger by the nursing station was. Were they expecting a new patient? Would he be staying here?

'I wouldn't be surprised,' she said, dimly aware that she was echoing a statement someone had made here very recently.

'Scant?' said Dr. Armentrout.

Cochran sat up in his chair and blinked at the doctor, who was seated at the desk and leafing through the file of Cochran's transfer notes from Norwalk Metro.

At first Cochran had followed him to what the doctor had described as the conference room, which had proved to be just a back office cluttered with stacked plastic chairs and a blackboard and a bulky obsolescent microwave oven; but the patient sitting at the table in there, a bald, round-faced old fellow with only one arm, had just grinned and begun quoting dialogue from the tea-party scene in *Alice in Wonderland* when Armentrout had asked him to leave, so the doctor had given up on it and led Cochran down a hall to this locked office instead.

Now Armentrout raised his bushy eyebrows and tapped the stack of transfer notes. 'Why does it say "Scant" here?'

'Oh – it's a nickname,' said Cochran. 'From when I broke my leg as a kid.'

'So is that leg ... *shorter* than the other?'

'No, Doctor.' Armentrout was staring at him, so Cochran went on, helplessly, 'Uh, I limp a little in bad weather.'

'You limp a little in bad weather.' Armentrout flipped a page in the file. 'You don't seem to have been limping on Vignes Street Sunday. After you broke the liquor store window, you took off like an Olympic runner, until the police managed to tackle you.' He looked up at Cochran and smiled. 'I guess it wasn't bad weather.'

Cochran managed to return a frail grin. 'Mentally it was. I thought I saw a man in that liquor store—'

'You probably did.'

'I mean this man – a man I met in Paris. A couple of days earlier. *Mondard*, his name was ... unless I hallucinated that whole thing, meeting him and all. And he changed into a bull – that is, he had a bull's head, like the minotaur. I imagine it's all in those notes, I told the doctor at Metro the whole story. And I thought that policewoman was—' He laughed unhappily. '—was going to kill me, that is tear me to pieces, and take my head back to him.' He took a deep breath and let it out. 'How is she?'

'You knocked out two of her teeth. Hence the Ativan and Haldol ... which I'll leave you off of, if you behave yourself.'

'I'll tell you the truth, Doctor, I don't *know* if I'll behave myself. I didn't mean to go crazy on Vignes Street, Sunday.'

'Well, you left the airport during your layover. You were supposed to catch a connecting flight back up to San Francisco, right? And you ditched all your ID.'

'It ... seemed urgent, at the time. I guess I thought he might find me ... he *did* find me, at that liquor store.'

Armentrout nodded. 'And you had seen this man before.'

'In France, right. In Paris. On Friday.'

'No, I mean ... where is it.' The doctor flipped back a couple of pages. 'Four years ago last April, in 1990. *Also* on Vignes Street – hmm? – right after you had a "breakdown" on your honeymoon.'

Cochran's heart was pounding, and he wanted to grip the arms of his chair but his hands had no strength. '*That was him too?*' he whispered. 'He had a wooden mask on then, that time. But – yeah, I guess that was him, that time. Big.' He shook his head. 'Wow,' he said shakily. 'You guys are good. And I didn't remember that it was on the same L.A. street. I guess the police report's in there from that time too, right?'

'What happened on your honeymoon?'

'I ... went crazy. We got married on the sixth of April in '90, at a place on the Strip, and—'

'The Strip? You mean on Sunset?'

'No, the Las Vegas Strip, Las Vegas Boulevard. We—'

'*Really?* Well well well! And here I'd been assuming you were married in Los Angeles!'

'No. Las Vegas. And—'

'At the Flamingo?'

'No.' Cochran blinked at the doctor. 'No, a little place called the Troy and Cress Wedding Chapel—'

'Oh, better still!' exclaimed Armentrout happily. The fat doctor looked as though he wanted to clap his hands. 'But I should shut up. Do go on.'

'I'm not making that up. It's probably in your file.'

'I'm sure you're not making it up. Please.'

Psychiatrists! thought Cochran, trying to put a tone of brave derision into the thought. '*And* – at dawn the next day, it was a Saturday, I guess a car honked its horn right outside our motel-room door, a *loud* car horn; the chapel was a motel too, see, with rooms out in the back. They told me later that it was just a car horn. But I was hungover, or still drunk, and in my dream it was the man in the mask, very big, roaring like a lion, and blowing up a building he'd been locked up in, just by the force of his will. A *loud noise*. And he was loose, and he might do, anything.'

Armentrout nodded and raised his eyebrows.

'So ... we left Vegas. I was in a panic.' He looked at the psychiatrist. 'Having a panic attack,' he ventured, hoping that conveyed it more forcefully. 'I made Nina drive back, across the Mojave Desert.' He held up his right hand. 'I was afraid that if I drove, we'd go ... God knows where. And then when I *did* go ahead and drive, after we'd got all the way back to California, we wound up in L.A. – on, I guess, Vignes Street.'

'Where you *saw* him.'

'Right. On the other side of the street. Right. He was wearing a wooden mask, and ... *beckoning*, like Gregory Peck on Moby Dick's back.' Cochran looked up, and saw that the psychiatrist was staring at him. 'In the movie,' he added.

'And you punched a store window that time too, and cut your wrist on the broken glass. Intentionally, the police thought, hence your 51-50. Standard with suicide attempts.'

'I wasn't trying to kill myself,' said Cochran defensively. 'This was nearly five years ago, and I don't really remember, but I think I was trying to cut off my right hand.'

'Oh, is that all.'

Armentrout put down his file and got up and crossed to a filing cabinet against the far wall. He pulled open the top drawer and came back to the desk carrying a spiral notebook and two fancy purple velvet boxes. He sat down again and put the boxes down by his telephone, well out of Cochran's reach, and then flipped open the notebook.

'You were married on the sixth of April,' he said.

'Ri-ight,' said Cochran, mystified.

'That's very interesting! A week later a lot of people went crazy there. Well, at Hoover Dam, which is nearby. Most of them recovered their senses by the next day, though two gentlemen fell to their deaths off the after-bay face of the dam.' He sat back and smiled at Cochran. 'We've got a woman on the ward here who also had a nervous breakdown in Las Vegas in April of 1990 – on the fifteenth, Easter Sunday.'

'Uh ... did she also go crazy in L.A.?'

'Yes! Or nearly. In Leucadia, which is ... well, it's almost to San Diego. But she called the police nine days ago and told them that she'd killed a man. She said he was a king, and that she killed him with a speargun spear. Do you believe in ghosts?'

'Shit, no,' snapped Cochran impatiently. He shook his head. 'Sorry – I

thought you'd be showing me Rorschach ink-blots here, or having me inter-
pret proverbs, like they did at Metropolitan in Norwalk. No, I don't believe
in ghosts.'

'Have you ever seen anything that seemed to be supernatural?'

'Well, I saw a man turn into a bull, on Vignes Street, day before yesterday.'

Armentrout stared at him for several seconds with no expression. 'You're
getting hostile.'

'No, I'm sorry, I—'

'You were being cooperative a few moments ago. You may be too labile
right now to participate usefully in group.'

'Too what?' Cochran wondered if he meant lippy.

'The charge nurse showed you your room? Where the cafeteria is, where
you shower?'

'Yes.'

'That was your roommate, the one-armed man I couldn't roust out of
the conference room. John Beach – we all call him Long John. It's almost
certainly not his real name; I think he chose it just because he was found in
Long Beach, get it? He's been with us since November of '92.'

Cochran felt empty, and hoped the one-armed old man didn't recite from
Alice in Wonderland all the time, at all hours.

'He'll be in group. So will Janis Plumtree – she's the one who had the
breakdown in Vegas in '90, and who believes she killed a king nine days
ago. You may as well participate. I'll ask you to leave if you start acting out
or getting too gamy.'

Gamy? thought Cochran, involuntarily picturing tusked and antlered
animal heads on the stone floor of an old smokehouse.

Armentrout led him back up the hallway to the TV lounge, but Cochran
hung back in the entry when the doctor strode out across the shiny waxed
floor and lowered himself into one of the upholstered chairs around the
conference table near the window. Four men and two women were already
seated around the table, visible only in silhouette from the hall entry –
Cochran thought it must almost be time for the lights to come on, or curtains to be pulled, for the evening sun was throwing horizontal poles of
orange light into the room through the shrubbery that waved outside the
reinforced glass.

'My civil rights are being violated,' a young woman at the table was saying
harshly. 'I haven't signed anything, and I'm being held here against my will.
What's nine days' impound fees on a car in the San Diego County municipal lot? I bet it's more than my car's worth, it's just an '85 Toyota Celery, but
I need it for my job, and I'm holding you people, you soy dissant doctors,
responsible.'

'It was a Toyota *Cressida*, Janis,' said Armentrout, and the backlit blob of his head turned either toward Cochran or toward the window. 'Unless you're thinking of some other vehicle. Perhaps a bus?'

'Fuck you, Doctor,' the woman went on, 'you're not scaring me away. It was legally parked, and—'

'Janis!' interrupted another man sharply. 'Personal attacks are not permitted, that's non-negotiable. If you want to stay, be good.' He raised his head. 'Are you here for the self-esteem group?'

Cochran understood that he was being addressed, and he shuffled forward uncertainly.

'Come in and sit down, Sid,' said Armentrout. To the group he said, 'This is a new patient, Sid Cochran.'

Cochran broadened his stride, squinting as he walked through the brassy sunbeams to the nearest empty chair, which was at the end of the table, next to the angry young woman, with the windows to his right and slightly behind him.

'Hi, Sid,' said the man who had rebuked the angry woman; he was wearing a white coat like Armentrout's, and seemed to be another doctor. 'How are you?'

Cochran stared into the man's youthful, smiling face. 'I'm fine,' he said levelly.

'Ho ho!' put in Armentrout.

'Well, my name is Phil Muir,' the younger man went on, 'and we're here this evening to address problems of self-esteem. I was just saying that you have to love yourself before you can love someone else—'

The young woman interrupted: 'And I was just saying, "Fuck you, Doctor."' She pointed at Armentrout. 'To him. "*Ho ... ho*." You big fat fag.'

Cochran looked at her in alarm – then found himself suppressing a grin. Under the disordered thatch of blond hair her sunburned face had a character he could only think of *as gamin*, with a pointed chin and wide mouth and high cheekbones, and the humor lines under her eyes and down her cheek made her outburst seem childishly valiant, just tomboy bravura.

Hoping to prevent her from being ejected from the group, he laughed indulgently, as if at an off-color joke.

But when she whipped her head around toward him, he quailed. Her pupils were tiny black pinpricks and too much white was showing around her irises, and the skin was tight and mottled on her cheeks—

Abruptly an old man who a moment ago had seemed to be asleep hunched forward and hammered a frail fist onto the table. '*The ... rapist!*' he roared as the pieces of a forgotten dominoes game spun across the tabletop. 'That's what it spells! Don't pronounce it therapist! You've raped me with your needles!' He twisted in his chair and suddenly smacked both of his palms around Muir's throat.

Muir was able to struggle to his feet with the old man's weight on him, but he wasn't succeeding in prying the hands free of his throat, and tendons were standing up like taut cables under his straining chin.

'*Staff!*' roared Armentrout, shoving back his chair and thrashing to his feet. '*Code Green! Help, get a chemical here!*'

The nursing-station door banged open and two nurses came sprinting out, and with the help of a couple of the patients who had leaped up from the table they pulled the old man off Muir and wrestled him face down to the floor.

'I'll be snap-crackling pork chops with Jesus!' the old man panted, his cheek against the linoleum tiles. 'You sons of bitches! Bunch of Heckle and Jeckles!'

Armentrout was standing beside the table. 'Thorazine,' he told the charge nurse, 'two hundred milligrams I.M., stat. Put him in four points in the QR till I tell you different.' Two uniformed security guards hurried in from the outer hallway; after taking in the scene, they slung their nightsticks and knelt on the old man so that the patients could return to their seats. The overhead fluorescent lights had come on at some point during the commotion, and as the doctors and patients sat down again the group seemed to be only now convening.

Cochran felt a touch on his shirt cuff, and he jumped when he realized that it was the woman Janis; but when he looked at her, she was smiling. She couldn't, he thought, be as much as thirty years old.

'With his hands and feet tied down,' she said, 'at the *four points* of a mattress, in the Quiet Room, he'll be back to himself in no time.'

Cochran smiled back at her, touched that she had worded her remark so that he would understand the psychiatrist's jargon without having to admit ignorance; though in fact he himself had spent time in four points in a QR back in 1990.

'Ah,' he said noncommittally. 'I hope so.'

Two mental-health workers had rolled a red gurney into the room, and the old man was lifted onto it and strapped down. Cochran saw a nurse walking away with an emptied hypodermic needle.

Muir was kneading his throat. 'And I think Janis—' He looked across the table at her and stopped. 'Janis,' he said again, 'maybe you'll be good now.'

'I do apologize to everybody,' she said. She watched the gurney being wheeled out of the room. 'I hope Mr. Regushi is going to be ail right ... ?'

'He just flipped out,' said Armentrout shortly, settling into his chair. 'Very uncharacteristic.'

'We feel vulnerable, threatened,' said Muir hoarsely, 'and we get defensive and lash out – when we don't *feel good about ourselves*. We feel like bugs on a sidewalk, like somebody's going to step on us.' He gave the patients a wincing smile. 'Janis, I think your recurrent dream of the sun falling on you from out of the sky is indicative of this kind of thinking. How do you feel about that?'

Cochran braced himself, but the woman was just nodding seriously.

'I think that's a valuable point,' she said. 'I've always been frightened, of everything – jobs, bills, *people*. I've wasted my whole life being afraid. My only constellation is that I'm finally getting good, caring, state-of-the-art help now.'

'Well,' said Muir uncertainly. 'That's good, Janis.' He looked at Cochran. 'I've, uh, looked at your file, Sid, and I think you're afraid of being hurt. I noticed that when poor Mr. Regushi attacked me, you didn't get up to help. I suspect that this is characteristic of you – that you're afraid to reach out your hand to people.'

Cochran shifted uncomfortably in his chair. 'Reach out your hand, you get it cut off, sometimes.'

Belatedly he noticed old Long John Beach at the other end of the table. The one-armed man bared his teeth, and a domino on the table in front of him quietly flipped over ... as if, it seemed to Cochran, he had flipped it with a phantom hand at the end of his missing arm.

No one else had noticed the trick, and Cochran quickly looked back at Muir. Long John probably tied a hair to it, Cochran thought, and yanked on the hair with his real hand. He's probably got a dozen such tricks. And he's my roommate! And now I've probably offended him with my get-it-cut-off remark. Swell.

Muir had apparently followed Cochran's brief glance. 'Long John can't remember how he lost his hand,' he said. 'His whole arm, that is. But he's okay with that, aren't you, John?'

'In *some* gardens,' said Long John Beach in a thoughtful tone, as if commenting on what had been said before, 'the beds are so hard that the flowers can't even put down roots – they just *run around* – right out into the street.'

'The dwarves in *Snow White*,' put in Janis, 'came home every night – because their little house was fixed up so nicely. Snow White made them keep it *just so*.'

Cochran thought of his own little 1920s bungalow house in South Daly City, just a few miles down the ... *the 280* ... from Pace Vineyards on the San Bruno Mountain slope; and he reflected with bitter amusement that these doctors would probably consider it 'valuable' for him to 'share' about it here, ideally with hitching breath and tears. Then all at once he felt his face turn cold with a sudden dew of sweat, as if he were about to get sick, for he realized that he *wanted* to talk about it, wanted to tell somebody, even these crazy strangers, about the tiny room Nina had fixed up in preparation for the arrival of the baby, about the teddy bear wallpaper, and the intercom walkie-talkie set they had bought so as to be able to hear the baby crying at night. Their whole lives had seemed to stretch brightly ahead of them; and in fact he and Nina had even bought adjoining plots at the nearby Woodlawn Cemetery, just on the other side of the highway – but now Nina's ashes were in France, and Cochran would one day lie there alone.

Janis touched his hand then, and he impulsively took hold of her hand and squeezed it – but his vision was blurring with imminent tears, and Armentrout was probably staring at him, and the mark on his knuckles was itching intolerably; he released her hand and pushed his chair back and stood up.

'I'm very tired,' he managed to pronounce clearly. He walked out of the room with a careful, measured stride – not breathing, for he knew his next breath would come audibly, as a sob.

He blundered down the hall to his room and flung himself face-down onto the closer of the two beds, shaking with bewildered weeping, his hands and feet at the corners of the mattress as if he were in four points again himself.

'She's did,' said Muir to Armentrout. He was sipping coffee and still absently massaging his throat. The two of them were standing by the supervision-and-privilege blackboard in the nursing station, and Muir waved his coffee cup toward Janis Plumtree's name, beside which was just the chalked notation SSF – supervised sharps and flames – which indicated that she, like most of the patients, was not to be entrusted with a lighter or scissors.

'Degenerate Incontinent … Dipsomaniac,' hazarded Armentrout. He wished the pay telephone in the lounge would stop ringing.

'*No*,' said Muir with exaggerated patience. 'Haven't you read the new edition of the diagnostic manual? "Dissociative identity disorder." What we used to call MPD.'

Armentrout stared at the intern. Muir had been resentful and rebellious ever since they'd heard the news about the overweight bipolar girl Armentrout had treated and released last week; the obese teenager had apparently hanged herself the day after she had gone home.

'Plumtree doesn't have multiple personality disorder,' said Armentrout. 'Or your DID, either. And I don't appreciate you running tests on her circadian rhythms, and giving her … *zeitgebers*! That silly watch that beeps all the time? You're not her primary, I am. I'm on top of her—'

'The watch is a grounding technique,' interrupted Muir. 'It's to forcibly remind her that she's here, and now, and safe, when flashbacks of the traumas that fragmented her personality forcibly intrude—'

'She's not—'

'You can practically see the personalities shift in her! I think the patients have even caught on – did you hear Regushi mention Heckle and Jeckles? I think he was trying to say Jekyll and Hyde … though I can't figure out why he seemed to *resent* her.'

'She's not a multiple, damn it. She's depressed and delusional, with obsessive-compulsive features – her constant demands to use the shower, the days-of-the-week underwear, the way she gargles mouthwash all the time—'

'Then why haven't you got her *on* anything? Haloperidol, clomipramine?' Muir put down his coffee cup and crossed to the charge nurse's desk.

To Armentrout's alarm, the man picked up the binder of treatment plans and began flipping through it. 'You don't know enough to be second-guessing me, Philip,' Armentrout said sharply, stepping forward. 'There are confidential details of her case—'

'A shot of *atropine*, after midnight tonight?' interrupted Muir, reading from Plumtree's chart. He looked up, and hastily closed the binder. 'What for, to dilate her pupils? Her pinpoint pupils are obviously just a conversion disorder, like hysterical blindness or paralysis! So is the erythema, her weird "sunburn," if you've noticed that. My God, atropine won't get her pupils to *normal*, it'll have 'em as wide as garbage disposals!'

Armentrout stared at him until Muir looked away. 'I'm going to have to *order* you, *Mister* Muir, in my capacity as Chief of Psychiatry here, to cease this insubordination. You're an intern – a student, in effect! – and you're overstepping your place.' The pay telephone in the patients' lounge was still ringing; in a louder voice he went on, 'I've been practicing psychiatry for nineteen years, and I don't need a *partial* recitation of the effects of *atropine*, helpful though you no doubt meant to be. Shall I … *dilate!* … upon this matter?'

'No, sir,' said Muir, still looking away.

'How pleasant for both of us. Were you going home?'

'… Yes, sir.'

'Then I'll see you – you're not working here tomorrow, are you?'

'I'm at UCI in Orange all day tomorrow.'

'That's what I thought. You're going to miss our ice-cream social! Well, I'll see you Thursday then. Bright-eyed and bushy-tailed, right?'

Muir walked out of the nurses' station without answering.

Armentrout looked after him for a moment, then made his way around the cluttered desks to the window and looked out into the TV lounge at the patients, who couldn't be bothered to answer the telephone. Plumtree and Long John Beach had stayed at the conference table after the foolish self-esteem group had broken up – Armentrout favored the quick 'buying the pharm' attitude toward mental illness over the long, tormenting, dangerous routines of psychotherapy – and he saw that Sid Cochran had got over his sulk and rejoined them. They appeared to be playing cards.

You've got a busy day tomorrow, he told himself; coordinating the paperwork on the nurse anesthetist and the attending nurses, and then dealing with Plumtree after she recovers from the procedure. A busy day, and you'll be lucky to get a few hours of sleep tonight. But tomorrow you may very well find out what happened on New Year's Day, and learn how to make it happen again.

Atropine, Philip – you fool – is used for more than just dilating eye pupils; it also dries up saliva and nasal secretions, which is desirable in the administration of . . . of what the patients sometimes call 'Edison Medicine.'

At first they had tried to play for cigarettes, but after Long John Beach had twice *eaten* the pot, snatching the Marlboros and shoving them into his mouth and chewing them up, filters and all, Cochran and Plumtree decided to play for imaginary money.

They were playing five-card stud, listlessly. To make up for the tendency of any sort of showing pair to automatically win in this short-handed game, they had declared all queens wild; and then Long John Beach had proposed that the suicide king be taken out of the deck.

'I second that emotion,' Janis had said.

'What's the suicide king?' Cochran had asked.

The one-armed old man had pawed through the deck, and then flipped toward Cochran the King of Hearts; and Cochran saw that the stylized king was brandishing a sword blade that was certainly meant to be extending behind his head, but, with the token perspective of the stylized line drawing, could plausibly be viewed as being stuck right *into* his head.

'Sure,' Cochran had said nervously 'Who needs *him*?'

Janis had just won a 'multi-thousand-dollar' pot with two queens and a king, which according to the rules of this game gave her three kings; Cochran had folded when she was dealt a face-up queen, but Long John Beach idiotically stayed to the end with a pair of fives.

'Hadda keep her honest,' the old man mumbled.

'I almost dropped out when you raised on third street, John,' Janis told him. 'I was afraid you'd caught a set of dukes.' Cochran realized that her doubletalk was a charitable pretense of having seen shrewdness in the old man's haphazard play.

Of course Beach couldn't shuffle, and Cochran had dealt that hand, so Janis gathered in the cards and shuffled them – expertly, five fast riffles low to the table so as not to flash any cards – and then spun out the three hole cards.

'Have you had your PCH scheduled yet?' she asked Cochran. 'That's probable cause hearing,' she added, 'to authorize the hospital to keep you for longer than two weeks.'

'*Longer* than two weeks?' said Cochran. 'Hell no, not even.' He had an eight down and an eight showing, and decided to keep raising unless a queen showed up. 'No, I'm just in on a 51-50, seventy-two hours observation, and that's up late tomorrow night, which I suppose means they'll let me go Thursday morning. I don't know why anybody bothered to have me transferred here from Norwalk. I've got a job to get back to, and Armentrout hasn't even got me on any medications.'

'I bet a thousand smokes,' said Long John Beach, who was showing an ace. The tiny black eyes in his round face didn't seem to have any sockets to sit in, and they were blinking rapidly.

'We're playing for imaginary dollars now, John,' Janis told him, 'you ate all the cigarettes, remember?' To Cochran she said, 'Has he *talked* to you yet? Dr. Armentrout?'

'For a few minutes, in his office,' said Cochran. 'She calls,' he told Long John Beach, 'and I raise you a thousand.'

'She calls,' echoed the old man, still blinking.

'He'll want to talk to you more,' Plumtree said thoughtfully. 'And he'll probably give you some kind of meds first. Do cooperate, tell him everything you know about – your problems, so you'll be of no further use to him. He – he *can* keep anybody he wants, for as long as he wants.'

'I been here two and a half years,' said the old man. 'My collapsed lung's been okay for so long now it's ready to collapse again.'

Collapsed brain, you mean, Cochran thought. But he stared out the window, and shivered at the way the spotlights on the picnic tables in the fenced-in courtyard only emphasized the total darkness of the parking lot beyond, and he thought about the wire mesh laminate that would prevent him from breaking that glass, if he were to try, and about the many heavy steel, doubly locked doors between himself and the real world of jobs and bars and highways and normal people.

The telephone was still impossibly ringing, but Cochran was again remembering the intercom he and Nina had bought to be able to hear their expected baby crying, and remembering too Long John Beach's hollow echo of *She calls*, and he wasn't tempted to answer it.

'Have you,' he asked Plumtree, 'had *your* ... PCH, yet?'

'Yes.' A rueful smile dimpled her cheeks. 'A week ago, right in the conference room over yonder. You're allowed to have two family or friends from outside, and my mom wouldn't have come, so my roommate Cody came. Cody hasn't got any respect for anybody.'

'Oh.' The one-armed old man had not called Cochran's raise, but Cochran didn't want to say anything more to him. 'What did Cody do?'

Plumtree sighed. 'I don't know. She apparently *hit* the patient advocate – the man had a bloody lip, I recall that. I think Dr. Armentrout was teasing her. But! – the upshot! – of it all was that I'm now 53-53 with option to 53-58 – the hospital was given a T-con on me, a temporary conservatorship, and I might be here for a year … or,' she said with a nod toward the distracted Long John Beach, 'longer. I'm sure my waitress job, and my car, are history already.'

'That's … I'm sorry to hear that, Janis,' Cochran said. 'When I get out, I'll see if there's anything I can do—' He could feel his face turning red; the words sounded lame, but at this moment he really did intend to get her out of this hospital, away from the malignant doctor. He reached across the table and held her hand. 'I'll get you out of here, I swear.'

Plumtree shrugged and blinked away a glitter of tears, but her smile was steady as she looked into Cochran's eyes 'All places that the eye of heaven visits,' she recited, 'Are to a wise man ports and happy havens.'

Cochran's arms tingled, as if with returning circulation, and he laced his fingers through Plumtree's. Those lines were from *Richard II*, from a speech his wife Nina had often quoted when she'd been feeling down, and he knew it well. The lines immediately following referred to being exiled by a king, and Cochran recalled that Plumtree had been committed for having claimed to have killed a king; so he skipped ahead to the end of the speech: 'Suppose the singing birds musicians,' he said unsteadily, 'The grass whereon thou tread'st the presence strewed, the flowers fair ladies, and thy steps no more than a delightful measure or a dance – '

Long John Beach opened his mouth then, and his harsh exhalation was a phlegmy cacophony like the noise of a distant riot; and then, in a *woman's* bitterly mocking voice, he finished the speech: 'For gnarling sorrow hath less power to bite the man that mocks at it and sets it light.'

—And then Cochran was standing on the linoleum floor several feet back from the table, shaking violently, his chair skidding away behind him and colliding with the wall – the woman's voice had been *dead Nina's* voice, and when Cochran had whipped his head around he had seen sitting beside him a massive figure wearing a wooden mask, and the golden eyes that stared at him out of the carved eyeholes had had horizontal pupils, like a goat's – and Cochran had instantly lashed out in an irrational terror-reflex and driven his right fist with all his strength into the center of the mask.

But it was Long John Beach who now rolled across the floor off of his overturned chair, blood spraying from his flattened nose and spattering and pooling on the gleaming linoleum.

Plumtree was out of her own chair, and she ran around the table to kneel by the old man – but not to help him; she drew her fist up by her ear and then punched it down hard onto a puddle of the blood on the floor. The crack of the impact momentarily tightened Cochran's scalp with sympathetic shock.

'Jesus!' came a hoarse shout from the nurses' station. 'Staff! Code fucking Green, need a takedown!'

Plumtree had time only to meet Cochran's frightened gaze and smile before the hallway doors banged open and an upright mattress was rushed into the room, carried by two of the security guards; then the guards had used it to knock Plumtree over backward on the floor, and had jumped onto it to hold her down.

'She,' choked Cochran, 'she didn't hit him, *I* did!'

Armentrout was hurrying in, and he glanced angrily at Cochran. 'Look at her,' he snapped.

Plumtree's bloody fist was thrashing tree ot the mattress for a moment, then one of the guards had grabbed her wrist and pressed her hand to the floor.

'And what hand did *you* hit him with?' Armentrout asked sarcastically.

Cochran held out the back of his right hand and saw, with a sudden chill in his belly but no conscious awareness of surprise, that the skin of his knuckles was smooth and unbroken, the old ivy-leaf discoloration not distended by any swelling at all.

'*No chemicals for her*,' called Armentrout sharply to the charge nurse, who had sprinted into the room with a hypodermic needle. 'Not tonight, she's, uh, due for a dose of atropine in a couple of hours. Don't argue with me! Put her in four points in the QR for tonight, with five-minute checks.'

One of the security guards looked up at him desperately. 'You're not gonna *sedate* her?' he asked, rocking on the mattress as he held down Plumtree's spasming body.

'I'm the one who hit the old man!' shouted Cochran. '*She* didn't do it, I did!'

'You've bought yourself a meds program,' Armentrout told him, speaking in a conversational tone but very fast, 'with this ... display of childish gallantry. No,' he called to the guard. 'PCP tactics. You're going to have to just wrestle her in there.'

Terrific,' the man muttered. 'Get hold of her other arm, Stan, and I'll get this busted hand in a hard come-along.'

'Watch she don't bite,' cautioned his partner, who was groping under the mattress. 'I got her hair too, but she's in a mood to tear it right out of her scalp.'

The guards dragged Plumtree to her feet. Her teeth were bared and her eyes were squinting slits, but the come-along hold on her wounded hand was effective – when the guard who held it rotated her wrist even slightly, her knees sagged and her mouth went slack. The three of them shuffled carefully out of the room. The charge nurse had got Long John Beach into a chair, where he sat with his face hanging between his knees and dripping blood rapidly onto the floor, while she talked into a telephone on the counter.

'Do you remember the way to your room?' Armentrout asked Cochran. 'Good,' he said when Cochran nodded, 'go there and go to sleep. Your room-mate is apparently going to be a bit late coming in.'

Cochran hesitated, not looking the doctor in the eye – his first impulse had been to tell Armentrout that he had just had a recurrence of the halluci-nation that had landed him in the state's custody, but now he was glad that Armentrout hadn't let him speak. Any shakiness he exhibited now would be considered just a response to this noisy crisis.

For his self-respect, though, he did permit himself to say, just before turn-ing obediently away toward the hall, 'I swear, on the ashes of my wife and unborn child, I'm the one that hit him.'

'I will heal you, Sid,' he heard the doctor say tightly behind him. 'That's a promise.'

The door to the Quiet Room was open, and Cochran waited until the yawn-ing psych tech had glanced in and then walked away down the hall before he stepped out of his own room and tiptoed to the open door. It would be five minutes before the man would be back to look in on Plumtree again.

She was lying face-up on a mattress in the otherwise empty room; and she rolled her head over to look at him when he appeared in the doorway.

'Mr. Cochran,' she said wearily, 'of the dead wife. Rah rah fucking rah. You *did* hit him, didn't you?'

'Yes,' said Cochran. 'I had to sneak in here and thank you for taking the blame, but I – I can't let you do it. I tried to tell Armentrout tonight what really happened; I'll make him … *get* it, tomorrow. Even though it'll prob-ably mean *I* get a –' What did she call it, he thought nervously, the highway through Laguna and Newport, '—a PCH. My God, Janis, your poor hand! You shouldn't have done that, not that I don't – not that I'm not grateful – I *do*.' I'm not making sense, he thought. But how can they leave her tied down on the floor like this? 'But I meant what I said, earlier – even if they keep me for two weeks, I'll get you out of here one way or another. I promise.'

'I punched the *floor*, didn't I? For *you*. Shit. You'd *better* get me out, I hope you can pull strings and you're not just a, like a burger-flipper somewhere. And see you do tell 'em what really happened – first thing tomorrow, hear? I've got troubles enough, in the name of the Father, the Son, the Holy Ghost. They're gonna give me some kind of *shot* here in a couple of hours, Christ knows what for.' Her mouth was working, and he wondered if she was about to start crying. 'This is *just* like twit Janis, to fall for some dorky tuna in the *nut hatch*.' She opened her mouth and licked her lower lip, and flexed her arms uselessly against the restraints. 'You want to have been of some use on Earth? Scratch my chin for me, it's itching like to drive me ... sane.'

Cochran stepped into the room and knelt by her head, and the lights dimmed for a moment. He reached out, with his trembling *left* hand, and gently drew his fingernails over the side of her chin she had apparently been trying to reach with her tongue.

She surprised him by lifting up her head and kissing his palm. 'I was sorry to hear about your wife's death,' she whispered. 'How long were you married?'

'... Nearly five years,' Cochran said. He had stopped scratching her chin, though his fingertips were still on her cheek.

'How did you meet her?'

'She ... fell down some steps, and I caught her.' He pulled his hand back selfconsciously. 'I'm a cellarman at a vineyard up in San Mateo County, by Daly City, Pace Vineyards, and she was visiting from France, touring all the Bay Area vineyards. Her family's in the wine business in the Bas Médoc – the Leon family, they've been there since the Middle Ages. And she was looking at the casks of Zinfandel, in fact she was just in the act of tasting the young vintage with a *tâte-vin*, thing like a ladle, and at that moment the big earthquake of '89 hit – 5:04 in the afternoon – and she fell down the steps.'

'And you caught her,' Plumtree said softly. 'I remember that earthquake. Poor Sid.'

'He,' exhaled Cochran, finally nerving himself up to broach the point of this midnight visit, 'the old one-armed man, he – I thought he talked with her voice, there, when we were quoting the Shakespeare. My dead wife's voice. And then he looked like a, a man who chased me in Paris. That's why I hit him, it was just a shocked reflex. But it *was* her voice, it was *her* – unless I'm a whole lot crazier than I even thought.'

'I'm sure it *was* her. He can channel dead people like a vacuum cleaner, and you were sitting right by him.' She glanced at the open doorway, and then back at Cochran. 'You'd better go. I'm not supposed to have visitors here.'

He managed to nod and stand up, though he was even more disoriented now than he'd been when he'd walked in. As he turned toward the door, she said quietly behind him, 'I love you, Sid.'

He hesitated, shocked to realize that he wanted to say that he loved her too. It *wasn't* possible, after all: he had met this woman only a few hours ago, and she did seem to be some genuine variety of crazy – though that only seemed to be something the two of them shared in common, actually – and in any case *Nina had been dead for only ten days*. And her ... *ghost* might be ...

He forced that thought away, for now.

'My friends call me Scant,' he said, without turning around; then, though he was aching to say something more, he made do with muttering, 'I'm as crazy as you are,' and hurried out of the room.

CHAPTER FOUR

'All sorts of people who are not in the least degree worthy of the pet, are always turning up,' said Miss Pross. 'When you began it –'

'I began it, Miss Pross?'

'Didn't you? Who brought her father to life?'

—Charles Dickens, *A Tale of Two Cities*

At dawn they awoke Plumtree by sticking another hypodermic needle into the vein on the inside of her elbow – this shot contained a potent mix of Versed and Valium, and she had only ten bewildered seconds to curse and swear at the two nurses and Armentrout, and strain uselessly against the damp canvas straps of the four-point restraints, before she collapsed into unconsciousness. After the nurses unstrapped the rubber tourniquet from around her biceps and unbuckled the restraints, Armentrout crouched beside her and held her swollen hand in both of his, rolling the bones under his thumbs and prodding between the knuckles with his fingertips; then gently, almost tenderly, he lifted the young woman's limp body onto the gurney.

The ECT clinic was at the other end of the building, and Armentrout was pleased to see that the hallway lights didn't dim as Plumtree was wheeled along under them. One of the nurses striding alongside was holding a black rubber Ambu face mask over Plumtree's nose and mouth and rhythmically squeezing the attached black bag to assist the comatose woman's weakened breathing.

The nurse anesthetist who was waiting for them in the fluorescent-lit treatment room was a bearded young man Armentrout had worked with many times before, and the man leaned back against a counter and frankly stared as the nurses unzipped Plumtree's jeans and pulled them down past her hips and then unbuttoned her blouse and lifted her up into a sitting position to tug her limp arms back and pull the blouse free; Armentrout allowed himself only a glimpse – for now – of Plumtree's pale breasts when the nurses removed her bra. When they had laid her back down, positioning her head carefully on the perforated plastic cushion, the anesthetist stepped forward.

'What happened to her hand?' the man asked as he looped a Velcro blood-pressure cuff around her left upper arm and then inserted an Intercath needle into the back of her bruised right hand and taped it down. The blush of red blood that backed up in the IV tube cleared instantly when he opened the valve to full flow.

'She punched a guy,' said Armentrout shortly. 'Just soft-tissue damage to her hand, no crepitation.'

'I hope he's not pissed off – very shortly now she won't remember doing it.' He taped onto Plumtree's right forefinger the pulse oxymeter that would shine a white light through her fingertip and monitor her oxygen level by changes in the ruby red color of her flesh.

'This guy can't remember his own name,' absently remarked the nurse who was peeling the backs off of the wire-tethered plastic disks that were the heart-monitor EKG electrodes. She began pressing the disks sticky-side-down onto Plumtree's skin at each shoulder and hip and then in a cascade pattern around Plumtree's left breast.

'Get her on the ventilator,' snapped Armentrout.

The anesthetist obediently pried open Plumtree's mouth and pushed in past her teeth the steel shaft of a laryngoscope that was guiding a balloon-tipped plastic tube into her throat; and when he had got the tube far down her trachea and inflated the cuff to get an occlusive seal, the ventilator began chugging and sighing as it forced oxygen in and out of her lungs.

'And inflate the blood-pressure cuff,' Armentrout said; 'it's time to get the succinylcholine running.' Armentrout was hunched over Plumtree's head now, ruffling the thatch of her blond hair and at measured intervals poking down into her scalp the tiny needles of the EEG electrodes that would measure her brain-wave activity.

Plumtree's semi-nude body shivered under the monitor wires as the succinylcholine hit, then relaxed totally – Armentrout knew that the motor end plates of all of her voluntary muscle fibers had now subsided in depolarization, and only the insistence of the ventilator was even keeping her lungs flexing.

A nurse now leaned over the unconscious woman to fit a bifurcated foam-rubber bite block around the endotrachial tube and between the teeth of Plumtree's upper and lower jaws.

Finally Armentrout smeared conducting jelly on the steel disks that would deliver the voltage, and he carefully stuck one onto each of Plumtree's temples – this would be a full bilateral square wave procedure, not one of the wishy-washy unilateral with one of the disks stuck onto the forehead. Armentrout knew it wouldn't damage her – he had undergone a series of full bilateral-wave ECTs himself, when he had been just seventeen years old, after his mother's death.

'Low voltage tracing,' said the nurse who was watching the EEG monitor; 'huh! – with some intermittent sleep spindles at about fourteen hertz.'

'That's to be expected,' said Armentrout, not looking at the anesthetist. 'You'll see some biphasics, too, if we make a loud noise.' He looked at his watch – it had been two full minutes since the muscle-disabling succinylcholine had gone coursing down the IV tube. 'Clear!' he called, and everybody stepped back from Plumtree's electrode-studded body. For a moment Armentrout let his eyes play over her breasts, the exposed nipples erect in the chilly air of the treatment room, and the wisp of blond pubic hair curling above the elastic waistband of her TUESDAY-stitched panties, and then he twisted the dial on the plastic monitor box to two hundred and fifty joules, took a deep breath, and flipped the toggle switch.

Instantly Plumtree's left hand twitched and clenched in a fist, for the tight constriction of the blood-pressure cuff had effectively prevented the neuro-muscular blocking drug from getting into her forearm.

'Total chaos,' calmly said the nurse who was watching the EEG monitor. Plumtree's brain waves on the screen were a forest of tight, wildly disordered peaks. 'A ten on the Richter scale.'

Then, slowly, the middle finger of Plumtree's tight-clenched left hand unfolded and extended out straight.

The anesthetist noticed it and laughed. 'She's flipping you off, Richard,' he told Armentrout. 'I've never seen *that* happen before.'

Armentrout kept his face impassive, but his belly had gone cold and his heart was knocking in his chest. I can't believe that's not involuntary, he thought – but – *who the hell* are *you, girl?*

'Me either,' he said levelly.

Cochran put on yesterday's clothes when he got out of bed – Long John Beach was in the other bed now, black-eyed and snoring like a horse behind a metal brace taped to his nose, and Cochran was careful not to wake him – but when he had sneaked out of the room he got one of the psych techs to let him rummage for fresh clothes in 'the boutique,' a closet full of donated clothing; and twenty minutes after he had got a nurse to unlock the shower room and give him a disposable Bic razor, he shambled into the windowless cafeteria, freshly bathed and shaved and with his wet hair combed down flat for the first time in twenty-four hours, wearing oversized brown-corduroy bell-bottom trousers and a T-shirt with A CONNECTICUT PANSY IN KING ARTHUR'S SHORTS lettered on it. All the other shirts had been too narrow for his shoulders or were women's blouses that buttoned right-over-left. He didn't think the crazy people, or even the staff, would read the lettering, and he nervously hoped Janis Plumtree might be able to find it funny.

But when he took a tray and got into the line for oatmeal and little square milk cartons and individual-size boxes of cereal, he looked around the tables and saw that Plumtree wasn't in the cafeteria.

He carried his tray to an unoccupied table and sat down, and began eating his cornflakes right out of the box, like Crackerjacks, ignoring the little carton of milk. He was breathing shallowly, and dropping as many cornflakes onto his lap as he got into his mouth.

He was wondering just how bad an infraction it was to break the nose of another patient; and he was giddily alarmed at his determination, even stronger this morning than it had been last night, to keep his promise to Janis Plumtree and get the true story across. Eventually Armentrout would be on the ward, and Long John Beach would be up to corroborate the facts. Cochran might very well even have to admit to having had another hallucination, and he supposed that would surely guarantee him a 'PCH,' an unfavorable one – which would mean not being able to see the *real* PCH, Pacific Coast Highway, for at least two weeks – but Cochran would be able, finally, to ... *take the blame.*

And she loves me, he thought as he licked his trembling finger to get the last crumbs out of the corn flakes box; or she did last night; or she said she did last night. I will take her out of this place.

But neither Plumtree nor Armentrout appeared in the cafeteria, and just as Cochran was reluctantly getting up to investigate the TV lounge, and brushing cornflake fragments off the crotch of his ludicrous corduroy pants, a young woman in a white lab coat came striding up to his table.

'Sid Cochran?' she said brightly. 'Hi, I'm Tammy Eddy, the occupational therapist, and if you're free I'd like to get your dexterity tests out of the way. Kindergarten stuff, really – the patients are always asking me if I majored in basket-weaving!'

Cochran managed to return her smile, though her cheer seemed as perfunctory to him this morning as the HAVE A NICE DAY admonition printed on the 'moist tow-elette' package on his tray, and she didn't notice his shirt.

He opened his mouth to tell her that he had something important to say to Dr. Armentrout first – but instead relaxed and said, 'Okay.'

'Let's go to the conference room, shall we?'

Maybe we'll meet him on the way, Cochran told himself defensively.

But there was no one in the sunny TV lounge as the young occupational therapist led him through it – Cochran noticed that the blood had been cleaned up, and the floor was a glassy plane again – and she had to fetch out her keys and unlock the conference room, for no one had been in it yet today.

'Sit down, Sid,' the woman said, waving at a chair by the table. 'Can you find a patch of clear space there? Good, yeah, that'll do. Today you're going to get a lesson in—' she had been moving things on a shelf over the microwave oven, and now turned around and laid on the table in front of him two five-inch square pieces of blue vinyl with holes around the edges, and a blunt white plastic yarn needle and a length of orange yarn. 'Can you guess?'

'Knitting,' said Cochran carefully, abruptly reminded of the book he'd read on the flight home from Paris three days ago.

'That's close. *Stitching.* This is called the Allen Cognitive Levels test, and it's just me showing you different ways to sew these two vinyl squares together. Here, the needle's already threaded – you go ahead and sew them together any way you like.'

Cochran patiently laced the things together as if they were the front and back covers of a spiral-bound book, and when he was done she beamed and told him that he'd just figured out the 'whipstitch' all on his own. She took back the squares and unlaced them and began showing him a different stitch that involved skipping holes and then coming back around to them, but though his fingers followed her directions, his mind was on the book he'd read on the plane.

The disquieting thing was that he had read Dickens' *A Tale of Two Cities* before; and though that had been a long time ago, he had eventually become aware that this book he was reading in the airplane seat by the glow of the tiny overhead spotlight – a Penguin Classics paperback, wedged between his cigarettes and the several little airline bottles of Wild Turkey bourbon – was a different text.

The variances hadn't been obvious at first, for he'd only been able to read the book fitfully, especially the Parisian scenes; he had still been shaky from his encounter the day before – in the ancient narrow streets south of the river Seine, by Notre Dame cathedral, where fragrant lamb koftes turned on spits in the open windows of Lebanese restaurants – with the man who had called himself Mondard ... and who had shortly stopped seeming to be a man, to be a human being at all ...

Cochran forced himself to concentrate on pushing the foolish plastic needle through the holes in the vinyl – not knitting, stitching—

The woman in the book had been knitting, *and* stitching, weaving into her fabrics the names of men who were to die on the guillotine. He'd remembered her name as having been something like Madame Laphroaig, but in this text all the French revolutionaries called her Ariachne – a combination of the names *Arachne* and *Ariadne*, given to her because she was always knitting and was married to the 'bull-necked' man who owned the wineshop. The notes in the back of the book explained that it was a *nom de guerre* of the revolution, like the name *Jacques* that was adopted by all the men. Cochran recalled that during the French Revolution they had even renamed all the calendar months; the only one he could remember was Thermidor, and he wondered what the others could have been. Fricassee? Jambalaya? Chowder?

He smiled now at the thought; and he tried to pay attention to the occupational therapist's cheery explanation of how to do a 'single cordovan' stitch, and not to think about the book.

But he realized now that the story he'd read on the airplane must have started to diverge from the remembered text very early on. In the scene in the Old Bailey courthouse in London, for example, in which the Frenchman Charles Darnay was on trial for treason, Cochran seemed to remember having read that the court bar was strewn with herbs and sprinkled with vinegar, an apparently routine precaution against 'gaol' air ... but in this text the bar was twined in living ivy, and splashed liberally with red wine.

And just because of the rhyme he had remembered 'Cly the spy,' whose death had been a hoax and whose coffin had proved to contain only paving stones – but he had remembered Cly as a *man*, and certainly the name had not been short for *Clytemnestra*.

His hand shook as he pushed the needle through the holes. In the book he'd read on the plane, Madame Ariachne's cloth had flexed and shivered as she had forced each new, resisting name into the fabric.

'You're not quite getting the hang of that one, are you?' said Tammy Eddy.

Cochran looked up at her. 'It's hard,' he said.

'Hard to remember what I said?'

'Hard to remember anything at all. But I can do it.'

He thought of the scene at the end of the book as he had read it years ago, in which the dissolute Englishman Sidney Carton redeemed himself by sneaking into the Conciergerie prison to switch places with his virtuous double, the Frenchman Charles Darnay who was condemned to die the next morning; and then Cochran made himself remember the scene as he had read it on the airplane three days ago—

In that variant version it had been a woman who furtively unlocked the cell door – the woman Clytemnestra, who was somehow the classical Greek Clytemnestra from Aeschylus' *Oresteia*, come to atone for having killed the high king Agamemnon.

And in this crazy version the prisoner was a woman too, though still the visitor's mirror-image double; and when she demanded to know the reason for this visit, this exchange of places, Clytemnestra had said, 'Forgive me. Madame has forgotten that we agreed to play in partnership this evening.'

Tammy Eddy was speaking sharply to him – and he realized that she had been repeating herself for several seconds. He looked up at her, and saw that she had retreated to the door and pulled it open. 'Put,' she said, obviously not for the first time, 'the needle ... *down*, Sid.'

'Sorry. Sure.' He opened his fingers and the needle dropped to the table-top. 'I wasn't listening.' He looked at the vinyl squares and saw that he had stitched them together and then with the blunt needle *torn a hole* in the center of each square. 'I guess I wrecked your ... your test,' he said lamely. And no doubt failed it, he thought. She'll probably testify at my PCH.

'They're not expensive. That'll be all for today, Sid.' She stepped back a yard into the TV lounge as he pushed his chair back and sidled around the table to the door. 'What,' she asked him as he walked past her toward the cafeteria, 'were you making, there at the end?'

He stopped for a moment but didn't look back at her. 'Oh, nothing,' he said over his shoulder. 'T just got bored and ... distracted.'

Perhaps she nodded or smiled or frowned – he kept his eyes on the cafeteria door as he strode forward. He might or might not tell Armentrout, but would certainly not tell this woman, that he had been unthinkingly making a frail mask in which to face the mask that the big bull-headed man would be wearing.

Probably because of his having hit Long John Beach the night before, the knuckles of his right hand stung, and he alternately made a fist and stretched his fingers as he walked through the cafeteria and back out into the lounge without having seen Plumtree or Armentrout – Tammy Eddy was nowhere to be seen now either – and then started down the hall, past the Dutch door of the meds room, to the wing of patient rooms.

At every corner and intersection of hall there was a convex mirror attached to the ceiling, so that anyone walking through the unit could see around a corner before actually stepping around it. At L-corners the mirror was a triangular eighth of a globe wedged up in the corner, and at four-way crossings it was a full half-globe set in the middle of the ceiling. Cochran didn't like the things – they seemed to be *whole* spheres, only part-way intruded here and there through temporary violations of the architecture, like chrome eyes peering down curiously into the maze of hallways, and he couldn't shake the irrational dread of rounding a turn and seeing two of them in the wall ahead of him, golden for once instead of silver, with a single horizontal black line across each of them – but he did reluctantly glance at a couple of them to get an advance look around corners on the way to Plumtree's room.

But when he finally arrived at her room he saw that her door, in violation of the daytime rules, was closed. He shuffled up to it anyway, intending to knock, and then became aware of Plumtree speaking quietly inside; he couldn't hear what she said, but it was followed by Armentrout's voice saying, 'So which one of you was it that took the shock?'

The question meant nothing to Cochran, and he was hesitant about interrupting a doctor-and-patient therapy session; and after a few moments of indecisive shuffling, and raising his hand and then lowering it, he let his shoulders slump and turned away and plodded back down the hall toward the TV lounge, defeatedly aware of the wide cuffs of his bell-bottom trousers flapping around his bare ankles.

'Somebody went flatline ten seconds after the shock,' Armentrout went on when Plumtree didn't immediately answer. 'We dragged the Waterloo cart into the treatment room, but your heart started up again before we had to put the paddles on you.' He was smiling, but he knew that he was still shaky about the incident, for he hadn't meant to call it a 'Waterloo cart' just now. Waterloo was the brand name of the thing, but it was known as a crash cart, or a cardiac defibrillator; the incident would probably have been *his* Waterloo, though, as soon as the idealistic Philip Muir heard about it, if Plumtree had died undergoing electroconvulsive therapy with forged permissions while just on a temporary conservatorship. Muir was surely going to be angry anyway, for ECT was not a treatment indicated for multiple personality disorder – or dissociative identity disorder, as Muir would trendily say.

And Armentrout couldn't pretend anymore that he didn't know she was a multiple – the ECT had separated out the personalities like a hammer, breaking a piece of shale into distinct, individual hard slabs. Armentrout could have wished that it was a little less obvious, in fact; but perhaps the personalities would blend back together a little, before Muir saw her tomorrow.

'Valerie,' said the woman in the bed. 'She always takes intolerable situations. It caught Cody by surprise.'

'And who are you?'

'I'm Janis.' She smiled at him, and in the dim lamplight her pupils didn't seem notably dilated or constricted now.

'How many of you are there?'

'I really don't know, Doctor. Some aren't very developed, or exist just for one purpose ... like the one called – what does he call himself? – "the foul fiend Flibbertigibbet!" What a name! He got it ... from Shakespeare, according to him. Is there a play called *Leah*? He claims to have been a Shakespearean actor. I – don't want to talk about him, he's who we've brought up when we've had to fight, to defend our life. He makes our teeth hurt like we've got braces on, and he gives us nosebleeds. I don't want to talk about him.' She shivered, and then smiled wryly. 'We're like the little cottage full of dwarves in *Snow White* – each of us with a job to do, while the poisoned girl sleeps. I used to sign my high-school papers "Snowy Eve White" sometimes.'

'Snow White, Eve White – you've seen the movie *The Three Faces of Eve*? Or read the book?'

She shook her head. 'No, I've never heard of it.'

'Hmm. I bet. And one of you is a man?'

She blinked – and Armentrout could feel the hairs standing up on his arms, for the woman's face changed abruptly, as the muscles under the skin realigned themselves; her mouth seemed wider now, and her eyes narrower.

'Valerie says you had all my clothes off,' she said in a flat voice. 'I'd be pissed about that if I didn't know you're a total queer. What did you hit me with?'

'Cody,' said Armentrout in cautious greeting, suddenly wishing Plumtree had been put back in restraints. She had recovered from the succinylcholine amazingly fast, and she didn't seem to be dopy and blurry, as patients recovering from ECT generally were for at least the rest of the day.

'You're the one,' he went on, 'speaking of hitting, who hit Long John Beach last night, aren't you, Cody?'

'I don't know. Probably.' Plumtree's forehead was dewed with sweat, and she was squinting. 'Was this while I had my clothes off? He probably asked for it, he's got a frisky spirit hand to go with the flesh-and-blood one. And I saw that Cockface guy's hand – I don't like his birthmark. A lot of tricky hands around here, and this place is a stinking flop.'

She was breathing through her open mouth, and she looked pale. Altogether she was acting like someone with a bad hangover, and it occurred to Armentrout that the Janis personality had been unimpaired because it had been Cody who had taken the shock treatment. Cody was the one who had given him the finger. Ten seconds had gone by before the Valerie personality, the one who took 'intolerable situations,' had taken over. He leaned forward to look at Plumtree's face, and he saw that her pupils were as tiny as pores. She definitely looked dopy and blurry now.

'What we're going to try to do is achieve *isolation*, Cody,' he said. 'We'll decide which personality is most socially viable, and then bring that one forward and … cauterize the others off.' This was hardly a description of orthodox therapy, but he wanted to draw a reaction from her. She didn't seem to be listening, though.

'How many of you are there, Cody?' Armentrout went on. 'I've met you and Janis, that I know of, and I've heard about Valerie.'

'God, I am still in the psych hospital, aren't I?' she mumbled, rubbing her eyes. 'I suppose a cold beer is out of the question. Shit. But no hair of *that* dog, thank you – that was the goddamn Wolfman.'

'That was ECT,' Armentrout said, leaning back in the chair beside the bed and smiling at her, 'electroconvulsive therapy – shock treatment, Edison Medicine.' He smiled reminiscently and said, 'Generally a course of treatment is six or twelve shock sessions, three a week.'

All the worldly weariness disappeared trom her lace, and for a moment Armentrout thought the Cody personality had gone away and been replaced by a little girl, possibly the core child; but when she spoke it was in response to what he had just said, so it was probably still Cody, a Cody for once frightened out of her sardonic pose.

She said, 'Again? You want to do that to me *again*?'

A genuine reaction at last! 'At this point I'm undecided.' Armentrout's heart was beating rapidly, and a smile of triumph kept twitching at his lips. 'I'll make up my mind after our conference later today.'

'Don't you need ... my permission, to do that?'

'One of you signed it,' he said with a shrug. She would probably believe that, even if shown the bogus signature. 'How many of you are there?'

'Oh, sweet Jesus, there's a lot of kids on the bus,' she said wearily, leaning back against the pillows and closing her eyes, 'all singing "Row, Row, Row Your Boat," and crying, with a smashed-up crazy man holding a gun on the driver.'

Armentrout recognized the image – it was from the end of the Clint Eastwood movie *Dirty Harry*, when the battered and hotly pursued serial killer hijacked a schoolbus full of children.

'Where is the ... the "foul fiend Flibbertigibbet" sitting?'

Plumtree's eyes were still closed – her eyelids were as wrinkled and pale as paper wrappers bluntly accordioned off drinking straws – but she managed to put derisive impatience into the shake of her head. 'He isn't *sitting*,' she said.

Then she was snoring through her open mouth. Armentrout reached out and switched off the lamp, then got up and opened the door to the hallway.

His belly felt hollow with anticipation as he pulled the door closed behind him – We'll surely get some tasty therapy done, he told himself smugly, in our therapy session at three.

An hour after lunch Cochran stood in the fenced-off picnic yard, smoking his third-to-last Marlboro, which the charge nurse had lit for him with her closely guarded Bic lighter when she had let the patients out here for the hourly, smoke break. The afternoon sunlight shone brightly on the expanse of asphalt and the distant palm trees outside the iron-bar fence, and Cochran was squinting between the bars at two men in the parking lot who were using jumper cables to try to start a car, and he was envying them their trivial problems.

Long John Beach was leaning on the fence a couple of yards to Cochran's right, gingerly scratching the corner of one swollen eye under the silvery nose brace. Cochran remembered the old man *eating* nine cigarettes last night, and he tried to work up some resentment over it; and then he tried to be grateful that the one-armed lunatic seemed to have no memory of, nor even any interest in, how his nose had been broken; but these were just frail and momentary distractions.

Cochran threw the cigarette down and stepped on it. 'Nina,' he said, loud enough for Long John Beach to hear but speaking out toward the parking lot, 'can you hear me?'

The old man had jumped, and was now craning his neck around to peer across the sunny lot at the men huddled under the shade of the car hood. 'You'll have to shout,' he said. 'Hey, was I snoring real bad last night? I got coughing when I woke up, thought I'd cough my whole spirit out on the floor like a big snake.'

Cochran closed his eyes. 'I was talking to my wife,' he told the old man. 'She's dead. Can you ... hear her?' After a moment he looked over at him. 'Oh—' Long John Beach shrugged expansively. 'Maybe.'

Cochran made himself concentrate on her bitter voice as he had heard it last night.

'Nina,' he answered her now, as awkwardly as a long-lapsed Catholic in the confessional; he was light-headed and sweating, and he had to look out through the fence again in order to speak. 'Whatever happened, whatever – I love you, and I miss you terribly. *Look*, goddammit, I've lost my *mind* over it! And – Jesus, I'm sorry. Of course you were right about the Pace Chardonnays—' He was talking rapidly now, shaking his head. '—they are too loud and insistent, and they do dominate a meal. Show-off wines, made to win at blind tastings, you're right. I'm sorry I called your family's wines flinty and thin. Please tell me that it wasn't that silly argument, at the New Year's Eve thing, that – but if I am to blame—'

He paused; then glanced sideways at his attentive companion. Apparently aware that some response was expected of him, Long John Beach shuffled his feet and blinked his blackened eyes. 'Well ... I was never much of a wine man,' the old man said apologetically. 'I just ate smokes.'

Cochran was clinging to a description of lunatics a friend had once quoted to him – *One day nothing new came into their heads* – because lately he himself seemed to be able to count on at least several appalling revelations every day.

'"Think not the King did banish thee,"' he said unsteadily, quoting the lines he'd skipped last night, '"but thou the King."'

Long John Beach opened his mouth, and the voice that came out was not his own, but neither was it Nina's; and it was so strained that Cochran couldn't guess its gender. '"The bay trees in our country are all withered, and meteors fright the fixed stars of heaven,"' the voice said, clearly quoting something. '"These signs forerun the death or fall of kings."'

'Who are you?' Cochran whispered.

'"I am bastard begot,"' the eerie voice droned on, perhaps in answer, '"bastard instructed, bastard in mind, bastard in *valor*, in everything illegitimate."'

Cochran was dizzy, and all at once but with no perceptible shift the sun-light seemed brassy amber, and the air was clotted and hard to push through his throat. 'Where is my wife?' he rasped.

'"Her bed is India; there she lies, a pearl."'

'Wh – *India*? Are you – talking to me? Please, what do you mean—' He stopped, for he realized that he was looking *up* at Long John Beach, and the base of his spine stung. He had abruptly sat down on the pavement beside one of the picnic tables.

There had been a startled shout from out in the parking lot, and the power lines were swinging gently far overhead. When Cochran peered out at the men, he saw that the car hood had fallen onto one of them; the man was rubbing his head now and cussing at his companion, who was laughing.

'Whoa!' said Long John Beach, also laughing. 'Did you feel that one? Or are you just making yourself at home?'

Cochran understood that there had been an earthquake; and, looking up at the power lines and the leaves on the banana tree in the courtyard, he gathered that it was over. The sunlight was bright again, and the jacaranda-scented breeze was cold in his sweaty hair.

He got to his feet, rubbing the seat of his corduroy pants. 'I suppose you've got nothing more to say,' he told Long John Beach angrily.

The one-armed man shrugged. 'Like I say, I was never a wine man.'

The charge nurse was standing in the lounge doorway, waving. The smoking break was apparently ended.

Cochran turned to trudge back to the building. 'You don't know what you've been missing,' he said.

When the two of them had shuffled up to the door, the nurse said, 'Dr. Armentrout wants to see you.'

'Good,' said Cochran stoically. 'I want to talk to him.'

'Not you,' the nurse said. 'Him.' She nodded toward the one-armed old man.

Long John Beach was nodding. 'For the Plumtree girl,' he said. 'He wants me on the *horn*. On the *blower*.'

'The usual thing,' said the nurse in obvious agreement as she flapped her hands to shoo the two men inside.

Armentrout knew it wasn't Cody that knocked on his office door at three, because when he peeked out through the reinforced glass panel he saw that Plumtree had walked down the hall and was standing comfortably; Cody would have needed the wheelchair he had told the nurses to have ready.

He unlocked the door and pulled it open. 'Come in … Janis?'

'Yes.'

'Sit down,' he told her. 'Over on the couch there, you want to relax.'

The tape recorder inside the Faraday cage in the desk was rolling, and the telephone receiver was lying on the desk, with Long John Beach locked into the conference room on the other side of the clinic, listening in on the extension – Armentrout was psychically protected, masked. Beside the receiver on the desk was the box that contained the twenty Lombardy Zeroth tarot cards, along with a pack of Gudang Garam clove-flavored cigarettes and a box of strawberry flavor-straws, so he was ready to snip off and consume at least a couple of Plumtree's supernumerary personalities – escort some of the girls off the bus, he thought with nervous cheer, kidnap a couple of Snow White's dwarves. *The better to eat you with, my dear.* And if Cody chose to step out and get physical, he had the 250,000-volt stun gun in the pocket of his white coat. A different kind of Edison Medicine.

When she had sat down on the couch – sitting upright, with her knees together, for now – he handed her the glass of water in which he had dissolved three milligrams of benzodiazepine powder. 'Drink this,' he said, smiling.

'It's … what?'

'It's a mild relaxant. I'll bet you've been experiencing some aches and pains in your joints?'

'In my hand, is all.'

'Well … *Cody* will appreciate it, trust me.'

Plumtree took the glass from his hand and stared at the water. 'Give me a minute to think,' she said. 'You've jumbled us all up here.'

Armentrout turned toward the desk, reaching for the telephone. 'Never mind, I'll have them give it to you intravenously.'

The bluff worked. She raised her bruised hand in a *wait* gesture and tilted up the glass with the other, draining it in four gulps; and if the desk lamp had flickered it had only been for an instant.

She now even licked the rim of the glass before leaning forward to set it down on the carpet; and when she straightened up she was sitting forward, looking up at him with her chin almost touching the coat buttons over his belt buckle.

'This is a highly lucrative position,' she said. 'But I guess nobody can see us right here, can they?'

'Well,' said Armentrout judiciously, glancing from the couch to the door window as if considering the question for the first time ever, 'I suppose not.' The drug couldn't possibly be hitting her yet.

She reached out with her right hand and winced, then with her left caught his left hand and pressed it to her forehead. 'Do you think I have a fever, Doctor?'

She was rubbing his palm back and forth over her brow, and her eyes were closed.

His heart was suddenly pounding in his chest. Go with the flow, he told himself with a jerky mental shrug. Without taking his hand away from her face he sat down on the couch beside her on her left. 'There are,' he said breathlessly, 'more reliable ... areas of the anatomy ... upon which to manually judge body temperature. From.'

'Are there?' she said. She pulled his palm down over her nose and lips; and when she had slid it over her chin and onto her throat she breathed, 'Tell me when I'm getting warmer, Doctor.'

He had got his fingers on the top button of her blouse when the desk lamp browned out and she abruptly shoved his hand away.

'Shouldn't there be a nurse present for any physical examination?' she said rapidly.

He exhaled in segments. 'Janis.'

'Yes.'

'Who ... was that?'

'I believe that was Tiffany.'

'Tiffany.' He nodded several times. 'Well, she and I were in the middle of a, a useful dialogue.'

'Valerie has locked Tiffany in her room,'

'In the ... dwarves' cottage, that would be?'

Plumtree smiled at him and tapped the side of her head. 'Exactly.' She had begun shifting uncomfortably on the couch, and smacking her lips, and now she said, 'Could I go take a shower?'

Of course there was no tone of innuendo at all in the remark. 'Your hair's damp right now,' Armentrout told her shortly. 'I bet you took a shower since lunch. You can take one after we're done here.' He slapped his hands onto his knees and stood up, and crossed to the desk. With shaky fingers he fumbled a clove cigarette out of the pack and lit it with one of the ward Bics. He puffed on it, wincing at the syrupy sweet smoke, and then flipped open the purple velvet box.

'Well!' he said, spilling the oversized tarot cards face up onto the desktop, though not looking directly at them. 'I did want to ask you about New Year's Day. You said you killed a man, remember? A king called, somehow, the Flying Nun? A week later Mr. Cochran saw a man who had a bull's head, in Los Angeles. On *Vignes* Street, that means "grapevines" in French; there used to be a winery there, where Union Station is now.' Pawing through the cards and squinting at them through his eyelashes and the scented cigarette smoke, he had managed to find the Sun card, a miniature painting of a cherub floating over a jigsaw-edged cliff and holding up a severed, grimacing red head from which golden rays stuck out like solid poles in every direction.

Now he spun away from the desk and thrust the card face-out toward her. 'Did your king have a bull's head?' He sucked hard on the cigarette.

Plumtree had rocked back on the couch and looked away. And Armentrout coughed as much from disgust as from the acrid smoke in his lungs, for there was no animation, no identity, riding the smoke into his head – he had missed catching the Janis personality, the Plumtree gestalt had parried him.

'Hi, Doctor,' Plumtree said. 'Is this a come-as-you-are party?' She stared at him for a moment, and appeared to replay in her head what had last been said. "Are you talking about the king we killed? Look, I'm being cooperative here. I'll answer all your questions. But – trust me! – if you hit us with the … Edison Medicine again, none of us will tell you anything, ever.' Her shoulders had slumped as she'd been talking. 'No, he didn't have a bull's head. He was barefooted, and had long hair down to his shoulders, and a beard, like you'd expect to see on King Solomon or Charlemagne.' She rubbed her hand over her face in an eerie and apparently unwitting re-enactment of what she had done with Armentrout's hand. 'But I recognized him.'

Armentrout knew his shielded tape recorder would be getting all this, but he tried to concentrate on what the woman was saying. You let that Tiffany girl get you all rattled, he told himself; you don't *want* to eat the *Janis* personality, you idiot, she's the one you want to leave *in* the body, to show how successful the integration therapy was. You're *lucky* you didn't get her, in the clove smoke. 'You … say you recognized him,' he said, nodding like a plaster dog in the back window of a car. 'You'd seen him before?'

'In that game on the houseboat on Lake Mead in 1990. Assumption – it's a kind of poker. He was dressed as a woman for that, and the other players called him the Flying Nun. Our mental bus navigator Flibbertigibbet was trying to win the job Crane was after, the job of being the king, which is why he had us there, playing hands in that terrible game; and he didn't succeed – and he went flat-out crazy on Holy Saturday when Crane won … it, the crown, the throne.'

'Crane?'

'Scott Crane. I didn't know his name until we all got talking together today; I thought Flying Nun was, like, his *name*, it might be a Swedish name, right, like Bra Banning? He was a poker player in those days.'

'I remember another man who wanted to be this king,' said Armentrout thoughtfully, 'a local man called Neal Obstadt. He died in the same explosion that collapsed Long John Beach's lung, two and a half years ago. And Obstadt was looking for this Crane fellow back in '90 – had a big reward offered.' He looked at her and smiled. 'You know, you may *actually have* killed somebody, ten days ago!'

'What good news,' she said hollowly.

'Whatever you did could be the *cause* of everything that's been different since New Year's Day – I thought you were just delusionally *reacting*, the way Mr. Cochran almost certainly is.' He held up one finger as though to count off points of an argument. 'Now, you couldn't have got through all of Crane's defenses, and abducted his very *child*, as you say you did, without powerful sorcerous help; you'd need virtually another *king*, in fact. Who could that be?'

'You got me.'

'I thought you said you'd be honest with me here. We can schedule another ECT *tomorrow*.'

'I – I'm being honest. I was alone. I don't *know* whose *idea* the whole thing was.'

'One of you might have been acting on someone's orders, though, right? On someone's careful instructions.' He was sitting on the desk now drumming his fingers excitedly on the emptied velvet box. 'There was a boy around, a couple of years ago, living in Long Beach somewhere. He was a sort of proto-king, as I recall.' Armentrout wished he had paid more attention to these events at the time – but they had been other people's wars in the magical landscape, and he had been content to just go on eating pieces of his patients' souls on the sidelines. 'His name was something goofy – Boogie-Woogie Bananas, or something like that. *He* could probably kill a king, or bring one back to life, even, if he wanted to. If he's kept to the disciplines. Somebody, your man Crane, probably, brought the gangster Bugsy Siegel back to life, briefly, in 1990. You've seen the Warren Beatty movie, *Bugsy*? Siegel was this particular sort of supernatural king, during the 1940s. Yes, this kid would be fifteen or so now – he could be the one that sent you to kill Crane. Does a name like Boogie-Woogie Bananas ring any bells?'

Plumtree visibly tried to come up with a funny remark, but gave up and just shook her head wearily. 'No.'

'His party had a lawyer! Were you approached by the lawyer? He had a pretentious name, something *Strube*, like J. Submersible Strube the third.'

'*I* never heard of *any* of these people.' Plumtree was pale, and perspiration misted her forehead. 'But *one* of us went to a lot of trouble to kill Crane. Obviously.'

Armentrout pursed his lips. 'Did you say anything to him, to Crane?'

'Sunday before last? Yeah. I wasn't going to hurt his kid, this little boy who couldn't have been five years old yet – God knows how I lured him out of the house, but I had the kid down on his back in this grassy meadow above the beach, with the spear points on his little neck – I suppose Flibbertigibbet *would* have killed the kid! – and when I found myself standing there after losing some time, I looked at the kid's *father* standing there, Crane, and I just said, almost crying to see what a horrible thing I was in the middle of, I said, "There's nothing in this flop for me."' There were tears in Plumtree's eyes right now, and from the angry way she cuffed them away Armentrout was sure that she was Cody at the moment. 'And,' she went on hoarsely, 'Crane said, "Then pass." He must have been scared, but he was talking gently, you know? – not like he was mad. "Let it pass by us," he said.'

'And what did you say?'

'I lost *time* then. When I could see what was going on again, Crane was lying there dead, with the spear in his throat, sticking up through his Solomon beard like a fishing pole, and the kid was gone.' Plumtree blinked around at the desks and the couch and the foliage-screened window. 'Why did Janis leave, just now? You made her peel off, didn't you?' Her expression became blank, and then she was frowning again. 'And she's crying in her bus seat! What did you do to her?'

Armentrout held up the card. 'I just showed her this.'

But Plumtree looked away from it. And when she spoke, it was in such a level voice that Armentrout wondered if she'd shifted again: 'Strip poker, we're playing here?' She looked past the card, focussing into his eyes, and Armentrout saw that one of her pupils was a tiny pinprick, as was usual with her, but the other was dilated in the muted office light. The mismatched eyes, along with the downward-curling androgynous smile she now gave him, made him think of the rock star David Bowie. 'I can be the one that wins here, you know,' she said. 'I can rake in your investment, or at least toss it out into the crowd. Strip poker. How many ... *garments* have *you* got?'

Armentrout was annoyed, and a little intrigued, to realize that he was frightened. 'Are you still Cody?' he asked.

'Largely.' Plumtree struggled up off of the couch to her feet, though the effort made drops of sweat roll down from her hairline, and she stumbled forward and half fell onto the desk. She was certainly still Cody, who had taken the succinylcholine and the electroconvulsive therapy at dawn this morning. Armentrout hastily slid the delicate old tarot cards away from her.

She shook out a Gudang Garam cigarette and lit it.

'This phone is your mask, right?' she gasped through a mouthful of spicy smoke, grabbing the telephone receiver and holding it up. 'Your nest of masks? What's your name?' Armentrout didn't answer, but she read it off the name plaque on his desk. 'Hello?' she said into the telephone. 'Could I speak to Richard Paul Armentrout's mom, please?'

Armentrout was rocked by the counter-attack – she was trying to get a handle on his *own* soul! *That* handle! What personality in her was it that knew how to do this? – but he was confident that Long John Beach was psychotically diffractive enough to deflect this, and many more like it. 'I t-took a vial of your blood,' Armentrout said quickly, 'when you were first brought in here, because I thought I might put you on lithium carbonate, and we have to do a lot of blood testing to get the dosage right for that. I never did give you lithium, but I've still got the vial of your blood.' He was breathing rapidly, almost panting.

'That's a big ace,' Plumtree allowed, 'but you've lost one garment now, and I've only lost my ... oh, call her one silly hat.'

Armentrout looked down at the cards under his hands, and his pelvis went quiveringly cold, followed a moment later by a bubbly tingling in his ribs, for he had no time here to squint cautiously sidelong at the distressing things, and was looking at them squarely. He snatched up the Wheel of Fortune card, the miniature Renaissance-style painting of four men belted to a vertical wheel – *Regno*, Latin for 'I reign,' read the word-ribbon attached to the mouth of the man on top; the ones to either side trailed ribbons that read *Regnabo* and *Regnavi*, 'I shall reign' and 'I reigned' – and he shoved the card into Plumtree's face as he took a cheek-denting drag on his cigarette.

The bulb in the desk lamp popped, and shards of cellophane-thin broken glass clinked faintly on the desk surface; the room was suddenly dimmer, lit now only by the afternoon sunlight streaking in golden beams through the green schefflera leaves outside the window.

Again Armentrout had got nothing but a lungful of astringent clove smoke. And he wasn't facing Cody anymore. Plumtree had twitched away the card-concussed, vulnerable personality before he could draw it into the barrel of his flavored cigarette, had swept the stunned Cody back to one of the metaphorical bus seats or dwarf-cottage bunks, and rotated a fresh one onstage.

'Hello?' said Plumtree into the telephone again. 'I'm calling on behalf of Richard Paul Armentrout – he says he owes somebody there a tre-men-dous apology.' The coal on her cigarette glowed in the dimness like the bad red light that draws loose souls in the underworld in the Tibetan *Bardo Thodol*.

Armentrout dropped the card and fumbled in his coat pocket for the stun gun. I think I've got to put an end to this, he thought; punch her right out of this fight with 250,000 volts and try again, tomorrow, after another ECT session in which I'll give her a full 500 joules of intracranial juice. If she really can summon, from across the hundreds of miles of mountain and desert wilderness, my m – or *any* of my potent old guilt ghosts, and lead them all the way in past Long John Beach's masks *to* me, they could attach, and collapse my distended life line, *kill* me. They're all still out there, God knows – I've never had any desire for the Pagadebiti Zinfandel, *confiteor Dionyso*.

Nah, he thought savagely, that one-armed old man is a better sort of Kevlar armor than to give way under just two shots – and I *will have* this woman. The damp skin of his palm could still feel her chin, and the hot slope of her throat. *Tell me when I'm getting warmer, Doctor.*

He snatched up one of the tarot cards at random with one hand and the lighter with the other, and he spun the flint wheel with the card blocking his view of the upspringing flame; the card's illuminated face was toward her, while he saw only the backlit rectangle of the frayed edge. Gaggingly, and fruitlessly, he again sucked at the limp cigarette – sparks were falling off of it onto the desk like tiny shooting stars.

'Let me talk to *your* m-mom,' he wheezed, knowing that multiples generally included, among their menagerie, internalized duplicates of their own abusive parents. Surely Plumtree's distorted version of her mother wouldn't be able to maintain this fight!

Plumtree's body jackknifed forward off the desk and tumbled to the carpet. 'Behold now,' she gasped in a reedy voice, 'I have daughters which have not known man.' Armentrout recognized the sentence – it was from Genesis, when Lot offered the mob his own daughters rather than surrender the angels who had come to his house. 'Name the one you want, Omar,' Plumtree's strained voice went on, clearly not quoting now, 'and I'll throw her to you! Just don't take *me* again!'

Armentrout was confident that he could consume this one, this cowardly, Bible-quoting creature – but this was only Plumtree's approximation of her mother, not a real personality; so he said, 'Give me ... Tiffany.'

'Tiffany,' said the woman on the floor.

And when Plumtree got back up on her feet and leaned on the desk with one hand while she pushed her tangled blond hair back from her sweaty forehead with the other, she was smiling at him. 'Doctor!' she said. 'What bloody hands you have!'

Armentrout glanced down – he had cut his hand on a piece of the broken light bulb in grabbing for the lighter, and blood had run down his wrist and blotted into his white cuff.

'With you, Miss Plumtree,' he panted, managing to smile, 'strip poker is something more like flag football.' I can have sex with her now, he thought excitedly. Janis snatched Tiffany away from me before, but Janis is off crying in her dwarf bunk now; and I routed Cody too, and whoever that third one was; and the mother personality has outright *given* Tiffany to me!

'Strip poker?' she exclaimed. 'Ooh—' She began unbuttoning her blouse. 'I'll raise you!'

The clove cigarette was coming to pieces in Armentrout's mouth, and he pulled it off his lip and tossed it into the ashtray and spat out shreds of bitterly perfumy tobacco. He wouldn't be able to consume any of her personalities this session, it looked like, but he could at least relieve the aching terror-pressure in his groin.

'Sweeten the pot,' he agreed, fumbling under his chin to unknot his necktie.

The close air of the office smelled of clove smoke and overheated flesh, and the skin of his hands and face tingled like the surface of a fully charged capacitor. This psychic battle had left him swollen with excitement, and he knew that the consummation of their contest wouldn't last long.

She reached out and tugged his cut hand away from his collar, and again she pulled his palm down across her wet forehead and nose and lips – her eyes were closed, so he couldn't see whether her pupils were matched in size or not—

And then she sucked his cut finger into her mouth and *bit* it, and in the same instant with her injured hand she grabbed the bulging crotch of his pants and *squeezed.*

Armentrout exhaled sharply, and the heel of one of his shoes knocked three times fast against the side of the desk as his free hand clenched into a fist.

'Gotcha, doctor,' said a man's voice flatly from Plumtree's mouth. 'I got the taste of your blood now, and the smell of your jizz. In voodoo terms, that constitutes having your ID package.'

Plumtree had stepped lithely away from the desk, and now stared down at Armentrout with evident amused disgust as she wiped her hands on the flanks of her jeans.

When Armentrout could speak without gasping he said, 'I suppose you're ... the foul fiend Flibbertigibbet, is that right?'

Plumtree frowned. 'That's what I've told the girls to call me. You were just talking to their mom, weren't you? Playing "Follow the Queen."'

'Your name's Omar,' Armentrout said. 'What's your last name?' He was still sitting on the desk, but he straightened his white coat and frowned professionally. 'I can compel you to tell me,' he added. 'With ECT and scopolamine, just for example.'

'I reckon you could. But I ain't scared of a little white-haired fag like you anyway. My name's Omar Salvoy.' Plumtree's pupils were both wide now. She picked up the telephone receiver, then smiled and held it out toward the doctor.

From the earpiece a faint voice could be heard saying, *'Let me up, Richie darling! Pull the plug!'*

With a hoarse whimper, Armentrout grabbed the receiver and slammed it into its cradle, and then he opened the second velvet box – but Plumtree had stepped around the desk and crouched by the chair.

'*You* got a *gun* in the box there, haven't you?' said the Salvoy personality jovially while Plumtree's hand fumbled under the desk. 'Think it through, old son. You kill us and you've got some fierce ghosts on your ass – we got your *number* now, no mask is gonna protect you from us. Call your momma back and ask *her* if I ain't telling you the truth.'

Armentrout's heart was hammering in his chest like a jackhammer in an airplane hangar, and he wondered if this was capture, death. No, he thought as he remembered to breathe. No, she can't have – got *a fix* on me – in that brief moment, with Long John Beach diffracting my hot signal.

After a moment, Armentrout let go of the derringer and closed the box. Had he been planning to shoot Plumtree, or himself?

'And I'll bet this button right *he-ere*,' Plumtree went on, her arm under the desktop, 'is the alarm, right?'

An instant later the close air was shaken by a harsh metallic *braaang* that didn't stop.

Still too shaken to speak, Armentrout stood up from the desk and fished his keys out of his pocket to unlock the door and swing it open. Security guards were already sprinting down the hall toward the office, and he waved his bleeding hand at them and stood aside.

CHAPTER FIVE

No fight could have been half so terrible as this dance.
—Charles Dickens, *A Tale of Two Cities*

'His little boy may have *watched* me kill him,' said Janis Plumtree in a quiet, strained voice.

A waterproof Gumby-and-Pokey tablecloth had been spread on the big table in the TV lounge, and she and Cochran were standing in line, each of them holding a glossy little cardboard bowl and a napkin that was rubber-banded around a plastic spoon.

'*You* didn't kill him,' whispered Cochran earnestly. 'Cody did.' He looked nervously at the patients on either side of them, but the old woman ahead of Plumtree and the morose teenager behind Cochran were just staring ahead, anxiously watching the ice cream being doled out.

Plumtree had been escorted to the Quiet Room again, directly after her conference with Dr. Armentrout this afternoon, and confined there for an hour, and when she had found Cochran afterward she had told him about the morning's costly discovery of her multiple personalities, the 'dwarves in Snow White's cottage.' He had listened with unhappy sympathy, withholding judgment but taking the story as at least a touching apology for her occasional rudenesses, which supposedly had all been the doing of the ill-natured 'Cody personality.' Apparently there was no Cody-the-roommate, really.

The appalling thing, the stark fact that still misted his forehead every time he thought of it, was that she had actually undergone shock therapy this morning; he was clinging to her insistence that it had been scheduled for her even before Long John Beach had been hit, and he was happy to be talking about topics that had nothing to do with the hospital, for he had not yet found a chance to tell Armentrout what had really happened last night.

'Well,' Plumtree said now, 'Cody didn't kill him either, directly. But we all knew we were going to that Leucadia estate to do somebody harm. Old Flibbertigibbet kept saying that we were just going to stab somebody in the leg. But we all knew what he could do, what he probably *would* do, and we all cooperated. We didn't care.' She sighed shakily. 'We do what he wants, ever since we got him to ... *kill* a man in '89.'

Cochran was inclined to doubt that; and he was fairly sure that she hadn't killed anybody on this last New Year's Day, either, for she'd surely be in a prison ward somewhere right now if the police or the doctors had found any reason to take her story seriously.

But *she* clearly believed these things, and was troubled by them – and Armentrout had given her *shock therapy* this morning! – so he said, with unfeigned concern, 'Poor Janis! How did that happen?'

They had got to the front of the line, and a nurse scooped a ball of vanilla ice cream into Plumtree's bowl and tucked a wafer cookie alongside it. Plumtree waited until Cochran had been served too, and then they sidled off to the window-side corner, by unspoken agreement choosing the far end of the room from where Long John Beach sat blinking and licking a spoon. At their backs, beyond the reinforced glass, a half-moon shone through the black silhouettes of the palm trees outside the courtyard.

'We were in a bar in Oakland,' she said quietly when the two of them had sat down on the linoleum by the nursing-station-side wall, 'and Cody got real drunk. I was twenty-two, and Cody was drinking a lot in those days, though I always stayed sober to drive home. And we lost time – or maybe Cody had an actual alcoholic blackout! – and when I could see what was going on again, I was on my back in a van in the alley parking lot, and the boyfriend I was at the bar with was trying to pull my clothes off. Cody had passed out, and he figured he could do what he wanted with an unconscious woman. This was only ... well, it was five-oh-four in the afternoon, wasn't it? Across the bay, you were just about to catch your wife, wife-to-be, when she fell down the winery stairs. Anyway, this guy gave me a black eye but I was able to fight him off because he hadn't expected me to ... *wake up*. I scrambled out of the van, with him still grabbing at me and me not able to run, with my clothes all hiked up and down. I probably could have got away from him then with no trouble, 'cause I was awake and outside and I think he was apologizing as much as anything; but I ... *got so mad* ... at him thinking he could do that to me when I was passed out that way, that I called a real serious *sic 'im!* in my head. You know? Like you would to a pit bull that was real savage but was *yours.* I can see now that all of us, even drunk Cody, helped call it. We hadn't ever been *that mad* before. We knew it was bad, and that it would cost us, but we called anyway. And we woke up Flibbertigibbet.'

Cochran recalled that this was another of her supposed personalities, a male one. Janis had told him that she didn't know much of what had happened at the therapy session with Armentrout today – she'd said she had 'lost a lot of time' after he had showed her some miniature painting that she couldn't bear to look at – but that she was pretty sure Flibbertigibbet had been out. Probably Flibbertigibbet had been the one who had reportedly broken the doctor's desk lamp and bitten his finger, earning Plumtree her most recent stay in the Quiet Room. She had said that she was grateful that Flibbertigibbet hadn't done anything worse.

'And … Flibbertigibbet—' Cochran was embarrassed to pronounce the foolish name. '—killed the guy?'

She shivered. 'He sure did. The big earthquake hit right then, and I suppose the cops thought it was falling bricks that smashed his head that way. It was never in the papers, anything about a guy being murdered there. I ran to my car, and it took me two hours to drive the ten miles home. Nobody at my apartment building, what was left of it, said anything about the blood on me – a lot of people were bloody that day.'

'… I remember.'

The Franciscan shale of San Bruno Mountain hadn't shifted much in that late-afternoon quake, and only a couple of Pace Vineyards' oak casks had fallen and burst, spilling a hundred gallons of the raw new Zinfandel like an arterial hemorrhage across the stone floor of the cellar, which Cochran had eventually had to mop up; but when he and a couple of the maintenance men had immediately driven one of the vineyard pickup trucks down to the 280 Highway, they had found cars spun out and stalled across the lanes, and in the little town of Colma hillsides had toppled onto the graves in the ubiquitous cemeteries, and he remembered stunned men and women standing around on the glass-strewn sidewalks, many of them in blood-spattered clothes and holding bloody cloths to their heads. Paramedic vans had been slow and few, and Cochran had driven several people to the local hospital in the back of the pickup truck before eventually returning to the vineyard. The visitor from France, young Mademoiselle Nina Gestin Leon, had been stranded there, and had stayed for the subdued late dinner in the Pace Vineyards dining room. They had all drunk up innumerable bottles of the '68 late-harvest Zinfandels from Ridge and Mayacamas, he remembered; the night had seemed to call for big wild reds implausibly high in natural alcohol content and so sharp with the tea-leaf taste of tannin that Cochran had thought the winemakers must have left twigs and stems in the fermenting must.

'I had blood and wine on my clothes when I went to bed that night,' he said now.

'Cody's more of a vodka girl,' said Janis. She leaned back against the TV lounge wall and sang, '*You can always tell a* vodka *girl* ...'

'That's the tune of the old Halo Shampoo ads,' Cochran said. 'That's before your time, isn't it? *I* barely remember that.'

'Geber me no zeitgebers,' she said shortly. She looked at the nearest of the other patients – poor old Mr. Regushi a dozen yards away, eating his ice cream with his hands – and then she said quietly, 'We've got to escape out of this place.'

'I think it'd be better to get *released* out of here,' Cochran said hastily. 'And I do think we can do it. I have a lawyer up in San Mateo County—'

'Who couldn't get us out before tomorrow dawn, could he? Dr. Armentrout is going to give me the electroconvulsive therapy again tomorrow – I can tell, I was told not to eat anything after ten tonight. He says he's elected *me*, Janis, to be the dominant personality inside this little head, and he's going to ... *cauterize* Cody away, like you would a wart.'

Cochran opened his mouth, wondering what he should say; finally he just said, 'Do you *like* her?'

'Cody? No. She's a, a *bitch* is the only word for it, sorry. She thinks I'm crazy to be – well, she doesn't like you. And I think her story about being a security guard somewhere at nights is a lie – I think she does *burglaries*.'

'Well ... I hope not. But if you don't like her, why not *let* Armentrout ... do that?' He could feel his face reddening. 'I mean, he *is* a doctor, and you certainly don't need—'

'She's a real person, Scant, as real as me. I don't like her, but I can't just stand by and let *her* get killed too.' Her lips were pressed together and she was frowning. ''Cause it would be the death penalty for her, and that without an indictment or jury or anything. Do you see what I mean?'

Cochran doubted that Cody was any more real than a child's imaginary playmate, much less as real as Janis. But, 'I follow your logic,' he said cautiously. Then, recklessly, he added, 'I'm ashamed of myself for saying just now to let Armentrout do it again. I can't bear thinking that it happened to you even once.'

'I'm sure he's got something planned for you, too,' she told him. 'You and me and Long John Beach – we're not specimens he's going to let go of.'

Cochran still hoped to get some rational planning done here. 'This lawyer of mine—'

'This what? This *lawyer*? You think old Dr. Trousertrout hasn't got lawyers? He'll sneak some meds into your food that'll make you such a five-star skitz you'll be running around naked thinking you're Jesus or somebody, or even easier just show you a few tarot cards to do it.' She glanced around then looked back at him and noticed, and stared at, his T-shirt. 'A Connecticut Pansy? Unbelievable. Unbelievable! Hell, *you* he could probably just show the *instruction* card to.' She flexed her jaw and winced. 'My teeth hurt. I hope I'm not gonna have a nosebleed.'

One of the nurses had brought a portable stereo out and set it on the table and was now trying to get all the patients to sing along to 'Puff the Magic Dragon.' Plumtree was humming something different in counterpoint, and after a moment Cochran recognized it as 'Row, Row, Row Your Boat.' 'Listen,' she said suddenly, '—what we've got to do? – is escape – tonight.'

Cochran was still sure that his lawyer would be able to secure his release, and very possibly Janis's too, with some routine legal maneuver; and the man might even be able to get some kind of stay-of-shock-therapy for her tonight, if Cochran could get him on the phone. He slapped the pockets of his corduroy bell-bottoms and was reassured to feel the angularity of coins.

'I'm going to call this lawyer—' he said, bracing himself to stand up.

Plumtree grabbed his upper-arm with her good hand. 'It won't work, we've got to escape—'

'Janis,' he said irritably, 'we *can't*. Have you seen the doors, the locks? How quick the security guards show up when there's trouble? Unless your Mr. Flibbertigibbet can come up with another earthquake—'

Her hand sprang away from his arm, and she was gaping at him. 'Has he … *called* you?'

The group sing-along was already getting out of hand – Long John Beach was improvising lyrics at the top of his lungs, and the other patients were joining in with gibberish of their own, and the nurse had switched the music off and was now trying to quiet everyone – but Cochran was staring at Plumtree in bewilderment.

'Who?' he said, having to speak more loudly because of the singing and his own alarmed incomprehension. 'Flibbertigibbet? No, you told me about it, how you were in that Oakland bar on October seventeenth—'

'I never did, not that *date*, *none* of us would!' She was shaking. 'Why would we?'

'Wh – Jesus, Janis, because I told you I met my wife that day, she fell down some steps when the earthquake hit, and I caught her. What's the matter—'

'My God, not *this* way!' She blinked, and Cochran saw tears actually squirt from the inner corners of her eyes. Her pupils were tiny, hardly discernible. 'Why did you mention him, you fucking idiot? I can handle locks – in the name of the Father, the Son, the Holy Ghost! Rah rah rah, you Connecticut pansy, I hope you get in his way!'

Cochran wasn't listening to her – he had scrambled to his feet, and now he reached down and pulled Plumtree up too. 'Get ready to run,' he told her. 'I think we're going to have a riot in here.'

Long John Beach and a couple of other patients had grabbed the window side of the table, lifted it, and, still singing raucously, now pushed it right over; the bowls and spoons and ice cream cartons tumbled as the colorful tablecloth flapped and billowed, and then the tabletop hit the floor with an echoing knock.

'*Pirate ships would bloom with vines,*' the one-armed man was singing, '*When* He *roared out his name!*'

'Code Green!' yelled a nurse. 'Hit the alarm!'

Cochran could hear a roaring now, a grinding bass note that seemed to rumble up from the floor, from the very soil under the building's cement slab foundation. He had to take a quick sideways step to keep his balance.

'Aftershock,' he said breathlessly, 'from the one this afternoon.' He glanced at Plumtree, and took hold of her forearm, for her face was white and pinched with evident terror, and he was afraid she would just bolt. 'Stay with me,' he said to her loudly. The fluorescent lights on the ceiling flickered.

'Code Green, code fucking Green!' shouted the nurse, retreating toward the hallway door.

The building was shaking now, and from the nursing station and the conference room echoed the crashes of cabinets and machinery hitting the floors.

'*—the magic flagon,*' sang Long John Beach, whirling the tablecloth like a bullfighter's cape, '*lived by the sea, and frolicked in the Attic mists in a land called Icaree!*'

And all the lights abruptly went out. Glass was breaking inside the building somewhere, beyond the waving and thrashing shapes dimly visible in the reflected moonlight in the room, but Cochran spun toward the reinforced window, yanking the unseeing Plumtree with him.

The window was glittering like the face of the sea, for silvery cracks were spreading across it like rapid frost and shining with the captured radiance of the moon – and a cloud of plaster dust curled and spun at the far corner.

'Get me Cochran and Plumtree!' came Armentrout's panicky call through the shouting, lurching bodies jamming the room. 'Stun guns *and* Ativan!'

Cochran looked back toward the hall doorway. The fat, white-haired doctor was standing just inside the room, waving a flashlight in random circles that momentarily silhouetted clawed hands and tossing heads and vertical siftings of plaster dust; two men Cochran had never seen before were standing closely on either side of the doctor, with their arms around his shoulders – and of the whole chaotic, crashing scene, the one element that chilled Cochran's belly was the sight of those two blank-faced men swivelling their heads back and forth in perfect unison, and flapping their free arms in swings that were awkward and disjointed but as perfectly synchronized as the gestures of a dance team.

Cochran bent down to shout in Plumtree's ear, 'Don't move, stay right where you are – we're getting out of here.' And he let go of her arm and lifted one of the upholstered chairs in both hands.

The floor was still flexing and unstable bur he took two running steps toward the far corner of the window, muscling the chair around him in a wide loop, and then he torqued his body hard, at the expense of keeping any balance at all, and slammed the chair with all his strength into the reinforced glass at that end.

The window *bent*, like splintering plywood, popping out of its frame at that corner.

'*One dark night it happened,*' the voice of Long John Beach roared on somewhere behind him, '*Pakijaper came no more—*'

Cochran's full-tilt follow-through had thrown him headfirst against the buckling sheet of glass, tearing it further out of its frame, and tumbled him to the gritty floor; but he scrambled to his feet and wobbled back to where Plumtree stood dimly visible in the roiling, flashlight-streaked dimness, and he pulled her toward the window. 'Both of us hit the glass with our shoulders,' he gasped, 'and we're out of here. Keep your face turned away from it.'

But a hand gripped Cochran's right hand strongly, and he was jerked around against the solid restraint of the big hard fingers clenched on his knuckles and wrist. He looked back – and whimpered aloud when he saw that there was no one anywhere near him. Then in a flicker of the flashlight beam he saw Long John Beach a dozen feet away, staring at him and hunched forward to extend his amputated stump.

Cochran tugged hard, and the sensation of clutching fingers was gone; Long John Beach recoiled backward into the crowd.

A number of the patients had lifted the table over their heads like a float in a parade, all of them singing now, and Cochran and Plumtree were able to step away from the wall and get a running start toward the bent sheet of glass.

It folded outward with a grating screech when they hit it, and then the two of them had fallen over the sill and were rolling on the cold cement pavement outside. Plumtree had hiked up her legs as she'd hit the glass, and had landed in a controlled tumble, but Cochran's knees had collided with the sill and he had jackknifed forward to smack the pavement with his outstretched hands and the side of his head, and in the moment when his legs flailed free and he was nearly standing on his head he was sure that his spine was about to snap.

But then he had fallen over and Plumtree had dragged him to his feet, and he was able to limp dizzily forward across the dark courtyard, pulling her after him; the exterior spotlights had gone out too, and Plumtree kept whispering that she couldn't see at all, but the dim shine of the half-moon was bright enough for Cochran to avoid the wooden picnic tables as he led her to the parking-lot fence, where he and Long John Beach had stood talking six hours ago.

'*Grape leaves jell like rain …*' came a wail through the broken window behind them.

The winter night air was as harsh as menthol cigarette smoke in Cochran's nose, but it cleared his head enough so that he could lift one of the picnic-table benches and prop it firmly against the spike-topped iron fence; and though he saw two of the security guards furiously pedalling their bicycles across the lot from the main hospital building, they were clearly heading for the clinic entrance, and no one shouted or shined a light at Cochran as he boosted Plumtree up the steeply slanted boards of the bench seat.

The fingers of her good hand caught the top edge, and with a fast scuffling she was at the top, and leaping; and Cochran was already scrambling up the bench when her sneakers slapped the pavement. Then he had jumped too, and though he almost sat down when he landed, he was ready to run when he straightened up.

But Plumtree caught his shoulder. 'Don't be a person in a hurry,' she said breathlessly. She linked her arm through his, wincing as her swollen knuckles bumped his elbow. 'It's lucky we're a couple. Just be a guy out for a stroll by the madhouse with his girlfriend, right?'

'Right.' With his free hand he reached back through the bars of the fence and pushed the bench away; the clatter of it hitting the cement pavement in the yard was lost in the crashing cacophony shaking out through the sprung window. 'What's my girlfriend's name?' he asked as they began walking – a little hurriedly, in spite of her advice – along the tree-shadowed fence toward the lane that led out to Rosecrans Boulevard.

'I'm Janis again. Cody came back just now like somebody fired out of a cannon, so don't tell me what happened – okay? – or you'll just have Valerie on your hands. It's enough to know that you agreed about escaping, and that we've done it.' She gave him a frightened smile. 'Let's make like a tree, and leave.'

He nodded, and though his breathing was slowing down, his heart was still knocking in his chest. 'Put an egg in your shoe and beat it,' he responded absently. He could see the corner of the fence ahead, and it was all he could do not to walk even faster. 'I did agree, in the end.'

He was remembering a pair of shoes Nina had bought for him, actually leather hiking boots. They were only about an eighth of an inch bigger than his ordinary shoes at any point, but he had constantly found himself catching the sides of them against furniture, and tripping on the tread edges when he'd go upstairs, and generally kicking things he hadn't realized were in his way; and it had occurred to him that in his ordinary old shoes, as he had routinely walked through each day, he must have been only narrowly missing collisions and entanglements with every thoughtless step.

What size shoe am I wearing now? he thought giddily. I'm not walking any differently, but lately I've collided with a man who can talk with my dead wife's voice, and who can reach out and grab you across a room with a hand he hasn't got; and I've run afoul of a doctor who wants to keep me locked up in a crazy ward and give electro-shock treatments to a woman I … am growing very fond of; and *she* claims to actually be several people, one of whom doesn't like me and another of whom is reportedly a man, who can—

He took a shuddering breath and clashed her arm tighter, for he was afraid he might fling it away and just run from her.

—who apparently can, he went on, finishing the thought, call up actual earthquakes at will.

Maybe I'm not wearing any shoes at all now, he thought, in that manner of speaking. It's mostly barefoot people that break their toes.

'You've … seen this stuff too, right?' he said softly. 'Ghosts? And—' She didn't want to hear about the earthquake right now. '—supernatural stuff?' He had spoken haltingly, embarrassed to be talking about the very coin of madness; but he needed to know that he really did have a companion in this scary new world.

'Don't make me lose time here, Scant.'

'Sorry.' Her abrupt reply had brought heat to his face, and he tried to keep any tone of hurt out of his voice. 'Never mind.' Don't be *disturbing* her, he told himself bitterly, with talk of something distasteful that might be *important* to you, like your mere *sanity*.

'I'm sorry, Scant,' she said instantly, hugging his arm and leaning her head on his shoulder, 'I was afraid you'd say something more – something specific! – that would drive me away from you here. You and I can't have misunderstandings between us! Yes – I've seen this stuff too, undeniably. Sometimes it's hard for me to tell, because even normal things … *change*, if I take my eyes off them. I never cross the street on the green light, because an hour – a week! – might have gone by between the moment I saw the WALK sign flash and the moment I step off the curb; I always cross with people, almost hanging on to their coats. When I was twelve, my mother took me to her sister's funeral, and halfway through the ceremony I found out that it was her *mother's* funeral, and I was *fourteen*! I think if she hadn't ever brought me to another funeral at that same cemetery, so I could recognize it, I wouldn't have found my way back at all, ever, to this day!'

She laughed helplessly. 'But I've seen ghosts, too, sure. I *attract* them, they come to me crying, often as not, telling me they're lost and want help finding their mothers, these transparent little … *cellophane bags*, like cigarette-pack wrappers! Or they're … feeling romantic, and whisper nasty things in my ear, as if they could *do* anything about it. But they can't grab me, I always just lose time. And Cody and Valerie have different birthdates from me, so each of us that comes up is a fresh picture, and the ghosts slide off, can't get a grip.' He felt her shudder through his arm. 'I think they'd hurt me, I think they'd *kill* me, if they *could* get a grip.'

Cochran kissed the top of her head. 'Why are they attracted to you?'

'Because I have "wide unclasped the table of my thoughts." Don't ask me about that,' she added hastily, 'or you'll be kissing Valerie's head.' She smacked her lips. 'I wish I'd brought my mouthwash.'

They had rounded the fence corner now, and they were walking on a sidewalk under bright streetlights. Cars were driving by, and he could see the traffic signal for Rosecrans Boulevard only a hundred yards ahead of them.

'I think I could call my lawyer now,' he said, 'when we find a Denny's, somewhere we can sit down and they have a pay phone. I've got change for the call, and I think I can slant the story a little to make sure he'll wire us money and then legally, get us out of Armentrout's control.'

'A Denny's would be nice,' Plumtree agreed, 'I've got a twenty in my shoe, and Ra only knows when I last ate. But we don't need your lawyer – Cody can get us money and a place to stay, and we've got … things to do, locally, people to see.'

Cochran could imagine nothing now but getting back to his house in South Daly City up in San Mateo County as quickly as possible. 'People?' he said doubtfully. 'What, family?'

'No. I'll tell you when we've got drinks in front of us. Don't most Denny's serve liquor?'

'I don't know,' Cochran said, suddenly very happy with the idea of a shot of lukewarm Wild Turkey and an icy Coors for a chaser. 'But most bars sell food.'

CHAPTER SIX

'Tell me how long it takes to prepare the earthquake?'

'A long time, I suppose.'

'But when it is ready, it takes place, and grinds to pieces everything before it. In the meantime, it is always preparing, though it is not seen or heard. That is your consolation. Keep it.'

—Charles Dickens, *A Tale of Two Cities*

'Do you know about "making amends"?' Plumtree asked as she led him across a dark parking lot in the direction of the white-glowing facade of a fast-food icecream place called the Frost Giant. Cochran thought she sounded a little uneasy.

'I suppose,' he said, trudging along beside her and wondering when they would get their drinks and talk. The night air was chilly, and he wished he'd been wearing a jacket when they had escaped from the mental hospital, and he wanted to get someone in San Mateo County to wire him some money tonight, or at least use a credit-card number to get him a motel room. That should be feasible somehow. 'Restitution,' he said. 'Taking the blame, if you deserve it; paying back people you've cheated, and admitting you were the villain, and apologizing,' He smiled. 'Why, did that guy in the 7-Eleven give you too much change?' They hadn't bought anything at the convenience store three blocks back, but Plumtree had cajoled the clerk into giving her seventeen one-dollar bills and a double fistful of assorted coins in exchange for the crumpled twenty-dollar-bill that had been in her shoe. When they had got outside, she had made Cochran give her too four quarters from his pants pocket.

'No. The thing is, making amends is ... good for your soul, right?'

He shrugged. 'Sure.'

'But before you can *do* it, you've got to cheat somebody.'

'I—' He laughed as he exhaled. 'I guess. If you want the sacrament of Confession, you do have to have some sins.'

'Whatever.' She gave him a blank, tired look in the white glow. 'Don't speak, here, okay? Do you know any foreign languages, besides plain old Mexican?'

'*Qui, mademoiselle je parl Français, un peu.*'

'That's French, right? Cool, you be a Frenchman. They'd figure you don't know what your stupid shirt says.'

She pulled open the glass door of the Frost Giant, and a puff of warm, vanilla-scented air ruffled Cochran's hair.

There was only one customer in the brightly lit restaurant, a woman in a Raiders sweatshirt in a booth by the far window. Plumtree scurried to the counter, and she was laughing with evident embarrassment as she dumped her pile of bills and change onto the white formica.

'Could you do me a *big* favor?' she asked the teenage boy who was the cashier. 'My friend paid me back twenty dollars he owed me, but he doesn't understand about American money – I can't fit all this in my pockets! Could you *possibly* give me one twenty-dollar bill for all this?'

'I – don't think so, lady.' The young cashier smiled nervously. 'Why don't you get rid of some of it by buying some ice cream?'

A muted crack sounded from the far booth, and the woman in the sweatshirt said, 'Shit. You got any spoons that are any damn good?'

Plumtree gave the young man a sympathetic smile as he fetched another white plastic spoon from under the counter and walked around to give it to the woman.

'I understand,' Plumtree said when he was back behind the counter, 'and we can come back tomorrow and buy some. But my friend here doesn't speak any English at all, and he thinks all Americans are stupid – especially me. I told him I could get this money changed into one bill, and if you don't do it, he'll call me a, a *haricot vert* again. That means damn fool. You can tell he's thinking it already, look at him.' She waved at Cochran. '*Momentito,* Pierre!'

'*Ce n'etait pas ma faute,*' said Cochran awkwardly. '*Cet imbecile m'est rentre dedans.*' It was a bit he remembered from the Berlitz book: *It wasn't my fault, this imbecile crashed into me.*

The name badge on the cashier's shirt read KAREN, and Cochran, perceiving him as a fellow-victim of ludicrous men's wear, sympathetically wondered when the boy would notice that he had put on the wrong badge. 'Well,' said the young man, 'I guess it'd be okay. We could use the ones, I guess.'

'Oh, thanks so much,' said Plumtree, helpfully spreading the bills out on the counter for him to count.

The young cashier opened the register drawer and handed her a twenty-dollar bill, his eyes on the ones and the change.

'What are you giving me this for?' asked Plumtree instantly.

The bill in her outstretched hand was a one-dollar bill.

The young man stared at it in evident confusion. 'Is that what I just gave you?'

'Yeah. I wanted a *twenty.* You must have had a one in your twenty drawer.'

'I … don't think that's what I just gave you.'

'You're gonna take all my money and just give me a dollar?' wailed Plumtree in unhappy protest.

The woman in the Raiders sweatshirt broke her spoon again. 'Hey, shithead!' she yelled. 'You'd think with all the money you make cheatin' folks, you could afford decent spoons!'

After a tense pause, the young man took back the dollar and pulled a twenty out of the drawer. He stared at it hard for a moment before looking up.

'I really hope,' he said quietly as he handed the twenty to her, 'we're not twenty short at cashout. You seemed nice.'

Cochran's teeth were clenched, and he could feel his face heating up. This was abominable. He knew he should make Plumtree give back the other twenty-dollar bill, the one she had palmed, but all he could think of was getting *out* of this place. 'Uhh,' he said, feeling a drop of sweat run down his ribs. '*Merde.*'

'I'll come back tomorrow and make sure,' said Plumtree, pocketing the fresh twenty and hurrying away from the counter. She took Cochran's elbow and turned him toward the door. 'Thanks again!'

Cochran was dully amazed that she could maintain her cheery tone. When they were outside again, he tried to speak, but she shook his arm, and so he just pressed his lips together. His foolish shirt was clammy with sweat now, and he was shivering in the chilly breeze.

At last she spoke, when they had scuffled away out of the radiance of the Frost Giant. 'Now we've got a clear twenty for food and drink.' Her breathing was labored, and she was sagging against him, as if the conversation in the ice-cream place had exhausted her.

'The kid's right,' he said tightly. 'You *did* seem nice. He'll probably lose his job.'

'He might lose his job,' she said flatly, apparently agreeing with him. 'I'll understand – I'll respect it! – if you decide you don't want anything to eat, anything that's bought with this money.' She frowned at him. 'Is that what you're saying?'

'No. Now that it's done—'

'I could go back.' She straightened and stepped away from Cochran, though she still seemed sick and wobbly on her feet. 'Do you want me to give it back to him?'

Cochran shivered; and as he shoved his cold hands into his pants pockets he wondered how energetically the police might be looking for Plumtree and himself, and how easy or difficult it might actually be to get money 'wired' to him from the Bay Area at this hour. Where would he go to pick it up? Wouldn't he need a driver's license or something? And he was very hungry, and he desperately wanted the warm relaxation and comfortable perspective that a couple of shots of bourbon would bestow. 'Well – no. I mean, now that it *is* done—'

'Right;' she interrupted dryly. 'You're just like Janis.'

'I hear you're not really a security guard,' he said – absently, for he had noticed a red neon sign ahead of them, on the same side of Rosecrans, that read MOUNT SABU – COCKTAILS. 'I hear what you really do is burglaries.'

'She just tells you every damn thing, doesn't she?'

A mirror studded disco ball was turning under the ceiling over the dance floor in Mount Sabu, but none of the people in the bar were dancing – possibly because the stone dance floor was strewn with sand as if for a soft-shoe exhibition. Even over here on this side of the long room, by the street door, Cochran could feel grit under his shoe soles as he led Plumtree to an empty booth under a lamp in the corner. The warm air smelled of candle wax and mutton.

'Hi, Scant,' Plumtree said when they had sat down. 'Are we going to have a drink? What—' She paused, staring at his T-shirt. 'Stand up for a minute, will you?'

He slid back out of the booth and stood up, and she started laughing.

'A Connecticut pansy in ... King Arthur's *shorts!*' she gasped. 'I love it! By Marky "Choo-Choo" Twain, I suppose.'

Cochran managed a sour grin as he sat back down, but her obviously spontaneous reaction to the shirt had shaken him. He had to ask: 'Do you, uh, happen to feel like dancing?'

'Sure!' she said brightly. 'Is that why we came in here?'

'No.' He sighed. 'No, and I don't want to dance, actually. A shot of Wild Turkey, please, and a Coors chaser,' he said to the dark-haired woman who had walked up to the booth with a tray. 'And ... ?' he added, turning to Plumtree.

'A Manhattan, please,' Plumtree said.

'And a couple of menus,' put in Cochran.

The waitress nodded and clunked down a fresh ashtray with some slogan printed around the edge of it before striding back toward the bar, her long skirt swishing over the sandy floor. Two men in rumpled business suits were playing bar dice for the price of drinks, banging the leather cup on the wet, polished wood.

'What does Cody drink,' asked Cochran, 'besides vodka?'

'Budweiser.' She smiled at him. 'This is fun! She's letting me sit and talk to you. Usually I just get to go to the bathroom – over and over again, throwing up there sometimes, while Cody gets to sit and talk to the man, and she never has to get up and leave him at all.'

'Well, she doesn't like me, you said. And,' he added, still shaken by the realization, 'she seemed exhausted, a few moments ago. *She* wouldn't have wanted to dance.'

Plumtree nodded. 'That treatment this morning hit her hard. She might appreciate a drink or two herself, before we leave here.'

Cochran thought of mentioning how they would be paying for the drinks and eventual food, but decided he didn't want to break Janis's cheerful mood.

A frail electronic beeping started up, and he remembered that her watch had made a noise like that when she had been talking the 7-Eleven clerk into giving her all the ones and change for her original twenty-dollar bill. 'What do you have that set for?' he asked.

'Oh, this silly thing. You have a watch, don't you? I think I'll just leave this one here. One of the doctors gave it to me – it's supposed to keep me in *now*, and not in the past ... or future, I suppose.' She had unstrapped the watch as she'd been speaking, and now held it up by one end, as if it were a dead mouse. 'It's my last link with that stupid hospital. If I leave it behind, I'll bet

I can leave all of their depressive-obsessive doo-dah with it. They *want* you to be sick, in hospitals. I bet I won't even have my old nightmare as much, away from that place.'

In spite of himself, Cochran said, 'About the sun falling out of the sky?'

'Right *onto* me, yeah.' She shook her head sharply. 'Filling up the sky and then punching me flat onto the sidewalk. I was in the hospital when I was two, and I guess there was no window in my room, 'cause I somehow got the idea that the sun had died. My *father* died right around that time, and I was too young to grasp what exactly had happened.' She frowned at her fingernails. 'I still miss him – a lot – even though I was only two when he died.'

The waitress had returned, and she set their drinks down on the table-cloth and then handed Cochran and Plumtree each a leather-bound menu. 'Could I borrow a pen?' Cochran asked her. When he raised his hand and made doodling motions in the air the woman smiled and handed him a Bic from her tray. Cochran just nodded his thanks as the woman turned away and strode back toward the bar.

'Prassopita,' said Plumtree, reading from the menu. 'Domatosoupa. This is a Greek restaurant.' She took a sip of her drink and audibly swished it around in her mouth before swallowing.

'Oh.' Cochran thought of Long John Beach singing *frolicked in the Attic mists ...*, and then remembered that Janis hadn't experienced that part of the evening. 'I guess that's all right.' He opened his own menu and stared at the unfamiliar names as he took a sip of the warmly vaporous bourbon. Finally he looked squarely at her. 'I believe you, by the way,' he began.

'We're not talking about the menu now, are we?'

'That's right, we're not. I mean I believe you about you being a genuine multiple personality.' He took several long gulps of the cold beer. '*Whew!* You obviously hadn't noticed my dumb shirt before a minute ago, and Cody saw it back at the hospital; and she didn't get that it was a joke about a Mark Twain book title.'

'You should believe it, it's true. I don't think Cody's much of a reader. I am – and I love books about King Arthur, though I've never been able to read *One Flew Over the Cuckoo's Nest*.' She rolled her eyes. 'You're taking a whole crowd of girls out to dinner!'

Cochran decided not to ask what she thought *One Flew Over the Cuckoo's Nest* had to do with King Arthur. A slip of paper with daily specials on it was clipped to the inside of the menu, and he tugged it free and poised the pen over the blank back side of it. 'Who all are you? Just so I'll ... know what names to write on the thank-you card.'

'Oh, Cody's paying for dinner, eh? I don't want to hear about it. Well, you know me and her ... and there's Tiffany ...' She paused while Cochran wrote it down. 'And Valerie ...' she added.

He wrote it down the way it was generally spelled, but she leaned over and tapped the paper with her finger. 'It's spelled with an *O* – Valorie.'

Cochran smiled at the idiosyncrasy. 'Like *calorie*. If you had an overeater in there, you could call her Calorie, and they could be twins.'

Plumtree bared her teeth in a cheerless grin. 'Valorie isn't a twin of anybody.' She stared at the names on the paper. 'Then there's *him*. Just write "him," okay? I don't like his name being out, even on paper.'

As he wrote the three letters, it occurred to Cochran that this Flibbertigibbet character was probably as real as Cody and Janis ... and might very well actually have killed a man in Oakland, a little more than five years ago.

And then he wondered about the king that Plumtree claimed to have killed ten days ago.

'That's a birthmark,' Plumtree said, 'not a tattoo – right?'

Cochran put down the pen and flexed his right hand, and the ivy-leaf-shaped dark patch below his knuckles rippled. 'Neither one. It's ... like a powder-burn, or a scar. Rust under the skin, I suppose, or even stump-bark dust. I was seven years old, and I got my hand between a big set of pruning shears and a stump-face. I guess I thought it was an actual, live face, and I tried to block this field worker from cutting the old man's head off.'

Plumtree was frowning over the rim of her glass. 'What?' she said when she'd swallowed and put it down

Cochran smiled. 'Sorry – but you obviously didn't grow up in the wine country. It's as old as "Ladybug, ladybug, fly away home," or the Man in the. Moon. *Le Visage dans la Vigne*, Froissart called it. The Face in the Vine Stump. See, in the winter, when it's time to prune back the grape vines, sometimes the lumpy budwells in the bowl of an old head-trained vine look like an old man's face – forehead, cheekbones, nose, chin. People used to be real superstitious about it, like in France in the Middle Ages – they'd uproot the one that looked most like a real face, and take it out on a mountaintop somewhere and burn it. In the middle of winter, so spring would come. The old man had to die.' Throw out the suicide king, he thought.

'As long as you do not die and live again, you are a stranger to the dark earth,' Plumtree said, obviously quoting something. 'Don't ask me what that's from, I don't even know which of us read it. Have you ever thought of having the mark removed? Doctors could do that now, I bet.'

'No,' said Cochran, making a fist of the hand to show the mark more clearly, 'I'm kind of proud of it, actually – it's my winemaker's merit badge, an honorable battle scar.'

Plumtree smiled and shook her head. 'I think I'll get this Ami Kapama thing, if I can chew it.'

Cochran looked at the menu. 'Lamb cooked with sugar and cinnamon? Yuck. I guess I'll go with the Moskhari Psito. At least that's beef, according to this. I wish they had plain old cheeseburgers.'

'Well, yeah. We don't have all night. Are you still set on calling *your* lawyer? What is it you'd be wanting him to *do*?'

The waitress came back then, and they placed their orders; Cochran ordered another bourbon and beer chaser, too, and Plumtree ordered another Manhattan.

'I'd want the lawyer,' he said when the woman had gone sweeping away, 'to ... *wire me some money* ... so that I could get back home. And I' – he looked straight into her tiny-pupilled eyes – 'I hope you'd be willing to come with me, Janis. The lawyer would be able to work for you better if you were up there, and you'd be that much farther away from Armentrout.'

Plumtree sang, *'I'll take you home again, Kathleen ...'* and then sighed. 'What's the hurry? About you getting back home?'

Cochran blinked at her. 'Isn't that song about a girl who's going to die?'

'I forget. So what is the hurry?'

Cochran spread his hands. 'Oh ... a paycheck.'

'What's the work, in January, in a vineyard?'

He barked out two syllables of a laugh, and flexed his right hand again. 'Well – pruning. It's winter. Get our guys to cut each vine back to two canes, with two buds per cane, and save what they call a goat-spur, a water-sprout replacement spur, closer to the stump for fruit a year or two from now – and then drive around to the vineyards we buy off-premises grapes from, and see how they're pruning their vines. If they're leaving three or four canes, and a lot of buds for a water-fat cash crop, I'll make a note not to buy from them come harvest.' He looked at the gray ivy-leaf mark on the back of his otherwise unscarred hand, and he remembered the vivid shock-hallucination that had accompanied the childhood injury, and it occurred to him that he didn't want to be there for the pruning – not this year. *Grape leaves fell like rain ...* 'Why, what's on your agenda?'

Plumtree eyed her cola-colored drink as the electric light over their heads flickered, and then she waved at the waitress. 'Could I get a Budweiser here?' she called. 'Two Budweisers, that is?'

Cochran heard no reply, just the continuing thump and rattle of the bar dice.

After a few moments he spoke. 'Janis mentioned that you might want a couple of drinks,' he said, levelly enough. He was annoyed to see that his hand trembled as he lifted his beer glass. He made himself look squarely at her, and the skin of his forearms tingled as he realized that he could *see* the difference, now that he knew to look for it; the mouth was wider now, the eyes narrower.

'My agenda,' said Cody. 'I've got a lawyer of my own to look up. His name is Strube. He'll be able to lead me to a boy who's about fifteen now, a boy-who-would-be-king, apparently, named something like Boogie-Woogie Bananas.'

Cochran raised his eyebrows as he swallowed a mouthful of beer and put his glass down. 'Uhh ... ?'

'This boy apparently knows how to restore a dead king to life. What's that you're drinking?'

'Wild Turkey and Coors.'

'Coors. Like screwing in a canoe. Oh well.' She reached across the table-cloth and lifted his glass and drained it in one long swallow. 'And two more *Coorses* too,' she called without looking away from Cochran.

'You can afford it,' he said.

'*Fuckyou!*' yelled a woman in the booth by the door; and for a second Cochran was so sure that she had been yelling at him that his face went cold. But now a man in the same booth was protesting in shrill, injured tones, and when Cochran looked over his shoulder he saw the blond woman who had shouted shaking her head and crying.

''Nuff said,' remarked Plumtree.

If Long John Beach's crazy lyrics for 'Puff the Magic Dragon' had not still been jangling in his head, if Beach had not clasped Cochran's hand tonight with a hand that he didn't have, if the bang and rattle of the dice-players at the bar hadn't been emphasizing the fact that nobody in this bar had seemed to speak above whispers until the woman had shouted, Cochran would never have thought of what he said next; and if he hadn't downed the bourbon on a nearly empty stomach he would not have spoken it aloud; but,

'You *throw* it, don't you?' he said wonderingly to Plumtree. 'Anger. Like, it can't be created or destroyed, but it can be *shifted*.' Over the aromas of lamb and mint and liquor, the humid air was sharp with the smell of wilted., chopped vegetation, like a macheted clearing in a jungle. 'Is that part of your *dissociative* disorder, that you can stay calm by actually throwing your anger off onto somebody nearby? The lady who kept breaking her spoon in the ice-cream place, and cussing, when the kid wouldn't give you a twenty ... and Mr. Regushi jumping up to strangle Muir yesterday, when Armentrout pissed you off.' He was dizzy, and wished the waitress would hurry up with the beer.

'*What gives you the right—*' choked the blond woman by the door.

Cochran exhaled, and gave Plumtree a frail, apologetic smile. 'Nothing, I guess,' he said.

'You still got any quarters?' asked Plumtree calmly.

Cochran squeezed his thigh under the table. 'At least one.'

'Let's go make a call.'

They stood up out of the booth and crossed the sandy floor to the pay telephone by the rest rooms in the far corner, and after Plumtree had hoisted the white-pages telephone book up from a shelf under the phone and flipped through the thin leaves of it, she said, 'No Strube listed. Not in L.A.'

Cochran was peering over her shoulder at the STR page. 'There's a ... "Strubie the Clown,"' he noted. 'He's listed twice, also as "Strubie the Children's Entertainer."'

She nodded. 'It's a good enough flop for a call. Gimme your quarter.'

Cochran dug it out for her, and she thumbed it into the slot and punched in the number. After a few seconds of standing with the receiver to her ear, she said, 'It's a recording – listen.'

She leaned her head back and tilted the receiver, and Cochran pressed his chin to her cheek to hear the message with her. His heart was pounding, and he let himself lay his hand on her shoulder as if for balance.

'... *and I can't come to the phone right now,*' piped a merry voice from the earpiece. '*But leave your name and number, and* Strubie *will right back to you be!*' A beep followed, and Plumtree hung up the phone and shook off Cochran's arm.

'He's, uh, not home, I guess,' said Cochran to cover his embarrassment as they scuffed back to the booth. Their dinners had been served – two plates sat on the tablecloth, the meat and vegetables piled on them steaming with smells of garlic and lamb and onion and cinnamon, along with another Manhattan and a fresh shot glass of bourbon and five fresh glasses of beer.

'Where *would* we be without you to figure these things out?' Plumtree said acidly as she slid into the booth.

Cochran sat down without replying, and as he began hungrily forking up the mess of onions and tomatoes and veal on his plate he looked around at the bar and the other patrons rather than at Plumtree. He hoped she'd be Janis again soon; and he resolved to catch her if she got up to go to the ladies' room.

The bartender was a woman too, and as Cochran watched she drew a draft beer for one of the men who had been playing bar dice. The man pulled a little cloth bag from his coat pocket and shook from it a pile of yellow-brown powder onto the bar. The bartender scooped the powder up with a miniature dustpan and disposed of it behind the bar.

Gold dust? wondered Cochran with the incurious detachment of being half-drunk. Heroin or cocaine, cut with semolina flour? Either way, it seemed like an awful lot to pay for one beer.

A black dwarf on crutches was laboriously poling his way out of the bar now, and when he had braced the door open to swing his crutches outside, Cochran caught a strong scent of the sea on the gusty cold draft that made the lamps flicker in the moment before the door banged shut behind the little man. And under the resumed knock and rattle of the dice he now heard a deep, slow rolling, as if a millwheel were turning in some adjoining stone building.

He became aware that his food was gone, along with the bourbon and a lot of the beer, and that Plumtree had a cigarette in her mouth and was striking a match. Cochran's cigarettes were still back at the madhouse.

When she threw the match into the ashtray it flared up in a momentary flame; an instant later there was just a wisp of smoke curling over the ashtray, and a whiff of something like bacon.

'Brandy in the ashtrays?' said Cochran, in a light tone to cover for having jumped in surprise. 'What's the writing on it say? "No smoking near this ashtray"?'

Plumtree was startled herself, and she reached out gingerly to tilt the ashtray toward her. 'It says – I think it's Latin – *Roma, tibi subito motibus ibit amor.* What does that mean?'

'Lemme see.' Cochran tipped the warm ashtray toward himself. 'Uh … "How romantic, to be … submitting … in a motor bus, having … a bit! … of love."'

'You liar!' She actually, seemed frightened by his nonsense. 'It doesn't say that, does it? In a motor bus? You're such a liar.'

Cochran laughed and touched her arm reassuringly. 'No, I don't know what it says.' He took a sip from one of the beer glasses, and to change the subject he asked, 'Why did you say Coors is like screwing in a canoe?'

'Because it's fuckin' near water. *Ho ho.* Let's get out of here. Strubie the Clown ought to be home by now. I'll go copy down the address listed for him and call us a cab.' She had got out of the booth and was striding away toward the telephone before he could protest.

'Strubie the goddamn *Clown* … ?' he muttered to himself. 'It won't be the right guy, not this lawyer you want. Tonight?'

He at least managed to finish the beers before she got back and pulled him up onto his feet; but when she had marched him to the door and pulled it open – there was no sea scent on the breeze now – she hurried back inside so that she could speak to the blond woman who had been shouting, and who by this time was very drunk and crying quietly.

When Plumtree rejoined him and pushed him out across the Rosecrans sidewalk, she immediately began looking anxiously up and down the street. 'I hope the cab gets here quick,' she muttered.

'Oh hell. Me too,' said Cochran, for he saw that she was now holding a purse.

Strubie the Clown's house was a little one-story 1920s bungalow off Del Amo and Avalon in the Carson area of south Los Angeles, and after the taxi dropped them off Cochran and Plumtree hurried out of the curbside streetlight's glare, up the old two-strip concrete driveway to the dark porch.

No lights seemed to be on inside the house, but Plumtree knocked on the door. Several seconds went by without any sound from inside, and Cochran blinked around at the porch.

A wooden swing hung on chains from a beam in the porch roof, and Cochran wobbled across the Astroturf carpeting and slumped into it – and instantly one of the hooks tore free of the overhead beam, and the swing's streetside corner hit the porch deck with an echoing bang.

'Christ!' hissed Plumtree; she reeled back and bumped a ceramic pot on the porch rail, and it tipped off and broke with a hollow thump and rattle on the grass below. Cochran had rolled off the pivoting and now-diagonal swing, but his arm was tangled in the slack chain, and it took him several seconds to thrash free of it. The fall had jolted him. His face was suddenly cold and damp, and his mouth was full of salty saliva; beside the front door sat a wide plastic tray heaped with sand and cat turds, and he crawled over and began vomiting into it, desperately trying to do so quietly.

'You shithead!' Plumtree gasped. 'We're wrecking his place!'

Cochran was aware of the sound of a car's engine idling fast out at the curb as it was shifted out of gear, and then the noise stopped and he heard a car door creak open and a moment later clunk shut.

'He's home,' whispered Plumtree urgently. 'Stop it! And get up!'

Cochran was just spitting now, and he got his feet under himself and straightened up, bracing himself on the wall planks. ''Scuse me,' he said resentfully with his face against the painted wood. ''Scuse the *fuck* out o' me.' He pulled his shirt free of his pants and wiped his mouth on it, then turned around to lean his back against the wall.

'Who's there?' came a man's frightened voice from the front yard.

'Oh,' muttered Plumtree, 'I got no time for this flop.' A moment later she turned toward the front steps. 'Mr. Strube?' she said cheerily. 'My friend and I need your help.'

'Who are you?'

Cochran pushed the damp hair back from his face and peered out into the yard. The figure silhouetted against the streetlight glare wore baggy pants and a tiny, tight jacket, and great tufts of hair stood out from the sides of the head. The shoes at the ends of the short legs were as big as basketballs.

'We're people in trouble, Mr. Strube,' Plumtree said. 'We need to find a boy whose name sounds like ... well, like *Boogie-Woogie Bananas*. He'll be able to help us.'

'I ... don't know anybody whose name sounds ... even remotely like that.' The clown walked hesitantly up to the porch steps, and his gaze went from Plumtree to Cochran to the broken swing. 'Is he a clown? I know all the local clowns, I think—'

'No,' said Plumtree. 'He's ... a king, or a contender for some kind of throne ... it's supernatural, a supernatural thing, actually ...'

Strubie's bulbous rubber nose wobbled as he sniffed. 'Did you two get sick here? Are you drunk? What have you done here? I'm going to have to ask you to leave. I'm in the entertainment business, and my schedule ...'

Cochran jumped then, for suddenly *a man's* voice came grinding out of Plumtree's mouth, gravelly and hoarsely baritone: 'Frank, you got a show-biz friend in the bar here!' the voice drawled amiably. 'Nicky Bradshaw, his name is. Shall I tell him where you live?'

Cochran gaped at Plumtree, totally disoriented. There had been a TV star called Nicky Bradshaw – he had starred in some situation comedy in the fifties. Was this voice Flibbertigibbet talking? Cochran was pretty sure that Nicky Bradshaw had died years ago. What *bar* was Flibbertigibbet talking about?

'Bradshaw doesn't ... blame me,' said the clown quietly, 'for his death.'

Again the man's voice boomed out of Plumtree's throat: 'Then you don't mind if I tell him where you live, right?'

The clown sighed shakily. 'Don't do *anything*.' He clumped up the steps to the porch, digging a set of keys out of the pocket of his baggy trousers, and he unlocked the front door. 'Come inside, if you've got to talk about these things.'

Plumtree followed the clown into the dark house, and after a light came on inside Cochran stepped in too, pulling the door closed behind him.

The green-carpeted living room was bare except for some white plastic chairs and a long mahogany credenza against the far wall; impressionistic sailboat prints and unskilled oil paintings of clowns hung in a cluster over it, as if Strubie had once, briefly and with limited resources, tried to brighten the empty expanses of mottled plaster walls.

Plumtree sat down in one of the plastic chairs and crossed her legs. Her jeans were tight, and it made Cochran dizzy to look at her legs and at the same time remember the voice she had just now been speaking with.

In the glare from the lamp on the credenza, the clown was hideous; the white face-paint was cracked with his anxious frown, and the orange tufts of hair glued onto the bald wig above his ears emphasized the exhausted redness of his eyes.

He didn't sit down. 'Who are you?' he asked, shakily pulling off his white gloves.

'That's not important,' said the man's voice from Plumtree's throat. A sardonic grin made her cheekbones and the line of her jaw seem broader, and Cochran had to remind himself that it *was* a woman's face.

Strubie cleared his throat. 'Who's your friend, then?' he asked, nodding toward Cochran, who, daunted by this attention, let himself fold into one of the chairs.

'I'll tell you the truth, I don't know.' Plumtree's face turned toward

Cochran, and the wide-pupilled eyes squinted at him. 'I gotta say I don't much like the look of him. However, he may kiss my hand, if he likes.'

Cochran shook his head and licked beads of sweat off his upper lip.

Strubie took a deep breath, and then hugely startled Cochran by reaching both hands behind his ears and peeling the white scalp, with the tufts of orange hair still attached to it, forward and right off of his head. 'Who is this bananas person,' the clown asked wearily, 'and how can he help you out of whatever trouble it is that you're in?' He tossed the white bald wig onto the wooden floor. His thinning hair was gray and tangled, and the inch of unpainted forehead below his hairline was the color of oatmeal.

The light dimmed out, then brightened.

And when Plumtree spoke, it was in a woman's voice: 'Don't tell him,' she said. 'You didn't tell him yet, did you?' Cochran glanced at her quickly, but was unable to guess which personality was up at the moment.

'Tell who,' said the clown, 'what?'

'The ... the man who was speaking through me,' she said. 'Valorie has blocked him, for now. Did you tell him how to find the boy?'

'No,' said Strubie.

'Good. I'll go away, and you'll never hear from ... that man, again. Or me.' Cochran thought it was Cody speaking. 'Tell me how to find the boy, and no harm will come to him, I promise.'

Strubie laughed softly, exposing yellow teeth in the white-painted face. 'I used to be a divorce lawyer,' he said. 'I've hurt enough children. Today I try to ... give them some moments of joy, if only in a frail, half-assed way. It's what I can do. How do I know you're not going to go hurt this boy, or kill him? Other people have wanted to, in the past.'

Plumtree spread her hands. 'I need to find him because he can restore a dead king to life. I killed ... or at least, the man you were just listening to, I helped *him* kill ... a king, and I need to make it right.'

'A king,' echoed Strubie. 'And if I tell you nothing ... ?'

'Then I'll hang around. I'll be back tomorrow. The bad man will get it out of you one way or another, and incidentally you'll have a terrible time. Everybody will.'

'God help everybody,' said Strubie softly.

Strubie reached under the lapel of his midget's jacket and slid out of an inner pocket a flat half-pint bottle Roses whiskey; he unscrewed the deep swig of the brown liquor; his long exhalation afterward was almost a whistle.

'The boy's name is Koot Hoomie Parganas,' he said hoarsely. 'His parents were murdered just before Halloween in '92, because they were in the way. The Parganas boy had another person inside his head with him – you should be able to empathize! – and a lot of ruthless people *wanted* that person, wanted to *consume* it into themselves. For them to do that, incidentally, would have involved killing the boy.'

He sat down on the credenza and lowered his face into his hands. 'The last I heard of him,' came his muffled voice, 'he was living in an apartment building in Long Beach. I don't remember the address, but it's a big old rambling three-story place on the northwest corner of Ocean and Twenty-first Place, run-down, with a dozen mailboxes out front, and he was living there with a man named Peter Sullivan and a woman named Angelica Elizalde.' He raised his head and pried off his bulbous red nose; his real nose was textured and scored with red capillaries. 'The building used to belong to Nicholas Bradshaw, the man who played the Spooky character in the old "Ghost of a Chance" TV show – he owned the building under the alias Solomon Shadroe – but it was quit-claimed to his common-law wife, who had some Mexican last name.'

'Valorie's got all that,' said Plumtree. 'Do you owe this Koot Hoomie any money?'

'Owe him—?' said Strubie, frowning. 'I don't think so. No. In fact, I got gypped out of a reward, when I led the bad people there; they were offering a reward to whoever could find Bradshaw, find the Spooky character, and I used to work for Bradshaw when he was a lawyer, after he quit being an actor, so I was able to track him down there. I never got—'

'It sounds like you made Koot Hoomie's life harder, doing that,' said Plumtree. 'Would you like me to take any money to him, from you, as a token of restitution?'

The clown put down his bottle and stared at her out of his red, watery eyes. 'I couldn't,' he said finally, stiffly, 'give you more than a hundred dollars. I swear, that's the absolute—'

'I think that'll do,' said Plumtree.

The clown stared at her for another few seconds, then wearily got to his feet and shuffled out of the room in his blimp shoes. Cochran could hear him bumping down an uncarpeted hall, and then a door squeaked and clicked shut.

Cochran exhaled through clenched teeth. 'This is very damned wrong, Cody,' he whispered. 'This poor man can't afford your ... extortion, or protection, or whatever it is. Hell, I'm sure that lady in the bar couldn't afford to lose her purse! I'm going to – first chance I get, I'm going to pay these people back—'

'Talk the virtuous talk, by all means,' Plumtree interrupted. 'Janis can give you tips on it. I'll make my own restitutions, like always. In the meantime, I don't need to hear *your* estimates of how much cash is *enough* to finance the resurrection of a dead king.' Her lip curled in a smile. 'No offense, pansy.'

Cochran shook his head. 'Janis is right about you. Did you know she escaped to save your life?'

'Well sure. She needs me a whole lot more than I need her.'

The door down the hall creaked open again, and the clown soon reappeared with a sheaf of crumpled bills in his hand.

'I'm paying not to see you people again,' he said.

'We'll see you get your money's worth,' Plumtree told him, standing up and taking the bills. She even counted them – Cochran could see that it wasn't all twenties, that there were at least a couple of fives in the handful.

Strubie crouched with an effortful grunt, and picked the latex bald wig up off the green carpet; and when he had straightened up again he tugged it back over his hair, and retrieved the rubber nose from where he had set it down on the credenza and planted it firmly on his face again. 'You've stirred old ghosts tonight,' he said hoarsely. 'I'll sleep in my full mask.'

'Let's for Christ's sake go,' said Cochran, struggling back up onto his feet.

Plumtree pushed the bills into the newly acquired purse and strode to the door.

When she and Cochran had stepped out onto the devastated dark porch, and then made their unsteady way down the driveway to the halo of street-light radiance at the curb, Cochran squinted back at the house: and in spite of everything that had gone before he jumped in surprise to see five – or was it six? – thin little girls in tattered white dresses perched like sickly cockatoos on the street edge of the roof, their skinny arms clasped around their raised knees. They seemed to be staring toward Plumtree and him, but they didn't nod or wave.

'Look at me!' said Plumtree in an urgent whisper. When Cochran had jerked his head around toward her, she went on, 'Don't look them in the eyes, you idiot. You want to be bringing a bunch of dead *kids* along with us? And *you're* not even *masked*! You'd just flop down dead, right here. Those are Strubie's concerns, whoever they might once have been, not ours.'

Cochran's head was ringing in incredulous protest, but he didn't look back at the girls on the roof.

Plumtree had started scuffling along the street in the direction of the gas-station and liquor-store lights of Bellflower Boulevard, and he followed, shivering and pushing his hands into the pockets of his corduroy pants.

Cochran forced himself to forget about the ragged little girls and to focus on Plumtree and himself. 'We've got plenty enough money for a motel,' he said. 'To sleep in,' he added.

'Maybe it's a motel we'll wind up at tonight,' Plumtree allowed, 'but it'll be in Long Beach, I think. We need to find another cab.'

Cochran sighed, but broadened his stride to keep up with her. Perhaps because of Long John Beach's upsettingly wrong lyrics to 'Puff the Magic

Dragon,' misunderstood rock lyrics were now spinning through Cochran's head, and it was all he could do not to sing out loud,

Had a gold haddock,
Seemed the thing to do,
Let that be a lesson,
Get a cockatoo,
Wooly bully ...

Plumtree called for a taxi from a pay phone at an all-night Texaco station on Atlantic, and when the yellow sedan rocked and squeaked into the shadowed area of the lot where the phone was, out by the air and water hoses, Cochran and Plumtree shuffled across the asphalt and climbed into the back seat. The driver had shifted into neutral when he had stopped, but even so the car's engine was laboring, and it stalled as Plumtree was pulling the door closed; the driver switched off the lights, cranked at the starter until the engine roared into tortured life again, and then snapped the lights back on and clanked it into gear and pulled out onto the boulevard before either of his passengers had even spoken.

'Long Beach,' said Plumtree flatly. 'Ocean and Twenty-first Place.' She was gingerly rubbing the corners of her jaw with both hands.

'It'll be costly,' observed the driver in a cheeful voice. Cochran saw that the man had a full, curly beard. 'That's a lo-o-ong way.'

'She can afford it,' muttered Cochran, feeling quarrelsome. He was breathing deeply; the interior of the car smelled strongly of roses, and he was afraid he might get sick again.

'Oh,' laughed the driver, 'I wasn't doubting your reserves. I was doubting mine.' The man's voice was oddly hoarse and blurred, and over the reek of roses Cochran caught a whiff of the wet-streets-and-iodine smell of very dry red wine. Their driver was apparently drunk.

'What,' Cochran asked irritably, 'are you low on gas?'

'What gas would that *be*?' the man asked in a rhetorical, philosophical tone. 'Hydrogen, methane? Not nitrous oxide, at least. An alternative fuel? But this is an electric car – I'm running on a sort of induction coil, here.'

'Swell,' said Cochran. He looked at Plumtree, who was sitting directly behind the driver, but she was holding a paper napkin to her nose and staring out the window. She's missing some scope for her sarcasm here, Cochran thought. 'You *can* find Long Beach, though, right?'

'Easy as falling off a log, believe me.'

Plumtree was still sitting up rigidly on the seat and staring out at the dark palm trees and apartment buildings as if desperate to memorize the route, and Cochran slumped back in the seat and closed his eyes. The tires were thumping in an irregular drumming tempo, and he muttered sleepily, 'Your tires are low on air.'

The driver laughed. 'These are experimental tires, India rubber. Hard with hard vacuum. Has to be a very hard vacuum, or I'd combust.'

The driver's nonsense reminded Cochran of Long John Beach's remark this afternoon: *Her bed is India; there she lies, a pearl.* Cochran frowned without opening his eyes, and didn't make any further comments. In seconds he had fallen asleep.

CHAPTER SEVEN

'My credentials, entries, and memoranda, are all comprehended in the one line, "Recalled to Life;"' ...

—Charles Dickens, *A Tale of Two Cities*

Dogs were howling out in the alleys and dark yards of Long Beach, and unless the ringing air was particularly distorted – which Koot Hoomie reflected that it might very well be – they were howling out on the beach sand too, possibly mistaking the electric glow of the *Queen Mary*'s million lights across the harbor for the moon, or a close-passing comet.

Kootie stepped out onto the front porch and pulled the door closed behind him. Or, he thought as the night breeze swept the echoes of amplified wailing around from the parking-lot side of the old apartment building, maybe the dogs are tired of our music. The tenants in the neighboring complexes would probably have come to complain about it a week ago if they could locate the source.

For ten days now, all day and all night, there had been some person or other dancing in the Solville parking lot; Elizalde's clients had spontaneously conceived and taken on the eccentric task, and many of them had missed work to do their individual four-hour shifts, each successive businessman or tattooed *cholo* or portly matron dutifully hopping and scuffing to the music banging out of the portable stereo that was connected by extension cords to an outlet in the kitchen. On Sunday and Monday of last week it had been a randomly eclectic sequence of sixties rock, mariachi, rap, and Country-Western musics, but by this last weekend they had somehow found and settled on one song – a hoarse, haggardly persevering thing called either 'Lay Down' or 'Candles in the Wind,' by Melanie, recorded more than a decade before Kootie had been born – and Arky Mavranos had dubbed a cassette of nothing but that song, repeated over and over again, for the dancers to play endlessly.

And his foster dad and Arky Mavranos had located and busted open an old fireplace behind the drywall in the bathroom down the hall from the office, and had climbed up on the roof and knocked the layers of tar paper off the obscured chimney, and so a fire of pine and oak logs had been kept continuously burning. There were enough people in residence to keep the fire tended, but Mavranos had in recent days begun to complain about having to drive all over town for more wood, and Kootie was afraid he would soon insist that they cut down one of the shady old carob trees around the parking lot.

Ten days so far on this deathwatch, and not even a whiff of decomposition yet. Kootie wondered if they would be able to keep on maintaining all these observances even until the weekend.

Kootie sighed, staring out at the dark rooftops.

And whenever the old king *did* begin to show some sign of decay, and could thus be formally acknowledged as dead, Kootie would apparently … be the next king. His poor naive dead parents had raised him to be some kind of Indian holy man, the new Krishnamurti, the *jagadguru*, and that discipline had been close enough to what was required here, what with all the well-remembered fasts and the meditations and the sacramental meal of smoked salmon and whitefish at Canter's Jewish delicatessen on Fairfax, one Friday in 1988 – and he was a virgin, physically, and he had the perpetually bleeding wound in his side.

That was why Arky Mavranos and Diana were here – to transfer the mantle, to pronounce *Le Roi c'est mort, vive le Roi.*

These recent mornings – in the sunny cool-breeze moments between waking and getting out of bed, when he seemed to thrill to the vertiginous flights of crows all over the L.A. basin, and flex with the powerful iron tides roaring along the San Diego and Harbor and Pomona freeways, and be able to just tap his feet in rhythm with the heartbeat of the continent – he found himself very much wanting this job the people in the red track had brought for him; it was only after the sun had gone down over the smokestacks of the *Queen Mary* a quarter mile away across the harbor that he seemed to catch the tang of fresh blood and stale beer on the taste buds of the broken asphalt, and cramp with the hopeless hunger and unknown withdrawals in the mazes of cracked plaster and parking garages and electric rainbows in glass on street corners, and shiver with the grinding of fast, shallow panting, or of some subterranean *gnawing*, that invisibly agitated all the pavements.

Kootie would soon have to either accept it, or refuse it; and he couldn't get rid of the thought that he would be accruing some debt either way – that a consequence, a price, would be demanded of him at some future time.

Tonight he just wanted to be Kootie, the fourteen-year-old boy who lived in Long Beach and studied astronomy and went in-line skating down the sidewalks of Bluff Park in the afternoons.

He leaned back against the clapboard wall and closed his eyes, and he cautiously let his attention expand just to include the building here. Most strongly he felt the presence of Scott Crane, the still-undecaying dead man in the kitchen, robed in white now and laid out across a dining-room table, with the sawed-short spear segment standing up from his shut-down, pulse-less throat; but Kootie was also aware of his foster mom Angelica and the pregnant, bald-headed Diana lady fussing over the big pot of bouillabaisse on the stove near the dead man's bearded head, and of his foster dad Pete crouching by the television set in the long office room, talking to Diana's two sons, Scat and Oliver; and of Johanna, who owned the buildings that were Solville, sitting out on the back steps drinking Tecate beer and eating homemade enchiladas with the girlfriend of the teenage boy who was currently keeping the dance going.

Now Pete had straightened up and was looking for Kootie – but it was probably just to ask about the pans full of bean sprouts, and Kootie didn't bother to open his eyes or step away from the shadowed wall. After Angelica had been convinced that these uninvited houseguests had to stay, and that in some vague but compelling way they needed and merited Kootie's coop-eration, she had done some research into their problem and come up with, among other troublesome measures, her 'Gardens of Adonis' – five shallow aluminum pans with half an inch of damp dirt and a handful of beans in each of them; the things had sprouted and quickly died again and had to be re-sown twice already, and Kootie knew that Pete was of the opinion that this third crop had about had it too. Let this lot go one more day, Dad, Kootie wearily thought now.

But Pete had leaned out the back door and spoken to Johanna, and had walked back through the office and was now striding up the hall toward the front door.

Kootie stepped away from the wall and opened the door just as Pete was reaching for the inside knob.

Kootie smiled. 'Let 'em go till tomorrow, Dad.'

'You're talking about those beans, aren't you?' said Pete Sullivan impa-tiently. 'To hell with the beans. We've got a line on the TV.'

'Oh. Okay.' Kootie followed his foster father back into the hall, and made sure to slide the feather-hung security chain into the slot on the inside of the door.

The hallway, and the office when they walked in there and stood beside the television set, smelled strongly of burnt coffee again. The smell had been untraceably hanging around the whole place for the last ten days, generally stronger at night, even with all the windows open and people cooking for a crowd and smoking and often not having bathed. Arky Mavranos had only joined in the general puzzled shrug when people remarked on the odor, but privately he told Kootie that when Scott Crane's first wife, Susan, had died of a heart attack in 1990, she'd been drinking a cup of coffee, and it was unfinished and still hot after the paramedics had taken her body away – and that Crane, unable to bear the thought of it too eventually cooling off, had put the cup in his oven over the lowest heat setting, and that it had baked dry in there, apparently filling the house with the burned smell. After a while, Arky had said, a crippled and malevolent facet of the wine god Dionysus had come to Crane in the apparition of Susan's ghost, incongruously heralded by the hot coffee reek. All this had apparently happened before Crane had become ... *king of the west* ... on Holy Saturday of 1990.

Tonight the coffee smell had a sharper edge to it, like hot, vapory Kahlua.

Kootie ignored the smell for now, and stared at the television on the desk. For the past ten days the set had been left on, with the brightness control turned down far enough to dim the screen to black. Now, though, a steady horizontal, white streak bisected the black screen.

'Well,' Kootie said slowly, 'it's a ghost, somewhere nearby. According to Sol Shadroe, disembodied personalities are an electromagnetic commotion in the fifty-five-megahertz range – which is roughly the frequency of Channel Two, which this set is tuned to.' He breathed a shallow, hitching sigh and ran his fingers through his hair, then glanced nervously at the bookshelves on the back wall, where the weather-beaten stuffed-toy pig sat on the top shelf. 'Has the line got brighter since you first saw it?'

'Yes,' said Diana's son Scat, who was Kootie's age, and who liked to sit in front of the TV even though the screen was generally blank. 'Uh ... twice as bright already, in this minute or so since it first showed up.'

'Then it's getting closer.'

Diana's first son, Oliver, was a year older than the other two boys, but the eyes in his tanned face were wet as he looked up at Kootie. 'Our dad,' he said, 'our stepfather, I mean, he took all the ghosts with him, when somebody ... killed him. The ghosts are *gone*.' He said it proudly, as though Scott Crane had gone down under an onslaught of ghosts, and only after heroically decimating their ranks.

'The local ones, yeah,' Kootie agreed gently, 'whatever "local" means, exactly, in this business.' He sighed, and went on, almost to himself, 'It's hard to judge their distance, just from their apparent brightness here, like trying to figure the absolute magnitude of stars. This here ghost could be one that was insulated – clathrated – when the king died, or it could be a visitor from outside the local area. Or of course it could be the ghost of somebody that died in this week-and-a-half *since*.'

For several moments no one spoke, and the only noise in the room was the steady plink and splash of water from the leaking ceiling falling into the pots and buckets around the couch, though it was not raining outside. Then Kootie heard a clatter and footsteps from the kitchen, and at the same instant a loud, mechanical burping started up behind and above him. He looked toward the kitchen doorway, though he did dart a glance down at Oliver, who was crouched on the floor, and say, 'That's the pig, right?'

'The toy one on the shelf,' said Oliver steadily, 'right. Burping.'

'There's an old man out front,' snapped Angelica, wiping her hands on a kitchen towel. 'He's caught in the pyrocantha bushes.' She glared across the office at the bookshelf. 'Of course this would be when the pig decides to put in its two cents' worth.'

'Two cents' worth …' echoed Kootie, catching an urgent thought from outside the building's walls; then it was gone. 'Get Arky Mavranos, will you, Oliver?'

'Right.' Oliver straightened up lithely and sprinted out toward the back parking lot.

Diana, the pregnant wife of the dead man in the kitchen, said, 'Is this a ghost, out front?'

She was standing beside Angelica; Kootie was getting used to her appearance – all the hair on her scalp had fallen out during the first night the dead king's company had spent in Solville, the first night after the king's murder. Probably her sudden baldness was an extreme reaction to grief and loss, but at times Kootie had uneasily wondered if it was instead somehow a consequence of his having asked the wrong question, when their party had driven up in the red truck ten days ago.

Why is your truck the color of blood? he had asked, instead of *Who does it serve?* Damn all this magical minefield, he thought.

'Probably,' he answered her. 'Tangled in the bushes – he sounds like one of what Johanna calls the "beasties" – the old ghosts that don't dissipate, and accumulate substance from bugs and spit and cigarette butts and stuff, and then walk around panhandling money for liquor. Snips and snails and puppydog tails. He doesn't sound like being … whoever it is we've been waiting for.'

'The Three Kings,' said Scat. 'With gold and frankincense and myrrh.'

Arky Mavranos had stepped into the office from the back yard, followed by Oliver. 'And *they're* supposed to show up on Epiphany,' Mavranos said gruffly, 'to venerate the new king. They're five days late already.' He took a sip from the can of Coors beer in his hand, leaving foam on his salt-and-pepper mustache. 'You got a line on the TV and a ghost out in the bushes by the driveway, is how I hear it.' He glanced disapprovingly at the stuffed pig on the bookshelf, which was still noisily retching. 'Ollie, take the batteries out of that suffering beast, will you? Kootie, let's you and I go out and talk to his ghost, see if he's got any news for us.'

'Do you want to bring him anything?' asked Diana, who was still holding the ladle from the pot of bouillabaisse.

'Keep a plate of rocks ready,' said Kootie, 'in case he hasn't had dinner yet.'

Mavranos was laughing at that as he and Kootie walked down the hall to the front door; by unspoken agreement they had avoided the quicker route, through the kitchen and the presence of the dead, bearded king.

The dogs were still howling, and the breeze off the ocean was colder, when Kootie undid the chain and opened the door; and when the two of them had trudged around to the driveway, Kootie jumped back with an involuntary yelp at the sight of the old man who was thrashing in the pyrocantha bushes.

In the fragmentary yellow light from the kitchen window the old man appeared to have a lot of long insect legs or antennae waving in the air around him, as if he were a gigantic daddy-longlegs spider. Then Kootie got a clearer look at the white-bearded figure in the middle of the tangle, and he saw with relief that the waving, flexing filaments were metal, and were attached to the old man's belt.

'Shit, I *know* this guy,' said Mavranos, striding forward. 'And he's still wearing his silly damn curb-feelers. Easy, there, Joe,' he said to the old man. 'you're just making it worse. Hold still.' Mavranos pulled the old man out of the bushes and began yanking the metal filaments free of the branches. Twigs and leaves spun across the driveway pavement. 'This guy ain't a ghost. I don't *think* – you didn't, like, *die*, did you, Joe?'

'Fuck you,' sputtered the old man, thrashing his hands against the bushes as if to help free himself. 'No, I'm not dead. Are *you* dead? If you know me, then I must have found the right place, so there's a dead guy here *somewhere*, right?'

'Yeah, but inside, we don't keep him out here in the shrubbery. Where's Booger?'

The old man was panting but standing still now, letting Mavranos pull him free. '*She* died,' he said harshly. 'She walked out into the desert, the day after your Easter of 1990. I went after her, calling – but I'm blind, and she was mute. Somebody found her body, after a while.'

'I'm truly sorry to hear that,' Mavranos said. He tugged the last filament free, and now old Joe was swaying on the driveway in the middle of his cluster of bobbing antennae, like, thought Kootie, a sea urchin left here by a high tide, or a big old dandelion seed carried here by the night wind.

From the dark street at Kootie's back came a shrill whisper: '*You ask them.*'

Kootie spun toward the voice, peripherally aware that Mavranos had quickly turned that way too.

A lanky, dark-haired man in a T-shirt was shuffling up the driveway, visibly shivering in the breeze. 'Excuse me,' he said, 'but—' His gaze fell on the old man, and he took a quick step backward. Then, after peering more closely, he exhaled hard, took another breath, and went on: 'Sorry. Why not? 'Specially tonight, huh? We're—' He barked a nervous, mirthless laugh and spread his hands. '—looking for a boy named Koot Hoomie Parganas. He lived here, at one time.'

A slim blond woman had sidled up behind the man, and was peering wide-eyed over his shoulder. Now she nodded.

'Kootie's living in Pittsburgh these days—' began Mavranos, but Kootie interrupted.

'I'm Koot Hoomie Parganas,' he said.

Abruptly Kootie could feel the old man whom Mavranos had called Joe staring at him, and Kootie glanced sideways at him in surprise – and the old man *was* obviously blind, his eyelids horribly sunken in his dark, furrowed face – but nevertheless the old man was suddenly paying powerful attention to him.

Kootie looked back at the man and woman shivering on the driveway.

Kootie heard footsteps rapping down the steps from the kitchen door, and he sensed that it was Angelica. *'Tiena la máquina?'* he asked, without looking around: *Do you have the machine?*

'Como siempre,' came Angelica's voice coldly in reply. *As always.*

'No need for your *máquinas*,' said the blond woman, stepping out from behind her companion. Her tight jeans emphasized her long slim legs, and her flimsy white blouse was bunched up around her breasts as she hugged herself against the cold. 'Sorry, I can't have been listening. Did you all say Koot Hoomie Parganas is here, or not?' She laughed, rocking on the soles of her white sneakers. 'Have we even *asked* yet?'

'*I'm* him,' Kootie said, irritated with himself for being distracted by her figure. 'What did you want me for?'

'I – Well, short form, kiddo, I need you to tell me how to find a dead king and restore him to life. Does this make any sense to you? Could we talk about it inside?'

'No,' said Angelica and Mavranos in unison; but a moment later Mavranos muttered, 'Restore him to *life*?'

Kootie gave the woman a quizzical smile. 'Why is it *your* job?' he asked quietly, 'to restore this dead king to *life*?'

She tossed her head to throw her thatch of blond hair back from her face, and she stared at Kootie. 'Amends,' she said in a flat voice. She raised her hands, palms out, as if surrendering. 'These are the hands that killed him.'

Kootie's heightened senses caught not only the rustle of Angelica's hand sliding up under her blouse, but also the tiny *snick* of the .45's safety being thumbed off.

Kootie glanced sideways and caught Mavranos's eye, and nodded.

'You two don't appear to be armed,' Mavranos said cheerfully, 'but we are. I reckon you can all come in, but keep your hands in sight and move slow.'

*

Plumtree didn't pull her injured hand away when Cochran gently took it, and the two of them followed the boy with the funny name across the dark lawn to the apartment building's open front door. Cochran was walking slowly and keeping his free hand open and away from his body – he had glimpsed the black grip of the automatic under the blouse of the tall, dark-haired woman who had come out of the kitchen, and he was suddenly sober, and taking deep breaths of the cold night air to keep his head clear.

We've blundered into some kind of crazy cult, he thought, and Janis – or Cody, probably – has got them mad at us. Watch for a chance to grab her and sneak out, or find a phone and call 911.

His heart was pounding, and he wondered if he might actually have to try to prevent these people from injuring Janis, or even killing her.

'How did you find this place?' called the man with the graying mustache from behind them as they stepped up to the front door and began walking up a carpeted hall. The place smelled like some third-world soup kitchen.

Cochran decided to protect poor Strubie, who had paid them the hundred dollars to keep out of this. 'A psychiatrist at Rosecrans Medical Center gave us the address—' he began.

The hall opened into a long room with a couch against the near wall and a desk with a TV set on it against the opposite wall. The TV set's screen was glowing a brighter white than Cochran would have thought possible, and as the others crowded in behind him one of the two teenage boys on the couch leaped up and snatched the plug out of the wall socket.

'Thanks, Ollie,' said the man who had followed them in. 'The ghost that was torquing the TV is apparently the deceased wife of my old pal Spider Joe here, this old gent with the curb feelers on his belt.' He now stepped to the bookshelves behind the couch and reached down a stainless-steel revolver, which he held pointed at Cochran's feet. 'Everybody sit down, hm? Plenty of room on the floor, though the carpet's wet in spots. And don't move those pots, they're catching leaks.'

The old man who was apparently called Spider Joe shambled across the threadbare carpet and slid down into a crouch beside the kitchen doorway, and the antennae standing out from his belt scraped the wall and knocked a calendar off a nail; and as Cochran sat down beside Plumtree in front of the desk he wondered if the ghost of the old man's wife might be snagged on one of the metal filaments. The woman with the automatic and the boy with the funny name stood beside the couch.

'Let's get acquainted,' said the man holding the revolver. 'My name's Archimedes Mavranos, and the lady in the kitchen is Diana, the guy beside her is Pete, and this lady with the *máquina* is Pete's wife Angelica. The boys on the couch are Scat and Ollie. Kootie you know.' He raised his eyebrows politely.

Cochran had resolved to give false names, but before he could speak, Plumtree said, 'I'm Janis Cordelia Plumtree, and this is Sid *Cochran*.' She pronounced his name so precisely that Cochran knew she had restrained herself from saying *Cockface* or something. For God's sake behave yourself, Cody, he thought. The long room was hot and smelled of garlic and fish and Kahlua, and he could feel sweat beading on his forehead.

Water was thumping and splashing into a saucepan by his feet, and he looked up at the mottled, dented, dripping ceiling, wondering how heavy with water the old plaster was, and whether it might fall on them. 'It's, uh, not raining,' he said inanely. 'Outside.'

'It's raining in San Jose,' spoke up a heavy-set woman who had stepped up to an open door at the far side of the room. She spoke shyly, with a Spanish accent.

'Oh,' said Cochran blankly. San Jose was three hundred and fifty miles to the north, up by Daly City and San Francisco. 'Okay.'

'And that's Johanna,' said Mavranos, 'our landlady. I wasn't asking how you got this address,' he went on, 'just now, but how you physically *got* here.'

'In a taxi,' said Plumtree. When Mavranos just stared at her, she added, 'We were in Carson. We told the driver the address, and he ... drove us here.'

'Dropped us at the corner,' put in Cochran. 'He didn't want to drive up to the building.'

'So much for our *protections* here,' said the pregnant woman in the kitchen doorway. Cochran focussed past the bobbing antennae of Spider Joe to get a look at her, and was startled to see that she was completely bald.

'No,' said Kootie, 'the space is still bent, around this building. The driver must have *been* somebody.' He stepped forward now, and leaned down to extend his right hand to Cochran, 'Welcome to my house, Sid Cochran,' he said.

Cochran shook his hand, and the boy turned to Plumtree. 'Welcome to my house, Janis Cordelia Plumtree.'

Plumtree gingerly reached up with her swollen right hand, and the boy clasped it firmly; but Plumtree's cry was one of surprise rather than pain.

'It doesn't hurt!' she said. She held up her right hand after the boy released it, and Cochran could see that the swelling was gone. She flexed the fingers and said, 'It doesn't hurt anymore!'

Cochran made himself remember the hard *crack* of her fist hitting the linoleum floor last night, and how this evening her knuckles had just been dimples in the hot, unnaturally padded flesh of her hand. He looked from Plumtree's metacarpal bones, now visible again under the thin skin on the back of her hand as she bunched and straightened her fingers, to the face of the boy standing in front of him, and for a moment in the garlic-and-Kahlua reek the boy was taller, and the brown eyes under his curly hair seemed narrowed as if with Asian epicanthic folds, and the unregarded blur of his clothing had the loose drapery of robes. Cochran's abdomen felt hollow, and he thought, This is a Magician. A real one.

'No,' said Kootie to him softly, once more just a teenage boy in blue jeans and a flannel shirt, 'something different than that.'

Cochran closed his own right hand, still warm from the boy's grip; and he relaxed a little, for he no longer believed that these people meant to harm him or Plumtree.

Kootie looked past him. 'Ah, my dinner,' he said. 'I hope you all don't mind if I eat while we talk.' He patted the flannel shirt over his left ribs. 'I'm bleeding, and I've got to keep up my strength.' He hiked himself up onto the desk and crossed his legs like a yogi. 'If any of you are hungry, just holler – we've got lots.'

The bald woman was carrying in a steaming, golden bowl cast in the form of a deeply concave sunfish, and the rich smell of garlic and fish broth was intensified; Angelica followed her back into the kitchen, and reappeared with a bottle of Mondavi Chardonnay and a bowl of some sauce for Kootie, while Diana brought steaming ceramic bowls for the two teenage boys who were sitting on the far end of the couch. Kootie was pouring the wine into a gold goblet that was shaped like a wide-mouthed fish standing on its tail.

Had a gold haddock, thought Cochran. 'What is it?' he asked.

'Bouillabaisse,' Kootie answered, stirring some orange-colored sauce into his bowl. 'According to old stories, a bunch of saints named Mary – Magdalen, Mary Jacob, Mary Salome, maybe the Virgin Mary too – fled the Holy Land after the crucifixion and were shipwrecked on the French Camargue shore, at a place that's now called Les-Saintes-Maries-de-la-Mer, and the local fishermen served them pots of this. Ordinarily I just have grilled sole or tuna sandwiches or H. Salt or something, but—' He waved his spoon toward Diana and the two boys on the couch. '—it's the traditional restorative dinner for fugitive holy families.'

'I heard you can't make real bouillabaisse in this country,' said Plumtree. 'There's some fishes that it needs that you can only get in the Mediterranean.'

'Rascasse,' Kootie agreed, 'and conger eel, and other things, yeah. But there don't seem to be any kinds of loaves and fishes that can't show up in the back of Arky's old red truck after he's driven it around town.'

'This lady,' Mavranos broke in, waving his revolver in the direction of Plumtree without quite pointing it at her, 'says she's the one who killed Scott Crane.'

In the silence that followed this statement Cochran stared down at the carpet, wishing he had a glass of Kootie's wine. He could feel the shocked stares of the bald lady and the teenagers on the couch and the Mexican lady in the back doorway, and he knew they were directed at Plumtree and not at him; and he found himself thinking about the twenty dollars Plumtree had swindled from young 'Karen' at the ice-cream place, and the purse she had stolen from the lady at the bar, and wishing he weren't sitting next to Plumtree here.

'Benjamin, our four-year-old,' said bald Diana softly, 'did say it was a woman, at first. He says it was a man that did it, but that it was a woman who walked up, and then changed into a man.'

'Benjamin's my godson,' said Mavranos, 'but he's a ... chip off the old block. Half of what he *sees* is more like stuff that's going on in some astral plane than stuff going on in any actual zip code. Still, he did say that. *And*,' he went on, 'Miss Plumtree claims that she's come here *now* to ... restore the king to *life*.'

'*Is that possible?*' asked Diana quickly. Cochran suddenly guessed that Diana was this Scott Crane person's widow, and in vicarious shame he kept his eyes on the carpet. 'Well, I want to listen to what she has to say,' said Mavranos, 'but I'm pretty sure it's not, no. Sorry. Scott's gone on to India, we established that right away – obviously there's no pulse or respiration, and there are no reflexes, and the pupils are way abnormally dilated and don't respond at all to light. And he's cold. And the spear is in his spine. We haven't been able to do an EEG for brain-wave activity, but the electron brush-discharge in Pete's carborundum bulb doesn't flicker when the body is wheeled past it with nobody else in the room, and the Leucadia place isn't sustained anymore, not even the rose garden – his *ashe* is completely gone. And he hasn't risen on the third day or anything.'

Johanna spoke from the back doorway: 'Did you try to call up his ghost?'

'Any *ghost* of him wouldn't be *him*.' Mavranos said wearily, stepping back and rubbing his eyes with his free hand, 'any more than a – goddammit, an old video or tape recording, or a pile of holograph manuscript, or an old pair of his pants, would be him.'

'I was possessed by the ghost of Thomas Alva Edison for a week in '92,' said Kootie, looking up from his golden bowl, 'and that ghost was as lively as they come; and I have some understanding now of what the king is ... what he does, what he monitors. And I've got to say that even *Edison's* ghost wouldn't have had the *scope* for the job.'

'Jesus, lady,' Mavranos burst out, 'if you *are* the one that killed him, how did you *get* to him? He was castled!'

'A knight's move,' said Plumtree flatly. 'I'm not the same person, neces-sarily, from moment to moment, so I can't be psychically tracked if I don't want to be. And I approached from around below the grounds, from the beach, with the whole half-globe of the Pacific's untamed water at my back.

And I used a spear that was already inside his defenses – I was told that he had injured himself with it, once before – and my own blood was on the spearpoints, so I was in the position of overlapping his aura.' She frowned. 'And I – there was something about a phone call – he was in a weakened state. And it was midwinter, the shift of one year to the next – the engine of the seasons had the clutch out, coasting.' She looked up at Mavranos and shrugged. '*I* – this person talking to you now – I didn't set it up, or *do* it. *I* just … cooperated, went along with somebody else's plan. And I don't know who that "somebody else" was.'

'He accidentally shot himself in the ankle with a speargun, in '75,' said Diana. She visibly shifted her weight from one foot to the other, as if in sympathy. 'I remember it.'

'So,' said Mavranos, 'did you have any … *ideas*, about how you'd go about bringing the king back to life?'

'Yes,' Plumtree said. 'And then I was told that Koot Hoomie Parganas could probably do it too. I came looking for him – figuring he could at least help me, somehow. See, I don't know *exactly* how I'll go *about* it.'

'How did you *plan* to do it?' Mavranos asked with heavy patience. 'Approximately.'

'Where is the body?' Plumtree countered.

'Do you need the body, to do your trick?' She shivered. 'I hope so. But I suppose not.'

'If you even reach out toward his foot,' Mavranos told her, 'I'll shoot you away from him, please trust me on that.' He gestured toward the kitchen doorway with the revolver, which Cochran estimated was at least .38 caliber, and which appeared to be fully loaded – he could see the holed noses of four hollow-point bullets in the projecting sides of the cylinder.

'Let's adjourn to the next room,' Mavranos said.

Cochran stood up when Plumtree did, and followed her into the fluorescentlit kitchen.

The white-robed body of a powerfully built, dark-bearded man was lying on a long dining-room table in there. A three-inch metal rod stood up out of his beard above his throat.

'Shit!' exclaimed Cochran. 'Is this *him*, is this guy *dead*?' His mouth was dry and his heart was suddenly pounding. Forgetting Mavranos's threat to Plumtree, he stepped forward and touched the figure's bared forearm – the flesh was impossibly cold, as cold as an ice pack, and he stepped back quickly. 'You can't keep a dead guy in here. Have you called the police? Jesus! Are you all—'

Angelica had walked up to him, and now put her hands on his shoulders and pushed down hard. His knees buckled, and he sat down abruptly on a chair that Diana had slid behind him a moment before.

'He is dead,' Angelica said to him clearly. 'The only symptoms he doesn't show are livor mortis, which is the discoloration caused by blood settling in the lowest areas of the body, and any evidence of decomposition. These *may* be signs that your girl *can* do something. Take a deep breath and let it out – would you like a drink?'

'No! I mean – hell yes.'

Cochran heard a clink behind him, and then Diana was pressing a glass of amber liquid into his shaking hand. It proved to be brandy.

'*Do* something?' he said breathlessly after he'd drunk most of it and help-lessly splashed the rest onto the front of his T-shirt. 'What you can *do* is call the – the coroner. All this supernatural talk is just – entertaining as hell, but it's all *crap*, you've got—'

'This is *all* supernatural,' said Pete Sullivan loudly, overriding him. 'From this undecaying body here all the way down to the TV in the other room. It's all real, independent of whether you believe it or not.'

Pete smiled tiredly and went on in a quieter voice. 'Hell, we had a – a piece of ordinary cotton string, and you could have cut it or burned it in two with a match, or just pulled it apart in your hands – if you could have got *around* to it! But somehow every time you'd try, something would interrupt – the phone would ring, or you'd cut yourself with the scissors and have to go get a Band-Aid, or the cat would start to throw up on some important papers, or you'd accidentally drop the string down behind the couch. I suppose if you really cornered it and forced it, you'd find that you'd suffered a stroke or a heart attack, or got knocked down by a random bullet through the window – and the piece of string would be on the floor somewhere, still whole.' He shook his head. 'None of these things make logical sense, but they're true *anyway*. If you insist on the world being *logical* at every turn, you'll even-tually be forced to retreat all the way into genuine insanity, I promise you.'

'Bring *me* the goddamn piece of string,' said Cochran loudly. 'I'll break the son-of-a-bitch for you!'

Angelica stood back and crossed her arms. 'We lost it.'

After a tense moment Cochran let his shoulders slump; he sighed, and rubbed his face with both hands. 'I suppose he's really a king, too. What's he king *of*, what *was* he king of?'

'The land, for one thing,' said Kootie, who had followed them into the kitchen, 'the American West. If he's well, the land is well – right now he's dead, and we're in winter and having earthquakes all over. God knows what the spring will be like, or if there'll even be one.'

Cochran raised his head and stared at the dead man's strong, bearded face. It was pale, and the eyes were closed, but Cochran could see humor and sternness in the lines around the eyes and down the cheeks. 'How could *he* have been ... in a weakened state?' he asked softly.

Mavranos was frowning, and he passed the revolver from his right hand to his left and back again; Cochran could hear the bullets rattle faintly in the chambers. 'We didn't know how. He and Diana were having healthy babies – though this last couple of years the kids were getting bad fevers in the winter – and the land was yielding several crops a year! But there were signs – the phylloxera—'

'The phylloxera had nothing to do with anything,' snapped Diana angrily from behind Cochran.

'Okay,' Mavranos said. 'Then I haven't got a clue.'

'What the hell's a phylloxera?' asked Plumtree.

'It's not important,' Diana said. 'Don't talk about it.'

Cochran said nothing – but he knew what phylloxera was. It was a plant louse that in the 1830s had inadvertently been brought from America to Europe, where it had eventually nearly wiped out all the vineyards – the fabulous old growths in Germany, and Italy, and even France, even Bordeaux. The louse injected a toxin that killed the roots, six feet under, so that the vine and the grapes up on the surface withered away and died; the eventual desperate cure had been to graft the classic old European *vitis vinifera* grapevines, everything from Pinot Noir and Riesling to Malvasia and the Spanish Pedro Ximenez, onto phylloxera-resistant *vitis riparia* roots from America. But now, just since about 1990, a new breed of phylloxera had been devastating the California vineyards, which were mostly grown on a modern hybrid rootstock known as AxR#1. Most of Pace Vineyards' vines were old Zinfandel and Pinot Noir on pre-war *riparia* rootstocks, so the subterranean plague hadn't hit them, but Cochran knew personally a number of winemakers in San Mateo and Santa Clara and Alameda Counties who were facing bankruptcy because of the expense of tearing out the infested AxR#1 vines and replanting with new vines, which wouldn't produce a commercial crop for three to five years.

He thought of what Kootie had said – *If he's well, the land is well.* And he thought of the billions of minute phylloxera lice, busily working away … *six feet under.* The land, Cochran thought, has not been truly well for several years.

'And he was always … less powerful, in winter,' Mavranos said, shrugging, 'and stronger in summer. One of the tarot cards that represents him is *Il Sole*, the Sun card.'

'This really is Solville,' said Angelica quietly, 'while he's here.'

Kootie pointed at the withered bean sprouts in Angelica's Gardens of Adonis pans on the counter by the door. 'Solville in eclipse,' he said.

'Not runnin' a carny peep-show here,' said Mavranos gruffly. 'Back into the office, now.'

'Wait a minute,' mumbled old Spider Joe, who had been peering in blindly through the doorway. 'I've got to … put in my two cents' worth.' He pushed his way into the kitchen now, his projecting curb-feelers dragging noisily through the doorframe and then twanging free to wave and bob over the dead man's bare feet. One of the metal filaments whipped across Plumtree's cheek, and she whispered 'Shit, dude!' and batted it away.

The white-bearded old blind man dug two silver-dollar-size coins out of the pocket of his stained khaki windbreaker, and for a moment he held them out on his outstretched palm. They appeared to be dirty gold, and were only crudely round, with bunches of grapes stamped in high relief on their faces, along with the letters TPA.

'Trapezus, on the Black Sea,' exclaimed Kootie, 'is where those are from. Those are about two thousand years old!'

Spider Joe closed his hand, and when he opened it again the coins were United States silver dollars. 'These are what he paid me with, nearly five years ago, for the tarot-card reading that led him to the throne.'

'I remember,' said Mavranos quietly.

'Well, he's gonna need them again, now, isn't he? – to pay for passage across the Styx, and for the drink of surrender from the Lethe River, over on the far side of India.' In spite of being blind, the old man shuffled forward, reached out and accurately laid one of the coins on each of the dead man's closed eyelids.

Mavranos's face was stiff. 'We okay now? Right, everybody out.'

They all began shuffling and elbowing their way through the doorway back into the office, while Mavranos hung back with the revolver; a couple of Spider Joe's antennae hooked one of Angelica's bean pans off the counter and flung it clattering to the floor, spilling dirt and withered bean sprouts across the linoleum.

CHAPTER EIGHT

Mark, silent king, the moral of this sport:
How soon my sorrow hath destroyed my face.
—William Shakespeare, *Richard II*

Kootie was back up on the desk beside the inert television, sitting cross-legged and finishing his fish stew. When everybody had resumed their places, he refilled his wine cup and said, 'Who was this person who gave you my name and address?'

'And when did he give 'em to you?' added Mavranos.

'Dr. Richard Paul Armentrout, at Rosecrans Medical Center in Bellflower,' said Plumtree, who was sitting on the floor beside Cochran in front of the couch now. 'This afternoon.' Apparently she too was respecting Strubie the Clown's hundred-dollar bid to be left out of this picture.

Mavranos frowned, his high cheekbones and narrowed eyes and drooping mustache making him look like some old Tartar chieftain. 'He *sent* you here?'

'No,' Plumtree said. 'Sid and I broke out of the hospital, when the earthquake hit, a couple of hours ago. Armentrout didn't even believe there *was* a king, much less that I had ... helped to kill him, until he talked to me this afternoon. Then he said, "Oh, you must have had help, from somebody who was practically a king himself, like this kid from a couple of years ago."' She looked up past Cochran at Kootie. 'Which was you.'

Kootie put the bowl aside and took a sip of the wine. 'Why did you escape?'

'Armentrout wants to find out what happened on New Year's Day,' Plumtree told him, 'and he wasn't going to let us go until he was totally satisfied that he'd found out everything, using every kind of strip-mining therapy that his operating room and pharmacy have available; and even then I don't think he'd have wanted us to be able to talk, after. He wouldn't have killed us, necessarily, but he'd have no problem fucking up our minds so bad that between us we couldn't string together one coherent sentence. This afternoon, just as a warm-up, he tried to break off and ... *consume* a couple of my personalities.'

'Your personalities,' said Angelica.

'I've got MPD – that's multiple—'

'I know what it is,' Angelica interrupted. 'I don't think the condition *exists*, I think it's just a romanticizing of post-traumatic stress disorder, best addressed with intensive exploratory psychotherapy, but I do know what it is.'

'My wife was a psychiatrist,' remarked Pete, 'before she became a *bruja*.'

Plumtree gave Angelica a challenging smile. 'Would you advise Edison Medicine for the condition?'

'ECT? Hell no,' snapped Angelica, 'I've never condoned shock therapy for *any* condition; and I can't imagine *anyone* prescribing it for PTSD, or a hypothetical MPD.'

'Edison Medicine,' came Kootie's wryly amused voice from above Cochran. 'It knocked *me* right out of my own head – and killed my dog.'

One of Spider Joe's antennae popped up from the carpet with a musical twang, making Plumtree jump against Cochran's shoulder. He put his arm around her, and in the moment before she shrugged it off he noticed that she was trembling. Well, he was too.

'Whatever,' said Pete, who had sat down on the couch. To Plumtree he went on, 'You say he tried to eat some of your personalities. Was he masked, when he did this?' He absently tapped a Marlboro out of a pack and flipped the cigarette into the air; it disappeared, and then he reached behind his ear and pulled out what might have been the same cigarette, lit now, and began puffing smoke from it. 'Like, did he have a ... a *pair of twins* present, or a schizophrenic?'

'He had a crazy guy on the extension phone, listening in,' spoke up Cochran. To Plumtree he said, 'The old one-armed guy, Long John Beach.'

For a moment no one spoke, and the only sound was the chaotic drumming of water splashing into the pots on the floor. Then, 'A one-armed guy,' said Kootie steadily, looking hard at Pete Sullivan, 'named after a local city.'

'I – I thought he died,' said Angelica, who was standing beside the desk. 'You mean the one who called himself Sherman Oaks, who wanted to kill you so he could eat the Edison ghost out of your head?'

'Right, the smoke-fancier.' Kootie glanced at Plumtree. 'Ghosts are known as "smokes" to the addicts who eat them, and he used to eat a lot of them.'

'Shit, he still does,' put in Cochran. 'Though he's down to Marlboros these days.'

'I thought he was dead,' insisted Angelica. 'I thought he blew up along with Nicky Bradshaw, when they both fell off the *Queen Mary*, two years ago.'

'With "a local man called Neal Obstadt," right?' said Plumtree. 'Who was looking for Scott Crane in 1990? Armentrout mentioned this. The explosion killed the Obstadt person, according to him, but just collapsed a lung of this Long John Beach, or Sherman Oaks.' She grinned, breathing rapidly between her teeth. 'I wonder what other names he's used. Wes Covina. Perry Mount.'

Cochran was embarrassed by her incongruous merriment, and nudged her. She nudged him back, hard, in the ribs.

'Or in drag, as Beverly Hills,' Pete agreed absently. Then he stood up abruptly and looked around the room. 'Well, he's been here before – he knows the way here, too. We'd better get ready for him, and for this psychiatrist.'

Angelica visibly shivered, and she touched the gun under her blouse. 'We should just run, right now.'

'We need to know *where* to run, first,' Pete told her. He stepped to the television set and clanked the channel switch a couple of notches clockwise. 'Could you plug this thing in again, Oliver? We need some readings, Angie. Pennies, I'd think, for a fine-grain closeup-type picture. What year was Crane born in?'

'Nineteen forty-three,' said Diana.

The tanned teenager hopped up off the couch and plugged the TV set's cord into the wall while Angelica pulled open a desk drawer and bumped glass jars around in it. 'Pennies,' she muttered. 'Nineteen ... forty ... three, there we are.' She lifted one of the little jars out and sat down on the couch. The set's screen had brightened, and a woman in a commercial was talking about some new Ford car. Cochran and Plumtree hiked themselves forward on the carpet to be able to see the screen.

Angelica shook the jar, and the half-dozen old gray pennies in it rattled and clinked – and the TV picture shifted to a newscaster reading the day's winning lottery numbers. She shook the jar again, and now they were watching the portly, bearded figure of Orson Welles sitting at a restaurant table, waving a glass of wine and quoting the Paul Masson slogan about selling no wine before its time.

Pete Sullivan caught Cochran's glance and smiled. 'Plain physics so far,' Pete said. 'This is an old set, from the days when the remote controls used ultrasound frequencies to change channels and turn the sets on and off. The remote was a tiny xylophone, in effect, too high in frequency for anybody but dogs and TVs to hear. Nowadays the signals need to carry more information, and they use infrared.'

'I get it,' said Cochran, a little defensively. He was still shaking, still enormously aware of the dead man on the table in the kitchen. He nodded. 'The TV thinks her jingling pennies are a remote. Who are you, uh, hoping to consult, here?'

Pete shrugged. 'Not who – what. Just ... the moment; right now, right here. The pennies she's shaking are a part of now with a link to Crane's birth year, and the pictures they'll tune the TV to will be representative bits of now in the same field of reference – just like a piece of a hologram contains the whole picture, or a drop of your blood contains the entire physical portrait of you. It's what Jung called synchronicity.'

'Synchronicity!' sneered Angelica, who was shaking the jar again and staring at the screen. She stepped back and sat down on the couch, still shaking the pennies.

'Angie thinks there are actual, sentient entities behind this sort of thing,' said Pete. 'A querulous old woman, in this case – the same party that's behind the Chinese I Ching, according to her.'

'A straitlaced and disapproving old party,' said Angelica without looking away from the screen. 'Sometimes I can almost smell her lavender sachet. Ah, we're online.'

Cochran peered at the screen curiously, but it was just showing a grainy black-and-white film of a blond woman brushing her hair.

'It always starts with this,' said Pete, visibly tenser now. 'That's Mary Pickford, the old silent-movie star. A guy name Philo T. Farnsworth was the first guy in the American West to transmit images with a cathode-ray tube, in

San Francisco in 1927, and he used this repeating loop of Mary Pickford as a demo.' He sighed shakily. 'This isn't a real-world, 1995 broadcast – we're into supernatural effects now, sorry.'

'You were getting spook stuff even *before*,' said young Oliver nervously. 'Paul Masson hasn't aired that Orson Welles ad for years.'

'I think he's right,' murmured Angelica from the couch.

Spider Joe had been sitting silently against the kitchen wall, but now he reared back, and half a dozen of his antennae sprang up from the carpet. 'Who just came in?' he barked, the sunken eyelids twitching in his craggy brown face.

Cochran glanced fearfully at the open back door, but there was no one there; and Plumtree and Diana and Angelica were craning their necks down the hall and toward the kitchen, but there was no sign or sound of any intruder.

Kootie had directed an unfocussed stare at the ceiling, and now he lowered his head. 'There's no one new on the whole block.'

Mavranos cleared his throat. 'But, uh ... your *Mary Pickford* has changed into a *negro*.'

'And she got older,' noted the teenager who had been introduced as Scat, and who hadn't taken his eyes off the screen since they'd all trooped back in from the kitchen.

On the TV screen, the figure was in fact a thin old black woman in a high-necked dark dress now, sitting at a mirrored vanity table and brushing her hair – and though her jawline was strong and unsagging, her kinky hair now looked more white than blond.

As if in response to Angelica's hard shaking of the penny jar, the grainy black-and-white picture sharpened in focus, and an open window with a row of eucalyptus trees beyond it was visible in the wall behind the old woman; and sounds were audible – a faint, crackling susurration as the old woman drew the brush through her hair, an insistent knocking of the raised window shade bar against the window frame, and a clanging bell from outside.

'The knocking, and the bell, those are to confuse ghosts,' said Plumtree.

Angelica was shaking the jar harder, as if trying to drive the image off the TV screen, and she seemed irritated that the pennies weren't doing it, were instead just jangling in rhythmic counterpoint to the bell.

'It's San Francisco, all right,' said Pete. 'That's a cable-car bell in the background.'

'This film clip is seventy years old,' panted Angelica. 'Everyplace probably had streetcars then.'

'It isn't the old clip anymore,' objected Pete. 'This here has got sound.'

'Pete,' said Kootie loudly as he clanked his empty bowl down beside the television set, 'dig out the Edison telephone and get it hooked up again. We're in a new game now, with this restoration-to-life talk, and even an idiot shell of Scott Crane might have something to say worth hearing. And I reckon Janis Plumtree should be enough of a link for us to reach him, her being his own personal murderer.'

'And his wife,' said the bald Diana from the kitchen doorway. 'You've got his wife here, too.'

'Right,' said Kootie hastily. 'Sorry, Diana – I was thinking in terms of the new arrivals. I meant *murderer* now *too*.'

Angelica finally leaned forward and set the jar of 1943 pennies down on the carpet. 'I'm not dealing with the I Ching old lady here,' she said, wiping her hands on her jeans as she leaned back against the couch cushions. 'And it's not being run by just your *synchronicity* either, Pete. It's ... I sense some *other* old woman.'

Cochran saw Mavranos, glance at Spider Joe. Clearly he was wondering if the crazy old blind man's dead wife might be taking over the show here. Cochran wondered if Booger had been a black woman.

'If you say so, Kootie,' said Pete. 'Scat, Ollie – you guys can help me carry some boxes in from the garage.'

After Diana's two boys had followed Pete out the back door, Angelica Anthem Elizalde Sullivan stared resentfully at the Plumtree woman sitting in front of the desk with her drunk Connecticut pansy boyfriend. MPD, thought Angelica scornfully. I didn't even think that was a hip diagnosis anymore, I thought everybody was busy uncovering suppressed memories of childhood sexual abuse these days.

'Kootie,' Angelica called, 'toss me my *Loteria* cards.'

Her adopted son twisted around on the desk and dug through a pile of utility bills and check stubs, then tossed over the heads of Cochran and Plumtree a little deck of cards held together with a rubber band.

Angelica caught the bundle and pulled the rubber band off the cards. 'Miss Plumtree,' she said, having forgotten the woman's first name, 'come sit by me on the couch here and chat.'

Plumtree stared back at her. 'Why should I answer your questions, lady?'

Angelica smiled at her as she deftly shuffled the cheap paper cards. 'I know about ... *making amends* to people you've allowed to die; people you're linked with by chains of guilt, hm? *Real* guilt and shame, the kind you've got to go back and *fix*, not just "get past" or "put behind you" or get "okay with." You think you can do it without help, but that's like thinking one hand can fix what it took two hands to break. If that dead man in the kitchen *can* be resurrected, it might be some thing you can tell us that'll help us all to get the job done.' She looked around the room affectionately. 'I wonder if we've got even one person here who doesn't believe, with some validity, that he or she is directly responsible beyond any excuse for the death of someone.'

'Shee-it,' snarled Plumtree; but she struggled wearily to her feet and shambled over to the couch, which thumped the floor with an uneven leg when she dropped onto it beside Angelica. Her boyfriend, Cochran, got to his feet and leaned attentively on the corner of the desk.

Angelica scooted back and spread the cards messily facedown on the couch cushion between them; the blurry black-and-white plaid patterns on the backs of the cards blended together so that it seemed to be one puddle on the cushion. In Mexico these cards were used to play a gambling game similar to bingo, but Angelica had long ago found that the mundane pictures on the fronts of them were useful for eliciting free association from patients. 'Pick me three of them,' Angelica said.

Pete and the boys came clomping back in, carrying cardboard boxes, as Plumtree carefully drew three of the cards out of the pile; and Angelica leaned forward to be heard over the clanking of telephone and radio parts being lifted out of the boxes and spread out on the desk. 'Now flip one of them face up,' she said.

With a trembling hand Plumtree turned over ... card 51, El Pescado, a picture of a red fish upside down in smoky water, holding a tethered hook in its mouth.

'I guess you know what that one indicates,' Angelica said in a carefully confident and dismissive tone.

'"I'll bite" is what it ... *means*,' Plumtree said, nodding. 'But if this is a reading of me, it's wrong. I won't bite. Maybe it's a warning for me, huh? Don't let yourself get pulled out into the air, get separated from the school – Off the school bus! – get cooked and eaten and digested by somebody out there. "Full fathom five my father lies."'

Angelica just nodded, but she was surprised – she had expected that this serendipitous picture would evoke some mention of the Fisher King, whom Plumtree claimed to have killed.

Angelica looked up and made a *ch-ch!* sound; Kootie had climbed down from the desk, but instantly looked around toward her.

'St. Michael the Archangel,' Angelica told him, 'with High John the Conqueror ready.'

The boy nodded and pulled open one of the desk drawers; he lifted out two aerosol spray cans and handed the purple one across to his foster mother.

'Your father's in the other direction, then,' Angelica said to Plumtree, hefting the can, 'from whoever's dangling the line into the water, is that right? Tell me about your father.'

'Well, he's dead. Is that Scotchgard? I wasn't going to piss on your couch, lady.' When Angelica didn't reply or change her expression, Plumtree sighed and went on. 'He died when I was two, but I was in the hospital, so they didn't tell me about it right away, about him being dead. Janis doesn't remember him any more than I do, but she claims to miss him real bad. All she knows about him is what she's heard from Valorie.'

'Valorie's older?'

'*Yes*,' said Plumtree tightly. 'Valorie's been – around from the beginning.'

'She remembers a lot of stuff?'

'She remembers everything. But all her memories,' Plumtree added, glancing at the TV set, 'are in black and white, and always with some drumming or banging going on in the background.'

'Can I talk to Valorie?'

Plumtree shifted uncomfortably and shot a nervous glance toward Cochran. 'Not unless she wants to talk to you.'

'What were you in the hospital for? When you were two?'

'I don't remember. Measles? Stress? Some kid thing.'

Pete had unplugged the TV set and was lifting it down off the desk to make room for the Ford coil box and the battered old field frequency modulator. 'I hope mice haven't got into all this stuff in these two years,' he muttered to Kootie.

'It'd be *ghosts* of mice that'd be attracted to it,' said Kootie, who was still holding the other spray can.

'How did he die?' Angelica asked Plumtree. 'Your father.'

'Jesus, lady!' said Plumtree tightly. 'You're just *asking* to have me lose time here.'

Angelica held up the purple spray can and let Plumtree look at the picture on the label, a crude drawing of a winged, sword-wielding angel kicking a bat-winged devil into a fiery pit. The directions advised, *Spray all areas of your surroundings. Make the sign of the Cross.* 'This is just air-freshener, really,' Angelica said, 'but the chlorofluorocarbons in it, and this groovy *label*, repel ghosts. After I spray it around us, you can talk freely.'

Angelica held the can over Plumtree's head and pushed the button on the top of it; a mist that smelled like bus-station rest rooms hissed out, drifting over Plumtree and Angelica both.

Plumtree took a deep breath and let it out. 'Well!' she said when Angelica had lowered the can. 'He fell off a building, is what happened, in San Francisco, one of the old wino buildings south of Market. *Soma*, they used to call that area, from *south* of Market, get it? *In Soma's realm are many herbs, and knowledge a hundredfold have they.* That's from the Rig-Veda. I hope you're right about that spray stuff. He was the chief of a hippie commune, like the Diggers, you know? A group that fed homeless runaways. My father's commune was called the Lever Blank, they're mentioned in a couple of the books about the Manson family. I suppose the name meant *vote-for-nobody* or something. My mom left the commune a couple of years after he died, and she always said that they killed him, because it was the summer solstice and he had failed to become this king of the west at Easter. '69 was a competition year for it, just like '90 was.'

Pete had sent Ollie back outside to fetch a car battery from one of the Solville vehicles, and was now brushing the dust off the pencil lines and screw holes still in the wood surface of the desk from the time they had set up this telephone in October of 1992.

'Okay,' Angelica said cautiously. She pointed at the two cards that were still face down. 'Hit me again.'

Plumtree turned over the second card, and it was the unnumbered El Borracho card, The Drunk – a picture of a man in laborer's white clothing walking bent-legged and carrying a bottle, with a dog snapping at his heels.

'That was you, tonight,' Plumtree said to Cochran, picking up the card and showing it to him.

Cochran peered at the picture on it, then jerked his head back, frowning. 'I may have been drunk,' he said, 'but I wasn't *bestial*. That there is more like who Long John Beach was singing about.' He rubbed his hand clumsily over his face, and Angelica noticed a leaf-shaped birthmark on his knuckles. 'And who was it that drank the Manhattans,' he went on, 'and all the Budweisers?'

'We're talking about *you*, here,' Angelica told Plumtree. 'How do you feel about this picture?'

'I hate drunks,' said Plumtree. 'I'd never let Janis get involved with one.' Apparently to end discussion of the Borracho card, she reached down and flipped over the third card.

It was number 46, El Sol, a drawing of a bodiless round red face encircled by a jagged gold corona.

Plumtree's eyes slammed shut and she flung herself back hard against the couch cushions, with her fingers clawed into the disordered thatch of her blond hair; her nostrils were tensely white as she whistlingly inhaled a deep breath, but her face was reddening visibly even under her sunburn – and fleetingly Angelica wondered how a patient in a mental hospital could acquire a sunburn. Plumtree was whispering some rapid-cadenced phrase over and over again.

From long practice Angelica resisted the impulse to participate in her patient's panic. 'I think we'd better titrate up our St. Michael dosage,' she said calmly, raising the purple can and spraying two more long bursts of the stuff over their heads.

Pete and Kootie had paused in their phone-assembly work to stare at Plumtree, and Mavranos was frowning and tapping the revolver barrel against his thigh.

Now Angelica could hear what Plumtree was whispering: '—Ghost! In the name of the Father, the Son, the Holy Ghost! In the name of—'

'What is it that this *reminded* you of?' Angelica asked the woman in a voice just loud enough to override the frantic whispering. 'Whatever it is, it's not *here*. Only this little drawing is *here*.'

'Let me,' said Cochran. He stepped forward and knelt beside the stiff, shaking Plumtree. 'Janis,' he said to her, 'this is 1995, the eleventh of January, Wednesday, probably getting on for midnight. You're in Long Beach, and you're twenty-eight years old.' He looked at the Sol card that was still face up on the couch cushion; he turned it face down, and then he glanced up at Angelica. 'She has a recurrent nightmare, of the sun falling out of the sky onto her, knocking her flat.'

Plumtree's eyes opened and she lowered her hands, and she blinked around at everyone staring at her. 'I'm sorry,' she said. 'Was I yelling?'

Angelica smiled at her. This, she thought, must be one of her other *personalities*. How I do love the histrionics and theatricalities of dissociatives. 'No,' Angelica said patiently. 'The gentlemen were wanting help with their telephone.' Plumtree's mention of herbs a few moments ago actually had reminded her of a crucial part of the telephone; she looked over at Johanna and said, 'You remember the mix we cooked on the stove, two years ago? You'd better get a pot of it going – Pete would have forgotten it, being all wrapped up in his hardware. The mint – the *yerba buena* leaves – you can pick out back by the garage, and there's tequila in the cupboard, unless Arky's drunk it all up.'

'It's your bourbon I drank up,' Mavranos said defensively. 'I don't touch tequila.'

Angelica clasped her hands and turned back to Plumtree. As casually as she could, she asked, 'Do you remember much about the hospital you were in, when you were two? Did it have ... lawns, playrooms, a cafeteria? Try to picture it.'

'I only remember the room I was in,' Plumtree said. 'There were get-well cards on the table by the bed,' she added helpfully.

'Close your eyes again, but this time relax.' When Plumtree complied, Angelica 'you'll find you can remember details very clearly, especially from when you were young, if you clear your mind of every distraction and just *relax*. And you're safe here with us, so you *can* relax, can't you?'

Without opening her eyes, Plumtree said, 'You're right here, Scant?'

Cochran clasped her shoulder. 'Right here.'

'Then I can relax.'

'So ... remember the hospital room,' said Angelica. 'What did it smell like?'

'... Fresh-peeled adhesive tape,' Plumtree said dreamily, 'and laundry baskets, and the woody taste of Fudgsicle sticks once you've sucked all the ice cream off, and shampoo.'

'And what did the room look like?'

'There was a window – there *was* a window! – with metal venetian blinds to my left, but I could only see part of a tree branch through it; the wallpaper was lime green, and there were dots, little holes, in the white tiles on the ceiling—'

Plumtree's eyes were still closed, and Angelica permitted herself a faint nod and a tiny mild smile of triumph. 'Why,' she asked in a voice she forced to sound careless, 'couldn't you see anything more out the window?'

'I didn't go over to it, to look out.'

'Were you ... *afraid* to?'

'No, it was on the ground floor. I just didn't get out of bed at all, even to go to the bathroom. I had to use a bedpan, though I was certainly not wearing diapers anymore, by then.'

'Can you see the room? All the details?'

'Sure.'

'Look at yourself, then, at your arms and legs. Why didn't you get out of bed?'

'I – I couldn't! – not with a cast on my leg and my arm in a sling – !'

Plumtree's eyes sprang open, and it was all Angelica could do to maintain her gentle smile – for she was abruptly, viscerally certain that it was an entirely different person now behind the Plumtree woman's eyes. Angelica made herself go on to note the physical indications – the tightened cast of the woman's mouth and jaw, the wider eyes, the newly squared shoulders – but the conviction had come, indomitably, first.

Plumtree turned her head to look at Cochran, who flinched slightly but kept his hand on her shoulder.

'How're you taking all this?' he asked her nervously.

'Upon my back,' Plumtree said in a flat voice, 'to defend my belly; upon my wit, to defend my wiles; upon my secrecy, to defend mine honesty; my mask, to defend my beauty; and you, to defend all these. And at all these wards I lie, at a thousand watches.'

'Now who just *left*?' demanded Spider Joe from the corner.

'Wow,' said Angelica humbly.

Plumtree had lowered her face into her hands, and now she looked up, squinting 'Wha'd I miss?' she asked irritably 'Do you people have such a thing as a *beer* around here?'

The woman has shifted again, Angelica thought. I may talk myself out of it eventually, but right now I'm a believer in MPD.

'Yes,' she said, just to get away from this woman who was such an affront to her professional convictions. 'Right. A beer. I'll get one of Arky's for you.'

But she was still too shaken by what she had deduced about Plumtree's condition to stand up right away; and she was wondering if the telephone call would even be possible with Plumtree here on the premises.

'Coors, that means,' sighed Plumtree.

'This stuff on the desk here is the antenna,' Pete was telling Scat and Oliver, 'but we can't be in the room with it, or the carborundum bulb and the rectifying lens will just pick up on our living auras. Let's set up the actual telephone receiver in the laundry room. That used to be the kitchen, before one of our remodeling campaigns, and it's where we did it before.'

And you don't want to do it in the current kitchen, right in the presence of the dead king, Angelica thought as she finally stood up, dizzily, from the couch. Well, neither do I.

She paused in the kitchen doorway, standing back against the doorframe to avoid getting tangled in Spider Joe's arching antennae. 'How are you planning to scramble the call?' she asked Pete. 'Even if Sherman Oaks and this bad psychiatrist already know where we are, there's no use in lighting a beacon for every *other* smoke-fancier in the L.A. area, if we can help it.'

Pete held up his hands and made dialling motions with his forefingers. 'I've still got antique hands.'

'Yeah,' said Angelica uncertainly, 'but they're *yours* now.'

Pete lowered his hands. 'I guess you're right. I've even put a few new scars on 'em in the last two years.'

'You do hand transplants, lady?' Plumtree asked Angelica. 'You sound more like Dr. Frankenstein than Dr. Freud.'

'Yeah,' said Mavranos, frowning like someone having health-insurance billing explained to them, 'what's all this Beast-With-Five-Fingers talk?'

'Sorry,' said Pete. 'The magician Houdini had a customized mask made in the twenties, see, sort of a decoy with a magical spell on it, to make it look like he was where he wasn't. It was plaster casts of his hands, and his actual cut-off dried thumb, and if you were carrying the lot when bad magicians focussed on you, you'd suddenly take on the physical appearance of Houdini – short stature, dinner jacket with break-away sleeves, curly hair, the whole outfit. And—'

Plumtree's boyfriend made a suppressed snorting sound.

'I wish we did still have that magical string from Mexico,' Angelica told him scornfully; 'I'd love to see you suddenly notice that your goddamn *shoes* were on fire, or you suddenly had a live *bat* in your hair, when you tried to snap it.'

'On Halloween day of '92,' Pete went on, 'we were dragged out of our apartment here at gunpoint by the people who wanted the Edison ghost that was in Kootie's head then – you got any problems with *that*, mister?

– and the dried thumb was somewhere else, the bad guys found that; but I grabbed the plaster hands – and they disappeared – and suddenly I had *Houdini*'s hands.' He held his hands up and wiggled the short, strong fingers. 'And I've had 'em ever since. They won't hold a weapon – I guess Houdini didn't want his decoy hurting anyone – and I'm more comfortable now writing with a fountain pen, and shaving with a straight razor; but at least I can do lots of parlor-magic stunts.' He clenched the hands into fists. 'Angie's right, though – they are mine now. They wouldn't disguise the source of the call.'

For a moment no one spoke, and the drumming of water falling from the leaky ceiling into the pots and pans was the only sound.

Then, 'Arky has the dried eyeball of a dead Fisher King,' said Kootie. 'That would be a fine scrambler.'

'Make it two beers,' called Plumtree, 'if I gotta sit here and listen to all this creepy shit.' Angelica could hear the tremor of fear under the woman's bravado.

Angelica decided that she would have a beer herself; and maybe some of the tequila, which she could now smell heating up in the kitchen, if there was any still left in the bottle. She rocked her head back against the doorway frame with a firm knock 'I suppose you really do have that,' she said wearily to Mavranos. 'And I suppose a one-time Fisher King's ghost might not have been banished by the current Fisher King's death, because of standing *behind* the shotgun, as it were.' She sighed. 'An eyeball. So is it *activated* at all, in any sense? I mean, is there any *ashe* in it, any vitality? How far away is the *rest* of this … dead Fisher King? If his body is real far away, or under water, then your … *dried eyeball* … won't be a whole lot of use.'

'Oh well,' said Mavranos, shrugging and shaking his head, 'as a matter of fact, I think the rest of him is in Lake Mead. And I think he's used up anyway.'

'Oh, well,' agreed Angelica, and she strode into the kitchen and walked around the dead king's feet to the refrigerator. Johanna was stirring the aromatic pot of mint leaves and tequila on the stove, and the sharp smell of it reminded Angelica to snag a beer for herself along with the two for Plumtree.

She heard Pete ask Mavranos, 'Who was it?'

'Bugsy Siegel,' came Mavranos's rueful answer. 'The eye was shot out of his head when he was killed in '46, and Scott's father had it stashed away in a hidey-hole in the basement of the Flamingo Hotel in Vegas. Scott's father was king, from '46 until '90.'

'No shit? Hey, Angie!' called Pete then. 'We're in business after all.'

CHAPTER NINE

The wine was red wine, and had stained the ground of the narrow street in the suburb of Saint Antoine, in Paris, where it was spilled. It had stained many hands, too, and many faces, and many naked feet, and many wooden shoes. The hands of the man who sawed the wood, left red marks on the billets; and the forehead of the woman who nursed her baby, was stained with the stain of the old rag she wound about her head again. Those who had been greedy with the staves of the cask, had acquired a tigerish smear about the mouth; and one tall joker so besmirched, his head more out of a long squalid bag of a nightcap than in it, scrawled upon a wall with his finger dipped in muddy wine-lees – BLOOD.

—Charles Dickens, *A Tale of Two Cities*

And now they're all drinking, thought Cochran, and cooking up a pot of some kind of noxious mint-and-tequila punch; and young Boogie-Woogie – *Kootie* – has refilled his wine cup at least once; and if there's a crazier brand of bullshit being talked in California tonight, it's gotta be in a loony bin for far worse cases than any at Rosecrans Medical. But *I'm* supposedly the one who's the *drunk*.

'Bugsy Siegel's ashes are in the Beth Olaum Mausoleum at the Hollywood Cemetery on Santa Monica, only about twenty miles from here,' the man called Pete was saying now. 'His ghost was a pal of my dad's ghost – Angie, you remember, it was Siegel's ghost that rapped back *knock-knock* when I rapped *knock, knock, knock-knock, knock*, when we were there to pick up my dad's ghost, day before Halloween in '92.'

'I do remember that,' allowed the woman who was coming back from the kitchen with three cans of Coors. Two for Cody and none for me, Cochran thought. He thought of going into the kitchen and fetching a couple for himself, but couldn't face the thought of seeing the dead man again.

And he was still unsettled by the picture on the card that Cody had shown him – with the comment *This was you tonight* – the fat, bearded, idiot face of the drunken figure in the drawing, the crown of roses that seemed to conceal horns, the animal-skin cloak, the sketchy legs that bent the wrong way like a goat's and ended in sketchy stumps like hooves!

Kootie had lifted out of one of the cardboard boxes an electric pencil sharpener, and now the boy carefully unsnapped its wood-grain printed plastic cowl. Underneath, instead of the crossed grinders of a pencil sharpener's works, a thick stick of yellow chalk was attached to the rotor.

'This middle section is pretty deeply grooved from the last time,' Kootie said peering at the chalk. 'But we can attach the spring to a different section, closer to the motor, and I remember how Edison set it up.'

'I'm not sure Edison himself knew what he was doing,' said Pete.

'I remember how he set it up,' said Kootie.

'Fine,' said Pete. 'Good.' He glanced at Cochran and smiled. 'That's our speaker, our receiver – that pencil sharpener. Most speakers use induced changes in the field of a magnet to wiggle the diaphragm; we can't do that, because an actual physical magnet would draw ghosts the way a low spot on a pavement collects rainwater. If we did this a lot, I'd hook up a piezo-electric quartz, or an electrostatic setup with perforated condenser plates, but this arrangement actually does work well enough. We'll soak the chalk with water, and then attach the diaphragm spring to the surface of the chalk, which will be spinning when we turn on the pencil sharpener – wet chalk is toothy and full of friction ordinarily, see, but it gets instantly slick when there's an electric current going through it. The changes are variable enough and rapid enough to get decent low-quality sound out of the attached diaphragm.'

Cochran understood that the man was sociably trying to let him in on what was going on, so he returned the smile, jerkily, and nodded. 'Clever,' he said.

'It was better sound quality than a lot of the headphones out there,' said Kootie.

'I'm not dissing your old orisha, son,' Pete said mildly. In one hand he picked up a rack of glass tubes and in the other a glass cylinder that had a little metal rod rattling in it like a bell clapper. 'I'm gonna take the vacuum pump out to the kitchen and hook it to the faucet to evacuate the Langmuir gauge. You might get everybody crowded into the laundry room, Kootie, or out in the back yard. Out of this room, anyway.'

'While you're in the kitchen,' spoke up Cochran, trying not to speak with passion, 'could you get me one of those beers?'

Behind him Plumtree snickered. Pete looked at Kootie, who shrugged and nodded.

'Okay,' Pete said.

Young Oliver was leaning against the couch, and now he hesitantly spoke. 'You're gonna call our father's ghost, now? Not him, himself, but his ghost?' The boy's face was stiff, but Cochran could see the redness in his eyes.

'That's right, Oliver,' said Mavranos. 'You're the man of your family now, you can be there for it, if you like.'

Oliver shook his head. 'No,' he whispered. 'It'd—'

'It'd just be him dead in that room too,' said his brother Scat solemnly. 'Like it is the kitchen.' He looked at Oliver and then said, 'We'll wait in the back yard.' Their mother, Diana, just bit her knuckle and nodded.

Cochran followed Plumtree and Angelica and Diana into the flower-wallpapered little laundry room, and he sat down beside Plumtree at the foot of a sink in the corner. Kootie had climbed up on top of the washing machine, which was one of the heavy-duty commercial kind that had a push-in slot for quarters; the pencil sharpener sat on a shelf beside his shoulder, attached now to the frame of a disassembled pasta machine with a spring and a paper loudspeaker cone attached to it.

Pete had set up a TV table and a lawn chair in the middle of the linoleum floor, and almost ceremoniously had placed on the table an old black Bakelite rotary-dial telephone that was connected with phone cords trailing one way to the pencil sharpener and strung along the linoleum floor the other way to the assembly on the table out in the office. Johanna had stayed in the present-day kitchen to keep an eye on the pan of mint-and-tequila, though the astringent smoke from it was making Cochran's eyes water. Probably she just forgot about it, he thought, and went outside to listen to the music some more, and the pan's on fire. He sipped his freshly opened beer cautiously, not having any idea how long this procedure might take; crazy old Spider Joe had elected to join the boys outside in the yard, where the music was, and Cochran was wishing he had gone along with the old blind man.

'Can I have the … eye?' Pete asked Mavranos, who was standing by the washer and puffing on a Camel cigarette as if to drive away the burning mint smell. With the hand that wasn't holding the gun, Mavranos dug a wad of tissue paper out of his shirt pocket and passed it across to him. 'And,' Pete said as he carefully unwrapped it, 'we've got Crane's … murderer, and his wife, here, which should one way or another work as a homing beacon. Kootie, start up the speaker; and Angie, would you do the honors in the next room?' He looked at Cochran as Angelica sidled past the TV table out into the office. 'We're out past physics again,' he said. 'She's got to light some candles, and pronounce certain Spanish rhymes and splash *Vete de Aqui* oil over the door lintel.' He looked at Diana, who was standing beside Mavranos. 'I need Crane's full name, and his birthdate. I realize it seems like bad security, to be dealing in his real psychic locators, but we can't have any masks at all in the way, for this.'

'Scott Henri Poincaré Leon Crane,' said Diana – who, even in the harsh electric light from the single naked bulb dangling from the ceiling, looked to Cochran's befuddled gaze like a luminous preliminary Botticelli painting of Venus, before the hair was brushed in. 'February 28, 1943.'

The pencil sharpener was spinning the wet chalk cylinder now, and a featureless hiss was rasping out of the paper speaker. Angelica hurried back into the little laundry room, wiping her hands on her blouse and exposing for a moment the grip of the automatic pistol in her waistband.

Pete grimaced as he lifted out of the tissue paper an angular black lump like an oversized raisin; but he sat down in the lawn chair and started to dial.

But even before he had carefully pulled the 7 hole of the dial around to the stop, a buzzing sounded from the speaker; it stopped, then started up again.

'Uh ... that's an incoming call,' Angelica said helplessly. 'You may as well answer it.'

Pete picked up the receiver. 'Umm ... hello?'

The frail voice of an old woman came shaking out of the paper speaker cone: 'Pirogi,' it said. 'That's a bayou boat, barely big enough for a body to kneel in. It's a thing you can cook, too, looks like a boat – stuff an eggplant with *seafood* once you've gouged away the ... the *core* of the vegetable like a dugout canoe. If he hollers, don't let him go, right? You all need to come here, I can guide your boats. I betrayed the god, I desecrated his temple, but this is my day of atonement. Today is January the eleventh, isn't it?'

For several seconds nobody spoke, then Kootie said, 'Yes, ma'am.'

'Ninety-one years ago today,' rasped the old woman's disembodied voice, 'I died. Three Easters and three days later he came for me, out of the sea, and he knocked down all the buildings and took all the other ghosts to himself, burned them up. *Yerba buena*, burning.'

The telephone speaker hissed blankly for nearly half a minute, and at last Angelica said, 'Well, she's right, the *yerba buena* does smell like it's burning. Johanna,' she called through the doorway, '*atenda a lo fuego!*' Then she looked at Pete. 'You're getting the party-line effect Hang up and try again.'

'You are to come and fetch me,' insisted the old woman's amplified voice, 'and another dead lady, too, who is hiding in a tight little box.'

'I – I think it's the old black lady,' ventured Kootie. 'Who was on the TV.'

'I think it is too,' said Angelica. 'Will you hang *up*, Pete? We don't need help from stray ghosts drawn by the electromagnetic field here, wanting to celebrate their *deathdays*. Fetch two old women ghosts! – it sounds like a sewing circle. Hang up, and dial Crane's number.'

'Rightie-o,' said Pete flatly, hanging up the receiver. He leaned forward again with the dark lump – which was apparently someone's eye! – and used it to rotate the dial. 'And I'm enough of a mathematician to know how to spell *Poincaré*.'

Altogether, for Crane's name and birth date, Pete dialled thirty-four numbers into the phone. 'It's very long distance,' muttered Kootie, which got a smothered laugh from Plumtree.

Again from the speaker sounded the measured buzz that apparently indicated ringing, and then a click sounded. Pregnant Diana's hands clenched into fists against the tight fabric of her jeans.

'Hello,' came a man's baritone voice from the pencil-sharpener apparatus, 'you've reached Scott Crane, and I'm not able to come to the phone right now. But if you leave your name and number and the time that you called, I'll get back to you as soon as possible.'

'The woman who killed you,' said Diana loudly, 'says she can restore you to life. Cooperate in this, Scott! And do give us a call, if you can.'

At the first syllables of the man's voice, Plumtree's elbow had bumped Cochran's knee; he glanced at her now and saw that though she was still sitting slumped against the pipes below the sink she had gone limp, her hands open and palms-up on the linoleum floor and her head bowed forward so that her blond hair had fallen over her face. He didn't bother to try to rouse her.

'Nearly midnight, Scott,' called Mavranos, 'on the eleventh of January, '95; Arky and Diana, and some allies; and we'll have to try you again somehow, or you'll have to catch us at some pay phone we might be near, okay? – I don't think we're gonna be by this phone much longer.'

Now that he had sat down again, Cochran found that he was hardly able to keep his eyes open. The voices of these strangers, and his cramped posture, and his nervous exhaustion, all strongly called to mind the sleepless twelve-hour flight home from Paris four days ago – he could almost hear again the faint brassy big-band music that had seemed to whisper perpetually from some forgotten set of earphones several rows ahead; and his eyes were aching now as they had when he had kept trying to read *A Tale of Two Cities*, while fatigue had been persistently casting faint, hallucinatory green bands across the bottoms of the pages; and he squinted in the glare of this laundry-room lightbulb and remembered how the horizontal white light of dawn over the north Atlantic had lanced in through the 747's tiny windows, and been reflected in wobbling flickers onto the white plastic ceiling by the compact-mirrors of ladies fixing up their slept-in makeup.

When the jet had landed at LAX in Los Angeles, he had got off and walked right out of the airport, abandoning his luggage.

Summoning all his strength now, he struggled to his feet and mumbled, 'Which way to the head?'

Mavranos, still holding the revolver, pursed his lips and scowled at him. 'Hold tight, sonny,' he said. 'Your bladder won't pop.'

'You're not Speedy Alka-Seltzer,' agreed Pete absently as he hovered over the phone, 'you won't dissolve.'

'It's not—' Cochran swayed in the smoky air. 'I think I'm gonna puke again.'

'Oh hell,' Mavranos said, glancing for reassurance at the unconscious Plumtree 'Down the hall to the right. If I see you turn left, toward the kitchen, I'll shoot you, okay?'

'Okay.'

Cochran stepped carefully over the telephone cords to the doorway, and glanced at the ivy-leaf mark on the back of his right hand to make sure he didn't turn the wrong way by mistake.

He followed his hand sliding along the wallpaper to the hallway corner. As he had done at the airport, he was forcing himself not to think about the consequences of this course of action; all his concentration was on the im-mediate tasks: step quietly down the side hall, unchain the street door, and then hurry away into the night, away from the dead body in the kitchen and *everybody* here, never looking back.

But when he had shambled around the hallway corner he froze.

Instead of the remembered narrow hall through which he and Plumtree had entered the building, with its threadbare carpeting and low, flocked ceiling—

—he was in a broad, dark entry hall, at the foot of a spiral staircase that curled away upward for at least two floors; rain was drumming on a skylight far overhead, and drops were free-falling all the long way down the stairwell to splash on the parquet floor at his feet. In the taut, twanging moment of astonished vertigo he rocked his head forward to look at the floor, and saw in the wood a stain that he was viscerally certain was old blood.

Then he had no choice but to look behind him.

A gilt-framed mirror hung on the panelled wall, and in the mirror, behind the reflection of his own wide-eyed face, stood the man he had met in the streets of Paris five days ago, who had called himself Mondard.

Cochran whirled to face the man, but there was no one there; he was still alone in the empty baroque hall; and so he had to look back into the mirror.

The man in the reflection had the same curly dark beard he'd had when Cochran had first spoken to him in the courtyard of the Hotel L'Abbaye, around the corner from the Church of St. Sulpice, but now it reminded Cochran of the bearded dead king who lay somewhere behind him; and these liquid brown eyes had shone with this same perilous joy even when they had stared at Cochran from a living bull's head on the man's shoulders, later that same morning in the narrow medieval Rue de la Harpe; and when

Cochran had fled, stumbling over ancient cobblestones past the Lebanese and Persian restaurants with whole lambs turning on spits in the windows, the thing that had pursued him and finally tripped him up on the Quai Saint Michel pavement by the river had been a man-shaped bundle of straw, with dried ivy for hair and split and leaking grapes for eyes.

In the hotel courtyard the man had introduced himself as Monsieur Mondard having to lean close to be heard over the glad baying of the dog in the lobby, and he had frightened Cochran by speaking of the dead Nina and offering him an insane and unthinkable 'surcease from sorrow' – and as Cochran stared again now into the reflection of those horizontally pupiled eyes, he knew from their unchanged hot ardor that Mondard was still holding out the same offer.

'*Donnes moi le revenant de la femme morte*,' Mondard had said, '*buvez mon vin de pardon, et debarrassez-vous d'elle*.' *Give the dead woman's ghost over to me, drink my wine of forgiveness, and be free of her.*

In that old Paris courtyard, under the marbled winter sky, Cochran had believed that the man could do what he offered: that he could actually relieve him of the grief of Nina's death by taking away Cochran's memories of her, his useless love for her.

And he believed it again now. The figure in the mirror was holding a bottle of red wine, and in the reflection the letters on the label were something like I BITE DOG AP but Cochran couldn't read it because of the sudden swell of tears in his eyes. Why *not* take a drink of the sacramental wine, and by doing it give over to this creature his intolerable memories of Nina – give to this thing that called itself Mondard his now cripplingly vestigial love for his killed wife?

When he looked up into Mondard's face, the goat-pupilled eyes were looking past him, over Cochran's shoulder; a moment later they were warmly returning his gaze, and he knew that Mondard was promising to provide the same solace, the same generously ennobling gift, when Cochran's grief would be for the death of Plumtree.

And Cochran wondered exactly *how* Nina had come to run out into the lanes of the 280 Freeway at dawn, ten days ago; had she been chased? ... Lured?

Nina was dead, and Cochran was suddenly determined not to betray his love for her by disowning it; and Janis was alive, and he was not going to sanction her death, abandon her to this thing, even implicitly.

The bottle of wine, 'Biting Dog' or whatever it was called, gleamed in the long-nailed hand in the mirror's reflection, and on the back of the hand was a mark that might have corresponded to the mark on Cochran's hand – but Cochran shook his head sharply, and turned away and blundered back the way he had come.

CHAPTER TEN

'You know that you are recalled to life?'
   'They tell me so.'
   'I hope you care to live?'
   'I can't say.'
   'Shall I show her to you? Will you come and see her?'
                  —Charles Dickens, *A Tale of Two Cities*

Plumtree was still huddled under the sink when Cochran stepped carefully back into the stark yellow light of the laundry room, but she was blinking and looking around now and Angelica was crouched beside her, talking to her.

Pete was hunched over the telephone, tapping the hangup button; the paper speaker cone on the shelf was silent in the instants when the phone was hung up, but always came back again with the same noise, which was distant mumbling and laughter and vitreous clinking, as if the phone at the other end had been left unattended in a crowded bar somewhere. Perched up on the washing machine, Kootie was frowning in the mint-and-tequila smoke from the kitchen, and holding his bleeding side.

As Cochran stepped over the telephone and electric cords to get back to his place beside the sink, he found that he was straining to hear, among the slurred babble crackling out of the speaker, the rattle-and-bang of someone playing bar dice.

'Oh, Scant!' said Plumtree when he sat down beside her. 'I was afraid you ran out on me.'

Cochran managed to smile at her. 'Decided not to,' he said shortly.

Angelica glanced at him, and then stared at him. He wondered what his expression looked like. 'Good,' she said. 'Did you get … lost, at all, looking for the bathroom?'

Cochran realized that he'd been holding his breath, and he let it out. 'Yes,' he said. 'Never did – find it.' Now that he had resumed breathing, he was panting, as if he had run a long distance back here.

'Big Victorian halls?' Angelica asked him in a neutral tone. 'Rich-looking?'

Cochran caught his breath with a hiccup, both relieved and frightened to learn that she knew about the hall he had found himself in, that he had not been hallucinating. 'Yes,' he admitted. 'Grand once – decrepit now.'

Angelica was nodding. 'For the last week and a half,' she said slowly, 'we've been getting print-through, here, overlay, overlaps, of two other houses, old

Victorians. One's dark and mildewy, and the other's clean and got electric lights. This building was put up in 1923, partly constructed of lumber salvaged from the Winchester House in San Jose. The top couple of floors of that house collapsed in the big earthquake in 1906—'

'When *he* came for the black lady's ghost, out of the sea,' said Janis in a helpful tone, 'and knocked down all the buildings. Valorie told me that part.'

'Oh, do be quiet, girl,' whispered Angelica, closing her eyes for a moment. 'The Winchester House is still standing, of course,' she went on to Cochran, 'big haunted-house tourist attraction on the 280 south of San Fran ... but lately when it's raining in San Jose, the roof leaks here.'

'It was – leaking there, too,' panted Cochran. 'Through a skylight.' He didn't feel able to tell her about the man he'd seen in the mirror. 'Talk to Kootie about it, he's seen—'

A clunking sounded from the speaker, then breathing; clearly someone at the unimaginable other end had picked up the telephone.

'Whooo wawnts it?' came a man's drawling voice from the speaker. 'Your daddy's home, baby! That bad old doctor wanna play *strip poker*, I'll see he gets his ashes hauled for real.' A high, razory whine had started up in the background.

Cochran's face went cold, for he was certain that this was the voice that had come out of Plumtree's mouth at Strubie the Clown's house.

Plumtree had sat up and stiffened. 'That *is* my daddy!' she said hoarsely, her voice seeming to echo faintly out of the speaker. 'Daddy, can you hear me? I'm so *sorry* I let you die, I tried to catch you—'

'Course I can hear—'

The whine grew abruptly louder and shriller, as if Dopplered by the source of the carrier-wave signal accelerating toward them at nearly the speed of light; a blue glow was shining now in the dark office beyond the laundry-room doorway, and the drumming of water into the pots out there was a barrage; then the speaker abruptly went silent and the blue glow was extinguished. Cochran couldn't hear the roof dripping in the other room at all now.

In the silence, Pete pushed back his chair and shuffled carefully to the doorway and looked into the office.

'The carborundum bulb *exploded*,' he said, turning, back into the brightly lit little room. He gave Plumtree an empty, haggard stare. 'Your dad's ghost is one muscular son of a bitch.'

'He's not a ghost,' said Angelica in a shaky tone as she lithely straightened her legs and stood up. 'And it wasn't Spider Joe's dead wife that whited out the TV. Let's go in the other room and get the *Vete de Aqui* oil splashed around.'

Cochran knew enough Spanish to understand that the phrase meant, roughly, *Go Away*; and in spite of his recent resolve to stay with these strange people, he forlornly wished he could rub some of that oil onto the soles of his shoes.

'I've got to make a couple of ordinary phone calls before we settle down again,' said Angelica when everybody had filed back into the office and turned the lights back on and Johanna and Kootie had begun shaking yellow oil from tiny glass bottles onto the doorframes and the windowsills. Angelica hurried into the kitchen, and Cochran heard a pan clank in a sink, and then running water and the sudden hiss of steam. Pete had unplugged the electrical cords and was twisting the clamps off the terminals of the car battery that was sitting on the desk.

'I'll bet he's an angel,' Plumtree was saying, 'if he's not a ghost. I'll bet he's my guardian angel.'

Cochran drained the last third of his can of beer in several deep swallows. Has she not even *considered*, he wondered, the likelihood that her father's personality is the famous Flibbertigibbet? – who battered the would-be rapist to death in 1989 on October the unforgettable seventeenth? An angel, maybe, Cochran thought, but one with a harpoon rather than a harp.

The thought of a harpoon reminded him of the sawn-off spear in the neck of the dead king in the kitchen; he darted a nervous glance in that direction, and then peered up at Kootie, who had climbed back up onto the desk and was sitting cross legged among the wires and radio parts.

Kootie was looking at him. 'Call me Fishmeal,' the boy said, softly and not happily. Cochran blinked at him. 'Uh ... sorry, you said what?'

'Never mind,' sighed Kootie.

Angelica came striding back into the office from the kitchen, her dark hair swinging around her pale, narrow face. 'Your Bugsy Siegel eye worked,' she told Mavranos. 'The two L.A.-area *santeros* I just called were aware of some powerful ghost agitations a few minutes ago, but Alvarez in Venice registered it as northeast of him, and Mendoza in Alhambra clocked it as just about exactly west.'

'The Hollywood Cemetery ... ?' ventured Pete.

'Unmistakably,' said Angelica. 'So we're no more vulnerable than we were before. At least.'

She threw herself down on the couch and stared hard at Plumtree, who was sitting on the floor beside Cochran. Impulsively Cochran put his arm around Plumtree's shoulder; and she leaned back against him, which led him to believe that she was currently Janis.

'And I'm pretty sure. I've got you diagnosed, girl,' Angelica said to her, 'though I'd love it if you could have brought your admission notes with you from the madhouse.' She looked around at the other people in the long, smoky room – just Cochran and Kootie and Mavranos and Diana – and she said, 'I'm afraid I'm going to be violating doctor-patient confidentiality in what I say here. But everybody here is concerned in this – and anyway, you never paid me forty-nine cents.'

Angelica shook her head and smiled then, though she was frowning. 'You know when I was a practicing psychiatrist, I learned real quick that the regular doctors the surgeons and all, were cowards when it came to giving their patients bad news. They'd call one of us shrinks over to their wing of the hospital to "consult" on a case, and it always just meant ... "Would you explain to my patient that his cancer is fatal? Would you tell his family?" So a lot of times I had to be the one to tell some stranger that his leg had to be amputated, or tell some girl her father had died. I always felt bad to be the one breaking the news.' She coughed out two syllables of uncomfortable laughter. 'I'm rambling, aren't I? What I mean is, I don't want to say what I've got to say now – though in a way I've got the opposite sort of news.' Plumtree must have opened her mouth to speak, for Angelica held up her hand. 'Let me talk, Miss Plumtree. You are, genuinely, a multiple personality,' Angelica said, 'but that's not all that's ... peculiar about you. How do I start? For one thing, I'm just about sure that you were present when your father ... well, let's call it *died*.'

Cochran belatedly noticed that Angelica had brought a glass of something with her from the kitchen, tequila probably, and he watched her take a solid gulp of it now. 'I think,' she went on, 'that you were standing on the pavement below the building he fell from – I think he partly *landed on you*, which is why you were in the hospital with broken bones. And it was almost certainly a sunny day, because you seem to have identified him with the sun, hence your dream of the sun falling out of the sky onto you, and hence too your no doubt stress-triggered hysterical sunburn and constricted pupils. Conversion disorders, we call that class of physical symptoms.'

Angelica leaned forward – but her head was now over one of the drip-catching pots, and the next drop spattered on her scalp. She leaned back again on the couch. 'That much is orthodox – Angelica Anthem Elizalde the doctor talking. Now it's *Bruja Angelica, del "Testículos del León"*: I think that in the instant before his body died, when you were both lying there on the sidewalk or whatever, he managed to look into your eyes, and then he ... *jumped across the gap*, threw his soul into your two-year-old body.' She was frowning deeply, staring at the liquor in her glass. 'So at the tender age of two you lost your psychic virginity, in what must have been a traumatic violation of your *self.* I doubt that your home life in the hippie cult-commune was real conducive to mental health, but this virtual rape by your own father was undoubtedly the event that triggered your multiplicity.'

'I'm still here,' said Plumtree cautiously. 'Valorie hasn't made me lose time. So this must not be bad news.'

'We-ell,' said Angelica, raising her eyebrows, 'the news is that your father is discorporate, but he's in you; like one of those flanged wedges they use to split logs into several pieces. And he's *alive*, he's not a ghost; he never did die, never did experience the psychic truncation of death. He *is*, though, almost certainly the person that killed Scott Crane.'

'My father is alive,' said Plumtree, clearly tasting the thought. 'I *didn't* let him die! I *did* catch him – save him!'

And he's Flibbertigibbet, thought Cochran nervously. Don't lose sight of that, Janis.

A jangling metallic screech at the back door made Cochran jump and almost shout; Spider Joe was coming back inside, and the long, stiff wires that projected from his belt were scraping paint chips from the doorframe. 'Goddammit,' the blind old man was muttering. Once through the narrow doorway he plodded across the floor, as Mavranos stepped out of his way and the antennae bunched and snagged the carpet and whipped through the air, and finally he sat down heavily on the floor beside the couch. Perhaps self-consciously, he groped around until he found Angelica's deck of *Loteria* cards, and began shuffling the frail cards in his brown-spotted hands.

Angelica turned back to Plumtree. 'Do you know what those lines were that you quoted a few minutes ago?' she asked Plumtree sharply. 'A list of defenses, all provisional and makeshift-frail – "Upon my back, to defend my belly," and so forth?'

'Don't say any more,' said Plumtree hastily, 'please. No, I don't even recall quoting anything.'

'Well, they happen to be from *Troilus and Cressida*,' Angelica said, 'a Shakespeare play that isn't considered one of his good ones, mainly because it doesn't seem to make a whole lot of sense. But some spiritualists, mediums *brujas y magos* – the real ones – are very aware of the play.'

'What's it about?' asked Cochran – in a strained voice for it had been at the Troy and Cress Wedding Chapel in Las Vegas that he had married Nina Gestin Leon – his beloved dead Nina – and had next morning had his first debilitating hallucination of the big, masked man.

Angelica sighed and finished her drink. 'Only a few people know what I'm about to tell you,' she said. 'See, Shakespeare didn't write the play for the general public – its only intended performance was for a small, sorcerously hip audience in London in 1603 – and in the published version he had to add four or five lines to the end of the first scene, tacked on after the rhyming couplet that originally ended it, in order to take away the real point of the play – which is that Troilus didn't go out and fight, but got his wound at home – fatally, by his own hand. Hardly anybody knows, anymore, that it's really a play about ghosts.'

She glanced at Plumtree, with what might have been sympathy. 'I'll have to reread it, but it takes place during the Trojan War you know? Like in Homer? – and it's about a Trojan girl, Cressida, who is being prepared to be a vehicle for the ghost of her dead father. The Greeks who are besieging the city have got hold of the ghost, and they want to use it against the Trojans, but they've got to get the ghost into a living body that's both compatible with it and not a virgin, psychically. It's a dirty-pool move, like using biological warfare, and some of the Greeks such as Ulysses don't approve of the tactic; the Greek soldiers are suffering disorientation from the powerful ghost's proximity, and they're using masking measures – "emulation," Ulysses calls it – to insulate themselves. So anyway, a traitor spiritualist in Troy is talking Cressida into having sex with the ghost of her dead *boyfriend*, Troilus, who near-decapitated himself with his sword before the action starts. In the play it's never outright stated that Troilus is dead, a suicide ghost, but his very name should have been a clue to the theater-going public, really – in Homer's *Iliad*, the Troilus character is dead long before this point in the story, though Homer doesn't say he killed himself out of unrequited love of Cressida, as Shakespeare secretly has it. Anyway, a trade is set up – the clueless Trojans agree to turn over Cressida in exchange for some VIP prisoner-of-war Trojan, and the spiritualist manages to get Cressida into bed with Troilus's ghost just barely before she's got to leave the city. And, of course, the Greek scheme works: Troy falls, the noble prince Hector is killed. Though,' she added, visibly restraining herself from glancing toward the kitchen doorway, 'Apollo and Aphrodite preserved Hector's body from corruption.'

Mavranos was still holding the revolver. He looked across the room at Plumtree and asked, 'What was your plan for reviving Scott Crane?'

She shivered under Cochran's arm and muttered, 'In the name of the Father, the Sun, the Holy Ghost.' The lights flickered; then she squinted at Mavranos. 'Okay, sorry – what did you say?'

'I asked you how you planned to restore Crane to life.'

A time for hard questions. She took a deep breath and let it out. 'I believed a *living* king would be able to restore him. A king in a living body. I knew he was a, a magic guy, and I figured he knew how to do shit like that. So I wanted to find the Flying Nun's – Crane's – presently disembodied spirit, and let him take my body, so he'll *be* occupying a living body – *this* one – and he'll be able to do the magical trick, whatever it involves. *I know* how to ... open myself up, "wide unclasp the table of my thoughts," step aside and let another personality take control of my body – I do it a hundred times a day. And he wouldn't be compromising himself by violating my spiritual virginity – I'm a regular Grand Central Station for personalities passing through this little head. So far they've all been homegrown, as far as I know, but I'm confident that any … psychic hymen! … is long gone.'

Truer than you yet know, Cody, thought Cochran. You should have been here for what Angelica said about your father a minute ago.

Plumtree was still holding Mavranos's gaze, though Cochran could see the glitter of tears in her eyes. 'And,' she went on steadily, 'if he can't manage the trick of getting himself back into his own body – even though it *does* happen to be so perfectly preserved *right here* in your kitchen! – then he can simply, God, simply stay in mine, *keeep* it. Mine's not perfect, and it's the wrong sex, but it's young, and it's all I have to give him, by way of atonement.' She wiped her eyes impatiently on her shirtsleeve. 'That was my plan. Dr. Armentrout said Koot Hoomie Parganas might know a way to do it, maybe another way.' She looked up at the boy on the desk. 'Hanging around here tonight, I get the idea you *don't*, in fact, know a way to do it. Is that … true?'

Angelica spoke up in answer, angrily. 'Of course it's true! If Kootie could revive the dead king, do you think he wouldn't have done it?'

After staring at Kootie for another second or two, Plumtree turned a tired smile on Angelica. 'No, lady,' she said quietly.

Mavranos swivelled his bleak gaze to Angelica. 'Now I know how you feel,' he said hoarsely, 'delivering the bad news to people.' He cleared his throat, but when he spoke again his voice was still as gritty as boot soles on sandstone: 'I think Miss Plumtree's plan might work.'

Angelica was visibly tense. 'Who is that bad news for?'

'You all, goddammit. You and Pete and Kootie. Shit. What Diana and I meant to do by coming here was to confer the kinghood onto the man with the bleeding wound in his side. That office, the kinghood, would have carried with it a lot of protections – Miss Plumtree can tell you again how much work she had to do to get through the defenses to Crane. *But* – if Crane can be revived, even though he's dormant and powerless right now, then Kootie doesn't become the king after all. There are no protections. And you people are fatally compromised – you've invited us in, you've voluntarily taken the dead king's very *body* in, given it shelter and respect! You've eaten bread and drunk wine in his corpse's presence, you've declared allegiance and fealty to his reign, like it or not. The bad guys know your address, this bad psychiatrist and—' He glanced at Plumtree, '—and other villains. And they won't let you live, you all being sworn-in soldiers in the routed side's army now, and knowing what you know. These two,' he said, waving at Plumtree and Cochran, 'found you tonight – hell, their *taxi driver* found you. And old Spider Joe had no problem, apparently, and he's *blind*. By morning you may have armored assault vehicles pulling up out front. You've blown your mask-gaskets by letting us in, and I don't even think you could run and hide somewhere else, now, and stay effectively hidden for long.'

Angelica had stood up from the couch during this, and paced to the kitchen doorway and back. 'Then anoint Kootie,' she said. 'Make Kootie the king, as you originally planned. We'll have the protections of the true living king then.'

Mavranos reached up to the side and laid the revolver on the bookshelf beside the inert stuffed pig, and he wiped the palm of his hand on his jeans. 'I deliberately killed a man once, at Hoover Dam, to protect my friends, and it has weighed cruel hard on me ever since. I won't – I *won't* kill a living person to protect a *dead* man; especially a living person I've become indebted to. You can march into the kitchen there and, I don't know, chop Scott's head off with a carving knife, if you like. I won't shoot you, Angelica. Kootie would become king then, even without the blessings of me and Diana, which it would damn sure *be* without. But Kootie will have become king by being an accessory to the murder of his predecessor … as, in fact, most of the previous kings have done. And his will be – trust me! – a reign poisoned at its root.'

Cochran thought of the phylloxera lice, killing the sunny grapevines from the darkness six feet under.

'I … won't do that,' said Kootie softly.

'Then I take back our invitation!' shouted Angelica. 'I hereby annul it! *I* never invited you in, and all we did for your damned *king* was lay him out on the kitchen table! Pete and Kootie will carry him right back out to your abracadabra truck – and you can wipe your fingerprints off the doorknobs and take your kids and your toothbrushes and get out of here – take a broom with you and sweep your footsteps off the walkway as you leave!' She looked at Pete and lifted her open hand, and caught the little bottle of *Vete de Aquí* oil that he obediently tossed across the room to her.

'Go,' said Plumtree with a giddy wave, 'and never darken our towels again.' Mavranos smiled sadly at Angelica. 'You took my forty-nine cents, that first day.' 'Cheerfully refunded!' Angelica stamped to the desk, pulled open the top drawer, and pawed through a pile of scattered change. Then she turned and threw seven coins at Mavranos.

The coins tumbled to a Wiffle-ball halt in mid-air; and they seemed to pop there, silently, like big grains of puffed rice; and then they fluttered away on dusty white wings toward the dripping ceiling.

Cochran watched them, and cold air on his teeth made him aware that his mouth was hanging open. The coins had turned into live luna moths, and a chilly draft had sprung up in the room.

Angelica was panting audibly as she dug seven more coins out of the drawer, and she flung them too toward Mavranos.

Again the coins dragged to a halt in mid-air, and twitched and puffed out in the moment that they hung suspended, and became live white moths that fluttered away in all directions. The long office room was cold now.

Pete stepped forward then, and he caught Angelica's wrist as she was scrabbling in the drawer for more coins; and she collapsed against him, sobbing. 'Why did you people have to ... *come* here?' she wailed, her hot breath steaming in the chilly air.

Mavranos spread his hands. 'Why did Kootie have to be the one with the qualifications, the unhealing cut in his side?'

Blind Spider Joe held up two of Angelica's *Lotería* cards; Cochran leaned forward to peer at them, and saw that they were a pair, two copies of a picture of a woman in a narrow canoe, labeled LA CHALUPA.

'Nobody's brailled these cards for me,' the old man said irritably. 'What are these?'

'They're both the same,' said Kootie. 'A lady in a little boat. She's got, uh, baskets of fruit and flowers by her knees, jammed in the bow.'

'Two boats,' Spider Joe said. 'You were in a boat on a boat, a boat aboard a boat, when you got wounded, boy, isn't that right? And you had a guide who protected you through the ordeal, somebody like Merlin, or Virgil who escorted Dante through the Inferno. That was a *rite de passage* – he didn't just save you, he saved you *for* something. That's when you swung around to point here, to this.'

'When my side got cut?' said Kootie. 'Not boats – I was in a van that some bad guys had driven up inside a truck, on Slauson, by the L.A. trainyards. I was being kidnapped. And the ghost of Thomas Edison saved my life.'

'And you had been prepped,' Spider Joe went on, 'like a piece of amber rubbed with a cloth, charged – fasting and observances as a child, that's obvious, and then you were violently severed from that life, and then you must certainly have renounced your name and your race; and you were a passenger, helpless. And what's a little charged boat floating aboard a boat?' asked Spider Joe. 'It's a compass. You've got to get to the boats now, point north, find a new Merlin or Virgil – or Edison. An *intercessor*.'

Pete Sullivan was squinting at the old man, and now he looked at Mavranos. 'You know this old guy, Arky. Is there value in this?'

Mavranos opened his mouth and closed it, and shrugged. 'He seemed to give Crane some good advice, before the big poker game on the houseboat on Lake Mead.'

'It sounds like the old black lady's boat, her pirogi,' said Diana. She glanced at Angelica. 'Do you still think she was just a ... random ghost drawn by your telephone?'

'This is the blind leading the blind,' Angelica said.

Cochran stood up, though he had to lean on the desk, and he crossed his arms to hide the foolish writing on his T-shirt. 'You tried to get your man Crane an the phone, and he wasn't there,' he said. 'North, says the, the *oracular* Mr. Spider Joe here; and you said that TV signal originated in San Francisco, and the old black lady's ghost was talking about San Francisco – obviously she was talking about the 1906 earthquake and fire, and she said "Yerba Buena burning," and Yerba Buena isn't just the Spanish term for mint, it was the original name for San Francisco, because of all the wild mint that used to grow on the north-shore dunes there. Your very *house* leaks because it's raining in *San Jose*, which is next door to San Francisco. And she said, "You all need to come here, and I'll guide your boats," remember?' And back up in the Bay Area, he thought yearningly, I can get my bearings, get to my house and get some *clothes*, pick up a paycheck, talk to my lawyer. 'For all sorts of reasons, none of us wants Crane to just *keep* Janis's body. We all have a stake in him getting his own back.' Or, better, him just going untraceably *away*, he added to himself. 'And Mr. Mavranos points out that we can't stay here. If we all leave now, we can be at the Cliff House in San Francisco for breakfast.'

'To the boats,' said Plumtree gaily.

CHAPTER ELEVEN

PANDARUS: ... Is it not birth, beauty, good shape, discourse, manhood, learning, gentleness, virtue, youth, liberality, and such like, the spice and salt that season a man?

CRESSIDA: Ay, a minced man; and then to be baked with no date in the pie, for then the man's date is out.

—William Shakespeare, *Troilus and Cressida*

As Johanna was banging around in the reeking steamy kitchen, insistently making snacks to sustain the travellers during the proposed long drive, Archimedes Mavranos was standing in the middle of the office floor and giving orders. He had taken his revolver down from the shelf again, and with his finger outside the trigger guard was now slapping his thigh with the barrel to emphasize his points.

'Diana,' he said, 'you take one of the Sullivans' cars and go back to Leucadia with the boys – Nardie and Wendy will be tired of taking care of all the young'uns by themselves. Mr. King-Arthurs-Shorts and Miss Plumtree can sit up in the front seat of the truck with me, and Kootie and

Pete and Angelica can sit in the back seat, with Angelica holding—'

'*Kootie* certainly won't go along,' interrupted Angelica, who had sat down on the couch and crossed her arms. 'And Pete and I aren't cowards, but I don't see why we should go along either.' She blinked around belligerently. 'And you can't take one of our cars. Pete or I can drive Diana and the boys back to Leucadia.'

'I thank you for the offer,' said the woman Cochran had begun to think of as the cue-ball madonna, 'but we'll take a bus. I would be honored to die with you, Angelica, if it were necessary, but I wouldn't let my boys or my unborn baby go anywhere with someone who was targeted to die.'

Angelica drummed her fingers on the arm of the couch. 'Why,' she asked Mavranos, 'would you even think of bringing a fourteen-year-old boy?' One of the moths fluttered past her face, and she waved it away impatiently.

'He's more than that, Angelica,' Mavranos said. 'He's an apprentice king – no, a *journeyman* king; he can see and sense things we can't. And if we fail, he's *the* king – he should be up to speed for that, be able to land running. And I'll tell you another bit of bad truth, I'm not at all sure that this restoration-to-life will work, without him.'

'*Meaning what?*' Angelica demanded.

'I don't know at *all* what it means,' said Mavranos, baring his teeth. 'But he's *here*, he's *empowered*, as you shrinks like to say. He's a uniquely potent soldier in the king's meager army.' He shrugged. '*But,* if the boy doesn't want to go, I certainly won't try to compel him.'

Cochran couldn't help sneaking a sidelong glance at Kootie.

The boy was frowning and holding his wounded side. 'My mom and dad will die if this doesn't succeed,' he said carefully.

Angelica leaped lithely to her feet. 'Kootie, that's not—'

'*Or* hide real damn low,' assented Mavranos. 'Moving frequently, not keeping souvenirs. For the rest of their lives.'

'What have we *been* doing but hiding real damn low?' Pete said to Kootie. 'The cops have been looking for us since '92, and for your mom since before that. Kootie, we don't—'

'Well what about *him*?' Mavranos said, turning to face Pete Sullivan. 'Kootie himself? He was brought up to be king, groomed for it – by the plain *universe*, apparently, if not by any specific person. Weren't you listening to Spider Joe at all? Even if Kootie never gets to take the crown, the ambitious guys will want him dead, like a valid pretender, and his is a soul they'll want to eat; they'll want it bad. You think he can keep his belt and his watchband Möbiused all his life one edge and one side get along forever with half his strength?'

'I *will* go with them,' said Kootie. He had picked up the bottle of Mondavi Chardonnay from the back corner of the desk, and now refilled his gold fish-cup. He smiled at Angelica. 'And I won't insult you and dad by asking whether or not you'll come along.'

The bald woman's lower lip was pulled away from her teeth in what might have been profound relief or pity, or both; and she hurried into the kitchen and came back with a ratty pale-yellow baby blanket. 'Kootie,' she said hoarsely, 'this belonged to my mother, who was ... such a successful avatar of the Moon Goddess that she was killed for it in 1960, at the order of Scott's natural father, when *he* was king. Spider Joe could tell you about it. Carry it with you, and she'll help you do ... whatever it might be that you have to do.'

Kootie started to say something, then wordlessly took the little blanket and began slowly folding it.

'Okay,' said Mavranos. 'Good. We'll have Crane's body in the back of the truck, like under a tarp, and Angelica will be sitting just forward of that, in the back seat, with a gun: Miss Plumtree is our tool for restoring Crane, but at the same time she's a potential Trojan Horse, she *contains* the man that *killed* him – so Angelica has to be ready to shoot her if her father should take over and try to mess things up.'

Plumtree was nodding absently, shaking a cigarette out of a pack from her purse.

'If I *shoot* her,' noted Angelica shakily, 'she won't be much use in restoring Crane.'

'You might not *kill* her,' said Mavranos.

'And even if you did,' put in Kootie, who seemed tensely distracted as he tucked the folded-up baby blanket into his hip pocket, 'we might find another way.'

Angelica opened her mouth as if to demand an explanation of that, but Cochran overrode her. '*She!* – came here *voluntarily!*' he said loudly. His face was hot, and he was trying not to stutter. 'At some peril to herself.' He turned to stare into Angelica's hostile brown eyes. 'You're Spanish,' he said breathlessly. 'Okay, that counts. But I'm Irish. If you decide to kill her, or hurt her, you'd be smart to kill me first.'

'Noted,' said Mavranos stolidly. 'Joe, do you need a ride anywhere that's along the 101 north? We won't want to take a route that strays too far inland – I think proximity to the sea is part of what's been sustaining Crane's corpse.' He grinned at Angelica. 'Along with Apollo and Afro-Dydee, natch.' He stared toward where Spider Joe sat on the floor beside the couch, then turned to Pete.

'The, uh, "beasties,"' Mavranos went on. 'Those strange dead guys that you had stacked in your trashed old van last week – we're gonna have to delay long enough to rip up the turf again over where we planted 'em.'

Pete Sullivan frowned with evident distaste. 'What the hell for? I let all the air out of the old Chevy Nova's tires after we parked it over them; and those were old tires, they might not take air again.'

'All of us together can push it,' said Mavranos softly, 'even on a flat or two.' He had been steadily slapping his thigh with the gun barrel, and now he struck himself hard enough with it to make Cochran wince. 'Shit,' Mavranos said in an almost conversational tone. 'The thing is, Pete, we gotta ... well, a Dumpster in back of some gas station wouldn't be right; we do owe Spider Joe a *burial*.'

Cochran watched everybody else turn to stare toward the couch before he looked away from Mavranos's stony face.

Spider Joe's head was rolled back, and above his slightly opened mouth the sightless eye sockets gaped at the ceiling; and the metal filaments that stood out from his belt were bent double, folded back across his khaki shirt like a dozen crossed fencing foils.

'He did traverse afar,' said Mavranos, 'to bring his gifts to the king – to return those two silver dollars.'

'Poor old fucker,' said Plumtree quietly. 'You got lots of dead guys around here, huh.'

For a long moment the dripping in the pans was the only sound. Cochran's teeth ached with the desire to be away from this building.

'Go with my blessings, Spider Joe,' said Kootie softly, 'whoever I may be in this.'

After a pause, 'His wife was the one who lured my mother to her death,' said Diana. 'I wonder if I—' She shook her head. 'His last words,' she went on, 'were, "Get to the boats, point north, find a new Merlin or Virgil or Edison. An *intercessor*."' She had been rubbing her eyes as she spoke, and now looked tiredly around at the others in the steamy, smoky room; drops of water fell from the ceiling and plunked in idiot drumming into the various pots, and the moths were bumping against the shade of the lamp on the desk. 'An intercessor is for dealing with somebody else – a person more powerful. Who,' she asked, 'do you imagine *that person* would be?'

'Wake up and smell the Kahlua,' said Mavranos. 'That person would be nobody else but Dionysus.'

'Ah, God,' said Angelica softly. 'I was really hoping it wouldn't be. I didn't want this to involve the Bay Area – that country's all ... *vineyards*.'

The word *vineyards* caroled in Cochran's head, echoed by the syllables of *Vignes*; and insistent memories flooded his mind – of the pre-dawn rolling clatter of the stainless-steel Howard winepress cylinder during the October crush, always run before daylight to elude *las moscas*, the flies and bees and whatever influences they might carry into the wine; of the fresh, sharp smell of new wine fermenting in a two-hundred-gallon redwood tank when he would pump the awakening juice over the cap of grape skins, the new-born red vintage splashing and spurting out of the hose and flinging up spray; and of the cathedral silence in the eight-foot-wide lanes between the vines, roofless holy aisles carpeted with yellow mustard-weed flowers in the spring, plowed under in the fall and sown with the yeast-rich pomace of spent grape skins to assure continuity of benevolent wild-yeast strains on the skins of the next season's grapes.

And he lifted his right hand now and started at the gray ivy leaf mark on the back of his knuckles ... and reluctantly he called up his impossible childhood memory of what had happened on the day his hand was cut.

'I think he's right,' Cochran said hollowly. 'I think it is Dionysus.' He looked at Plumtree, and had no idea who might be behind her eyes at the moment. 'When they were talking about shooting you, just now,' he said to her, 'did you ... do your stay-calm trick, did you throw your anger over onto me?'

'No,' Plumtree said. 'They weren't insulting me, I wasn't mad. That was all *you* – but hey, I gotta say I liked your style.'

'Well, good for me. But a person can throw other things, anybody can. What I mean is, you can throw away grief for dead people you loved, if you're willing to disown along with it all you have of them, all your memories and all your – all the feelings you had about them ... which are arguably of no use to you anymore anyway, they're just stuff in your head that there's nothing to be done with anymore, like a collection, a very damn *costly* collection, of eight-track tapes after all the stereos are gone that ever played 'em.'

'Yeah,' said Plumtree quietly, 'they just make you unhappy. All you could do would be dust off the big old cassettes; whistle the tunes from memory and try to remember the instruments, and the vocals.'

Pete closed his eyes for a moment and shook his head. 'This is all just – deep and moving as hell, you know, but it's near midnight and—'

'Let the guy talk,' said Mavranos.

'You can disown the dead person,' Cochran went on, 'but not just into a void; I suppose that'd ... like, violate the law of conservation of grief, right? The god wants you to give it all to *him*.' He smiled, but didn't dare look at anyone but the dead body of Spider Joe. 'And it's a gift, that the god takes it – in exchange he gives you "surcease from sorrow."'

'Euripides?' said Mavranos.

'That's what the tailor says,' put in Plumtree with hectic cheer, 'when you bring in a torn pair of pants; and then *you* say, "Eumenides!"'

'That's mighty funny,' said Mavranos patiently. 'But Euripides wrote a play that deals with what Mr. Cochran is talking about.' He glanced at Angelica. 'It's another play with a secret hidden in it, like your *Troilus and Cressida*.'

Cochran sighed, with a shiver at the bottom of his lungs. 'This would be

Les Bacchants, wouldn't it,' he said. This soaked ceiling may as well fall in on me, he thought; everything else is.

'I guess so,' said Mavranos. 'That's French? I mean what in English they call *The Bacchae*, this ancient play about a guy named Pentheus, who was king of Thebes, and his mom, Agave, who cut his head off and brought it to town.'

'Agave is the cactus they make tequila from,' noted Plumtree. 'Often enough I've felt like it cut *my* head off.'

'I never read the play,' Cochran told Mavranos. He yawned, creaking his jaw and tipping tears from the corners of his eyes. 'But as a matter of fact my in-laws were reading bits of it to me just last week, in France.'

Cochran wished for another cold American beer, to chase away the palate-memory of the flinty claret with which Monsieur Leon had kept topping up his glass – the family's most prized *vin de bouche*, the old 1945 vintage, picked from vines that had gone unpruned during the Nazi occupation – while Madame Leon had droningly read page after leisurely, age-yellowed page of the old play; and he remembered how his weary brain had eventually stopped struggling to translate the French sentences, and had begun simply letting the syllables come through as random near-miss English, and how it had all seemed then to be phrases of idiot obscenity, both childish and shocking at the same time. There had been some moral the elderly couple had wanted him to derive from the play, and though he had come to their fifteenth-century farmhouse in Queyrac to turn over to them the urn that contained the ashes of their daughter and unborn grandchild, it had soon become clear that they were trying to get him into bed with their other, younger daughter, the slow-witted Marie-Claire. The thought that had sent him running from the house to his rented car and speeding away down the D-1 across the low country of the Bas Medoc toward distant Paris was *It's only January – they want a second try at a grandchild crop out of me in this thirteen-moon year.*

'At the start of the play,' said Mavranos, 'Dionysus comes to Thebes disguised as a stranger from Phrygia, but he gets all the local women to go dancing off into the hills in his honor, wearing animal skins and waving these staffs that are wrapped in ivy and topped with pinecones—'

'Easy on the *vino* there, Kootie,' interrupted Angelica.

But the boy didn't put the bottle down until he had refilled his gold cup; and when he spoke, it was to Mavranos: 'Was there blood on these staffs too?'

'After a while, there was,' Mavranos told him. 'The old retired king, Cadmus, he puts ivy vines in his hair and goes out to honor Dionysus too; but the present king, Pentheus, disapproves of all this crazy behavior and has the stranger arrested and thrown in jail. But since the stranger is really the god Dionysus, it's no problem for him to conjure up an earthquake and blow the jail to bits and get out. Pentheus asks him who set him free, and the stranger says, "Him who provides mortal man with the grapevine." And Pentheus says something argumentative back, which makes the stranger laugh and say, "That's hardly an insult to Dionysus!"'

Dutifully, Cochran asked him, 'What did Pentheus say?'

'Well, officially that line has been lost. In all the modern editions the editors have put in something like, "The god who makes men and women act like lunatics." But Scott Crane's dad had a real old copy, in Latin, and in this old version the original line's still there – and it translates to "An unjust gift – that lets men forsake their wronged dead." Then the stranger talks Pentheus into putting on a dress so he can go spy on the women, disguised as one of them. Pentheus is like somebody with a concussion at this point – he's seeing double, and he asks the stranger, "Were you an animal a minute ago? You've got a bull's head now."'

Cochran could feel Plumtree's gaze on him, but he didn't glance at her; instead he strode into the kitchen and managed to fumble three cans of Coors out of the refrigerator without looking squarely at the dead man on the table. Perceived only in his peripheral vision, the body seemed huge.

'Sorry,' he said when he had stepped back into the office and popped open one of the cans. He took a deep sip of the stinging cold beer and gasped, 'Do go on.'

'Well,' Mavranos said, 'the women aren't fooled by Pentheus's disguise, and they chase him down and just tear him apart. His own mom, Agave, is the worst – she's, like, delirious, and doesn't recognize him, she thinks they've caught a mountain lion or something, and she cuts off his head and carries it back to town, real pleased with herself. Old Cadmus, who's her dad, *he* sees that this is his grandson's head, and he talks her out of her delirium so that she sees it too; they're both horrified at what she's done – and then there's another missing section, a whole couple of pages. Modern editors have put in made-up speeches from Cadmus and Agave saying what a terrible thing this is and how bad they feel. And then when the old, real text picks up again, Dionysus is condemning Cadmus and his wife to be turned into snakes, and sending Agave off into destitute exile. '

'Is that how it ends?' asked Plumtree. 'Downer play, if you ask me.' Angelica closed her eyes and sighed, obviously weary of Plumtree's remarks but reluctant to snap at her.

'Well, yeah,' Mavranos agreed. 'You do wonder why the god treats 'em so rough, when they were apparently just doing what he wanted 'em to do. It doesn't make sense – the way it's published these days. But in the original version, after Cadmus and Agave realize what she's done, the god offers them a sacramental wine, called the debt-payer; he tells them that if they drink it, they will lose all memory of Pentheus, and therefore all guilt and unhappiness and grief over his bloody murder. They'll be turning over Pentheus's ghost to the god, and in return he'll give them forgetfulness and peace. And the reason the god is being so harsh to them at the end of the play is that in the last bit of the omitted section they *refuse* his offer, his gift – they can't bear to renounce their love of Pentheus, can't make themselves disown him, even though he's dead.'

Angelica was frowning, and looked as though she was ready to spit. 'Dionysus wants to take grief, and then more of it – and he won't wait for it to occur accidentally.' She visibly shivered. 'We *don't* want to deal with him face-to-face, visit him where he lives – if we've got to deal with him at all, we want to deal with his borders.'

Pete was half-sitting against the desk, and he looked up at Angelica with raised eyebrows. 'He takes in boarders?'

Diana had sat down on the couch and was holding her distended belly. 'It doesn't sound like Dionysus will want to help us, does it?' she asked. 'We want to do the *opposite* of renounce Scott.'

'That's why we need an intercessor, I reckon,' said Mavranos. He squinted at Cochran. 'How did you get that mark on the back of your hand?'

'I was—' Cochran began.

'Jesus!' yelled Pete Sullivan suddenly, leaping away from the desk. 'Angle! Get me the can of brake-parts cleaner!'

Angelica had jumped when he shouted, and now she spoke angrily. 'No. What is it, a wasp?'

Kootie had scrambled down from the desk, so fast that his forgotten bouillabaisse bowl flew off too and hit the carpeted floor with an echoing clang and a spray of tepid fish broth.

'Yes!' said Pete without looking away from the lamp. 'Your goddamn moths are turning into wasps. Get me the goddamn brake-parts cleaner, this wasp's as big as my head!'

Angelica was just staring at him, and frowning impatiently. 'It's not that big.'

'It is! Will you hurry!'

'Well, it's not as big as a *normal* person's head.'

'If a normal person comes in here we can check. Get me the goddamn brake-parts cleaner!'

'I'll get it,' said Kootie. Before stepping into the kitchen, the boy grinned nervously up at Cochran. 'Best thing for killing bugs, brake-parts cleaner spray is.'

'I bet,' said Cochran to his receding back. Absently he licked fish broth off his shaking fingers.

Plumtree took Cochran's other hand and led him away from the confusion, past Spider Joe's corpse to the far end of the couch; then, while Pete and

Angelica went on arguing about the wasp, Plumtree stepped quietly into the entry hall, pulling Cochran along after her.

The wasp must have made a break for it, or else another one had manifested itself, for Cochran heard renewed banging and cursing from the office behind them; but Plumtree calmly used the noise as cover while she drew back the chain in the doorframe slot and pulled the heavy door open.

The cold night air was potent with the briny smell of the wild sea as the two of them sprinted down the walk and across the lamplit asphalt to the corner of Ocean Boulevard; and when they had dashed through a gap in the surging headlights across the lanes of Ocean, Plumtree dragged Cochran around a parking lot to a set of iron stairs that led downward toward the beach sand. The majestic old liner *Queen Mary* was moored permanently as a hotel now at the Port of Long Beach peninsula a quarter-mile away across the dark harbor water, and her yellow lights glittered on the low waves like a windy lane of incandescent flowers.

Plumtree's blond hair was blowing around her face as she stepped off the last of the iron stairs onto the sand. 'Untamed water,' she said, waving at the sea. 'They won't be able to sense us here, even if they've got time to look. Which they don't. They're crazy even to think of delaying long enough to bury the poor old buggy man.'

Now that they were below the seaside cliffs, Cochran could see a couple of fires down the beach, a hundred yards or so to the south, and he wondered uneasily who might be sustaining them out here in the middle of this night. Faintly on the breeze he could hear drumming.

'Uh,' he said, shivering, 'where to?'

'Frisco,' Plumtree said. 'Why the Cliff House?'

'It's—' he said with a shrug, '—a nice place for breakfast. Tourist spot, good cover.' He shoved his hands into his pockets and tried to figure out why the Cliff House had seemed such an obvious place for them all to reconnoiter. 'I don't know, Cody, it just came to me. It's right by the ruins of the old Sutro Baths, and that's a good area to talk, down on the plain among the ruins, right by the water, the *untamed* water, because you can see anybody coming a long way off; nobody could eavesdrop, and the wind and the sea would even fox a shotgun microphone; and—' He laughed self-consciously. 'And on the cliffs of Sutro Heights Park, there used to be rows and rows of Grecian statues. They're all buried in the park somewhere now. I guess I was thinking they'd be a, a protective influence. All the stone people, to distract attention from us.'

He glanced to the side at her shadowed face, wondering if she would make fun of him, but she was just nodding. 'Why did they bury 'em?'

'It was during World War Two,' he said. 'The government was afraid they'd draw the attention of Japanese submarines.'

'Sure,' she said absently as they trudged through the loose sand north, away from the fires. 'Guy at the periscope sees a bunch of naked white guys standing on the cliffs in the middle of the night – "This mussa be Flisco, Captain-san!"'

Cody's crude witticism depressed Cochran, and he hoped Janis would be up again soon. 'For this,' he said stiffly, 'I think we could call my lawyer, and have him wire us some money. We could rent a car then—'

'And leave a paper trail for Armentrout to follow,' she said, nodding again. 'Fuck that noise, as the poet said. I'll get us a car.'

Armentrout had never stayed this late on the ward. The patients had all long since been put to bed, and the lights in the common rooms were dimmed; after the final clang of the door closing behind the last of the staff who would not be staying all night, the silence was whole, and tense – the occasional breathless, yiping scream, or raucous laugh, was a welcome collapse-to-one of the standing wave that seemed to fill all the rooms and corridors when the silence was unbroken.

Armentrout was sitting in one of the upholstered chairs at the re-righted table in the TV lounge. The television screen overhead was an opaque dark green, and he knew that the view of the courtyard behind him was blocked by the two board sheets of plywood that had been bolted over the window through which Cochran and Plumtree had escaped.

The *views*, the extensions to the outside world, were truncated. The pay phone had stopped its incessant ringing, and he was afraid that if he were to get up and cross to it and lift the receiver, he wouldn't even hear a dial tone.

Every couple of minutes he slapped his pants pockets, and twice in the last couple of hours he had actually had to dig out his keys and look at them to reassure himself that he could leave this locked ward if he wanted to. So far he was resisting the impulse to *try* the key in the door; what if it should fail to fit the lock, and none of the nurses or staff admitted to knowing who he was? What if they made him take off his white coat and put on clothes from the boutique closet, and forced him to take some subsistence-pharmer dose of meds, and showed him a bed in one of the rooms and told him it was his? What if it *was* his? He *had* been a patient in a place like this, in Wichita, at the age of seventeen ...

Atropine again for Richie ...

The charge nurse had given him a bewildered look when he had burst into the demented ice-cream social, hours ago, wearing his awkward two-figure mannikin appliance. He had mumbled something about it being a tool to reintegrate dissociatives – well, he could stick with that. He might *try* it on a dissociative sometime!

But he had needed the masking effect of the contraption. Long John Beach had been dangerously preempted during that ice-cream-social bedlam, and Armentrout had needed every masking measure he could put on, what with the god apparently *right in here*, breaking the place up with an earthquake and freeing inmates from their captivity.

Armentrout rocked his head back to look up at the raw cracks in the ceiling. All at once he stood up, shuddering. His fully charged cellular telephone was a weight in his jacket pocket, but suddenly he couldn't bear being in the TV lounge any longer. He waved at the night charge nurse through the station window as he hurried past.

Plumtree and *Cochran*, Armentrout thought as he strode down the dark hall toward his closed office door. Why would the god have freed Cochran *too*?

Armentrout wondered uneasily if he ought to have paid more attention to the deluded widower. How *had* the man come to have that ivy-leaf mark on the back of his right hand? Cochran hadn't reported having any delusional episodes – or visitations – while he was here; Armentrout would have been alerted by anything like that; but was the dreary fellow more than just psychically sensitive, could he have some *link* with the god?

Armentrout's key unlocked his office door, but he was too distracted to be pleased by the little vindication. I should have had him on hard meds, he thought as he blundered across the linoleum floor and sat down at the desk; hell, I should have given *him* benzodiazepine and ECT! I lost more than I gained, working them out on Plumtree, even if my – even if no distant ghost got a fix on me.

I got the taste of your blood now, and the smell of your jizz. In voodoo terms, that constitutes having your ID package. True, Armentrout thought now. But I do have a vial of your blood, Mr. Salvoy.

He stared at the two-figure mannikin appliance that was canted against the couch. With shirts, jackets, trousers, and shoes hung and hooked onto the aluminum poles, and the pair of clothing-store mannikin heads stuck on the swivelling neck-posts, the thing did look like two blandly smiling men with their arms around the shoulders of an invisible third man in the middle; and when he strapped the framework onto his own shoulders, Armentrout would become the third man, the man in the middle. A lever in the chest of the left-hand dummy permitted him to work the mechanical outside arms, and one in the right-hand dummy let him swivel the heads this way and that. And he had cored out holes in the backs of the Styrofoam heads, under the Dynel wigs, and stuffed into the holes dozens of paper towels spotted with patients' blood samples. The thing weighed about twenty pounds and was awkward to wear, and in public it drew *far* too much derisive attention, but on several occasions it had proven to be an effective multi-level psychic scrambler, a terrifically refractive and deflecting mask.

Even some moron with a plain old *gun*, Armentrout thought, would be likely to hit the wrong head.

The telephone on his desk rang, making him jump in his chair, and in the instant before he realized that the vibration in his ribs was just his cellular phone ringing too, he thought he was having some sort of cardiac arrest.

'Yes?' he said into the receiver when he had fumbled it up to his ear. Not long-distance, he thought fervently, please. Let it just finally be the cop.

And, thankfully, it *was* the cop.

'Doctor?' came the man's voice. 'Officer Hamilton here. Sorry it's so late, I called as quick as I could after I got off work. Got a pencil? I've got the location of the place where your Appleseed girl said she killed the Flying Nun king.'

Armentrout shakily wrote down an address on Neptune Avenue in Leucadia. 'And did you come up with anything about Neal Obstadt's death two years ago?'

'More or less. Something damn peculiar was going on that week, and the L.A. cops are still trying to figure it out. Obstadt's body was found in the water off the ocean side of the *Queen Mary* after some kind of bomb went off in the water there, on October 31 of '92, though no traces of any kind of explosive chemicals were found in the water, and no bomb fragments at all were recovered; he was blown to pieces, but they found a small-caliber bullet in his guts too. And the body of a film producer named Loretta deLarava was found up on one of the tourist decks with a .45 slug in her heart. She was filming some kind of TV special there, and we questioned a lot of her employees. Apparently deLarava had brought six people aboard *at gunpoint, as handcuffed prisoners.* One was that one-armed amnesiac nut you took charge of, who still had a pair of cuffs hanging from his wrist when they found him half-dead on the shore of the lagoon. And I've got the names of the other five, if you want 'em.'

'Yes, please.'

'Okay. Nicholas Bradshaw – he was the actor who played Spooky the ghost in that old TV show, "Ghost of a Chance," which was cancelled in 1960; a lawyer named J. Francis Strube, who spoke to detectives only through a lawyer of his own and basically had nothing useful to say; an itinerant electrical engineer named Peter Sullivan, whose twin sister had killed herself in Delaware five days previous; a lady psychiatrist who's been wanted on manslaughter charges since November of 1990, named Angelica Anthem Elizalde; and an eleven-year-old kid named Koot Hoomie Parganas, whose parents were torture-murdered the same night Sullivan's twin sister killed herself. All these people got free of their handcuffs, as if one of 'em had a key or was an escape artist.'

Hamilton sighed over the line. 'Bradshaw and Sullivan and Elizalde and the Parganas kid haven't been found since,' he went on, 'even though they're seriously wanted for at least questioning. DeLarava was offering a big reward for the fugitive Parganas boy, and the boy apparently called nine-one-one on the evening of the 27th, but the call was interrupted, and *I* think he's probably dead; and the Elizalde woman apparently shot at a woman in the Westlake area on the 28th. And then after Halloween the LAPD was deluged with calls about all this – from *psychics*! Unhelpful.'

Elizalde! thought Armentrout with a stir of remembered admiration. What a deluded pioneer that woman was! And a dark, long-legged beauty, too – I used to see her a lot when she was on the staff at the County Hospital in Huntington Park in '88 and '89.

But the mention of one-armed Long John Beach had reminded him that the crazy old man was presently in 'three-points' in the Quiet Room, and that if he was going to have to take Beach out of the hospital, it would be far easier with just the night staff to get past.

'So, have there been,' Armentrout asked, knowing that this was his main question, and not at all sure what answer he wished for, 'any of the peculiarities I asked about, going on at the Leucadia address, or near it?' Do I get to go home now and catch a few hours of sleep, and visit the Neptune Avenue place at my leisure and alone, he thought – or must I rush off there now, bringing all my cumbrous psychic-defense impedimenta along?

'Well,' said Hamilton, 'nobody's *reported* any "sudden growth of vegetation" to the cops ... nor the opposite ... but they wouldn't hardly, would they?'

'I suppose not,' said Armentrout with a smile, beginning to relax and think of his bed.

'But there've been a *whole* lot of calls about crazy teenagers driving through the neighborhood honking their horns and shooting off firecrackers – guns too, we've found ejected shells on the street. And either them or some other crowd of teenagers has been dancing on the beach at all hours, real noisy. You did mention "other disturbances." And,' Hamilton added, chuckling through a yawn, 'you didn't ask about this, but *two separate people* have called the *Union Tribune* to announce that Elvis Presley is going to be coming to town to stay with them for a few weeks. Oh, and you know the way evangelists are always saying the world's about to end? Well, a nut Bible church on the 101 there, one of the charismatic-hysterical types that rent space in failed laundromats, has announced that the world *already* ended, on New Year's Day. We're all living in some kind of delusional Purgatory right now, they say.'

While the man had been talking, Armentrout had abandoned all thought of going home to bed, and was now wearily planning how he would get Long John Beach and the two-figure appliance out of the clinic past the security guards.

'These ... teenagers,' Armentrout said, just to be sure, 'are they ... dressed nice? Seem to have money?'

'Not in particular. But hey, their cars all look like solid gold! They drive anything at all, Volkswagens, beat old Fords, Hondas, see – but a whole lot of them are painted metallic gold, and they've got wreaths of flowers hung over the license plates; even on the back plates, which is a violation. The neighborhood residents say it'd look like a parade if they weren't tearing through so fast. The kids on the beach, it's hard to tell – get this, they bring big pots of *white clay*, and smear themselves up with it for their dancing. Can't even tell what race they are, I gather.'

Armentrout sighed. 'Thank you, Officer Hamilton. I think that will be all.'

'Okay, Doc. Say, how's your crazy girl working out? Was her name Figleaf? I hope she was worth the money'

Armentrout thought of telling Hamilton that the woman had escaped, then discarded the idea. I don't really want the cops in on this now, he thought. 'Miss Figleaf has been a valuable addition to our team,' he said vaguely.

'Softball league, sounds like. Well, if you use electric scoreboards, no-body'll know when you lose – right? – with her playing for you.'

Armentrout agreed absently and hung up the phone. 'And if the referee's got a pacemaker, he'd better not declare her out,' he said softly, to no one but the Siamese-twin mannikins leaning against the couch.

Well, she really did kill the king, he thought, our Miss Plumtree, our Miss Figleaf ... who certainly held tight to her fig leaf while she was here. And a new king is apparently in readiness. Those people expecting Elvis sense it – *the undying King is coming here!* – and the gangs of teenagers are clearly, some kind of spontaneous embodiment of the Maruts who are mentioned in the Rig-Veda: noisy, armed youths from a culture so primitive that dance served the purpose of devout prayer, who – helpfully in this instance, while the king is temporarily out of the picture – aggressively embody fertility; and they're assuming too the role of the Cretan Kouretes, who hid the vulnerable infant Zeus from his murderous father Kronos by performing their Sword Dance around the baby, and masked his crying with the noise of their clashing weapons.

It's in Leucadia that I'll get a line on the new king, Armentrout thought, whoever it turns out to be. I wonder if dawn is close enough yet for Venus to be shining like a star in the eastern sky.

The telephone rang again. Armentrout assumed Hamilton had forgotten some detail, and he picked up the receiver. 'Hello?'

And then his lungs seemed to freeze – because over the phone he was hearing once again, for the first time in eleven days, the familiar phantom bar sounds, laughter and clinking glass and moronic jabbering. Then a well-remembered voice came on the line – loud, as the very fresh ones always were: 'Doctor?' whined the teenaged bipolar girl who had killed herself last week. 'I walk all crooked now – where's the rest of me?'

He hung up the phone without saying anything. There was no use talking to ghosts anyway, and he didn't want to give the thing the confirmation of having found him.

But she *had* found him, and no doubt would again. Hers was the first local death for which he'd been responsible since the mysterious and apparently one-shot amnesty that had been granted at dawn on New Year's Day. How long could it possibly, reasonably be before he would need to send more people – or even just idiot mumbling fragments of people, which would clump together – to that incorporeal bar?

As he stood up and crossed to the file cabinet to fetch out the two purple velvet boxes and the unrefrigerated blood sample from Plumtree, he was mentally rehearsing his imminent departure from the clinic. I can avoid some carrying-hassle by strapping the two-figure appliance right onto Long John Beach, he thought; he's already established as crazy.

I'll write him a pass, say we're going on a field trip ... to early-morning mass at some Catholic church. I'll tell the guards that the old man thinks he's the Three Wise Men, overdue at Bethlehem.

CHAPTER TWELVE

My father hath a power; inquire of him,
And learn to make a body of a limb.

—William Shakespeare, *Richard II*

'Watch for a Mobil station,' said Plumtree, leaning back in the driver's seat and squinting through cigarette smoke at the onrushing dark pavement of Highway 101.

Cochran nodded and peered through a wiped-clean patch of the steamy windshield, though there was nothing at the moment to see but the end-less ellipsis of reflective orange lane-marker dots and the perilously close night-time fog hanging on the road shoulder. They were north of Oxnard, out of L.A. County, and had just driven past the exit for something called Lost Hills Road. *Why would anyone take that exit?* Plumtree had wondered aloud. *If* hills *get lost out there, they'd certainly lose* you.

'The Jenkins woman's not gonna be cancelling her credit cards till ten,' Plumtree went on now, 'at the earliest. Hell the way she was knocking back the margaritas, she probably won't get up before noon.'

Jenkins had proven to be the name of the woman whose purse Plumtree had stolen at the Mount Sabu bar. After searching the Belmont Shore area for an older-model car, and then finding and quickly hot-wiring a '69 Ford Torino that had been parked off Redondo Avenue, Plumtree had used the Jenkins woman's Visa card in an all-night Ralph's market to buy a carton of cigarettes and a dozen cans of soup and a can opener and a fistful of Slim Jim packages and two twelve-packs of Coors and two bottles of Listerine and three 750-milliliter bottles of Popov vodka. A vodka bottle was opened now, wedged between her thighs and occasionally rattled by the bumps on the steering wheel when she changed lanes.

One of the lane changes was a sharp enough swerve to press Cochran against the passenger-side door and make him drop his cigarette, and Plumtree only remembered to click on the turn signal after she was in the left lane and yanking the car back straight. The vodka bottle had rattled like a mariachi band's percussion gourd. 'You want me to drive?' Cochran asked, fumbling on the floor for his cigarette.

'You're drunk,' said Plumtree. 'And don't … *point out to* me … that I'm drinking. Alcohol makes me a better driver, keeps me alert. We need an alert driver, for this fog.'

Cochran sat back in the passenger seat and hoped she was right. Certainly he wasn't sober … and at least they both had their seat belts on. He didn't want to have to stop and get out of the car, anyway – the car had a heater, and Plumtree had blessedly turned it up to full blast.

Past her silhouetted head he could faintly see the line of the surf glowing gray as it silently rose and fell out past the State Beach, under stars haloed by the incoming fog so that they looked like the stars in Van Gogh's *Starry Night*.

'I wonder if the dead king's crowd has even got started yet,' he said.

'All the dead king's horses and all the dead king's men …' Plumtree said softly.

Couldn't put Scott Crane together again, Cochran mentally finished the rhyme.

'I think—' Plumtree began; then she went on quickly, 'this car runs pretty smooth, doesn't it? I'd like to have done a compression check before we took off on an eight-hour drive, but I don't hear any bad lifters or rocker arms.'

Cochran bent over to reach into the bag between his feet, and he tore open the top of one of the beer cartons and lifted a can out. '*What* do you think?' he asked casually as he popped the top and took a leisurely sip.

'You may as well start working on those,' said Plumtree with a nod, 'they'll only warm up, sitting down there by the heater vent.' She hiked up the vodka bottle and took a hearty gulp. 'I think *I* turned those moths into wasps.'

The lights and exit ramps of Ventura had swept past now, but Cochran hadn't noticed a Mobil sign. Oh well, he thought, Santa Barbara is coming, up fast, and – he peered at the lighted dashboard – we're only a little under a quarter tank. 'Really?' he said, his voice quiet but not skeptical. 'Good enough so they could actually sting?'

'Well, I don't know if they could really *sting*. And it would be Valorie that did it, not actually this here *me*. But I think it was because that Mavranos guy asked you about the mark on your hand, and I – we – didn't want him to find out about it. Is that a birthmark?'

'I – told Janis about it,' Cochran whispered hoarsely after another gulped sip.

'She and I don't speak to each other much.'

Cochran sighed. 'In 1961, when I was seven, I thought I saw a face, a whiskery little old head, in an old Zinfandel stump that was being pruned back for the winter, and, without thinking, I shoved my hand out to stop the shears from cutting the old man's head off.' The steady green glow of the instrument-panel dials was a cozy contrast to the night and the fog and the rushing lane markers outside, and he took another sip of the cold beer, secure in the knowledge that there were twenty-three more full cans between his ankles. The coal of his cigarette glowed as he inhaled on it, and a moment later exhaled smoke curled against the windshield.

'*Actually*,' he said slowly, then paused; 'I think it's old rust or bark dust, under the skin. Like a powder-burn. Anyway, it's not a birthmark.'

Plumtree nodded and had another couple, of swallows from the vodka bottle. 'Actually what?' she asked.

Her question forced a short, awkward laugh out of Cochran. It made him dizzy to realize that he was teetering on the brink of telling this Plumtree woman – *this* one! – a secret he had kept for thirty-three years; and to realize too that, in the warm nest-like secrecy of this anonymous car flying along in the middle of cold dark nowhere, he *wanted* to; so he choked down a big impulsive mouthful of beer and used the sudden dizziness to get himself over the hump.

He spoke rapidly: 'Actually – as I remember it, anyway, maybe I'm confusing it with dreams I had later – the shears cut right through my hand, cut it most of the way *off*. No kidding – there was blood squirting everywhere, and the vineyard worker with the shears was in shock, looking like … like his face was carved out of bone, with a big bullet-hole for a mouth.' He tilted up the can to finish the beer in three deep gulps. 'Then, about one full second later, there was an almighty bang – a, a crash like you dropped a Sherman tank from thirty thousand feet onto the roof of the Astrodome – and when I could *think* again, maybe another second or two later, my hand was fine, whole, not a scratch, and not a drop of blood anywhere – my hand didn't even have this mark on it yet; that was there when I woke up one morning about exactly a year later – but the old vine was standing there in full, bushy, *impossible* summertime bloom.' Jerkily he leaned forward again to put the empty can onto the floor mat and tug another can free of the carton.

'Mobil station,' he said briskly when he had straightened up again and looked out through the windshield. 'Next exit, it looks like,' he added, nodding and squinting like a navigator. He popped the can open, but just held it. 'And,' he went on gently, shaking his head, 'it had ripe grape bunches hanging all over it, but also … pomegranates, and figs, and I don't know what all else. This was in the *dead* of winter.' He took a deep breath and let it out, then glanced at Plumtree with a wry smile. 'You'd better let me deal with pumping the gas, and paying for it. You're gonna reek of liquor.'

'That's Santa Barbara,' Plumtree said, switching on the turn-signal indicator and scuffing her tennis shoe from the gas pedal to the brake. 'After this we turn inland at Gaviota. The fog'll be worse then. Vodka doesn't have half the smell that beer's got. You probably stink like an old bar towel. What did the guy with the shears do, the vineyard worker?'

'He got very damn drunk.'

Plumtree nodded as she steered off the highway and rattled across an intersection on a green light. 'That shows respect.'

The left-side tires bounced up over the curb when she swung the big old Ford into the white-lit Mobil station, but she managed to park it next to one of the pumps. Cochran had dropped his cigarette again, but he just stomped it out on the floorboards. Before he could remark on the way she'd handled the driveway, she said, 'I gotta disconnect the coil to turn this off. That's good, though – a modern car, with the ignition in the steering column, I'd have had to bust it out, and cops look for that, in parking lots, and then … they wait for whoever to come back to the car. Who's driving it.'

She enunciated the syllables as carefully as if she were pushing silver dollars out of her mouth one at a time, and Cochran realized that she herself was very drunk; and when he levered open the passenger-side door and stood up and took several deep breaths of the icy air, he was so dizzy that he had to hang on to the door to keep his balance.

He swung his unwieldy gaze over the car's roof, and watched Plumtree shuffle to the front bumper, frowning and holding on to the vibrating fender with both hands. When she had hoisted up the hood and pulled free the wire that connected the coil to the battery, the engine shook twice and then wheezed to a halt; and in the silence he said, 'I think we should … let Janis drive.'

'She'd get lost,' said Plumtree shortly. 'I'm gonna go give the man the card, sign for it – you pump the gas when I wave.' She wobbled across the damp asphalt toward the glass door, then halted and looked back at him. 'On the Torinos the gas cap is behind the rear license plate.'

Cochran squeaked the license plate down, unscrewed the gas cap, and shoved the nozzle of the premium pump into the filler hole, and then he leaned heavily on the trunk as he held the aluminum trigger squeezed and numbly watched the wheels behind the little gas pump window roll around to, finally, fifteen dollars and sixty cents. The aromatic reek of gasoline on the cold night air did nothing to sober him up. He had hung up the nozzle but was still trying to get the cap threaded back on when Plumtree reattached the coil wire and jumped the solenoid again to start the engine. When he heard the hood slam down he just dropped the cap and let the license plate snap up over it, and then hurried to the passenger-side door and got in, glad of the interior warmth even if they were both about to die in a Driving-Under-the-Influence one-car crash in the foggy canyons beyond Gaviota.

She clanked the engine into gear and drove right over the curb onto Milpas Street, swinging wide in a chirruping left turn to get back to the 101.

'Oh, *okay*,' she said, and the engine missed for a moment, coming back strongly when she fluttered the gas pedal. 'Whoops! When do I turn?'

'Take that on-ramp on the right,' said Cochran through clenched teeth, pulling the seat belt across himself. '101 north.'

She glanced at him after she had made the turn. 'Scant! What day is it?'

He relaxed a little, and didn't attach the seat belt. 'It's the morning of the twelfth by now,' he said cautiously, 'of January. It's been a couple of hours since we left Solville.'

'My father is alive,' she said. 'I *did* catch him!'

'That's ... right, I guess. According to that Angelica woman.' He tried to remember when it had been that Janis had last been up.

She leaned back in the seat now, straightening her arms and flexing her fingers at the top of the wheel. 'This is disorienting – I don't have to watch for cues, I can just *ask* you! How did we get away from there? I don't think they wanted us to just leave.'

'No – we snuck out. They were talking about – holding a gun on you. We're still working with them, I guess, but at arm's length.'

She was gingerly licking her lips and grimacing. 'I'm glad to get away from that burnt-liquor stink ... Nobody got hurt, I hope?'

'Oh no.' He let the seat belt reel back up into the slot above the door, and finally sat back and let himself exhale. 'Well, not *hurt* – but that old man with the windshield wipers all over him died. But it – was just, like, a heart attack, I guess. Nothing to do with us. And then in the confusion Cody just grabbed my hand and we walked out. And stole us this car.'

'My father spoke to me over the telephone.'

Cochran thought of someone who had to maintain a '69 Torino, going out to work on a Thursday morning and finding the car gone; but at least Janis was a sober driver. She hadn't had anything to drink since ... what? A Manhattan or two at dinner, hours and hours ago. Of course it was the same bloodstream, really, but it did seem that Cody had taken the alcohol away with her. 'Yes,' he said. 'I heard him.'

She was still smacking her lips, and now she said, 'Did Cody get mouthwash?'

'As a matter of fact, she did. A big bottle of Listerine.'

'Could you pass it to me?'

Cochran did, and she unscrewed the cap and took a swig of the mouthwash; she swished it around audibly in her mouth for a few seconds, then rolled down the window to spit it outside.

'We're going to San Francisco, aren't we?' she said as she rolled the window back up.

'Yes.' Cochran blinked in the new Listerine fumes, trying to remember whether Janis had still been on when San Francisco had first been proposed. He was sure she had not, that Cody had already been in control then. 'How did you know that?'

'That's where he ... fell off the building. And I caught him.'

'We're going there because it's where they all – you all – hell, we all, can get Scott Crane restored to life.' According to a crazy old dead black lady, at least, he thought.

'They're bringing his body along, I hope?' It seemed to Cochran that she spoke anxiously.

He thought of the vague plan Cody had described for getting Crane back into his own undecayed body – or, failing that, into hers permanently; and he discarded the idea of asking her about it, for she would probably just lose time if he did ask, and leave the drunk Cody to drive.

'They said they were,' he told her. 'We're probably going to be meeting them at a place called the Cliff House Restaurant, on the northwest shore.'

'I'll be hungry by then – Cody ate most of my dinner. Did she pick up any snacks?'

'Some Slim Jims,' said Cochran, trying to remember if he had been as unconcerned as this when he had learned that Spider Joe was dead; of course he had actually seen the body, and Janis had not.

'Could I have a pack?'

Cochran leaned down and dug a Slim Jims package out of the bag; and he got out too another beer for himself. He opened the can, and, before he took the first sip, he said, 'Here's to poor old Spider Joe. May he rest in peace.'

Plumtree nodded, staring ahead. 'His wife died, though, right? Recently?'

'They did say that,' agreed Cochran. He took another, deeper sip.

At the gas-station-and-motel town of Gaviota the 101 curled sharply to the east, inland, and soon they were climbing through the dark canyons of the Santa Ynez Mountains. The fog was a blurry wall close ahead of them, glowing gray with the diffracted radiance of the headlights, and the short patch of pavement that was visible in front of the fog seemed to Cochran's tired eyes to be stationary, so that the black lines of skid marks were standing waves shimmying in place, and the point-of-impact of a long-ago dropped can of white paint seemed to be the beak of a diving white bird. They passed big semi-trailer trucks that were stopped on the shoulder, visible through the fog only by yellow light seemed to Cochran to trace the rigging of tanker ships more remote in the night than the trucks could possibly really be.

Cones of light, luminous triangular shapes in the darkness, resolved themselves into spotlit billboards, or steep hillside shoulders with headlights approaching from the other side, as he watched them gradually materialize out of the night; and rotating spoke-like fingers of light would turn overhead when an unseen car in the southbound lanes approached behind invisible tree branches. Sometimes Plumtree would change lanes to get around the ghostly red eyes of brake lights ahead of them, and in those transitional moments when the tires were thumping across the lane-divider bumps the turn-signal lights would strobe deeply into the fog on the shoulder, illuminating a bottle or a weed or a shoe for a brief, startled instant.

From time to time Cochran glimpsed moonlit forests off to the side, and the sterile extents of deserts, but it wasn't until he twice saw a vast castle in the remote distance, with rows of yellow and green-lit windows, and then saw that it was only a reflection of the instrument panel lights in the close window glass, that he realized that nothing he saw beyond a distance of about six feet could be genuine. The realization didn't stop his weary, smoke-stung eyes from registering new wonders; in fact it seemed to free his optic nerves to present him with wilder things, ships and towering siege engines and dirigibles.

The old Ford's engine had begun to cough when they were driving past the isolated lights of the Madonna Inn in San Luis Obispo, but began to run smoothly again after that – and Plumtree, who for some miles had been folding her left leg and straightening it again and scooting forward and back in her seat as if trying to stay awake, reached out to the side and squeezed Cochran's leg just above the knee.

'Do we have any more cigarettes?' she asked.

'A – whole carton,' Cochran said, suddenly very aware of the close flex of her legs in the tight jeans. He gripped his current beer between his thighs and bent forward to grope by his feet for a fresh pack of Marlboros.

But when he straightened up she glanced at it and shook her head. 'I meant More, the brand name. I suppose Cody just thought of herself, and got just the Marlboros.' Her fingers were curled around his leg now, palpably brushing against the dashboard-facing side of the beer can, and her thumb was absently rubbing the top of his thigh. 'And I don't suppose she bought any Southern Comfort.'

'No,' said Cochran. 'Just beer and vodka.' He stubbed out his cigarette in the ashtray and then, as if for a sip of beer, lifted away the impeding can. Her hand slid halfway up his thigh, her fingers kneading the worn secondhand corduroy.

'All alone in the middle of nighttime nowhere,' she said, barely loud enough for him to hear. 'Some people would consider this a highly lucrative situation.'

Cochran didn't see how some people would, but he shifted closer to her and put his arm around her shoulder to stroke her coarsely cut blond hair. She rolled her head back against his forearm and her right hand slid up his leg until her little finger was brushing the tight fabric over his crotch.

'We should,' he said hoarsely, 'probably pull over and park on the shoulder for a while. Till the fog clears a bit.' His heart was thudding in his chest, and he wished there was somewhere he could put down the beer he was holding in his right hand. And I should try to get a slug of that mouthwash, he thought.

Her kneading hand was fully on his crotch now, and he simply let go of the beer can; it thudded to the carpeted floorboard as he reached across to cup the unfamiliar hot softness of her left breast through the thin fabric of her blouse.

'Nobody can interrupt us out here,' she whispered, and snapped the turn signal lever up to indicate a lane change. 'Nobody knows where we are.' The right tires were rumbling on the shoulder, and Plumtree's leg flexed as she pressed the brake pedal. 'There's no phone here, so nobody can say we should have taken the time to call anyone.'

'You're a big girl,' Cochran agreed dizzily. 'You don't have to call your mother and let her know where you are.'

'Ah!' she said, and her voice sounded sad; then she had whipped her right hand up so hard that it struck the head liner and nearly broke his elbow. Her foot slammed onto the gas pedal, and the back tires screeched and burned rubber as she steered the bucking old Ford back out into the slow lane.

'Fog, take it easy!' Cochran yelled, clasping his elbow.

She hit the brake hard enough to throw him forward against the padded black dashboard. He could hear his dropped beer can rolling on the floor.

'I will drive this car straight into a wall if you try to touch me, Omar!' Plumtree said loudly. 'In arousing ways! Jesus will not blame me – He will take me into His bosom, and throw *you* into the fires of Gehenna! You know I will, and you know He will!'

'Fine!' Cochran gasped. 'Drive normal! What's the matter with you, Janis?'

She straightened the wheel, and though the engine was coughing again she quickly accelerated the car to a steady twenty miles an hour, glancing harriedly from the road to the rear-view mirror and back. 'I'm sorry, Scant!' she said. 'I must have dozed off! God, I might have got us killed! Okay, fog still, okay. Did I hit anything? God, my arms are shaking! Are you all right?'

'Well you nearly broke *my* arm,' he said, harshly. 'Jesus, girl!' He could see that there had been at least one personality shift, and that the erotic moment was long gone. 'No, you didn't hit anything.' He leaned down and yanked a fresh beer out of the box. The floorboard carpeting was marshy under the soles of his tennis shoes, and the hot air was fetid with the smell of the spilled beer. 'Who's Omar?"

'That's my father's name! Be careful now, Scant, I don't want to lose time with you – but – was *he* here?'

'No,' Cochran said. Thank God, he added mentally. He popped the tab on the beer can. 'Another woman – did I ... ? Do you, uh, recall putting your hand on my leg?'

'Oh, God, Tiffany,' she said ruefully. 'That would be Tiffany. I bet. She made a pass at you, right? And you thought it was me! Poor Scant!'

He had been panting, but now began to relax. 'I wouldn't mind,' he said cautiously, 'if it was you.'

'It will be, Scant, I promise you, soon, and not in the back of an old car, either.' She patted at the seat around her legs. 'Did she eat my Slim Jim? God, that woke me up, at least – I could feel that I was slipping in and out, back there. I guess Tiffany was slipping out and in.'

Her guileless last couple of lines were echoing in his head, and he tilted up his fresh can of beer for a distancing, objectivity-inducing mouthful.

'If you get sleepy again,' he said, 'just pull over. You can catch a nap on the front seat, and I'll do the same in the trunk.'

'Did Cody get a key to the trunk?'

He sighed. 'I was kidding. And no, she didn't – she hot-wired the car somehow.'

'She is mechanically inclined,' Plumtree allowed, diligently watching the road. Her mouth was working, and she rolled down the window; cold night air blew into the car and twitched Cochran's sweaty hair. 'My mouth's full of Tiffany's spit,' Plumtree said, her voice frailer with the open window beyond her. 'Could I have the mouthwash?'

Cochran passed it to her, and again she swished a sip of the sharp-smelling stuff and spat it out the window. He was glad when she rolled the window up again, though the sudden scents of diesel exhaust and spicy clay and the dry-white-wine smell of the fog had been a relief from the warm-beer fumes.

'You okay to drive?' he asked.

'Oh, sure. I kind of did catch a nap there, I guess, while she was on. Besides, you're a little – you're more than point-oh-eight blood alcohol, I'd guess.'

'Technically, I suppose, yeah,' he said. 'We'd better,' Cochran went on steadily, 'take the 280, to the city, rather than follow the 101 all the way up. We can stop at my house, and I can pick up some clothes and money.' And think all this over, soberly, he thought. And check the phone messages, and take in the mail. And clip the holstered .357 onto the back of my belt, if I decide we should indeed go on and meet the others.

'Tell me when to turn,' Plumtree said.

'Oh, it won't be for hours yet.'

'Won't it ... bother you, seeing the place where you lived with your wife?'

Cochran took a long drag on his cigarette. 'I suppose so. Sure it will. Gotta be done, though. Faced.'

Plumtree shivered. 'It must be scary, not having anyone you can turn the wheel over to, in bad situations.'

Cochran smiled bleakly. 'I never—'

Both of them jumped when for an instant a big brown owl swooped into the flickering headlight glow and then disappeared over the roof.

Cochran forced a laugh, embarrassed to have been so startled but pleased that he had not dropped his cigarette. 'I wonder what owls think of this highway of light running through the middle of their mountains.'

'They're hoping for a crash, a fire that'll drive the mice and rabbits out of hiding.'

After a moment, he said, 'A plausible answer, Cody, but I was talking to Janis.'

She exhaled as if trying to whistle. 'Listerine! Who else was on?'

'Somebody called Tiffany. And then—'

'You pig.' She rocked on the seat and then brushed the fingers of one hand from the buttons of her blouse to the fly of her jeans. 'What did you two *do* with me?'

'Nothing.' He tried to say it as though he had resisted Tiffany's advances. This was a disorienting basis for conversation, and it occurred to him that it might be difficult to manage any intimacy even with Janis, without Cody objecting and interfering in humiliating ways. 'Anyway, she was interrupted by somebody else, a woman who cussed me out – called me Omar.' He wondered how much Cody might have sobered up in the time she was gone, and he half-hoped something he said might drive her away and let Janis back on.

'Follow the Queen, you were playing,' said Plumtree. 'You must have mentioned our ... female parent, right? She comes up sometimes when somebody even just mentions her, and *always* when somebody *asks* for her. You ever play Follow the Queen?'

'The poker game? Sure – seven-card stud, where the next card dealt face up, after a face up queen, is wild.'

'Wild, right – that is, it's *whatever you declare it to be*. And when our parent-of-the-fair-sex is up, the next girl is whoever you ask for. Who did you ask for? Not me, Mom doesn't do the mouthwash bit.'

'I guess I called for Janis.'

'Not Tiffany? That was noble of you. Of course you didn't understand the rules yet. Do you *swear* you two didn't do anything with me?'

Cochran realized, to his surprise, that he didn't want to swear to a lie. 'I swear there was no kiss,' he said, 'and not a button was undone or a zipper unzipped.'

'Oh, you pig. I bet you groped me. I bet you were ready to go all-in on that flop.'

'Flop,' said Cochran, thinking in poker terms now, and remembering that she had used the word several times before this. 'That's what the three communal cards are called, in Hold-'Em: the flop. You hope they make some good hand, combined with your two personal down-cards. Sometimes you just pass even if you've got ace-king down, if the flop is all the wrong suit, 'cause somebody's surely got two of the flop's suit, for a flush.'

'When it's ... *real life* ... you can't pass,' she said grimly, 'it's like you're the perpetual Big Blind, gotta make the bet whether you want to or not.'

Cochran remembered Janis telling him, just a few moments ago, that he must find it 'scary' not to be able to turn a bad situation over to another personality; and he laughed softly with dawning comprehension. 'You girls are like a ... squad, a relay-team, at the big Poker Table of Life, though, aren't you? If a flop comes that's no good to Cody's hole-cards Janis or Tiffany or somebody will be holding two different cards, ones that'll make a flush or a full boat or something. And so the girl with the playable cards steps in.'

'It still calls for some hard bluffing sometimes. But so far they haven't dealt us a flop *one* of us couldn't play.'

Cochran tilted up his beer to get the last swallow, and sleepily wondered whether to bother opening another. And he thought again about Janis's remark: *Wont it bother you, seeing the place where you lived with your wife?*

'Must be convenient, though,' he said now, 'nevertheless. "Somebody yelling at me? I got a headache? I'll split, and be back when it's been taken care of."'

Plumtree's vodka bottle was on the seat between them, and he impulsively picked it up and unscrewed the cap. 'I – *I* had to go identify my wife's run-over pregnant body,' he said, suddenly speaking loudly, 'in the morgue. She was *pregnant*. We bought stuff for the kid-to-be – the stuff's in that house now, that I'm gonna be breaking a window to get into in a few hours – a crib, goddammit, teddy-bear wallpaper. And Nina and I had adjoining plots, in a cemetery there, we picked out a spot we liked and paid for it – but I had to have her cremated and take her ashes to France, so I'll be buried there alone.' He gulped a mouthful of the warm, scorching liquor and burningly exhaled through his nose. 'I haven't had the option of *going away* during *any* of this. I've got to *pay* for what I take, sometimes as much as all I've got. I've got to, like *most* people, I've got to take the wounds and then just keep playing, wounded, shoving all my chips out with one hand while I – hold my burst guts in with the other.' The fumes in his nose were making his eyes water. 'My hole cards are two dead people, and the, the *flop* I'm facing is – is those three merciless ladies in Greek mythology who measure out life and fucking cut it off.'

'Clotho, Lachesis, and Atropine,' said Plumtree blandly, watching the road. 'Let's play a game – I'll name a paper product, and you guess what it is.'

Cochran's heart was hammering, and his mouth was dry and hot in spite of the vodka, but he didn't go on shouting. 'What?' he said, his voice cracking. 'That doesn't make any sense.'

'Why don't you take a nap, then, champ? It might sober you up, and I'll be ready to be spelled off, come dawn.' She glanced at him and smiled. 'Little man, you've had a busy day.'

'... Maybe I will.' His anger had evaporated as quickly as it had come, leaving him deflated. Slowly he screwed the cap back on the bottle. 'You want some of this?'

'I'm fine for now. Leave it on the seat there, in case of emergencies.'

Cochran stretched his feet out and leaned his head against the cool, damp window glass. 'You did that trick just now, didn't you?' he said emptily, closing his eyes. 'What I said made you mad, and you threw the anger over onto me. I – I'm sorry if I hurt your feelings.' Though as I recall, he thought, everything I said was true.

'Go to sleep. You can say anything you want, and yeah, if it pisses me off I'll just throw it back at you. "I'm rubber, you're glue, whatever you say bounces off me and sticks to you." All I care about is looking out for Number One.' She laughed softly. 'I'm just trying to figure out who that is.'

Cochran's last thought before he went to sleep or passed out was that her remarks about his interval with Tiffany must not, after all, have represented real anger.

'Mad as a March herring,' observed Kootie, agreeing with Mavranos's assessment of Janis Cordelia Plumtree. They were sitting in the front seat of Mavranos's truck, barrelling along at a steady seventy miles per hour north on the 101 out past Oxnard, with the surf a rippling line far away in the darkness on their left. Mavranos's view of the right lane was partly blocked by a new Buddha-like stone statue on the dashboard, but he was getting used to that.

'That would be the technical term, yes,' said Angelica Sullivan from the back seat, where she was loading a stack of extended-round .45 ACP magazines – pressing each Eldorado Starfire hollow-point bullet down against the spring pressure with the forefinger of her left hand while she tucked the next into the cleared top of the magazine with the fingers of her right.

Mavranos could see her working in the rear-view mirror. She must have loaded a dozen of those illegal twelve-round magazines by now, he thought. Even with her .45 Marlin carbine, handily built to take the same size magazine, that's a whole lot of back-up ammo.

She looked up, and in the mirror he could see a glint of highway light reflect from her eye. 'You think I'm over-preparing?' she asked.

Mavranos shrugged. 'Better than under.'

Pete Sullivan lifted three of the loaded magazines and tucked them into the canvas knapsack at his side. 'And these bullets have each got a drop of a rust-based *omiero* soup in the tip,' he said, '—my pacifist Houdini hands have been capable of that much work, at least – so these'll stop a ghost as readily as a live human.'

'Good thing,' said Mavranos, watching the traffic ahead and wondering what sort of vehicle Plumtree and Cochran might be driving in. 'For the Plumtree woman you'd want both functions. I know, Angelica, you already said her murderer father's actually not a ghost – but I swear there's a ghost in that blond head *too*.' He glanced at the dashboard. 'We're gonna need gas again, next chance – maybe switch in one of the fresh batteries too.'

'We should have taken one of the Solville cars,' said Pete Sullivan; saying it in fact for about the sixth time since they'd buried Spider Joe in the parking lot behind the Solville buildings.

'We need this truck,' said Kootie.

'*Why* exactly?' asked Pete.

'It's—' Kootie sighed, and Mavranos caught the boy's brief, frail grin out of the corner of his eye. 'Because when I sensed it coming north to us, Sunday before last, I sensed it as a cup, a chalice. And when Arky takes it to town, it always comes back full of as much food as we're needing – all this last week and a half, there's been enough tortillas and bananas and fishes and ground beef and cheese and beer and all, when we unload it, for all the people who've been coming over, even though we don't know in advance how many there'll be.'

'And it turns red during Holy Week, or any local equivalents,' said Mavranos. 'And,' he added ruefully, 'so many ghosts are drawn to it and sucked into the air cleaner and burned up in the carburetor that their cast-off charges screw up the electrical system.'

'And it's used to serve the king,' said Kootie quietly, as if that settled it.

Right now, thought Mavranos as he glanced in the rearview mirror at the draped tarpaulin in the back, it's being used to *carry* the king.

Mavranos remembered another time Scott Crane had lain stretched out in the back of the truck while Mavranos drove. It had been very nearly a year ago, on January 19th of last year.

Scott had been wearing sweatpants for that painful mid-morning trip up the 405 to Northridge, with not even a bit of twine for a belt, but still his legs had been as weak and racked with cramps as if he'd been wearing a Mobius-twisted belt during a solar eclipse; and he had been as sick – vomiting blood, seeing double, hearing voices – as if he had eaten a rare steak cooked in an iron pan on a Friday in Lent.

He had been that way for two days – ever since 4:31 in the pre-dawn morning of January 17th, when the Northridge earthquake had struck Los Angeles with a force of 6.4 on the Richter scale and 6.7 on the more modern moment-magnitude scale. It had been one of the newly recognized 'blind thrust faults,' punching the land upward from a previously unsuspected subterranean fault line.

Mavranos had even noticed several white strands in the coppery bushiness of Scott's beard.

Scott had been too weak to talk loudly enough for Mavranos to hear him up in the front seat of the rackety truck, and the intercom set they had brought along for the purpose was drowned in the static-fields of thousands of ghosts awakened to idiot panic by the quake, and so they had stopped at a Carl's Junior hamburger place on the way and put together a string-and-paper-cup 'telephone.'

Mavranos had specially 'stealth-equipped' the truck for the trip, with sea-water in the windshield-washer reservoir and clumps of anonymous hair from a barbershop floor taped onto the radio antenna supplementing the usual tangle of ultrasonic deer-repelling whistles pined in conflicted patterns on the roof and hood, and he was sure they couldn't be traced while they were in the moving vehicle; but he was uneasy about Scott's determination to struggle out of the truck and walk around among the fractured and concussed buildings.

'It's the *date*, Pogo,' Mavranos had finally said, turning his head to speak into the paper cup while keeping the string taut, 'that makes me nervous about this. It seems like a ... almost a warning.' Mavranos had routinely addressed Scott by the name of the possum character in the Walt Kelly comic strip.

'Today is the 19th,' had come Scott's faint, buzzing answer through the cup.

'Sure it is,' Mavranos had replied impatiently, 'but the earthquake was on the 17th. St. Sulpice and all that.'

Scott hadn't answered right away, but even through the unvibrating string Mavranos had been able to feel the ill king's irritation. Mavranos still believed that his point had been relevant, though.

A Vietnamese woman who lived at the Leucadia estate had been given the job of tracing historical events having to do with the secret history of the Fisher Kings and their rivals, and she had discovered a peculiar reactionary vegetation-king cult that had appeared in Paris in 1885, four years after a special congress in Bordeaux had, reluctantly but officially, advised grafting all French grapevines onto imported American rootstocks, which were resistant to the phylloxera louse that looked likely otherwise to obliterate all the vineyards of Europe. The dissenting cult had centered around the seminary and cathedral of St. Sulpice in the St. Germaine district of Paris, and had included among its members the writers Maurice Maeterlinck and Stephane Mallarme, the composer Claude Debussy, and eventually the writer and film-maker Jean Cocteau – but it appeared to have been started by a village priest from a parish in the rural.Languedoc Valley south of Carcassonne. The priest, Berenger Sauniere, had in 1885 uncovered some documents hidden in the foundation stones of his church, which stood on the site of an ancient Visigoth winery dating back at least to the sixth century, and of a Roman mysteries-temple before that; Sauniere's discoveries had led somehow to his getting substantial payments from the French government and a Hapsburg archduke; and Sauniere had suffered a stroke on January 17th of 1917, and died five days later, after an attending priest had found it impossible to give the dying man the sacraments of confession and Extreme Unction. January 17th was the feast day of St. Sulpice.

The Vietnamese woman, a one-time cabdriver and casino night manager called Bernardette Dinh, had flagged this particular cult because it had shown signs of continuing well into the twentieth century in several splintered branches. In the Bibliotheque Nationale in Paris she had traced a network of obscure items published from the late 1950s through the 1970s – pamphlets, and issues of a rare magazine called *Circuit*, and a privately printed booklet called *Le Serpent Rouge*, which had been published on January 17th of 1967 and whose three authors were found hanged at separate locations less than two months later. All of these publications mentioned the cathedral of St. Sulpice and contained cryptical essays on the science of multi-generational, almost genealogical, viticulture and vine-grafting. Some researchers had evidently considered that *Le Serpent Rouge* dealt with a long-preserved bloodline, but Dinh had speculated that it referred to a secretly cultivated varietal, snaking its way in concealment down through the centuries, of *red wine*.

One branch of the cult survived in the village of Queyrac in the Bas Medoc, and another had taken the name of a fifteenth-century Dionysiac cult called L'Ordre du Levrier Blanc and appeared to have relocated to the American west. In all the branches – and in fact in many other cultures, from the Estonians on the Baltic Sea who sacrificed sheep and oxen on that date, to the Egyptian Copts who observed the day as the anniversary of the death of the tormented visionary St. Anthony – January 17 was a date to be both celebrated and, feared.

'At least,' Scott had said finally, his voice humming in the paper cup linked to where he had lain in the back of the truck on that day, 'if I have a stroke, I won't have any trouble remembering some sins to tell the priest.'

'I can help you out there,' Mavranos had agreed; and the tense moment had passed, but they had still been driving north toward the wounded city.

Traffic on the 405 had slowed to a stop near the intersection with the Ventura Freeway, northwest of Los Angeles, and Mavranos had got off onto the crowded surface streets; plywood covered many shop windows along these sunlit blocks, and hasty curtains of chain-link fencing had been hung across the breezeways of several of the apartment buildings they passed, and finally on a side street off Reseda and Roscoe he had simply let the truck engine's idle-speed drift them to a parking space at the curb, where he stepped on the brake and, almost as an afterthought, switched off the ignition.

His attention sprang out to the surroundings when the clatter of the engine subsided into silence, and he heard Crane hiking himself up to look out too.

The opposite curb was crowded with empty cars parked bumper-to-bumper, glittering in the bright midwinter sunlight; and the roof of every one of the cars was crushed in, the windshields twisted and white with crazed cracking, the side windows just gone. Beyond the block-long line of

Bronco and Jetta and Eldorado hulks, across a lot somehow already brown with dead grass, stood the ruptured apartment complex from whose collapsed carports these cars had been extricated – the outer walls had sheared away, exposing interior rooms and doors, and when Mavranos cranked down the driver's-side window he could smell the faint strawberry tang of garbage on the breeze.

Mavranos had got out and swung open the back of the truck to help Scott down, uneasily noting the fresh blood blotting Scott's shirt from the unhealing wound in his side, and though Mavranos had been afraid that they'd be arrested as looters, Scott had insisted on hobbling across the empty street and inspecting the damage.

They had climbed in among the apartments picking their way over the drywall and joist beams and aluminum window frames that had fallen across beds and couches, and shuffled carefully across springy, uneven floors, and stared at the body counts spray-painted by rescue workers on the pictureless walls.

When they had clambered outside again, Scott had sat down on the metal box of a fallen air-conditioning unit. Harsh, shouting rap music echoed from some open window on the other side of the street. 'My lands are in disorder,' Crane said. 'Broken.'

'From underneath,' said Mavranos stolidly. He had agreed with Dinh that the resurgent phylloxera plague in the north California wine country was a bad sign for Scott's reign, a message of discontent 'from six feet under.'

Scott squinted toward the far side of the empty street. 'Sitting on a, an air-conditioning unit, weeping again the king my father's wreck, this music gibbered by me upon the pavement.' He laid his bare wrist on a torn edge of metal. 'So what am I *not doing*? Just five weeks ago the old Flamingo building in Las Vegas was torn down – that was my father's castle, when he was king, before I killed him – wasn't that a victory? Las Vegas is turning into a family place, a kid's place. And Diana and I have had four children, and we … get three crops a year at the Leucadia place …'

'Why don't you ever prune back the grapevines, in the winter?'

'They don't *need* it …' He looked up at Mavranos and gave him a wasted grin through his disordered beard. 'Well, they *don't*, you know. But okay, that's not the reason. I *did* prune 'em back, in that first winter after Las Vegas, but later I – I dreamed about it. In the dreams, the branches *bled* where they were cut; and I dreamed about Ozzie, turned to dust at the touch of Death and blowing away across the desert.'

Mavranos just nodded, and wished he'd brought along one of the beers from the truck Scott and Diana weren't related, but they had both been informally adopted by the same man, an old-time poker player named Oliver Crane but known in the poker world as Ozzie Smith. He had disappeared in the desert outside Las Vegas during the tumultuous Holy Week of 1990, and Scott had always maintained that the old man had died in saving Scott from a murderous embodiment of Dionysus and Death that had taken the physical form of Scott's dead wife Susan.

'Maybe you're *s'posed* to dream about Death, Pogo,' Mavranos said. 'It's one of the Major Arcana in the tarot deck, and I get the idea that in your dreams you practically go *bar-hopping* with the rest of that crowd.'

'I humanize them,' Scott said. 'A perfect Fisher King wouldn't just have a wounded side, he'd have no left arm or leg or eye, like the *santeria* orisha called Osain – *his* other half was the land itself. I take the archetypes into myself, and they stop being just savage outside influences like rain or fire, and start to be allies – family, blood relations – a little.'

'Poor old Death sounds like the bad witch in Sleeping Beauty,' said Mavranos. 'Pissed off because she was the only one not invited to the christening.'

'You haven't ... *been* there, Arky. Death isn't a ... it doesn't embody a characteristic that shows up in humans, the way the others do, so you can't *relate* to it at all. There's no common ground. It has no face – and I can't just arbitrarily assign the face of, say, poor Susan to it, 'cause that was just my own personal closest death mirrored back at me; anybody else there would have seen some face from *their* past.' He coughed weakly and shook his head. 'In the court of the tarot archetypes, Death's just a blobby black hole in the floor.'

Mavranos had taken a deep breath then – and he wondered if he could bring himself to say what he thought he had to say here, for Scott Crane was his closest friend, and Mavranos was godfather of Scott and Diana's first child – but he made himself say it: 'Seems to me there *is* ... *one* face you could put on Death.'

Crane sat there on the air conditioner and stared at the dead grass and didn't speak, and Mavranos wondered if he had heard him. Then Crane shifted, and coughed again. 'You mean the fat man in the desert,' he said softly. 'My father's bodyguard, my father's emotionless hired assassin. And I killed *him*, in cold blood – the first shot was in self-defense, to save you as much as me, but he was still alive after that. The last five shots, when he was lying in the gully below the road, were to make sure he didn't wind up recovering in a hospital.'

Mavranos nodded, though Crane couldn't see the gesture. The fat man had at some time become a localized embodiment of one of the oldest, possibly pre-human archetypes, a cold figure of almost Newtonian retribution which showed up spontaneously in desert swap-meet legendry and country-western songs and insane-asylum artwork and even, as a repeating obese silhouette, in certain iterative mathematical equations on the complex number plane. Diana's mother had been an avatar of the Moon Goddess, and the fat man had killed her outside the Sands Hotel in Las Vegas – 'shot the moon in the face' – when Diana had been an infant, in 1960. Mavranos had not been sorry when Crane had killed the fat man, but that homicide was surely Crane's letter of introduction, his indenture, to the kingdom of death.

'No,' said Crane finally. 'It can't be done. It doesn't *need* to be done.'

Mavranos had thought of reminding him of the phylloxera, had considered mentioning the many species of tropical fish that had recently stopped being born with any distinct sexes, and the rapid decline in the sperm count of modern male humans – even the slow, progressive collapse of Hollywood Boulevard down into the catacombs being dug for the MTA Metro Rail – but at that point an unkempt middle-aged couple and their two blank-eyed children had come shuffling up through the brown grass to where the bearded king sat, and had hesitantly asked Scott if everything was going to be okay. They were living in their car, they told him, and had hung curtains in the windows, and were wondering if they shouldn't simply keep living in those cozy quarters forever, even after the houses had been put back up again.

Scott had wearily told them that he would do what he could; and they had showed no surprise, only sympathetic gratitude, when Scott had pushed his own wrist down onto the jagged piece of metal and then held out his hand so that his blood dripped rapidly onto the dry dirt.

Mavranos had muttered a panicky curse and sprinted to the nearby truck for the first-aid kit. And he had noted bleakly, after he had tied a bandage around Scott's wrist and helped him up for the walk back to the truck, that no flowers had sprung up from where the king's blood had fallen.

'It's what Nardie Dinh calls the Law of Imperative Resemblance,' said Mavranos to Angelica and Pete now.

Fog was beginning to roll in off the ocean, and Mavranos knew that it would be getting worse as the night wore on toward dawn and their route led them inland at Gaviota; maybe he'd get Pete to drive for a while. 'There are eternal potent *forms* out there,' Mavranos went on, 'idiosyncratic outlines, and if you take on enough characteristics of one of the forms, if you come to resemble it closely enough, knowingly or not, you find that you're wearing the whole damned outfit – you've *become* the thing. It *arrives* upon you.'

'Like critical mass,' said Kootie sleepily, rocking on the passenger seat.

'Well, *hijo mio*,' said Angelica sternly to the boy as she went on loading her .45 magazines, *you're* not going to be taking communion at this Mass.'

CHAPTER THIRTEEN

The bay trees in our country are all withered,
And meteors fright the fixed stars of heaven,
The pale-faced moon looks bloody on the earth,
And lean-looked prophets whisper fearful change;
Rich men look sad, and ruffians dance and leap,
The one in fear to lose what they enjoy,
The other to enjoy by rage and war.
These signs forerun the death or fall of kings.
            —William Shakespeare, *Richard II*

Bernardette Dinh, known as Nardie to her few close friends, was perched crouched on a dead peach-tree limb, staring down the flagstone steps that led away between rows of dead grapevines to the beach and the dawn-gray sea. Five years ago she had got into the habit of climbing a tree when she was very scared or disoriented, and during these last eleven days she must have spent nearly a full day's worth of hours up in the branches of this or that dead carob or apple or avocado tree in different corners of the Fisher King's Leucadia estate, in the periods when she could get Wendy to keep an eye on the kids.

Twenty years ago, when Nardie had arrived at Clark Air Base in Manila on the rainy morning of April 29 in 1975, airport personnel and travellers alike had exclaimed over her and the other passengers that got off the plane with her: *Oh, thank God you're safe!* She had then learned that the Saigon airport had been heavily shelled at 5 A.M., just four hours after her plane had taken off; but rockets had been shelling Saigon for two months before her American father had got her a ticket, and for the whole ten years of her life to that point, as she recalled it now, there had always been the background noise of planes and bombings. Her luggage had been mailed ahead, but never did show up anywhere – when she finally arrived at Camp Pendleton in Southern California, all she had had was the clothes she'd been wearing and the cellophane-thin sheets of gold leaf her father had managed to stuff into her pockets.

California had been bewildering, even with the help of other immigrant Vietnamese; *Here the poor eat beef every day*, she had been told, *and the rich people are all vegetarians.* And when her new American half-brother had taken her to a modern shopping center in Costa Mesa, the thing that had most struck her had been the pennies and nickels and even quarters scattered in the pool around an indoor fountain; she had struggled with the two ideas of it: that people had tossed the coins in there, and that other people didn't climb in to get them out.

Nardie was thirty now – but since the first of this month, when Scott's dead body had been found in the canted meadow down here between the house and the beach, she had been dreaming of those days again. But the fountains in her dreams were dry and bare, and the rockets came plummeting out of the night sky before the airliner she was in could take off.

The last time Nardie had seen Scott Crane alive, he had been trudging away barefoot down these flagstone steps to rescue his four-year-old son, Benjamin; Scott had got some kind of formal threatening challenge over the telephone only ten minutes earlier, and when he had hastily awakened and summoned to the atrium everybody that lived here at the compound – Arky and Wendy and their two teenage daughters, and Diana's two teenage sons by her first marriage, and Nardie herself, and Diana and the four young children she and Scott had had together – Benjamin had proved to be missing, and the three-year-old girl had said that a black crow had flapped down onto Benjamin's bedroom windowsill and told the boy that a magical woman in the meadow needed to see him right away.

It was a woman, on the phone just now, Scott had told Nardie and Arky and Diana in the kitchen as he'd pulled off his shoes and tugged his still-dark-brown hair out of the rubber-banded ponytail and let it fall loose onto his shoulders; *she claimed to have spoken to the ghost of my first wife, Susan, who was the embodiment of Death in the Las Vegas desert five years ago; and she knows I was called the Flying Nun in the big game on Lake Mead, and she said she was going to 'assume the Flamingo,' which must mean that she's some 'jack,' some rival, from the game five years ago, when the Flamingo Hotel was still the king's bunker-castle. I told her that it had been torn down, but I guess she's got a piece of the physical building – and that would be a potent ... charm, talisman. She must have a lot of other things, too, protections and masks and even maybe a tethered ghost or two, to have got in here past our wards without showing up as a consistent, solid intruder. And we have to assume that she's got Benjamin now. I've got to go meet her alone, or it's too likely that she'll kill him.*

Arky Mavranos had tried to insist that it was his own clear duty to go and rescue the child – *I'm Benjamin's godfather, Scott,* he had said forcefully, *and I'm not wounded.*

Scott Crane had refused to let Arky go, and had then had to flatly forbid the man's offers of 'armed back-up support, at least.'

And so Scott had gone padding down that set of steps alone, to the tilted meadow below the house ... and a few minutes later Benjamin had come running back, sobbing about a woman who had knocked him down and held a spear to his throat and who had changed into a man. *Daddy stayed to talk to the man*, the boy had said. *It's a very bad man.*

At that moment the pans had begun rattling in the cupboards, and the overhead light had begun swinging on its chain.

Arky Mavranos and Diana had simply bolted outside then, and skipped and hopped down the shaking steps after Scott ... and by the time they had got to the slanting meadow, the earthquake had stopped, leaving only smokelike clouds of raised dust hanging over the cliffs to mark its passage, and they had found Scott's supine body on the grass, speared through the throat.

They had half-carried and half-dragged the body back across the meadow to the steps before going to get Nardie to help carry, and apparently blood had fallen copiously from Scott's torn throat, like holy water shaken from a Catholic priest's aspergillum—

—And, from every point where the blood drops had hit the grass, a spreading network of flowers and vines had violently erupted up out of the soil in a ripping spray of fragmenting dirt clods, as if in some kind of horticultural aftershocks – so that Arky and Diana had in effect been shuffling along at the advancing, untrusting edge of a dense thicket of vibrant grape and ivy and pomegranate. An hour later Nardie had seen a couple of uniformed police officers escorting a blond woman around the edge of the newly overgrown meadow, but they had gone away again without even ringing the bell at the outer gate.

Mavranos had lifted Crane's body into the back of the – tragically, prematurely! – *red* truck, in preparation for driving away with Diana to search in the north for *another* man who would have an unhealing wound in his side: the man whom they would acknowledge and bless as the next Fisher King.

Nardie had given Mavranos a baseball-sized white stone statue of Tan Tai, the Vietnamese god of prosperity, to put on the truck's dashboard; and only after the truck had gone creaking and rattling away down Neptune Avenue did she recall that her half-brother had given her one very like it, back in the brightly familial days before he had tried to break her spirit and mind to further his own bitter Fisher Kinghood ambitions. Arky Mavranos had had to *kill* her half-brother eventually, at Hoover Dam during the terrible Holy Week in 1990 – Nardie hoped now that her gift had not been an unwitting expression of some lingering subconscious resentment. She had never ... *blamed* poor, staunch Arky for the death of her only blood sibling.

All the magical new plants had wilted and withered during the following week, along with all the other plantings on the whole sprawling estate; and now the grounds were drifted with, dry leaves – among which, if she looked closely, she could discern husks of perished bees and the stiffened, lifeless forms of the million earthworms that had come corkscrewing up out of the ground on that morning – and Nardie could only hope that a new good king would somehow be appointed before the Tet celebration at the end of the month.

Crane had kept a rose garden near the house, and when all the red petals had fallen to the brick pavement last week, they had looked to Nardie like the exploded scraps of firecracker paper that used to litter the Saigon pavements on Tet Nguyen Dan, the festival of the first day of the Vietnamese New Year. She had put a photograph of Scott Crane on her Tet altar, and now she whispered a prayer to the Kitchen God, a humble entreaty for, somehow, prosperity and health for her friends during this disastrous new year.

All she could see ahead of her, in the notch between the brown grapevines, was a triangle of the distant gray sea ... but now she heard the scuffle of someone, possibly several people, climbing the cement stairs that led up the sloping cliff from the beach sand to the slanting meadow. Nardie watched the flagstone steps, but the visitors were probably just more of the white-clay dancers, come to solemnly jump rope with trimmed lengths of kelp for a while in the blighted meadow below the steps – though generally the unspeaking white figures kept that softly drumming vigil at the end of the day, when the red sun was disappearing below the remote western horizon.

At her back she could often hear the cars of the crazy local teenagers racing up the street, and she heard at least one screeching past now, and heard too the *pop-pop-pop* of automatic weapons fire. In this last week and a half she had sensed a kind of vigilant protection in their constant racket, but an impatience too. Absently, Nardie touched the angular weight in her sweater pocket that was her ten-ounce Beretta .25 automatic.

The dry leaves on the peach-tree branches rattled in the chilly wind from the sea, and Nardie caught the familiar wild strains of the music from the beach. Arky had telephoned the Leucadia estate several times from pay phones, and he had laughed once – dryly – when she had described the music to him, and he had told her the name of the constantly repeated song: 'Candles in the Wind,' by somebody called Melanie. Apparently the disattached people near where the killed king was were spontaneously playing the same song as were the disattached people near the king's broken castle.

Definitely there was more than one person in the meadow – Nardie could hear excited voices.

The white-clay dancers had never spoken.

Silently Nardie swung down from the branch, and her tennis shoes crackled only faintly in the dry grass as she landed and then stole to the top of the steps and looked down.

At the edge of the new wilderness of dead vines in the meadow, by the top of the stairs that led down to the beach, four figures stood silhouetted against the vast gray sea. Three stood together with their arms around each other, though the effect was more as if they were handcuffed that way than comradely; the fourth figure, standing apart, was an old man who had only one arm.

The middle figure of the trio, whose styled hair was white, reached out toward a dead pomegranate bush – and when his two dark-haired companions twisted their heads up toward her and clumsily grabbed their crotches in perfect unison Nardie shivered and bared her teeth, for she understood abruptly that only the middle figure was a real person, and that the outer two were some kind of mobile mannikins.

As if following the gaze of the two artificial heads, the one-armed old man looked up the slope at Nardie.

'Heads up, Doc, all three,' the old man said, loudly enough for Nardie to hear. 'The homegrown Persephone yonder don't want you triflin' with her *seed pods.*'

Nardie realized that she had drawn her tiny gun, so she lifted it and pointed it down the steps toward the two living men and the two dummies, though she kept her finger outside the trigger guard.

The one-armed man turned his shoulder stump to her, as if hiding behind the upraised, missing arm; and the trio shifted position, so that one of the dark-haired mannikins was blocking her view of the white-haired man in the middle – who now shakily reached out and plucked the dried gourd of a dead pomegranate from the bush.

Then, in a crackling of trodden dry leaves, all four of the figures in the meadow were lurching away back toward the stairs that led down to the beach, the two mannikins waving their free arms in perfect synchronization, like, Nardie thought giddily, a couple of Gladys Knight's Pips.

Her teeth stung as she sucked in the cold sea air. Should I shoot at him? she wondered. What, she thought then, for stealing a *pomegranate*? A *dead* one? And at this range with this stubby barrel, I'd be doing well to put the bullet in the meadow at all, never mind hitting a head-size target. And she remembered Arky's assessment of her weapon: A *.25's a good thing to have in a fight, if you can't get hold of a gun.*

The four figures tottered away down the beach stairs, the mannikin arms waving in spastic unison over the two fake heads.

Nardie straightened up when they had descended out of her sight, and she smiled derisively at herself when she noticed that she was standing hunched, and looking around for cover between nervous glances at the sky. The rockets fell a *week and a half ago*, she told herself; and you're *living* in the dry, coinless fountain.

She pocketed her little gun and turned to trudge back uphill toward the house. She'd have to tell Arky about these intruders, whenever he next called from wherever he was.

She really did hope Arky was safe.

Tan Tai be with you, she thought blankly.

The dozen white dancers who appeared to be made out of clay had been high-stepping around in a solemn ring on the flat sand a hundred yards to the south when Dr. Armentrout and Long John Beach had originally walked up the beach to the Crane estate's stairs, but now they were skipping and hand-clapping back this way. The dawn wind was cold, but Armentrout felt a drop of sweat roll down his ribs under his shirt as he scuffed down from the last cement step onto the sand.

'Keep walking,' Armentrout whispered to Long John Beach as he began plodding away north under the weight of the two-mannikin appliance, 'back to the stairway that'll take us up to the Neptune Avenue parking lot, and don't look back at those … those white people.'

The one-armed old man immediately turned to gape at the figures following, and his eyes and mouth were so wide that Armentrout turned around to look himself, fearing that the dancers might be silently running at them, perhaps armed with some of the smooth black stones that studded the marbled black-and-gray sand.

But the white figures, though closer, were just walking purposefully after Armentrout and Long John Beach now, and staring at them with eyes that seemed yellow and bloodshot against the crusted white faces. The clay plastered onto their swimsuit-clad bodies made them seem to be naked sexless creatures animated out of the wet cliffs.

Armentrout let go of the lever that controlled the mannikins' heads, in order to reach into his jacket pocket and grip the butt of the .45 derringer. The Styrofoam heads now nodded and rolled loosely with every jouncing step toward the cement pilings of the wooden municipal stairway that led up to the parking lot, and to the car, and away from this desolate shoreline.

But Long John Beach stopped and pointed back at the advancing mud-people.

'No outrageous thing,' he cried, his voice flat and unechoing in the open air, 'from vassal actors can be wiped away; then kings' misdeeds cannot be hid in clay.'

For a moment Armentrout considered just leaving the crazy old man standing here, as a cast-off distraction to occupy the dancers while he himself trotted away to the car; but he knew now that he needed to find Koot Hoomie Parganas, and he would need every scrap of mask for that.

So Armentrout stopped too, and he turned to face the advancing animated statues; and with deliberate slowness he tugged the fist-sized gun free and let them see it. He gripped the ball-butt tightly, for he remembered that the little derringer tended to rotate in his hand when he pulled the hammer back against the tight spring, and now he cocked it with a crisp, ratcheting click.

'What business,' Armentrout said, '*exactly*, do you have with us?'

One of the figures, breastless and so probably a young man, stepped forward. 'You took something,' came a high voice, 'from up the stairs.'

'I did? What did I take?'

The figure's blue eyes blinked. 'You tell me.'

'Answer my question first. I asked you what *exactly* your business is here.'

The stony figures shuffled uneasily on the wet black-veined sand, and Armentrout suppressed a smile; for these were young people whose random propensities for music and dancing and the beach had happened to constitute a compelling resemblance to an older, mythic role in this season of insistent definition – but they *were* just San Diego County teenagers of the 1990s, and when they were challenged to *explain* their presence here, the archaic hum of the inarticulate purpose was lost beneath the grammar of reason.

'No law against dancing,' the figure said defensively.

'There *is* a law about concealed weapons,' another piped up.

The modern phrases had dispelled the mythic cast – they were now thoroughly just modern kids on a beach, with mud all over them.

'Scram,' said Armentrout.

The white figures began to amble away south with exaggerated nonchalance. Armentrout put the gun away and turned toward the stairs. A blue sign on the railing said,

WARNING
Stay Safe Distance
Away From Bluff Bottom
FREQUENT BLUFF FAILURE

Not today, Armentrout thought with satisfaction as he shooed Long John Beach ahead of him up the stairs.

In the parking lot between landscaped modern apartment buildings, Armentrout unstrapped the two-mannikin appliance and stowed it in the back seat of his teal-blue BMW.

Then he opened the passenger-side door and pushed Long John Beach inside. 'Belt up,' he said breathlessly to the old man.

'"The purest treasure mortal times afford,"' the one-armed old man wailed, the strange and eerily flat voice echoing now between the white stucco walls, '"is spotless reputation; that away, men are but gilded loam or painted clay."'

'I said *belt up*,' hissed Armentrout between clenched teeth as he hurried around to the driver's side and got in. 'Anyway,' he added in shrill embarrassment as he started the engine, 'there's no hope anymore for our reputations in *this* town.'

As he drove back down Neptune Avenue, in the southbound lane this time, Armentrout could see a plywood sign attached to a pine tree beside the gates of the field-stone wall on his right. Black plastic letters had been attached to it once, but weather or something had caused most of them to fall away; what remained was accidental Latin:

E T IN

ARC

ADIA

EGO

Et in Arcadia ego.

And I am in Arcadia, he thought, tentatively translating the words; or, *I am in Arcadia, too*; or, *Even in Arcadia, I am.*

Armentrout reflected uneasily that the word Arcadia – with its resonances of pastoral Greek poetry and balmy, quiet gardens – probably had applied to this place, before Our Miss Figleaf had come here and killed the king; but who was the *Ego* that was speaking?

Even when he had got back on the 5 Freeway, heading north through the misty morning-lit hills below the Santa Ana Mountains, Armentrout found himself still noticing and being bothered by signs on the shoulder. The frequent GAS-FOOD-LODGING 1 MI AHEAD signs had stark icons stenciled on them for the benefit of people who couldn't read, and though the stylized images of a gas pump and a knife-and-plate-and-fork were plain enough, the dot-dash figure of a person on a long-H bed looked to him this morning disturbingly like a dead body laid out in state; and while he was still south of Oceanside he saw several postings of a sign warning illegal Mexican immigrants against trying to sprint across the freeway to bypass the border checkpoint – the diamond-shaped yellow sign showed a silhouetted man and woman and girl-child running hand-in-hand so full-tilt fast that the little girl's feet were off the ground, and under the figures was the word PROHIBIDO. Armentrout thought it seemed to be a prohibition of all fugitive families.

And when he became aware that his heartbeat was accelerated, he recognized that he was responding with defiance, as if the signs were reproaches aimed at him personally. I didn't kill any king, he thought; I haven't uprooted any families. I'm a *doctor*, I—

Abruptly he remembered the voice of the obese suicide-girl as he had heard it over the telephone a few hours ago: *Doctor? I walk all crooked now – where's the rest of me?*

But I certainly didn't mean *that* to happen, he thought, her *killing* herself. I don't give anyone a treatment I haven't undergone and benefited from myself; and from my own experience I know that cutting the problem right out of the soul, rather than laboring to assimilate it, really does effect a cure. And even when these misfortunes do result – goddammit – aren't I allowed some sustenance? I genuinely do a lot of good for people – is it wrong for me to sometimes take something besides money for my payment? Does this make me a, a *sicko*? He smiled confidently – *Not ... at ... all.* The whole notion of intrinsic consequences of 'sin' is just infantile solipsism, anyway: imagining that in some sense you are everybody and everybody's you. Guilt and shame are just the unproductive, negative opposites of self-esteem, and I feel healthily *good* about everything I do. That's *okay* today.

Then he thought of what it was he now planned for his patient Janis Cordelia Plumtree, whenever he might catch up with her, and for Koot Hoomie Parganas, if the boy was still alive – and he heard again the flat howl that had burst from Long John Beach's throat: *gilded loam or painted clay.*

It occurred to him, with unwelcome clarity, that the idealistic dancers on the beach had carried the rainbow of living flesh on the *inside*, and dry, cracked clay on the *outside*.

His cellular telephone buzzed, and he fumbled it up from between the seats and flipped open the cover. 'Yes?' he said furiously after he had switched it on.

'Get your *toes* aft of the *white line*, please,' drawled a man's humorous voice, 'and sit your ass down in one of the seats! I'm in control of this bus, and you're upsetting the children!'

In his first seconds of confusion Armentrout knew he recognized the voice, but he seemed to remember it as disembodied – a ghost? – and this was clearly not a ghost call. The voice and the background breeze-hiss were real, unlike the eternal clattering busy-mess of the group-projected ghost-bar.

'You was comin' on to my *daughter*, man,' the voice said now. 'You can't blame me for having got a bit *testy*, now can you?' Before Armentrout could stammer out anything, the voice went on: 'This is Omar Salvoy, and I can't talk for long. Listen, you and I each got a gun pointed at the other, haven't we? Mexican standoff. I think we can work together, both eat off the same plate. Here's the thing – you'd like to get Koot Hoomie Parganas locked up in your clinic, wouldn't you, in a coma and brain-dead, on perpetual life-support? Or haven't you thought it through that far?'

It made Armentrout dizzy to hear this voice on the phone speaking his recent, somewhat shameful, thought aloud. 'Y-yes,' he said, glancing sideways at Long John Beach and then in the rear-view mirror at the two placid Styrofoam heads. 'What you describe is ... it could, I guess you've figured out that it could, benefit you and me both. But not *yet* – it would have to be after he had been induced to, uh, officially ... *take the crown*, if you know what I mean. I was just at the Fisher King's castle, this morning, and it's very evident from the look of things there that no new king has been consecrated yet. But after that's occurred, I could set things up so that you and I could both benefit. As you know, I'm uniquely able to set up that scenario, just as you describe it.'

'Ipse dipshit. Now the girls have got some cockamamie idea about restoring the dead king, the *old* one, to life – I gotta monkeywrench that scheme, that guy is really *old*, he's hardened in his thought-paths and likely to be resistant, not like the kid would be.'

'All ROM and no RAM,' agreed Armentrout, though he didn't see how any of this would matter in a brain-dead body.

'Rom? Ram? Gypsies, sheep? Easy on the mystical, there, Doctor, I want you for *science*. You do know about how the spirit-transfer thing works, knocking a personality out of somebody's head?'

'Uh.' Armentrout wiped his forehead and blinked sweat out of his eyes to be able to watch the freeway lanes. 'Yes.' I wasn't being mystical, he thought – doesn't Salvoy know anything about computers? Oh well, give him the science. 'The force that, that holds them *in*, works the opposite of forces like gravity and electromagnetism and the strong nuclear force, which all get weaker as the, the *satellite*, say, moves further away from the primary; ghost personalities are more strongly *restrained*, the further they get out, especially in sane people, but feel no clumping-together force at all if they stay within the mind's confines. It's much the same situation as is theorized for the quarks that make up subatomic particles – if they stay close together, they experience what's called asymptotic—'

'Speaking of which, I'm gonna have to pick up my ass and tote it out of here. I'm at a pay phone – we've stopped for gas in King City, and her boyfriend has just ducked off to visit the gents' and pump the gas. You'd better get up here, right now; and then on to San Fran, apparently – this thing will go a lot smoother if we've got a real licensed psychiatrist along, for authority-figuring in case any locals should object to anything. Wave the stethoscope, flourish the prescription pad. I'll make a point of getting out here again and calling you with more specific directions as we proceed, so Lake your telephone with you, you can do that, can't you?'

'King City? San Francisco? Certainly, I've got the phone with me now. Obviously. But the P – the boy – he's alive, I gather? Is *he* in San Francisco? We need—'

'He's alive, and on his way there. Gotta go – stay by the phone.'

The line was dead, and Armentrout clicked the phone off, closed the cover, and wedged it carefully between the seat and the console. He would have to dig out of the trunk the phone-battery recharger that could be plugged into the cigarette lighter.

His lips were twitching in a brittle, almost frightened grin. There's no reason why this shouldn't work, he thought. When the king died eleven days ago, his death opened a temporary drain in the psychic floor locally, so that all my vengeful old California ghosts, at least, were sucked away, leaving me with their abandoned memories and strengths intact and harmless. I was *fifty miles away*, and my ghosts were banished! That drain has since closed up – but imagine if I could be *in the same building* with a flatline Fisher King! If we can get the new king on perpetual brain-dead life-support, the drain could be held propped open for … for decades. I'll be able to outright *terminate* patients, consume their whole lives, without fear of being hassled by their outraged ghost personalities afterward. And Omar Salvoy will be able to – what? I suppose to evict all the girls from Plumtree's head, so that he'll have that youthful body all to himself, to live in.

It'll be the best of both worlds, Armentrout thought, nodding and smiling twitchily. All the forgiveness that Dionysus's *pagadebiti* wine offers, but with the profit from the sin retained intact too!

He glanced again at Long John Beach and the two heads in the backseat. I may be able to outright *ditch* the three of you in San Francisco, he thought.

'Who were you calling?' asked Cochran, frowning.

They hadn't found a Mobil station here in King City, and so they were using some of the Jenkins woman's cash at this Shell station, and apparently the Torino's fuel tank hadn't had room for a whole twenty's worth of gas – Cochran was stuffing a couple of ones into the pocket of his corduroy bell-bottoms. He must have bought the cheapest gas.

Plumtree blinked at him around the aluminum cowl of the pay telephone. There was only a dial tone to be heard from the thoroughly warmed earpiece of the receiver she held in her hand. Cochran looked tired and bedraggled, she noted, in the cold morning sunlight, and she could see strands of white hair among the disordered brown locks tangled over his forehead.

'It was ringing,' she said, in the old reflexive dismissal of a patch of lost time. 'Nobody on when I picked it up.' She reflected that this *might* be the literal truth; but she wasn't happy to find herself reverting to the helpless shuck-and-jive evasions, the poker-table calls that were bluffs because she didn't know what her hole cards were, so she went on spontaneously, 'Let's get breakfast now, there's a Denny's a block back – we can just have coffee with the others at the Cliff House place – and maybe a dessert, if they have some kind of sweetrolls there. And listen, if there's a Sav-On or someplace open in this town, I'd like to buy some fresh underwear – these panties I've got on still say Tuesday on 'em – and *Tiffany's* been wearing them.'

'… Okay.'

They got back into the beer-reeking warmth of the car and drove around, but didn't find any open store at all in the whole town, and so eventually she had to go into the ladies' room in Denny's, pull off her jeans, and wash the panties in the sink – with hand soap, wringing them halfway dry in a sheaf of paper towels after she'd rinsed them out – and then shiveringly pull them back on.

Now she was eating scrambled eggs and shifting uncomfortably on the vinyl booth seat, bleakly sure that the dampness must be visibly soaking through the seat of her jeans, and remembering reading *On Her Majesty's Secret Service* in another restaurant booth eleven days ago. She had had the aluminum spear taped to her thigh during that breakfast, the points of it cutting her skin.

'I can't ever sit comfortably in restaurants,' she complained. She remembered that a telephone had started ringing then, too, on that morning, right in the restaurant; it was Janis's job to answer telephones, and Cody recalled flipping her lit cigarette into the open paperback book, intending to slam the cover firmly closed and extinguish the coal, since there had been no ashtray on the table and Janis didn't smoke. But Janis had come on more quickly than usual, apparently, and hadn't known about the lit Marlboro between the pages.

Cody grinned sourly now. *Excu-u-se* me!

At least my teeth don't hurt much right now – not any worse than usual, anyway. And I certainly don't have a nose-bleed! If Flibbertigibbet was on, it wasn't for very long.

She looked up. Across the table, Cochran was, smiling at her gently, out of his tired, red eyes. 'Who were you calling?' he asked again.

Okay – perhaps the gas-station pay phone had *not* already been ringing when she had picked it up, and Cochran knew it. Okay. 'I call time,' she said, 'a *lot*. That's UL3-1212 everywhere. In England they call it "the speaking clock," which always makes me picture Grandfather Clock, from the "Captain Kangaroo" TV show, remember? *Wake up, Grandfather!* Even when I have a watch on. Those liquid-crystal displays, you can't ever be—'

He was still smiling tiredly at her.

'I—' She exhaled and threw down her fork with a clatter. 'Oh, fuck it. *I* don't know, Sid. The receiver was warm, we must have been talking to somebody. My teeth are hurting, but we *do* call time a lot.'

'Not for extended conversations, though, I bet.' He took a sip from his glass of V-8, into which he'd shaken several splashes of Tabasco. 'In this hippie commune you grew up in,' he said; 'what was it called?'

'The Lever Blank. My mom and I lived at their farm commune outside of Danville for another couple of years after my lather died.'

'Did they let you watch a lot of TV?'

Plumtree stared at him. 'This was mandala yin-yang hippies, Sid! Organic vegetables and goat's milk. Old mobile homes sitting crooked on dirt, with no electric. My father was the only one that even read *newspapers*.'

'So how did you ever see "Captain Kangaroo"? And Halo Shampoo ads? And I'm not sure, but it seems to me that neither one of those was still being aired in '71. I'm an easy ten years older than you, and I hardly remember them.'

Plumtree calmly picked up her fork and shovelled a lump of scrambled egg into her mouth. 'That's a, a terrible point you make, Sid,' she remarked after she had swallowed and taken a sip of coffee. 'And I don't seem to be losing time over it, either, do I? This must be my flop. Do you think I'm an alcoholic? Janis thinks so.'

'Of course not,' he said, with a laugh. 'No more than I am.'

'Oh, *that's* good, *that's* reassuring. Jesus! The reason I ask is, I need a drink to assimilate this thought with. Let's pay up and get out of here.'

'Fine,' Cochran said, a little stiffly.

Oh, *sorree*, Plumtree thought, restraining herself from rolling her eyes.

As Cochran took their bill to the cashier, Plumtree walked out of the yellow-lit restaurant to the muddy parking lot. The sky had lightened to an empty blue-gray vault, but she felt as though there were the close-arching ceiling of a bus overhead, and that the battered madman who had hijacked the bus and cowed the driver had now turned and begun to advance on the hostage children, all the brave little girls.

The chilly dawn wind was throwing all sounds away to the south, and she was able to hum 'Row, Row, Row Your Boat' until Cochran had come out of the restaurant and shuffled up to within a yard of her, before she had to stop humming for fear he might hear.

North of King City they were driving up through the wide Salinas Valley, with green fields of broccoli receding out to the far off Coast Range foot-hills. Long flat layers of fog, ragged at the top, hung over the ruler-straight dirt roads and solitary farmhouses in the middle distance, and Cochran began to notice signs for the Soledad Correctional Institute. Don't want to be picking up any hitch-hikers around there, he thought. We've got enough of them aboard right now. Neither he nor Plumtree had spoken since getting back into the car in the parking lot of the Denny's in King City, though she had taken a quick, bracing gulp of the vodka after she had started the engine, and, after a moment of resentful hesitation, he had shrugged and opened one of the warm beers. The sky had still been dark enough then for her to turn on the headlights, but she reached out now and punched the knob to turn them off.

'Smart thinking,' he said, venturing to break the long silence. 'We'd only forget to turn them off, once the sun's well up.'

'And it's cover,' she said, speaking indistinctly through a yawn. 'You can tell which cars have been driving all night, because they've still got their lights on. Everybody with their lights *out* is a local.' She yawned again, and it occurred to Cochran that these were from tension as much as weariness. 'But we can't hide – *I* can't, anyway – from my father. Those are *his* memories, those TV things. Captain Kangaroo, that shampoo. He was born in '44.' A third yawn was so wide that it squeezed tears from the corner of her eye. 'If we're compartmentalized, in this little head, then he's leaking into my compartment. I wonder if he's leaking into the other girls' seats too.'

Seats? Cochran thought.

'Like in a bus,' she said. '*You* could step off, you know, Sid. Like the driver in that movie, *Speed*, who got shot, remember? The bad guy let him get off the bus, because he was wounded. When we stop at your house. I could drop you off at some nearby corner, in fact, so Flibbertigibbet won't even know where you live.'

After a long pause, while he finished the can of warm beer and reached down to fetch up another, 'No,' Cochran said in an almost wondering tone; 'no, I reckon I'm … along for the ride.'

Plumtree laughed happily, and began drunkenly singing the kid's song, 'Row, Row, Row Your Boat.' After she had finished the trite lyric and started it up again, frowning now and waving at him, his face heated in embarrassment as he gave up and joined in, singing the lyric in the proper kindergarten counterpoint. And until he put out his hand to stop her, the vodka bottle between her knees was rhythmically rattled as she swung the wheel back and forth, swerving the big old car from one side of the brightening highway lane to the other in time to their frail duet.

CHAPTER FOURTEEN

… blood, like sacrificing Abels, cries
Even from the tongueless caverns of the earth
To me for justice and rough chastisement …
                    —William Shakespeare, *Richard II*

After more distant sort of pop-pop-pop *sounded from the cliffs above the plain of ruins, and while echoes of the rapid knocks were still batting away between the old broken walls, Plumtree swung her ponderous gaze to Cochran, and she saw his face change from the robust color of damp cement to an ashier gray.*

It was certainly an external noise, she reasoned. It must have been gunfire. Cody always springs away at sudden dangerous sounds – telephones, gunfire.

Plumtree skipped lightly ahead down the muddy path, almost tap-dancing in instinctive time to the constant hammering noise in her ears, and she beckoned Cochran forward, downhill, toward the ruins and the wide, still lagoons that were separated by eroded walls from the crashing sea beyond. The lush, steel-colored vegetation on either side of the path shook in the ocean breeze.

'Further down?' she heard him say. His voice was shrill and uncertain. 'Toward the baths?'

'A seething bath,' Plumtree pronounced, 'which yet may prove against strange maladies a sovereign cure.'

'Valorie,' he said as he hurried after her.

The clatter and thump that rang ceaselessly in her head increased its tempo, and she knew that an emotion was being experienced. 'She that loves her selves,' she called, 'hath not essentially, but by circumstance, the name of Valorie.' The emotion was something like shame, or cowardice – or fear of those.

On an impulse but resolutely, she halted and pulled from the pocket of her jeans the object she had prepared at Cochran's house, when they had stopped there earlier this morning; and she held it out to him in a hand that shook with the rhythmic cracking in her head. 'This form of prayer can serve my turn,' she said: '"Forgive me my foul murder."'

Still glancing up at the cliffs and the road, Cochran took the folded cardboard from her hand.

And Cochran paused to stare obediently at the green-and-tan 7-Eleven matchbook Plumtree had handed him, but it was just a matchbook. 'Thanks, Valorie,' he said 'but could I talk to Janis?' Neither Janis nor Cody, he reflected fretfully, had ever mentioned that Valorie was crazy. '*Jan-is*,' he repeated.

He shifted impatiently from one foot to the other, grateful, in this chilly mist or sea spray, for the jeans and boots and flannel shirt and London Fog windbreaker he had changed into at his house; and he was nervously reassured by the angular bulk of the holstered .357 Magnum clipped onto his belt in the back.

'Scant!' Plumtree exclaimed; and then she stared around at the fog-veiled amphitheater into which they had by now halfway descended. 'Wow, I'm glad I don't have to pretend with you, Scant! Are we still in California, at all?'

'Yes,' he said, taking her arm and hurrying her forward. 'San Francisco – that building up on the promontory behind us is the Cliff House Restaurant, Cody and I were just in there. It's only been a few hours since you were last up. But let's get ... *behind a wall*, okay? I swear I heard gunfire up on the highway – not a minute ago.'

She trotted along beside him, and he was tensely glad that the bouncing blond hair and the lithe legs were Janis's again, and that the deep blue eyes that blinked at him were those of his new girlfriend, in this strange landscape under this rain-threatening gray sky.

He could see why she had doubted that they were still in California. The Sutro Baths had only burned down in 1966 but these low crumbled walls and rectangular lagoons – all that was left of the baths, overgrown now with rank grass and calla lilies – fretted the plain in vast but half-obliterated geometry between the steep eastern slope and the winter sea like some Roman ruin; long gray lines of pavement cross-sections showed in the hillsides in the misty middle distance, and every outcrop of stone invited speculation that it might actually be age-rounded masonry. Fog scrimmed the cliffs to the north and south to craggy silhouettes that seemed more remote than they really were, and made the green of the wet leaves stand out vividly against the liver-colored earth.

'Who was just up?' Plumtree panted. 'Were you going to light a cigarette for somebody?'

A low roofless building with ragged square window gaps in its stone walls stood a few hundred feet ahead of them, where the path broadened out to a wide mud-flat, and Cochran was aiming their plodding steps that way. 'Valorie,' he said shortly. 'No, she gave me these matches.' He flipped the matchbook open, and then he noticed fine-point ink lettering, words, inscribed on the individual matches.

'She's *written* something on 'em,' he said; and he felt safe in stopping to squint at the carefully printed words, for the popping from the highway had been distant and hadn't been repeated. He read the words off each of the matches in order, aloud: '"*Si bene te tua laus taxat, sua laute tenebis.*" Latin, again.'

'Again?'

'There was some Latin writing on the ashtray last night, in that bar, Mount Sabu—'

'Scant!' she interrupted, seizing his arm and staring at the top of the northern cliff wall. 'God, you almost lost me, almost got Valorie back!'

Cochran had spun to look up that way, his right hand brushing the back of his belt; but he could see nothing up on the fog-veiled cliff top.

'What?' he said tensely, stepping sideways to catch his balance on the slippery mud. 'Should we run?'

'There was a wild man up there, looking down here!'

'Shit. Let's – let's get inside this,' he said, stepping up onto the undercut foundation of the roofless stone structure and crouching to fit through one of the square window gaps. Grass and gravelly sand covered any floor there might have been inside, and when he had glanced around and then helped Plumtree in, they both crouched panting against one of the graffiti-painted walls. Cochran had pulled the revolver free of the holster, and he belatedly swung the cylinder out and sighed with relief to see the brass of six rounds in the chambers.

'What's a wild man?' he asked, snapping the cylinder closed.

'Bearded and naked! In this weather!'

'A *naked* guy?' Cochran shook his head. 'I don't know how scared we've got to be of a *naked* guy.'

'I looked away. I didn't want to look at his face.'

'Didn't want to look at his face,' Cochran repeated tiredly. He stared up into the gray sky that from where he sat was bisected by low stone cross-beams. 'I wonder when the others will show up here. I wonder *if* they will. I did give the hostess at the restaurant ten bucks to tell them we'd meet 'em down here, in the ruins.'

'If? You said they would, Scant!' She glanced up wide-eyed at the ragged top of the wall close above their heads – as if, Cochran thought, she was afraid her wild man might have bounded down from the cliff and be about to clamber right over the wall. 'They're bringing the king's body, right?' she asked.

'Yes.'

'And it's still okay? They didn't drop it on its head or anything?'

Cochran smiled. 'It's still apparently inhabitable, Janis.'

'Good. I did help kill him, and I do owe him his life back, but ... I'd just as soon get to keep my own life afterward, not let him just *have* me ... even though that's what I deserve.' She shivered visibly and, after another fearful glance at the close top of the wall, leaned against Cochran. 'Of *all* things,' she said in a small voice, 'I don't want what I deserve.'

'None of us wants that,' he agreed quietly.

He draped his left arm around her shoulders, and he wondered if she might be mixing up the death of Scott Crane, for which she had been to some extent responsible, with the death of her father. A question for Angelica to wrestle with, he thought; though in fact Angelica, and now Janis, don't believe Janis's father died at all. Somehow.

Her shoulder was pressing into his ribs the tape cassette he'd taken from the telephone answering machine in his house a couple of hours ago, and he shifted his position – not to relieve the jabbing, but to keep the cassette in his pocket from possibly being broken.

When he had punched in his kitchen-door window with an empty wine bottle that had been standing on his back porch, he had heard his wife's voice speaking inside the house – '... *and we'll get back to you as quickly as posseebl'* ...' – and even though his mind had instantly registered the fact that the voice was coming from an electronic speaker, his spine had tingled with shock, and his hands had been clumsy as he had unlatched the chain and pushed the door open.

Whoever had called had not stayed on the line to leave any message.

He had gone to the telephone answering machine and popped the cassette out of it, without letting himself think about why he was taking it; and then he had gone to her sewing room to find a sample of Nina's handwriting. Cody had followed him, and in a surprisingly humble tone had asked if she might 'borrow' some of Nina's clothes. Cochran had curtly assented, and as Cody had gone through Nina's closet and dresser, he had pulled out the drawers of her desk. And while Cody carried away underwear and jeans and blouses and a couple of jumpsuits and sweaters, Cochran took from one of the desk drawers an old French-language Catholic missal, on one page of which Nina had written a lot of presumably important dates, including their wedding day; several snapshots, with Nina's inked notes on the back, were tucked in between the missal's pages, and he tamped them in firmly before tucking the book into his jacket pocket. And from the bedroom he had retrieved the gun and half a dozen twenty-dollar bills and Nina's wallet.

Cochran had driven the stolen Torino out into the back yard and parked it between the garage and the greenhouse, and then draped a car cover over it.

He and Plumtree had driven the rest of the way up the 280 to San Francisco in Cochran's '79 Ford Granada. Getting off the freeway onto Junipero Serra Boulevard, and then driving past the lawns of the San Francisco Golf Club and Larsen Park, had made him think of his many bygone trips to the city in this car with Nina sitting beside him, and he had been glad that the car had no tape player, for he might not have been able to resist the temptation to play Nina's phone-machine greeting over and over again.

Allo – you 'ave reached Sid and Nina, and we are not able to come to ze phone right now ...

From far away up the amphitheater slope, someone was whistling a slow, sad melody. Cochran recognized it – it was the theme music from the movie *A Clockwork Orange*. And that had been some old classical piece, a dirge for the death of some monarch ...

Cochran straightened up, still holding the black rubber Pachmayr grip of the revolver, and he peeked over the top of the crumbling wall.

Arky Mavranos was plodding down the path from the road above, with Kootie hopping and scrambling along behind him. The two of them looked

like a father and son out for a morning stroll, the father whistling medita-
tively – but Mavranos's right hand was inside his denim jacket, and even
at this distance Cochran could see the man's eyes scanning back and forth
under the bill of the battered blue Greek fisherman's cap.

'They're here,' Cochran told Plumtree. He lifted the revolver and clicked
the barrel twice against a stone that protruded from the top of the wall.

The sound carried just fine in the foggy stillness; Mavranos's gaze darted
to the structure in which Cochran stood, and he nodded and turned to
speak to Kootie.

'We'll negotiate with them,' Cochran said quietly to Plumtree. 'They'd
like to have you in captivity, but we'll make it clear that's not an option. We
can get a motel room, and have him give us a phone number where we can
reach them. *Go* on meeting like this, on neutral ground.'

'My aims don't conflict with theirs,' she said bleakly. 'If you'll come with
me, I don't mind being in captivity, for the … duration of this. All of us
are here, their friend is dead, because of what I did, what I let happen. *Mea
maxima culpa.* I'm just ashamed to meet them.'

It's not entirely why *I'm* here, Cochran thought, aware of the angularities
of the cassette and the French missal in his pockets. 'Well – let me do the
talking, okay?'

'What?'

'I said, let me do the talking.'

'Oh, blow me.' She looked, around at the roofless stone walls. 'What are
we paying for this room?'

Cochran bared his teeth. 'We're in San Francisco, Cody, and Mavranos
and the Kootie kid are walking up. I've got a gun, and so does Mavranos, but
if you don't do anything stupid here we won't have to all shoot each other,
okay?'

'Was it him that was shooting at us before? I guess I dove for cover.'

'No, that wasn't him, I don't know who that was.' Cochran peered again
over the wall. Mavranos was close enough now to be eyeing the stone structure for a place to step up. 'I don't *think* it was him.' To Mavranos, he called,
'I've got a gun.'

'So does everybody this morning, seems like,' Mavranos said. He used
both hands to climb up onto the exposed foundation ledge a few yards to
Cochran's left, and Cochran noted the deepened lines around the man's eyes
and down his gaunt cheeks. 'We got shot at, on the road up there, as we were
driving up to that restaurant – maybe you heard it. Semi-auto, definitely,
because of how fast the shots came; looks like nine-millimeter, from the
holes. We drove on past the restaurant, eluded 'em with some magical shit
and some *return fire* in the numbered streets east of here and parked in an
alley off Geary, and Kootie and took a cab back here.' He noticed Plumtree

crouched below him on the inner side of the wall, and touched the bill of his cap. 'Mornin', Miss Plumtree.'

'Was the king's body hurt?' she asked.

'It – yeah, it was shot in the thigh.' He rubbed one brown hand across his face, leaving a streak of mud down his jaw. 'Live blood was leaking out, till we bandaged it tight. I mean, it was purple venous blood, but it turned bright red in the air. Got oxygenated, according to Angelica. It's a good sign, that the blood is still vital. Not so good that he's got a bullet in his leg now.'

Cochran glanced down at Kootie, who was still standing on the mud-flat. The boy's face under the tangled black curls was tired and expressionless.

'Who was it that shot at you?' Cochran asked.

'Local jacks,' spoke up Kootie. 'Boys who would be king. The world's been twelve days without a king, and it's getting impatient. If we wait long enough, the *trees* will be trying to destroy Crane's body. The *rocks* will be.'

'Kootie's ... sensory apparatus works better up here,' said Mavranos. Plumtree had stood up to be able to see over the top of the wall, and he squinted belligerently at her. 'You still up for the restoration-to-life stunt, girl?'

Plumtree gave him an empty look.

And down on the ground Kootie stepped back, his face suddenly paler, and he glared at Plumtree. 'Don't,' he said, almost spitting, '*ever ... do that to me again.*' He took a deep breath and let it out. 'Just because neither of us is a virgin, psychically, doesn't make both of us ... *sluts.*'

Cochran glanced at Plumtree. She was looking down now, and she said, 'Well, you just tell your fucking pal – oh, hell, I'm sorry, kid! But Mavranos just now asked me – with a straight face! – if I wasn't a coward and a liar and a cheat, on top of being a, a murderer. Murderess. "Are you still up for it, girlie!" After I came to you people.'

'And then ran out,' added Mavranos stonily.

Cochran caught on that Cody had thrown her anger to Kootie – who had instantly known where it had come from! 'If she was really trying to "run out,"' Cochran said to Mavranos reasonably, 'we wouldn't have come here to meet you, would we? Let's not waste time. What do we do next, now that we're in San Francisco?' How, he thought, does a restoration-to-life *work*?

Mavranos reached into one of the outer pockets of his denim jacket, and Cochran tightened his grip on his own gun – but what Mavranos pulled out was a can of Coors, which he popped open one-handed. 'Okay. Angelica says we gotta call up that black lady that talked to us on the phone, the one who was brushing her hair on the TV. She's our *intercessor*, though Angelica doesn't totally trust her, doesn't want her taking over. And Angelica brought along a lot of ... beacons and landing lights, for Dionysus's remote attention as well as Crane's soul: those two silver dollars Spider Joe brought, and a gold Dunhill lighter that some hired assassin gave Crane one time – Angelica says the guy was a representative of Death, so it's a significant gift – and a bunch of myrtle-bush branches from the back garden. What other stuff we may need we'll—'

Plumtree interrupted him with a sharp, startled laugh – she was staring over the edge of the wall in the direction of the north cliff – and then she shivered and closed her eyes; Cochran glanced where she'd been looking, and his eyes widened in surprise to see a powerfully built naked man standing on the mud a couple of hundred feet away, facing them, with shoulder-length brown hair and a curly reddish beard that fell over his chest.

And Cochran's rib-cage went cold, for he recognized the man. 'That's our taxi driver!' he exclaimed. 'The guy that drove us to Solville!'

'That's Scott Crane,' said Mavranos hoarsely. 'Or his ghost.'

'Catch him in a bottle,' said Kootie.

Cochran stifled a nervous laugh at the foolishness of the boy's unconsidered remark – but then the naked man turned away, toward the cliff, and suddenly the distance and perspective were problematic. The man seemed to be smaller, tiny, as if he were some kind of elf standing on the rim of the wall a yard in front of Cochran's face, and a moment later he seemed to be immensely far away, and huge; and when he moved – away, presumably, for his form appeared to shrink – he shifted without any apparent contact with the ground. For one instant he seemed to jump from side to side like a figure in patchy animation – and Cochran grabbed one of the shoulder-height stone crossbeams, viscerally certain that the figure had been holding still and that it had been the whole world that had jumped.

Cochran's straining eyes focussed by default on the cliff face, and he noticed that a deep shadow at the base of it was the mouth of a cave; and when the naked figure flickered away out of sight it seemed to disappear into the shadowed opening.

Mavranos was sprinting away around the coping of a sunken mud lagoon, toward the cliff and the cave.

'It's just his ghost,' yelled Kootie, starting after him.

'It's the ghost of my friend!' Mavranos shouted back.

Cochran shoved his revolver into his belt, then crouched to climb back out through the crusted-stone window hole. 'Come on,' he gasped at Plumtree, 'we should go along.'

She wailed softly as she followed him out. Then, 'He drove our *taxi*?' she said as she hopped down after him from the foundation ledge to the mud. 'He must have *known who I was*. I held a fucking *spear* to his baby boy's *throat*!' Even though she was Cody, she took his hand as the two of them trotted after Mavranos and Kootie. 'If it comes to *facing* him, I think it'll have to be Valorie. She's the one who plays intolerable flops.'

*

The cave opened into a roughly straight tunnel, high enough for a person to walk upright in. The passage appeared to be natural, floored with wet gravel and bumpy with stone outcroppings on the rounded walls and ceiling, though Cochran could dimly see a metal railing installed along part of the seaward wall, halfway down the shadowed tunnel. By the time Cochran and Plumtree had come scuffing and panting into the broad entrance, Kootie was a dark silhouette far down the length of the tunnel and Mavranos stood in chalky daylight out beyond the far side, perhaps thirty yards distant. Reflected gray sky glittered in agitated puddles that filled low spots of the floor, and the moist breeze from the vitreous corridor was heavy with the old-pier smell of tide pools.

'Come on,' Cochran said, tugging Plumtree's cold hand as he stepped into the darkness.

'Take Valorie,' she said tightly, 'I hate caves.'

Cochran thought about the dead-eyed woman Plumtree had been right after the hollow knocking of the gunshots, and he shuddered at the prospect of walking through this dim, wet tunnel with her. 'I'd rather have you along, Cody,' he said, 'actually.'

She shrugged irritably and stepped forward, her sneakers crunching in the wet gravel. 'I'm here at the moment.'

The mushy rattle of their shoes on the yielding humped floor echoed from the stone walls, but Cochran could hear too the hissing rise and gutter of contained surf – and when he and Plumtree had trudged to where the metal railing stood against the seaward wall, he saw that two jagged holes opened out from floor level to the outer air, where waves could be seen foaming up over rocks that glittered in the gray daylight outside.

A seething bath, he thought, *which yet may prove against strange maladies a sovereign cure.*

Up ahead, Kootie too was out in the leaden light now, and Mavranos's voice came reverberating down the tunnel: 'Get your girlfriend out here.'

'Come on, girlfriend,' Cochran said.

She yanked her hand free of his, and hurried past him so that he had to splash along after her.

'Wait for moron Tiffany, asshole,' she called back to him.

He touched the lump in his jacket that was the cassette tape from the telephone answering machine. Tiffany, he thought, or someone else.

There was only a wide ledge under the open sky at the other end of the tunnel, and no way to go farther without climbing over wet, tilted boulders.

Cochran blinked around in the relative glare when he was standing out there beside Kootie and Mavranos and Plumtree, and he pointed at the tan boulder nearest to them, across a narrow gap that had sea water sloshing in it. 'That one looks like George Washington,' he said, inanely. It did, though – the broad face turned out to sea in profile, the nose and the jawline and even the edge of the wig, were all rendered in weather-broken stone.

'The father of our country,' said Plumtree brightly.

Kootie was peering down into the water, staring at the foamy scum on the waves. 'He's gone,' he said.

Cochran frowned at Plumtree to stop her from asking if he meant George Washington.

Mavranos was squinting up at the northern cliff face and then out across the huge tumbled stones. 'He's not corporeal,' he said, speaking loudly to be heard over the waves crashing on the rocks farther out. 'That's good, right? He's not one of the solidified ghosts, like those "beastie" things your dad had in his van.'

'He wasn't corporeal just *now*,' Kootie said. 'And I think it generally takes a fresh ghost a while to firmly gather up enough ... spit and bubble gum and bug blood and plaster dust ... to form a reliably solid body. Still, he ...' Kootie yawned widely. 'Excuse me. Did Crane *drink* a lot?'

'Drink, like alcohol?' Mavranos scowled at the boy. 'Well, he used to. He cut back hard after Easter in '90 – since then it's been a glass or two of wine, with the bread fish he has for breakfast, lunch, and dinner. Why?'

In a fruity, affected voice, Plumtree said, 'I *enjoy* a *glass of wine* with my meals.'

Ignoring her, Kootie said, 'I think ghosts of drunks solidify faster. And then they keep drinking, buying cheap wine with money they get panhandling – but they can't digest the alcohol, and it comes bubbling out of their skin like sweat. It's like the *habit* is what animates them.' He turned a cold gaze on Plumtree. 'Do *you* drink a lot?'

'Well,' she said, 'one's not enough and a thousand is too many, as they say. Why do you ask?'

'If he *was* your taxi driver,' the boy said, 'he must have had some substance for that. Turning the steering wheel, pushing the pedals. You met him then, and you were the first to see him today. Sometimes a ghost clings to the person responsible for his death, especially if the person has a lot of guilt about the death. Al – Thomas Edison – he had a couple of 'em hanging on him, at one time and another.'

'You're saying what, exactly?' said Plumtree quickly.

'I'm saying your dad may have had help screwing up our TV set. I'm pretty sure you've got the ghost of Scott Crane riding in your head like ... like a bad case of lice. And you're only making the ghost develop faster by drinking all the time.'

Cochran couldn't tell if Plumtree relaxed or tensed up at this statement;

then her mouth opened and she droned, 'Sometimes she calls the king, and whispers to her pillow, as to him, the secrets of her overcharged soul: and I am sent to tell his majesty that even now she cries aloud for him.'

'Valorie,' Cochran said.

'She that loves her selves,' Plumtree said woodenly, 'hath not essentially, but by circumstance, the name of Valorie.'

Cochran shivered in the chilly ocean breeze, and he was glad Mavranos and Kootie would be accompanying him and Valorie back through the tunnel to the ruins and the mud-flats and the long zigzagging path back up to the normal-world San Francisco highway; for this was the same thing Valorie had said half an hour ago, when he had mentioned her name, and it had just now occurred to him that the Valorie personality was to some extent a kind of reflex-arc machine ... dead.

Mavranos had been nodding rapidly while Plumtree spoke, and now he said, 'Groovy. Scott sure picked a well-ventilated head to *occupy*.' He turned a pained look on Kootie. 'But in fact *he* doesn't know anything about it, does he?'

'Right,' said Kootie. 'Crane *himself* is ... somewhere else. Wherever the actual dead *people* go. Somewhere I guess only Dionysus has the key to. This ... "beastie," this naked thing we saw today, it's like a ROM disk. Not useless, if we could talk to it, but hardly more a real person than the Britannica on CD-ROM would be. No, Crane himself wouldn't know about this thing we followed down here, any more than the real Edison knew about the ghost I had in my head two years ago.'

'No doubt.' Mavranos stared at Cochran. 'So are you and Miss ... Miss Tears-On-My-Pillow coming with us?'

Cochran touched the butt of his revolver. 'No.' His heart was beating fast. 'No, we're gonna get a motel room somewhere. You and Angelica can cook up the restoration procedure, and we'll join you for that. You go get a place to stay, and meet me tomorrow at ... Li Po, it's a bar on Grant Street. At noon. If you forget the name, just remember where we are right now – the street entrance to the bar is stuccoed up to look like a natural cavern. You can give me, then, the phone number of whatever place you're staying at; and we can set up a time and place where Janis and I can meet you all.'

Mavranos smiled. 'You don't trust us.'

'Somehow I just don't,' Cochran agreed, struggling to keep his voice level. 'I think it must have something to do with,' he added with a jerky shrug, 'you all discussing *shooting* Janis, last night.'

'That's noble,' Mavranos said. 'But she just did one of her personality changes right now, didn't she?' He smiled at Plumtree. 'You're Dr. Jekyll, or Sybil, or the Incredible Hulk now, right?' To Cochran he went on, 'Any time you leave her alone – hell, any time at all – she could change into her father, who murdered Scott Crane. Do you think he wouldn't kill you?'

Cochran quailed inwardly when he remembered the man who had spoken out of Plumtree's body last night at Strubie the Clown's house; but aloud he said, 'I'll take my chances.'

'You'll be taking all of our chances,' said Kootie.

Cochran jumped when Plumtree spoke again, but the flat voice was still that of the Valorie personality: 'How chances mock, and changes fill the cup of alteration with diverse liquors!'

And Cochran remembered the bottle of wine that the Mondard figure had generously offered him in the hallucinated mirror last night. *Biting Dog*, or something, the label had seemed to read, in the reflection. And he thought too about Manhattans, and Budweisers and vodka, and Southern Comfort; and about flinty French *Graves* wine thoughtlessly disparaged at a New Year's Eve party.

Mavranos had already shrugged and started slogging back down the tunnel; Kootie followed him, after shaking his head and saying, 'Liquor, again.'

Cochran took Plumtree's elbow and led her after them. And all he was thinking about now was the – admittedly warm – twelve-pack of Coors he had transferred from the stolen Torino to his Granada, parked now just up the hill.

BOOK TWO

Diverse Liquors

O God! that one might read the book of fate,
And see the revolution of the times
Make mountains level, and the continent,—
Weary of solid firmness, – melt itself
Into the sea! and, other times, to see
The beachy girdle of the ocean
Too wide for Neptune's hips; how chances mock,
And changes fill the cup of alteration
With divers liquors! O! if this were seen,
The happiest youth, viewing his progress through,
What perils past, what crosses to ensue,
Would shut the book, and sit him down and die.

—William Shakespeare, *Henry IV, Part II*

BOOK TWO

Diaries: Log 206

CHAPTER FIFTEEN

It was an inconsistent and ubiquitous fiend too, for, while it was making the whole night behind him dreadful, he darted out into the roadway to avoid dark alleys, fearful of its coming hopping out of them like a dropsical boy's-Kite without a tail and wings. It hid in doorways too, rubbing its horrible shoulders against doors, and drawing them up to its ears, as if it were laughing.

—Charles Dickens, *A Tale of Two Cities*

For five days now the skirts of the storm clouds had swept across the fretted hills and smoky lowlands of San Francisco. At the northeast corner of the peninsula the intermittent downpours had saturated the precipitous eastern slope of Telegraph Hill, loosening wedges of mud that tumbled down onto the pavement of Sansomme Street, where old wooden cottages still stood from before the 1906 earthquake, having been saved from the subsequent fire by bucket brigades of Italians who had doused the encroaching flames with hundreds of gallons of homemade red wine; and the rain had swelled the waters of Stow Lake in Golden Gate Park, making a marsh of the playground to the south and completely submerging the strange old stones that edged the lake's normal boundaries; and in the southeast corner of the city the rain had frequently driven customers out of the open-air Farmer's Market on Alemany Boulevard, and kept the Mexican children from playing in the streets of the Mission District east of Dolores. In the blocks of run-down post-war housing in Hunter's Point, east of the 101, gunfire from passing cars was more common than usual.

In fact, incidents of random gunfire had increased all over the city in the five days since a burst of semi-automatic weapons fire had startled tourists outside the Cliff House Restaurant on the northwest shore, on the morning of January 12th. Of less general concern, the wild monkeys that lived in the sycamore trees on Russian Hill had begun a fearsome screeching every evening at sunset, and in the sunless dawns vast flocks of crows wheeled silently over the old buildings at the south end of the Embarcadero by the China Basin. The *Chronicle* ran a brief human-interest article about the spontaneous street-dancing that had started in these South-of-Market streets and alleys around the French restaurant whose name translated as *I Am Starving*, the rain-soaked dancers were described as neo-Beatnik youths and unreconstructed old hippies, and the dance was supposed to be a revival of the French *carmagnole*, and the preferred dance music appeared to be the 1970 Melanie song 'Candles in the Wind.'

The newspaper had noted that the *carmagnole* dancers liked to toss lit strings of firecrackers around their feet as they stamped and spun in the ferocious dance, but to Archimedes Mavranos, standing now on the second-floor balcony of the apartment he had rented on Lapu Lapu Street in the shadow of the elevated Bay Bridge Freeway, the staccato *pop-pop-pop* sounded like volleys of full-auto machine-gun fire.

He was tapping his current can of Coors on the wet iron balcony rail. 'I don't like it,' he said over his shoulder.

'*Duh*,' said Kootie from the living room behind him.

After frowning for another moment down at the shiny car roofs trundling by on the wet pavement, Mavranos smiled and turned back to the room. 'I guess I have made it clear that I don't like it,' he allowed. 'But dammit, it *is* the day the earthquake blew up L.A. The one-year anniversary.'

Kootie was sitting against the door of the unfurnished room, holding a red-blotted face-cloth to his side, and Pete and Angelica Sullivan stood over the old black-and-white television set they had brought along from Solville. It was sitting on top of another TV set, newer but non-functioning, that they had found in the street.

'We drove up there too, a day or so later, to Northridge,' said Pete, without taking his eyes from the images on the working screen, which were just a modern Ford ad at the moment, 'to look at the wreckage. Kootie insisted.'

'Of *course* the seventeenth of January is a day to be scared of,' Kootie said to Mavranos. 'I saw what happened to L.A. But that would be why the French people you told us about made such a big deal *of it*. How could Dionysus's mid-winter death-day be anything *but* scary?' He smiled unhappily. 'He's the earthquake boy, right?'

'Our pendulum stuck over the thirty-first, too,' pointed out Angelica – wearily, for she had pointed it out many times already. 'Tet.'

'Our *pendulum*,' said Mavranos in disgust as he drained his beer and strode in through the living room to the kitchen, which fortunately had come with a refrigerator. 'Our *scientific apparatus*,' he called derisively as he took a fresh can from the refrigerator's door-shelf.

Angelica had brought along several jars of pennies to shake at the TV, and over the last five days the old black woman had several times been induced to intrude on the TV screen here in San Francisco, though the reception of her inserts was scratchy here with some unimaginable kind of static. And she had spoken, too, though her opening words each time had been just an idiot repetition of the last phrases spoken on the real channel before her image had crowded out the normal programming.

At first the old woman had said that they must find her house, and 'eat the seeds of my trees,' so that one of their party could be 'indwelt,' which apparently meant inhabited by the old woman's ghost. The disembodied image on the television had insisted that this was the only way she could properly guide the dead king's company.

Angelica had vetoed that. *We have no hosts to spare,* she had said. *This is just identity-greed, she wants a body again, and she probably would cling. She can advise us just fine from the TV screen, and do her interceding from there.*

And the old black woman had had a lot to say, even just from the television speakers. She had babbled – uselessly, Mavranos thought – about being a penitential servant now of Dionysus, whose chapel she had apparently desecrated during her lifetime; she had said that they needed to call the god beside untamed water, and had talked uncertainly about some banker friend of hers who had drowned himself 'near Meg's Wharf.' Pete had gone to the library and established that her drowned friend had been William Ralston, who had founded the Bank of California, and who had drowned near Meiggs Wharf in 1874 after his bank went broke. And she had said that a calendar would have to be consulted with 'a plumb line' to determine a propitious date.

Angelica had called on her *bruja* skills and made a pendulum of hairs from Scott Crane's beard, weighted with the gold Dunhill lighter a professional assassin had once given to Crane; and, after Mavranos had been sent out to buy a calendar, Kootie had dangled the makeshift pendulum over the January page.

The glittering brick-shaped lighter had looked like some kind of Faberge Pez dispenser with its mouth open, for Angelica had had to open the lid to knot the hair around it – and the lighter had visibly been drawn to the square on the calendar that was the seventeenth, continuing to strain toward it, as if pulled magnetically, even after Kootie's hand had moved an inch or so past it. And, as Angelica had noted, the swinging lighter had been tugged toward the thirty-first, too, which was the Vietnamese Tet festival and the Chinese New Year. The Year of the Dog was ending, the Year of the Pig due to start on the first of February – and *that* date was the first day of Ramadan, the Moslem holy month of fasting.

Mavranos drank the fresh beer in three very big swallows, then popped open another can to carry with him into the living room.

'The thirty-first would probably work,' he told Angelica stolidly. 'I'm with you, I like it better; for one thing, we might be able to get more of a showing from this dead lady that's supposed to be our *intercessor*. But the thirty-first is two weeks from now. The seventeenth is tomorrow. We've been in San Francisco five days today. Scott's body is still in the back of the truck, and we'll be getting warm weather eventually. And as Kootie says, if we're going to ask Dionysus for a favor, it does make sense to do it on his own ... terrible ... day.'

He looked out the window at the gray concrete pillars of the elevated 101, and he remembered the newspaper photos of the collapsed double-deck I-880 in Oakland, after the big quake in October of '89; and he remembered too the flattened cars he and Scott Crane had viewed in Los Angeles a year ago. 'Shit,' he said mildly. 'I guess we do have to try it tomorrow, intercessor or no intercessor. You should have picked up a football helmet for each of us, along with your skeleton wine.'

'And some Halloween masks,' said Kootie quietly, with a somber glance at Marvranos. 'Two or three apiece, ideally.'

Mavranos returned the boy's look, and thought, *You've known all along how this will have to go, haven't you, kid? And you came along anyway, to save your parents.* Aloud, he said, 'Yeah, they're probably real cheap this time of year.'

Angelica darted a suspicious look from her foster-son to Mavranos. 'That Plumtree woman had *better* still be willing to go through with this,' she said. 'Does Cochran say anything about her, what she's been *doing* for four days? I don't suppose he'll bring her along today.'

'No chance of that,' said Mavranos. 'Just like I haven't, for example, been bringing Scott's body along when I've met Cochran at the bar. They-all and us-all don't trust each other; he thinks I'll try to shoot Plumtree, and I think Plumtree's dad will try to finish the job on Scott's body.' He took a sip of the beer and licked foam off his graying mustache. 'I bet Cochran takes as *circuitous* a route back to wherever he's staying as I do when I come back here.'

'Wherever *he's* staying?' spoke up Angelica. 'Isn't she staying with him?'

'Well, I assume,' Mavranos began; 'he tells me that she is—' Then he exhaled and let himself sit down cross-legged on the wooden floor. 'I think she ran away from him, actually,' he admitted in a level voice, 'and he doesn't want to tell me. I think Cochran doesn't have any clue where she is. Sorry. I think her father came on sometime, and just ... ran away with her body.'

Cochran had been visibly drunk at their last two noon meetings at the Li Po bar, and too hearty in his assurances that Plumtree was still eager to get the dead king restored to life; and Mavranos had got the uneasy impression that Cochran was hoping to hear that *Mavranos* had somehow heard from her.

Kootie winced as he got to his feet. 'Consider phlebotomy,' he said.

'"—Who was once as tall and handsome as you,"' added Mavranos, automatically making a pun on the line in T. S. Eliot's *The Waste Land* about Phlebas the drowned Phoenician sailor.

Angelica's face was suddenly pale as she, whirled to glare at Kootie, and her voice was low: '*I forbid it absolutely.* We've got money – We're going home. Or somewhere. To hell with this king.'

Pete Sullivan was blinking at the woman and the boy in alarm. Clearly no one had got Mavranos's pun, not that it mattered. 'What?' said Pete. 'Lobotomy? For who?'

'Phle-botomy,' said Angelica, still scowling at her foster son. 'Venesection, bloodletting; from Crane's body into a, a wine glass, I suppose. You are simply *not* going to let the, that *dead man who we don't even know*, occupy your head, Kootie! You're not going to let him have *your* body! Pete, tell him that we—'

'Mom,' said Kootie stonily. '*Angelica*. We've *all known*, we haven't talked about it but we've all known – come on! – that the king would probably have to take *my* body to do this, not that woman's.' His eyes glistened, but he seemed even angrier than Angelica. 'Look at my qualifications – I'm a *male*, for one thing. I'm not a virgin, psychically; and I *am* a virgin, physically, which Plumtree probably is not; and I've been living the king's discipline, fish and wine, and rituals, and visions! Call me fucking Fishmeal, excuse me. I've got to be … served to him.' His shoulders relaxed, and he rubbed the face-cloth across his eyes, leaving a brushstroke of fresh blood on his cheek. 'And who knows, it might work out just the way the Plumtree woman said – he might just use my body to do the magical stuff that'll let him get back into his own.'

'His own?' shouted Pete. 'His own is over fifty years old! And two weeks dead! You've been *planning* this? Your mother's right. Even if he *wanted* to, the Fisher King probably *couldn't* shift back out of an adolescent body into an old one! Any more than water can run uphill! How would this "bloodletting"—'

'Even if—?' Mavranos interrupted harshly; then he took a deep breath and started again. '"Even if he wanted to"? You – goddammit, you didn't know the man, so I guess I got no right to take offense. But you know me, and I'm telling you now that he wouldn't, ever, save his own life at the expense of somebody else.' He glared at the TV. 'Hey, turn it up – our lady's on again.'

Angelica gave the screen a startled look, then twisted the volume knob.

In the grainy black-and-white picture, the old black woman was standing beside her chair now, and staring directly out of the screen. 'Gotta get the *bugs* out of your *house*,' she quavered, apparently reciting the tail end of some exterminator commercial she had interrupted. Mavranos hoped she wouldn't, this time, go on for several minutes with the parroted recitation.

'But I didn't – I wasn't even shaking the pennies,' said Angelica softly.

A crackling had started up inside the dead TV set that they were using as a table for the working one.

'The bugs that work six feet under,' said Kootie in a tense voice.

Mavranos couldn't tell if the boy was responding to what the old woman had said, or was sensing something nearby, or was speculating on the source of the noise in the dead TV; and he realized that his heart was pounding.

'Too late!' said the old black woman. 'The bugs win this round! *You* get out.'

It's not an exterminator ad, thought Mavranos.

Black smoke abruptly began billowing up from the back of the bottom television set; but its speakers came to booming life, croaking right along with the top TV set's, when the old woman shouted, 'Boy-king, witch, escape artist and family retainer, I am speaking to you all! *Get out now.* They're coming up the stairs, the ones who hate the California vines! You four go out the window – I will distract the intruders with conversation and difficult questions.'

Before she was finished speaking Mavranos had dropped his beer and stepped forward, and he grabbed Kootie and Angelica by their shoulders and propelled them stumbling across the floor toward the balcony. Pete Sullivan had reached through the black smoke to snatch the car keys off the top TV set, and he stepped along after his wife and foster son.

'There's a fire escape on the right side,' Mavranos said, trying not to inhale the sharp-smelling smoke. He paused to grab his leather jacket and Angelica's purse, because their handguns were in them, and then he was standing on the balcony beside Angelica and Pete, taking deep breaths of the fresh air; he shoved the purse at Angelica with one hand while he flexed his free arm into the sleeve of the jacket. 'You got a live one in the chamber?' he gasped.

She nodded, frowning.

'Take the time to aim,' he said, boosting Kootie over the railing.

Behind them, a knock shook the hallway door. As if jolted to life by the knocking, the room's smoke alarm finally broke into a shrill unceasing wail.

'Who is it?' demanded the old woman's voice loudly from the two sets of speakers. 'Be damned if I'm lettin' any *bug men* into my home!'

Kootie was halfway down the iron ladder now, but Angelica had only swung one leg over the rail, and Pete was standing behind her, uselessly flexing his hands.

Mavranos's mouth was dry, and he realized that he was actually very afraid of meeting whoever it might be that the old woman was referring to as bug men. 'Pete,' he said gruffly, 'we're only on the second floor here.'

Pete Sullivan gave him a twitchy grin. 'And it's muddy ground below.'

Both men clambered over the long rail of the balcony and hung crouched on the outside of it – like, thought Mavranos, plastic monkeys on the rims of Mai Tai glasses – then kicked free and dropped.

After a windy moment of free-fall Mavranos's feet impacted into the mud and he sat down hard in a puddle, but he was instantly up and limping to the curb, his hand on the grip of the .38 in his pocket as he stared back up at the balcony. 'Keep 'em off to the side of me,' he called to Pete, who had got to his feet behind him.

Over the distance-muted siren of the smoke alarm Mavranos could hear the loud, cadenced voice of the old woman – she seemed to be shouting poetry, or prayers.

Kootie had hopped down onto a patch of wet grass, and as soon as he had sprinted to the sidewalk Angelica sprang away from the ladder and landed smoothly on her toes and fingertips. As she straightened up and followed Kootie to the sidewalk, she caught her swinging purse with her left hand and darted her right hand into it.

Pete herded them down the sidewalk past a tall bushy cypress tree and a brick wall; Mavranos followed, but stopped to peek back through the piney branches of the cypress.

Across the lawn and above him, wisps of black smoke were curling out of the open balcony doorway and being torn away by the rainy breeze, but he saw no people up there; and he was about to step away and hurry after his companions when all at once three figures shuffled clumsily out onto the balcony, and from the second-floor elevation looked up and down Lapu Lapu Street. The middle figure, a white-haired man in a business suit, was clearly holding a weapon under his coat; but it was the pair of men flanking him that made Mavranos's belly go cold.

The two figures were bony and angular inside their identical lime-green leisure suits, and their bland faces swung back and forth in perfect unison – and though they didn't appear to say anything, and their theatrically raised hands didn't move to touch the white-haired man, Mavranos was certain that the pair had somehow perceived him. And at the same time he was sure that they were inanimate mannikins.

Mavranos turned away and ran; but by the time he had caught up with Pete and Angelica and Kootie he had reined in his momentary panic and was able to plausibly force his usual squint and grin. The old red truck with Scott Crane's tarpaulin-covered body in the back of it was at the curb in front of them, and there was no use in spooking these people – though before long he would have to tell them what he had seen.

Not right now, though – not for several minutes, several miles, at least. Whatever it is, it's what Nardie saw in Leucadia last week.

'It looks like we *all* go meet Cochran today,' he panted as he held out his hand to Pete for the car keys. 'And,' he added in a voice he forced to be level, 'I hope there aren't any bug men at Li Po.'

In an upstairs room at the Star Motel in the Marina district of the city, Sid Cochran was sitting on the bed, gently nudging a clean glass ashtray across the back of a yellow enameled-metal National Auto Dealers Association sign he had salvaged two days ago from a gas-station Dumpster at Lombard and Octavia.

The sign was lying face down on the bedspread, but he knew that the front of it read NADA, and he found that oddly comforting. On this blank side he had inked the twenty-six letters of the alphabet and numbers from 0 to 9, in a bow-and-string pattern like what he remembered seeing on Ouija boards. Up by the pillows, next to an ashtray full of cigarette butts, lay half a dozen sheets of paper covered with lines of lettering tentatively divided into words by vertical slashes.

He had been trying for some time now to conduct a lucid conversation with the ghost of his wife.

Now the ashtray appeared to have stopped moving again, and he sat back and wrote down the last letter it had framed, and then he stared uneasily at the latest answer the ashtray had spelled out for him: CETAITLEROIETPUISSONFILSSCOTTETAITLEROI.

After driving away from the Sutro Bath ruins on Thursday in his old Granada, and then looping around and around the blocks of the Marina district until he was sure they were not being followed, Cochran and Plumtree had checked into this motel on Lombard Street. Cody had used Nina's Visa card, signing 'Nina Cochran' on the credit-card voucher.

Plumtree had stayed up all that night and into Friday the thirteenth, watching television with the sound turned low enough so that Cochran could at least try to sleep; Cochran's only clue as to which personality might be up at any time had been the choice of programs. Cochran had gone sleepily stumbling out to meet Mavranos at noon, and when he had got back to the motel at about two in the afternoon, Plumtree had been gone. Cochran had slept until nearly midnight, by which time she had not reappeared.

And he had not seen her since. Twice on Saturday the telephone had rung, but when he had answered it there had been only choked gasping on the line.

On both of the days since her disappearance he had gone out to meet Arky at the Chinese bar at noon, and a couple of times a day he had trudged to the deli on Gough for coffee and sandwiches and bourbon and beer, but he had spent most of his time drunkenly studying the French Catholic missal he had found in Nina's sewing room when he and Plumtree had stopped at his house early on Thursday morning.

One page of the little volume was clearly a family tree. Cochran learned that Nina had not been the first of her family to have emigrated to the United States – a grand-uncle, one Georges Leon, had moved to New York in 1929, and then onward west to Los Angeles in 1938, and had had a son in 1943. Old Georges had apparently been a black sheep of the Leon family, had *n'avait pas respecte le vin*, disrespected the primordial French rootstocks. In tiny, crabbed script someone had declared that, precisely because the Bordeaux wines were terrible from 1901 through 1919, these were the times when all true sons of *père Dionysius Français* should show their loyalty, not go running off to *les dieux étrangers*, strange gods.

In fact, just about all of the notes in the missal concerned viticulture and wine-making. On the *dates importantes* page, 1970 was noted because Robert Mondavi of California's Robert Mondavi Winery had in that year met with Baron Phillipe de Rothschild of Bordeaux – in Honolulu, of all the remote places. 1973 was listed just for having been the year in which the Baron's Chateau Mouton Rothschild claret was finally promoted to the official list of First Growth Bordeaux wines; this development was apparently viewed as bad news by Nina's family because of the Baron's association with the Californian Robert Mondavi. One marginal scrawl described the two men as acolytes of the damnable California Dionysus.

Some of the notes were too brief and cryptic for him to make any sense of at all. For 1978 was just a sentence which translated as, 'Mondavi visits the Medoc – failure.' The following year was pithily summarized with the French for 'Answered prayers! The new phylloxera.'

For 1984 was simply the words *Opus One*, but because of his profession he did know what that must refer to.

'Opus One' was the '79 vintage California wine that Mondavi and Phillipe de Rothschild had finally released in 1984 as a joint venture between their premier Californian and French vineyards. It had been a fifty-dollar-a-bottle Cabernet Sauvignon with some Cabernet Franc and Merlot blended in, to soften the roughness imparted by the Napa hot spell in May of '79, fermented in contact with the skins for ten days and aged for two years in Nevers oak casks at Mouton, in the Medoc. Cochran remembered the Opus One as having been a subtle and elegant Cabernet, but the person who had scribbled the notes in the missal didn't approve of it at all: *le sang jaillissant du dieu kidnappe*, she called it, 'haemorrhage blood of the kidnapped god.'

The 1989 entry was on the next page, and it was just *J'ai recontre Adrocles, et c'est le mien* – 'I have met Androcles, and he is mine.'

A photograph of Sid Cochran was laid in at that page.

Sitting drunk in the Star Motel room, Cochran had taken some comfort from the fact that Nina had treasured his picture this way … until he noticed that in it he was posed with his chin on his right fist, and the ivy-leaf mark on the back of his hand was in clearer focus than his face was.

And so he had improvised the makeshift Ouija board.

Using the glass ashtray as a planchette, he had spelled out a call for Nina's ghost, and then had let the ashtray drift of its own accord from one letter to another after he had spoken questions aloud to it.

To his shivering nausea and breathless excitement the device had appeared to work. The indicated letters, which he had painstakingly copied down one by one on sheets of Star Motel stationery, had been resolvable into French words.

The very first words had told him that he was indeed the 'Androcles' the missal note had referred to – and his initial suspicion that he had unknowingly propelled the planchette himself, just subconsciously spelling out what he'd wanted to read, had been dispelled when further words appeared: *TU TEXPOSES AU DANGER POUR SAUVER LE DIEU DANGEREUX*, 'You put yourself in danger to save the dangerous god.' That part made no sense to him.

Twice he had told his wife's ghost – aloud, in stammering self-conscious syllables – that he loved her; and both times the slowly indicated letters had advised him to turn all his feelings for her over to the god who died for everyone. The wording had been exactly the same both times, and he had been reminded of the repetitive answers he had got from Plumtree's Valorie personality.

In spite of that, he had carefully wrapped the cassette from the telephone answering machine in a clean sock and stashed it in the bedside table drawer, beside the Gideon Bible – and he had stayed here at the motel, running up Nina's credit-card debt, in the hope that Plumtree would come back here, ready to do her mind-opening trick. He had called Pace Vineyards and got them to agree to let him have an unspecified amount of vacation time.

Yesterday morning he had got around to asking the Ouija board about one of the missal notes that had puzzled him – and then, in horrified alarm, he had chosen to regard the resulting answer as delusional, a fever-dream notion induced in the unimaginable sleep of death.

He'd had no choice: for in answer to his question about the unspecified 'failure' during Mondavi's 1978 visit to the Medoc, the planchette had given him the letters JAI ESSAYE MAIS JAI MANQUE A TUER LHOMME DE CALIFORNIA, which worked out to spell, 'I tried but failed to kill the man from California' in French.

After getting that answer on Sunday morning, he had stayed away from the planchette all the rest of that day – he had spent most of the gray daylight hours on a long, agitated walk among the incongruously peaceful green lawns of nearby Fort Mason. Nina would have been only fourteen years old in 1978 – he had assured himself that the Ouija-board statement could not be anything more than a sad, morbid fantasy.

But this morning he had nevertheless helplessly found himself consulting the NADA sign and the ashtray once again, and a few minutes ago, at lonely random, he had got around to asking about her disgraced granduncle Georges Leon.

The answering string of letters that he had just copied down was easily translatable as, 'He was the western king, and then his son Scott was the western king.'

And he now remembered Pete Sullivan dialling out Scott Crane's full name on the old rotary telephone in the laundry room in Solville, six days ago – Cochran had noticed at the time that one of the two last names had been Leon.

It could hardly be a coincidence – apparently the dead king in the back of Mavranos's truck was some remote cousin of Cochran's dead wife.

Abruptly there was a hard knock at the motel-room door, and Cochran jumped so wildly that both ashtrays sprang off the bed; then he had dived to the closet and fumbled up the .357 with hands so shaky that he almost fired a bullet through the ceiling.

'Who is it?' he demanded shrilly. He hoped it was Plumtree at last, or even Mavranos – and not the police, or Armentrout with a couple of burly psych-techs and a hypodermic needle, or whoever it had been that had shot at Mavranos by the Sutro ruins last week.

'Is that you, Sid?' came a woman's hoarse voice from outside.

Carrying the gun, Cochran hurried to the door and peeked out through the little inset lens. It was Plumtree's flushed face staring at him – in fact, in spite of the apparent sunburn and the tangled blond hair across her face, he could recognize her as being specifically Cody. And even through the peephole he could see dried blood on scratches below her jaw and at one corner of her mouth.

He pulled the chain free of the slot and swung the door open. 'Cody, I'm damn glad to—' he began, but guilt about his recent schemes stopped his voice.

She limped in past him and sat down heavily on the bed. She was wearing clothes he hadn't seen before, khaki shorts and a man's plaid flannel shirt, but she smelled of old sweat, and her bare legs were scratched and spattered with mud and burned a deep maroon. As he closed the door and reattached the chain, Cochran remembered dully that the Bay Area sky had been solidly overcast this whole past week.

Plumtree was shaking her head, swinging her matted hair back and forth, and she was mumbling, perhaps to herself, 'How do I *hang on*, how do I *keep him down*? I feel like I've been stretched on the *rack*! Even Valorie can only pin him down *sometimes*.' She looked at the gun in Cochran's hand, and then her bloodshot eyes fixed on his. 'Shooting me might be the best plan, that Mavranos guy's no idiot. But right now you better tell me you've got something to drink in here.' She sniffed and curled her grimy lip. 'Jeez, it stinks! Talk to the school nurse about *hygiene*, would you?'

'I—' Cochran stopped himself, and just tossed the gun down on the bed and fetched the current pint bottle of Wild Turkey from the windowsill.

After he had handed it to her he hesitantly picked the gun up again and tucked it into his belt.

Plumtree tipped the bottle up and took several messy swallows, wincing as the whiskey touched the cut at the corner of her mouth; but she nodded at him over the neck of the bottle as she drank, and when she had lowered it and gingerly wiped her mouth, she wheezed, 'Don't be shy about it,' breathing bourbon fumes at him. 'Put one through my thigh if you've got the leisure and elbow room, but – if I turn into my dad? – you *stop* me.' The bottle had been half full when he'd handed it to her, but there was only an inch or so left when she gave it back to him. 'How long have I been gone?' she asked. 'Not too long, I guess, if you're still here. I was afraid you wouldn't be – that, like, everything happened a year ago, and the king was dead past recall.'

'Today is Monday the sixteenth,' he said, 'of January, still. You've been gone ... two full days.' He thought of wiping the neck of the bottle, then just tilted it up for a sip. The whiskey will kill any germs, he thought. 'Where *were* you?' he asked after he had swallowed a mouthful of the vapory, smoldering liquor.

'You're a gentleman, Sid. Where was I? I—' She inhaled sharply, and then she was sobbing. She looked up at him and her eyes widened. '*Scant*! You found me!' She clawed the bedspread as if the room might begin tossing like a boat; then she grabbed his arm and pulled him down beside her, and buried her face in his shirt. 'God, I hurt all over – my teeth feel like somebody tried to pull them all out – and I'm a mess,' she said, sniffling. 'Hold on to me anyway. Don't let me run away again! You might have to handcuff me to the plumbing in the bathroom or something.' He had both his arms around her now, and felt her shaking. 'But don't – Jesus, don't *hurt* him, if he comes out.'

He patted her dirty hair and kissed the top of her head. I've got to just throw away that cassette from the phone-answering machine, he thought. Even if it *would* serve as a potent lure, how could I possibly have thought of – pushing this woman out of her own head, in order to get Nina back? – or even just compounding Janis's problems by adding one more ghost to her sad menagerie? And Nina is *dead*, she'd only be what Kootie called a ROM disk, like Valorie. I swear I will *not* settle for that!

The bottle was in his right hand, behind her, and he wished he could get it up to his mouth.

'Where have you been, Janis?' he asked softly.

'Where—?' She shuddered, and then shoved him away. 'Right back to me, hey?' she said. 'Janis can't face this flop? Or did you have Tiffany here, is that why you're on the bed? How much time's gone by *now*?'

Cochran stood up. 'It was Janis,' he said wearily, 'and just for a few seconds. Cody, I wish you – never mind. So *where were* you all?'

'I *was* – well, I was out in the hills. *I've* got to remember this, huh? Out in the woods with people wearing hoods, killing goats.' Tears spilled down her cheeks, and smeared the grime when she cuffed them away, but when she went on her voice was animated, a parody of vivacity: 'One of the goat heads wound up on a, a *pole*, and I was on for just a couple of heartbeats when it was, in the middle of *speaking* to us, in what I think was Greek. The goat head was speaking, in a human language. Goats have horizontal pupils because they look from side to side, mostly, and cats have vertical pupils because they're always looking up and down. My pupils are … staying after school for detention. I don't know who the hooded people were.' She nudged the NADA sign with her hip. 'Whaddaya got, a Ouija board? Ask *it* who they were.' She smiled at him. Her nose had begun bleeding. 'The hooded people.'

Cochran glanced at the clock radio on the bedside table. He still had an hour and a half before he was to meet Mavranos. In the last couple of days he had got into the habit of walking up Russian Hill on Lombard to Van Ness and catching the cable car down to California Street and then taking another one east to Chinatown, but today he could drive the old Granada, and hope to find a parking place. He might even get Cody to drop him off at a corner near Grant and Washington. No, she'd be way too drunk – maybe Janis could drive him.

'Okay,' he said. He stepped into the bathroom and hooked a face-cloth off the towel rack, then tossed it to her as he bent down beside the bed to retrieve the clean ashtray. 'Your nose is bleeding, Cody,' he said, placing the ashtray on the metal sign. 'Put pressure on it.' He sat down on the bed and laid his fingertips on the round piece of clear glass. 'Who has … Miss Plumtree been with, during these last few days?' he asked.

As soon as he spoke, it occurred to him that Cody should be touching the ashtray too, and that he should have cleared the ghost of Nina off the line; but the ashtray was already moving.

'Write down the letters as they come,' he told Plumtree nervously.

'I can remember 'em,' she said, her voice muffled by the towel.

'Will you please – here we go.' The ashtray had paused over the L, and now moved sideways to the E.

'Letterman,' mumbled Plumtree. 'I knew it. I was with David Letterman.'

When the ashtray planchette had spelled out L-E-V-E-R, Plumtree inhaled sharply and stumbled back to the Wild Turkey bottle and took a gulp from it, wincing again. 'Fucking Lever Blank,' she gasped as blood spilled down her chin, 'that's what I was afraid of. Goddamn old monster, he can't leave that pagan hippie cult alone, even though they threw him off that building in Soma.'

'It's not "lever," dammit,' interrupted Cochran loudly without looking up from the metal sign. 'Will you please write this stuff down? It's L-E-V-R, with no second E. And now an I, and an E ... get the goddamn pencil, will you?' He glanced quickly at her. 'And you're bleeding all over the place.'

'Okay, okay, sorry. Just, my hands feel like I've got arthritis.' The alcohol was visibly hitting her already – she was weaving as she walked back to the bed, as if she were on a ship in choppy water. She fumbled at the paper and pencil. 'What ... ?'

'L-E-V-R-I-E-R-B,' he spelled out. 'And another L – and an A.'

She was goggling blearily at the board now. 'And N ... and C ...' she noted, painstakingly writing the letters.

After several tense seconds, Cochran lifted his fingers from the ashtray. 'That's it. What, Levrierble ... ?'

'Levrierblanc.' She held out the blood-spattered sheet of paper and gave him a scared, defiant glare. 'That's still Lever Blank, if you ask me. The French version.' She pressed the towel to her nose again.

'My wife is French,' he said, nodding, realizing even as he spoke that it was an inadequate explanation. 'Was.'

'I know. Sorry to hear she died, dirty shame.' She snapped a grimy fingernail against the paper, spiking the blood drops on it. 'It's two words. Blanc's the second word, like Mel Blanc.'

Cochran nodded. Obviously she was right – and he suspected that if Nina hadn't been their ... *operator* here, it would have come out in plain English as LEVERBLANK.

'A goat head,' he said, 'speaking Greek.' In his mind he heard Long John Beach's crazy lyrics again ... *and frolicked in the Attic mists in a land called Icaree*. 'I think you'd better write down everything you can remember about this Lever Blank crowd.' He glanced again at the clock radio. 'Not right now. I've got to meet Mavranos in a little over an hour. Let's get Janis to drop me near the place, she—' isn't falling-down drunk, he thought; '—isn't having a nose-bleed, and then you can come back here and—'

'Janis drive? Fuck that. I can drive, and I'm meeting Marvos – dammit – *Mavranos* with you, too. We'll get this *done*. I don't want to have that little kid's dad's blood on my hands one hour more than I have to.' Her own blood was running down her wrist. 'He just wants, my father, he wants to become king, like he failed to do when he was in a body of his own. A *male* body, he needs. If we can get Crane solidly raised from the dead. I think my father will have no reason to hang around, he'll just go back into hibernation, like a case of herpes in remission. You don't have herpes, do you?'

Cochran blinked at her. 'No.'

'Tiffany does. You should know. I won't even drink out of a glass she's used. How far away is it, where you're meeting Marvy-Arvy?'

'Oh – no more than twenty minutes, if we drive. Of course if we've got to find a place to *park the car*, I don't know how long that might take. No, I really think it's too dangerous for you to be there, Cody – if Mavranos gets hold of you, he's liable to do something like—'

'Nothing I'll object to. Nothing I won't deserve. I got his friend killed.' She struggled up from the bed, still pressing the bloody face-cloth to her nose. 'You got coffee? Good. Make me a cup, and pour the rest of that bourbon into it. I'm gonna,' she said with a sigh, as if facing a painful ordeal, 'take a shower.'

'Could I talk to Janis about all this?'

'No. And what do you mean, "she doesn't have a nosebleed"? It's her nose too, isn't it?'

Cochran opened his mouth to point out some inconsistencies in the things she'd said, but found that he was laughing too hard to speak; tears were leaking from the corners of his eyes, and his chest hurt. 'I'll,' he managed to choke, 'have the coffee ready when you ... get out of the shower.'

Her mouth twitched. 'Laugh it up, funny boy,' she said sourly, then lurched into the bathroom and closed the door with a slam. From the other side of the door he heard her call, 'And don't be peeking in here to see if Tiffany's on.'

Cochran was still sniffling when he pulled open the bedside table drawer, and he lifted out the cassette and stared at it.

Two full seconds over a lit match would destroy the thing.

But, *It's her nose too, isnt it?* – and, if it comes to that, *his*, too. Her terrible father's. A lot of jumping around, reshuffling and discarding, might happen before we all get out of San Francisco.

He tucked the cassette carefully into his shirt pocket.

CHAPTER SIXTEEN

Besides that all secret men are men soon terrified, here were surely cards enough of one black suit, to justify the holder in growing rather livid as he turned them over.

—Charles Dickens, *A Tale of Two Cities*

Dr. Armentrout knew he was lucky to have got out of the smoky apartment building and back down to the street, and his car, and to Long John Beach, before encountering this ... *very shifty* woman.

The day had started propitiously, but this last half hour had been a rout.

*

Late last Thursday his teal-blue BMW had finally limped off the 280 at Junipero Serra Boulevard and sputtered up Seventh to Parnassus to the UCSF Medical Center, where he had got a couple of colleagues to make some telephone calls for him; the upshot was that he had been allowed to take over house-sitting duties at the nearby Twin Peaks villa of a neurologist who was on sabbatical in Europe.

The first thing he had done at the empty house was to change the phone-answering message. Then, very quickly, he had made a photocopied blank sheet of letterhead from the nearby Pacifica minimum-security psychiatric facility, and he'd altered the phone and fax numbers on it to those of the absent neurologist's house; he had addressed the sheet to Rosecrans Medical, and typed on it a transfer for Long John Beach, along with a request for Beach's records – to make it look plausible he had had to ask for everything: nursing progress reports, psychosocial assessment, treatment plan, financial data, the legal section. He hoped the neurologist was in the habit of keeping a lot of paper in his home fax printer. Long John Beach was 53-58, on a full conservatorship, but the old man's 'conservator' had been a fictitious entity from the start, so there'd been no risk in signing the remembered made-up name.

Then Armentrout had telephoned Rosecrans Medical and peremptorily announced his application for immediate administrative leave. He'd explained that he was temporarily working as a consultant at UCSF Medical, and pointed out that he was entitled to six weeks a year of vacation, and had never taken any of it. He had named one of the other doctors, an elderly Freudian, to serve as acting chief of staff in his absence. Nobody had argued with him, as he had known they would not – a chief of psychiatry could pretty well do as he liked in a clinic.

To his surprise, he had felt bad about violating their trust, breaking the rules – and not just because he would lose his career and probably be charged with a felony if he were to be caught. He had pursued a psychiatric career largely out of gratitude for his own long-ago deliverance from guilt and shame, and he regretted the necessity of this dishonesty far more than he had ever regretted the killing of a patient.

While waiting vainly to hear from Plumtree's Omar Salvoy personality on the cellular telephone, Armentrout had printed up a flyer and posted it in various bars and surf shops and parks around the city; REWARD FOR INFORMATION, the flyer had read, followed by a picture of Koot Hoomie Parganas – an old school photo, the same one that had been on billboards in Los Angeles when the boy had dropped out of sight in '92 – and one of Angelica Anthem Elizalde, also from that year, blown up from a newspaper photo, and unfortunately showing her with her mouth open in surprise and her eyes closed. He had printed the absent neurologist's phone number at the bottom, and let the answering machine take all calls to it.

There would have been no point in listing the number of his cellular phone – it rang all day long now, with apparently every idiot ghost in the country wanting to threaten him or weep at him or beg him for money or rides to Mexico. He had to answer it every time, though, because it was the line Salvoy would call in on; and at times during this last couple of days, tired of Long John Beach's insane rambiings, Armentrout had even stayed on the line and had disjointed conversations with the moronic 'ghostings,' as the old writers had referred to the things. They certainly were more gerund than noun.

The woman he was facing now, though, seemed to deserve a noun.

This morning a call had come in on the neurologist's line, and Armentrout had picked it up after hearing a few sentences. It was an old man calling from a pay phone at the Moscone Convention Center, and he was excitedly demanding the reward money. Armentrout had driven over there and paid him fifty dollars, and the man had then told him that the woman and boy on the flyer, and two other men, were living in an upstairs apartment on Lapu Lapu, a block away.

And probably the old informant had been right. When Armentrout had burst into the indicated apartment, wearing his clumsy two-figure manni-kin appliance, the occupants had apparently just fled out the window. Two smoking television sets sat one atop the other in the middle of the room, chanting crazy admonitions at him like Moses' own burning bush. He had shambled past them out onto the balcony before fleeing the room, but, though the two mannikins he was yoked with had seemed to twitch spon-taneously as he had stood out there in the rainy breeze, he had seen no one on the street below.

And so he had shuffled sideways back down the stairs and outside to the car. Fortunately Long John Beach had got tired of waiting in the back seat and had got out to urinate on the bumper – for Armentrout had no sooner opened his mouth to yell at the one-armed old man than he became aware of someone standing only a yard away from Long John Beach and himself.

Armentrout had jumped in huge surprise, the two mannikins strapped to his shoulders twitching in synchronized response, for there had been no one standing there a moment earlier. The impossible newcomer was a lean dark-skinned woman in a ragged ash-colored dress, and her first words to him were in French, which he didn't understand. In the gray daylight her face was shifting like an intercutting projection, from bright-eyed pubescence in one instant to eroded old age in the next. Armentrout knew enough not to meet her eyes.

'*No habla Français*,' he said hoarsely. This is a ghost, he told himself. A real one, standing beside my car on this San Francisco sidewalk. His shirt was suddenly clammy, and the heads and arms of the mannikins yoked on either side of him were jiggling because his hands were shaking on the control levers inside the jackets of their green leisure suits.

'No habla Français,' echoed Long John Beach, stepping forward and shoving his still-swollen nose against the outside ear of the right-hand mannikin, 'today. No grandma's cookies, so de little mon say. Madame has forgotten that we agreed to play in partnership this evening.'

The flickering woman goggled at the four heads in front of her – teeth were appearing and disappearing inside her open mouth – and clearly she was uncertain as to which head was which. Armentrout was careful to look away from her eyes, but as her gaze brushed past him he felt his attention bend with the weight of her unmoored sentience, and he shuddered at the realization that he had come very close to dying in that instant – in a group therapy session once he had seen a patient meet the eyes of a ghostly figure that had been loitering out on the lawn for several days after an in-house suicide, and the ghost figure had disappeared in the same moment that the patient had toppled dead out of his chair.

Now Long John Beach raised the amputated stump of his left arm, and the two Styrofoam mannikin heads began nodding busily. Armentrout wasn't doing it – he could feel the control lever in his nerveless right hand jiggling independently of him.

'If she hollers, let her go,' Long John Beach chanted as the heads bobbed, 'my momma told me to pick this verry one, and out ... goes ... *you*.'

He sneezed at the woman, and her face imploded; and with a disembodied wail of '*Richeee!*' she all at once became nothing more than a cloud of dirty smoke tumbling away down the sidewalk.

'G-good work, John,' stammered Armentrout, spitting helplessly as he spoke. The ghost-woman's final cry had sounded like Armentrout's *mother's* voice – invoked by Long John Beach saying *my momma*? – and he was afraid he was about to wet his pants; well, if he did, he could switch trousers with one of the mannikins, and people would think the Styrofoam-man had wet *his* pants. That would work. But then Armentrout would be wearing lime green pants with a gray tweed jacket.

He assured himself that what he feared was impossible. How *could* his mother's ghost be here? He had left his loving mother in that bathtub in Wichita thirty-three years ago, drunk, *dead* drunk; and then intensive narcohypnosis and several series of ECT had effectively severed that guilt-ghost from him, way back in Kansas. 'John, what do you suppose—'

'We better motate out o' here,' interrupted the one-armed old man. 'That was several girls in one corset. I sneezed a ghost at 'em to knock 'em down, but they'll be back soon, with that ghost glued on now too.'

'Right, right. Jesus.' Armentrout was blinking tears out of his eyes. 'Unstrap me, will you?'

With the deft fingers of his one hand – or maybe, it occurred to Armentrout now, with help from his phantom hand – Long John Beach unbuckled the two-mannikin appliance, and Armentrout shrugged it off and tossed it into the back seat and got in behind the wheel and started the car. After the old man had gone back to the bumper to finish pissing, and had finally got in on the passenger side, Armentrout drove away through the indistinct shadow of the elevated 80 Freeway.

'Let me tell you a parable,' said Long John Beach, rocking in the passenger seat. 'A man heard a knock at his door, and when he opened it he saw a snail on the doorstep. He picked up the snail and threw it as far away as he could. Six months later, he heard a knock at his door again, and when he opened it the snail was on the doorstep, and it looked up at him and said, "What was *that* all about?"'

Armentrout was breathing deeply and concentrating on traffic. 'Don't *you* start getting labile and gamy on me, John,' he said curtly.

He was driving north on Third Street, blinking through the metronomic windshield wipers at the lit office windows of the towers beyond Market Street. Beside him Long John Beach was now belching and gagging unattractively.

'Stop it,' Armentrout said finally, as he made a left turn and accelerated down the wet lanes southeast, toward Twin Peaks and the neurologist's house. 'Unroll the window if you're going to be sick.'

In a flat, sexless voice, Long John Beach said, 'I would be blind with weeping, sick with groans, look pale as primrose with blood-drinking sighs, and all to have the noble king alive.'

Armentrout blinked at the man uneasily. Ghosts were harmless in this form, channelled through the crazy old man, but their arrival often made the car's engine miss – it had stalled almost constantly on the drive up here – and he worried about what the ghosts might overhear and carry back to the idiot bar where they seemed to hang out – 'India,' the old writers had called that raucous but unphysical place. And this particular ghost, this sexless one that seemed to quote Shakespeare all the time, had been coming on through Long John Beach frequently lately, ever since their visit at dawn last Thursday to the beach below Scott Crane's Leucadia estate.

There was something oracular about this ghost's pronouncements, though, and Armentrout found himself impulsively blurting, 'That last cry, from that ghost out on the sidewalk – that might have been my mother.'

'My dangerous cousin,' came the flat voice from Long John Beach's mouth, 'let your mother in: I know she is come to pray for your foul sin.'

'My foul sin?' Armentrout was shaking again, but he forced a derisive laugh. 'And I'm no cousin of yours, ghosting. Don't bother holding a chair for *me*, in your ... moron's tavern.'

'Most rude melancholy, Valerie gives thee place.'

'Shut up!' snapped Armentrout in a voice he couldn't keep from sounding petulant and frightened. 'John, come back on!' The one-armed figure was silent, though, and just stared at the streaks of headlights and neon on the gleaming pavement ahead; so Armentrout picked up the telephone and switched it on, meaning to punch in some null number and talk to whatever random ghost might pick up at the other end.

But someone was already on the line – apparently Armentrout had activated it in the instant before it would have beeped.

'Got no time for your ma nowadays, hey Doc?' came a choppy whisper from the earpiece. 'She's back here crying in her drink, complaining about you sneezing in her face. Shall I put her on?'

The cellular phone was wet against Armentrout's cheek. 'No, please,' he said, whispering himself. He knew this caller must be Omar Salvoy, Plumtree's ingrown father, and Armentrout had no decent defenses against the powerful personality. The tape recording he had made last Wednesday had been magnetically erased by Salvoy's field – even in the Faraday cage inside his desk! – and the vial of Plumtree's blood had come open in Armentrout's briefcase, and soaked the waxed-paper wrapper of a sandwich he'd stowed there for lunch; he couldn't imagine how he could use a dried-out bloody sandwich as a weapon against the Salvoy personality. 'You need my clinic,' he ventured weakly. 'You need my authority for commitment of the boy, and ECT treatment, and maintenance on life-support.'

'I don't need this black dog,' came the whisper. 'When it barks, the whole India bar shakes out of focus. Is this your dog?'

In the passenger seat beside Armentrout, Long John Beach rocked his gray old head back against the headrest and began jerkily *whining* up at the head-liner, in an eerily convincing imitation of a dog.

'*Stop* it!' Armentrout shouted at him, accidentally swerving the BMW in the lane and drawing a honk from a driver alongside.

'Take it slow, Daddy-O,' Salvoy said through the telephone. 'I only got a minute, boyfriend is in the shower, and anyway I'm *not ... seated* properly here, I'm steering from the back seat and can't reach the pedals – *as it were*. Valerie is surely gonna kick me out again any time now. This isn't the Fool's dog, is it? *Get away!* Listen, my girl got away from me hard today, and that's bad because tomorrow is a Dionysus death-day, it's their best day to do the restoration-to-life trick with Scott Crane's body. And my girl Janis tells me that they were talking last week to a ghost black lady in the Bay Area who claimed to have died in like 1903; that can only be this old voodoo-queen ghost known as Mammy Pleasant, who's been screwing with TV receptions around here ever since there's been TVs to screw with. If the Parganas crowd is still in touch with Pleasant, they might be getting some real horse's mouth. Better than half-ass goat head. It'll be by the water, in any case, at dawn – oh shit, stay by the phone.'

With a click, the line went dead. Then, seeming loud in contrast to Salvoy's whispering, a girl's nasal voice from the earpiece said, 'Doctor, I'm eating broken glass and cigarette butts! Is this normal? I eat till I jingle, but I can't fill myself up! Won't you—'

Armentrout flipped the phone's cover shut and slammed it back into its cradle. That last speaker had probably been the obese bipolar girl who had killed herself last week – but who was the flat-voiced one who had spoken through Long John, the *one* who seemed always to quote Shakespeare and who apparently called herself Valerie? Could it be *Plumtree*'s Valerie personality, astrally at large and *spying* on him? Good God, he had told her about his mother!

And the voice on the sidewalk *had* been his mother's – Salvoy had said she'd been in the bar weeping about someone sneezing in her face.

Armentrout sighed deeply, almost at peace with the realization that he would have to perform a seance, and an exorcism, today.

Long John Beach had hunched forward over the dashboard now, sniffing in fast snorts punctuated by explosive exhalations.

It was so convincing that Armentrout almost thought he could smell wet dog fur. Long John had been doing this sort of thing periodically for the last couple of days, sniffing and whining and gnawing the neurologist's leather couch – was the crazy man channeling the ghost of a *dog*?

This isn't the Fools dog, is it?

It occurred to Armentrout that in most tarot-card decks the Fool was a young man in random clothes dancing on a cliff edge, with a dog snapping at his heels; and certainly Long John's crazy speech, his 'word-salad' as psychiatrists referred to skitzy jabbering, did sometimes hint at a vast, contra-rational wisdom.

But surely, the crazy old man couldn't be in touch with one of the primeval tarot archetypes! Especially not *that* one! The Fool was a profoundly *chaotic* influence, inimical to the kind of prolonged unnatural stasis that Armentrout needed to establish for the life-support confinement of the Parganas boy.

Could the old man possibly channel someone – or something – that big?

A Dionysus death-day.

Armentrout remembered the catastrophic ice-cream social at Rosecrans Medical Center last week. Long John Beach had seemed to be channeling – had seemed to be *possessed* by – the spirit of the actual Greek god *Dionysus* on that night. It was hard for Armentrout to avoid believing that Dionysus had somehow been responsible for the earthquake that had permitted Plumtree and that Cochran fellow to escape.

Armentrout thought he knew now why the death of the Fisher King had eliminated all the ghosts in the Southern California area. Murdered in the dead of winter, the slain Fisher King had become compellingly identical to the vegetation-god Dionysus, whose winter mysteries celebrated the god's murder and devourment at the hands of the Titans and his subsequent return from the kingdom of the dead. Being a seasonal deity of death and the underworld – and incarnate this winter in this killed king – the god had taken all the local ghosts away with him, as a possibly unintended entourage, just as the death of summer takes away the vitality of plants, leaving the dried husks behind. In the case of the ghosts, it was their memories and strengths that had lingered behind, while their lethal, vengeful *sentiences* were conveniently gone.

If you like dead leaves, Armentrout thought as he drove, it's good news to have a dead Fisher King; and I like dead leaves. I *sustain myself spiritually* on those dear dead leaves.

But eventually, he thought, if nature follows her cyclical course, Dionysus begins his trek back from the underworld, and a Fisher King again becomes evident; and the plants start to regain their life, and the ghosts – quickly, it seems! – are again resistant, dangerous presences. The god wants to *rake up* the dead leaves, he wants to gather to himself not only the ghosts but all the memories and powers and loves that had accrued to them ... which scraps I don't want to let him have. He wants us to figuratively or literally drink his *pagadebiti* Zinfandel, and let go of every particle of the cherished dead, give them entirely to him ... which I don't want to do.

When Armentrout and Long John Beach had finally got off the 280 Freeway last Thursday, the crazy old man had suddenly and loudly insisted that they take a right turn off of Junipero Serra Boulevard and drive five blocks to a quiet old suburban street that proved to be called Urbano; and in a grassy traffic circle off Urbano stood a gigantic white-painted wooden sundial on a broad flat wheel with Roman numerals from I to XII around the rim of it. After demanding that Armentrout stop the car, Long John Beach had got out and plodded across the street and walked back and forth on the face of the sundial, frowning and peering down around his feet as though trying to read the time on it – but of course the towering gnomon-wedge had been throwing no shadow at all on that overcast day. The passage of time, as far as this inexplicable sundial was concerned, was suspended.

And if Armentrout could succeed in getting the new Fisher King main-tained flatline, brain-dead, on artificial life-support in his clinic, Dionysus's clock would be stopped – at the one special point in the cycle that would permit Armentrout to consume ghosts with *impunity* – with no fear of con-sequences, no need for masks.

The two-mannikin framework shifted and clanked in the back seat now as Armentrout drove fast through the Seventeenth Street intersection, the car's tires hissing on the wet pavement. Market Street was curving to the right as it started up into the dark hills, toward the twin peaks that the Spanish settlers had called *Los Pechos de la Chola*, the breasts of the Indian maiden.

'There was still *time*,' Long John Beach said, in his own voice.

'For what?' asked Armentrout absently as he watched the red brake lights and turn-signal indicators reflecting on the wet asphalt ahead of them. 'You wanted to get something to eat? There's roast beef and bread at the house – though I should feed you in the driveway, the way you toss it around.' He passed a slow-moving Volkswagen and sped up, eager to put more distance between himself and that shifting maternal ghost on Lapu Lapu Street. 'I should feed you Alpo.'

'I mean there *was* still *time*, even though I couldn't see it. It doesn't stop because you have something blocking the light. If we coulda seen in infra-red,' he went on, pronouncing the last word so that it rhymed with *impaired*, 'the shadow woulda been there, I bet you anything.' The BMW was abruptly slowing, because Armentrout's foot had lifted from the gas pedal, but the old man went on, 'Infrared is how they keep patty melts hot, in diners, when the waitress is too busy to bring 'em to you right when they're ready.'

'Stay,' said Armentrout in a voice muted to a conversational tone by the sudden weight of fear; he took a deep breath and made himself finish the sentence, 'out … of … my … mind. God damn you.' But his thoughts were as loud and rapid as his heartbeat: You can't read *my* mind! You can't start channelling *me*! I'm not dead!

Long John Beach shrugged, unperturbed. 'Well, you go around leaving the door open …'

From the backseat came a squeak that could only have been one of the Styrofoam heads shifting against the other as the car rocked with resumed acceleration – but to Armentrout it sounded like a hiccup of suppressed laughter.

Tall Cypresses hid from any neighboring houses the back patio of the neu-rologist's villa on Aquavista Way, and the green slope of the northernmost Twin Peak mounted up right behind the pyrocantha bushes at the far edge of the lawn. After Armentrout had parked the car in the garage and made

Long John Beach carry the two-mannikin appliance out to the patio, he fixed a couple of sandwiches for the one-armed old man and then carefully began scouting up paraphernalia for a seance and exorcism in the back yard.

The neurologist's house didn't afford much for it – Armentrout found some decisive candles in glass chimney shades, and a dusty copper chafing dish no doubt untouched since about 1962, and a bottle of Hennessy XO, which was almost too good to use for plain fuel this way. *Popov vodka* would be more appropriate to his other's—

He hastily drank several mouthfuls of the cognac right from the bottle as he made himself walk around the cement deck of the roofed patio, shakily lighting the candles and setting them down in a six-foot-wide circle. Then he picked up a hibachi and walked around the circle shaking clumped old ash in a line around the perimeter; after he tossed the hibachi out onto the lawn, where it broke like glass, he walked around the circle again, stomping and scuffing the ash so that the line was continuous and unbroken. The chafing dish he set on a wooden chair inside the circle, and, needing both hands to steady the bottle, he poured an inch of brandy into it.

Then for several minutes he just stood and stared at the shallow copper pan while the morning hilltop breeze sighed in the high cypress branches and chilled his damp face. I *can* face her, he told himself firmly; if it's for the last time, and if she's concealed behind the idiot shell-masks of Long John Beach's broken mind, and if I'm armed with the Sun card from the monstrous Lombardy Zeroth deck – and there's brandy to lure her, and then burn her up.

A hitch that might have been a sob or a giggle quivered in his throat.

Will this mean I'll have committed matricide *twice*?

He shivered in the cold wind, and took another big gulp of the brandy to drive away the image of the old face under the surface of the water, the lipsticked mouth opening and shutting, and the remembered cramps in his seventeen-year-old arms.

He looked up at the gray sky, and swallowed still another mouthful and mentally recited the alphabet forward and backward several times.

At last he felt steady enough to go back inside and fetch out from under the bed the two purple velvet boxes.

'Finish your sandwich and get out here,' he told Long John Beach as he carried the boxes through the kitchen to the open back door. 'We've got a ... a call to make.'

When Long John Beach came shambling out of the house, absently rubbing mustard out of his hair and licking his fingers, Armentrout had to tell him several times to go over and stand inside the circle, before he finally got the old man's attention. 'And step *over* the ash line,' he added.

At last the old man was standing inside the circle, blinking and grinning foolishly. Armentrout forced himself to speak in a level tone: 'Okay, John, we're going to do our old trick of having you listen in on a call, right? Only this time, you're going to be the telephone as well as the eavesdropper. 'Kay?'

Long John Beach nodded. 'Ring ring,' he said abruptly, in a loud falsetto.

Armentrout blinked at him uncertainly. Could this be an *incoming* call? But this couldn't start *yet*, he hadn't lit the brandy yet! 'Uh, who is this, please?' he asked trying to sound stern so that the old man wouldn't laugh at him if he'd just been clowning around and this *wasn't* a real call.

'Dwayne,' said Long John Beach.

Armentrout tried to remember any patient who had ever had that name. 'Dwayne?' he said. 'I'm sorry – Dwayne who?'

'Dwayne the tub, I'm dwowning!'

Armentrout reeled back, gasping. It wasn't his mother's voice, but it had to be a sort of relayed thought from her ghost.

'J-John,' he said too loudly, fumbling in his pockets for a match or a lighter, 'I want you to light the brandy – light the stuff in that pan there.'

He found a matchbook and tossed it into the circle, then fell to his knees on the wet grass beside one of the purple velvet boxes. I can't *shoot* him, he thought, it wouldn't stop her, she's just passing through Long John's train-station head.

He flipped open the other box and spilled the oversized cards out onto the grass, squinting as he pawed through them until he found the Sun card.

When he looked up, Long John Beach had lifted the copper chafing-dish pan in his one hand and was sniffing it. And now it *was* Armentrout's mother's voice that spoke from the old man's mouth: '*Oh, how I wish I could shut up like a telescope!*'

'Put that down,' Armentrout wailed.

The pan tipped up toward the old man's mouth.

'Mm—' Armentrout choked on the word *mom,* and had to make do with just shouting, 'Don't drink that! John! Kick out that woman's ghost for a minute and listen to me!'

Suddenly, from the gate by the garage, a man's voice called, 'Dr. Armentrout?'

'Get out of here!' Armentrout yelled back, struggling to his feet. 'This is private property!'

But the gate clanged and swung open, and it was the young intern from Rosecrans Medical Center, Philip Muir, who stepped out onto the backyard grass. He didn't have his white coat on, but he was wearing a long-sleeved white shirt and a tie. 'John!' he exclaimed, noticing the one-armed old man standing in the ash circle on the patio. Long John Beach was noisily drinking the brandy now, and slopping a lot of it into the white whiskers that bristled on his cheeks and neck these days. Muir turned to Armentrout. 'He's supposed to be at Pacifica.'

'I – have him out on a day pass,' Armentrout panted. 'This is none of your—'

'*Richie!*' called Armentrout's mother's voice from Long John Beach's throat, bubbling around the last gulp of the brandy. '*Can you hear me under water? I've got a* beard! *Did they have to give me ...* hormones? *Pull the plug, darling, and let me breathe! Where's some more of this whiskey?*'

Muir sniffed sharply. 'And you're giving him whiskey? Doctor, I—'

'It's not whiskey,' babbled Armentrout, 'it's brandy, she doesn't know the difference—'

Muir was frowning and shaking his head. '"She"? What's the matter with you? Have you got Plumtree and Cochran up here too? I know Cochran is in the area, he telephoned the vineyard he works at—'

Armentrout interrupted him to call out, 'I'll get you more liquor in a moment! just – *wait* there!'

But Long John Beach blinked at him and spat. 'I was never a liquor man,' he said. 'I just ate smokes.'

Armentrout sighed deeply and sank down cross-legged beside the two velvet boxes. At least his mother was gone, for now. But Muir surely intended to report this, and investigate Beach's transfer, and end Armentrout's career. 'Come over here, Philip,' he said huskily, lifting the lid of the box that contained the derringer. 'I think I can show you something that will explain all of this.'

'It's not me you need to be explaining things to. Why on earth did you give Plumtree ECT? What the hell happened during the ice-cream social last Wednesday? Mr. Regushi swallowed his *tongue!*'

Armentrout again got wearily to his feet, one hand holding the box and the other gripping the hidden derringer 'Just look at this, Philip, and you'll understand.'

Muir angrily stepped forward across the grass. 'I can't imagine what it could be.'

'I guess it's whatever you've made it.'

The flat, hollow boom of the .410 shot-shell was muffled by the cypresses and the hillside.

CHAPTER SEVENTEEN

TROILUS: What offends you, lady?
CRESSIDA: Sir, mine own company.
TROILUS: You cannot shun yourself.
CRESSIDA: Let me go and try.

　　　　　　—William Shakespeare, *Troilus and Cressida*

'Cochran said he's been walking and taking the cable cars to get down here into Chinatown,' said Archimedes Mavranos. 'Maybe the cable cars were full today, and he's gotta hike the whole way.'

Shadows from a slow ceiling fan far overhead swept rhythmically over the red Formica tabletop.

'He might have sold us out,' said Kootie. 'Maybe bad guys are just about to come busting in here.' He had asked for a straw with his Coke, and now he glanced over his shoulder; the bartender was looking at the television in the corner above the bar so Kootie stuck his straw into Angelica's glass of Chardonnay and took a sip of it. 'It's sacramental,' he explained to his foster-mother when she frowned at him. 'The king needs a sip at noon, especially if bad guys are due.'

'I don't need Coke in my wine,' Angelica said.

'If bad guys want to open a hand in a no-limit game like this,' said Mavranos with more confidence than he felt, touching the front of his denim jacket and glancing at Angelica's purse, 'they're liable to see some powerful raises.'

Pete Sullivan was sitting beside Angelica at the table by the stairs that led down to the rest rooms, and he was deftly, one-handed, cartwheeling a cigarette over the backs of the knuckles of his right hand; it had been unlit, fresh from the pack, when he'd started, but the tip was glowing when he flipped it into the air off his last knuckle and caught it by the filter in his lips.

'Wow,' said Mavranos.

'Yeah, wow,' agreed Pete irritably as he puffed smoke from the cigarette. 'Magic tricks. But if I try to hold a *weapon*, my hands are no good at all. Even a pair of scissors I drop, if I think about stabbing somebody.' He wiggled his fingers. 'Houdini made sure his mask wouldn't be capable of hurting anybody.'

Kootie grinned wanly. 'He can't even play video games,' the boy told Mavranos. 'The hands think he's really trying to shoot down enemy pilots.'

Mavranos opened his mouth to say something, then focussed past Kootie toward the front door of the bar. 'Heads up,' he said.

Sid Cochran had just stumbled in from the street, and Mavranos felt his face tighten in a smile to see the blond Plumtree woman lurching along right behind him.

Mavranos pushed his chair back and stood up. 'I was afraid we weren't ever going to see you again, ma'am,' he said to Plumtree.

Plumtree's hair was wet, and Mavranos thought she looked like someone going through heroin withdrawal as she collapsed into the chair beside Kootie. There were cuts under her chin and at one corner of her mouth, and her face had a puffy, bruised look. 'Shove it, man,' she said hoarsely. 'I'm an accessory to a murder today. More than anything else in the world, I want *not* to be. Soon, please God.'

'A murder *today*?' asked Kootie.

Plumtree closed her eyes. 'No. I'm *still*, today, an accessory to Scott Crane's murder. Is what I meant. But tomorrow I might not be.'

'Tomorrow you might not be,' Mavranos agreed.

'She insisted on coming,' said Cochran nervously as he took the chair opposite her, next to Pete Sullivan. 'We're laying our cards on the table here, but we can see yours too. We saw your truck in the Portsmouth Square parking structure, and saw what had to be your, your *dead* guy under a tarp in the back of it. If we'd wanted to screw this up, we'd have put a bullet through Crane's head right then.'

Plumtree was blinking around now at the gold-painted Chinese bas-reliefs high up on the walls, and she squinted at a yard-wide, decorated Chinese paper lantern hanging from a string above the bar. An old Shell No-Pest Strip dangled from the tassel at the bottom of the lantern.

'Can I get a drink in this opium den?' she asked. 'What is all this shit? The entrance to this place looks like a cave.'

Mavranos could smell bourbon on her breath right across the table. 'It's named after a famous eighth-century Chinese poet,' he told her. 'The pictures painted on that lantern are scenes from his life.'

'What'd he do to earn the No-Pest Strip?' she asked. 'Somebody get me a Bud, hey?'

I guess there's no need for her to be sober, thought Mavranos; he shrugged and leaned over to pick up his own beer glass, which was empty.

'I'll have a Singapore Sling,' Cochran said. He glanced at Plumtree. 'They make a good Singapore Sling here.'

'Said the Connecticut Pansy,' remarked Plumtree absently. 'Did flies kill him?' she asked Mavranos. 'Your eight-cent poet, I mean – that yellow plastic thing is to kill flies, if you didn't know.'

'*Las moscas*,' said Cochran, and Mavranos realized that he wasn't totally sober either. 'That's what they call flies at a vineyard. They can get into the crush, if you do it after sunup – the Mexican grape-pickers think flies will carry little ghosts into the fermenting must, make you dizzy and give you funny dreams when you drink the wine, later. I suppose you might die of it, if enough ghosts had got into the wine.'

'I'm sure each of us has a funny story about flies,' said Mavranos patiently, 'but right now we've got more important ... *issues at hand*.' He turned away toward the bar, then paused and looked back at Plumtree. 'The poet is supposed to have drowned – the story is he fell out of a boat, drunk, in the middle of the night, reaching for the reflection of the moon in the water.'

'Rah rah rah,' said Plumtree.

When Mavranos got back to the table with the three drinks and sat down, Plumtree greedily took the glass he pushed across to her and drank half of it in one long, wincing sip. 'I should have told you to get two,' she said breathlessly when she had clanked the glass back down. 'Do you people have a set of handcuffs? My father took over control of my body three days ago, and I just this morning got free of him; and I feel like he spent the whole time body-surfing in avalanches. But he might come back on at any time.' She opened her mouth and clicked her teeth like a monkey.

Mavranos stared at her. We should just ditch these two losers, he thought. Get back to the truck now, and just drive away.

'No, Arky,' said Angelica sharply. She was glaring at him. '*She's* the one that's going to do the ... that's going to let Crane assume her body.'

Plumtree glanced at their faces. 'Well, *yeah*. What, were you—' Her bloodshot eyes widened in sudden comprehension. 'My God, you were gonna have the *kid* do it! Shit, did you people even consider the possib-lil – possibility that Crane might not be able to get back *into* his old body, afterward? – that he might have to *keep* the one he takes for this?'

'We did consider that,' said Kootie. 'I did consider that. But we're *all* gonna get *killed* if this doesn't get settled. Our TV burned up today, and – well, you had to be there. And,' he added with a scared glance at Mavranos, 'I'm taking Arky's word that Crane won't keep my body, if he can help it at all.'

'Well, he won't get a chance,' Plumtree told him with a haggard but possibly kindly meant smile. '*I'm* going to do it.'

'Damn right,' said Angelica.

'Kootie's correct,' said Mavranos, 'in saying that we've got to settle this situation – we've got to collapse this probability wave, let the daylight into Schrodinger's shitty cat box. As long as there's no real king working, we're all exposed – hell, *spotlighted* – and pretty near totally defenseless. You're staying at a motel or something?'

'Ye-es,' said Cochran cautiously.

'Well congratulations, you now have four houseguests. I hope the management won't mind. We're gonna do this thing tomorrow at dawn, it looks like, this *restoration-to-life*, so there's no point in us getting a different room at the same motel. We just this morning got rousted out of our place by some kind of walking department-store dummies, and—'

Cochran choked on his Singapore Sling. 'Did they,' he said after he'd wiped his mouth redly on his sleeve, 'move in synch, like they were puppets working off the same strings?'

'They did,' said Mavranos stolidly. 'And suddenly I don't like the idea of Scott's body sitting out there in the truck, you know? Let's finish up here, and get to your motel. With you and me and Pete, we should be able to get Scott into the motel room. And then we've got some preparations to make.'

Kootie nodded, and Angelica scowled at him.

'Finish every drop of your drinks,' said Plumtree with a ghastly, exhausted gaiety, 'there's poor people sober in China.'

Chinese New Year was still two weeks off, but Asian boys on ribbon-decked bicycles tossed strings of lit firecrackers ahead of the six of them, as they walked south on the Grant Street sidewalk under the red-and-gold pagoda-roofed buildings, so that their ears rang with the staccato popping, and their noses burned with the barbecued-chicken smell of gunpowder, and Kootie was treading on fragments of red paper that crumpled and darkened on the wet pavement underfoot like fallen rose petals; and when they trudged across the wet grass of Portsmouth Square, the hoboes and winos hobbled out of their path and seemed to bow, or at least nod, as they passed.

And when they had piled into the two vehicles – Plumtree riding in the front seat of Mavranos's truck, and Pete riding in the Granada with Cochran, for mutual trust as much as to make sure both parties knew the way to the Star Motel – crows and mockingbirds swooped over them as the old car and truck labored up Van Ness, the darting birds seeming to be fighting in the gray sky.

At Lombard Street at the top of Russian Hill, where a right turn would have led them down the ornamental, brick-paved 'crookedest street in the world,' they turned left instead, and drove down the straight lanes between bars and car-repair shops and liquor stores and motels, and after three blocks both vehicles ponderously turned left up the driveway into the Star Motel parking lot.

When they'd parked and all climbed out onto the asphalt, Angelica and Plumtree crowded around the tailgate of Mavranos's dusty red truck to block the view as Pete and Cochran and Mavranos slid Scott Crane's body out from beneath the tarpaulin. The body was dressed now in jeans and a white shirt, though with no shoes or socks, and Cochran tried not to look at the bloody bandage knotted around the thigh, over the denim.

The body was limp, not stiff, but they managed to tilt it into an upright posture and march it right past the ice and Coke machines and up the stairs to Cochran's room; Plumtree had got her key out and scrambled ahead of them, and had got the door open by the time they had carried the dead king to the room.

They flopped Scott Crane down onto the bed that didn't have Cochran's homemade Ouija board on it, and Mavranos straightened the body's arms and legs and unlooped the graying beard from the sawn-off stump of spear that stood up from the throat. The room was still humid from Plumtree's and Cochran's showers this morning, and smelled like old salami and unfresh clothing.

'Just like Charlton Heston in *El Cid*,' said Kootie bravely. 'Dead, but leading the army.'

'He is d-damn cold,' panted Cochran as he stood back and flapped his cramping hands. His heart was pounding more than the couple of minutes of effort could justify, and he was shivering with irrational horror at having touched the dead man again. 'How can you – *think* he—' His voice almost broke, and he turned toward the TV set and just breathed deeply.

'Your place – could use some airing,' said Angelica, smoothly calling everyone's attention away from his momentary loss of control. 'Kootie, see if you can't open the windows, while I go back down to the truck for our witchy supplies.'

'Don't blame me for this pigpen,' said Plumtree, 'I been away.'

'Witchy supplies,' put in Cochran in a carefully neutral tone. He gave Plumtree a resentful glance, very aware of the cassette tape in his shirt pocket and the French-language missal in the bedside table drawer. Kootie had ducked under the curtains and was noisily yanking at the aluminum-framed window.

Mavranos had his hands in the pockets of his denim jacket as he stared at Cochran. 'I got to ask you to give me your gun,' he said. 'I almost apologize, since we're all really on the same side here and my crowd is taking over your place this way, for tonight – but Miss Plumtree said herself that her dad came on three days ago and she just this morning came back to herself; and you appear to have a ... loyalty to her. I can't justify—'

'Sure,' said Cochran, speaking levelly to conceal his reflexive anger. Slowly, he reached around to the back of his belt and tugged the holster clip free. Then he tossed the suede-sheathed gun onto the bathroom-side bed.

Mavranos leaned forward to pick it up with his left hand, keeping his right in his jacket pocket. 'Thanks,' he said gruffly. 'If we run into outside trouble, I'll give it back to you.'

Cochran just nodded. I can see his point, he insisted to himself. I'd do the same, in his place.

Angelica came tromping back upstairs lugging a green canvas knapsack, and Cochran had to move his NADA sign and papers as she began unpacking its contents onto the bedspread.

She lifted out some springy shrub branches that smelled vaguely of eucalyptus, held together by a rubber band. 'Myrtle,' she said. 'Sacred to Dionysus, the books say. And a bottle of wine for us all to drink from, to show him respect.'

With shaky fingers Cochran took from her the bottle she had dug out of the knapsack. It was, he saw, a Kenwood Vineyards 1975 Cabernet Sauvignon, and the stylized picture at the top of the label was of a skeleton reclining on a grassy hillside.

Cochran's ears seemed to be ringing with a wail that he was afraid he might actually give voice to, and for the moment he had forgotten the dead king and his confiscated gun. 'This – was never released,' he said, making himself speak slowly. 'This label, I mean, with this picture on it. I remember hearing about it. David Goines originally did one of a nude woman on the hill, and the BATF rejected it because they said it was indecent, so he did this one of the same woman as a skeleton; and they rejected *it* because of fetal alcohol syndrome or something. Finally Goines did one of just the hillside, and that got okayed, and Kenwood printed it.' He looked up into Angelica's concerned gaze, and let himself relax a little. 'But this was never released, this label was never even printed! – except, I guess, for this one. Where the hell did you find it? And why did you get *it*? I mean, it's a twenty-year-old Cab! There must have been cheaper ones.'

Angelica opened her mouth, then closed it. 'I,' she said finally, 'don't remember what it cost. But I got change back from a twenty, and we got ice and some canned green beans in the same purchase, I remember. This was the only fancy wine they had, at this little place called Liquor Heaven in the Soma neighborhood – Arky, you drove us there and waited in the truck, remember? – the only other wine was one of those bum's-rush specials, Hair-of-the-Dog or some name like that.'

Mavranos had been watching Plumtree and Cochran, but now he slowly turned to Angelica. '... Bitin Dog?' he asked.

Cochran sat down on the bed heedlessly crushing Angelica's myrtle branches and he was remembering the Mondard figure in the mirror in the vision he'd had last week in Solville. 'That's how it looks in a reflection,' he said dizzily. 'You must have been in Looking-Glass Land. The right-way name is something like *pagadebiti*.'

'Get your butt off the boughs of holly,' Plumtree told him.

'No,' said Mavranos, 'stay where you are, Dionysus probably likes it a bit crushed, like cats do catnip. Miss Plumtree, you sit beside him. You got your *maquina*, Angelica?'

Angelica touched the untucked tail of her blouse. 'Yes, Arky,' she sighed.

'Stand over here and keep your hand on it, and watch those two. Pete and I gotta go to the truck, drag up some of our *scientific apparatus*, more of our *high-tech defensive hardware*.'

Kootie sniffed the air after Arky and his foster-dad had shuffled outside and pulled the door closed behind them. He sensed at least a couple of fragmentary personalities buzzing clumsily around the room.

'The king's body is drawing ghosts,' he told his foster-mom. 'A couple got in when Arky opened the door just now.' He sniffed again. 'Just little broken-off bits, probably shells thrown off of somebody who didn't even die of it.'

Kootie knew that people, especially very neurotic people whose personalities spun in wide and perturbed orbits, often threw ghost-shells in moments of stressfully strong emotion. Kootie could feel the insistent one-note resonance of these, and his hands were shaky and he wasn't able to take a deep breath.

He found himself staring at Janis Plumtree's loose blouse and tight jeans, and he snorted and shook his head to dispel the induced lust. Easy to guess what the unknown source-person was up to, he thought, when he shed *these* ... psychic snake-skins! And the man must have been left bewildered and abruptly out-of-the-mood after they'd broken away.

The vibrations of the ghost fragments did have a strongly male cast; Kootie wondered what his own response would have been if the source-person had been a woman – would he have found himself looking at ... at *Cochran*? – or would he have been so out-of-phase with them that he wouldn't have sensed their presence at all?

'I'm okay,' he told Angelica, who had taken her eyes off Cochran and Plumtree long enough to give Kootie a raised eyebrow. 'I hope Arky's bringing up the St. Michael and High John the Conqueror sprays.'

'I packed 'em,' she said.

In spite of himself, Kootie was staring at Plumtree again. She was clearly nervously excited – she had pulled a little order pad out of her pocket and was flipping through the pages, nodding and mumbling to herself.

She looked up and caught his gaze, and her sudden smile made his heart thump. 'Tomorrow,' she said through her teeth, 'no matter what it may cost me, I *won't* be a murderer anymore!'

Her companion seemed less happy about the idea – Cochran was frowning as he shook a cigarette out of a pack and flipped open a book of matches. Probably he's worried that this attempt tomorrow will work the way she thinks it will, Kootie thought, and his girlfriend's body will suddenly have a fifty-two-year-old *man* in it. Talk about out-of-phase!

Kootie wasn't aware of the ghost fragments now – probably his lustful response had blunted his latent Fisher King ability to sense them. As if I took a long sniff of a rare hamburger that was cooked in an iron pan, he thought ruefully, or spent the day at the top of a modern high-rise building, far up away from the ground, or gargled with whiskey on a Friday in Lent.

Cochran struck a match – and the matchbook flared in a gout of flame, and Cochran had dropped it and was stamping it out on the carpet.

Cochran and Plumtree both exclaimed 'Son of a bitch!' and Plumtree went on to add, 'You clumsy stupid shit!'

But Kootie had caught a whiff of cooked bacon on the stale, humid air, and he said 'I think you burned up the ghosts, Mr. Cochran. Toss me the matches, would you?'

Cochran bent over, pried the matchbook from the carpet, and tossed it to Kootie who juggled the hot thing around in the palm of his hand to look at it.

The moment of flame had not obliterated the letters inked onto each match. Kootie read the words carefully, then looked up at Cochran. 'The match you lit has "*tenebis*" written on it, doesn't it?'

Cochran bent down again and brushed his hand over the carpet until he had found the match he had struck; then he straightened and stared at it.

'"*Tenebis*,"' Cochran read. He looked at Kootie. 'You've seen this inscription before? It's Latin, right?'

'I suppose it's Latin,' Kootie said. 'I've never seen it before, but I can tell what the missing word must be – 'cause it's a palindrome. See?' He tossed the matchbook back to Cochran. 'The letters read the same backward as forward.'

'On a matchbook,' said Angelica with a wry smile. 'That's like the people who letter *LA. Cigar – Too Tragical* around chimneys and frying pans – or gun muzzles,' she added, touching the grip of the automatic in her belt. 'Ghosts are drawn to palindromes, and these tricks burn 'em up – dispel 'em into the open air, unlike in the coal of a cigarette, which sends their broken-up constituent pieces straight into your lungs, for a nasty predatory high. The palindrome torchers send them safely on past India.'

This seemed to jar Cochran. 'What exactly the hell do you people mean by "India"?' he asked.

A measured thumping sounded at the motel-room door, and Kootie could hear Arky Mavranos impatiently call something from outside

'Peek out before you unlock it,' Angelica said as Kootie stepped toward the door.

'Right, Ma.' Kootie peered out through the lens, then said, 'It's just them,' as he snapped back the bolt and pulled the door open.

Mavranos came shuffling in carrying one of his spare truck batteries in both hands; Pete Sullivan followed, carrying a stack of boxes balanced on top of the ice chest. An electric plug dangled from one of the boxes.

'On the table by the window,' said Mavranos to Pete. 'Hook up the charger to the battery, a quick charge on the ten-amp setting – if it's not too dead you might have time to drag one of the others up here and charge it too.'

'What's India?' insisted Cochran.

'Uh – ghosthood,' said Angelica, frowning at the boxes Pete was putting down. Then she glanced at Cochran and apparently noted the man's anxious squint. 'In Shakespeare's time,' she went on patiently, '*India* was sorcerously hip slang for a sort of overlap place, a halfway house between Earth and Heaven-or-Hell. It's the antechamber to Dionysus's domain – the god was supposed to have come to Thebes by way of Phrygia from northern India, around Pakistan.'

'*Pakijaper came no more,*' sang Plumtree, to a bit of the tune of 'Puff the Magic Dragon.'

Mavranos barked out two syllables of a laugh at that, wiping black dust off his hands. 'I'm gonna—' he began.

'So what would it mean,' Cochran interrupted shakily, 'to say ... "Her bed is India, there she lies, a pearl"?'

Angelica was frowning at him with Kootie thought, puzzled sympathy. 'That's a line from *Troilus and Cressida*,' Angelica said. 'It would mean "she" is in that India ; space – a ghost associating with a living person, or vice versa. The overlap, see? And the "pearl" reference would probably mean she's accreting stuff from the other category – physical solidity, if she was a ghost to start with, or ghosts, if she was a living person. The Elizabethan slang for ghosts was "ghostings" – by way of folk etymology from "coastings," meaning coastlines, outlines, silhouettes; traced replicas – and later in the play—'

'I'm gonna go trace the coastline here,' said Mavranos, 'the north coast from Fort Point by the bridge to where those three old ships are moored at the Hyde Street Pier: the area where the wild mint used to grow, that gave the city its original name of Yerba Buena. I've got a *piedra iman*, and a—'

'A *magnet*?' said Angelica, turning toward Mavranos. 'But that's only good for drawing *ghosts*, Arky, you don't want Crane's *ghost*—'

'Why aren't you gonna check west of the bridge?' demanded Plumtree. 'The Sutro Baths ruins is where we saw his naked ghost, last week, and that's west of the bridge. I think you should—'

'But you don't *want* his ghost—' Angelica went on and Kootie was interrupting too: 'We should see what the old black lady has to say about it—'

Arky had lifted one of Angelica's weather-beaten stuffed toy pigs out of the box Pete had carried in, and now he shoved a C battery into the compartment in its rear end; and the pig's sudden harsh mechanical burping silenced the two women and Kootie.

After three noisy seconds Mavranos pulled the battery out, and the croaking stopped. 'I'm not gonna look for his ghost,' he said clearly, 'nor where we saw his ghost. What I want to do first is search around the area where your old black lady's banker friend drowned, back in 1875; that's near the Hyde Pier. And I'm gonna use the magnet *along with a magnetic compass* – I figure that when the compass needle ignores both the magnet and the real magnetic north pole, I'll have found the spot ; where we can yank Scott back here from the far side of India. Wherever the spot is, it's got to be a regular *black hole* for plain-old ghosts, and they've got to add up to a pre-emptive magnetic charge – especially now, on the eve of Dionysus's day.' He bared his teeth in a smile. '*Okay?*'

'Just asking,' said Angelica.

'I have no idea how long this'll take,' Mavranos went on. 'I'm gonna walk it, and leave you people the truck. If I get no readings at all, I'll just come back here, well before dawn, and we can do the restoration-to-life right at the spot where the banker jumped in.' He swivelled an unreadable stare from Kootie to Angelica to Plumtree. 'You all are gonna want to figure out your tactics. Don't go out – order a pizza delivered, and if you need beers or something, send Pete. Angelica,' he added, with a nod toward where Cochran and Plumtree sat on the bed, 'if they try anything at all, don't you hesitate to—'

'I know,' said Angelica. 'Shoot our hosts.'

'Right,' agreed Mavranos. He slapped the pocket of his denim jacket and nodded at the solid angularity of his revolver. Then he was out the door, and the clump-clop of his boots was receding down the stairs.

'What happens,' asked Plumtree bleakly, 'if you untie that bandage from around Crane's leg?'

'He bleeds,' said Angelica. 'He's got no pulse, but fresh blood leaks out of him.'

'Not forever,' Plumtree said. 'Where we stabbed him ... his throat stopped bleeding after a while, right? I mean, I doubt they tied a tourniquet around his neck, then." She sighed hitchingly, and ran her fingers through her disordered hair. Her lips were turned down sharply at the corners. 'Tilt a few good slugs of his blood into that empty Wild Turkey bottle. Tomorrow I'll – probably have to—' Her eyes widened in evident surprise and her face went pale. 'Scant! Why am I—'

Plumtree stood up and wobbled to the bathroom then, barely managing to slam the door behind her before Kootie heard her being rackingly sick in there.

'Who's in the mood for a pizza?' he asked brightly.

'Hush,' said Angelica quietly. She opened her mouth as if to say more, then just repeated, 'Hush.'

*

At sunset the entirely discorporate spirit of Scott Crane stood on a cliff over a sea, and it was no longer possible for him to overlook his sin of omission. The call of the one neglected tarot archetype could no longer be drowned out in the busy distractions of life. It had been beckoning during three winters – whispering from six feet under in the agitation of the lice that blighted the vineyards, wheezing in the fevered lungs of Crane's young children in the winter months, and roaring like a bull in the cloven earth under Northridge a year ago tomorrow. And on New Year's Day of this year it had come to his house.

It had worn many faces – that of Crane's first wife, and that of his adopted father, and a hundred others; but today it wore the face of the fat man he had shot to death in the desert outside Las Vegas in 1990. A bargain had been made, and his part had not been fully paid.

CHAPTER EIGHTEEN

'Afraid?'

'It's plain enough, I should think, why he may be. It's a dreadful re-membrance. Besides that, his loss of himself grew out of it. Not know-ing how he lost himself, or how he recovered himself, he may never feel certain of not losing himself again. That alone wouldn't make the subject pleasant, I should think.'

—Charles Dickens, *Tale of Two Cities*

The sky beyond the curtains had been dark for hours, and the clock on the bedside table read 10:30, when the traditional Solville knock sounded on the door: *rap-rap-rap, rap*, in the rhythm of the Rolling Stones' 'Under My Thumb.'

Angelica was sitting on the carpet in front of the television, and she put down her jar of pennies. 'Peek out anyway,' she told Kootie as she straight-ened her legs and stood up. It was a relief to be able to look away from the grotesque, distressing images on the screen.

Kootie hurried to the door and peered out through the lens. 'It's him,' he said as he unchained the door, 'alone.' He pulled the door open.

Mavranos brought in with him the smells of crushed grass and cold pier pilings, and Angelica thought she could see the stale room air eddy behind him as he strode to the ice chest and crouched to lift out a wet can of Coors.

'I found our place,' Mavranos said shortly, after popping the top and taking a deep sip. 'It's hardly more than walking distance from here. I found it at sunset, but I've spent all this time making sure I wasn't followed back here. There was a lot of local hippies dressed up as druids there – or druids dressed as hippies? – and I kept on *seeing* them after I left the place.'

He finished the can and crouched again to get another. 'I'd see 'em on *rooftops*, and in passing *buses*, but each of 'em was looking at *me*, I swear, with no expressions at all on their faces, under the hoods. I finally lost 'em by buying a – hah! – a Jiminy Cricket latex rubber mask in Chinatown, and then *wearing* it while I rode the cable cars Washington-to-Mason-to-Jackson-to-Hyde in a windshield circle for about an hour.' He glanced at Angelica. '"Windshield" – the olden-times word was "widdershins."' He twirled a finger in the air. 'It means moving counterclockwise, to elude magical pursuit.'

'I know what widdershins is,' said Angelica. '*Contra las manecillas.* So where is this place? Is it where the banker drowned?'

'No, it's – well, you'll see it tomorrow at dawn. It's out at the end of the peninsula at the Small Craft Harbor, on the grounds of some yacht club; I had to step over a "No Admittance" sign on a chain. It looks like an old ruined Greek or Roman temple. I asked about it at the yacht club – apparently the city planners had a whole lot of cemetery marble left over after they cleared out all the graveyards in the Richmond District in the thirties, transplanted the graves south to Colma, and so somebody set up this pile of ... steps and seats and pillars and patchwork stone pavements ... out at the end of the peninsula. Very windy and cold – and the compass needle had no time for my magnet or the north pole; I swear I could feel that compass twisting in my hand, so the needle could point *straight down.*'

His eyes moved past Angelica to the body on the bed, and when he gasped and darted a glance toward the Plumtree woman, Angelica knew he had seen the fresh blood smeared on Scott Crane's jeans.

'She go messin' with him?' Mavranos demanded. 'Did her dad, I mean?'

Angelica took hold of his arm. 'No, Arky. We decanted some of Crane's blood into a bottle. We think she'll have to—'

'Phlebotomy,' put in Kootie.

'Right,' Angelica agreed nervously; 'it looks like she'll probably have to, to *drink* some of Crane's blood, to summon Crane, to draw him into her body tomorrow.'

Mavranos's nostrils widened in evident distaste at the thought, and Angelica sympathetically remembered how the poor Janis personality had found herself suddenly in a body that was convulsing with nausea, after the Cody personality had first proposed the idea and then fled.

Mavranos glared around the room and ended up staring at the television, which for the last five minutes had been insistently showing some French-language hardcore pornographic movie.

'So you decided to distract yourself with some T-and-A,' he said sourly. 'You psychiatrists figure this is wholesome entertainment for fourteen-year-old boys, do you?'

'T and ... ?' echoed Angelica. 'Oh, tits and ass, right? Sorry – to me T-and-A has always been tonsillectomy-and-adenoidectomy.' With a shaky hand she brushed a damp strand of hair back from her forehead. 'No, damn it, we've been trying to get this *off* the screen – we had the old black lady, for a few seconds – but now shaking the pennies and even pushing the buttons on the set won't shift us from this channel.' She glanced at Kootie, who was studiously looking away from the screen but who had clearly been upset – even haunted, she thought – when the desperate, contorting figures had first appeared on the screen.

From far away out in the chilly darkness came the metronomic two-second moan of a foghorn.

'I been hearing that all day, seems like,' Mavranos said absently, 'it's the horn on the south pier of the Golden Gate Bridge. Two seconds every twenty seconds.' He sat down on the carpet and put down his beer can so that he could rub his eyes. 'Okay,' he said with a windy sigh, 'so did the old black lady have anything useful to say? She's supposed to be our *intecessor*, and she's been awful scarce.'

'She,' Angelica began; then, 'No,' she said. I'll tell you later, Arky, she thought. 'Cochran and Plumtree have been working his homemade Ouija board, though, and—'

But Kootie spoke. 'She said, "The debt-payer is always a virgin, and must go to India still a virgin."'

Angelica could feel her face go slack with exhaustion; she was certain that this was a verbatim recollection of the old woman's words. Then she made herself raise her head and put on a quizzical expression. 'Yes,' she said briskly, 'that's what she said.' Oh, it won't be you, Kootie, she thought. I won't *let* it be you, don't worry. Oh, why the hell are we even—

'*Damn* this garbage!' she burst out, and she sprang to the wall and yanked the television's plug right out of the wall socket.

And then she just blinked from the cord in her hand to the television screen, on which the sweaty bodies still luminously strained and gasped. Her chest went suddenly hollow and cold a full second before she was sure she had pulled out the right plug.

Mavranos had got to his feet and stared at the wall behind the dresser the television sat on, and now he even waved his hand across the back of the set as through cerifying a magic trick.

'Lord,' he said softly, 'how I do hate impossible things. Pete, let's carry this abomination down to the truck, and—'

But at that moment the screen went mercifully dark at last.

'Bedtime for the satyrs and nymphs,' Mavranos said. 'And for us too, I think.' He looked toward Plumtree and Cochran. 'What did the Ouija board say?'

Plumtree shifted on the bed. 'We asked to talk to anyone who knew about this ... situation of ours, and – well, you tell him, Scant.'

Cochran reached behind Plumtree to pick up one of the many sheets of Star Motel stationery. '"Canst thou remember a time before we came unto this cell?"' he read. '"I do not think thou canst, for then thou wast not out three years old."'

'I do think that's your subconscious speaking,' Angelica said to Plumtree. 'Or the core-child, the traumatized personality: the poisoned comatose girl in your Snow White scenario, or the battered lady bus driver in Cody's *Dirty Harry* version.' Angelica looked at Mavranos and shrugged. 'God knows why it's in that Shakespearean language Pete's pretty sure it's from *The Tempest*, the exiled king Prospero talking to his daughter Miranda.'

'Valorie always talks that way,' said Cochran. 'She's the oldest personality, and I think she may be—' He hesitated, and then said, 'I think she may be the core-child.'

You were going to say *dead*, weren't you? thought Angelica. You were right to keep that idea from her, whether or not it's true.

Quickly, so as not to let Plumtree think about Cochran's momentary hesitation Angelica asked him, 'Why does Janis call you Scant?'

Cochran glanced at the back of his right hand and laughed uncomfortably. 'Oh, it's a childhood nickname. I grew up in the wine country, doing odd jobs around the vineyards, and when I was ten I was in a cellar when one of the support beams broke under a cask of Zinfandel, and I automatically stepped forward and tried to hold it up. It broke my leg. The support beams are called scantlings, and the cellarmen told me I was trying to be a proxy scantling.'

'*Atlas* would have been a good name, too,' remarked Kootie.

'Or *Nitwit*,' said Mavranos, stepping away from the television. 'Angelica, you and Miss Plumtree can sleep on the Ouija-board bed by the bathroom after you clear the pizza boxes off it, with her on the bathroom side, away from Crane's body; and we'll tie a couple of cans to her ankle so as to hear her if she gets up in the night. Cochran can sleep on the floor on that side, down between the bed and the wall. Kootie can sleep over by the window, and Pete and I will take turns staying awake with a gun; well, I'll have a gun, and Pete can wake me up fast. At about five we'll get up and out of here.'

'If that TV comes on again during the night,' said Kootie in a small voice. He sighed and then went on, 'Shoot it.'

'I bet my hands would let me do that, actually,' said Pete.

Valorie's perceptions and memories and dreams were always in black-and-white, with occasional flickers of false red and blue shimmering in fine-grain moire patterns like heat waves; and always there was a drumming or knocking, which she understood was an amplification of some background noise present in the soundtrack – or, if there was no actual sound to exaggerate, was simply imposed arbitrarily on the scene. Her dreams never had any fantastic or even inaccurate elements in them, aside from the constant intrusive percussion – they were just re-run memories – and her default dream was always the same, and all the Plumtree personalities experienced at least the last seconds of it whenever she did:

Her mother was wearing sandals with tire-tread soles, but in the dream they rang a hard clack-clack *from the sidewalk concrete, and Plumtree's little shoes and shorter steps filled in the almost reggae one-drop beat.*

'They've painted a big Egyptian Horus eye on the roof,' said her mother, pulling her along by the hand. 'Signaling to the sun god, Ra, he says. All the time Ra Ra Ra! But he blew his bigplay at Lake Mead on Easter, and nobody can pretend anymore that he's gonna be any kind of king.'

Plumtree couldn't see the men dancing on the roof of the building ahead of them, but she could see the bobbing papier-mache heads that topped the tall poles they carried.

The sun burned white like a magnesium tire rim, straight up above them in the sky, at its very highest summer-solstice point.

'You stay by me, Janis,' her mother went on. 'He'll want to do the El Cabong bang-bang, but he won't try anything with me today, not if his own baby daughter is watching. And – listen, baby! – if I tell you to run along and play, you don't *go, hear? He won't hit me, not with you there, and he can't ... well, not to talk dirty, let's just say he* can't *– okay? – unless he's knocked me silly, kayoed me past any ref's count of ten. As close to dead as possible. I never even met* him *before he – I didn't even* meet *him during, I was in a coma when he – when you stopped being just a glitter in your daddy's evil eye.* Dead *would've been better, for him, but if you knock 'em dead you can't knock 'em up, right? Never mind.'*

On the sidewalk in front of the steps up to the door her mother stopped. 'And what do you say,*' her mother demanded, 'if he says, "Baby, do you* want *to leave with your mother?"'*

Plumtree was looking up at her mother's backlit face, and the view blurred and fragmented – that was because of tears in her eyes. 'I say, "Yes,"' Plumtree said obediently, though the cadence of her voice indicated an emotion.

Plumtree's eyes focussed beyond her mother – above her. Way above her.

This was the part of the dream that the other Plumtree personalities always remembered upon awakening.

There was a man in the sky, his white robes glowing in the sunlight for a moment; then he was a dark spot between the girl on the pavement and the flaring sun in the gunmetal sky. Plumtree opened her eyes wide and tried to see him against the hard pressure glare of the sun, but she couldn't – he seemed to have become the sun. And he was falling.

'Daddeee!'

Plumtree pulled her hand free of her mother's, and ran to catch him.

The clattering clopping impact drove her right down into the ground.

Cochran was jolted out of sleep and then rocked hard against textured wallpaper in the darkness, and his first waking impression was that a big truck had hit whatever this building was.

Carpet fibers abraded his face, and a mattress was jumping and slamming on box springs only inches from his left ear; he couldn't see anything, and until he heard shouting from Mavranos and abruptly remembered where he was and who he was with, Cochran was certain he was back in the honeymoon motel room behind the Troy and Cress Wedding Chapel in Las Vegas in 1990, again enduring the tumultuous escape-from-confinement of the big man in the wooden mask.

'Earthquake!' someone was yelling in the pitch blackness. Cochran sat up, battered by the mattress that was convulsing beside him like a living thing, and then he scrambled forward on his hands and knees until his forehead cracked against some unseen piece of furniture – the dresser the television had been sitting on, probably. The pizza boxes tumbled down onto his head, spilling crumbs and crusts.

'Mom!' yelled Kootie's voice. 'Mom, where are you?'

Two shrill voices answered him: '*Here!*'

Light flooded the room, just yellow electric lamplight but dazzling after the darkness. Squinting, and blinking at the trickle of blood running down beside his nose, Cochran saw that Angelica was standing beside the door with her hand on the light switch, and that Mavranos was crouched between the beds holding his revolver pointed at the ceiling. Kootie and Pete Sullivan stood beside Angelica, staring at the bed with Plumtree on it.

The bed was still jumping, the bedspread flapping like manta-ray wings, and Plumtree's body was tossing on it like a Raggedy Ann doll – even though the rest of the room had stopped shaking.

'Omar!' grated a shrill, keening voice from between Plumtree's clenched teeth. 'Damn your soul! Stop it, take one of the girls, Tiffany or Janis, just let me go!' The three empty beer cans that Mavranos had wired to her ankle with a coat hanger were shaking and clattering.

Kootie has provoked the Follow-the-Queen sequence, Cochran thought; he did it when he yelled for his mother. Next card up is wild, whatever you declare it to be. Dizzy and light-headed, Cochran opened his mouth.

'Nina!' he called hoarsely.

'Omar, I will kill any child conceived in this way!' screamed the voice out of Plumtree's mouth. 'God will not blame me!'

It hadn't worked.

Cochran's bruised forehead was chilly with sweat. 'J—' he began; then, 'Cody!' he called.

At first he wasn't sure the card he had declared would be honored, for though Plumtree's eyes sprang open she was now gasping, 'In the name of the father, the sun, the holy ghost!' Then she had rolled off the spasming mattress and scrambled across the carpet to the front door, the beer cans snagging in the carpet and hopping behind her.

'Whoa,' said Mavranos.

The mattress flopped down flat and stopped moving.

Mavranos stared at the bed with raised eyebrows. 'I,' he said, as if speaking to the bed, 'was talking to Miss Plumtree.'

Cochran half-expected the bed to start jumping again at this explanation, but it just lay sprawled there, the mattress at an angle now to the box springs, the pillows and blankets tumbled in disorder.

'Get back by boyfriend,' Mavranos told Plumtree.

Somewhat to Cochran's surprise Plumtree had no rude retort, but just obediently stepped back toward the bed; though she did shake her ankle irritably, rattling the attached cans. She was smacking her lips and grimacing. 'Jeez, was my *female parent* on? I hate her old spit. I gotta gargle, excuse me.' She hurried past Cochran into the bathroom, and he could hear her knocking things over on the sink.

The light in the room was flickering, and when Cochran looked around he saw that the television had come on again, possibly because of having been jolted in the earthquake. Again the screen showed a glowing nude man and woman feverishly groping and sucking and colliding.

Mavranos stepped back to see behind the set, and frowned; clearly the cord was still unplugged.

'Could you get me a beer, Angelica?' he said, holding out his left hand and not taking his eyes off the television. He was gripping the revolver in his right hand, and Cochran wondered if he might actually shoot the TV set, and if he'd think of muffling the shot with a pillow.

Angelica leaned over the ice chest and fished up a dripping can; she popped it open and reached over to slap it into his open palm.

'Thanks.' Mavranos tilted the beer can over the ventilation slots on the back slope of the television set, and after a few seconds of beer running down into the set's works the picture on the screen abruptly curdled into a black-and-white pattern like a radar scan, with a blobby figure in one corner that looked to Cochran like a cartoon silhouette of a big-butted fat man with little globe limbs, and warts all over him; and the sound had become a roaring hiss that warped and narrowed to mimic whispered words: *et ... in ... arcadia ... ego ...*

Then it winked out and was dark and inert, a wrecked TV with beer puddling out from the base of it. Mavranos absently drank the rest of the beer and clanked the can down on the dresser.

For several seconds no one spoke, and the distant foghorn moaned out in the night.

Mavranos raised the gun barrel for silence while he stared at the watch on his left wrist.

Cochran began to let the muscles in his shoulders relax, and he gently prodded the bloody bump on his forehead.

The foghorn sounded again, and Mavranos lowered his arms. His face was expressionless. 'What time is it?' he asked.

'You were just staring at your watch!' said Angelica.

'Oh yeah.' Mavranos looked at his watch again. 'Quarter to five, apparently that's showtime.' He sighed shakily and rubbed his left hand over his face. 'Let's mobilize. Angelica, get your witchy shit together and have Pete carry it downstairs and into the truck while you cover him with your .45, and don't forget to bring that Wild Turkey bottle with Scott's blood in it. Don't put stuff in the back bed, though – we'll be carrying Scott down and putting him back there. I'll drive the truck, and Pete can drive Mr. Cochran's Granada—'

Plumtree had stepped out of the bathroom, and Cochran could smell the Listerine on her breath from a yard away, though he was ashamed to meet her eye. She dug in the pocket of her jeans and pulled out a bundle of bills.

'Kid,' she said to Kootie. When he looked up, she thrust the bills out toward him. 'This is yours. A hundred bucks – long story, don't ask. I want to give it to you now, in case we get ... in case we don't quite meet again.' Cochran thought there was gruff sympathy in her voice. 'No hard feelings.'

Kootie was holding the little yellow blanket that bald-headed Diana had given him back in Solville, but he reached across the bed with his free hand and took the money. 'Thank you, Janis Cordelia Plumtree,' he said.

'And Janis Cordelia can ride shotgun in the Granada,' Mavranos went on rapidly 'with Angelica behind her ready to shoot. Come on, everybody, up! I want us out of here in five minutes.'

Angelica snatched up her knapsack and grabbed the Wild Turkey bottle.

'What's the hurry, Arky?' she asked irritably. 'Sunrise isn't for another hour or so, and you said the place is walking distance from here.'

Mavranos had peered through the peek hole and now unchained the door and pulled it open. 'That foghorn, just now – it's sounding every *fifteen* seconds, not twenty, and it's a different tone. It's a different foghorn.'

Pete was squeezing the battery charger's clamps off the terminals of one of Mavranns's car batteries and then lifting the battery in both hands. 'So?' he asked breathlessly. 'Maybe the wind's from a different direction.'

'They don't vary that way, Pete,' said Mavranos impatiently, 'or they wouldn't be any good as foghorns, would they? We're – we're Scott's army, this king's army, and in that sense we won't truly exist until the potential of his resurrection becomes an actuality. Our wave-form has to shake out as *one* rather than as *zero*. And I think – this wrong foghorn makes me think – that we're a fragmented waveform right now, that psychically we're *somewhere else* too, as well as here in a motel on Lombard Street.'

'So,' said Angelica, spreading her hands, 'what do we *do*?'

'What are you asking *me* for?' Mavranos snapped. 'All I can think of is for us to go to this crazy cemetery temple on the peninsula, in the wrong gear and without even our TV-star intercessor, and hope we can catch up to ourselves.' He darted a glance around the room. 'Where'd Kootie go?'

'He's right outside,' said Angelica. 'He waved his hand in front of his face like he wanted fresh air, and he stepped out.' She hurried to the door, calling, 'Kootie?'

She leaned around the doorjamb to look, and then she had lunged outside, and Cochran heard her voice from out on the railed walkway: 'A note!' she yelled. 'Shit – "*Can't be with you for this – sorry—*" Pete, he's run away!'

Kootie had already tiptoed down the stairs and sprinted across the dark parking lot the Lombard Street sidewalk, and was now hurrying to a cab that had pulled in the curb after he had, without much confidence, waved to it. He levered open the back door and scrambled in. Better than hiding behind a Dumpster somewhere, he thought nervously, and I can *afford* this now, thanks to Miss Plumtree. He hiked up the seat to stuff Diana's baby blanket into his hip pocket.

The cab driver was an elderly black man who stared at him dubiously over his shoulder. 'You okay, kid?'

'Yes,' panted Kootie. 'Drive off, will you?'

'I don't like hurry.' As if to prove the point, he cocked his head to listen to a dispatch on his radio. "And I don't like driving people who turn out to not have any money,' he went on finally. 'Where did you want to go?'

Kootie bared his teeth in impatience and tried to remember the name of any place in San Francisco. 'Chinatown,' he said.

'You better give me ten dollars up front, kid – I'll give you the change when we get there.'

Hurriedly Kootie dug out of his pocket the money Plumtree had just given him, and he held the bills up to the window to be able to see the denominations by the glow of the nearest streetlight. He peeled off two fives and thrust them over the top of the front seat to the driver.

At last the driver shifted the car into gear and accelerated away from the curb. Kootie pressed his lips together and blinked back frightened tears, but he didn't look out the back window.

Angelica trudged back up the stairs from the parking lot. Many of the motel rooms had their lights on after the earthquake, and the doorway at which Mavranos stood wasn't the only one that had been opened.

'No sign of him,' she told Mavranos when she had stepped inside and closed the door. 'There was a taxi driving away – he might have been in it, or not, and I couldn't see what company it was anyway.' She gave Plumtree a look that was too exhausted to be angry. 'Thanks for giving him getaway money.'

Plumtree narrowed her eyes, then visibly relaxed and just pursed her lips. 'He was going anyway – read the rest of the note! – and if the money did let him take a cab, you should be glad he's not walking, in this neighborhood at this hour.'

'Gimme the note.'

Pete Sullivan wordlessly passed to Angelica the piece of Star Motel stationery that had been weighted down with a motel glass on the walkway outside the room, and Angelica forced her tired and blurring eyes to focus on the clumsy ballpoint-ink letters:

> MOM & DAD & EVERYBODY – I CAN'T BE WITH YOU
> FOR THIS. I'M SORRY. I KNOW ID HAVE TO DO THE
> BLOOD DRIKING – HOPE YOU CAN READ THIS, I DON'T
> TURN ON THE LIGHT – JESUS I HOPE TV STAYS OFF – I'D
> HAVE TO DRINK THE BLOD, & I CANT DO IT AGAIN:
> LET SOMEBODY HAVE ME – & ME BE OUT OF MY HEAD.
> EDISON IN 92, NEVER AGAIN, ID GO CRAZY. I ~~HAVE~~/
> HAVE NOT TAKEN THE TRUCK. I DO ~~NOT~~ HAVE A KEY
> TO THIS ROOM BUT I'LL BE BACK AFTER. I'VE GOT ~~A~~
> ~~LITTLE~~ MONEY, ENUFF. I LOVE YOU DONT BE MAD
> KOOTIE

Angelica looked up at Mavranos. 'I've got to stay here.'

Mavranos started to speak, but Pete Sullivan overrode him. 'No, Angie,' he said loudly. 'We've got to go through with this thing, this morning. We've got Plumtree, and we've got the dead king – and we need a *bruja*. And Kootie knows where we'll be, he heard Arky describe the place – if he wants to find us, that's where he'll go, not here.'

'Just what I was gonna say myself,' growled Mavranos.

Plumtree had sat down on the bathroom-side bed, and was untwisting the coat-hanger wire from around her ankle. 'You don't mind if I get rid of the house-arrest hardware now, do you? Me, I'm glad the kid's out of it.'

She tossed the wired beer cans aside and straightened up, then looked around and chuckled softly. 'Do you all *realize* what we've done to this room? Burnt the rug and now stomped old pizza crusts into it, blasted the bed, poured beer in the TV – at least Janis made it to the toilet to puke last night. There's even a lot of shed black dog *hair* on the beds! I'm glad it's no credit card of mine this is on.' For a moment her face looked very young and lost, and Angelica thought of the little girl who had been hospitalized because the sun had fallen out of the sky onto her. 'Get your Wild Turkey bottle and let's go,' Plumtree whispered. 'And please God I still be here by lunchtime, and Crane be alive again.'

'All of us still alive at lunchtime,' said Mavranos, nodding somberly. 'Amen.'

CHAPTER NINETEEN

I would be blind with weeping, sick with groans,
Look pale as primrose with blood-drinking sighs,
And all to have the noble duke alive.
>   —William Shakespeare, *Henry VI, Part II*

The pavement of the yacht club's empty parking lot was wet with sea spray and pre-dawn fog, and the low overcast looked likely to drop actual rain soon. The clouds were moving across the sky from the direction of the Golden Gate Bridge, but the eastern horizon was still open sky – a glowing pearl-white, making black silhouettes of the long piers at Fort Mason a mile away.

In spite of the dim light, Angelica Sullivan was wearing mirror sunglasses – *Standard precaution,* she had told Cochran curtly when she and Plumtree had climbed out of Cochran's Ford Granada; *the mirror surface throws ghosts back onto themselves, prevents 'em from being able to fasten on your gaze. Don't you look squarely at anything.*

Cochran remembered the half-dozen little girl ghosts he had glimpsed on the roof of Strubie the Clown's house in Los Angeles, and how Plumtree had yelled at him for looking at them. Right, he thought. I won't look at anything.

Driving the Granada with Cochran and Plumtree and Angelica in it, Pete had followed Mavranos's red truck up Divisadero to Marina and Yacht Road, and the two vehicles were now parked side by side in the otherwise empty lot. Beyond the curb and a short descending slope of tumbled wet boulders, the gray sea of the San Francisco Bay looked as rolling and wild as open ocean.

On a shoulder strap under her tan raincoat Angelica was carrying a compact black Marlin .45 carbine, its folding stock swivelled forward to lie locked against the left side of the trigger guard; and as she stepped away from the Granada she pulled back the rifle's slide-lever and let it snap back, chambering a live round. The extended base of a twelve-round magazine stuck out from the magazine-well, and back in the motel room Cochran had seen her stuff a couple of extra magazines in the pocket of her jeans and a couple more in the raincoat's left pocket.

You expecting an army? he had asked her.

I want to have plenty of the ghost-killer hollow-points, she had answered in a flat singsong voice, as if talking to herself, *but I want hardball too, full jacket, 'cause if I shoot off the first magazine's dozen rounds and need more, I'm likely to be shooting at a distance after that, or through car doors, and hardball's more reliable for that kind of thing; and adrenaline's likely to make me shaky, loosen my grip, and hollow-points don't feed through smoothly sometimes if the gun's not being braced firmly. Hardball in the raincoat, hollow-point omieros in the jeans.*

You've given it thought, Cochran thought now as he watched her pull the raincoat around herself and loosely tie the belt in front.

Plumtree was wearing a cranberry-colored cashmere sweater of Nina's, and she was huddled against the Granada's front bumper beside Cochran and blowing into her cupped hands. 'I don't see any of Mavranos's hippie druids,' she said quietly.

'With luck they don't get up this early,' said Cochran. I hope nobody does, he added to himself. Mavranos said we'll be trespassing, going on out to the end of this peninsula.

And what about coming back? Is it really conceivable that Scott Crane will be *walking back* here with us? Limping, I guess, with the bullet in his thigh now. And—

'My God,' he said; then, speaking more loudly, 'Angelica? You're gonna remember to pull the spear out of his throat, right? It'd be no good if he *did* come back to life, if—'

He saw two reflections of his own pale face in Angelica's mirror sunglasses when she smiled at him. 'We've thought of that, Sid. Thanks, though.' She looked past him. 'Arky? How wide is the path to the cemetery temple place? I think you should just back the truck right out to it.'

Mavranos had opened the back of the truck and was kneeling on the tailgate. '*Back* it out there?' he said, squinting over the Granada's roof at her. 'Well, it would mean we don't have to *carry* Scott's body ...'

'Nor the rest of the crap,' Angelica agreed. 'And I like the truck's exhaust – with the muffler all fucked up the way it is, it's kind of a spontaneous *bata* drumbeat, and it's the pulse of the king's vessel.'

'There's a chain across the path,' Mavranos went on. 'Probably padlocked.'

'What's another dent? What's some more scratches in your paint?'

'Quicker exit afterward, too,' allowed Mavranos. 'That's worth a lot. Okay.' He hopped down to the pavement and hoisted the lower half of the tailgate shut, though he left the top half raised. 'Pete will walk backward ahead of me, waving directions so I don't go off into the water; Plumtree and Cochran ahead of Pete, so I can keep an eye on 'em over Pete's shoulder; Angelica behind, watching for pursuit.'

'I should have my gun,' said Cochran.

Mavranos frowned at him. 'Actually, I suppose you should. Okay.' He walked around to the open drivers-side door and leaned in, then walked back to the rear of the truck with Cochran's holstered revolver. 'Just keep it away from Miss Plumtree,' he said as he handed it to Cochran. 'And put it away for now.'

Cochran reached behind himself with both hands to clip the holster to the back of his belt.

Mavranos pointed to the northeast corner of the parking lot. 'The path starts behind that building, as a paved service road. All of you meet me there.'

He got into the driver's seat and closed the door, started the engine again, and audibly clanked it into reverse; the truck surged backward out of the parking space and began yawing away across the asphalt in a broad circle.

'After you two,' said Angelica to Cochran and Plumtree, punctuating the request by letting the hidden rifle barrel briefly tent the tan fabric of the raincoat in front of her knee.

They all began trudging after the receding red truck. When Plumtree took his hand, Cochran glanced at her in surprise, for Cody had been on a moment before; but then he saw that it was still Cody – by now he could recognize her stronger jaw and the deeper lines around her flinty eyes

Her nostrils flared as she inhaled deeply. 'Kahlua,' she said, 'burning.'

Cochran too had caught a whiff of hot-coffee-and-alcohol on the cold sea breeze. 'Just like down in Solville.'

She squeezed his hand. 'I guess that means *something* is gonna happen.'

He looked at her again, but the humble and subdued voice had still been Cody's.

The battering exhaust of Mavranos's truck rolling along at idle speed in reverse behind them set the pace of their walk.

'Don't fall over the chain here, Pete,' called Cochran over his shoulder.

After Plumtree and Cochran stepped over the chain with the rusty no admittance sign hanging from it, their shoes were crunching in sandy red dirt, and they could see a cluster of low, rectangular stone structures and an iron light pole a hundred yards ahead of them at the end of the narrow spit of land; and a few seconds later they heard the chain creak and snap and then thrash into the dry wild-anise bushes that fringed the road.

'What chain?' came Pete Sullivan's voice from behind them, speaking loudly to be heard over the indomitable drumming of the truck's exhaust.

Cochran and Plumtree kept walking along the dirt path, their hands in their pockets now because of the chill. Puddles in the road reflected the gray sky, and the red dirt was peppered with fragments of brick and marble.

They were close enough to see the structures ahead now – Cochran and Plumtree were already walking past ornate broad capitals of long-gone Corinthian columns that sat upside-down on the dirt like heroic ashtrays, and spare blocks of carved and routed granite that lay at random among the weeds; but though the low walls and stairs and tomb-like alcoves ahead had been cobbled together out of mismatched scavenged brick and marble, the site had a unified look, as if all these at-odds components had come to this weathered, settled state together, right here, over hundreds of years.

A motorboat had been crossing the choppy water of the yacht harbor to their right, between the peninsula and the distant white house-fronts on Marina Boulevard; it had rounded the tip of the peninsula and was coming back along the north side, several hundred feet out, and now Cochran heard a rapid hollow knocking roll across the waves.

And behind him, much closer, he heard the rattling pop of car-window glass shattering. Brick fragments exploded away from a stairway head in front of them even as he had grabbed Plumtree's forearm and yanked her forward into a sliding crouch behind a low marble wall.

He looked back – Pete was running back toward Angelica, who had flung open her raincoat and raised the short pistol-grip rifle, and the open back end of the red truck was jumping on its old shock absorbers as it picked up speed.

Angelica fired three fast shots, then quickly unfolded the stock and had it to her shoulder and fired two more even as the ejected brass shells of the first three were bouncing on the red dirt. Out here under the open sky the shots sounded like sharp hammer blows on a wooden picnic table.

The truck ground to a halt with its back bumper rocking only a couple of yards from where Cochran and Plumtree were crouched, and two more hard gunshots impacted the air – Cochran realized that Mavranos was now shooting at the boat through the hole where his passenger-side window had been.

The motorboat had paused, out on the gray water; but now its engine roared, and its bow kicked up spray as it turned north and began curving away from the peninsula, showing them nothing but wake and a bobbing transom.

Pete and Angelica came sprinting up as Mavranos hopped down out of the truck.

'Let's get him out,' Angelica gasped, 'and down these stairs to that cobble-stone lower level there. I should have had hardball rounds first up. You all carry him, I'll fetch the *bruja* stuff.'

Cochran stood up, and realized that he had drawn his revolver at some point during the confrontation, and that it was cocked; and after he had carefully lowered the hammer he had to touch the cold barrel to be sure he hadn't fired it. His right hand was shaking as he reached around behind him and stuffed the gun back into its holster. He brushed a buzzing fly away from his ear, and then, with huge reluctance, stepped toward the truck.

Robed and whole and in some sense still barefoot, the spirit of Scott Crane stood beside the lapping gray water. It wasn't precisely where Mavranos and the Plumtree woman and the two silver coins were – he was just as immedi-ately aware of the capering naked ghost of himself that was flickering like a hummingbird at the ruins by the sea, where the foghorn moan came for two seconds every fifteen seconds – but what confronted him either way was the water, the obligation to cross the cold, unimaginable water.

Obligation but not inevitability. He could with only moderate difficulty blunt and truncate himself enough to animate the ghost, become no more than the ghost but at least be wholly that, and stay here, with real physical mass; free to shamble around in the familiarity of noisy human streets, and bask in the earthly sun, and pour the coarsening common short-dog wine down his shabbily restored throat. He would be a poisoned and diminished quantity, but still a real quantity.

Or he could take the two silver dollars that Spider Joe had brought back to him, at such cost, and spend them on the oblivion that the Greeks had represented as Charon's ferry over the River Styx – and then drink from what the Greeks had called Lethe, the river of forgetfulness and surrender.

No guarantees of anything there, that way, not even of nothing. Total abject and unconditional surrender, to whoever or whatever it might ultimately be behind the busy, clustering gods and archetypes that humanity had tried to hold up to it for size. He could hope for mercy, but there would certainly be justice, a justice older and more implacable than the forces that kept the suns shining and the galaxies wheeling in the nighttime sky.

Sitting in the steamy BMW idling in the Star Motel parking lot, Long John Beach turned to the two-mannikin appliance in the back seat. 'Let me tell you a parable,' he said.

'Talk to me, goddammit,' said Armentrout hoarsely, gripping the sweat-slick steering wheel. *They were here during the Marina 3.2 earthquake last night*, one of the motel guests had told him. *They were all yelling at each other, and yelling, 'Where's Kootie?' They carried a guy down the stairs to a truck, and drove away, some of 'em in the truck and some in a beat old brown Ford.*

'I'll tell you all,' Long John said equably. 'A man's car drove over a cliff, and in midair he jumped out, and caught hold of a tree stump halfway down the cliff. Below him is only fog, and he can't climb up or down. He looks into the sky and says, "Is there anybody up there? Tell me what to do!" And a big voice says, "Let go of the tree." So after a few seconds the guy says, "Is there anybody *else* up there?"'

Armentrout nodded impatiently, and finally turned to Long John. 'So? What did he do?'

The one-armed man shrugged. 'That's the end of the story.'

Down a set of mismatched brick-and-marble stairs, under the shadow of a scrollwork-roofed marble alcove that looked as if it should shelter the carved effigy of a dead king, a broad cobblestone-paved crescent with a raised stone edge-coping projected out over the sea like an ancient dock.

At the moment the only dead king present was laid out on the pavement below the alcove, his jeans and white shirt blotting up moisture and grime from the puddles between the uneven paving stones; and all that was on the broad table-like slab under the alcove roof was a couple of sheets of corrugated cardboard, bedding for some absent transient.

In the direction of the peninsula point and the iron light pole another set of steps led back up to road level from this stone floor, flanked against the open gray sky by a bench that was a marble slab laid across two broken granite half-moons. Cochran realized that he badly wanted to feel that this shelter was an enduring, solid edifice – but it was too obvious that what distinguished this place from a real, old ruin was the fact that all the stone edges here, even the ones fitted up against each other as part of some wall or seat, were broken and uneven. A line from some poem was tolling in his head: *These fragments I have shored against my ruins …*

Plumbing pipes projected up out of the muddy ground at every shelf and wall-top, their open-mouthed ends bent horizontal to project the echoing sound of sea water rising and falling in their buried shafts, a deep twanging like slow-fingered ascending and descending slides on slack bass-guitar strings. Cochran's thudding heartbeat and his shallow panting seemed to provide a counterpoint, and it was only Plumtree's evident, valiant desperation to accomplish the task at hand, and his own queasy shame at having called for Nina's ghost during the Follow-the-Queen episode, that kept him from wading out into the cold sea on the Marina side and trying to swim to shore.

His face was chilly with sweat, and not just because of having had to help carry the cold dead body a few moments ago. In his mind he was again seeing the carbine jolting in Angelica's fists and flinging out ejected shell casings, and the brick stairway-top exploding into dust and high-speed fragments, and he was shaking with a new, visceral comprehension of velocity and bullets and human mercilessness. He couldn't help but be glad that he hadn't fired his own gun.

Angelica had fetched her canvas knapsack from the truck while Mavranos and Pete and Cochran had been carrying Scott Crane's body down the steps, and now she was spreading out on the damp stones her paltry-looking tools – there was, along with the assorted garage-sale litter he'd seen last night in the motel room, an empty H. Upmann cigar box, a can of Ronsonol lighter fluid, a pair of pliers, a Star Motel postcard … Cochran shook his head in bewilderment.

Mavranos cussed and slapped at his own neck. 'No hippie druids this morning,' he said, 'but we got flies up the butt.'

'Here, at this hour,' said Angelica in a strained voice, 'those can't be anything but ghost-flies; *las moscas*, little essences of dead people, either brought in on us or already here. Ordinarily they'd just be an implicit cloud, but they're condensed to individuality this morning by the sudden low pressure of having the dead king right here.' She glanced up, frowning. 'Try not to breathe them – and if any of you have got any bleeding cuts, cover them.'

She handed Mavranos the bottle of 75 Kenwood Cabernet. 'You hold this, Arky,' she told him; 'open it when I tell you.'

'Go ahead and do this thing right,' Mavranos said, 'but as much on fast-forward as you can, okay? Those guys in the boat will be back, or their friends.'

'Right, Arky,' Angelica said, 'but it's important for this procedure that all the minds present understand what's going on, assent to it.' Speaking to all of them, she went on rapidly, 'See, we're gonna be doing a kind of ass-backward honoring-of-the-dead here. Usually the procedure is to have a heavily masked guy, a Lucumi *ogungun*, let himself be taken over by the ghost of the deceased; it's to let the ghost see the funeral and mourners and flower displays and all, and everybody being sorry, so that the ghost can go away, can dissipate happily and not hang around and cause trouble.'

While she'd been talking she had laid the cigar box on the stones and draped it with a white linen handkerchief, and now she set on it a water glass from the motel. As she hoisted a plastic bottle of Evian water out of the knapsack and began twisting off the cap, she said, in a formal tone, 'This is an altar, a *bóveda espiritual*.' It seemed to be a declaration, and she poured the glass half full of water as she spoke.

She looked up at Plumtree then, and her mirror glasses were lozenges of glowing gray sky. Cochran could see the butt of the slung carbine under her open raincoat. 'The way it ordinarily works,' Angelica went on at her previous quick pace, 'is you set out a glass of some nice kind of water, and everybody dabs some on their hands and temples, as a kind of cleansing, so the guest-of-honor ghost will have a transparent medium to focus on but won't *fixate* on anybody.' She took the Wild Turkey bottle out of the canvas sack and twisted out the cork. 'But,' she said hoarsely, 'we don't *want* his *ghost*, we want *him*. And we want to make sure that he *does* fixate, that retreat is not even an option for him.'

She poured the still-liquid red blood into the water, about three tablespoons, and then covered the glass with the Star Motel postcard to keep the ghost-flies out of it. 'So you're going to *drink* this.'

Plumtree was biting her lip, but she nodded. 'This has to work,' she was whispering, 'please let this work, this has to work...' The sunburn was spotty over her cheekbones, as if the skin was stretched tight, and Cochran guessed that her hands would have been trembling if she had not been clenching them tightly together, as if in prayer.

Cochran remembered the note Kootie had left, when he had run away last night. *I can't do it again ... me be out of my head ... I'd go crazy.* This woman, Cochran thought, underwent electroconvulsive therapy six days ago this morning. She was knocked out of her own head, and has been evicted again several times since then by her terrible father ... most recently for more than two whole days, and she got herself back just yesterday morning. Cochran remembered her saying yesterday, in a falsely bravely cheerful voice, *The goat head was speaking, in a human language* ... But she's here doing this, voluntarily. *Assenting,* and then some.

He stepped closer to her and reached out and squeezed her hand. Without glancing away from the glass of streaky red water on the draped cigar box, Plumtree shook her hand free of his.

'No offense,' she said faintly. 'This is our flop.'

Cochran took a step back. Over the wavering drone of the flies he heard a faint pattering on the stones behind him, and when he turned he saw Mavranos brushing tiny cubes of truck-window glass out of his hair.

'I could drive back for coffee and doughnuts,' Mavranos said.

'We're almost ready here,' said Angelica.

She now laid the myrtle branches on the stones and squirted them with the Ronsonol lighter fluid; and she laid out as well the gold Dunhill lighter and the two silver dollars that Spider Joe had brought to Solville.

At last Angelica straightened up, with a visible shudder, and elbowed the slung carbine back behind her hip. 'Okay, Arky,' she said, 'open that skeleton-label wine. We're each going to take a sip of it, and then I'm going to light the myrtle. This stuff will get – God help us! – it'll get the attention of Dionysus, his *remote* attention, I trust, and that will give us a line-of-sight link to the underworld.'

'And from the underworld right back to us, here,' said Mavranos stolidly as he twisted the corkscrew of his Swiss Army knife into the cork. 'Pogo?' he called loudly into the gray sky. He yanked the cork out with a frail pop. 'That's a sound you ought to recognize, old friend.'

He tipped the bottle up to his lips, and after a couple of bubbles had wobbled up inside it he lowered it and passed it to Pete Sullivan, who also drank from it.

'Plumtree last,' said Angelica, taking the bottle from her husband and handing it to Cochran. The harbor breeze was tossing her black hair around her face. 'And out of the glass.'

Cochran raised the cold bottle and took several deep gulps, and he was so hungry for the blurring effect of alcohol on his empty stomach, on this terrible morning, that he had to force himself to hand it back without swallowing more.

'Thirsty boy,' said Angelica bleakly. 'You're not through yet, by the way.' She drank a token mouthful herself, then crouched again by her little altar and, flicking the postcard away, topped up the water glass with purple Cabernet. She clanked the bottle down on the stones and lifted the glass, and straightened up and handed it to Plumtree.

'Not quite yet,' Angelica said to her. 'You,' she told Cochran, 'hold up that right hand of yours, toward the water, with that birthmark facing out.'

Cochran's ears were ringing, and he distinctly felt a drop of sweat roll down his ribs under his shirt. 'Why?' he whispered. I won't, he thought. He heard again what he had said in the self-esteem group at Rosecrans Medical Center, on that first day: *Reach out your hand, you get it cut off, sometimes.* And he remembered seeing the red blood jetting from his chopped wrist, when he had put his hand between the old Zinfandel stump and the pruning shears thirty-three years ago. He was about to say I *won't* out loud, but Mavranos spoke before he could:

'I got no affection for your girlfriend,' Mavranos said gruffly, 'but I gotta say that she's bought a lot of ... plain cold admiration in my rating. Not that she cares, I'm sure. What she's ready to do ... I don't think I *could* do. None of the rest of us can claim our part's too hard in this, compared to hers.'

'That mark on your hand is some kind of Dionysus badge,' Angelica said gently, 'isn't it?'

Le Visage dans la Vigne, Cochran thought. The Face in the Vine Stump. 'I suppose it is,' he said helplessly, and then in his mind he heard again the hard *crack* of Plumtree's fist hitting the bloody madhouse linoleum floor, right after he had punched Long John Beach in the nose. His teeth ached now as he took a deep breath of the sea air and let it out in shaky segments. 'I'm ... with you. Okay.' Slowly he lifted his right arm, with the palm of his hand turned back.

'Okay,' echoed Angelica. To Plumtree she said, 'Now when I get the myrtle burning, you call to – damn it, you brought this on yourself, you know, girl, I'm so sorry, but – call to Scott Crane; and then drink—' She shook her head quickly and waved at the glass of rusty-colored liquid in Plumtree's hand, then whispered the last word, '—it.'

Cochran noticed that the peak of the alcove roof and the top of the marble stair were shining now in the cold pink light of dawn. Mavranos stood on tiptoe and looked back down the peninsula.

'Sun's coming up,' he said, 'over Fort Mason.'

'Get the pliers,' Angelica told him. 'Pull the spear out of his throat.'

Mavranos swallowed visibly, but his face was impassive as he nodded. 'Happy to.' He picked up the pliers and then knelt beside Scott Crane's body, with his back to the others; Cochran saw his shoulders flex under the denim jacket, and then he was straightening up, holding the closed pliers out away from himself, and the red-stained three-pointed spearhead quivered between the pliers' jaws.

'Can I pitch it into the ocean?' he asked hoarsely.

'You have to,' said Angelica, nodding and not looking at the thing.

Mavranos reached back over his shoulder and then snapped his hand forward, letting the pliers spring open at the last moment, as if he were casting a fishing fly. The little bloody metal fork spun away, glittering for a moment in the horizontal sunlight, and then disappeared behind a wave.

Cochran looked back at the body of Scott Crane. A spatter of fresh red blood stood out on the dark beard, but the pale, lined face was as composed and noble as before, and he reminded himself that at the moment Crane was incapable of feeling pain.

The two silver dollars were lying on the stones near Scott Crane's bare feet. 'Aren't you gonna put the coins on his eyes?' Cochran asked.

'No,' snapped Angelica. 'They're his fare *over*. We want him to come *back*.'

Then why have them here at all? thought Cochran defensively. His raised arm was getting tired.

Angelica crouched to pick up the myrtle branches and the gold cigarette lighter, and she opened the lighter's lid and flicked the striker; the myrtle caught and burned with an almost invisible flame, though Cochran could smell the incense like smoke.

Angelica nodded to Plumtree.

Plumtree faced the now-glittering gray water, and when she had lifted the glass she paused. 'Not even Valorie?' she asked in a quiet voice, clearly not addressing any of the others present. 'This is *mine*?'

Standing to the side of her with his arm stiffly raised, Cochran could see windblown tears streaming back across her cheek.

'Scott Crane,' she called strongly out toward the waves and the glowing fog. '*I know you can fucking hear me! Come into me, into this body of your murderer!*' And she tipped the glass up and drank it down in three convulsive swallows.

With a drumming roar like the sound of a forest fire sudden solid rain thrashed down onto the peninsula, flinging up a haze of splash-spray over the stones and blurring the surface of the sea. The sudden haze of flying water was lit by two rapid white flares of lightning, and the sudden hard crash of close thunder battered at the marble walls and rocked Cochran back on his heels.

Plumtree's hair was instantly soaked, and it flew out like snakes when she flung her head back and shouted out three syllables of harsh laughter.

'*Four-and-twenty blackbrides baked in a pie!*' roared the voice of Omar Salvoy from her gaping mouth. '*When the pie was opened, the brides began to sing! Wasn't that a dainty dish to set before the king!*'

Cochran had lost his footing, and he twisted as he fell so that his knees and elbows knocked against the wet stones.

He could see the remains of Scott Crane, only a couple of feet in front of his face. It was a bare gray skull that now lolled above the collar of the shirt, and the already-wet fabric was collapsed against stark ribs and no abdomen at all, and the hands that spilled from the cuffs were long-fingered gray bone.

Plumtree turned away from the sea, and even through the dimness and the retinal afterglare from the lightning Cochran could see the white of her bared teeth, and he knew this was Plumtree's father, Omar Salvoy. He might have been looking straight at Cochran.

'*Moth-er!*' Cochran yelled, and though he was only trying to induce the Follow-the-Queen effect in her, to his surprise the wail powerfully evoked his own dormant childhood fear of being heartbreakingly lost and monstrously found, and he was glad that the rain would hide the tears he felt springing from his eyes. For his self-respect more than from any particular hope of its efficacy, he shouted, '*Janis's mom!*'

Perhaps it had worked – at any rate the figure that was Plumtree was allowing itself to be hustled back up the stairs by Mavranos, and Angelica was now crouched on the other side of the dressed skeleton, hastily folding the stick-like arms and legs.

Angelica looked up at him over the arch of the cloth-draped breastbone. 'Get the Wild Turkey bottle!' she said.

Cochran nodded, and crawled across the stones and snatched up the pint bottle in the moment before Pete Sullivan grabbed him under the arms and hauled him to his feet. Cochran had almost dropped the bottle in surprise – it was as hot as if scalding coffee had just been poured out of it, and he shoved it into the pocket of his windbreaker.

Another flare of lightning lit the weathered stones through the thick haze of rain, and the instant bomb-blast of thunder fluttered the wet hair on the back of Cochran's head.

Things like beanbags were falling out of the sky and hitting the stones all around him – he squinted at a couple of them as Pete hurried him across the pavement, and he saw that they were dead seagulls. Over the roar of the rain battering the pavement he could hear bestial groans and howls shaking out of the mouths of the deeply moored pipes now.

He and Pete followed Angelica up the slippery stone steps to the roadway mud, and after Angelica had unceremoniously dumped the armful of clothes and bones in through the open back window of Mavranos's truck they all scrambled around to the side doors and piled in, kicking out old clothes and McDonald's take-out hamburger wrappings.

Cochran and Plumtree and Pete were all wedged uncomfortably in the back seat; but Cochran relaxed a little when he heard Plumtree muttering about Jesus. Apparently the Follow-the-Queen invocation had worked, and this was the personality of Plumtree's mother.

Mavranos had started the truck and levered it into gear before they had got the doors shut, and he clicked the headlights on as the truck rocked forward along the dirt path back toward the yacht-club parking lot. Tools and frying pans clanked in the truck bed, and Cochran wondered if Crane's skeleton was being broken up back there.

Then he leaned forward over the back of the front seat to peer ahead past the squeaking whips of the windshield wipers. Translucent human figures waved and grimaced out on the road in the yellow headlight glare, and stretched or sprang away to the sides as the massive bumper and grille bulled through them.

Angelica was crouched in the front passenger seat with her carbine across her knees. 'I see lights, ahead,' she said, speaking loudly to be heard over the rain and wind that were thrashing in through the broken window by her right elbow. 'Don't waste time focussing on these ghosts.'

'Motorcycles,' said Mavranos, squinting through the streaming windshield. He took his right hand from the steering wheel long enough to draw the revolver from under his belt and lay it across his lap. 'They're on Yacht Road, turning into the parking lot.' He tromped on the accelerator, and the old truck bounced violently on its shocks, clanging the tools and pans in the back. 'I'm gonna stop,' he called, 'sudden, when we're past the Granada. You all jump out and get into it – I'll use this truck to clear a path through these guys.'

'No, Arky—' Angelica began, but then the truck had slammed down over a curb and had passed the parked Granada, and was braking hard and slewing around to the right on the wet asphalt. Cochran was pressed against the back of the front seat, but he shoved the right-side door open while the truck was still rocking from side to side, its left side facing the oncoming glare of motorcycle headlights.

He dragged Plumtree out onto the pavement after him, and he was fumbling in his pants pocket for the Granada's keys. Pete had followed him out and had opened the truck's front passenger door, but Angelica was arguing with Mavranos and wouldn't get out.

'I'll shoot ahead while you drive,' she was yelling. 'Pete, go get in the Ford! Arky, *drive us out of here!*'

Over the stadium-roar of the rain Cochran heard several hard bangs, and the truck's long right rear window became an opaque spiderweb in the moment before it fell out onto the asphalt in a million tiny pieces.

He saw Mavranos lunge up and across the front seat, blocking Angelica from the gunfire. 'Angelica,' Mavranos was yelling, 'get down, get back to—'

Five more fast bangs hammered at the truck, and Angelica tumbled backward out of the truck and sat down hard on the puddled pavement. As Pete Sullivan ran toward her, Cochran spun away, toward the Granada.

He frog-marched Plumtree around to the passenger side, opened the door, and shoved her into the back seat; then he ran around the front and got in behind the wheel and started the engine.

Angelica was on her feet, and Pete was hurrying her to the passenger side of the Granada. They got in, and Cochran shifted the engine into gear.

'Don't go!' Angelica was yelling in his ear as he stepped on the gas, 'Drive into them, Arky's been shot, we've got to get him—'

'He's driving,' Cochran told her. He took his eyes off the advancing pavement ahead for just long enough to give her a quick up-and-down glance, but he didn't see any obvious blood on her rain-soaked jeans and blouse. Apparently she had not been hit.

Ahead of them the truck had surged around and roared forward, and with an audible slam a motorcycle headlight beam whirled up across the dark sky as the truck rocked right over the fallen machine and rider; Cochran swerved his lower-slung car around the body and the spinning, broken motorcycle, and then he tromped on the accelerator to keep up with the racing truck as it sped out of the parking lot. Dead seagulls thumped under the tires.

The motorcycles were behind them now, their headlights slashing the walls of rain as they turned around, and Angelica was lying across Pete's lap to hold the carbine outside of the car, its black plastic stock wedged against the still-open passenger door.

She pulled the trigger five times – the concussions of the shots were stunning physical blows inside the confined cab of the car, and the flashes of hard yellow muzzle-flare made it impossible to see anything more than the truck's taillights in the dimness ahead, but the headlights behind didn't seem to be gaining on them, so Cochran just bit his lip and hummed shrilly and kept squinting through the rain-blurred windshield.

Over the ringing in his ears and the roaring of the engine, he became aware that Plumtree was shouting in a quacking voice in the back seat. 'You can't kill him with bullets,' he dimly heard her say. 'Even when his Lever Blank acolytes threw him off a building in Soma, he didn't die. He is the Anti-Christ.'

'Oh hell,' he whispered. Who to call up, he thought – not Janis nor Cody, there's no point in breaking the bad news to them yet. '*Valorie!*' he shouted.

At least it shut her up. Angelica had pulled the door closed and folded the stock of her carbine, but now she had popped out the old magazine and rammed a new one in – hardball rounds, Cochran guessed – and had rolled down the window and was sitting on Pete's knees with her head and shoulders, and the rifle, out the window.

She fired six measured, presumably aimed shots – the explosions rang the car roof, but were much less assaulting than the previous five had been – and then she hiked herself back inside and rolled the window back up. Cochran glanced at the rear-view mirror and couldn't see any headlights back there.

'Arky's shot,' Angelica said breathlessly. 'He got shot in the head.'

Cochran nodded at the truck ahead of them, which had just caught the tail end of a green light and turned left onto Marina Boulevard. 'He's driving fine.' Cochran sped up and honked his car horn to catch the yellow light and stay behind the truck; the tires squealed on the slick asphalt but didn't lose traction.

Angelica rubbed her fist on the steamy inside surface of the windshield and peered out through the glass. 'I don't *see* him, though – do you see his *head* at all, if he's driving?'

Cochran tried to see details of the truck in the moments when the windshield wipers had swept aside the blobs and streams of rain. 'No,' he admitted finally, 'but he might be sitting real low.' With the feedback-like ringing in his abused eardrums he had no idea how loud he might be talking.

'But—' he went on shakily, in a louder voice. Hadn't Pete or Angelica noticed? 'But the truck is blue, now.'

'It's—?' Angelica stared expressionlessly at the boxy truck bobbing in the Ian ahead of them. Even in the dim gray light, the truck's color was unmistakably a dusty navy blue. 'And it's – that's him, that's the same truck, we haven't taken our eye off it.' She sat back between Pete and Cochran, looking all at once small and young behind the wet black metal of the gun in her arms. 'The local Holy Week is over, that means – and nobody rose from the dead. We really did fail here today.'

Plumtree wailed in the back seat, and for a moment Cochran thought the mother personality was still on; then she spoke, in the flat cadence of Valorie: '*What would you have me be, an I be not a woman? Manhood is called foolery, where it stands against a falling fabric. And tell the pleasant prince this mock of his hath turned his balls to gun-stones.*'

For a moment no one spoke; then, 'I reckon Kootie was right,' said. Pete. 'I guess the receiver had to be somebody of the same sex.'

Cochran's right shoe sole squeaked back and forth between the brake and the gas pedal, and the engine roared and slacked, roared and slacked, as he swerved from one to another of the eastbound lanes to keep the speeding truck in sight ahead of them, and the word *sex* hung in the steamy air.

CHAPTER TWENTY

The night wore out, and, as he stood upon the bridge listening to the water as it splashed the river-walls of the Island of Paris, where the picturesque confusion of houses and cathedral shone bright in the light of the moon, the day came coldly, looking like a dead face out of the sky. Then, the night, with the moon and the stars, turned pale and died, and for a little while it seemed as if Creation were delivered over to Death's dominion.

—Charles Dickens, *A Tale of Two Cities*

Though he couldn't see her in the shadowy alley ahead of him, Kootie sensed that the woman in the hooded white raincoat had found the *other* mouth of this interminable unroofed passage, and was picking her way down the rain-slicked cobblestones toward him, patient as a shadow.

Even if there had not been wooden crates full of cabbage heads and big green onions stacked against the ancient brick walls, the alley would have been too narrow for any car to drive down it; and the scalloped eaves of the pagoda-style roofs were four or five stories overhead, and Kootie was certain that even on clear days the sunlight had never at any season slanted all the way down to these wet paving stones, which had probably not been dry of rain water and vegetable juices and spit and strange liquors since the pavement was laid – and Kootie giddily thought that must have been before the 1906 earthquake.

If that earthquake ever even happened, he thought, here.

He was crouching in the deeper shadows under an iron stairway, and all he was doing was breathing deeply and listening to his own heartbeat, which for several minutes now had been alternating between scary rapid bursts and even scarier three-second dead stops. Like bad-reception images on a TV, every object he looked at seemed to have a faint twin half-overlapping it to one side, and he suspected that the rainbow-edged twins weren't precisely identical to the actual objects; and the cold, oily air seemed to be shaking with big dialogues he couldn't quite *hear*, like the faint voices you can catch on a turned-up stereo in the moments between tracks.

He wasn't at all sure he was still entirely in the real, San Francisco Chinatown.

When he had first noticed the Chinese woman in the white hooded raincoat he had been standing out of the downpour under an awning in an alley called Street of Gamblers; and he had ducked through a touristy souvenir shop to evade her, hunching through aisles of woks and wisdom hats and plastic back-scratchers, and when he had pushed through the far door and stepped out into the rain again, he had sprinted right across the narrow neon-puddled street, between the idling, halted traffic, into the dark slot of this alley. He hadn't looked back, for when he had caught the woman's eye in the Street of Gamblers she had for one hallucinatory moment seemed to be the globular black silhouette that had showed up on the motel TV screen this morning in the instant after Arky had poured beer into the set; and he had guessed that, whoever she was, she had assumed a psychic posture that had made her compellingly identical to one of the wild archetypes.

He had hurried down this alley – jogging past inexplicable open-air racks of whole barbecued ducks, under ornate balconies and indecipherable banners and clotheslines crazily hung with dripping squid, and stared at by ancient women smoking clay pipes in open doorways – and he had skidded to a panting halt here when it had finally occurred to him that no real alley in San Francisco could stretch this far without crossing a street.

He hadn't eaten anything since a few slices of delivery pizza late yesterday afternoon, and he had been wearing this now-wet flannel shirt for twenty-four hours. He was dizzy, and exhausted without being at all sleepy, and he knew by the aching fractures in his mind that something awful had happened this morning. Something besides industrial pollution and dead sparrows was coming down hard with this rain, and the cooked ducks and raw squids were, he thought, probably being exposed to it intentionally, for some eventual bad sacramental purpose.

He jumped in surprise – and a moment later,

'You caught me,' came a high, lilting voice from close by.

He looked up to his left, and there she was, smiling down at him where he crouched under the stairs.

He had been startled a moment before she had spoken. He was on bar-time again, experiencing events a moment before they actually happened. That meant that she, or somebody, was paying a magical sort of attention to him – but he had bleakly guessed that already.

Her face under the white plastic hood was younger than he had thought, and the faint aura he saw off to one side of her was rainbow-colored now, and was clearly just a reiteration of her real shape.

He noticed that her feet were bare on the wet stones, and that the long black hair that trailed across her chest between the lapels of her raincoat seemed to be clinging to bare skin, rather than to any clothing.

He hiked himself forward and stood up in what he now thought of as the duck-and-squid-basting rain; and he opened his mouth to say something, but she spoke first:

'What are you looking for?' she asked.

Kootie thought about that. 'Shelter, I guess,' he said. 'Food, rest.' He glanced fearfully up and down the alley, clenching his fists against another burst of rapid heartbeat. 'Real streets,' he added breathlessly.

'Go to this place,' she told him, pulling a folded sheet of white paper out of the raincoat pocket and handing it to him. Her fingertips were as cold as the rain.

Then she had hurried past him and away, and the wings of her raincoat spread out wide in the rainy wind, so that she was a white triangle receding away with eerie speed between the close, dark walls.

Kootie unfolded the piece of paper, trying to shield it from the rain with one shaky hand. It was a poorly photocopied line drawing of a scowling Chinaman with tiny smudged images of ships and animals all over his shirt and trousers. In the bottom margin of the paper, ballpoint-ink numbers were arranged unevenly:

60

31 10, 78 53:
   49 80, 86/100 90 91.

—12

Kootie looked after the vanished woman. He understood this code, but he wondered how she had known that he would. It was the Cuban *charada china*, a lottery and rebus system that had been brought to Havana by Chinese contract laborers in the mid-nineteenth century. Originally of thirty-six characters, it had been expanded during the twentieth century to include a hundred symbols.

This reproduction of the famous drawing was so poorly copied that not even the little images on the *chino*'s clothing, much less the tiny numbers beside each one, could be made out – but Kootie's foster-mother Angelica had done so much divination work with the antique system that Kootie effortlessly remembered what picture each number traditionally referred to.

Now he tried to read the indicated images as a message, a letter to him, and after a few moments he had mentally arranged them into phrases, filling in gaps with words that seemed probable:

(On this day of) *dark sun*

Deer Big Fish, Bishop of (Thomas Edison's) *electric light:*
   (Look for a, you'll find a) *drunk physician* (or *physician for drunks*), (at the) *hotel* (or *convent*) (where you saw the) *big mirror and the old man*, (by the) *gemstone tortoise.*

—Saintly woman (or *prostitute*)

How long, Kootie wondered, was she following me? Right around sunrise, when the dead sparrows fell out of the sky with the sour rain, I *did* see an old man propping up a big gilt-framed mirror against a brick wall and staring at me in the reflection. I think he was in front of a Chinese restaurant, though, not a hotel or a convent – though in fact this was right next to a shop called ... *Jade Galore*, with a big jade tortoise in the display window. It had been near the Street of Gamblers ... Washington and Stockton.

Even as he wondered how he might find his way back to the normal San Francisco streets, he heard the rippling throb of car tires on wet pavement; and when he stepped forward and looked to his left, he saw the muted colors of cars moving past across the alley from left to right. A real street! – ask and ye shall receive, he told himself.

He thought about the old man he'd seen with the mirror ... and about the woman in the white raincoat.

Saintly woman (or *prostitute*).

Angelica would see danger in this invitation, spiritual peril even more than physical peril. *Not everybody that uses magic is bad*, she had told him more than once over the past two years, *but it's always bad for them – even if you're masked and working for the good of others or in self defense, it coarsens and blunts your soul.*

Kootie was trudging toward the cross-street ahead, not taking his eyes off the vision of the passing cars, but he was very aware of the paper crumpled in his hand. Angelica would expect him to run away from whatever it was that this letter offered – run to a Catholic church, or to the police, even; ideally, of course, she would expect him to run to her and Pete, if he could find them.

But he knew what his psychically concussed symptoms this morning meant. As Mavranos had pointed out, Kootie was a member of Scott Crane's magical army now – and he knew, in his guts and his spine and the primitive base of his brain, that their army had within the last hour suffered the equivalent of a nuclear strike.

All he could sense with his stunned powers was injury and absence. The attempt to restore Scott Crane to life had palpably failed. Mavranos and Plumtree and Cochran were very likely dead.

Kootie's thoughts just exploded away into chaos whenever he tried to think about his foster-parents. He couldn't believe that Pete and Angelica were dead, but he knew too that his individual capacity for belief wouldn't affect whatever was. His natural parents had been tortured to death only a little more than two years ago; and now the fugitive couple who had taken him in, and had loved him and cared for him and been loved by him, might very well be dead too.

He could only postpone that thought, for now.

For now, Kootie was alone and conspicuous in a hostile, awakened city. *49 80,* he thought. *12.*

He had emerged at last from the dimness of the alley – his sneakers were scuffing on the wet cement of the street sidewalk now, and the passing cars were so obviously real that he could see the momentarily clear tread-prints of their tires on the puddled asphalt as they rolled past, and so close that he could see faces behind the rain-beaded window glass. This street was Stockton. Washington should be the next street down to his left.

He shoved the crumpled paper into his jeans pocket. His legs were shaky, and he had to actually glance down at his belt to make sure he had not buckled it in a Möbius twist – he had not – but he sighed and began shuffling south, toward Washington Street.

The blue truck hadn't been stopping for red lights as it led the Granada on a swerving, skidding chase through the dawn streets of the Richmond district. The truck had braked for cross-traffic, but then gunned through the rainy intersections as soon as a gap between oncoming cars appeared, as if the red lights were just yield signs. Cochran had been hard-pressed to keep the vehicle in sight through the slapping windshield wipers, and even so he had had to run a couple of red lights himself, cursing and sweating as he did it. He had told Angelica to stash her gun under the seat in case they were pulled over by a cop.

On the long westbound stretch of Geary Street, Cochran had briefly been able to pull up in the left lane alongside the racing blue truck, and Pete had hiked himself up nearly to a standing position in the Granada's passenger seat, with his head and shoulders out the window; and when he had slumped back down in the seat and looked across Angelica at Cochran, his rain-wet face was pale.

'He's lying across the seat,' Pete had said flatly. 'Face down, with blood on the seat by his head.'

Cochran had hissed angrily as the truck had edged ahead again. Both vehicles had at times reached speeds of at least fifty, probably sixty – at green lights flying right across the stepped intersections and clanking the abused shock absorbers on the downhill slopes – and he'd been glad these Chinese restaurants and secondhand clothing shops weren't open yet, and that traffic was sparse. 'So who's *driving*?' he'd demanded.

'Nobody is,' Pete had said. 'The truck is.'

'I don't mean to be—' Cochran had begun. 'Damn it, do you mean the *truck* is driving? Driving *itself*?'

'That's what he means,' Angelica had told him, chewing her knuckles. 'If he'd stop – if *it* would stop – at a red light, Pete could get out and get behind the truck's steering wheel.'

'No chance of that, it looks like,' Cochran had said grimly. 'Maybe the thing'll run out of gas.'

Now the truck and the car were on the Great Highway, headed south along the western coast under the lightening gray sky, having screeched through the twisting promontory lanes of Point Lobos Avenue and gunned past the Sutro Bath ruins and the Cliff House Restaurant.

Last week we saw Crane's naked ghost on the seaside rocks down there, Cochran had thought as he had leaned the speeding car around that bend of the highway. Today we're chasing a runaway truck with Crane's skeleton dumped in the back of it and the Kootie kid is gone and Mavranos is probably dead. The king's army has been pruned back right down to the dirt.

The open lanes of the Great Highway stretched straight ahead, with the slate-colored sea to the right and the massive greenery of Golden Gate Park and the stumpy tower of an old windmill rolling past to the left beyond the northbound lanes. Ahead of the Granada the truck was barrelling along, staying in its lane.

Pete Sullivan was sweating. 'Pull up right behind him,' he told Cochran, 'and kill the wipers. We left the back window of the truck's tailgate open, see?'

Cochran switched off the windshield wipers and carefully edged up behind the truck, watching its close bumper rock nearer by inches as the two engines roared on and the lane markers whipped past under the wheels. The raised horizontal window at the back of the truck bobbed on its struts.

'Hope he don't brake,' said Cochran through clenched teeth, 'or—'

'What the hell are you going to do, Pete?' interrupted Angelica. 'You can't!'

'*I* can't,' said Pete Sullivan, flexing his hands and staring at the close back of the truck through the rain-stippled windshield, 'but I bet Houdini can.' He glanced at Angelica. 'Arky might be dying in there'

'Or *dead*, she told him shrilly, 'and *you* might be dying right on this highway! Under the wheels of this very car I'm driving in! Pete, *you can't*. You may have Houdini's hands, but you haven't got his ... the *rest* of his body!' Out of the corner of his eye Cochran saw her pat Pete's knee, as if the subject were closed. 'We'll wait for the truck to run out of gas.' To Cochran she said, 'Hey, back off, you're gonna run right up his tailpipe. And turn the wipers back on.'

The seat jerked hard then as Plumtree grabbed it from behind, and Cochran lifted his foot away from the gas pedal to keep from being jolted into accidentally ramming the truck. Plumtree seemed to be trying to climb over the seat – and then she was clawing at the open passenger-side window as if she intended to climb right out of the speeding car.

'*Take these rats thither,*' she was saying loudly, '*to gnaw their garners. Worshipful mutineers, Valorie puts well forth; pray, follow.*'

Pete Sullivan pried her wet hands loose from the window frame. 'I'll go,' he said, speaking distinctly into her blank face. 'I *will* go. You stay.' He pushed her backward against evident resistance until she was again sitting stiffly in the back seat.

In the rear-view mirror Cochran saw her lean back in the seat, watching Pete steadily.

'Catch up,' Pete told Cochran as he turned around in the front seat and again peered out through the rain-blurred windshield. 'Get closer. Angie, what you can do is say a prayer to ... Ogun, right?' He was panting, almost laughing. 'Isn't he the orisha of iron – Detroit iron, I hope! – and the guy who takes people who die in traffic accidents? Tell him to hold off, here.'

Angelica held up the hand she'd been chewing on, and Cochran saw blood on her knuckles. 'I've been,' she said. 'There's iron in blood. But – Kootie needs you! I need you, goddammit!'

Pete rocked his head toward the back seat. 'Imagine the scene in here if I don't. Anyway it's gonna work.'

Angelica was nodding, and biting her knuckle again. She took her bloody hand away from her face long enough to say, 'I can see you're going to do it. If you die – listen to me! – if you die here I *will not* forgive you.'

Pete dragged his knees up until he was crouching on the seat. 'I'm not gonna die.' He threw a bright glance at Cochran and said, 'Watch me, and the truck. Compensate.'

Cochran was dizzy with the realization that there was no way out of this. 'Get it over with,' he said tightly, gripping the wheel and gently fluttering the gas pedal to keep the car's bumper close to the truck's. He didn't dare glance away from the truck's horribly close back window to look at the speedometer, but the lane markers were hurtling past and he knew the two vehicles must be doing sixty miles per hour.

Pete hiked himself up to sit on the windowsill, with his whole upper body out of the car, out in the battering rain; then he raised his left knee outside and braced the sole of his shoe against the doorpost. He leaned forward against the headwind, and peripherally through the windshield Cochran saw his right hand grip the base of the radio antenna; then Cochran was aware of the fingertips of Pete's left hand pressed against the top edge of the windshield glass.

'Fucking lunatic,' Cochran whispered absently. The steering wheel and the gas pedal seemed to be living extensions of himself, aching with muscular tension, and he felt that he was using the car to reach out and *hold* the speeding truck.

And he was balanced in the driver's seat, ready for it, when Pete jackknifed forward and slammed prone against the outside of the windshield; Cochran just raised his head to be able to see over the blur of Pete's shoulder against the glass, and the speeding car didn't wobble in the lane.

Angelica was muttering syllables in which Cochran heard the name *Ogun* several times; and in one corner of his mind he realized that the words droning in his own head were the Lord's Prayer.

Outside the glass, Pete's hands were braced out to the sides and in front of him as he slowly drew in his feet and edged forward across the car's hood on his knees. His weight was on his fingertips, and it seemed to be his hands that were maintaining his balance.

Houdini's hands, Cochran thought.

Now the fingers of Pete's right hand were curled over the front edge of the car hood, and the left hand slowly lifted in the rushing headwind ... and beckoned.

Cochran increased the pressure of his foot on the gas pedal by an infinitesimal degree; and he felt a nevertheless solid clang shake the car as its bumper touched the truck's.

And in that instant Pete's hands had both lifted away from the hood, and his legs had straightened as he lunged forward in a dive.

Angelica exhaled sharply, and Cochran could only guess at the control it had taken for her to make no greater sound.

But now Pete's shoes were clearly visible kicking in the dark gap under the raised back window of the truck. He had gone into the truck rather than under the car's wheels.

Cochran was shouting with hysterical laughter as he snatched his foot off the gas pedal and trod on the brake, and Angelica was laughing too, though the sudden deceleration had thrown her against the dashboard.

'He must have landed *right on* Crane's skeleton!' Cochran yelled delightedly.

'He'll come up wearing the skull like a hat!' agreed Angelica.

'A *skullcap*!' crowed Cochran, and then he and Angelica were both laughing so hard that he had to slow down still more to keep from weaving in the lane.

'A kamikaze yarmulke,' choked Angelica. 'Catch up, catch up, you don't want to lose 'em now. And turn the windshield wipers back on.'

Cochran's hands were shaking on the wheel now, and the tires thumped over the lane markers as the car drifted back and forth. When he switched the windshield wipers back on, he could see the dim silhouette of Pete Sullivan inside the truck, clambering over the seats.

When Pete seemed to have got up to the driver's seat the truck wobbled visibly and then backfired like a cannonshot, with two flashes of bright yellow flame at the exhaust pipes by the back wheels.

Then Cochran saw Pete Sullivan's hand wave out of the driver's-side window, and the truck swayed smoothly back and forth in a clearly deliberate S-pattern.

Angelica exhaled. 'He's got control,' she said softly. 'He'll be pulling over real quick.'

'Not here,' said Cochran, 'there's no shoulder.' He let himself finally take his eyes off the truck and look around at the landscape. The gray surf still streaked the sea beyond the fence to the right, but at some point they had passed the green forest wall of Golden Gate Park, and now it was low pastel-colored apartment buildings and bungalows that fretted the gray sky to the left. 'He'll want to turn inland to find some place we can park,' he said, and he clicked his left-turn indicator to give Pete the idea.

Pete steered the blue truck in a careful left turn onto Sloat Boulevard, and then drove slowly through half a dozen residential blocks of old white-stucco houses to the parking lot at the South Sunset Playground. There were no other cars in the lot as Cochran swung the Granada into the parking space next to the truck, and Angelica was out of the car before he had even come to a full stop. When Cochran turned off the ignition and got out, she was already standing at the opened passenger-side door of the truck. The rain had stopped and the clouds were breaking up in the east, and the mirror lenses of Angelica's sunglasses flashed as she leaned into the truck cab over Mavranos.

'Can you push against Pete's hands with your feet?' she was saying to Mavranos. 'Both feet? Good! Open your eyes, Arky, I want to check your pupils.' She looked up toward Pete, who was still behind the wheel of the truck. 'We'll need to get him to a hospital, stat. He's conscious, with no bleeding from the ears or nostrils, and this isn't a bullet wound, but ... he was knocked out, it *is* a concussion.'

She doesn't want to say *possible subdural hematoma*, thought Cochran nervously. Mavranos is probably in shock, and doesn't need to hear that there might be blood leaking inside his skull, lethally pressing against the brain.

Plumtree had climbed out of the back of the car now, and she was leaning on the front fender, blinking around at the lawns and swing sets and the two vehicles. 'Did it work?' she asked hoarsely.

'Not a bullet wound?' said Cochran, reluctant to answer Plumtree. He could see that the truck's windshield was starred with cracks radiating from a hole low down on the passenger side. 'What is it then?'

Angelica turned her mirror lenses toward him, then held out a fragment of polished white stone. 'A bullet hit this statue he had on his dashboard – some kind of Buddha – and part of *it* hit him, to judge by the fragments in his scalp. A glancing blow to the back of the head, above the occipital region.' She turned back to Mavranos, whose head Cochran could just see on the truck seat. 'Arky,' she said. 'Open your eyes for me.'

'Did it fucking *work*?' Plumtree demanded. 'Is Scott Crane alive now?'

Cochran bared his teeth in irritation and pity. 'No, Cody. It – failed, I'm sorry.'

'I think the truck was heading back to Leucadia,' said Pete, who had opened the driver's-side door and had one foot down on the pavement. 'I think it would have driven all the way back there, like a horse that knows the way home – if somebody would have filled the gas tank every hour.'

Plumtree had taken a wobbling step back across the asphalt. 'Did it work?' she asked. 'Where's Scott Crane?'

'Radioactive!' Mavranos seemed to say, loudly but in a slurred voice.

'No, Janis,' Cochran said. 'I'm sorry, but it didn't work.' It occurred to him that Plumtree was sounding like a concussion victim herself.

Look at me,' Angelica said to Mavranos.

'You're upside-down,' Mavranos said in a high, nasal voice, 'but I'll look at you all you want.' To a tune that Cochran recognized as some old Elvis Costello song Mavranos sang, 'You better listen to your radio.' But he slurred the last word, so that it seemed to be *ray-joe*.

Angelica had jerked back against the open door, her forehead wrinkled above the sunglasses. 'You – your pupils are normal,' she said uncertainly. 'But we've got to get you to a hospital, Arky, you've got a—'

'Bitch broke my nose!' Mavranos braced himself on his elbow and sat up, feeling his face. 'Is my traitor sister here?' He blinked at Angelica. 'Who the hell are you people? My nose *isn't* broken! Am I – did I do it, am I the king?'

Angelica held out the white stone fragment. 'This was a statue of a, a fat Buddha,' she said, and Cochran could tell that she was trying to keep her voice level. 'Do you – recognize it?'

'Buddha,' said Mavranos in his new, high voice, 'it's not Buddha, it's Tan Tai, gook god of prosperity. I gave her one like it once, when she was still my loyal half-sister.'

Angelica stepped slowly away from the truck, glancing worriedly at Cochran and Plumtree. 'Look only at me please,' she said to them in a quiet, professional tone. 'Pete? Eyes front. We won't be going to a hospital after all, unless I see a deterioration in Arky's vital signs.'

Cochran could feel goose bumps rasping the fabric of his damp shirt-sleeves, and not because of the dawn chill. He understood now that a ghost had got punched into Mavranos's head back there; and he wondered if it was one of the ones that had clustered ahead of the truck on the drive back from the ruins at the end of the yacht-club peninsula, or if it was one that Mavranos had been carrying with him all along, like an old intolerable photo in a sealed locket.

To Cochran, Angelica said, 'You're a local boy – where is there water nearby? Tamed water, contained water. With – we need to get Arky and me into a boat, very quick.'

'A *boat*?' echoed Cochran, trying not to wail in pure bewilderment. 'Okay. Well! Golden Gate Park, I guess. Stow Lake. You can rent boats, I think.'

'Close by?' asked Angelica.

'Two or three miles back the way we came.'

'It's not – famously *haunted* or anything, is it?'

Cochran rocked his head uncertainly. 'There's supposed to be druid stones on the island in the middle of the lake,' he said, 'and I heard that there were stones from a ruined Spanish monastery around the shore; but my wife and I went looking for this stuff a couple of years ago, and couldn't find any of it. Anyway, no, I've never heard of any hauntings or murders or anything.'

Remotely, as if from some previous life, he remembered the picnic he and Nina had unpacked on the Stow Lake island one sunny weekday morning, and how in the bough-shaded solitude at the top of the island hill they had soon forgotten the sandwiches and overturned the wine as they had rolled around on the dewy grass. They had made a sort of bed of their cast-off clothing, and when they had finally collapsed, spent, Nina had said that it had been as if they'd been trying to *climb through* each other.

And now he jumped, for Plumtree had slid her hand up the clinging seat of his jeans.

'Can we go?' she asked quietly. 'Did they get the dead man back alive again?'

'No,' Cochran said, blinking away tears of exhaustion, 'Tiffany. It failed. The dead man is – deader than he was before.'

Her hand was snatched away, but he didn't look at her to see who she might be now; he just stepped to the side to block her view of Mavranos and said, rapidly, 'Remember the little girls we saw on the roof of that clown's house? I think we're in the same sort of – situation now. Look only at Angelica. Do you follow me?'

'Mirrors can ricochet,' she said bleakly, in the voice he now recognized as Cody's. 'I'm looking no higher than the ground.'

Angelica gently pressed the truck door closed until it clicked, as if to keep from waking someone up. 'You lead the way to this lake,' she told Cochran as she pulled open the truck's back door to get in. 'And when we get there, you walk ahead of us and buy the tickets or whatever.'

'Right.' Cochran turned back to the Granada, jerking his head at Plumtree to follow.

'What's left for us?' Plumtree asked dreamily as she got in on the passenger side and Cochran started the engine again. 'After this?' Perhaps she was talking to herself.

'Getting drunk,' he said anyway, clanking the shift lever into reverse. 'What did you think?'

'Oh,' she said, nodding. 'Right. Of course.'

'Boats first.'

'To the boats,' she said, emptily.

CHAPTER TWENTY ONE

CRESSIDA: ... he is himself.
PANDARUS: Himself? Alas, poor Troilus, I would he were.
CRESSIDA: So he is.
PANDARUS: Condition, I had gone barefoot to India.
                           —William Shakespeare, *Troilus and Cressida*

At the corner of Stockton and Washington, Kootie had found only the Chinese restaurant he remembered having passed at dawn, next door to the Jade Galore shop; the restaurant wasn't open, and the old man who had been peering into a mirror propped against the restaurant wall was gone now, and the big old gilt-framed mirror too. Someone had even swept up the dead sparrows. Kootie had turned away toward the wet intersection, stepping to the curb and mentally cursing the Chinese woman who had given him the useless message, when he sensed a change in the light from behind him.

And when he turned around, the restaurant was gone.

In its place stood a three-story plaster-fronted building with narrow arched windows. At a wrought-iron gate to an enclosed patio garden, the woman in white stood staring out at him, and behind her he could see the big framed mirror, propped now against a knotty tree stump in the rainy garden. On a white sign over the gateway arch, plain black letters spelled out, PLEASANT BOARDING HOUSE.

Oh, this is magic, Kootie thought, his spine suddenly tingling with a chill that wasn't from the cold rain. I should run away.

Run away to what place, he asked himself bitterly then, that hasn't been conquered? To what people, that haven't been defeated and probably killed?

His breath was hitching and catching in his throat.

The Chinese woman beckoned with constrained urgency, and touched a finger to her lips. Kootie noticed that though she was still draped in white, it was a frail linen robe she was wearing now, and the fabric appeared to be dry.

At least she's offering shelter, he told himself as he shrugged and stepped back across the sidewalk from the edge of the curb. His sneakers squished on the pavement, and he could feel cold water spurting between his toes.

The woman tugged the gate open on hinges that made no sound over the clatter of the rain, and then pushed it closed again after Kootie had stepped through onto the round paving stones laid out across the patio mud. 'What is this place?' he whispered to her.

Her face was tense as she shook her head again and pressed her cold lips to his ear. 'Later,' she breathed, and at least her breath was warm. 'Don't wake up the master of the house.' As she pulled her face back she nodded out toward the garden without looking that way.

Kootie had to look. He glanced over his shoulder as the woman took his elbow and hurried him toward a pair of windowed doors ahead – but all he saw in the walled garden, aside from the dripping ginger stalks and rose vines on the far side of the rain-stippled puddles, was the tree stump with the mirror leaning against it.

Squinting against the rain, he saw that the stump was a gnarled and hairy old grapevine, a full yard thick, with jagged, chunky outcrops where old canes had been pruned back. A soggy animal fur had been draped around two of the truncated woody limbs as if around shoulders, and to Kootie the bumpy bark between the cane stumps looked, in the moment before the woman pulled him through the doors into a dry, pine-floored hallway, like the whiskery gray face of an aged man.

The woman in the white robe was leading him quickly toward a set of polished black wood stairs that led upward. 'What is this place?' Kootie whispered again.

'It's his boardinghouse,' she whispered back. He takes in boarders? Kootie thought. 'It's not here all the time,' she went on, 'but it's always here on January seventeenth, for people with the right kind of eyes – and with this bad checkmate rain, the place would certainly have been here today in any – case or else this rain couldn't have happened except on this day, St. Sulpice's Day. If you're a fugitive, you're welcome here.' They had reached a shadowy upstairs corridor with narrow gray-shining windows along one wall, and she led Kootie by the hand to an open interior door.

'Are you hungry?' she asked. 'I've cooked you a king's breakfast.'

Kootie could smell some kind of spicy roasting meat on the musty air. 'Hungry as a bedbug,' he said, quoting an old Solville line that had somehow evolved from *Don't let the bedbugs bite.*

'Me too!' she said with a breathless laugh as she stepped into the dimly lit room. 'This Death-card rain will bring out a *lot* of fugitive places in the city, like toadstools, that won't be there anymore after the sun comes out again. But the eating is best here.'

Kootie followed her into the room, and quickly stepped across onto a knitted rug so as not to drip rain water onto the polished wood floor. There were no windows in the room, but flames in oil lamps on the walls threw a soft illumination across dark old tapestries and a battered white make-up table and a huge, canopied bed. A black-brick fireplace took up most of the far wall, and though there were no logs on the grate, a tiny brass brazier stood on the broad hearthstone, with coals glowing under a grill draped with strips of sizzling, aromatic meat. A basket of thick black bread slices stood on a carpet nearby.

'The Loser's Bar is surely out there somewhere today,' the woman said as she tossed her head back, freeing her long black hair from the linen hood, 'serving pointless seafood today – though they might as well be serving cooked sandals and baseball caps, for all the good it can do anyone on a day like this.'

Her hair was lustrously dry now, and Kootie wondered how she could have dried it, and changed her clothes, and prepared this food, in the few minutes since he had seen her in the long alley off the Street of Gamblers. And he remembered how her silhouette had seemed for a moment to be the knobby round figure that had shown up briefly on the motel television.

I don't care, he thought. I can take care of myself. He saw a bottle of dark wine by the mirror on the make-up table, and he was able to cross to it and pick it up without stepping on bare floor.

The label just said, BITIN DOG.

'I shouldn't,' he said uncertainly, 'be eating … meat.' Or drinking alcohol, he thought.

'Here's a dry robe for you,' she said. 'You don't want to meet the lord of this house in those clothes anyway. Take them off and get warm.' She looked at the bottle in his hand and smiled at him. 'You can have a drink of that … after. It's the wine of forgetfulness, you know. And it's all right – *it* you can swallow with impunity, as much as you like, the whole bottle.' She knelt in front of him and began prising loose the knots in his soaked sneaker laces. She looked up at him. 'You'd like some of that, wouldn't you? Impunity?'

'God,' said Kootie softly, 'yes.' *After*, he thought. After what?

'The peppered venison is still raw in the middle,' she said. 'We can eat it, too, after.'

'Okay,' he said, and began unbuttoning his shirt with shaking fingers. He hoped the cut over his ribs wasn't bleeding through the bandage.

Fleetingly to his mind came an image of himself buttoning his shirt as he stumbled sleepily out of his Solville bedroom, sniffing onions and eggs and coffee on jasmine-scented morning air, yawning and replying *As a bedbug!* to Angelica's cheery *Are you hungry?*

Good-bye to all that, he thought despairingly.

The boathouse in Golden Gate Park was locked up and the boats were inert and chained to the dock when the five bedraggled figures trudged across the lake lawn to the shuttered rental window, but the two teenaged park employees who'd been banging around inside agreed to open early after Angelica made Cochran offer them a hundred dollars; and by the time the sun was coming up over the cypresses, two electric boats were buzzing slowly out across the glassy surface of Lake Stow – Pete and Angelica and the distracted Mavranos in one, and Cochran and Plumtree closely pacing them in the other.

The boats were small, with not quite enough room on the padded benches for three people to sit comfortably. A toggle switch on the right side by the steering wheel turned the electric motor of each boat on and off, and with no windshield the long flat hood was a sort of table. Cochran wished they could have stopped to get beer in addition to his hundred dollars, he had paid twenty-six dollars for the minimum full hour for two boats, and it looked as though it would take the tiny engines the whole hour to coax the boats all the way around the wooded island in the middle of the lake. The unrippled water ahead was studded with ducks and seagulls who all might have been asleep. Cochran remembered the dead birds that had fallen out of the sky after Crane had turned into a skeleton, and so he was relieved when a couple of these ducks awoke and went flapping away across the lake, their wing tips slapping rings in the water like skipped stones.

The boat with Angelica and Pete and Mavranos in it buzzed along at a dog-paddle pace only two yards to the right of Cochran's elbow, which hung out over the low gunwale of the boat he shared with Plumtree.

'Angie, shouldn't we be going the other way around?' asked Pete Sullivan in a near-whisper. 'This is clockwise, not ... windshield.'

'I wish we could,' Angelica muttered. 'But that's an evasion measure, we don't dare – we might wind up losing the wrong one.' She shook her head. 'God, this is slow! The motor on this boat sounds like a *sewing machine*.'

Cochran thought of the woman who had been called Ariachne in the version of *A Tale of Two Cities* that he had read on the plane home from Paris a week and a half ago – the woman who sewed into her fabrics the names of people who were to be beheaded on the guillotine.

Angelica sighed and squared her shoulders. 'What's your name?' she said now, speaking to Mavranos. Her voice was clear in the still air.

'Ray-Joe Pogue,' Mavranos said quietly. 'I'm not okay, am I? I remember now – I fell off of Hoover Dam. I was blind, and a man told me it was the *water* below me, Lake Mead, but he lied. It was the *other* side of the dam below me, the tailrace, the power station roof – way, way down, with a hard, hard landing.'

'It's the water below you now, though,' Angelica said gently. 'You can see it, can't you?' She dipped her hand in the water, lifted a palmful and let it trickle back into the lake.

'I'm seeing two of everything,' said Mavranos. He looked at Angelica. 'There are two bulls in your glasses! Did you have animals in your glasses before? You do now.' He was visibly shivering.

'Now you're seeing as you should be seeing,' said Angelica. 'The pairs will get rather apart – like bars in a prison – until you can escape between them.' She smiled. But you should lose some weight! Tell me how your sister betrayed you.'

Cochran remembered Angelica's description of a conventional honoring-of-the-dead ritual. Clearly she was trying now to lift the ghost away from Mavranos's mind, over this giant cup of relatively transparent water so that the ghost wouldn't … *fixate*. And, in asking the ghost to talk about itself, she was apparently trying to get it to relax its psychic claws out of *Mavranos's* mind and memories. It probably helped that Mavranos's mind was still concussed and disorganized – that must have been why he'd been in such a hurry to get here.

'Nardie Dinh,' came the high, nasal voice from Mavranos's mouth. *'Bernardette* Dinh. She was my half-sister, our dad married a Vietnamese woman after he divorced my mom. I was supposed to become the king, at the succession in '90, and Nardie was supposed to be my queen. I kept her a virgin, until I should take the crown, the cown of the American West … but she rebelled against me, she was ungrateful for what I had made her into, with diet and discipline and exposure to the gods behind the Major Arcana tarot cards … she *killed* the woman I had placed her with, *escaped* me. Nardie threw in her lot with the Scott Crane faction—'

All at once, with a chill, Cochran remembered Mavranos saying back in Solville that he had once killed a man at Hoover Dam.

'—and she hit me in the nose, broke my nose, five days before Easter. Swole up, black eyes. I couldn't become the king with the injury, and for sure there wasn't time for it to heal. I drove out to the dam to stop the succession, use magic to throw it off for another twenty years … and she sent – this man!—' Mavranos's hand touched his face '—to kill me.'

Mavranos's head rocked back to stare into the overhanging alder branches against the sky. 'It's true,' he said in a harsher voice, 'that I killed you. On purpose, knowing what I was doing – because you would have killed my friends, if I hadn't. But Nardie didn't want me to do it.'

He inhaled hitchingly, and when he spoke again it was in the nasal voice: 'But she thanked you for doing it. I was aware of that.' And Mavranos's natural voice said, 'It's true.'

Angelica's mouth was open and she was frowning, as if she wanted to convey a message to Mavranos without letting the Pogue ghost hear; and Cochran wondered if Mavranos had ruined Angelica's plan by awakening now and conversing with the ghost; but Mavranos was speaking again in his own voice:

'Ray-Joe Pogue, the bars are nearly wide enough apart for you to leave, to jump, and it *is* water below you, this time. I've carried you, in guilt, for five years, nearly – and Nardie has too, I've seen it pinch her face when people talk about ... *family* I bet we've both thought of you every day, your death has been like a bad smell that I can't get rid of, that I notice just when I've started to forget about it and have a nice time.' Mavranos yawned, or else Ray-Joe Pogue did. 'Before you go free,' Mavranos said, 'can you forgive us?'

'Do you want that?' came the other voice from his throat.

Angelica dipped her hand into the water again.

Mavranos inhaled to be able to reply. 'Yes. We do both want that – very badly'

'Mess with the bull, you get the horns,' said the high voice. 'It's enough to know that you do want it.'

Mavranos sighed deeply, and his head rocked forward – and Angelica whipped her hand across and slapped him in the face with a handful of water.

'*Now,* Arky!' she, said urgently. 'What's my name? Where were you born? Who's president of the United States?'

Mavranos was spitting. 'Angelica Sullivan, goddammit. Muscoy, San Bernardino County, California, in 1955, okay? And William Jefferson Airplane Clinton.'

Both boats had stalled in the water.

'Get these boats moving out of here,' said Angelica sharply, 'the ghost is off him but it'll be a standing wave here for a while. Everybody lean out and paddle, if you have to.'

Cochran flipped the toggle switch on his boat off and on again, and the motor resumed its buzzing and his boat surged slowly ahead of Angelica's until she copied his move and got hers running again too.

Pete Sullivan exhaled as though he'd been holding his breath. 'Good work, Angie.'

Angelica pushed her hair back from her face, and Cochran saw that she was sweating. 'He might have forgiven you, Arky,' she panted, 'but I had to swat him off right then – he had let go of your mind for a moment, in something like real serenity, but he might have gripped on again at any moment, and clung. It would have killed you.' She looked around, and spun the steering wheel to avoid tangling the boat in the arching branches of an oak tree that had fallen from the island bank into the water. 'Sorry, if I was too hasty.'

Mavranos cleared his throat and spat mightily out past the bow. 'I'll ... get along without it,' he said hoarsely. 'Damn, I can still taste his ghost. Motor oil and *Brylcreem*.'

Plumtree spoke up from beside Cochran. 'You want people to *forgive* you?'

Cochran steered the boat ponderously out toward the middle of the water. 'Some people want that, Cody.'

'I'm Janis. I'd rather buy a new tire than drive on one with a patch.'

The boats were trundling around the east end of the island in the middle of the lake. Seagulls wheeled above a waterfall that poured over tall stone shelves on the island, and closer at hand Cochran saw some kind of Chinese pavilion on the shore, among the green flax stalks that crowded right down into the water. At the top of the island hill he could see the trees around the clearing where he and Nina had made love, so terribly long ago.

'We're going to watch you closely, Arky,' said Angelica. 'If your pupils start to act funny, or your pulse, or if your speech gets slurred or disconnected – "waxing and waning mentation" – then you *are* going into a hospital, and we can do our level best to keep you masked in there. But you've – right now you'd be much better off out of such a place.'

Mavranos nodded grimly, touching the cut in the back of his scalp. His hair was spiky with bourbon as well as blood, for Angelica had sterilized it with a few hasty splashes from a pint bottle Mavranos had kept in his glove compartment, promising to put a proper bandage on it as soon as the wound had been 'thoroughly aired out.' Presumably it had been, now.

'Nardie Dinh gave me that statue I had on the dashboard,' Mavranos said. 'She probably did mean something by it, even after all these years, though she loves me like a – like a brother. Damn sure she didn't mean it to be shot into my head.' He looked at Angelica. 'But it was. And I think you mean ghosts would be attracted to me in a hospital ... now.'

'There are a lot of scared, lonely, hungry ghosts hanging around in hospitals,' Angelica said, staring ahead. The boats had rounded the eastern end of the island, and were now buzzing irresolutely in the direction of a double-arched stone bridge.

Mavranos laughed weakly. 'Keep your eyes on the course, by all means,' he said. 'Lose control of this torpedo and we're liable to plow right up onto the bank. What I mean is, I'm *particularly* vulnerable right now, aren't I?'

'*Yes*,' said Angelica. She gave Plumtree a haggard stare. 'What did you mean, Janis, about a new tire?'

'Oh, I meant like a ... relationship that's been ... fractured,' Plumtree said. 'I wouldn't try to patch it up, I'd just move on and meet somebody new, somebody who didn't yet have any disappointments with me.'

'Or cobble up a new personality out of some of the unused lumber of your soul,' Cochran said tiredly, 'one that hasn't even met the other person yet. Fresh start all around.'

Plumtree nodded. 'My father hath a power; inquire of him, and learn to make a body of a limb.'

That had sounded like Shakespeare. 'Valorie?' Cochran asked.

'Janis,' Plumtree said, glancing at him impatiently. 'I told you that, Sid.'

A lot of the tall oaks had fallen into the water on this side of the island, and the interior wood at the split stumps was raw and pale, and the leaves on the water-spanning branches were still green; clearly these trees had been felled in the storms that had battered the whole California coast two weeks ago, at dawn on New Year's Day ... when Scott Crane had been killed.

'Don't say anything specific,' Plumtree said hastily, 'about why we're here, or you *wil* have Valorie in the boat with you. But even in what we were trying to do, I – I wanted *him* to be *alive* again, but I didn't want his *forgiveness*. I didn't want one bit more of his attention on me than would have been necessary! And even that, Valorie would have taken.' There were tears in her eyes, and she let Cochran put his arm around her.

'Not your flop,' he said.

She buried her face in the shoulder of his damp windbreaker, and when his hand slid down to her waist his palm was on her bare, cool skin where Nina's sweater had hiked up away from her jeans; and he found himself remembering Tiffany's hand caressing him half an hour earlier – and the steamy sweater smelled of Nina's rose-scented perfume, blended once again here with the wild odors of pine sap and lake water, and for just a reflexive moment, before instant shame actually pulled his lips back from his teeth, he wondered if the rain had ruined the cassette in his shirt pocket.

None of them spoke as the boats buzzed quietly under the island-side arch of the old stone bridge. Cochran noticed one, then several, then dozens of black turtles perched motionless on the unnaturally horizontal branches of the felled trees – but as soon as he started to watch for them, all the dark ovals he focussed on proved to be pinecones.

He lifted his left arm from around Plumtree so that he could steer the boat with that hand; his right hand, with the ivy-leaf mark on the back of it, he stuffed into the pocket of his windbreaker.

To the left, beside the park road, a particularly big redwood tree had fallen this way across the lakeside footpath, and a segment as broad as the path had been sawed out of the six-foot-thick log so that strollers and bicyclists could pass unimpeded. Perhaps the tree was too heavy to move, and would stay there forever as a randomly placed wall, while its water-arching branches would eventually be overgrown by ivy and form a sort of new, hollow bank. After a while, like the cemetery construction on the yacht-club peninsula, it might look like part of the original plan.

With that thought Cochran looked ahead – and at last saw the carved stones of the Spanish monastery.

They were set low into the lakeside mud as an irregular segmented coping between the park grass and the water, each placed so that a broken-stone face was turned upward; only from this vantage point, low and out on the water, could the fretted and fluted carved sides be seen.

'Nina and I didn't search from out in a boat,' he said wonderingly. When Angelica gave him a weary, questioning look, he went on, 'There's the stones from the old monastery – from here you can see what they are.'

Mavranos blinked ahead uncomprehendingly. 'What are they?' He had still been unconscious when Cochran had mentioned them before.

'William Randolph Hearst bought a medieval Spanish monastery,' Cochran said, quoting what Nina had told him, 'and he had it dismantled and shipped to America to reassemble over here – but the crates and plans burned up, and nobody knew how to put the building back together again. And after a while the park maintenance guys began using the stones for ... odd little landscaping projects, like *that*.' He pointed ahead, at the half-submerged bits of forgotten pillars and porticoes.

'And you said there are druid stones on the island,' said Pete Sullivan. 'Maybe the monastery stones *counter* those, balance 'em – net zero.'

'A monastery building would have been formally blessed,' Mavranos muttered, nodding. 'Sanctified.'

'I'm glad you were along,' Angelica told Cochran. 'This lake *was* a perfectly balanced place to shake off the ghost.'

'Not the job those stones thought they'd have,' Mavranos went on, 'when they were carved up so pretty, I bet – just sitting here in the water, not even looking different from plain old fieldstones to anybody walking by 'em. But there's this purpose they can serve. Even broken. *Because* they're broken.'

Again Cochran thought of walls made of chance-fallen trees, and stairs and benches and pavements made of scavenged pieces of derelict cemetery marble.

'There's the dock,' said Pete, pointing ahead and to the right. 'Our tour's up. Where to now? Back to the Star Motel, see if Kootie's waiting for us there?'

'Not yet,' said Angelica. 'And not in the truck with Crane's skeleton in it. We—'

Plumtree jumped in the seat beside Cochran. 'His *skeleton's* in the truck? How did he—' She blinked around. 'What? What scared Janis?'

Cochran turned to her, wondering if he was about to summon Tiffany here, and if so, what he'd tell *her*. 'Crane's skeleton is in the truck, Cody.'

She blinked at him. Then, 'Fuck me!' she said, and in spite of himself Cochran smiled at the idea that he might take the exclamation as evidence of Tiffany's presence; but in fact he could see that this was still Cody. 'I'm still *on*?' she said angrily. 'How come *I'm* the one that gets to stay with all the horrible flops lately? His *skeleton*? Goddammit, Valorie's supposed to take the intolerable stuff!'

'I guess you can tolerate more than you imagine,' said Cochran gently.

'They say that God won't hit you with more than you can handle,' said Mavranos in a faint, shaky voice, possibly to himself. 'Like, if He made you so you can just take a hundred pounds per square inch, He won't give you a hundred and one.'

'We're still too hot,' Angelica went on. 'Magically, I mean. There's been a lot of fresh—' Her breath caught in her throat. '—fresh blood spilled, this morning. I think plain *compasses* will point at us for a while after all this stuff – and we can't be certain we haven't been followed, either. On the drive down here, we were all looking ahead at the truck, not back. If Kootie *is* at the motel, he'll wait for us, he's got a key. And I guess he's ... *the king*, now. He'll have the protections that come with the office.' She looked around among the trees at the anonymous pastel Hondas and Nissans that had begun to drive slowly past on the park road. 'We should drive somewhere, aimless, watching behind, and just sit for an hour or so. Give ourselves time to fall back to our ground states.'

'I'm a, a *citizen* of the ground state,' said Plumtree. 'And our – *community hall* – is a bar. I need a drink like a Minnie needs a Mickey.'

'The truck can go where it likes,' Cochran declared. 'The Ford is going to the first bar we find.'

'I'd be interested in finding something to chase that cabernet with,' ventured Pete.

'I *don't think*,' said Angelica judiciously, 'that I can stay sane for very long, right now, without a drink, myself.' She sighed and clasped her elbows. 'Arky, I guess you can have one, but you'd better stay sober. Doctor's orders.'

Mavranos didn't seem to have heard any of the discussion. 'But can we really imagine,' he went on quietly, 'that He'd give you anything less than ninety-nine-point-nine?'

Angelica frowned at Mavranos's disjointed rambling, probably thinking about *waxing and waning mentation*. 'If Kootie's at the motel,' she said again, absently, 'he'll wait for us. And he'll be safe. He's the king now.'

When he had tugged off his shirt and jeans and kicked his soaked sneakers heedlessly away across the gleaming floor, the woman had kissed Kootie, her arms around his neck and her robe open on nothing but bare, hot skin against his cold chest. Her tongue had slid across his teeth like an electric shock.

They had fallen across the quilt on the huge, canopied bed, and Kootie had been feverishly trying to free his hands to pull the robe off of her and tug his own damp jockey shorts off as she kissed his neck and chest – when he'd heard what she had been whispering.

'Give me you,' she'd been saying hoarsely, 'you're not a virgin – fill me up – you're so big – you can spare more than I can take – and not near die.'

Die? he had thought – and then her teeth had begun gently scoring the skin over the taut muscle at the side of his neck.

If she had been drawing any blood at all it had been from no more than a scratch, and the sensation had been only pleasurable ...

But he had suddenly been aware that his psychic attention and self was wide open and strainingly extended, and that with all the strength of her own mind she was trying to *gnaw off a piece of his soul.*

—In an instant's flash of intolerable memory he was again duct-taped into a seat in a minivan that had been driven up inside a moving truck in Los Angeles – 'a boat in a boat' – while a crazy one-armed man with a hunting knife was stabbing at his ribs, trying to cut out his soul, and consume it—

Abruptly the room seemed to tilt, and grow suddenly darker and hotter, and he was unreasoningly sure that he was about to fall bodily into her furnace mouth, which in this moment of vertiginous nightmare panic seemed to have become the gaping black fireplace below his feet.

He felt himself sliding—

And with all the psychic strength that the events of this terrible morning had bequeathed to him, he lashed out, with such force that he was sure he must have burst a blood vessel in his head.

He hadn't moved at all, physically, and only a second had passed, when he realized that her skin was impossibly cold and that her bare breasts were still – she was not breathing.

He tugged his arms out from under her chilly weight and scrambled off the bed. Sobbing and shaking, he clumsily pulled his jeans and shirt on, and he was thrusting his feet back into his sodden sneakers, when the hallway door was snatched open.

An old woman was standing silhouetted in the doorway.

'Call nine-one-one,' Kootie blubbered, 'I think she's—'

'She's dead, child,' the old woman said sternly. 'Both the telephones downstairs are still ringing themselves off their hooks with their poor magnets shaking, and the god's big mirror has got a crack right across it. She's dead and flung bodily right over the spires of India like a cannonball. What-all did the poor woman want, one little bit of the real you, and you couldn't spare it? Child, you don't know your own strength.' She shook her head. 'He can't meet you now, with or without the humble-pie breakfast, the wine and the venison. Later, and probably not affording to be as polite as it would have been now. You've clouded yourself beyond his sight here today.'

Kootie cuffed the tears from his eyes and blinked up at her – and then clenched his teeth against a wail of pure dismay. The figure scowling down at him was the old woman he and his parents had seen so many times on the magically tuned black-and-white television. Now he could see that her eyes were of different colors, one brown and one blue.

'I'm Mary Ellen Pleasant,' she told him. 'You may as well call me Mammy Pleasant, like everybody else. Now, boy, don't you fret about what you've done here, bad though it damn well is – hers won't be the first dead body I've disposed of in secret. Right now you get your clothes in order, and come down and talk to me in the kitchen.'

She stepped back out into the hall, mercifully leaving the door open. As her footsteps receded away along the wooden floor outside, Kootie stood up. Without looking toward the nearly naked body on the bed, he crossed to the make-up table and picked up the bottle of Bitin Dog wine.

You'd like some of that, wouldn't you? he remembered the woman saying. *Impunity?*

The humble-pie breakfast ...

Cochran had said, 'Couldn't have asked for a better place,' and swung the Granada across momentarily empty oncoming lanes into the uneven parking lot of a bar-and-restaurant that seemed to be a renovated cannery from the turn of the century, the walls all gray wood and rusty corrugated iron. Over the door nearest where he parked was a sign that read THE LOSER'S BAR, but Plumtree pointed out a sign over the main building: SEAFOOD BOHEMIA.

'Fine,' Cochran said as they left the car unlocked and hobbled to the bar door 'we can have bohemian seafood for lunch, if they take plastic here.'

The dusty blue Suburban was out in the center divider lane of Masonic Avenue, its left blinker light flashing.

Cochran plodded up the wooden steps, hiking himself along with his hand on the wet wrought-iron rail, and he held the bar door open for Plumtree.

She took one step into the dim interior, and then stopped and looked back over her shoulder at him. 'Sid,' she said blankly, 'this place—'

He put one hand on her shoulder and stepped in past her.

The mirror-studded disco ball was turning over the sand-strewn dance floor, but again there was no one dancing. The air still smelled of candle wax, but with a strong accompaniment of fish-reek this time instead of mutton. Two men in rumpled business suits, conceivably the same men as before, stood at the bar and banged the cup of bar dice on the wet, polished wood.

The dark-haired waitress in the long skirt smiled at them and waved toward a booth near the door.

'We shouldn't stay,' whispered Cochran. He was still holding the door open, and he glanced nervously back out at the car and the parking lot and the Suburban, which was now turning into the lot.

'You think if you go in and shut the door, we'll walk out and be on Rosecrans again?' asked Plumtree. 'Down in Bellflower?'

'It's possible,' he said, his voice unsteady. 'If it's possible for this place to be *here* at all.'

'Wait in the car, if you like.' She stepped away from his hand, into the dimness of the bar. 'I'll try to sneak you out a beer from time to time. I need a *drink*.' She was shaking, but clearly not because of the weird bar.

'—No,' he said. 'I'm with you.'

They both stepped inside, and as the door squeaked shut behind them they scuffed across the sandy wooden floor to the indicated booth and sat down, with Plumtree facing the front door. Cochran noticed two aluminum crutches propped on the seat of the booth beyond theirs, but neither he nor Plumtree were inclined to be peering around at their surroundings, and they just humbly took the two leather-bound menus the waitress handed them.

'Two Budweisers,' said Plumtree. She was breathing deeply, like someone hoping not to be sick.

'And I'll have two Coorses, please,' said Cochran. 'Oh, and there are three more in our party,' he added, holding up three fingers. The waitress nodded, perhaps understanding, and strode away back to the bar, her long skirt swirling the patterns of sand on the floor.

Plumtree had opened her menu, and now pried a slip of paper from a clip on the inside cover. She frowned. 'Do you remember if the specials were all fish things, before?'

'No, I don't,' said Cochran. 'I ordered off the printed menu that time.'

'I didn't look at the specials either, then.' She read, '*Barbunya, Morina, Levrek* – mullet, cod, bass – this is all fish. And it seems more Middle Eastern now, than Greek. If it was Greek before.'

'Then maybe this *isn't* the same place, because I do remember you saying it was—' he began; then he paused, for she had flipped the specials sheet over and then pushed it across the table toward him.

On the back of the sheet, in his own handwriting in ballpoint ink was written: CODY, JANIS, TIFFANY, VALERIE, HIM. The E in VALERIE had been crossed out, with an O written in above.

'Do you remember writing that?' she asked.

In spite of everything that had happened to him during this last two and a half weeks, Cochran's first impulse was to look around at the other people in the bar, to see who had set up this hoax; then he sagged, remembering how random and unconsidered had been their route to this place today.

'Sure,' he said dejectedly. 'It was only a week ago, and I wasn't that drunk.' His heart was thudding in his chest, and he stared at the paper and wondered if he was more angry or scared. 'I guess this is more … *magic*, huh.'

Plumtree tapped the word HIM. 'I can't,' she said, 'ever have *him* come on again.' She touched her face and her throat. 'Do you see these cuts? Razor nicks! I think *he* was *shaving*.' Behind Cochran the front door squeaked.

He opened his mouth, but Plumtree had looked past him, toward the front door, and now held up her hand to cut him off. 'The rest of the losers have arrived,' she said loudly; then she leaned toward him and whispered quickly, 'I think he *had* to!'

Mavranos and Pete and Angelica slid into the booth from Cochran's side, so that Pete Sullivan was now crowding him against Plumtree.

'Scott's skeleton is all busted to shit,' said Mavranos.

'Valorie says Pete jumped on it,' said Plumtree.

'Somebody should bury it,' said Mavranos, 'back at the Leucadia compound.'

'You can do that yourself, Arky,' said Angelica. 'Oh hell – a tequila *añejo*, neat, with a Corona chaser,' she said to the waitress who had walked up with a tray and begun to shift full beer glasses onto the table, 'and a – Coors Light, Pete? – for this gentleman, please. Arky? Dr. Angelica Elizalde says you can have one beer.'

Mavranos heaved a windy sigh. 'A club soda for me,' he said. 'That which I greatly feared hath come upon me.'

'What, sobriety?' said Pete Sullivan. 'I don't think that's a decision you should make right after a concussion.'

'At Spider Joe's trailer, out in the desert north of Las Vegas in 1990,' Arky said 'the Fool archetype took possession of everybody in the room, except me. J knocked the tarot cards onto the floor, broke the spell. I couldn't … have a personality in my head that wasn't me.'

Angelica touched his scarred brown hand. 'He's gone, Arky,' she said. 'I'd tell you he was inhabiting one of those ducks on that lake now, if I wasn't sure he went right on past India.'

Mavranos nodded, though Cochran got the feeling that Angelica hadn't addressed the man's real concern. 'I'll stick with water,' Mavranos said. 'It probably should be salt water, for the *leaching* properties.'

'Carthage cocktail,' came a gravelly voice from the table behind Cochran, away from the front door. 'In the winter and spring, surfers taste fresh water in the San Francisco Bay sometimes, from the Sacramento River.'

Cochran shifted around to see the speaker, and at this point he was only a little surprised to recognize the black dwarf who had made his way on crutches out of the Mount Sabu bar down in the Bellflower district of Los Angeles, when Cochran and Plumtree had been ... had been here, there; and Cochran recalled now that when the dwarf had opened the door then the draft from outside had smelled of the sea.

The little man's aluminum crutches stood on the seat next to him, the cushioned ends leaning against the electric light sconce over his gleaming bald head. An iron wok sat incongruously on the table in front of him, red-brown with rust and filled to near the rim with a translucent reddish liquid that seemed to be wine.

Cochran had braced his right hand behind Plumtree's shoulders, and now the black man was staring at the back of Cochran's hand. He met Cochran's eyes and exposed uneven teeth in a smile, then rang the rim of the wok with an oversized spoon. Ripples fretted the surface of the wine, for that's what it was – Cochran could smell it now, a dry domestic Pinot Noir or Zinfandel.

Plumtree on his right and Pete on his left were leaning forward, leaving Cochran to talk to the stranger.

'My name is Thutmose?' said the black man. 'Known as Thutmose the Utmos'? This year the surfers haven't tasted freshwater yet.' He ladled some of the wine into a glass with the spoon. 'Do you think they will?'

Cochran had already gulped down half of one of his beers, and he could feel the dizzying pressure of it in his head. 'No,' he said, thinking of the failure at dawn. 'I reckon they won't, this year.'

'That's the wrong attitude,' said Thutmose. 'Will you drink some of my wine? It's decent store-bought Zinfandel right now, and it *could* be ... *sacramento.*'

'No, I've – I'm working on beer,' said Cochran. His neck was aching from being twisted around toward the dwarf, and he was irritably aware that the others at his table were now talking among themselves.

Thutmose seemed disconcerted. 'Do you know where Zinfandel came from?' he snapped. The whites of his glittering eyes were as red as the wine.

'What, originally?' Cochran closed his tired, stinging eyes for a moment, then opened them. 'Sure, a guy named Count Haraszthy brought it to California from Hungary in the 1850s.' He was trying to keep track of both conversations – behind him he heard Angelica say, 'I picked up the lighter, but the two silver dollars were just gone.' And Plumtree helpfully said, 'Well, the lighter's worth a lot more than two bucks.'

'It showed up in the eastern Mediterranean in 1793,' declared Thutmose, 'right after the revolutionaries up in Paris desecrated Notre Dame cathedral – they deliberately stored *grain* there, in the place that had already been holy to the vine for thousands of years before any Romans laid eyes on the Seine River – and then they – filled the gutters of Paris! – with the blood of the aristocrats who had been using the holy wine's debt-payer properties too freely. "It is not for kings and princes to drink wine, lest they drink, and forget the law." Proverbs 13. So the Zinfandel grape all at once and appeared and started growing wild in all the god's old places, in Thebes, and Smyrna, and Thrace, and Magnesia. The Yugoslavian Plavac Mali grape is a strayed cousin of it. And the disrespected vine took its new Zinfandel castle right across the water to America, tossing the bad root-lice behind it like the Romans sowed salt in Carthage. A *mondard* of the *new* world now.'

Halfway through the little man's speech, long before even the word *mondard*, Cochran had nervously realized that Thutmose was somehow involved in the season's Fisher King contentions, and that he must be here at the Losers Bar for reasons related to those of Cochran's party; clearly too the dwarf had at least guessed that Cochran and his friends had been concerned in it.

As if confirming Cochran's thought, Thutmose said, 'You're the people who had the red truck, and the undead king.'

But it's all over now, Baby Blue, Cochran thought helplessly. The red truck's blue now, and the undead king is deader than a mackerel. Kootie will be king now, and Kootie isn't here.

'Do you know what *sin-fan-dayl* means, in classical Greek?' Thutmose went on, in a wheedling tone now. 'A sieve, washed clean and bright and joyous in the noonday sun. Drink the sacramental Zinfandel and *become* the sieve – all your loves fall right through you to the god, and you're cleansed and cheered in the process – you're refreshed, even under the harsh eye of the sun. "Give wine unto those that be of heavy hearts."' The little man was practically declaiming now, and Cochran hoped Plumtree hadn't heard the bit about the eye of the sun.

Again the dwarf rang the wok with his spoon, and it dawned on Cochran that Thutmose wanted him to acknowledge the rusty bowl, refer to it.

It's a half-ass Grail, Cochran thought suddenly; and Thutmose is some sort of near-miss, fugitive, underworld Fisher King – crippled by God-knows-what unhealing injury, and clearly hoping for some kind of vindication, some salvific Wedding-at-Cana miracle from Dionysus. This terrible New Year has probably brought hundreds like him to San Francisco. And now he's seen the 'Dionysus badge' on my hand – maybe he even saw it when we were in this place back in L.A., and he's somehow found me again.

At the Li Po bar on Sunday, Mavranos had told Cochran how Kootie had asked the wrong question when first confronted with the red Suburban truck – *Why is it the color of blood?* instead of *Who does it serve?*

'Why,' asked Cochran gently now, 'is your bowl the color of blood?'

Thutmose the Utmos' sighed, and seemed to shrink still further. 'When he was a baby-god, Dionysus was laid in a winnowing fan. You're being a dog in the manger.' He shook his head, and there were tears in his red eyes and the word *dog* seemed to hang in the air. 'It's rust, what did you think? Goddammit, I'm an ex-junkie, trying to turn my life around! I used wine to get off the smack, and now I just want to find the god's own forgiveness wine.' He tapped the wok with the spoon again, miserably. 'A heroin dealer used it to mix up batches, step on the product. When it got too rusty for him to use, he gave it to me. I scraped some of the red crust off and cooked it up in a spoon, and, I slammed it, even though I was sure I'd get lockjaw. It did do something bad to my legs – but I didn't die, and this red bowl kept me well for months.'

'None of us here can do anything for each other,' interjected Plumtree. Cochran saw that she had shifted around and was listening in. 'If we could, we'd be in a place called the Glad Boys Bar, or something, not here.' She slid out of the booth now and stood up. 'Come talk to me over by the phones,' she told Cochran.

Glad to get away from the unhappy dwarf, Cochran got up and followed her across the sandy floor.

Cochran hadn't heard the front door squeak while he'd been listening to Thutmose, but there were a lot of people in the long barroom now, though they were all talking in low whispers. Cochran thought they looked like people tumbled together at random in an emergency shelter – he saw men in dinner jackets or denim or muddy camouflage, women in worn jogging suits and women in inappropriately gay sundresses – and none of them looked youthful and they all looked as if they'd been up all night. Cochran reflected that he and his friends must look the same way.

As he and Plumtree passed the bar, Cochran saw a man pay for a drink by shaking yellow powder out of a little cloth bag – and before the lady bartender carefully swept the powder up, Cochran was able to see that it was some kind of grain, perhaps barley.

We walked in here through a door in Los Angeles once, he thought, and now through a door in San Francisco – how old *is* this place, and from what other places has that door opened, perhaps on leather hinges, over the centuries and even millennia? Boston, London? Rome, Babylon, Ur?

Cochran was relieved to see that the pay telephones were the same modern pushbutton machines he and Plumtree had used to call Strubie the Clown.

'Listen,' said Plumtree hoarsely. 'What we've got to do? Is escape.'

'Okay,' said Cochran. 'From what? To where?'

'You remember,' said Plumtree in a near-whisper, 'who the *he* on the menu-specials paper referred to, right? After he was on in '89, I ached in all my joints, and had nosebleeds. And in Holy Week of '90, when he tried to win the Kinghood in that poker game on Lake Mead, he was on for a day and a half, and I had a nervous breakdown so I can't remember *what I felt* like. But this time, ending yesterday morning, he had me for almost three full days, and I could hardly even walk, yesterday and today.' She touched her jaw and the corner of her mouth. 'And I swear he *shaved* while he was in this body!'

Cochran winced, and nodded. 'Probably meaning – like you said – that he had to.'

'Right. He's not a ghost, he's not dead – he imposes his natural form on this body when he's in it for any length of time, so it's … like I'm taking steroids. I grow fucking *whiskers*, and I'm sure he screws up my period.' She was blinking back tears, and Cochran realized that she was frightened, and possibly struggling to stay on for this flop. 'I think if he was to occupy me for too long—' She slapped her chest. '—this would turn all the way into a man's body – a clone of *his* body, the one that got smashed when it fell partly *on* me, on the Soma pavement in 1969.'

Cochran spread his hands. 'What can you *do*?

'God, I don't know. Figure out a way to *kill* him, don't tell Janis. Hide out, in then meantime, and stay away from that Kootic kid – *he* is very interested in that Kootie kid.'

'We can go to my house,' Cochran said. 'You remember it, you were on when we were there last week.'

She pushed back her ragged blond bangs and stared at him. 'You don't mind living with a murderess? Or even maybe one day a murderer?'

Cochran stared into Cody's frightened, squinting eyes – and admitted to himself that in these last eight nightmare days this rough-edged young woman had become, for better or worse, a part of his life. The jumpy infatuation he had initially felt for Janis was gone, but at this moment he couldn't imagine a life for himself that didn't abrasively and surprisingly include Janis Cordelia Plumtree.

'I think,' he said with a weary grin, 'we're partners, by now.'

'Shake on it.'

He shook her cold hand.

'Let's hit the road,' she said.

'Okay. But let's have lunch first.' He smiled. 'And then you can help me get rid of a stolen car in my back yard, when we get there.'

'I can deal with that,' she said. 'I hadn't forgotten it.'

Thutmose didn't look up from his bowl when Cochran and Plumtree returned to the booth. The waitress was just taking orders for food, and Cochran quickly asked for carp in wine while Plumtree frowned over the menu and grumpily settled for stuffed mussels.

By the time the food arrived, Cochran had finished both his beers and ordered two more. The fish tasted like pier pilings and the wine sauce was featureless acid and he hadn't realized the dish would have raisins in it.

All the people in the bar were still talking in whispers, and after his fourth beer Cochran noticed that the whispering was in counterpoint unison – a fast, shaking chant that took in the bang-and-rattle of the bar dice as punctuation. The exhausted-looking men and women were all jerkily walking back and forth and between each other, and after staring in befuddled puzzlement for a few moments Cochran saw that their spastic restlessness was a dance. The dancers didn't appear to be enjoying it, perhaps weren't even doing it voluntarily. Beneath the rapid shaking whispers and the noise of the dice there was a deep, slow rolling, like a millwheel.

Plumtree leaned toward him. 'Let's hit the road,' she whispered. 'And ... *to avoid complications* ... let's just walk out without saying anything.'

It was easy enough to slide out of the booth again and walk away across the gritty floor – in the booth behind them Angelica was clearly avoiding her own appalling recent memories by talking consolingly to Mavranos, and Pete Sullivan was waving his empty glass and trying to catch the waitress's eye – and soon Cochran and Plumtree had made their ducking, sidestepping way, helplessly participating in a few shuffling steps of the joyless group dance, to the front door.

Outside, in the fresh wet-greenery-and-topsoil breeze from Golden Gate Park, the sun had broken through the morning's overcast and glittered in the raindrops that still speckled the brown Granada and the blue Suburban. Oddly, there were no other vehicles in the lot.

As Cochran opened the Granada's passenger-side door for Plumtree, she paused by the back end of the truck to peer in through the dusty glass. Cochran had carefully avoided looking at that window at all, not wanting to see the tumbled, broken skeleton of Scott Crane.

Now Plumtree shuddered visibly, and stepped back to catch her balance; but a moment later she again stepped up to the back of the truck and looked in.

And again she staggered, and it was a blank look she gave him as she finally shuffled forward and got into the Granada.

'You okay?' he said as he got in himself and started the engine.

'Fine,' she said. 'Don't talk. On the way to – on the way – stop for some cigarettes and booze. Mores regular, and Southern Comfort.'

Cochran had said 'Okay,' before remembering that she had asked him not to talk. He nodded; and, because he was drunk it was easy for him to think only about how he would get from here over to Mission Street, which would take him south to the 280, seven miles down which he would find South Daly City – right across the highway from the little transplanted-cemetery town of Colma – and his empty, empty house.

*

Neither of them spoke at all as Cochran steered the old car down the straight, narrow lanes over South San Francisco and then looped west past San Bruno Mountain, with its highway-side Pace Vineyards Tasting Room billboards; and even with a wordless stop while he ducked into a strip-mall liquor store, it was only twenty minutes after leaving the Loser's Bar parking lot that he pulled into his own driveway and switched off the car motor.

Plumtree had her arm around his waist and her head on his shoulder as they trudged up the walkway to the front door; and when he had unlocked the door and led her in, then handed her the liquor-store bag and locked the door again behind them, it seemed only natural that they should both shuffle into the bedroom. The bureau drawers were still pulled out and disordered from their hasty visit five days earlier.

Plumtree twisted the cap off the bottle of Southern Comfort and poured several big splashes of the aromatic liqueur into the glass on the bedside table, and drained it in one swallow. Then as she unbuttoned her blouse with one hand she touched his lips with the forefinger of the other. 'No talk,' she whispered.

Cochran nodded, and sat down on the bed to take off his muddy shoes.

CHAPTER TWENTY TWO

> I would not deprive Col. Haraszthy of a moiety of the credit due him as the first among the first grape culturists of this state, but an investigation of the subject forces the conclusion, that the glory of having introduced [the Zinfandel grape] into the state is not among the laurels he won ... To who is the honor of its introduction due? To an enterprising pioneer merchant of San Francisco, the late Captain F. W. Macondray, who raised the first Zinfandel wine grown in California in a grapery at his residence, on the corner of Stockton and Washington streets, San Francisco.
>
> —Robert A. Thompson, *San Francisco Evening Bulletin*, May 1885

With no key to the motel room, Angelica and Pete and Mavranos just sat in the blue truck for an hour in the Star Motel parking lot. Mavranos hadn't eaten anything at the Loser's Bar, and at one point he got out and trudged across the street to get a tuna sandwich, but he came back to the truck to eat it, and when he had tossed the wrappers onto the floorboards there was still no sign of Cochran and Plumtree, nor of Kootie. Every five minutes or so one of them would impatiently get out and climb the stairs to knock at the room door, but there was never an answer.

They had driven back up here in a roundabout route that had taken them through the green lawns of the Presidio, with Pete at the wheel and Angelica watching behind to be sure they weren't followed. Cochran and Plumtree had sneaked out of the bar and driven away with Angelica's carbine still under the front seat of their car, but she still had her .45 handgun, and Mavranos's .38 was on the truck seat now, under an unfolded Triple-A map.

Angelica's flesh quivered under the .45 that was now tucked into her belt.

The full-throated bang, and after the blue-white muzzle flash faded from her retinas she saw one less motorcycle headlight in the dawn dimness behind the racing Granada ... and then she had steadied the jumping rifle sights on another headlight ...

'What's two times twelve, Arky?' she asked quickly.

Mavranos sighed and wiped the steamy inside surface of the windshield. 'Twenty-four, Angelica.'

'It's *your* mentation that's waxing and waning, Angie,' said Pete irritably from the back seat. 'You were saving our lives. If my stupid hands could hold a gun, it would have been me shooting out of the car window.'

'Oh, I know you would have, Pete,' she said miserably, 'and you came back for me both times when they were shooting at us. I'm glad it *wasn't* you. I wouldn't wish this on you.'

Mavranos was squinting at her sideways with what might have been knowing sympathy.

'Twice thirteen,' she snapped.

'Twenty-six,' said Mavranos. 'You told me you shot a lady on the *Queen Mary* two years ago, after you thought she had killed Pete. Today you thought these boys had killed me. Both times the bad people *would* have killed us, if you hadn't stopped them, if you hadn't killed them. What's half of two?'

'Oh,' she said with a sudden, affected breeziness, 'less than one, if it's me and Pete. Or even me and you, I guess.' She had been looking past Mavranos, and now she lowered her head and rubbed her eyes. 'How long has that turquoise BMW been parked over there? Its engine is running. See the steam?'

Pete shifted around in the back seat to peer. 'Four guys in it,' he said after a moment. 'The two in the back look ... funny.'

Mavranos had not taken his eyes from the Lombard Street sidewalk. 'There's Kootie,' he said suddenly.

Angelica whipped her head around – and the thin, scuffling figure walking down the sidewalk from beyond the motel office was indeed Kootie. She yanked open the truck door and hopped down to the asphalt, and as she began sprinting toward the boy she heard behind her the truck's other two doors creaking open as Pete and Mavranos followed.

She also heard a car engine shift into gear from idle, and then accelerate.

The Green Ripper, Kootie had been thinking insistently as he had trudged up the Octavia Street sidewalk toward Lombard – he was afraid to think about his foster parents, and whether or not he might find them still alive after this ruinous morning – *the Green Giant, the Green Knight. I owe him a beheading. The Green Ripper, the Green Giant*...

Hours earlier, in the upstairs room of the magical boardinghouse that had appeared at Stockton and Washington, Kootie had picked up the bottle of Bitin Dog in both shaking hands – and he had wondered helplessly how he could possibly keep from drinking it right there. He was sure that the dead woman on the bed had been telling the truth: that the bottle contained real impunity, that if he were to drink it he would simply *lose*, lose *track* of, the enormous sin that made even taking each breath seem like the shameful act of a horrifying impostor. Kootie had despairingly thought that *especially* if his foster-parents were still alive he should drink it – if they were somehow not dead, he couldn't encompass the thought of going back to them with the mark of a murder on his soul. Angelica would see it on his face as clearly as she would a tattoo.

But he knew that if he drank it, he would forget about them too. In good faith the wine would take all his loves along with all his guilts – and because he would be drinking it in this stolen, unsanctioned moment, the wine would certainly not ever give any particle of them back. It was a kind of maturity that the wine had to offer, which was to say that it was a renunciation of his whole youth – he would be a man if he drank it, but he would be the wine's man.

After what could only have been a few seconds, really, he had lifted the bottle past his shoulder and flung it into the cold fireplace. It disappeared in that darkness without any sound at all, and he thought that the house had reabsorbed it, and not with disapproval or offense. Only afterward did he fully and fearfully comprehend that he had chosen to remain Koot Hoomie Sullivan – the wounded foster-son of Pete and Angelica Sullivan – the fourteen-year-old who had committed a murder this morning.

That knowledge was like a boulder in the living room of his mind, so that his thoughts had to crawl over it first before they could get anywhere.

He had carried this new and all but-intolerable identity downstairs, where the old black woman had prepared him a different sort of meal than the peppered venison that was cooking to cinders upstairs. It was a spicy hot salmon that Mammy Pleasant set out for him on the kitchen table, served with the fish's tail and sunken-eyed head still attached; he forked up mouthfuls of it hungrily, and though it blunted no memories it reinvigorated him, made him feel implausibly rested and strong.

And as he had eaten it, he had learned things.

With some evident sympathy, Mammy Pleasant had told him her own story – and, in this impossible building on this catastrophic day, Kootie found that he had no capacity for disbelief left.

She told him that she had been born a slave in Atlanta in the winter of 1815, her mother a voodoo queen from Santo Domingo. At the age of ten Mary Ellen had been sold to a merchant who had placed her in the Ursuline convent in New Orleans, to be brought up by the nuns – but a Catholic convent had *not* been any part of the god's plan for her. The merchant soon died, and she was eventually sent to be a servant for a woman who ran a yardage and crockery store way up north in New England, on remote Nantucket Island.

In New England in those days a new variety of wine grape had appeared, brought in obscurely on the transatlantic schooners and cultivated in American greenhouses. Something terrible had already begun to devastate the great old European vineyards of the Herault and the Midi, but in America this new wine from across the sea flourished aggressively. It was variously known as the Black Lombardy and the Black St. Peter's, but in 1830, at the Linnaean Botanic Gardens on Long Island, it was tentatively dubbed the Black Zinfardel.

On wintry Nantucket Island the teenaged Mary Ellen had discarded the Caribbean voodoo systems her mother had taught her, and had begun giving her allegiance to an older god, a wild deity of woods and ivy. As a teenager she learned to tie strips of pine bark to the bottoms of her shoes, so as to mask her footprints when she stole fruit from neighboring farms at night, and she had only been caught when she had used the trick to steal exotic Brazilian peanuts.

The woman storekeeper had taught Mary Ellen how to ferment and bottle the new wine – and when Mary Ellen was twenty-four, and still a virgin, the store had caught fire and burned, and the storekeeper had died of shock, or possibly fright, after staring too intently at the tall, wildly dancing flames. Mary Ellen inherited hundreds of the miraculously undamaged bottles.

The new variety of wine was also called *pagadebiti*, Italian for debt-payer, and Mary Ellen had understood that the god had come to her in it, and that he was generously holding out to her the duty to drink it and become his American Ariadne, rescued by him from abandonment on a bleak island. She knew that the god was Dionysus, and that he was offering to take all her debts, past and future, in exchange for her individual will.

But her will had prevailed – she had *sold* the wine, for profane cash, to a local importer who had a lifetime of old crimes to forget.

A Hungarian emigrant called Agoston Haraszthy had arrived in America in that same year, 1840, and by 1848 had taken on the role of secret king of the American West in distant San Diego – the first of the New World kings – but Mary Ellen had already unfitted herself to be his destined queen, and his reign would now be unbalanced and obstructed.

For sheer concealment she went through the rituals of conversion to Roman Catholicism, and then married a man who owned a tobacco plantation in Charles Town, Virginia. She poisoned him with arsenic, and shortly after that married the plantation overseer in order to sacramentally take the man's fortuitous last name *Plaissance*, which derived from the French *plaisant*: – a jester, a joker. It was a name that was virtually a motley mask in itself.

She took her new husband back to New Orleans. Though ostensibly Catholic now, Mary Ellen bore little resemblance these days to the girl who had scampered through the halls of the Ursuline convent in muslin dresses and ribbon-tied sandals – she took up the bloody practice of real voodoo, under the tutelage of the infamous Marie Laveau, who got for Mary Ellen a high-paid position as cook for the household of a planter in nearby Bayou St. John.

Mary Ellen was a sincerely ardent abolitionist, and she used her privileged position to make contacts with negro slaves throughout the New Orleans area; and she managed to spirit away such a number of them to freedom through 'the Underground' that the authorities began looking for the light-skinned negro woman who always seemed to attend somehow at the escapes – and this slave-stealing woman was too-accurately described as tall and thin, with mismatched eyes.

And so one night Mary Ellen had fled, leaving behind in her bed a bolster wrapped in her nightdress with a wig on it. Marie Laveau booked steamship passage for her to San Francisco, by way of Cape Horn.

Mary Ellen arrived in San Francisco on April 7, 1852 – but Agoston Haraszthy himself came to the city only a few months later to establish his kingdom in nearby Sonoma; and of course he had brought with him cuttings of the god's New World wine, which by this time had already reached the Bay Area and was known, properly at last, as *Zinfandel*.

The god would still have forgiven her, on some basis – but she fought him.

She quickly got employment as a gourmet cook, serving Cajun *pirogis* and shrimp *remoulade* and exotic spicy *jambalaya* to the bankers and gold-dealers of San Francisco – and she made contact with escaped slaves and was able to find jobs for them in the households of affluent families; and then she used her beneficiaries as spies to garner valuable particulars of scandal ... murders, illicit births, embezzlements, abortions. Soon she owned several laundries, but blackmail was her real business.

'My life,' she had told Kootie ruefully this morning at the kitchen table, 'was based on the very *opposite* of any divine *pagadebiti*.'

In her voodoo procedures she didn't hesitate to *use* the power of alcohol, and even of wine, but always in spitefully broken or vitiated forms. The founder of the mercantile firm F. W. Macondray & Company had erected a grapery, a greenhouse-chapel to the god's holy vine, at the corner of Stockton and Washington – and so in 1866 Mary Ellen Pleasant, as she now called herself, bought the property and sacrilegiously converted it to the boardinghouse whose kitchen she and Kootie were now sitting in; and to the bankers and steamship owners who dined at her boardinghouse she served hot raspberry vinegar, and cowslip wine, and double-distilled elderberry brandies. When in 1892 she finally killed the man who had been her main benefactor in San Francisco, she first hobbled his ghost by serving him wine from which she had boiled off all the alcohol ... and then after she had pushed him over a high spiral stair railing she hurried down to where his body lay on the parquet entry-hall floor and pulled the hot brains out of his split skull, so that the ghost would be sure to dissipate in confused fragments.

'A surer trick than those ashtrays with *Madam, I'm Adam* or some such nonsense written around them,' Mammy Pleasant had told Kootie this morning.

'I bet,' Kootie had said hoarsely.

'But at the turn of the century the god caught up with me,' she had said, taking Kootie's empty plate to the sink, 'and took everything away – my great house on Octavia Street, my servants, my money – until at the last I was a plain homeless charity case, shambling around the Fillmore district like ... like a bolster with an old wig on it, in a nightdress. I had only one companion left by then, a negro giant who was actually my captor and guard, known to people as *Bacus*—' She spelled it out for Kootie. '—because people didn't ever see it spelled right, which would have been B-A-C-C-H-U-S. He – it – was a sort of idiot fragment of the god's attention. And finally, on January eleventh of 1904, in the spare room of a mere Good Samaritan acquaintance, I died.'

Kootie looked past her. He thought the strings of garlic and dried red peppers hung in the high corner of the ceiling had lost some of their color in the last few minutes, even become a bit transparent, but he wished forlornly that he could just forget his life and become one of the boarders here.

The old woman went on softly, perhaps talking to herself: 'For a while after that I just drifted in the gray daguerreotype-plate ghost-world version of the city, lost, mostly on the beaches by Sutro's Cliff House and Point Lobos and Land's End. It was a time of cleansing exile for me, like Ariadne abandoned on Naxos by her false human lover Theseus. At last, three Easters and three days after I died, the god mercifully did come back for my ghost, and he knocked down Yerba Buena when he came.'

She looked up at Kootie, and her mismatched eyes were again sharp. 'For me,' she said, 'January eleventh is the open door of the revolving year, and on that day I was able to call out to you people, to try to tell you all what you had to do. And I was interceding for you all with the god – he broke your two friends out of the madhouse on that night, and allowed the king's ghost to be called and drive them right to where you were, where his body was. You had every species of help.'

'I don't know that we've done very well,' said Kootie.

'You've all done very badly,' she agreed, 'and amassed huge debts.'

From a shelf stacked with old gray cookbooks and account ledgers she now pulled down a jarringly modern oversized paperback book with garish red and green swirls and the word FRACTALS in big red letters on the slick cover. She flipped it open to an inner page and showed Kootie a color picture of flames or ferns or octopus tentacles boiling away from a warty, globular black shape.

'Have you seen this silhouette before?' she asked gently, pointing to a clearer picture of the five-lobed silhouette, which resembled a fat person with a little round head and stumpy arms and round buttocks.

Kootie could only look away from the picture and nod and close his throat against sudden nausea. It was the silhouette that had appeared on the television screen in the motel this morning after Arky had poured beer into the set, and it was, too, the shape he had momentarily seen overlapping the pretty Chinese woman when he had first glimpsed her today in the Street of Gamblers.

Mammy Pleasant sighed and shook her head. 'Oh, it's death, child, the person of the god's unholy trinity that's retributive death, and you can testify yourself that it does love to have people enter into its terrible bargain. *It* was the person of the god that came for me *first*, on that cold January eleventh morning, demanding payment for chopping down the vine in Macondray's grapery – dethroning the vine god, killing the vegetation king, beheading the Green Knight. In olden-days history it was called the Quinotaur, and it gave power to the Frankish king Merovee in the Dark Ages – it came to him in the form of a talking bear, and Merovee cut its head off – and it came back under the name of' – she tapped the page – 'Pepin the Fat, to kill Merovee's greatly-greatly-grandson Dagobert, and that ended the Merovingian line of kings in that long-ago time. And it's been known as Bertilak of the High Desert, the Green Knight, who met Sir Gawain at the Green Chapel on New Year's Day, a year after Gawain had cut off Bertilak's head, to collect on that debt. Other folk, meaning to or not, have let the Quinotaur take over themselves to some degree, and always they come back to demand payment-in-kind for their deaths.'

Mammy Pleasant seemed to relax, though she was still frowning. 'You should go now, child. The New Year is close at hand. The Quinotaur doesn't always *take* the life he's owed – the Green Knight didn't behead Gawain, just nicked his neck, because he showed courage. Show courage yourself.'

'Courage,' echoed Kootie, and the word reminded him of the Cowardly Lion of Oz. The memory of watching that innocent movie on television in Solville, in the contented days before the red truck had arrived, before Kootie was a murderer, brought tears to his eyes.

She tugged a bookmark out of the volume's back pages and handed it to Kootie. 'You people should have come to me for this before. Your king is the suicide king now, you've got to keep him in your deck – he's unconditionally surrendered, you see, and is waiting for his instructions, any orders at all. But the god is merciful sometimes – these commandments haven't changed.' She handed Kootie the paper – he glanced at it, but it seemed to be poetry in Latin, which he couldn't read. 'You bring your people back here,' the old woman went on, 'and take me away with you. The god still looks with favor on your king, and wants you all to succeed in restoring him to life: the god owes a good turn to one of your king's company. But it will cost each of you much more, now, than it would have once. Child, it can't any longer be your *king* who comes under your curly-haired roof – and your *king* will have to come somewhere else.'

Mammy Pleasant put down the book and then moved some jars away from a breadbox on the counter, scattering dust and tearing cobwebs. Kootie looked around and saw that the kitchen had deteriorated in the last few moments – the windows were blurred with greasy dirt now and blocked by vines clinging to the outside of the glass, and the paint was flaking off of the sagging shelves. The old woman tugged open the lid of the breadbox, breaking old rust deposits – and then she lifted out of it Diana's yellow baby blanket. She reached across the warped table to hand it to him.

Kootie wordlessly took it and tucked it into the back pocket of his jeans. He knew it must have fallen out of his pocket in the bedroom upstairs, not an hour ago; and he couldn't even bring himself to wonder how it had wound up here.

Mammy Pleasant blinked around at the iron sinks and the cutting boards and the wire-mesh pantry doors, as if for the last time. 'This place won't stay visibly wedged into your electric new world much longer,' she said. 'I'll show you out.'

She led him out of the kitchen – into a huge shadowy Victorian hall, clearly once elegant but now dark and dusty and empty of furniture. A spiral stairway receded away up toward a dim skylight several floors above, and when Kootie looked down at his feet he saw a dark stain on the parquet floor.

'We're in my house on Octavia Street now,' Pleasant told him as she led him to a tall, ornate door at the end of the passage, 'not as it was in my arrogant days, and anyway *it* won't last much longer here either. You all come back here and get me. Look to the trees, you'll see how.' She twisted the knob and pushed open the door. 'Go left,' she said from behind him, 'up the street. Don't look back for a few blocks.'

Kootie blinked in the sudden gray daylight. Splintery old wooden steps led down to a yard choked with brown weeds, and beyond a row of eucalyptus trees he could see a street, with a cable car trundling up the middle of the pavement and ringing its bell.

He remembered this cable-car bell from the first time they had got Pleasant on the television in Solville, and he recalled Thomas Edison's ghost telling him once that streetcar tracks were a good masking measure – 'the tracks make a nice set of mirrors.' *For a while*, Kootie thought now as he stuffed the piece of paper into his pocket. *Not forever.*

Obediently he walked down the steps and across the overgrown yard to the sidewalk, where he turned left, kicking his way through the drifts of acorn-like seeds that had fallen from the eucalyptus trees.

He was sweating in the cold morning air, and he wasn't tempted to look back as he walked away from the house; he didn't even want to look around, for there were no traffic lights at all visible between the corniced buildings bracketing the narrow intersection ahead of him, and aside from the receding cable car all the vehicles on the street were horse-drawn carriages, and though he was aware of the clopping of the horses' hooves and the voices of the quaintly dressed people that he passed, he was aware too of breezy *silence* in the background. The air smelled of grass and the sea and wood smoke and horse manure.

After he had walked two blocks, the noise of the modern world abruptly crashed back in upon him: car engines, and radio music, and the sheer roaring undertone of the modern city. His nostrils dilated at the aggressive odor of diesel fumes.

Oh, this is magic, he thought, for only the second time in that whole morning.

Between the traffic lights swung a metal street sign – he was at the intersection of Octavia and California, and Lombard Street and the Star Motel lay a dozen steep blocks ahead of him.

If my mom and dad are still alive, I'll meet them there, he thought. If they're not, if they've been killed because I ran away this morning—

Recoiling away from the thought, and from a suspense that could not possibly be resolved either way without grief, he began a loud chanting in his head to drown out all thoughts as he strode north on the Octavia Street sidewalk: *The Green Ripper, the Green Giant, the Green Knight. I owe him a beheading. The Green Ripper, the Green Giant, the Green Knight ...*

CHAPTER TWENTY THREE

Gawain, stand ready to ride, as you bargained;
Seek in the wilderness faithfully for me,
As these knights have heard you to solemnly promise.
Find the Green Chapel, the same blow take bravely
You've given today – gladly will it be given
On New Year's Day.

—*Sir Gawain and the Green Knight*, lines 448–453

Angelica glanced jerkily back over her shoulder – the bumper of the turquoise BMW was scooping fast across the motel parking lot pavement toward her – no, it would miss her – it was accelerating straight at Kootie.

She tried to run faster toward the boy, and she managed to suck enough air into her lungs to yell to him, '*Get out of the way!*'

Kootie just stood and stared; but Mavranos was ahead of her now his arms and knees pumping and his dark hair flying as he lashed himself across the lot. As the low BMW roared past her, painfully clipping her left elbow with the passenger-side mirror and nearly spinning her off her feet, she saw Mavranos bodyblock Kootie right off his feet to a driveway-side planter as the car screeched to a halt where Kootie had been standing. The two heads in the rear seat flopped forward and back as if yanked by one string. Mavranos had rolled over Kootie and was struggling to his hands and knees the sidewalk past the planter, and Angelica saw a clenched hand poke out of the BMW's driver's-side window. A stubby silver cylinder was squeezed in the fist, and it was pointed toward where Kootie lay thrashing weakly among the flowers.

The icy recognition of *It's a gun* shrilled in Angelica's head, but as she sprang forward again she also thought, imperatively, *but he's! – the king now! – he's got protections against plain guns!*

The fist was punched back out of sight by the recoil, and the pop was loud enough to set her ears ringing and deafen her to the roaring of her panting breath and the hard scuff of her sneaker soles on the pavement.

Long John Beach tried to hold on to the seat-back with his phantom left hand but when Armentrout stood on the brake the psychic limb snapped like taffy and his head smacked the windshield; still, he was able to peer out the open driver's-side window as the doctor frantically contorted his own arm to get the little gun extended outside the stopped, rocking car.

Even in the passenger seat on the far side of the console, Long John Beach was only a couple of yards from the boy who was lying on his back among the pink geraniums ... and in the instant before the gun flared and cracked back against the doorframe, their eyes met, and Long John Beach and the boy recognized each other.

The rangy man in denim who had shoved the boy out of the car's path was on his feet, and he lunged at the car and slammed a tanned fist against the windshield hard enough to flash silvery cracks across it. Then he was reaching in through the open window and had grabbed a handful of the doctor's white hair—

But wailing Armentrout stamped on the gas pedal, and though his head was yanked violently back, the car had slewed out into the lanes of Lombard Street; horns were honking but there were no audible collisions, and in a moment Armentrout had wrestled the wheel into line and was steering the car fast down the eastbound left lane.

'That was the boy,' Armentrout was whispering rapidly, 'I *know* that was the boy! He was older, but the face was the same as the one in the picture.'

'That was Koot Hoomie Parganas,' said Long John Beach.

Peripherally he could see Armentrout glance at him, but Long John had seized on an *old* memory, and had no attention to spare for the doctor. The sight of the boy in the flowers had reminded him of some *old* event.

He nearly never remembered anything of his life before Halloween of 1992, when he had been found on the shore rocks beside the permanently moored *Queen Mary* in Long Beach. When the police and paramedics had found him he had had a ruptured spleen and a collapsed lung, with 'pulmonary hemorrhages' – as well as a set of handcuffs dangling from his bloody right wrist. He had spent weeks in a hospital, at first with a chest tube inserted between his fifth and sixth ribs. Apparently he had been in the lagoon around the old ship when an underwater explosion had occurred. The doctors had speculated that he must have been exhaling in the instant of the blast, and curled up into a ball, and that that was why he hadn't been killed; another man in the water *had* been killed ... and must have lost at least his shoe and all the skin off his left foot, for ... for somebody had previously handcuffed Long John Beach's wrist to the man's ankle!

But Long John Beach had been going by another name, then – another makeshift name based on a city he had found himself in.

Like a whisper the old name came to him: *Sherman Oaks.*

He had been hunting for Koot Hoomie Parganas in that long-ago season, and so had the man who had died in the underwater explosion ... and so had a fat woman who had been some kind of movie producer. Each of them had wanted to get hold of the Parganas boy, and kill him, and inhale the powerful ghost that the boy contained – the ghost of Thomas Alva Edison.

Sherman Oaks had failed, and of course the man who'd died in the explosion had failed. Perhaps the fat lady had succeeded in inhaling Edison.

No – she couldn't have, because that would have involved killing the boy, and Long John Beach had just seen the boy a minute ago, alive.

The boy's face, when the haunted brown eyes had locked on to Long John Beach's gaze just now, had been pale and gaunt, and openmouthed with surprise and apprehension – but the sick wrinkles around the eyes spoke of some imminent punishment feared but *expected*, even accepted. The expression was one of fearful guilt, Long John Beach thought.

The boy's face had been younger when Beach had first seen it, but it had worn that same look of pathetically anticipating and deserving punishment.

The Parganas boy had apparently run away from home one night in October of '92, directly after stealing the Edison ghost from whatever shielded hiding place his parents had kept the thing in. Long John Beach – Sherman Oaks, rather – had tracked the ghost's intense field to the boy's Beverly Hills home, and he had duct-taped the boy's mother and father into chairs and tortured them to find out where the ghost had gone. But they hadn't *known* where, and he had wound up killing them in a fury of hungry impatience, finally even gouging out their sightless eyes.

And then later that night the boy had come back home, repentant and sorry, visibly ready to take his punishment for having run away and stolen whatever glass container had held the ghost.

It had been Sherman Oaks, not his parents, who had awaited him; but the boy had eluded Oaks, and had run out of the house ... *right through the room in which sat his dead mother and father.*

And then a few days later Sherman Oaks had succeeded in briefly capturing the boy, in a van in the back of a moving truck – and after terrifying him nearly to madness Oaks had tried to kill him, and had in fact managed to stab him in the side with a hunting knife.

Long John Beach had never, since Halloween of '92, had much awareness of himself as a distinct person. The Edison ghost had lashed out at him somehow and broken something in his mind, so that he'd been left with nothing but the useless ability to channel stray ghosts, as inertly and promiscuously as a tree harbors birds. But now, in this swerving, speeding car, that tortured boy in the flowers back there was connected to his self. The boy's evident unhappiness was not – Long John Beach flexed the hoardings of his mind to be sure, and it was true – was not separable from the admittedly dim and decayed entity that was Long John Beach's own self.

He knew that as Sherman Oaks, and probably as other personalities before that one, he had killed people; and he remembered that in those old days he had been addicted to inhaling ghosts, consuming them rather than just channelling them, strengthening his own soul by eating those poor dissolving 'smokes' – but suddenly it was Koot Hoomie Parganas, whom he had not even killed, that was an intolerable weight on his frail mind.

There was no new sound in the humming BMW, and Long John Beach saw nothing but the drab motels of western Lombard Street through the windshield, but he was suddenly aware of a *change*.

A personality that wasn't a ghost, and might not even have been human, lifted him like a wave under a foundering ship; cautiously, still clinging to the prickly husk that was his identity, he nevertheless let the new person partway into his mind.

All at once he was speaking. 'I always have a dog,' Long John Beach found himself saying. 'For now he barks all night at the end of his tether. Chancy measures at the bowsprit of the million-dollar hot-air balloon, what you might call an exaltation of barks if you had to spit-shine a wingtip hanging upside down by one ankle.' He was laughing excitedly now. 'Just imagine! Shouting out of your liver and lights to hand-deliver these parables – pair-o'-bulls! – to the momma's boy who wants to put the salmon in the freezer.'

'You and your dog.' Armentrout was blinking rapidly at the traffic ahead, and breathing through his mouth. 'It doesn't matter now,' he whispered. 'It's all cashed out, I *killed* the boy back there.'

Long John Beach gathered back the shreds of his mind and pushed himself away from the big inhuman personality – and he got a quick impression of a young man in patchwork clothes, with a bundle over his shoulder, dancing at the edge of a cliff. He recognized the image – it was one of the pictures in the doctor's set of oversized tarot cards, the one the doctor called The Fool.

The doctor was afraid of that one. And Long John Beach was not ready to surrender himself to The Fool. The one-armed old man's identity was nothing more than a limp threadbare sack, angular at the bottom with the fragments of broken poisonous memories and short, rotted lengths of intelligence, but it was all he had.

In spite of his uneasiness with the memories of the Koot Hoomie Parganas boy, he was not ready to surrender himself to The Fool.

Kootie was sobbing and trying to get up when Angelica tumbled to her hands and knees in the muddy planter beside him; Pete slid to an abrading stop against the cement coping beside her.

Mavranos was kneeling on the other side of the boy, and holding him down with hands that were red with fresh blood. 'Let your ma look at you, first,' Mavranos said irritably, and then he squinted up into Angelica's face. 'He was rolling over when the bullet hit him – I don't think it was a direct hit.'

'Mom!' Kootie wailed. 'I thought you were all dead!'

'Check it out as a doctor, Angie,' said Pete breathlessly.

'*Hit* him?' she panted. 'We're fine, Kootie, we're – all just fine.' To Pete she snapped, 'It can't have *hit* him.' Gently but irresistibly she pushed Kootie down on his back in the snapping geranium branches and pulled his shirt up, and the familiar old unhealed knife cut over his left ribs was now a raw long gash with blood runneling down his side and pattering onto the green leaves.

Angelica's peripheral vision cringed inward so that all she could see was this gleaming red rip in Kootie's white skin; but she replayed what Pete had said and forced herself to look at it professionally. 'You're right, Arky – it's shallow, no damage at all to the muscle layer and hardly even scored the corium, the deeper skin layer – not life-threatening.' She grinned at the boy as confidently as she could, and gasped out, 'Welcome back, kiddo,' but she knew the look she then gave Mavranos must have been stark. 'Get the truck here right now. I don't want my boy in a hospital like this.'

'Right.' Mavranos scuffled to his feet and sprinted heavily away.

'Let's get you moving, Kootie,' Angelica said, grunting as she and Pete helped the boy stand up. Bright drops of blood spilled down the left leg of his jeans, and she mentally rehearsed grabbing the first-aid kit that Mavranos kept in a box beside the back seat. 'That must have been a magical gun—' she began. Then she looked into his eyes. 'You're not hurt anywhere else, are you? Physically?'

'No.' But Kootie was crying, and Angelica knew it was about something that had happened before this shooting ... and after he had run away in the pre-dawn darkness this morning.

'Tell your dad and me about it when we get clear of this,' she said gently.

'And I thought,' the boy sniffled, 'that I got you killed, by running away. I just *ran away* from you! I'd give anything if I could go back and do that different.'

'We're just fine, son,' said Pete, hugging the boy against himself. 'It's okay. And now you're back. We're all *alive* for our ... reconciliation here, and that's a very big thing.'

Angelica remembered Pete making a very similar apology to *his* father's *ghost*, on the night before Halloween in '92 – Pete too had run away once, when it counted – and she winced in sympathy and opened her mouth to say something; but the shrill whine of the truck engine starting up stopped her.

The truck came grinding up behind her and squealed to a halt, and Angelica helped Pete hustle Kootie around the front bumper to the back door. As soon as they had boosted him in onto the back seat and clambered aboard themselves, Pete in the front seat and Angelica in the back seat with Kootie, Mavranos gunned the dusty blue truck out of the parking lot; Kootie sprawled across the seat, and Angelica, crouched on the floorboards beside him, had to lean out over the rushing pavement to catch the swinging door handle and pull the door shut.

Then she hiked the first-aid kit down with one hand while she raised her other hand over the back of the front seat; and Pete had already opened the glove compartment, and now slapped into her palm Mavranos's nearly empty bottle of Jack Daniels bourbon.

Kootie was lying on his back, and Angelica knelt over him and popped open the first-aid kit. 'This'll hurt,' she told him as she tore open a gauze pad envelope and spilled bourbon onto the cotton.

'Good,' said Kootie. Then he said, 'The old guy in the passenger seat of that BMW – it was Sherman Oaks, the one-armed guy who killed my natural mom and dad. I recognized him. And he recognized me.'

Angelica suppressed a worried frown, and just pressed the wet bandage onto his wound. 'Drive right out of the city, Arky,' she called over her shoulder, 'in whatever direction you're heading. To hell with whatever we left in that motel room. When we're—'

'No,' said Kootie through clenched teeth. 'First we've got to go to Octavia Street – uh, two blocks south of California Street.'

'Tell me which,' growled Mavranos from the driver's seat.

'Why, Kootie?' asked Pete, hunching around to look back at the boy. 'If that Sherman Oaks guy is here in town—'

'We've got to do it *right* this time,' said Kootie hoarsely. 'We've got to *fetch* Mammy Pleasant. She's the old black lady from the TV, and her house is on Octavia there.'

'Oh, honey, that – didn't work out,' Angelica said as she peeled adhesive tape off a roll. She restrained herself from glancing over his head toward the bed of the truck. 'That's all over.'

'It's not,' Kootie said, closing his eyes as Angelica pressed the strip of tape tightly over the bandage 'He can still come back. To life. Dionysus *wants* him to.'

'South on Van Ness,' announced Mavranos as the truck leaned into a right-hand turn. 'I'm going straight on down to the 101 south unless somebody convinces me to do different.'

'*Arky*,' Kootie wailed, 'get over to Octavia! We won't ever be okay until we've paid this thing off. Does it look like we're done, here? Does it look like I'm the king now? *He can still be restored to life.*'

'You don't know the whole story, Kootie,' said Pete. 'We do. Trust me, there's no way—' He paused, for Mavranos had swung the truck into another hard right turn at Filbert, and the battering exhaust was echoing back from the close garage doors alongside the narrow, steep street. 'Arky—? The 101 is—'

'Talk to me, Kootie,' said Mavranos. 'If he *can* still come back, it can't be into his own body anymore. That turned into a skeleton, and got all busted up.'

'And it won't be into yours,' said Angelica, peeling off another strip of tape. 'I will sabotage any effort at that, I promise. So don't even—'

'No,' said Kootie, 'it *would* have been that way, if we'd done it right, and then he would have shifted back into his own. Arky and the Plumtree woman were right about that. But we were doing it wrong, we didn't get Mammy Pleasant to guide us like she told us to, and then I ran away—' He sniffed. 'Mammy Pleasant gave me a message for Crane, some Latin poetry on a piece of paper, from Dionysus.'

Angelica felt a thump through the front seat at her back, and she looked up – Mavranos had thrown his injured head back, though he was still squinting furiously ahead. 'So how *will* it work out?' he asked in a gravelly voice. 'Now?'

'I don't know at all,' said Kootie. His eyes were wide and he was staring up at the rust-spotted bare metal roof. 'I think we might all die, if it works out right this time.'

'Let's see this message,' said Pete.

Luckily Kootie had stuffed it into his right-hand pocket; he was able to dig it out without putting any strain on his bandaged side. 'Here,' he said, handing it to Angelica, who passed it over the seat to Pete.

Pete read it aloud, slowly:

'*Roma, tibi subito motibus ibit Amor,*
Si bene to tua laus taxat, sua laute tenebis,
Sole, medere pede: ede, perede melos.'

He handed it back to Angelica, who returned it to Kootie. 'It's a palindrome,' Pete said thoughtfully, rocking in his seat as the truck continued to climb the narrow street. 'Three palindromes, that is. Latin, and I don't read Latin.' He yawned. 'Palindromes draw ghosts.'

'I'd like to know what it means,' said Angelica defiantly.

'I think we better go pick up the old lady's ghost in the meantime,' sighed Mavranos. 'I'll stop at a pay phone on the way and read Kootie's note to Nardie Dinh; she'll be able to puzzle it out for us, if we give her time to go through her books – and she owes me one.'

At a tiny liquor store on the corner of Gough and Filbert, Mavranos found a parking space and then copied the text of Kootie's note onto the back of his car registration. Finally he got out of the truck, leaving it in park with the engine running.

After he closed the driver's door he leaned in the open window to say,

'Pete, if you see a blue-green BMW, you just ram it and then drive away, and meet me at Li Po at sunset.'

He trudged across the tiny lot into the liquor store, slapping his pockets for coins for the pay phone by the beer cooler.

He strode up to the phone and dropped a quarter into the coin slot, and then punched in the well-remembered Leucadia number; and after a recorded voice asked him to deposit another dollar and thirty cents, and he impatiently rolled six more quarters into the slot, he heard ringing, and then Nardie's voice saying, cautiously 'Hello?'

'Nardie,' he said, 'this is Arky, still up in San Fran, with – apparently! – still no conclusions.' His forehead was damp; he had almost said *concussions*. He wanted to touch the back of his head, and to ask her about the dashboard statue she had given him. But, *She didn't do it*, he told himself, and he only said, 'I got some Latin for you to translate, if you got a pencil—'

'It means, "And in Arcadia, I—"' came Nardie Dinh's voice. 'It's an unfinished sentence, like the story's not over, okay? I think the speaker is supposed to be Death, so it's like Death hasn't made up his mind yet what he'll do, here. Where have you seen it?'

Mavranos blinked, and discovered that the telephone cord was long enough for him to open the beer cooler and pull out a can of Coors. 'What?' he said. 'But it's longer than that. And where did *you* find it?'

Nardie Dinh paused. 'This is something that's lettered on a sign somebody put up on the big pine tree out front, by the driveway. *Et in Arcadia ego.* What Latin have *you* got?'

'Jeez. Well, mine's longer. Have you got a pencil?'

'Shoot,' she said.

He winced, and his finger hovered over the tab on the beer can, but he knew the owner was watching him and would throw him out if he opened it in the store. He read her the three palindromes slowly, spelling the words out. 'I'll have a translation for you in an hour,' she said. 'I suppose you're not at a phone I'll be able to call you at?'

'No,' he told her, 'I'll call you.' He shifted his weight from one foot to the other, and he wished he could open the beer, for his mouth was dry. 'Nardie, your brother—'

'Oh, Arky!' Her voice was startled and not happy. 'Do let it lie, please!'

'I – well, I discover I can't. Anymore. I know *he* doesn't forgive me, but I do have to ask you – ask you—' He was sweating. 'I have to tell you that I'm – sorry, for it.' He coughed, and though his eyes were squeezed tightly shut, his voice was almost casual: 'Always have been.'

'I know you are, Arky. Don't still trouble yourself about it – whatever my feelings were for my brother, or are now, I love you—' She laughed awkwardly. 'I was going to say "I love you anyway," but there's no "anyway" to it;

you did what you had to do, for all of us. So I'll just say, I love you.'

Mavranos discovered that he hadn't been inhaling or exhaling, and he let his breath out now in a long sigh. 'Thank you, Nardie. I love you too. Call you back in an hour or so.'

He remembered to pay for the can of beer before he walked out of the store, and he popped it open as he walked across the asphalt to the truck, which was still idling where he'd left it. In spite of his undiminished dreads of what was to come, his step was lighter, and after he had got back in and taken a deep sip of the beer, he wedged the can between his thighs and said, with a fair imitation of hearty cheer, 'Now we're off to pick up Kootie's old lady.'

In the rear-view mirror he saw the boy close his eyes.

Mavranos drove right by the place, because Kootie wasn't sure whether it had been two or three blocks he had walked up to get to California Street, and none of these office and apartment buildings looked familiar to him – and it was only after they had driven past the Bush Street intersection that he realized that the six huge, shaggy eucalyptus trees they had just passed must be all that was left of the long row of trees he had seen when he had walked out of Mammy Pleasant's run-down Victorian mansion an hour ago.

'Back,' he said. 'Her house is gone, but those six eucalyptuses are where it was.'

'She say meet you by the trees?' asked Mavranos as he signalled for a right turn to go around the block.

'She said "Look to the trees, you'll see how." To pick her up. And last week on the TV she said "Eat the seeds of my trees."' He shifted uncomfortably. 'She's just a ghost, remember – I don't think we'll have to make much room for her in here.'

Mavranos looped around Sutter and Laguna to Bush, and then turned right onto Octavia again and parked at the curb, putting the truck into park but leaving the engine running. Where Pleasant's dry brush yard had been was now a walkway-transected green lawn out in front of a Roman-looking two-story gray stone building. 'It's a ... a pregnancy counseling center,' said Angelica, staring at the big white sign out front as she opened the door and climbed down to the sidewalk. 'That's a ... pleasant ... use for the property.' Pete got out of the passenger side and stood beside her as she shaded her eyes to look up and down the street. Finally she stared down at the pavement and scuffed some leaves aside. 'There's a stone plaque inset in the sidewalk here – it says something about—' She frowned as she puzzled out the letters. '*Mary Ellen Pleasant Memorial Park,*' she read aloud, '... *mother of civil rights in California ... supported the western terminus of the underground railway for fugitive slaves ... legendary pioneer once lived on this site and planted these six trees.'* Angelica looked up.

'And it says she died in 1904. You were – here today, Kootie?'

Kootie was half sitting up in the back seat, staring out through the open back door.

'Her old house was still standing when I was here,' called Kootie, 'an hour ago, by my clock. There were more trees then, and they weren't so big and shaggy.'

'I should have had more respect for her ghost,' said Angelica. 'She sounds like she was a fine woman.'

'She had her faults,' said Kootie shakily. 'Like us all, I—' he let the sentence hang unfinished. 'Do any of the trees ... look funny?'

'Funny,' echoed Angelica out on the sidewalk. 'Well, they've all got strips of bark hanging off 'em ... and got bright green moss around their feet.'

'Around their *roots*,' Pete corrected her, standing by the truck bumper. 'Their *feet* are way up in the air.' He was standing by the second one from the corner, looking up at its thick, bifurcated trunk. 'This one looks like somebody buried head-down up to the waist, with their legs sticking up. Wasn't there a place in Dante's *Inferno*, where the damned souls were stuck head-downward?'

'In the Eighth Circle,' called Mavranos from the driver's seat. He was looking down, fumbling with both hands among the papers on the front seat, and Kootie heard a faint metallic rattle. 'The Simoniacs, who sold ecclesiastical offices and indulgences and forgivenesses. *Sold* is the key word there. But in the book they were stuck head-down in baptismal fonts.' Kootie heard the cylinder of the revolver click closed. 'Hurry up,' Mavranos said loudly. 'I haven't reloaded since this morning.' He sat back, not looking at Kootie. 'I've been ... distracted,' he said quietly.

Though she gave a deprecating laugh, Angelica had taken a step back from the gnarled old tree with its two bulky, skyward-stretching limbs. 'For what god is a *hole in the ground* a baptismal font?'

'The god of woods,' said Kootie, though probably only Mavranos could have heard him. He was remembering Mammy Pleasant's confession of having sold a fabulous cache of the *pagadebiti* Zinfandel for money, way back in her youth on Nantucket Island. More loudly, he called, 'Gather up some of those acorns or chestnuts or whatever they are, from around that tree. And peel off some strips of the bark; she can't go barefoot.'

A minute later Pete and Angelica climbed back into the truck, Angelica with two pockets full of the seeds and Pete with an armload of mustysmelling damp bark strips.

Mavranos clanked the engine into gear and steered out away from the curb. 'Out of town, now?' he asked.

'Yes,' said Angelica, 'but not by the 101.' She smiled. 'Take the 280 south.'

CHAPTER TWENTY FOUR

TROILUS: O, let my lady apprehend no fear; in all Cupid's pageant
there is presented no monster.
CRESSIDA: Nor nothing monstrous neither?
—William Shakespeare, *Troilus and Cressida*

After he got out of the hot shower Cochran wiped the steam off the medicine-cabinet mirror and thoroughly brushed his teeth, and as he stared at the reflection of his haunted face he kept thinking about Nina's green toothbrush hanging in its slot only inches behind the hinged mirror; and he decided not to open the medicine-cabinet door again to get out his razor. When he had fumbled out his own toothbrush he hadn't thought to note how dry Nina's must be, and he didn't want to now.

Plumtree had been asleep under the sheet when he had got out of bed to come in here. The shower, and now the shock of a mouthful of Doctor Tichenor's mouthwash, had sobered him up, and he was profoundly disoriented to realize that a naked blond woman whom he had met one week ago was at this moment inertly compressing the springs of the bed he and Nina slept in.

He was remotely glad that the cassette from the phone-answering machine was in the pocket of his shirt on the back of the dressing-table chair – he didn't want to know what his response would be if someone were to call now, and Nina's recorded voice were to speak from the machine.

Plumtree would certainly sleep for at least a couple of hours. Cochran hadn't been watching the bottle of Southern Comfort, but she must have refilled her glass half a dozen times, before, between, and after. His thoughts just slid away from memories of the details of their lovemaking; all he could really bring himself to remember right now – and even that shakily – was Plumtree's hot, panting breath, flavored with More cigarette smoke and the peach-liqueur-and-bourbon taste of Southern Comfort.

He spat in the sink, and rinsed out his mouth with cold tap water scooped up in his hand because the bathroom glass was in the other room, sticky with liqueur. He had closed the bathroom door when he had come in here, and now he paused before opening it again; and after a moment of indecision he picked up his jeans and pulled them on and zipped the fly before he turned the damp doorknob and stepped out onto the bedroom carpet.

And he blinked in surprise – Plumtree was sitting up in bed, anxiously holding the sheet up to her chin.

Her shoulders slumped when she saw him. 'Oh, *you*, Scant?' she wailed. 'Oh, why? I *told* you I'*d* go to bed with you, if you'd wait! I was *sure* it was going to be a *stranger* that would walk out of that bathroom! I was just waiting to see what sort of – creep! – it would be, so I'd know who to give this flop to! Oh, Sid – *Tiffany*?' She buried her face in the sheet, and her muffled voice went on, 'I loved you! And I thought you loved *me*.'

Cochran could feel his face get instantly hot, and at the same time chilly with evaporating sweat, for he suddenly had to fully admit to himself that what he was about to say was a lie. 'Janis,' he said, too shrilly, 'I thought it was you! Are you saying that it *wasn't* you? Good God, I'm sorry, how was I—'

'You *stole* – me! It's as if you had sex with me while I was knocked out, unconscious, like when I nearly got raped in the van behind that bar in Oakland. At least *that* guy didn't ... *have* me.' She shook her head furiously. 'How could I ever give myself to you now?'

'Janis, it was a, a horrible mistake, I swear I really thought we – you were *conscious*, for God's sake – we were both drunk—'

'I said "as if." You *knew*. Oh, God, I've lost you.' She lifted her tear-streaked face and stared at him; then she looked down at the sheet over her body, and flexed her legs. Finally she smacked her lips. 'Oh, you horny son-of-a-bitch. Do you have any idea how badly you've hurt her? She was in *love* with you, you asshole!'

'Oh, I know, Cody,' he said miserably. 'But goddammit, we *were* both drunk, and you *do* all look exactly alike!'

Cody was scowling at him with evident disgust. 'You're saying you didn't know it was Tiffany? Didn't even suspect it might be? Are you honestly telling me that?'

'I—' He sighed. 'No.' He lifted his shirt from the chair and slid his numb, leaden arms through the sleeves. 'No, I guess not – not the *didn't even suspect* part, anyway, I guess. You're right – she's right – I wasn't *thinking* about who it was, I was just ... what you said.' He could feel the fabric of the shirt clinging to his chest already. 'Jesus, Cody, I'm not being flippant, and I am sorry. You all deserved way more ... respect? consideration? ... from me. God, what can I—'

'Try getting out of here, so I can get dressed.'

'Okay. Of course.' He gave her a fragile smile as he buttoned the shirt. 'I'm asking for an insult here, and I deserve it – but I've got to say I hope you won't leave. I hope you'll stay, somehow.' He stepped toward the hallway door. 'I'll be in the kitchen, making some coffee.'

At least she didn't say anything as he walked out.

At the kitchen sink he filled the glass coffeepot with water and poured it into the back of the coffee machine; the action reminded him of that Mavranos guy pouring beer down the back of the Star Motel TV set, and he remembered that the room had been on Nina's credit card. Five nights, plus a wrecked TV set. God knew what it would cost.

As he spooned ground coffee into the filter he wondered who Tiffany might be, how complete a person – whether she was anything more than the Plumtree sex function, with no character details besides the sketched-in tastes for More cigarettes and Southern Comfort. Maybe she had been provided with one or two other props he hadn't discovered – some surface preferences in movies, or food. The ideal girlfriend, some sophomoric types would probably say with a snigger. He wondered if he had ever been shallow enough to say something like that. Well, he'd been shallow enough to *act* on it, today, which had to be worse.

He slid the filter funnel into the coffee machine and clicked it on and opened the cabinet to snag down a couple of cups. His hands were still shaking. Sugar was on the table, and he opened the refrigerator and took out a half full carton of milk.

Plumtree was like a family of sisters – with a scary, seldom-seen father, and a crazy mother. Cochran had been initially attracted to the nice sister, and now he had gone to bed with the nymphomaniac one; but the one he had come to rely on and even admire was the ... the tough one.

He tweaked open the milk carton and sniffed the contents. The weeks-old milk smelled cheesy, and he sighed and poured it down the sink. There was a jar of Cremora in the cabinet, he recalled.

The coffee machine had just started to sputteringly exhale air when Plumtree stepped into the kitchen from the hall. She was wearing her jeans and white blouse again, though she was still barefoot, and she was tugging one of Nina's hairbrushes through the disordered blond thatch of her hair.

'Coffee sounds good,' she said. 'I think spiking it would be a bad idea.'

'I think we've had enough to drink for today,' Cochran agreed cautiously.

'Well,' she said, pulling out one of the chairs at the kitchen table and sitting down heavily, 'as for the whole *day* I don't know. I kind of picture a glass or two of something at around sundown.' When Cochran had set a cup of steaming coffee in front of her, she added, 'Bring that milk over here.'

'It's empty,' he said, turning back to the cabinet. 'I've got Cremora, though.'

'Cremora,' she echoed, stirring sugar into the coffee. 'What do you keep the milk carton around for?'

'I just now poured it out, it was bad.' He glanced at the milk carton, thinking he might save it for the garden. 'At the vineyard we put half-gallon milk cartons around young vines,' he added absently as he poured his own cup.

'It keeps the rabbits from getting at them, and prevents sunburn, and makes the shoots grow straight, up toward the light at the top.' He carried his cup to the table and sat down across from her, and stared out the window at the roof of the greenhouse as he sipped it. 'They'll be putting out the new seedlings soon, at Pace, in the couple of acres down by the highway.' He used the Italian pronunciation for the vineyard name, *pah-chay*.

At last he looked at her. Plumtree seemed to be listening, and so he let himself go on about this neutral topic. 'And,' he said, 'the malolactic fermentation will be starting up soon in the casks of last year's wine – that's a second fermentation that happens at about the same time that the new year's leaves are budding out, as if they're in communication; it's bacteria, rather than yeast, and it converts the malic acid to lactic acid, which is softer on the tongue. You want it to happen, in the Zinfandels and the Pinot Noirs.' He smiled faintly, thinking about the vineyard. 'When I left for Paris, the grape leaves were all in fall colors – you should see it. The Petite Sirah leaves turn purple, the Chardonnays are gold, and the Cabernet Sauvignon leaves go red as blood.'

'You miss the work,' said Plumtree. 'Do you make good wine there?'

'Yeah, we do, actually. These last few years we've been having ideal marine-influence weather, and we're picking later in the season, and our '92 and '93 Zinfandels, not bottled yet, are already showing perfect old-viney fruit, with tannin like velvet.' He shrugged self-consciously. 'But, hell, since 1990, everybody in California's been making good wines, it seems like. Not just the names you've heard of, like Ridge and Mondavi, but Rochioli in the Russian River Valley and Joel Peterson's Ravenswood in Sonoma; everybody's producing spectacular harvests and vintages, in spite of the phylloxera bugs. It's almost as if the world-scale has to stay balanced – Bordeaux, all of Europe, in fact, have been getting way too much rain in these growing seasons, and *they've* been consistently *mediocre* since '90.'

'Well, Scott Crane became king in 1990. I bet '95 will be a terrible year.'

'That Kootie kid might be a good king. Maybe we'll be able to tell if he's okay, by how the wine turns out.'

Plumtree tasted the coffee and grimaced. 'Did your wife like wine? Just because I'm talking to you doesn't mean I've stopped thinking you're a heartless dickhead.'

He gave her a constricted nod to show that he understood. 'Nina,' he said, clearing his throat. 'Actually, she seemed to resent the big, vigorous California wines—'

Plumtree's mouth opened. 'Why should the god favor this coast on the wrong side of the world? Where none of the *Appellation Controlee* commandments are even being observed! Here you are free to mechanically irrigate, if no rain comes! And you may produce ... three, four, six tons of grapes per acre, with no penalty! In the Médoc our *vandangeurs* hold to the god's old laws, making no more than thirty-five hectoliters of wine from each hectare of land, and we nurture the sacred old Cabernet Sauvignon and supplicate the god to make it into his forgiving blood, as he did in the centuries before the Revolution – and for our pains we scarcely get a wine that's fit to drink with dinner! It's rejected like Cain's sacrifice. Here in barbaric California the desecrated Cabernet is turned into wines like, like cathedrals and Bach concertos, and *it's* not even the wine he *blesses* – he consecrates this unpedigreed upstart interloper *Zinfandel*.'

Cochran had stopped breathing, for this was Nina's voice. He could see his shirt collar twitching with his heartbeat, and he hardly dared to move, fearing that any motion might startle her ghost away.

He realized that he should speak. 'Uh, not always,' he said in a quiet, placating tone, peripherally reminded of poor Thutmose with his rusty grail full of Zinfandel that he craved to have transformed into the *pagadebiti*. 'Most Zinfandel is just red wine.'

'You called me,' said Nina's voice. She looked around at her own kitchen. 'When I was on the *lit marveil*, the jumping bed, in the room with all the people in it.' She shifted her chair back from the table and peered out the window at the midday glare on the greenhouse roof. 'When was that?'

Cochran remembered having called *Nina!* when Plumtree's mother had been controlling her body, right after the pre-dawn earthquake. 'That was this morning, early,' he said steadily. He had been ashamed of calling her name, immediately after he'd done it, and he didn't want to look squarely at the action now. 'I didn't think you heard me.'

'I had a long way to come, to answer.' She was frowning thoughtfully, and Cochran felt goose bumps rise on his forearms as he recognized the top-of-the-nose crease of Nina's characteristic frown, on Plumtree's sunburned face. 'I was in a – unless it was a dream? – a *bar*, with a lot of very drunk people.' She visibly relaxed, and smiled at him. 'But I'm home now.'

This isn't *her*, he told himself as his heart hammered behind his ribs, it's just her ghost. Wherever the real Nina is – *her bed is India; there she lies, a pearl* – she has no part in this. Still, this is a ghost of *her*, this is *her* ghost. Could she stay? Sleep in the bed, dampen the toothbrush? She was building a stone fountain in the garden, when she died; could she finish building it now?

But there was something wrong – something subtly but witheringly grotesque – about the idea of dead-reflex, mimic hands finishing the living woman's interrupted garden work.

And would the unborn *baby's* ghost come back, sobbing inconsolably in the darkness late some night?

And could he do this to Cody?

He lifted his coffee cup and stood up and crossed to the sink, pausing by the refrigerator to pry off of its door one of the little flat promotion-giveaway magnets stamped to look like a miniature bottle of Pace Zinfandel. 'I've decided to have the mark on the back of my right hand removed,' he said over his shoulder as he dumped the half-cup of lukewarm coffee into the sink. He was speaking carefully. 'Laser surgery, get it done in a couple of outpatient sessions.'

'*Ce n'est pas possible!*' she exclaimed, and he heard Plumtree's shoes scuff on the floor as she stood up. 'It is your Androcles mark! The lion owed Androcles an obligation after Androcles merely pulled the thorn from the lion's paw – but you at some time put out your hand to injury to save the god! I've never spoken of it; but the mark is for only the god to take away, as it was for him to bestow it. I would never have – I would not have your child, if its father were not marked by *him*. My family didn't send me here simply to—' She gripped his shoulder with Plumtree's strong hand. 'Tell me you won't do it, Scant.'

'Okay,' he said gently. 'Sorry. I won't do it.'

He filled the coffee cup with cold tap water and carried it back to the table. 'Sit down,' he told her, placing the cup of tap water on the table between them and stirring it with the forefinger of his right hand. After she had resumed her seat, he asked, 'What ... happened, on New Year's Day?' He touched his forehead with his wet fingertip. Then he took the cassette from the phone-answering machine out of his shirt pocket.

'In the morning, at dawn,' said Nina's voice with Plumtree's lips. 'I thought it might be him again, this morning, when you called me on the leaping bed. I was thrown awake at dawn on New Year's Day, and I knew he was calling me, from outside the house. My ... I was married to him, through you. And he was freed that morning, when the earth moved and the trees were all knocked down. I wrapped myself in a bedsheet, and tied ivy in my hair, and I ran out to meet him, down the backyard path to the highway. And I – did? – it was loud, and it hurt – but I knew that was how he would come.' She was staring into the clear water in the cup, and she sighed deeply.

Cochran felt empty. 'What's your name?' he asked, in a voice that he tried to keep from being as flat as a dialtone.

Slowly, he slid the little bottle-shaped magnet back and forth over the cassette.

'Nina Gestin Leon. Ariachne.' Plumtree's blue eyes met his. 'I see two of you, Scant. I *died* that morning, it seems to me now. Didn't I?'

'Yes, Nina.' Fighting to conceal the aching bitterness in his throat, he said hoarsely, 'You died that morning. I flew your ashes back to the Bas Medoc, to Queyrac, and I talked to your mother and father. We were all very sorry that you were gone, none sorrier than me. I loved you very much.' He pushed the erased tape away, until he felt it tap against the coffee cup.

She shivered visibly, and blinked away tears. 'Where do I go now?'

Her peace is the important thing here, he told himself wonderingly, not your betrayed love, not your pride. Let her rest in what peace there is to be had. 'To your real husband at last, not just to a symbol anymore.' He couldn't tell if the quaver in his voice was from rage or grief. 'I imagine you'll find the god ... in the garden.'

The frown unkinked from Plumtree's forehead, leaving her sunburned face expressionless; and Cochran closed his eyes and slowly lowered his face into his, hands. He was panting, his breath catching in his throat each time he inhaled, and when he felt hot tears in his palm he realized that he was weeping.

He heard the lifeless voice of Valorie: 'O he is even in my mistress' case, just in her case!' A cold finger touched his cheek. 'Stand up, stand up! Stand and you be a man.'

He raised his head and dragged his shirtsleeve across his wet eyes. And then it was recognizably Cody who sat across from him now, blinking at him in bewildered sympathy.

'Sid,' she said. 'There's a car pulling into your driveway.'

He pushed his chair back and stood up. He had left his revolver in the bedroom, and he started down the hall – but then, in the moment before the engine in the driveway was switched off, he recognized the sound of the rumbling exhaust.

He padded barefoot to the front door and squinted through the peephole.

The old Suburban in his driveway was bright blood red. An aura like heat waves was shimmering around it for a distance of about a foot, and the green box hedge on the far side of the driveway shone a brighter green through the aura band.

Pete and Angelica Sullivan were climbing out on this side, and he could see Arky Mavranos getting out from the driver's side. Kootie's head was visible in the back seat, and there was no one else with them.

Cochran unlocked the door and pulled it open, and the ocean-scented breeze was chilly on his wet face.

Pete and Angelica were helping Kootie step down from the back seat, but Mavranos plodded around the front of the truck and up the cobblestone walkway.

'Congratulations,' Mavranos said from the bottom of the porch steps. 'You've got four houseguests.' He looked over Cochran's shoulder and smiled tightly, and Cochran realized that Cody must have followed him to the door. 'It looks like the trick can still be done – somehow – on new terms that no one's got a clue about.' His smile broadened, baring his white teeth. 'I hope you're still feeling up for it, girl.'

'Oh, shut up, Arky,' Cody said. She stepped past Cochran, out onto the porch. 'Is Kootie hurt?'

'Somebody shot him,' said Mavranos. 'Probably your psycho doctor. But the boy's apparently gonna be okay.'

Cody gave a hiss of concern and hurried down the steps, past Mavranos, to help Pete and Angelica.

In Cochran's living room Angelica stitched up Kootie's wound with dental floss from a freshly opened box, Pete kneeling alongside to hand her scissors and cotton, while Mavranos paced back and forth at the front window with his revolver in his and, watching the road. Cochran and Plumtree retreated into the kitchen, where they threw together in a stockpot a big stew of canned clam chowder, crabmeat, chopped green onions, cheap Fume Blanc and curry powder. When it was hot, the aroma apparently convinced everyone that the late breakfast at Seafood Bohemia hadn't been adequate, and in half an hour all of them, even Mavranos, were sitting around Cochran's dining-room table mopping the last of the makeshift chowder out of their soup bowls with stale sourdough bread. By unspoken common consent they were all drinking Pellegrino mineral water.

Cochran had to remind himself that these people had treated him rudely – and abused his credit card – and got him into the middle of an actual *gunfight*, in which people had probably been *killed* – for he found that he was unthinkingly warmed to have the Sullivans and Kootie and Mavranos come fussing and suffering into his life again, somehow especially after his humiliations with Plumtree and Nina's ghost. Despite all their bickering and crisis, they always brought with them an urgent, sweaty sense of purpose.

'How long were you people planning to stay here?' Cochran asked now, forcing his voice to be flat and uncompromising. 'Overnight?'

Mavranos gave him a bland stare and Pete and Angelica Sullivan looked uneasy, but it was Kootie who answered: 'Until the end of the month,' the boy said diffidently. 'Until the Vietnamese Tet festival, or maybe the start of the Moslem fast, Ramadan. That's February the first. Our pendulum—'

'Two weeks?' protested Cochran. 'I've got a job! I've got neighbors! I've got – furniture that I don't need wrecked.'

'It's not *quite* two weeks,' said Kootie. 'Uh ... eleven days.'

'I saw Scott Crane's skeleton,' said Plumtree. 'How is it supposed to work this time? He takes me forever?' She raised her eyebrows. 'He takes *Kootie* forever?'

'Neither, I think,' said Kootie. Cochran noticed that the boy didn't seem happy to be exempted – in fact he looked haunted and sick. 'I don't know – we have to ask Mammy Pleasant. She's the old black lady from the TV.'

Angelica snorted. 'She's been no help up to now.'

'Maybe Crane will just ... *materialize* a body,' ventured Plumtree.

'No,' said Pete, 'where will he get stuff from? He'll need protoplasm, like a hundred and sixty or so pounds of it!'

'Edison conjured up a sort of body,' said. Kootie quietly, 'a mask, at least, when he took me over, in '92; he used the flesh of a dog I was friends with. I've dreamed of it, since. In one second, Fred – the dog – was suddenly just a bloody skeleton, and Edison had a flesh head and hands of his own, and even a furry black overcoat.' He gulped some of the mineral water. 'But the flesh was killed in the rearrangement. I'm sure it just rotted, after we shed it.'

Jesus, thought Cochran.

Angelica nodded. 'So he'll not only need protoplasm, but *unkilled* protoplasm. Are we supposed to bring some homeless guy along? A bunch of dogs?'

'Pigs are supposed to be very like humans, physically,' said Plumtree. 'Maybe we should bring a couple of good-size pigs.'

Mavranos was pale, and looked as though he wanted to spit. 'Kootie *talked* to old Pleasant today. Her ghost, but in person, not on a TV. She's apparently sort of an indentured servant, or prisoner serving out hard-labor time, of Dionysus, and she's – and the god is too – trying to help us. Apparently. She gave Kootie a message for Crane, some kind of summons and commandment, and it's in the form of a Latin palindrome. I don't like that, 'cause it's *ghosts* that are drawn to palindromes, and Crane's *ghost* is a naked imbecile running around at the Sutro ruins.'

'Is it the Latin thing I burned up the matchbook with,' asked Cochran, 'in the motel room? And there was another Latin bit that Cody and I saw, on an ashtray in L.A. I don't remember what it was.'

Mavranos hiked his chair back to dig a car registration slip out of his jeans pocket. He unfolded it, and read:

'Roma, tibi subito motibus ibit Amor.
Si bene te tua laus taxat, sua laute tenebis.
Sole, medere pede: ede, perede melos.'

'That first line is definitely the thing that was on the ashtray in L.A.,' said Plumtree.

Cochran could feel hairs stirring on the back of his neck. 'After I read that line out loud, there, Crane's ghost showed up as our taxi driver. And after I read out the second one, in the Sutro ruins, his crazy naked ghost appeared *there*.'

'Don't speak the third one now,' said Mavranos. 'A naked guy banging around in your kitchen would only upset the ladies. Wouldn't do me any good, either, seeing a semblance of my old friend in that totally bankruptious state.' He sighed, then glared at Cochran. 'Okay if I use your phone? I should see if Nardie's got the damn thing translated.'

'There's a speakerphone in the kitchen,' Cochran said. 'Talk to her on that, so we can all hear it.'

In the sunny kitchen, Cochran and Plumtree resumed their seats at the table, while Pete and Angelica leaned on the counter by the sink. Kootie slumped into a third chair, but looked at the counter as if he'd have liked to climb up on it if he hadn't had fresh stitches in his side. Cochran recalled that Kootie had sat up on a washing machine when they had tried to call Crane's ghost in Solville, and he wondered why the boy wanted to be distanced from the ground when important calls were being made.

Mavranos had walked straight to the telephone on the wall and punched in the eleven digits of the long-distance number, and now tapped the speakerphone button.

'Hello?' came a young woman's cautious voice out of the speaker; Cochran had seldom used the speakerphone function, and he now reflected ruefully that the sound wasn't as good as what Kootie's chalk-in-the-pencil-sharpener speaker had produced.

'Arky here, Nardie,' said Mavranos, 'with all the king's horses and all the king's men listening in. Whaddaya got?'

'Okay, your three palindromes are a pentameter followed by a hexameter followed by a pentameter,' said the woman called Nardie. 'That's a natural alternation in Roman lyric verse, like in Horace and Catullus. This could be very damned old, you know? And the lines do seem to relate to your – our – situation. You got a pencil?'

Mavranos pulled open a drawer under the telephone and pawed through it. 'Yes,' he said, fumbling out an eyeliner pencil and Cochran's January gas bill.

'Okay,' said Nardie's voice from the speaker, '*Roma*, with a comma after it, is in the vocative case, addressing Rome, which our context pretty clearly makes "spiritual power on Earth"; like a rogue version of the Vatican, okay? *Tibi subito* is "to you, suddenly, abruptly." *Motibus* is in the ablative case, indicating in what manner, so it means something like "with dancing motion," though Cicero uses it in the phrase *motus terrae*, which means an earthquake.'

'You told me *motibus* was "motor bus,"' Plumtree whispered to Cochran. She seemed relieved.

He nodded tightly and waved at her to be quiet.

'*Ibit*,' Nardie was saying, 'is the third-person future tense of "to go." Of course *amor* is "love," but the capital A makes me think it's a person, like some god of love; and in this suddenness-and-earthquake context very likely a harsh one.'

Cochran was thinking of the god who had awakened him with an apparent earthquake in the Troy and Cress Wedding Chapel in Las Vegas nearly five years ago, and of Nina, who had preferred that god's fatal love to his own.

'In the second line,' Nardie went on, '*taxat* is a first-declension verb, *taxo, tax-are*, meaning "hold, value, esteem." Literally, it's "if your praise values you well," but in English that'd be "if you value your praise well." *Sua* is a possessive pronoun – it has to be in the nominative case, though I'd have liked *suam* better; anyway, it's feminine, agreeing with the feminine *laus*, which is "praise" or "fame." I think "your fame" here is supposed to be actually, literally feminine in relation to this *Amor* person, who is fairly emphatically masculine. *Laute* is "gloriously." *Tenebis* is a second-declension verb: "to hold, to arrive at."'

Mavranos was impatiently waving the eyeliner pencil in front of his face. 'Nardie, what does the goddamn thing *mean*?'

A shaky sigh buzzed out of the speaker. 'I'm explaining why I think it means what I'm gonna tell you, Arky, okay? Now listen, the last line really does flicker between alternate readings; I just finished untangling this a few minutes ago. *Sole*, with a comma after it, is like *Roma* in the first line, it has to be the vocative of *sol*, direct address for "sun," as in "O Sun." *Medere* is an infinitive or a gerund – or, as we've got here, an imperative – of "cure, remedy"; it's not so much "to cure" or "curing" as it is an *order*, see – "fix it!" or "remedy it!" *Rede* is "louse," the singular noun, as in Pliny's use *pediculus* or the English word "pediculosis," which means an infestation of lice. Now the verb *Ede* is very interesting here; it's either from *edo, edere, edi, esum*, which is the usual Latin verb for "devour, consume, eat away" – or else it's another verb, *edo, edere, edidi, editum*, which means "breathe one's last, bring to an end," or at the same time "give birth to," or "give forth from oneself." Either verb works here, though the long *e* imposed by the trochaic meter makes me favor the second one. *Perede* is lemphasis, emphatic repetition of the previous verb, whichever that is. And *melos* is generally translated as "song," but it's a Latinized Greek word – obviously, from the suffix, right? – and the Greek for *melos* can also be "limb." As a Latin word it could be either nominative or accusative here, but with the Greek form it's got to be accusative, a direct object.'

'What,' said Mavranos, speaking with exaggerated clarity, 'does – the-damn-thing-mean?'

'Okay. In my interpretation, it means: "O spiritual power on Earth, the god of love will come to you suddenly and abruptly," either "with dancing movements" or "as an earthquake" – or as both, conceivably. "If you value your praise highly you will hold it" – or "arrive at it" – "gloriously. O Sun, remedy the louse: give forth from yourself, and give forth from yourself again, your limb." And with the confusion of the two *edo* verbs, there's the implication of "your *devoured* limb."'

'Leave the suicide king in the deck,' said Plumtree.

Mavranos frowned at her, but nodded. 'I think I tried to tell Scott that, when we went to Northridge after the earthquake a year ago. The subterranean phylloxera lice were a summons from ... under sanctified ground.'

'He never could bear to cut back the grapevines, in the midwinter,' said Nardie's voice from the speaker, 'after that first year. Even when the babies started to get fevers and pulmonary infections in the winters, and he had to eat No-Doz all day long, and his fingernails bled.' There was a pause while she might have shrugged. 'He was still strong in the summers.'

Cochran was remembering putting out his hand to keep the face in the stump from being beheaded. 'What we do next,' he said, glancing at everyone but finally fixing his gaze on Angelica, 'is what?'

Angelica gave him a tired smile. 'Thank you for the we,' she said. 'We won't ask you for your gun again. What we do next,' she said, stepping away from the counter and stretching, 'can't be anything else but summon Kootie's silly old black lady, I guess.' She dropped her arms and looked at Plumtree. 'We've got to talk to her in person.'

'In *this* person, you mean,' said Plumtree, though only in a tone of tired resignation. 'Jeez, if my own genetic *father*, imposed on me, gives me toothaches and nosebleeds, God knows what this strange old woman will be like.'

'No,' said Kootie, 'your father never died, but Mammy Pleasant did. She's a ghost. When Edison had possession of me, there was nothing like that afterward. Ghosts don't have the, the *psychic DNA* of a body anymore, they've got no vital structure to impose on the living body that hosts them.'

'Cool,' sighed Plumtree. 'Not really my idea of a fun date *anyway*, to tell you the truth, but I guess that's neither here nor there.' She stood up from the table. 'Tell me what I've got to do.'

'I'm Bernardette Dinh,' came the voice from the speaker, 'at the king's overthrown Camelot in Leucadia.'

'I'm Janis Cordelia Plumtree, and my *compadre* here is Sid Cochran. I hope we can all meet in person one day, in the presence of the king.'

'Back in Solville,' said Kootie hesitantly, 'Mammy Pleasant told us, "eat the seeds of my trees."'

Angelica now reached into the pocket of her denim jacket and pulled out a fistful of what looked like angular gray acorns. She dropped them onto the kitchen table, and their rattling was nothing like bar dice. 'We picked these up this morning, at the foot – sorry, at the *waist* – of one of her suffering trees. Koala bears eat this stuff, so it's probably not poison,' she said. 'I figure we can make an infusion in wine, with some of 'em, and grind up some others to mix with flour and make bread.'

BOOK THREE

Gout de Terroir

The vine by nature is apt to fall, and unless supported drops down to the earth; yet in order to keep itself upright it embraces whatever it reaches with its tendrils as though they were hands.

—Marcus Tullius Cicero

CHAPTER TWENTY FIVE

'I am afraid of it,' she answered, shuddering.
'Of it? What?'
'I mean of him. Of my father.'
—Charles Dickens, *A Tale of Two Cities*

In the Salinas and Santa Clara and Livermore valleys, on the jade green slopes that stretched away from the highways up to where the Santa Cruz Mountains in the west and the Diablo Range in the east met the gray sky, the newly head-pruned grapevines stood in rows like gnarled crucifixes, as if a tortured god hung at endlessly reiterated sacrifice in the cold rain.

The work in the vineyard cellars in late January was racking the wines, pumping the new vintages from one cask to another to liberate them from the freshly thrown sediments of dead yeast cells, and fining them with egg whites to precipitate cloudiness out. In the Pace cellars on San Bruno Mountain the suspension cloudiness in the casks was heavy this year, and bentonite clay as well as egg whites was needed to bring the wine to clarity, and the '*goût de terroir*,' the flavor of earth, was especially pronounced. On the slopes outside, tractors dragged harrows and cultivators through the old-standard eight-foot aisles between the rows, and this year the blades and disks were soon blunted to uselessness by the rocky soil and had to be replaced after having served only half of their expected life spans.

During the long days Sid Cochran oversaw the washing out of the drained casks with soda ash and hot water so that the wines could be racked back into them, and in the evenings he was kept busy in the lab, chilling some samples of the adjusted new wines to test for tartaric acid stability and heating others to provoke any incipient protein hazing. After his twelve days off, which the payroll clerk had listed as compassionate leave following the death of a family member, Cochran had now worked for seven days straight, as much for relief from his five houseguests as for catching up on the uncompromising vineyard chores and getting in some justifiable overtime pay.

Six or seven houseguests, he thought on Saturday afternoon as he steered the Granada up into his driveway and switched off the engine; at least. Though admittedly only five at any particular moment.

Mavranos's truck was parked at the top of the driveway. The new pair of tan car covers, weighted down with bricks, concealed the truck's red color, but did nothing to hide its boxy shape.

Cochran got out of the car and walked toward his 1960s ranch-style house across the lawn rather than on the stepping-stones, for Kootie had covered them with chalk detection-evasion patterns he'd apparently learned from Thomas Alva Edison two years ago; and up on the porch Cochran brushed aside Angelica's wind chimes of chicken bones and old radio parts, avoided stepping in the smears of pork-fat-and-salt that Mammy Pleasant had carefully daubed onto the concrete, then ignored the brass keyhole plate below the doorknob and crouched to fit his housekey into the disguised lock Mavranos had installed at the base of the door.

The warm air in the entry hall smelled of WD-40 spray oil and stewing beef and onions, and Cochran could hear Bob Dylan's 'It's All Over Now, Baby Blue' from the *Subterranean Homesick Blues* album playing on the stereo in the living room. The music told him that Mavranos was in the house, and the pair of treebark-soled Ferragamo pumps by the door indicated that Mammy Pleasant was not currently occupying the Plumtree body.

'Cody?' he called as he shrugged out of his rain-damp windbreaker.

'She's out working on the Torino,' came Pete Sullivan's voice from the kitchen. 'How goes the bottle?' He was sitting at the kitchen table, leaning over a couple of half-dismantled walkie-talkies with a screwdriver.

'Aging.' Yesterday Cochran had replied, *Cobwebby*. He stepped into the kitchen and tossed his windbreaker onto the counter and then opened the refrigerator to get one of Mavranos's beers. Freshly scratched into the white enamel of the refrigerator door were the numbers *1-28-95*; during this week of frustrating waiting Plumtree had got into the habit of key-scratching the current day's date on any surface that would show a gouge – wood tabletops, dry wall, book spines. When he had protested after finding the first few examples, last weekend, she had doggedly told him that she had to do it, that it was like the hospital surgery-ward policy of inking *NO* on limbs that were not to be 'ectomied,' cut off. And she had been using a black laundry-marking pen to letter the name of each day on whatever blouse of Nina's she was wearing. Probably she was doing the same to her underwear; Cochran was sleeping on the living-room couch these days, and didn't know.

Cochran carried his beer out through the laundry room to the back door, the window of which was still broken from the morning two weeks ago when he and Plumtree had let themselves in by breaking the glass with a wine bottle. When he unlocked the door and pushed it open against the cold outdoor breeze, the woman standing by the raised hood of the '69 Torino looked at him, and was clearly Cody.

'You've got to talk to Janis,' Cody said.

Cochran walked up to the old car. Cody had taken the carburetor and the distributor cap off of the engine, and had laid out wrenches and a timing-light gun on a towel draped over the fender. 'I've tried to,' he said.

Several times at their noisy buffet-style breakfasts he had noticed Plumtree eating poached or fried eggs, holding the fork in her right hand, and he had caught her eye – but each time her face had changed, and it had been Cody who had given him a blank, questioning look as she switched the fork to her left hand and reached for the bowl of scrambled eggs; and once Plumtree's posture, as she had stood on tiptoe to reach a volume of Edna St. Vincent Millay down from a high bookshelf, had clearly been Janis's shoulders-back stance – but, when he had called to her, Cody had blinked impatiently at the book and paused only long enough to dig her set of car keys out of her pocket and scratch the date into the cover before putting it back. 'She's avoiding me,' Cochran said.

'Well I wonder why.' Plumtree laid down a screwdriver she'd been twisting the idle screw with and held out her black-smeared left hand. 'Can I have your beer? I'm too dirty to be touching your doorknobs and refrigerator handles.'

Cochran handed it to her, without even taking a last sip of it. 'And I'll get you another if you want, just to save you the walk,' he said, 'but *mi casa es su casa*, Cody. Mess up anything you want.'

Plumtree took the beer with a grin. After a deep sip, she exhaled and said, 'Thanks, but Mammy Pleasant will make me clean up any messes I make. Have you *seen* those lists of chores she leaves for me? Not just shopping and cleaning – sometimes she tells me to go buy or sell houses! But I called about a couple, they're all pre-1906 addresses. It's a good thing she doesn't know the 1995 prices I'm paying for her groceries, she'd think I was embezzling. And in the notes she's always calling me Teresa.'

Cochran nodded. Cody and Mammy Pleasant were both strong presences in the household, and managed to get on each other's nerves in spite of the fact that they could never meet, taking turns as they did at occupying the same body. But Cochran had several times talked directly to the old-woman personality, and she seemed to be as senile as Kootie said most ghosts were. The Teresa person had evidently been a servant she'd had when she'd been alive.

The Mammy Pleasant ghost had first arrived upon Plumtree last Sunday, after Cody had consented to eat bread baked with ground Octavia Street eucalyptus seeds in it and drink wine in which the split seeds had sat soaking overnight. For an hour after taking the dubious sacrament, Plumtree had just sat on the living-room couch, flushing her mouth with vodka to kill the taste of the eucalyptus and watching the news—

And then she had blinked and reared back, staring with clear recognition into the faces of Kootie and Pete and Angelica and Cochran through eyes that momentarily seemed to Cochran to be mismatched in color. After a few seconds she had looked back at the television, and said in a strong, deep voice, 'I was talking to you people through that thing, wasn't I?'

'Yes, ma'am,' said Kootie, looking away from her.

'Courage, boy!' she said. 'Remember Gawain.'

'Yes, ma'am,' said Kootie again.

Angelica had begun asking the old woman questions, but Mammy Pleasant had immediately demanded to know if they had brought any eucalyptus bark from her tree; and, when she'd been assured that they had, that a pair of shoes be soled from the bark for her. And when Pete and Kootie had cut out bark soles and heels and Superglued them onto a pair of Nina's low-heeled Ferragamo pumps – Pleasant had haughtily dismissed the notion of using a pair of Reeboks after getting a look at them – the old woman had put the shoes on and walked outside in the crackling, fragmenting footwear, straight to the greenhouse.

Scott Crane's disordered skeleton was laid out in there on a shelf between Nina's orchids and a crowd of potted fuchsias, and the Plumtree hands were shaky as they touched the broken skull. 'He himself will lead you to the god's wine,' she had said. 'And by then you'll have learned where to go with it, and what to do.'

She hadn't said very much more about Crane's restoration to life than that – then or in the six days since. She generally came on within an hour to either side of noon, though the sun was seldom visible through the overcast, and often she seemed absent-minded, or senile, or even drunk – which, Mavranos noted, was only to be expected in a servant of Dionysus. She kept finding jobs around the house for 'Teresa' to do, and had to leave notes because she could never find the girl; and Plumtree had begun leaving notes in return, buggesting that the old woman clean the floors and windows herself. When Kootie or Angelica would stop the old woman and try to get information about the procedure they were supposedly going to perform on the day of the Tet Festival, Pleasant's drunkenness would seem to become more pronounced – and she would just insist that Crane would presently tell them what to do. Adding to the confusion was the fact that she generally slurred the name to *Cren*, and frequently pronounced it with a stutter, *C-cren*, so that she seemed to be referring to Cochran. Even her pronunciation of *Scott* sometimes seemed to slur nasally toward *Scant*.

Cochran now watched Cody spraying the carburetor with some very flammable-smelling aerosol.

'Janis is avoiding me,' he said again.

'Don't light a cigarette right now,' Cody said. 'I don't blame her. But I think she should talk to you.' She put down the spray can and squinted up at him, her face shadowed by the raised car hood. 'I saw into her dream for a couple of seconds last night. You were in both of our dreams, and the ... figure of you, your outline, must have sort of matched up and spun around at the partition between her mind and mine – like one of those secret bookshelf-walls in old movies, that rotate on a pivot when you pull on the right book.' Cody took another gulp of the beer. 'Her dream was in color, but barely – it looked fake, like a black-and-white photo touched up with watercolors, and the backgrounds were plain gray. And there was music, the dwarf music from *Sleeping Beauty*, but I could hardly hear the melody because the drumming was so hard and loud. It sounded like soldiers marching fast on an iron deck.'

Cochran bared his teeth unhappily. He couldn't forget the image of Janis valiantly punching the linoleum floor at the Rosecrans Medical Center nearly three weeks ago; nor her look of despairing hurt in his bed last Tuesday, when he had last spoken to her. 'What does that mean?' he asked Cody.

'*Valorie's* memories are in black-and-white, and always have drumming going on. I think Janis is draining away into Valorie.'

But Valorie's dead! he almost said. 'Can ... that happen?'

'As far as we're concerned, Sid, *anything* can happen. We went to a funeral once when we were twelve, and by the time the minister was done talking it was somebody else's funeral and we were fourteen; and what we thought was the emotion of rage turns out to be our male parent, who's alive and crouching inside our head; and I have to look at whatever I last scratched the date on to be sure—' She glanced at fresh scratches in the greasy curve of the manifold valve cover. '—to be sure that the goddamn Edison Medicine that broke us all into separate pieces, all finally *aware* of each other, happened only seventeen days ago!'

Cochran smiled with half of his face. 'I see what you mean. The word "impossible" isn't what it used to be, for any of us.' Cody was holding out the beer can toward him; he took it to throw away for her, but it was still more than half full, so he gratefully tilted it up for a sip and then handed it back to her. 'What can I say to Janis besides that I'm sorry? Besides that I know I was the bad guy and that she deserved better from even a total stranger, never mind from somebody she had got herself into bad trouble to protect?'

Cody laughed. 'Besides those things?' Then she sobered. 'I honestly don't *know*, but it might save her if you told her you love her.' She shook her head. 'My ... it's not sister; my *other half*? ... seems to be evaporating, *dying*.'

'I *could* tell her that, I suppose, if it would help,' he said cautiously. He glanced back at the kitchen door. 'But if it did help, and she came back, even though I'd – I mean, she'd be able to tell—'

Cody raised an eyebrow. 'You don't love her?'

'No.'

'Huh. She seems to me like the ideal woman, everything I'm not. So do you love *anybody*?' She coughed. 'I mean, anybody who's alive?'

At first Cochran thought he wouldn't be able to look at her. Then he did meet her eyes, though his voice was incongruously light when he answered, 'Yes.'

It was Cody that looked away. 'I don't think that's very smart.' She coughed again, rackingly. 'Well, go ahead and lie to her, and we can worry about the consequences once she's herself again. Better a car that's gonna let you down halfway home than one that won't run at all.'

Cochran considered, then rejected, the idea of drinking a couple of beers first. 'I don't know what I'll say. But go ahead – call her up.'

'I can't, she won't come voluntarily. *You've* got to call her up.'

'How am I supposed to – oh. Follow-the-Queen.'

'Right. Wait right here, I'll ... get my stupid parentess.' Plumtree closed her eyes. 'Mother!' she called.

Instantly her eyes sprang open, and she stepped back away from Cochran after grabbing up a screwdriver from the fender. 'You tell him,' she said, 'that if he comes out of that house I'll drive this straight into my own heart. He'll know I mean it.' The skin of her neck was suddenly looser, and her eyes seemed closer together.

'He's nowhere around here, Mrs ... .Plumtree,' said Cochran awkwardly. Why was he talking to this personality? According to Angelica it wasn't her real mother, nor even a real ghost, just an internalized version of her parent patched together from memories and overheard conversations. 'I do know who you mean,' Cochran went on. 'We're hiding from him.' He felt as though he had dialed six digits of Janis's number, and was afraid to dial the last one. 'We're protecting your daughter from him.'

'You can't *hide*, you can't *protect* anyone, from Omar Salvoy,' said the querulous voice, though her fist relaxed around the screwdriver handle. But Cochran's stomach was cold, and he wished she had not mentioned Salvoy's name. '*Especially* you can't protect *her*. He wants to have a child by a dead woman. I was nearly dead when he had intercourse with me, I was – unconscious – in a coma! – after a head injury!'

Cochran thought of his afternoon with Tiffany, then drove the horrifying parallel out of his mind.

The mother personality almost put Plumtree's eye out as she reached up to rub her eyes with the hand holding the screwdriver. 'Listen to me,' she went on. 'He studied the old books of the Order of the Knights Templar, and one of their secret mystery-initiation stories was about a man who dug up a dead woman out of her grave and had intercourse with her cold body; and after he had raped the corpse and buried it again, a voice from the earth told him to return in nine months and he would find a divine son. He came back then, and when he dug her up this time he found a, a blinking, grimacing

little black *head* lying on her thigh-bones. And the voice from the earth told him to guard it well, for it would be the source of all forgiveness. And so he took it away, and guarded it jealously, and he prospered with impunity.' There were tears in her eyes as she glared at Cochran. 'My baby died when he fell on her. There's some kind of … *kaleidoscope* girl that's grown up in there, in her head, but my *baby* died that day in Soma.' She was shaking her head violently and drawing the screwdriver blade across her chest. 'But she can still, my *dead daughter* can still become pregnant, if Omar is in a male body. He can become the father of the god.'

Cochran knew that it was his vision, and not the sky, that had darkened; but with a shaking hand he reached out and then suddenly, firmly, gripped the blade of the screwdriver.

'Don't kill her,' he whispered. Was this the same god? he wondered; was the horrible little homunculus she'd described the same person as the deity of groves and grapevines that offered the *pagadebitil*. The *mondard* that had spoken to him in Paris with such fatherly affection, before turning into a bull-headed thing and then into a tumbled straw effigy? The god that had made the Agave woman in Mavranos's Euripides play cut off her son's head? What kind of primordial proto-deity could be all these things?

He thought of the endless rows of gnarled crucifixes dripping out on the surrounding hills in the rain.

'Don't kill her,' he repeated. 'I'll protect her, I'll save her from him. I love her.' I love the *real* one, he thought, even if you don't know which that is.

Plumtree shook her head in evident pity. 'She'll come to the point where she'll tear you to pieces just for the honor of being able to bring your head to him. Who are *you* to the *god*?'

Cochran abruptly pulled the screwdriver out of her hands. Then, slowly, he turned his hand around to show her the mark below his knuckles. 'When I was a boy,' he said, 'I put out my hand to save him from the pruner's shears.'

Plumtree had gasped, and now nodded slowly. 'Send her away into the sea,' she said. 'She belongs in India, not here, not being the mother of the god. The god himself couldn't want that, to have an incarnate aspect of himself in filial obligation to a monster.' The smile she gave him was one he had not seen before on Plumtree's face, but it was brave. 'I love her too.'

'I'll do what's right,' he said, 'for her.' Then he took a deep breath and said, gently, 'Janis.'

Plumtree's features pinched in anxiety. 'Oh, it's Scant,' she said; then her voice quickened: 'Was *he* here? I can feel his name still on my tongue! *Daddy?*' she called, glancing around at the yard and the greenhouse. 'I'll never ditch you, Daddy! I'll always catch you! Listen to me! Where I go, you go, I swear on my life!'

'Shut up, Janis, please!' Cochran hissed, spinally aware of the vineyards and of the skeleton in the greenhouse. 'He wasn't here. I have to talk to you, Janis. You don't have to forgive me, but you do have to know that, that I know I was totally in the wrong, and I'm terribly sorry and ashamed of myself.' He smacked his fist against his thigh, angry with himself for saying this badly. 'All my excuses were lies, Janis. You were right about me, but I want to make it up to you, to whatever extent I can. Will you come back to us, please? Cody needs you. *I* need you. I—'

'To be or not to be, that is the question,' said Plumtree.

Cochran faltered. 'Valorie?'

'No ... no, I'm Janis, still.'

I should have known, Cochran thought, that it wouldn't be Valorie quoting the only Shakespeare line that everyone in the world knows. 'Janis, I—'

'Don't, Scant mustn't, I'll make myself deaf to him – we can do that. Leave me alone, if he wants to do something for me, he can leave me alone!' She hurried away across the concrete patio deck to the kitchen door, yanked it open, and slammed it behind her.

Cochran thought seriously for a moment about pursuing her. Then he sighed picked up Cody's abandoned beer, and leaned against the car fender. Maybe, he thought, I should tell it all to dead *Valorie*, and let *her* explain it to Janis.

What damn good is this person that's me? he thought, glancing from the kitchen door to the mark on the back of his hand. How in hell am I supposed to play this flop, when I'm gambling with so many people's bankrolls? And he remembered Kootie telling him, at the Sutro ruins two weeks ago, *You'll be taking all our chances.*

Omar Salvoy found himself in a bedroom with a telephone in it.

He knew he would have to be careful in what he said to Dr. Richard Paul Armentrout, and he crossed his arms under his daughter's breasts – *A divine offspring for you to nurse during this thirteen-moon year, baby, I promise*, he thought – and paced up and down the rag rug in front of the bedside table. *Bye, baby bunting, Daddy's gone a-hunting, gone to get a leopard-skin to bury baby bunting in.*

In his youth Salvoy had only wanted to find a king to serve. He had been a theater major at Stanford University, specializing in Shakespeare and finding startling clues in some of the obscurer plays, and living in a shabby little apartment in Menlo Park.

In May of 1964, when he had been nineteen, Salvoy had gone with a friend to the La Honda house of Ken Kesey, out in the redwood forests at the south end of State Highway 84. Kesey's *One Flew Over the Cuckoo's Nest* had been published only two years earlier.

And, in Kesey, Salvoy thought he had found his king. The burly, balding

Oregonian had gathered a whole tribe together at his remote hillside ranch in the canyon, and he spoke of the new drug LSD as the almost sacramental key to 'worlds that have always existed.' Hi-fi speakers boomed and yowled on the roof of the house, shattering the silence of the ancient redwood forest, and weird wind chimes and crazy paintings were hung on all the trees. Omar Salvoy had begun visiting the place on his own, driving his old Karmann Ghia down the 84 over the Santa Cruz Mountains to the La Honda ranch every weekend.

One day out in the woods someone had found a dozen oversized wooden chessmen, weathered and cracked, and Kesey's tribe had spontaneously begun improvising a dialogue among the figures – it had had to do with a king threatened with castration, and a girl with 'electric eel tits that ionized King Arthur's sword under swamp water' – and though the impromptu play was just a cheerful stoned rap from a bunch of distracted proto-hippies, Salvoy had believed he had heard mythic, archetypal powers manifesting themselves in the lines. When Kesey had set his people to painting random patterns in Day-Glo paint all over the 1939 International Harvester school bus he had just bought, Salvoy had climbed up to the destination sign over the windshield and painted on it the name ARTHUR.

That night he had managed to catch Kesey for a few minutes away from his followers, and he had told him about the magical kingdom of the American West, and how the current king – a castrated transplanted Frenchman! – could surely be overthrown when that cycle came around again, at Easter in '69, five years hence. And he had told Kesey about the supernatural power he would have if he took the throne, how he would be able to shackle and control the god of earthquakes and wine as the present king was doing, and raise ghosts to do his errands, and live forever. Omar Salvoy would be King Kesey's advisor.

But Kesey had just laughed and, as Salvoy recalled, had said something like, 'And if I jump off a cliff, angels will bear me up lest I dash my foot against a stone, right?' – and he had walked away. Salvoy believed it had been a quote from the New Testament, when Jesus was refusing to be tempted by Satan. *One Flew Over the Cuckoo's Nest* had been full of Christ-figure imagery. Salvoy had driven home over the mountains in a humiliated rage, and never returned. Later he had seen a photograph of Kesey's bus in *Life* magazine – someone had painted *FU* over his *A* on the destination sign, so that it now just read, idiotically, FURTHUR.

Salvoy had abandoned college, though he'd kept studying the plays of Shakespeare, and he began to sample the strange cults that were springing up in the Bay Area in the mid-sixties. From a splinter group of the Order of the Knights Templar he learned about the uses of the Eye of Horns symbol, the *udjat eye* that looked like a profile falcon, in countering the influences of the feminine Moon Goddess; and that it was possible actually to become the human father of a living, absolving fragment of the god who died with the grapevines every winter and was reborn in them every spring, by impregnating a dead woman; and for a few months he traveled up and down the coast on Highway I, from Big Sur to the state beaches between Santa Barbara and Ventura, with the agricultural human-sacrifice cult that was then still calling itself the Camino Hayseeds, not for two decades yet to be internally reorganized and have its name changed to the Amino Acids.

And then toward the end of the year he had found the Danville-area commune known as the Lever Blank, whose secret and very old real name was L'Ordre du Levrier Blanc, which meant The Order of the White Greyhound. The name had apparently been chosen as long ago as the thirteenth century as a repudiation of the dog that appeared on the Fool card in the tarot deck, which was always a mongrel and generally black. The Lever Blank grew vegetables and marijuana on part of its land, and dispensed food to indigent street people, and talked a lot about harmony with nature and celebrations of life; but the Levrier Blanc was concerned with the grapes that grew on the rest of the commune land, and with re-establishing the carefully preserved old pre-phylloxera vines that had borne Dionysus's sacramental wine before the French Revolution, and with the supernatural kingdom of the American west which Salvoy had already perceived. Salvoy had decided to join them and become the king, the earthly personification of the sun-god, himself. And, based on what he had learned from the Order of the Templars, he had resolved too to father an incarnate piece of the earthbound, annually dying vegetation god. He had failed at all that, then. This year he would do it.

But it would be a risky and probably one-shot procedure. He would have to learn from Armentrout how to exit a body without hurting it – he wanted to leave the Plumtree body alive, healthy, and fertile. The Koot Hoomie boy would have to be comatose, flat-line brain-dead; Salvoy would take the ventilator out of the boy's throat and then lean over him and jump across the gap in a moment when Koot was, ideally, inhaling. At that point, with no tenant-mind to overcome, Salvoy would simply *have* Koot Hoomie's body.

And Salvoy would quickly have to kill Armentrout, whose goal in all this was to have a *perpetually* flatline brain-dead king. If Armentrout were actually present, Salvoy would have to remember to put a gun or a knife into the boy's limp hand before throwing himself out of the Plumtree body into Koot Hoomie.

He punched the doctor's number into the telephone, and when the querulous voice said, hoarsely, 'Hello?' Salvoy forgot diplomacy and just said, 'You tried to kill Koot Hoomie, you fat freak!' He did remember to keep his voice down.

'But I failed,' said the doctor quickly. 'My mother – Muir – my ghosts are *still around*, they haven't been banished! The boy must still be alive – healthy, even! – I've been searching for him with the shadow of a pomegranate, but there's been so little sun—'

'Yeah, he's alive. He's with us, still. I'm in the same house with him right now! But I ain't tellin' you dick if you're just gonna try and kill him again.' He bared the Plumtree teeth and spat out, 'You fucking block, you stone, you worse than goddamn senseless thing!'

'No, I won't, I was desperate that day – of course I want to, we both want to, get him onto the perpetual life-support arrangement, brain-dead – but, try to understand this, my *mother's ghost* had found me! I was desperate – I was only thinking about – if I killed him outright it would at least get rid of *her*.'

'You fucking dumb – didn't you think *Koot Hoomie's* ghost would come after you?'

'It would have been a reprieve – and he's the king, and I think the king's ghost would have bigger concerns than to go after his murderer. Crane didn't come after your girls, did he? Anyway, I *didn't kill the boy*.'

'Well, you're on my shit-list, ipso fatso. The good news is that they did the restoration-to-life trick *all wrong*, and this Koot Hoomie boy is the king if anyone is. Anyway, nobody else is. Look, I'll cut the boy out of the pack here, but before I let you anywhere near him, you're gonna have to tell me everything you know about transferring a person from one body to another.'

'Why would you need to know that? All you need to know is that a dead Fisher King is a heat-sink.' Armentrout giggled breathlessly. 'He takes the heat.'

'Tell you what, why don't I just go find another doctor? There's gotta be more than one psychiatrist in this country who'd like to have in his clinic an engine for ... for eliminating the spiritual consequences of sin.' Salvoy clunked the receiver against the wall as if about to hang up – and then he heard a knock at the bedroom door.

It was recognizably Cody who pulled open the bedroom door after Cochran's knock, and she was holding the telephone receiver to her ear against the spring-tension of the stretched-out cord. Her face was spotty, and she touched a finger to her tight bloodless lips as she held the receiver out toward him.

Cochran twisted his head to listen, with her – and he heard Dr. Armentrout's unmistakable fruity voice coming out of the earpiece: '—can hear you breathing! You need *me*, Salvoy, don't kid yourself! What other psychiatrist is going to *know* that mind-shifting trick you want? Hah? Asymptotic freedom, remember? How to pick up your *ass and tote it* out of there? I'll tell you how to do it – I'll *help* you do it. I was just curious why you wanted to, that's all. And I'm her physician-of-record!' Armentrout was panting over the phone. 'You're listening, right? So tell me where you are, where *he* is.'

Cochran ventured to make a gravelly 'Hmm,' sound.

'You say they did the restoration-to-life trick all wrong,' said Armentrout, catching his breath. 'Are you afraid they might do it again, and do it *right* this time? I don't know why you should care about that, but if you want to screw them up, I can certainly help you, you know. You could *use* the physician-of-record being present. Is that Cochran guy there too?'

Nervous sweat itching under his eyes, Cochran replied with a careful whistling sigh.

'Oh shit,' whispered Armentrout. 'Janis?' he said then, strongly. 'Cody? This is your doctor. Please tell me where you're staying.'

Cochran saw Plumtree put her top teeth into her lower lip as though preparing to say a word that started with F, but instead she shook her head and stepped back to the phone to rattlingly hang up the receiver.

'Smart not to say anything,' Cochran said when the connection had been broken. 'This way he can't be *sure* it wasn't ... your father. I'm sorry I spooked him, there, at the end—'

'No,' she said, staring at the telephone as if she thought it might manifest some dire noise or light that would give them only seconds to flee the room, flee the house; 'you had to make *some* response, and that first *hmm* got a couple of extra sentences out of him.' When she looked up at him her pupils were pinpricks and her jawmuscles were working. 'Janis let him on. *Damn* her, it makes me *sick* to think of him—' She spread her fingers and then closed her hands into tight fists, '*in here*, in me.' Her mouth worked, and then she spat on the rug. 'I need Listerine. At least he wasn't on for long enough to give me a nosebleed or hurt my teeth much – and he didn't tell Armentrout where we are.' She glanced at the black plastic ten-dollar watch she'd bought to replace the hospital *zeitgeber* watch. 'How long ago was it that I called up my mother for you?'

'Oh – five minutes?'

Plumtree tossed her head in exasperation. 'Five minutes at the end for *some* of them,' she said sternly, 'but *they've* got to be sautéed *too*, and added in with the ones that have been cooking all along. You want onions that're still toothsome, surely, but others should be nearly melting, they've been in there so long.'

You saved me from a reproach, Mammy, Cochran thought after his first instant of puzzlement. 'Whatever you say, Mrs. Pleasant.' In fact the old-woman personality had unexpectedly proven to be a terrific cook, and during the past week had prepared a couple of black-roux jambalayas that had even drawn enthusiasm from the preoccupied Mavranos. Cochran now remembered smelling onions cooking when he had come into the house. 'Are you talking about what you've got simmering in there now?'

'Yes, a *beef bourguignonne,* and eggplant *pirogis,*' she said. Plumtree's eyes had a heavy-lidded, almost Asian cast when Mammy Pleasant was on. 'You've got three pirogis,' she went on. 'Do you know how they are to be filled?'

He knew she was no longer talking about dinner – and he was fairly sure of what she meant. 'I think I know how to fill *one,*' he said bleakly, 'temporarily, at least. I hope somebody else suggests it – I hope *she* thinks of it, herself! – so I won't have to.'

'Partly you're here to think of things,' came the old woman's strong voice out of Plumtree's mouth; 'yes, partly each of you has been chosen for your wits and cleverness. But each of you has a specific task as well. Each of you, like the three wise men, has brought a gift to your helpless king in this January season of Epiphany. Do you know what gift it is you've brought him, Scant Cochran? Do you know what it is that you're to give away?'

Cochran thought about that. Nina's ghost, his now objectless and always deceived love for her? Well, yes, the god did appear to want that, but that couldn't be his purpose here. 'Something to do,' he said, 'with the mark on my hand.'

Plumtree's blond head nodded. 'If all goes well this time, if you all generously do what the god generously asks, King Crane will be alive at midsummer, and you will no longer have in hand the god's marker.'

Cochran realized that his mouth was open; he closed it, and then said, 'That's why I'm here, involved in this? To give away the—' What had Angelica called it at the broken temple on the end of the yacht-harbor peninsula? '—the Dionysus badge?'

'Boy, it's the only reason you were allowed to volunteer to get the mark in the first place.'

'*Allowed* to—?' Cochran could feel his face heating up. In the Mount Sabu bar in Bellflower, when Janis had asked him why he didn't get the mark removed, he had told her, *I'm kind of proud of it … it's my winemaker's merit badge, an honorable battle scar.* And he remembered Nina's ghost telling him that when he had put his hand out to injury to save the god, thirty-four years ago, he had been like Androcles daring to pull the thorn from the lion's paw in the old story; the lion had thereafter owed Androcles a debt of gratitude. And Cochran was surprised now at the hurt of learning that in his own case he had apparently only been meant to hold the golden beast's favor for someone else, someone more highly esteemed – that it had never been for him. Like my wife's love, he thought.

'So all along the god meant,' he said, forcing his voice not to hitch ludicrously, 'for me to just hold the obligation in trust for Scott Crane? Why didn't the god let f – let precious Crane earn the obligation himself, get his *own* hand half cut off?'

'The god, and Scott Crane too, was yoked in the harness of another king then, a bad king. The god had to incur the debt outside the king's control but still within his own – that is, in a remote vineyard. I think that, as much as anything, you were chosen because of the similarity of your name to that of the favored boy who would one day be king.' She smiled at him, with no evident malice or sympathy. 'As if the god needed a sign even to remember you. And later, it was probably just so that you would get a name closer to *Scott* that he broke your leg under a cask of his wine.' She reached out and gently touched his marked hand. 'To be used by him – yes, even to ignominious destruction – is to be loved by him. You should be honored to have been judged worthy of being deceived and cheated in this way.'

Cochran let the hurt run out of himself as his shoulders relaxed. Spider Joe brought the two coins, he thought, and an oracular reading of Angelica's cards; and died to do it, and ended up buried under an old Chevy Nova in a Long Beach parking lot. 'And Cody brought her father,' he said dully.

'Yes. The king had to die, so that he would no longer be a stranger to the dark earth.'

Cochran frowned into the blue eyes that seemed for the moment to be of two slightly different colors. 'I meant for what we've got to do next: make him tell us what we did wrong, what we should have done differently, last week. I didn't mean – my God, woman, are you saying that Dionysus not only wants Crane restored to life, but wanted him to die too?'

'He's no real king, no real representative of the god, if he doesn't spend the pruning season of each year in the kingdom of darkness. Few kings have been thorough enough in their observations of the office to *do* that – to actually die, each year but the god does love Scott Crane.'

'To Crane's misfortune. To the misfortune of all of us.'

'Yes,' she agreed, 'the god loves all of us, in spite of our rebellions and failures.' She blinked around the room then. 'I'm too alert – I'll draw attention. Where are my penance shoes?'

'By the front door where you left 'em.'

She nodded and shuffled past him, her shoulders, too, slumped in unsought humility. 'I'll probably forget, once I've got them on – but the dinner will be ready to serve at sundown.'

And I'll have something to serve to poor Cody, Cochran thought as he followed the old woman out of the bedroom. A flop that even Valorie might quail at. *It makes me sick to think of him in here, in me.*

*

Angelica had taken a bus into the city early that morning, and had spent the day consulting *magos* and *santeros* in the run-down Mission and Hunter's Point districts south of Market Street. She came plodding back up the driveway just at sundown, and grabbed a beer from the refrigerator and slumped on the couch in the living room while the others ate Mammy Pleasant's beef bourguignonne. Angelica had had a late lunch of pork tamales and menudo and Tecate beer, and couldn't now face a plate of steaming, vinous beef stew and a glass of room-temperature Zinfandel.

When Kootie and Pele had begun clanking the emptied dishes together and carrying them out to the kitchen sink, Angelica walked into the dining room.

She hadn't looked behind the door when she had come in, to see if the eucalyptus-soled shoes were leaned against the wall, but by now she could recognize Cody Plumtree.

'Our supernatural escrow is about to close,' Angelica said, loudly enough for Pete and Kootie to hear in the kitchen. 'Tet is only three days off, and we have no clue about what we're supposed to do, this time. My people in the *barrios* and ghettos are getting signs of something big cooking, but for all their painted bells and chicken blood they don't know what or where. Our crazy old lady keeps saying that Crane or *C-cren* will direct us when the time comes – but the old lady's just a ghost.'

'Sid,' said Cody Plumtree, 'speak up.'

Sid Cochran pushed his chair back. '*C-cren* has got a, a horrible proposal,' he said, 'which as far as I'm concerned anybody here can veto – especially Cody.'

Angelica glanced at Cody, who was sitting across from Cochran in the corner against the kitchen-side wall and had just lit a cigarette – and she got the feeling that Cody knew what Cochran was going to say, and hated it, but was not going to interrupt now, nor veto later.

'Omar Salvoy,' said Cochran, 'that's Cody and Janis's dad, who killed Scott Crane, came on today, here – he was talking on the phone to our Dr. Armentrout.'

Armentrout! thought Angelica. That's the man who shot Kootie! She darted a fearful glance toward the front door as she touched the .45 automatic at her belt and opened her mouth to speak.

But Cochran had held up his hand. 'Wait. Salvoy faded off while they were speaking, and Cody and I heard Armentrout going on talking; Salvoy had *not* told the doctor where we are. But—' Cochran paused and shook his head. 'But, from what Armentrout was saying, it was pretty clear that Salvoy knows what we did wrong, when we tried to bring Crane back to life last week.' He glanced at Cody, who just stared straight back at him. 'I think,' Cochran went on stolidly, 'we've got to do the Follow-the-Queen trick to talk to Omar Salvoy.' Angelica whistled a descending note.

'Why should he tell us anything?' interrupted Pete from the kitchen doorway.

'Valorie can make him, I bet,' said Cody. 'She could be on with him, if you call her, like a second file showing in split-screen on a computer monitor.' Once again Angelica found herself admiring the woman. 'It's a – goddam-mit, it's a good idea. My father probably *would* know. He knew enough to nearly become the king, twenty-five years ago, and from the day he exited his smashed body he's had one foot in India.'

'And I think I could effectively threaten him,' said Kootie quietly from behind Pete.

Angelica stared at her adopted son warily. 'With what, *hijo mio*?'

Ever since the seventeenth, when he had run away from the Star Motel before dawn and reappeared in the afternoon, having spent some part of the morning talking with Mammy Pleasant in her boardinghouse kitchen, Angelica thought Kootie seemed somehow far older than his fourteen years. All he had told Pete and herself about that morning was that he had killed someone, but Angelica had known that much when she had simply met his eyes as he'd lain shot and bleeding in the planter outside the Star Motel office – behind the physical shock that had paled his face and constricted his pupils, independent of that injury, dwarfing it, the new horror and guilt had been clearly evident to her.

'In '92,' said Kootie, 'when Sherman Oaks or Long John Beach tried to eat the Edison ghost out of me, he had to lure it up toward the surface of my mind first. This was when we were in the "boat on the boat," the van inside the truck. And from what Miss Plumtree has said about her psychic striptease session with that doctor, he was trying to draw a personality to the surface, to bite it off. The one on top is the one that's vulnerable.' The boy bared his teeth in a humorless smile. 'It seems like a personality brought up by this Follow-the-Queen trick is ... stuck in the *on* position for at least a little while. I think I could validly threaten to ... bite *him off*.'

Angelica's ears were ringing. 'But,' she said, 'no, you can't – it's like slam-ming bad heroin, Kootie, you'd have, his memories in you like heavy metal – his poisonous life force—' Much worse than whatever you're carrying now, she thought helplessly, trust me.

'Besides,' said Pete Sullivan, staring in obvious dismay at his adopted son, '*he's* not a *ghost*. He's a full-power person. You'd – you'd probably blow up!'

'I said *validly threaten*.' Kootie sat down in the dining-room chair next to Plumtree, where Pete had been sitting. 'If *I* can't be sure I can't do it, neither can he. And I think I *could kill* him, depending on how strong he is – swat him off the top of Miss Plumtree's mind like driving a golf ball off a tee.'

Oh, don't be flippant and proud of it, Kootie, thought Angelica unhappily; and she would have said it out loud but for the knowledge that they might in fact need him to do it, and if so she didn't want to hamper him in advance.

'Without killing "Miss Plumtree"?' asked Cochran, his voice hoarse and his eyes wide with skepticism.

Kootie raised his eyebrows and squinted across the table at him – then peripherally caught Angelica's anguished, vicariously mortified gaze; and the boy instantly looked down at the tablecloth, his face reddening. 'I don't know,' he whispered. 'I don't know if he isn't stronger than me, even. He's older than me, and meaner, so he might be.' He looked up, clearly abashed. 'But – see? – I can believably *threaten* him with it.'

'Just don't kill me before he's said what to do,' said Plumtree with what Angelica recognized as hollow, exhausted bravado. Plumtree held up her hands, and her voice skidded up and down the scale as she said, 'Sid, do you have some duct tape?'

Kootie looked nauseous.

'We won't do it tonight,' Angelica said hastily. Plumtree was like a flexed piece of tempered glass, and Angelica was afraid one measured tap might actually shatter her mind into a *thousand* tiny personalities, no one of them more sentient than an infant. And Kootie wasn't looking much better himself. 'Not if he's already been out once today,' Angelica went on in her most self-assured doctor-tone. 'Tomorrow will be plenty of time.'

Both Kootie and Plumtree sagged in what looked like uncomfortable relief.

'Then for God's sake right now get me a drink,' said Plumtree in a husky voice. 'Sid, you got vodka?'

'Got vodka,' said Cochran, getting up out of his chair like an old man.

'Got a lot of it?'

Cochran just nodded as he shambled into the kitchen.

He paused by the sink before reaching up to the liquor cabinet overhead, and stared at the glittering white mound of tiny soap bubbles that stood motionless above the dish-filled sink. And he experienced a vivid memory-flash of how Nina had looked, so many times, wearing an apron and leaning over this sink; and all at once, silently except for a nearly inaudible hissing, the soap foam diminished away to nothing, leaving the dishes exposed poking out of the surface of the gray water.

Her ghost is gone, he thought giddily as he reached up for the vodka bottle, but my memories of her apparently still have some palpable force.

We're not ... *finished*, yet.

CHAPTER TWENTY SIX

I'll hide my silver beard in a gold beaver ...
—William Shakespeare, *Troilus and Cressida*

Cochran woke up in his own bed, alone, roused by the gunning of the Torino engine in the back yard. From the gray light filtering into the bedroom through the lace curtains, he muzzily judged that it must be about seven in the morning. He had sat up drinking with Plumtree until after midnight; and when at last he had got up unsteadily and announced his intention of retiring to the couch, Plumtree had told him to take the bed. *I'll sleep on the couch,* she had said, enunciating carefully. *I can see it from here, so I know I'll be able to find it.*

As much as anything, they had been discussing immortal animals. Cody had insisted that carp never died naturally, and survived the winter frozen solid in pond ice; and Cochran had told her about toads that had been found alive in bubbles in solid rock. When the animals in question began to be imaginary ones from children's books and science-fiction movies, like the Pushmi-pullyu and E. T., Cochran had just followed the drift of the conversation, and talked about Reepicheep the mouse in the Narnia books, and the bread-and-butter-flies from *Through the Looking-Glass.* Plumtree's voice had changed several times, and she had vacillated sharply between skepticism and credulity – but since Cochran was the only other person in the room she had not had to address him by name, and the nearest electric light that was on had been the one in the kitchen and Cochran couldn't tell when it might have flickered, and their talk had been abstract and speculative enough to keep him from guessing who he might have been talking to at any particular moment. He hadn't been aware of any obvious archaisms that would have indicated lines quoted from Shakespeare, though he hadn't by any means caught everything she had said; and if Tiffany had been on, she had been subdued, and content with vodka.

He got into a fresh shirt now and pulled his jeans back on and opened the bedroom door. The car noise had evidently awakened the Sullivans too – he could hear Kootie and Pete talking quietly behind the closed door of the spare bedroom.

Mavranos was sitting at the dining room table frowning over the Saturday *San Francisco Chronicle.* In front of him a cup of coffee sat steaming, and on the opposite side of the table stood fourteen mismatched cups and tumblers. Cochran padded over barefoot and peered at them;

each had a grainy white sediment puddled in the bottom.

'You better pick up some more Alka-Seltzer when you go out,' said Mavranos quietly, 'a big bottle. I guess each of the girls had a hangover, and couldn't stomach drinking out of another one's used glass.'

Cochran stared at the cups and glasses on the table. '*Fourteen?*' he whispered in awe.

'Each one for a different bad flop, I reckon,' Mavranos said with a shrug. 'Like chopping up a starfish.' He lifted his coffee cup in both hands to take a sip. 'I kind of admire her restraint in having only fourteen, after twenty-seven years. If I had the option, I'd be splitting off all the time.' Softly he sang a line Cochran believed was from a Grateful Dead song: '"I need a *mir*acle *ev*-ery day."'

Cochran began carrying the cups and glasses into the kitchen, gripping three with the fingers of each hand; and when he came back from carrying the first six out of the dining room, Kootie was wordlessly picking up four more.

When they had brought the last of the cups and glasses out to the counter, the Torino hood audibly slammed down outside; and after Cochran had rinsed out two of the cups and filled them with fresh coffee and carried them back to the dining-room table for himself and Kootie, he heard Plumtree come battering in through the kitchen door and run more water in the sink. A moment later she shuffled into the dining room with a steaming McDonald's mug and slumped down into the chair beside Kootie. She was clearly Cody, and her T-shirt was correctly marked SUNDAY in crude black letters.

'You're awake,' she observed as she lit a Marlboro.

'Somehow,' agreed Cochran.

'The Torino's running again, a lot better than before. Let's get this thing done.' She squinted at Kootie. 'Your mom and dad up yet?'

'I think they are,' said Kootie nervously. 'I think they'll be out in a minute.'

'Sid,' said Cody, 'if this goes real wrong, leave the Torino parked somewhere it's sure to be towed, will you? And leave the registration on the front seat. Oh, and the Jenkins purse is in the trunk – first mail that to the Jenkins woman.'

'I – won't hurt you,' said Kootie.

'It's not you I'm scared of, kiddo – but thanks.'

Pete and Angelica Sullivan came in then, and Angelica sat down at the table while Pete went into the kitchen.

'This chair is no good,' said Plumtree, wiggling the arms of her dining-room chair. 'My snips-and-snails parent could bust it to kindling. Let's go out back and use one of the iron patio chairs.' She had one more sip of her coffee and then stood up.

'What,' said Angelica, wide-eyed, 'right now? Before breakfast?'

'Well I'm just not hungry, somehow,' said Plumtree. 'And the sooner we get my job done, the sooner you can have your old lady in the wooden shoes cook you up some fucking *gumbo* or something, right?'

'Sorry,' said Angelica.

'Shit,' said Plumtree. 'If her nose isn't bleeding too bad for her to cook, by then.'

Five minutes later Mavranos, Angelica, Pete, Kootie, and Cochran were sitting, uncomfortably like judges, on one side of the long picnic table under the patio roof between the kitchen and the backyard greenhouse, facing the chair in which Plumtree now sat confined by strips of duct tape wrapped tightly around her wrists and waist and ankles. The sky was low and gray behind the pepper trees that overhung the yard; and though the breeze was chilly, Cochran knew that wasn't why Plumtree was visibly shivering. Inside Mavranos's open denim jacket Cochran had seen the checkered wooden grip of the revolver tucked under the man's belt.

For a few moments Plumtree waited blankly, relaxed enough for her teeth to chatter; then she rolled her head back to stare up at the beams of the patio roof, and she whispered, 'Valorie, whatever you make at your job, you're overpaid.' She took a deep breath, and Cochran did too. 'Mom!' called Plumtree hoarsely.

Then she lowered her head to stare at the five people sitting across from her at the table, and her shoulder muscles flexed under her T-shirt. At last her gaze fixed on Cochran. 'Are we near the sea?' she asked him in the shriller voice of Plumtree's mother. 'Are you going to call her up now, and send her to India?'

'No,' Cochran said. 'We need to learn some things Omar Salvoy knows. We're going to call *him* up, and question him. You can see that he'll be restrained.'

'I can *see* a car,' protested Plumtree's mother, 'and I can *smell* the ocean! Are you too squeamish to kill her body? You said you loved her!'

At the same time Angelica was leaning forward from between Mavranos and Pete to say, quietly, 'Sid, this isn't even a ghost of her mother, this is just a, an "internalized perpetrator," why are you talking to it—'

'As far as Cody's concerned,' Cochran interrupted, 'it's her mom.' He looked back at Plumtree taped into the chair. 'Trust me,' he said, 'I won't let him have her.'

'We won't let him have her,' Mavranos agreed.

'Oh, Jesus,' said the mother's voice. She looked back to Cochran. 'I hope you're a lot smarter than you look, mister.' She sighed shakily. 'Go ahead, and God be with you.'

'Omar Salvoy,' said Cochran, and he felt Kootie tense beside him.

Plumtree's eyes hadn't left Cochran's face, but now it was an amused, crafty, almost reptilian gaze. Again the arms flexed, but the tape held, even though the muscles had bulked out more. 'Hell-lo, baby!' said the man's voice from Plumtree's mouth. Cochran's nerves were twanging with the impulse to run, but his muscles felt as loose as wet cement.

'Valorie,' said Cochran then, breathlessly.

One of Plumtree's pupils visibly tightened down to a pinprick. *Split-screen*, thought Cochran.

Like a pole-vaulter visually picking out each spot his feet would touch on the run to the bar, Cochran prepared his words; then, carefully, he spoke: 'What did we do wrong twelve days ago, when we tried to get Scott Crane restored to life?'

'Oh, eat me.' The childish taunt rode incongruously on the deep, vibrating voice.

'I will, if you don't tell us,' spoke up Kootie. 'I can.'

'Ay,' came, a new, flat voice from Plumtree's lips, speaking to Kootie, 'sharp and piercing, to maintain his truth; whiles thy consuming canker eats his falsehood.' The face contorted and gasped for breath, and the man's voice added, 'Dammit, that's *Henry the Sixth, Part One*! Valorie, you traitorous bitch! Who do you think you got all your lines from, anyway? Do you remember *Love's Labour's Lost*? "We to ourselves prove false, by being once false for ever to be true to those that make us both – fair ladies, you."'

'Valorie is on our side,' said Kootie, 'and she'll know it if you lie.'

Plumtree's gaze fixed on Kootie, and her teeth were bared.

Kootie's shoulder jumped against Cochran's arm, and then the boy leaned tensely forward—

—The air was suddenly colder, and Cochran thought the pepper trees shook in no breeze—

And in the same instant Plumtree's head was rocked back as if from a physical blow. 'Easy, kid!' gasped the man's voice. 'Unless you want all the fair ladies dead!'

'I bet you can tell I pulled that punch,' said Kootie. His voice was calm and level, though Cochran could feel the boy shivering, 'I *have* used it full strength, before today. And I don't believe that punching you dead out of that head would hurt any of the Plumtree ladies.'

'You haven't yet seen *any* of *my* strength, boy.' Salvoy's voice seemed to vibrate in Cochran's ribs. 'That was a love-pat a moment ago. I *killed* your king, and I did *not* flinch when I did it. But I don't want you to be hurt.' The teeth were still bared, and now the lips curled in a smile. 'I'm prob'ly the only one here who doesn't want you to kill yourself.'

Angelica started to say something, but a rumbling, liquid growl from Plumtree's throat stilled her.

'You're the one with the wound in your side, boy,' the man's voice went on, loudly and almost anguished, 'it's always been you that would have to drink the real *pagadebiti*, even supposing you assholes could ever find a bottle of the stuff. It's *you*, Baby Gawain, that would have to be possessed by the actual god, abandon yourself to his ... bestial mercies. You sure you're up for that, Gumby Gunslinger?'

Cochran heard elbows shift on the wooden table somewhere to his right, and guessed it was Angelica.

Plumtree's gaze swung toward Angelica, and the flat Valorie voice said, 'Pardon me, madam: little joy have I to breathe this news; yet what I say is true.'

'Were we at the right *place*, at least?' asked Mavranos insistently. 'Out at those ruins by the yacht club? Mammy Pleasant was talking about a spot out on that shore.'

'You were in the right place,' said Omar Salvoy, 'but you didn't have the right wine, and I'm glad to say I don't even know where you would get—' Abruptly Plumtree choked; and then Valorie's voice said, 'Upon my soul a lie, a wicked lie. Touching this dreadful sight twice seen of us – you may approve our eyes, and speak to it. Looks it not like the king? Thou art a scholar; speak to it.' And immediately Salvoy's voice shook breathlessly out of the mouth: 'Valorie, when I have you alone under me—'

'At those other ruins, she means,' said Kootie, 'the ruins of the baths, by that restaurant. That's where we saw Crane's ghost. And it was the second time Plumtree had seen it.'

The Plumtree body leaned back in the chair and took a deep breath. 'You all were so embarrassed by that, I bet,' said Salvoy, grinning. 'Your exalted king, probably babbling nonsense and dressed like a bum, right? Or naked, looking like a crazy man. Brought down in the world, and how. Dizzgusting! And you sensible folks probably just ran away from him. Think how pleased he must have been with his *friends*.'

'I,' stammered Mavranos, 'ran after him—!'

'The palindrome should have been a clue,' Pete Sullivan interrupted, making a chopping gesture at Mavranos. 'The Valorie personality gave Cochran one line of that, at the ruins, and we knew that palindromes were good for nothing but drawing ghosts.'

'Palindrome?' said Salvoy. 'What palindrome?'

'Sit on a potato pan, Otis,' Kootie told him.

'And that foghorn was a clue,' said Mavranos. 'I bet the foghorn we heard in that motel room at dawn was the one you'd hear out at the Sutro Baths ruins. Shit, I even *noticed* it.'

Plumtree's face was red and twitching, but in a mockingly conversational tone Salvoy asked, 'Is one of you ready to *die*? That's part of it, you know. To get a life back, the god wants one in exchange. Even to repay an old debt-of-honor,' he said, with a scorching glance at Cochran, 'he can't violate his own math. And blood – fresh blood has got to be spilled. Splintered bone, torn flesh, before he'll consider it consummated. Ask apple-o'-my-eye Valorie if you think I'm lying about this.' Plumtree's head rocked back, and the Valorie voice said, 'That this is true, father, behold his blood. 'Tis very true.' Her head came down and Salvoy's furious gaze swept across them. 'And what *body* is your king going to take, now? Some bum's? That's another death, in addition to the god's bargain!' He gave a harshly jovial laugh, and then Plumtree's eyes squeezed shut. 'I'm fading out, thank Ra. Think about what I've said Koot Hoomie – and any of the rest of you that care—'

Plumtree's chin fell forward onto her chest, and for a moment she just panted. Then she looked up, in blank puzzlement; but when her eyes darted to Cochran she looked away again quickly. 'Oh, it's Scant,' she said. 'I can't stay here.' She flexed her arms and legs and then said again, in a voice shrilling with panic, 'I can't stay here! Arky, what's going on?' She smacked her lips. 'Was my *father* just here?'

'Can I talk to Cody?' said Cochran, standing up from the table. He was aware now that his shirt was clinging to his back with sweat.

'Nobody can talk to anybody, please,' said Plumtree quickly. Her hands were fists. 'Arky, get me *out of this*!'

Mavranos had stood up too, and was opening his lock-back pocket-knife one-handed as he strode around the table to the chair. 'Relax, Janis,' he was saying gruffly, 'you're gonna hurt yourself. Here.' He crouched in front of her iron chair to swipe the knife blade through the duct tape on her wrists and ankles, then got up and went around to the back of the chair to cut the strips that bound her waist. 'Sorry about this imposition,' he said to her as he helped her struggle to her feet. '*Inquisition*, even. We can explain it whenever you want to hear about it.'

'I just want to get inside,' she muttered quickly, 'away from him.'

Cochran wondered which *him* she meant as he watched her shakily peel cut flaps of duct tape from her wrists. She was limping past him toward the kitchen door, with one hand on Mavranos's shoulder and she looked at her wristwatch and then raised her elbow and tilted her head to hold the watch to her ear.

But of course it was a black Casio quartz watch, with a liquid-crystal display. Her gesture reminded Cochran of old black-and-white Timex ads on

TV, and in his head he heard the old shampoo-ad song: *You can always tell a* Halo *girl* ...

When, Cochran wondered, did I last see anybody with a watch that *ticked*?

Oh, Jesus, she's still *split-screen*!

But her mismatched eyes had been watching him, and caught his instant comprehension, and as he opened his mouth now she was snatching the revolver from Mavranos's belt and lunging, smashing the barrel and butt of the gun like brass knuckles into Cochran's belly.

Then Plumtree had danced back away as Cochran folded and sat down jarringly hard on the concrete, and she slapped both hands to her face, her left palm covering her eyes and her right hand pointing the gun up at the patio roof.

And she pulled the trigger. The *bang* was a ringing impact in Cochran's ears, and Plumtree's head smacked the stucco wall at her back.

But an instant later the gun barrel was horizontal, the muzzle pointed at Mavranos's chest. Mavranos stepped back, his hands open and out to the sides.

'Mom,' Cochran choked, not able to get air into his lungs. 'Janis's ... mom.' Fragments of wood and tar paper spun down from the new hole in the roof.

Angelica understood what he was doing, and called 'Janis's mom! Mother!' – before visibly wilting with the realization that Plumtree was deaf now.

As Mavranos shuffled backward across the patio deck, the gun muzzle swung toward Angelica. To Cochran's tear-filled eyes it seemed to leave a rippling wake in the air. 'Koot Hoomie,' said Salvoy, much too loudly, 'pick up the roll of duct tape and come here – or I put a big hole in your mom. Scant-boy – reach slow into your pants pocket and throw me the car keys.' Plumtree wasn't looking at Kootie directly.

Cochran thought he could feel ruptured organs inside himself ripping further open as he dragged his legs up under his torso and crawled across the concrete to Plumtree; he even had to reach out and brace himself with one hand on Plumtree's blue-jeaned thigh as he hitchingly got up onto his knees. His lungs were chugging in his rib cage, but he still wasn't able to draw any breath down his throat, and his vision had narrowed to a tunnel.

Plumtree had her back against the house wall, so she couldn't retreat; Cochran was looking up at her, and his dizzy focus shifted effort fully outward from the ring of the .38-caliber muzzle to her eyes. Both of her eyes were wide and staring at him, the tiny-pupiled one and the dilated one, and at the bottom of his vision he could still blurrily see down the rifled barrel of the gun.

'Troilus, farewell!' hissed Valorie as Plumtree's body shook with internal conflict against the stucco wall. The finger lifted out of the trigger-guard ring. 'One eye yet looks on thee, but with my heart the other eye doth see.' Then the Salvoy voice grated, 'No,' and the finger wobbled back down onto the trigger, and whitened.

Abruptly a youthful brown right hand sprang into Cochran's narrow field of vision and closed over the muzzle, and from above him Kootie's voice said, 'You want this to be your right hand one day, don't you? Will you shoot it off?'

Plumtree couldn't have heard what the boy had said, but her eyes lifted. And Kootie's gaze must have caught hers, for she suddenly convulsed sideways across the wall onto the projecting hose faucet as Kootie crouched along with her and violently twisted the gun in her hand.

Cochran threw himself onto her back as she rolled off the faucet and thudded heavily to the concrete, and he too was grabbing for the gun – and when he saw the hammer jump back he got his thumb in under it as it came down.

At last Kootie yanked it away, tearing a gash in the base of Cochran's thumb. Cochran was breathing at last, in abrading gasps.

With a solid boom Mavranos rebounded off the wall then and fell to his knees on Plumtree's right arm, and the roll of duct tape shrilled as he tore a long strip free and wrapped it around her wrist; then he had grabbed her other arm and wrapped tape around that wrist too.

Her back was rising and falling as she panted, and after a moment she rolled her head so that she could squint up sideways at Cochran. 'How'd it,' she gasped with a bloody rictus of a smile, 'go?'

Her nose was bleeding, though Cochran couldn't guess whether it was from the physical stresses of Salvoy's visitation or from having collided with the concrete deck. '*Can you hear me?*' he managed to croak loudly.

Cochran's heart ached to see how wrinkled her eyelids were as she closed her eyes.

'Yes, Sid, oh, shut up!' She was gasping for breath and her bloody upper lip was twitching away from her teeth. 'God, Sid, I hurt! Did I fall off the roof? What the fuck *happened*?'

'Cut her loose, Arky,' choked Cochran, in horror, as he braced his hands on the concrete deck and carefully climbed off her legs.

'She may still be split-screen,' came Angelica's voice from behind him.

'Not – Cody.' Cochran reached out his jigging, bleeding hand and gently touched Plumtree's shoulder. 'We can – trust Cody.'

And in fact Mavranos was already knifing the tape off of her wrists.

CHAPTER TWENTY SEVEN

Her bed is India; there she lies, a pearl.
Between our Ilium and where she resides
Let it be called the wild and wand'ring flood,
Ourself the merchant, and this sailing Pandar
Our doubtful hope, our convoy, and our bark.
                    —William Shakespeare, *Troilus and Cressida*

Angelica wanted to look at Plumtree's bashed ribs and possibly sprained hand, but when Cochran and Mavranos had helped Plumtree to her feet and walked her into the house, she shook them off.

'Leave me be,' she said irritably, leaning over the kitchen sink while blood dripped from her nose. 'It's just a spell of the spasmodics.' She grabbed a dishtowel and pressed it to her face. 'Get Teresa to fetch me a cup of Balm Tea,' she said through the rowel, 'with some gin in it.' Then she blinked around at the low-ceilinged white kitchen she was standing in, with its blocky white refrigerator and the gleaming black box of the microwave oven. 'I mean, a glass of Z-Zinfandel,' she amended querulously. 'And my bark-soled penance shoes.'

'No,' said Cochran sharply, 'not yet. Sit down, Mrs. Pleasant. Have some coffee. Arky, get her a cup of coffee. Listen, we've learned some things about Crane's resurrection.'

He felt goose bumps tickle against the sleeves of his shirt then, for when the woman looked at him, her forehead and high cheekbones seemed for a moment to be patrician with age, and momentarily her blond hair appeared white in the shine of the overhead fluorescent lights; then it was Plumtree's face, with both eyes the same shade of blue, though the eyelids were still full and vaguely Asian. She sat down in one of the kitchen chairs stiffly, dabbing at her nose with the bloody towel. Her nose wasn't bleeding anymore, and the Mammy Pleasant personality didn't appear to feel any pains in her ribs.

Raindrops began tapping against the window over the sink.

'I tried to tell you people everything,' said Mammy Pleasants cautious voice, 'right from the first, well in time for you to have done it correctly on St. Sulpice's Day. I was supposed to be your intercessor – I told you then that I would have to indwell one of you, but you thought I just wanted a body to take the fresh air in.'

'We're listening now,' said Angelica. 'And you've got the body now.'

'I'll tell you nothing, now,' said Pleasant's voice. 'Your Chinaman holiday isn't until the day after tomorrow. Ask me about it then, respectfully, and I might tell you what to do, and I might not. At any rate I can have wine for one more day, and my shoes'

Kootie had started toward the hall, but Cochran said, 'Don't get the shoes, Kootie. They apparently work as a damper to keep her personality from being conspicuous from being a beacon to this house – maybe she seems to be a *tree*, to psychic radar when she's wearing 'em – but I think they're also a damper on her intelligence. I think they're like dope.'

'Now I will *assuredly* tell you nothing.'

'But you've said that the god's purpose is your purpose too,' said Angelica in a tone of sympathetic concern. She knelt, beside Plumtree. 'And that the god's purpose is to bring Crane back, as king. We need to know what to do.' Cochran guessed that Angelica was already resolved to ditch this whole enterprise, and every person that resided in the Plumtree head, and simply wanted to find out as much as possible before fleeing; but he had to admit that she projected sincerity. Doctors are trained to do that, he thought.

'The god's *purpose*,' said Pleasant, stubbornly shaking Plumtree's tangled blond hair. 'You're to take two old women to the sea, and throw them in, because the god's *purpose* doesn't include poor frightened old ghosts trying to sleep in some frail shelter out of the rain.' She turned to Angelica, blinking rapidly. 'What if we *did* fight him? Who *won*?'

Two old women? thought Cochran. She mentioned another old woman right at the first, on the Solville TV – Angelica said it sounded like a sewing circle. Who's the other one? Plumtree's phantom mother?

'Could I have insisted?' the old woman went on. Plumtree's eyes were blinking rapidly. 'I tried to insist! Through your, your "boob tube"! You *could* have accomplished it then, on St. Sulpice's Day, if you had listened to me.'

'And if I hadn't run away,' said Kootie

'We were well down the wrong track already, by that morning,' Mavranos told the boy gruffly. 'Going to the wrong shore, with the wrong wine ...' To Plumtree's sunburned face, he said, 'You could have told us more. We might not have listened, but ...'

'I needed to be in a body! I told you that much! How could I *think*, without a *brain*?' Plumtree's eyes were blinking rapidly.

Mavranos's nostrils were flared and the corners of his mouth were drawn down. 'You wanted a body to take the fresh air in,' he said flatly.

Rain was drumming now against the window over the sink, and Cochran could see the bobbing stems of Nina's window-box basil outside. The back door was open, and the cold draft smelled of wet clay.

'I wanted some time to *rest*,' Mammy Pleasant said in a near-whisper, perhaps agreeing with him. 'This little time, these little days sitting with the orchids in the greenhouse, and cooking for people again! I don't see how anybody can describe *total oblivion as rest* – you couldn't even call it losing yourself, because for losing to go on there has to be a loser, and there wouldn't be even that. Oh, believe me, the god's purpose has only been delayed.'

'And made ... costlier,' said Mavranos, very quietly. His brown hands were clenched in fists against his thighs.

'Let me tell you about Omar Salvoy's purpose,' Cochran said, leaning back against the refrigerator. 'According to Plumtree's mom, he wants to get into the right male body and become this Fisher King, and then get Plumtree pregnant – specifically, get *Valorie* pregnant. Valorie is evidently the core child inside Plumtree, and she's apparently dead. I'm sure Cody and Janis don't know that. Salvoy believes that if he can father a child by a dead woman – well, not a whole child; I gather it would be just a sort of deformed, unconnected head – that partial child will be a living, obligated piece of Dionysus.'

'Jesus!' exclaimed Angelica, looking away from Plumtree to gape up at him.

Kootie was hugging himself, grasping his elbows; and Cochran thought that this revelation had somehow stirred the boy's memories of whatever devastating thing it was that he had done twelve days ago, after he had run away from the motel on Lombard Street before dawn.

For several seconds no one spoke.

Plumtree's head was bowed. 'Yes,' Mammy Pleasant whispered finally, 'if he was the king, he could force that. If he had the body with the wounded side, and if he made a mother of Death, he could stand *in loco parentis* to the god. Other kings have sometimes achieved degrees of domination over the god, in other ways.'

'Loco parentis is right,' said Mavranos hollowly.

Plumtree's head snapped back, throwing her blond locks back from her forehead. 'The god, in that form,' she said, 'and that king, would have uses for a couple of old ghost ladies.' Her face was impassive, but tears spilled down her cheeks. 'Thank you, Scant Cochran, for making me understand that the oblivion in the sea is one of the god's mercies. I do thank him for the offered gift of ceasing to exist. And I'm grateful, too, that it must be the last of his gifts to me.'

Cochran opened his mouth to speak, but Mammy Pleasant rapped Plumtree's knuckles on the kitchen table. 'I will speak, now, and you all will listen,' she said. 'When your king's castrated father was king, he ruled in Las Vegas. And your king ruled and may rule again in the place that rhymes with Arcadia. But there was a king who cultivated the miraculous Zinfandel vine in San Diego until 1852, and who then castled to Sonoma, north of San Francisco, where he grew the vines in the Valley of the Moon, between Sonoma Mountain and Bismark Knob. The god originally intended me to be queen to this king, but I had irretrievably rebelled against the god a dozen years earlier.'

'This was ... Harass-thee,' said Kootie.

'Haraszthy,' said Plumtree, subtly correcting the boy's pronunciation. 'Agoston Haraszthy, who took the title of "Count" for the grandeur in it. In 1855 he was made assayer and melter and refiner of gold at the United States Mint at Mission Street south of Market; and the furnaces burned all day and all night, and after he quit, the roofs of the surrounding houses were all deeply stained with misted gold.' The reminiscent smile on Plumtree's face somehow implied lines and creases that weren't actually there. 'That was a kingly thing, if you like! But, like most of the men who attain the throne, he refused to submit to real death in the winter. And so in the thirteenth year of his reign, 1861, the worst winter floods in the history of California devastated Haraszthy's precious grapevines; and in 1863, the surviving vines withered in the worst drought in twenty-five years. I was happy to help in undermining this king's power, and in 1868 I bought the Washington Street property that had housed the original greenhouse-shrine devoted to the Zinfandel in California, and I tore out the sacred old vines and converted the place to a boardinghouse.'

She stared curiously around at the kitchen, as if to fix the details of it in her memory. 'After that sacrilege,' she went on, 'Haraszthy was getting no spiritual power from the god at all, no psychic subsidy, and so he just abandoned his ordained throne and the American West altogether, and he fled south all the way to Nicaragua – to distill *rum*, from unsanctified *sugarcanes!*' She laughed gently and shook her head. 'He was hiding from Dionysus, who was without a king now, and therefore not as close to human affairs. I decided to put them both out of my picture – and so on the night of June 24th of the next year, on St. John's Eve, I celebrated the very first voodoo ceremony to be held in the American West, and in the woods out along the San Jose Road my people danced and drummed and drank rum and worshipped Damballa the Great Serpent, and I conveyed my prayers to him. And twelve days later, down in Nicaragua, the Dionysus who was no longer very human found his faithless king – Haraszthy was eaten by an alligator, which was Sebek-Re, a very crude, early Egyptian personification of the fertility-and-death god.'

Cochran looked away from the ophidian eyes and the somehow distinctly Egyptian-seeming smile, and saw that his companions too were avoiding looking into Plumtree's face. He thought of the broken skeleton out in the greenhouse in the rain, and he wished someone would close the back door.

'I did not know, at first,' Mammy Pleasant's voice went on carefully, 'that the kinghood had rebounded like a snapped rope when Haraszthy fled this continent in 1868. Dionysus,' she said, with a look that Cochran could feel on the skin of his face, 'places great stock in names, in clues and similarities in names; and a weapons manufacturer back East who was known as "the rifle king," and who, among other fortuitous resemblances, had the middle name "Fisher," became the unintended and unknowing and unsanctified focus of the kinghood. A ... measurable westward deflection! ... of my magics, made me aware of the obstruction of him, and in 1880 I held another voodoo ceremony – this time in the basement of my grand house on Octavia Street. Again my people drummed and danced to the Great Serpent, and in the December of that year this poor misplaced king-apparent died. He had a middle-aged son, and in the following March the son died too, of consumption, leaving behind a childless forty-one-year-old widow. They had had one child, a daughter, who had perished of the marasmus back in '66 at the age of a month-and-a-half.'

'Is she the ... other old-woman ghost?' asked Cochran.

Plumtree's head nodded. 'And she's a rebel, like me, now. She wasn't always – right after her husband died, she consulted a spiritualist, who told her that she was obligated to the god for the attentions he had so generously paid to her family, and that in return she must use her inherited fortune to build an infinite chapel: a gateway for straying ghosts to leave this world through, and go on to the next. And she did, only a couple of years after her precious husband had died. She set about building an enormous house designed to attract ghosts, and then not let them get out; construction of it never stopped for nigh forty years, there was hammering and sawing day and night, and new doors and halls every day – doors and stairways that led nowhere, windows in the floors, faucets way up where no one could reach – and about the only way the ghosts could get out was to be unmade and sent off to the god through one of the fireplaces. She had forty-seven fireplaces there, before she died.'

'I thought hammering repelled ghosts,' said Cochran.

'No,' snapped Angelica, 'banging, hammering sounds, the racket disorients 'em. It jolts them out of the groove, resets their controls back to zero – cashes out bets they'd have wanted to let ride.' She looked at Pete. 'Of course we know what this crazy house is.'

'And who the old lady was,' Pete Sullivan agreed. 'It's the Winchester House, a few miles down the 280 from here.'

'Winchester,' said Pleasant's voice out of Plumtree's mouth. 'Yes. And like me she was chosen to be a caretaker and communicant of the god's *paga-debiti* wine – the consecrated Zinfandel. But one night in 1899, even while I was being evicted from my own overthrown house and taken into custody by the idiot god-fragment known as Bacus, Winchester found a black hand-print on the wall of her chapel, in the wine cellar, and she knew that she was being called upon to give over to the god her own husband's ghost … and she couldn't bring herself to obey *that*, to forget *him*. And, even while know-ing that she'd be punished, she rebelled: she *walled up the wine cellar*. When the god came to take charge of my wandering ghost three days after Easter in 1906, he struck her too, *en passant*, with the earthquake of his arrival – the top floors of her house fell onto her bedroom, and she was trapped in there for hours. But she didn't repent her rebellion – after her servants freed her, she boarded up that whole wing of the house, and spent six months living on water, aboard a houseboat called *The Ark*, in the south bay here by the Dumbarton Bridge.'

'And the scrap lumber,' said Pete, 'from the collapsed upper floors, was used to build a maternity hospital in Long Beach in the 1920s; probably be-cause of the ghost-confusion influences in it.' He looked at Cochran. 'That hospital eventually became our apartment building – Solville.'

'When Winchester returned to her house,' Pleasant went on, 'she was masking herself against the god as well as the ghosts now. And when she eventually died she left instructions that her ghost was to be caught, and hidden. And so it was, and now the god wants you to bring her, and me, to him. You'll need to find a guide.'

Mavranos was rubbing his forehead.

'Omar Salvoy says that someone will have to die, probably more than one person, for our king to come back to life,' said Cochran. 'He says there will have to be bloodshed.'

'Of course,' said Pleasant.

Angelica straightened up beside Pleasant's chair. 'And he says that Kootie, the boy here, has to be possessed by Dionysus.'

'Everybody does, eventually,' said Pleasant calmly.

'Well, that's simply *out*, I'm afraid,' said Angelica, shaking her head. 'I don't know what's *going* to happen, but that's the thing that's *not* going to happen. We've got nearly two clear days to run away.'

Plumtree's shoulders bobbed with tired laughter. 'Don't try Nicaragua,' said Pleasant's voice.

'No, Mom,' said Kootie. 'What, should I save myself for Omar Salvoy?' He was speaking softly, not looking at any of the others in the kitchen, 'if the god is offering me his debt-payer wine, I'm very damn ready to take a drink.' He went on even more quietly, 'And I do owe a beheading. He might not *take* it, but I *owe* it.'

'We'll see about that,' said Angelica, bur her voice was too loud, and Cochran thought she looked lost and scared.

'How do we get a guide?' asked Mavranos.

Angelica threw him a surprised, hurt look. 'Arky, Kootie is not—'

'On the resurrection day,' said Pleasant, 'you are to give a ride to a hitch-hiker. In your motor-car. I have now told you this. And this woman,' she said, touching Plumtree's forehead, 'is to carry with her, at all times, that gold cigarette lighter. I have now told you this.' She nodded virtuously.

And of course you'd have told us two weeks ago, thought Cochran angrily, if we'd simply asked: *Should we be picking up hitch-hikers? Should Plumtree hang on to that Dunhill lighter?*

'Go ahead and get her goddamn shoes, Kootie,' he said. He crossed to the back door and pushed it closed, not looking out through the broken glass; he was afraid he might see the naked figure of Scott Crane's ghost out there, sitting in the wet grass and possibly even mournfully looking this way.

Cody came back on just as the sun was redly silhouetting the northernmost peaks of the Montara Mountains. Cochran was in the driveway, walking around the shrouded Suburban with a tire-pressure gauge, when through the open living-room window he heard a cry and a thudding fall.

He let the gauge clatter to the driveway pavement and just sprinted across the grass to the window, punched in the screen, and pulled the curtains up.

Plumtree was lying on her side on the carpet, huffing furiously and struggling up to a sitting position, trying to get traction with the crumbly eucalyptus-bark soles of Pleasant's penance shoes. Mavranos and Pete scuffed and bumped to a halt in the hall doorway a moment after Cochran leaned in the window.

'This is like the – end of the – fucking *Wizard of Oz*,' Cody panted, blinking away tears. 'Everybody leaning in to see if the – little girl is okay. After her knock on the head.' She was sitting up on the floor now, hugging her side and breathing deeply. 'She was – dancing! I came on in the middle of some – kind of goddamn pirouette, off balance. Don't help me up!' she said in a wheezing voice to Mavranos, who had hurried across the room to her. 'My ribs are like broken spaghetti in a cellophane bag. I'll get up on my own. In a minute.' She looked up at Cochran. 'She was dancing around in here, all by herself! *How* old is she?'

'Hundred and something,' said Mavranos.

'And now I bet I've got a broken hip, too,' Plumtree said, 'from falling on whatever she put in my pocket.' Bracing herself on an old overstuffed easy chair, she fought her way to her feet, then reached into the hip pocket of her jeans.

'Look at that,' she said, holding out the gold Dunhill lighter. 'The old dame was stealing the lighter!'

Cochran swung one leg over the windowsill and climbed into the room, thrashing out from under the curtain like, he thought sourly, a rabbit from under a magician's handkerchief.

'No she wasn't, Cody,' he said. 'That's *supposed* to be in your pocket.'

'We discover,' added Mavranos.

'Have Angelica earn her keep,' said Plumtree, 'and tape up my ribs or something. And for God's sake get me something to drink.'

Cochran started toward the hall. 'You want your mouthwash?' 'No,' she said, 'ghosts don't seem to have spit. I want vodka.' She squinted belligerently from Pete and Mavranos and Cochran to the window beyond the flapping curtain. 'The day's over, it looks like. Is it possible for you to tell me what's been going on?'

'We can try,' said Cochran. He took her arm, and she let him lead her down the hall toward the dining room. 'Have something to eat, with your vodka,' he said gently. 'The old lady made a fine-looking shrimp remoulade this afternoon, and I was going to make some sandwiches.' He was nodding solemnly. 'I think if we all take our time, and don't interrupt each other, we can actually explain what's gone on today.'

'Well don't goddamn strain yourselves,' she said, leaning on Cochran.

'Oh, well,' he said, his voice suddenly quivering with an imminent, mirthless giggle, 'I don't know that we can do it without straining ourselves.'

'It really calls for mood music,' said Pete from behind them. His voice too was tense with repressed hysteria. 'Wagner, I think, or Spike Jones.'

Mavranos gave a harsh bark of laughter. 'And I better make some hand-puppets,' he said.

Even Plumtree was snorting with nervous merriment as they came lurching and cackling into the living room, drawing puzzled stares from Angelica and Kootie.

Cochran made ham and pepper-jack cheese sandwiches, and Plumtree switched from vodka to beer when they ate, then went back to vodka after the dinner dishes were cleared away; and the occasional pauses in the tense and unhappy conversation were punctuated by horns and sirens wailing past on the highway at the bottom of the sloping backyard, the 280.

And seven miles to the northeast, in the Li Po bar in Chinatown, Richard Paul Armentrout sat at a table under the high, slowly rotating fans and nervously rolled the rattling pomegranate shell around the ashtray and the club-soda glasses. The two Lever Blank men had frisked him in the downstairs men's room, but after a quick, whispered conference between themselves they had decided to let him keep the pomegranate. Lucky for them that they did, Armentrout thought defiantly. I wouldn't be talking to them if they'd taken it, and on their own they would never figure out how to find the king with it.

Now they were sitting on the other side of the table from Long John Beach and himself. Armentrout was sure they had guns concealed under their tailored Armani suit coats somewhere. Plumtree had told him about the commune she had grown up in, and he was finding it difficult even to believe that these two gray-haired businessmen had been leaders of a Bay Area hippie cult in the sixties, much less that they were still somehow involved in it.

'We tried,' said the balding one who had introduced himself as Louis, 'to stop the resurrection out at the St. Francis Yacht. Club on the seventeenth of this month; some field men of ours did interfere, and in fact the attempted resurrection did fail. We would have acted more decisively if Mr. Salvoy had approached us sooner, and if there had not been unavoidable delays in establishing that the ... apparent young woman was Mr. Salvoy; that required summoning entities we don't usually hold congress with, and procedures, out in the remote hills around Mount Diablo, that the ASPCA wouldn't approve of.'

The other man, Andre, leaned forward. 'Had to kill some goats,' he said. 'Needed their heads, for the entities to speak through.'

'Let me tell you a parable,' said Long John Beach.

'Not now, John,' said Armentrout in embarrassment.

Armentrout knew that these two men wanted to intimidate him; and he was intimidated, but not by what *they* were saying. He forced himself not to focus on the television screen above and behind the men, and he tried not to listen to the two voices buzzing out of the television speaker.

'I gather,' said Louis, 'that you don't precisely *represent* Mr. Salvoy. You and he are not partners.'

'No,' agreed Armentrout. 'Our interests have overlapped, but my main goal right now is to get a drink of the—'

Andre coughed and held up his hand. 'No need to say it, we know you're not talking Thunderbird.'

On the television screen above the bar, Armentrout's mother said, 'I bet I swallowed gallons of that bath water.' She and Philip Muir were sitting in vinyl-looking padded chairs in front of a blue backdrop with big red letters on it that spelled out AFTERHOURS. She was wearing the same housedress she had been wearing when seventeen-year-old Armentrout had held her under the bath water in 1963, and the dress was still soaked, dripping on the studio floor; but she was opaque and casting a shadow, and when she spoke her teeth glinted solidly between the twisting red-painted lips. Muir, never a heavy drinker and only recently dead, was still a bit translucent, and his eyes were still very protuberant and his forehead visibly blackened in pseudosomatic response to the gunshot that had killed him. 'Thanks for sharing,' he croaked. Armentrout remembered greeting cards that audibly produced the syllables of *happy birthday or merry Christmas* when a thumbnail was dragged down an attached strip of textured plastic; Muir's voice reminded him of them. 'I can hold my breath for hours now,' Muir went on. 'In fact, I can't breathe.' Armentrout's dripping mother reached across the low table that separated the chairs and imploded Muir's shoulder with a sympathetic pat. 'Why would you want to breathe when everything smells so bad?' she said.

'Mr. Salvoy did good work for us,' said Louis, 'a long time ago – though he was unsuccessful in becoming the king, in 1969, and had to be retired.' Andre winked at Armentrout.

'We would be happy to take Mr. Salvoy on again,' Louis said, 'in this new *persona*, on the basis of his achieving the kinghood this time, and his being willing to comply with the harsher requirements of the office.' He took a sip from his glass of club soda. 'But when he spoke to us on the sixteenth he didn't tell us *quite all* about the Koot Hoomie boy. He simply indicated that there was a healthy young body he was ready to assume. If we had known that the boy was virtually the king already, we would not have risked harming him; a plain bullet wouldn't have been able to hurt the true king, but the truck could have rolled into the sea, and the king could drown in sea water. But as it happens the boy wasn't present, at that attempt at the yachts club. Our only urgency then was preventing the undesirable Scott Crane kinghood from being renewed.'

Andre spread his hands. 'We'll be happy with either one of them, Salvoy or Koot Hoomie, in the boy's body. We just want a king, an emissary to the god."

'A cooperative king,' added Louis. 'The boy alone might actually be easier to work with. He'd probably be more malleable.'

'Well,' said Armentrout, carefully not looking at the pomegranate and trying to project easy confidence, 'I've got a sort of *psychic dowsing rod* that's leading me to the boy, and Salvoy is committed to keeping me apprised of his own whereabouts by telephone. I can lead you to both of them.'

'A rabbi in a synagogue,' said Long John Beach, 'told his congregation, "I am ... *nothing!*" And after the service, a prosperous businessman from the congregation shook the rabbi's hand and said, with feeling, nodding and agreeing with the rabbi, "I am ... *nothing!*"'

'I'll tell you frankly,' Louis said to Armentrout, 'we haven't been able yet to ferment the real sacramental ... beverage you want, though we've preserved and cultivated the very oldest strain of *vitis sylvestris* vine, untouched by the phylloxera louse plague, and we do press a vintage from it every autumn; waiting for the year when the god will see fit to answer our prayers.'

Armentrout didn't follow all this – he only knew that if he should not be able to kill Koot Hoomie, his sole hope for immunity from the two ghosts who were now on the television screen would be to take a drink of the fabulous *pagadebiti* wine: disown the ghosts, let Dionysus have all of Armentrout's memories of them. But he hoped it wouldn't come to that, for the god might take all of the ghosts, and pieces of ghosts, that he had consumed over the course of his psychiatric career; and Armentrout wasn't sure he could mentally or even physically survive that loss. But it's just a backup, last-ditch measure, Armentrout told himself reassuringly; I'll almost certainly find an opportunity to kill the boy.

'And the custodian came up,' went on Long John Beach, 'and he said, real earnestly, "I am ... *nothing*!" And the businessman jerked his thumb at this guy and said to the rabbi, "Look who thinks he's nothing!"'

Armentrout was looking intently into Louis's eyes, but from the television he heard imbecilic laughter.

'But bottles of it do survive,' said Louis, a little impatiently. 'We still have several that were bottled on the Leon estates in the Bas Medoc in the early eighteenth century. And when the Scott Crane contingent tries to do their resurrection ritual again on Tet, they may very well have got hold of a bottle themselves. Bottles of it are around, especially in the Bay Area. We can make sure that you are given a drink of the god's forgiving blood, one way or the other.'

Andre said cheerfully, 'I imagine we'll have our people retire the whole party, except for the Koot Hoomie boy and, at least for a while, the Plumtree woman.'

'Certainly the one called Archimedes Mavranos,' agreed Louis. 'His commitment to restoring Scott Crane appears to be so strong that he would try to impede the coronation of anyone else.'

Armentrout had to force himself to comprehend that these men were talking about *killing* Cochran, Plumtree, and the Sullivan couple and Mavranos. Not therapeutically, nor as a regrettable necessity for personal sustenance, as he himself had sometimes had to do, but just because these people were inconvenient, in the way; and for a moment he was profoundly sickened at his alliance with them.

How, he wondered forlornly, and when, did I become indistinguishable from the bad guys?

When Louis and Andre had introduced themselves, they had told Armentrout that they were in the children's products business these days, and owned a controlling interest in the White Greyhound brand of toys. Armentrout had remembered the White Greyhound Solar Heroes action figures and the Saturn's Rings carnival set; and he had been unhappy to learn, in conversation this evening, that the toys had been designed to initiate children at least a little way into the Dionysian mysteries. Armentrout had learned that the toy figures in the carnival set had been designed to subliminally embody the Major Arcana figures from the tarot deck: with The Magician as the ticket seller, The Lovers on the Ferris Wheel of Fortune, Death as the janitor, and so forth; the White Greyhound people had carefully not included anything to represent The Fool, but they had had to stop production of the set anyway, because by 1975 children all over the country were spontaneously adding a Clown of their own, and suffering bad dreams at night and even banding together during the day to elude the hideously smiling painted figure of random madness that their consensual credulity had nearly brought into real, potent existence.

Louis and Andre had told him with satisfaction that their original five-year-old consumers were now in their late twenties, and as a segment of American society were beginning to show valuable symptoms.

These men are monsters, Armentrout thought. They've trekked much farther out into the dark than I ever have, and abandoned items from the original spiritual kit that I could not ever abandon.

And he might have spoken – but now Louis and Andre had hiked their chairs around and were staring at the television over the bar.

On the screen, Muir and Armentrout's mother had got to their feet and were doing an awkward dance around the studio floor; his dripping mother was making swimming motions, and Muir had pulled up his diaphanous pants cuffs and was walking on his heels. They were both staring right into the hypothetical camera, right out at Armentrout – he avoided looking squarely into their phosphor-dot eyes, even though he doubted that they could get a handle on his soul through the television screen – and they were chanting in unison, '*Why so stout, Richie Armentrout? Let 'em all out, Richie Armentrout!*'

Louis's face was pale as he turned back to stare at Armentrout, and his voice was actually shaky: 'They're ... talking to *you*?'

'Leftovers from the old Dale Carnegie days,' Armentrout said hoarsely as he shoved his own chair back and stood up. 'We've got a deal – let's get out of here.'

Outside, the Grant Street pavement glittered with reflected neon, and rippled like sketchy animation with the constant rearrangement of the falling raindrops.

CHAPTER TWENTY EIGHT

Brethren and sisters of the hold-door trade,
Some two months hence my will shall here be made.
It should be now, but that my fear is this,
Some galled goose of Winchester should hiss.

—William Shakespeare, *Troilus and Cressida*

The rain kept up all night, and into the morning.

In spite of Mammy Pleasant's wish for as much on-time as she might still be able to have, she didn't appear at all throughout the gloomy morning, and Pete Sullivan wound up making lunch – tacos of fried ground beef and chopped ortega chilis, with the corn tortillas heated in the grease and a hot red salsa splashed liberally over it all. There had been only one Alka-Seltzer cup on the table this morning, and at lunch it was just Cody who sweated and scowled as she ate the restoratively spicy Mexican food and washed it down with a succession of cold beers. She was wearing one of Cochran's dress white shirts, with MONDAY freshly inked over the pocket.

After Kootie had cleared away the dishes and Angelica had taken the ads from the *San Francisco Chronicle* out to the living-room couch, Cochran stood at the back door and looked out across the wet yard at the Torino, which for all of Cody's work still shook as its engine was gunned.

Cody herself had shambled back to bed right after lunch, declaring that she needed to rest the cracked ribs and sprained hand that Angelica had diagnosed and taped up yesterday evening; it was Arky Mavranos who was out revving the car engine in the rain – pointlessly, for the Torino was blocked in by the Granada that was parked behind it.

'He's near used-up,' said Pete quietly, standing with a freshly opened can of beer beside Cochran and looking too out the window. 'I don't know what his part in this thing tomorrow is supposed to be, but it better not call for liveliness. He doesn't even drink beer anymore, and he doesn't eat, either, except for rice and beans and tortillas. That shrapnel-hit to his skull, or else that ghost that was on him ...' he said, shaking his head, 'broke him down.'

'At least the engine's in park now,' said Cochran. 'A few minutes ago when I ran out there he had it in drive. I told him there's a mud track that curls down the slope to the 280 at the back of the yard, but that he'd have to drive right through the greenhouse to get to it.' He tossed his cigarette out through the hole in the door window onto the patio. 'Now I think of it, I'm glad he didn't just *do* that.'

'No chance,' said Pete with a faint, sad smile. 'He wouldn't run over Scott Crane's skeleton. And he wouldn't have the heart to move the bones, either.' He finished his beer and visibly thought better of throwing it out the window after Cochran's cigarette.

'*Morituri emere*, or something,' he said, stepping into the kitchen. '"We who are about to die go shopping." Angie and I are going to take the Suburban truck out to fill the tank and check the oil in preparation for whatever it is that's going to befall tomorrow, on resurrection day – and Angie's made a list of *bruja* items to shield Kootie with, so we're going to stop at a grocery store. Oils, candles, chalk, batteries for the stuffed toy pigs. Anything you want? Beer's already on the list.'

'A Kevlar suit and hat,' said Cochran absently, still staring out at the unhappy man sitting alone in the roaring, smoking car. 'A squirt gun full of holy water. A home skitz-testing and lobotomy kit.'

He turned away from the broken door-window and walked into what he still thought of as Nina's kitchen, littered now with Coors twelve-pack cartons full of empty cans, the shelves crowded with Angelica's morbid herb bundles and saint-decal candles. 'No, if you've got beer on the list, I guess I—' He sagged; all at once the whole house was too depressing to bear. 'Oh hell, I don't appear to be going to work today, and I'll just get in a fight with Mammy Pleasant if I hang around here. I'll go with you.'

'Oh.' Pete picked up his denim jacket from the pile of damp clothes and scarves on the kitchen table. 'Okay. We've told Kootie to stay away from Plumtree, and it looks like she's down for the day anyway. Angie'll want to leave him her .45, but she'd do that even if you were staying.' He pulled on his jacket and then lifted down one of Angelica's stuffed pigs from on top of the refrigerator. 'Get you fitted for a battery,' he said to it.

Kootie stepped into the kitchen now from the front hall, and Cochran could smell wine on the boy's breath. 'Is Mammy Pleasant planning on making dinner?' Kootie asked. 'I'd rather order in a couple of big American pizzas, actually, than have another Creole thing.' He shrugged. 'I believe tomorrow I'm gonna be eating in India.'

Cochran and Pete stared at him, and Pete began to stammer a response, waving the stuffed pig.

'I hear they have a New Delhi,' Kootie added hastily.

Pete exhaled. 'Here comes your mother. Don't upset her unless it's necessary, okay?'

Angelica stepped into the hall, carrying her stainless-steel .45 automatic in one hand and tucking a shopping list into the hip pocket of her jeans with the other. 'Good deal on Coors at Albertson's,' she said. 'Are you coming along, Sid?'

'Thought I would, instead of going to work.'

'Here, Kootie,' she said, handing the gun to the boy. 'Cocked and locked. Sid, we've got the carbine in the truck, but why don't you bring your .357 too.'

Pete took the truck keys from a hook by the door as Cochran nodded and hurried back into the living room to get his revolver out of the locked strongbox on the bookshelf. 'We should be back in an hour,' Pete told Kootie. 'If Pleasant shows up, tell her we're getting pizza. Tell her she might like it.'

Freed of the two car covers, the red truck was in good enough condition to drive. Last week Mavranos had pulled out the holed, starred windshield and sealed a new windshield in place, and scraped the broken glass out of the rear panel windows and replaced them with sawn pieces of plywood. Mavranos himself had not driven the vehicle since parking it in Cochran's driveway thirteen days ago, possibly because it would agitate the fragments of Scott Crane's skeleton that were scattered among the cubes of broken window glass in the truck bed.

Angelica got into the back seat, so Cochran climbed into the front and sat in the passenger seat while Pete started the engine and let it warm up. The truck interior smelled of fresh plywood and old beer. Cochran had just settled back in the seat against the hard bulk of the revolver at the back of his belt, and lit a cigarette, when through the rain-blurred new windshield he saw the front door of his house pulled open, and saw Plumtree step out.

She was wearing his old leather jacket now, and sneakers – and when she stared across the driveway at the truck, Cochran's face chilled in the instant before he consciously recognized the narrower face and higher shoulders.

'I guess Cody wants to come along too,' observed Pete, moving the stuffed pig so that Cochran could scoot over.

Cochran ground his cigarette out in the ashtray. 'It's Janis,' he said.

He stared toward her, and their eyes met with an almost palpable reciprocation through the glass; and Cochran was peripherally aware that a big raindrop rolling down the outside slope of the windshield stopped at the top edge of their linked gaze as if at an invisible barrier, then wobbled off to the side and ran on down to the black rubber gasket without having crossed between their eyes.

Then Janis was hurrying across the wet pavement with her head down and her hands in the pockets of the leather jacket, and she opened the front door and climbed in beside Cochran, who shifted to the middle of the long seat to give her room.

'Janis,' he said, 'I'm glad you—'

She touched her ear and shook her head. 'I'm deaf, Scant,' she said in a loud, droning voice.

'Oh.' All he could do then was look into her eyes and nod, as Pete clanked the gearshift into reverse and backed the truck around on the wide driveway, then drove down the road to Serramonte Boulevard and made a right turn onto the southbound lanes of the 280.

'Janis's mom!' said Angelica sharply from the back seat. And when Janis just kept looking ahead at the rainy highway lanes for several seconds, Angelica said, 'I guess she really is deaf.'

'Don't ... *tease* her,' said Cochran, 'even if she ... can't know you're doing it.'

Janis had seen him speaking, and looked at him; he looked into her eyes and lifted his right hand, and then held it raised even though after the first few seconds he thought Pete must be expecting him to thumb his nose at the traffic ahead. At last Janis brought up her unbandaged left hand and clasped his, creaking the sleeve of the leather jacket. For several seconds she squeezed his hand hard; then she had released it and looked away, out at the road shoulder rushing past outside.

'I wasn't teasing her,' said Angelica quietly. 'And I'm glad she's along. I wasn't thrilled to be leaving her back there with Kootie, and just poor Arky.'

Beyond the window glass the vivid green San Mateo County hills swept past under the low gray sky, with pockets of fog visible in the hollows, and columns of steam standing up like white smoke from behind the middle-distance hills.

Black crows were flapping low across the rainy sky, and for a panicky moment Cochran couldn't see any buildings or signs, and there appeared to be no other cars on the highway.

Then Janis spoke loudly: 'Why would someone be hitch-hiking on a day like this?'

The truck's engine seemed to roar more loudly after Pete had lifted his foot from the gas pedal. Obscurely reassured by a glimpse of a couple of cars passing the truck on the left, Cochran leaned forward to peer out between the slapping windshield-wiper blades – there was a lone figure in flapping white clothing on the misty highway shoulder a hundred yards ahead, trudging south, the same way they were going, with its highway-side left arm extended.

'Well, it can't be the hitch-hiker the old lady told us about,' said Angelica matter-of-factly, 'today's not the day. *Tomorrow's* Tet.'

Pete was pressing the brake. 'I'm not risking any more carelessness.'

'How far are we from Soledad?' protested Angelica. She was leaning forward across the seat, her breath hot on the back of Cochran's neck. 'That's probably an escaped prisoner!'

'Do they dress them in bedsheets?' asked Pete quietly.

The right-side tires were now hissing and grinding in the muddy shoulder gravel, and the mournful squeal of the brakes made the walking figure stop.

'We're a hundred miles north of Soledad,' said Cochran.

The hitch-hiker was barefooted and wearing a sort of stiff, blue-patterned white poncho, and when Cochran made out the letters ARLI on the fabric and looked more closely, he realized that the garment was a big painted-canvas banner from one of the roadside garlic stands down in Gilroy. The person was still facing away from them.

'Long dark hair,' said Angelica. 'Is it a man or a woman?'

'There's a beard,' said Pete.

The figure had turned its head in profile to look back at the vehicle, and Cochran recognized the high forehead and chiselled profile. 'It's—' he began.

Beside him, Plumtree jumped violently. 'The Flying Nun!' she wailed.

'—Scott Crane,' said Angelica, after giving Plumtree a startled glance. 'I remember the face from when he was stretched out, dead, on my kitchen table down in Solville. Well, we're really in the animal soup now.' She levered open her door, and the sudden chilly breeze inside the truck carried the earthy smells of wet grass and stone. 'Uh ... hop in,' she called over the increased hissing of the rain, squinting as she leaned out of the still slowly moving truck. Obvious fright made her speak too loudly. 'Where you headed?'

With shaking hands, Plumtree cranked down the passenger-side window, and Cochran flinched at the damp wind in his face.

Scott Crane's ghost turned to face them – it might have been naked under the makeshift poncho, but it was decently covered at the moment. Its beard and long hair were dark and ropy with rain water. 'Jack and Jill went up the hill,' the figure called back, 'to fetch a chalice of *aquamort*. To the grail castle, to take away the container of the god's reconciling blood.' Its voice was baritone but faint, like a voice on a radio with the volume turned down. 'I will brook no ... trout,' the ghost said.

'Before its time,' agreed Plumtree. The voice was Cody's, and fairly level, though Cochran could hear the edge of hoarse strain in it. 'We can drive you there,' she cried. 'But you got to tell us where to turn:"

Can we get there by candlelight? thought Cochran, quoting the old nursery rhyme; *aye, and back again.*

'And we might need to stop for gas,' said Pete shakily.

Cochran was shifted around with his right elbow down the back of the front seat now, and he saw Angelica visibly consider climbing into the back of the truck or even over the front seat and right onto his lap; but by the time the king's ghost had limped to the truck's side door she had simply slid all the way over to the left.

The ghost was as solid as a real person as it climbed in – the truck even dipped on its shocks – and when the dripping bony face turned toward the front, Cochran could feel cold breath on his right hand. 'What gas would that be?' the ghost asked. 'Not nitrous oxide, at least. I'm running on a sort of induction coil, here.' Its eyes squinted ahead through the rainy windshield. 'Straight on south,' the ghost said, pulling the door closed with a slam. The thrashing of the rain on the highway shoulder was shut out, and there was just the drumming on the truck's roof.

'I know the way,' said Cochran nervously as he shifted back around and clasped his hands in his lap, 'and we won't need to stop for gas, if it's the Winchester House in San Jose.' He was breathing fast, but he wasn't panicking; and it occurred to him that Crane's ghost wasn't nearly as scary as his dead body had been.

'Find the green chapel,' said the ghost. 'Take what you've dished out; there's a New Year's Eve party coming that'll square all debts.'

When Scott Crane's ghost directed Pete to take the Winchester Boulevard off-ramp, following the signs meant to lead tourists to the 'Winchester Mystery House.' Cochran nodded. 'Be ready to take a left onto Olsen,' he told Pete quietly. 'The parking lot's right there.'

Cody pointed at a bleak hamburger-stand marquee sign that read STEAK SAN/PASTRAMI. 'I think we're supposed to go to the San Pastrami Mission,' she whispered to Cochran. He could feel her shivering next to him.

But, 'Take a left onto Olsen,' said the ghost in the back seat. Its voice was deeper now, and louder. 'The parking lot's right there.'

Cochran remembered that ghosts tended to be repetitive. And the same thought might have occurred to Cody, for beside him she whispered, 'I never need mouthwash, after Mammy Pleasant has been on. Ghosts don't have spit.' Cochran looked at her in time to see teardrops actually fly out from the inner corners of her eyes.

'Valorie never has spit – I – never have to gargle, after Valorie.'

'I don't think you need to—' Cochran began.

'Valorie's dead!' said Cody wonderingly. 'Isn't she?'

Cochran took her hand. 'It's – it's not,' he stammered, 'I mean, you—' The truck interior was steamy since the dead king had got in, and Cochran was sweating under his windbreaker. He wanted to say, *If it works, don't worry about it.* 'Whatever Valeria's status is, Cody,' he said finally, '*you're* certainly not dead.'

'But she's the oldest of us!' Cody gripped his hand, hard, as if the truck was tipping over and she might fall out. 'All the rest of us are at least two years younger! *She's* the one who has our, our *birth!*'

Angelica leaned forward across the dead king's ghost to squeeze Plumtree's shoulder. 'Cody,' she said strongly, 'lots of people are divided from their births by some kind of fault-line. Most of them aren't fortunate enough to know how it happened, or even *that* it happened – they're just aware of a pressure-failure back there somewhere.' She paused, obviously casting about for something else to say. 'Plants often can be safely severed from their original taproots, if they've developed newer roots further along the vine.'

Cody was hurting Cochran's gashed thumb, and even her bandaged right hand was pulling on the door handle so hard that Cochran thought the handle must be about to break off. Her feet were braced against the slippery wet floorboards. 'But *have* I, have any of us?' she whispered. 'Janis is deaf now, and her dreams were fading to black-and-white even on Friday night! Tiffany, Janis, Audrey, Cody, Luanne ... are we all going to slide into the, the booming black-and-white *hole* that's Valorie?'

The king's ghost spoke now, clearly addressing Cody: 'In the midsummer of this year,' said the deep voice, gently but forcefully, 'you and I will be standing in happy sunlight on the hill in the lake.'

Cochran looked back at him – and didn't jump in surprise, only experienced a dizzying emptiness in his chest, to see that the ghost was draped in a white woolen robe now, apparently dry, conceivably the same robe Crane's body had worn when it had been lying in state in Solville. The full, King Solomon beard was lustrous and dry.

The truck rocked as Pete steered it into a parking space and tromped on the brake. 'The grail castle,' he said. 'The green chapel.' A tall hedge blocked the view of the estate from here, but they could see a closed gate, and signs directing tourists toward the low, modern-looking buildings to the right.

Pete Sullivan led the way across the parking lot, but he took his four be-draggled companions toward the locked gate instead of in the direction of the little peak-roofed booth and the Winchester Products Museum beyond it.

He had pulled his comb out of his pocket, and he appeared to be trying to break the end of it off. 'I suppose they count the guests, on the guided tours,' he said to Cochran over the hiss of the rain.

'Yes,' Cochran told him. 'Even *one* couldn't sneak away, let alone five. And I bet they wouldn't let a barefoot guy go anyway.'

'I don't expect anybody's looking this way,' Pete, said, 'but the rest of you block the view of me; act like you're taking pictures of the house.'

Cochran took Plumtree's elbow and stood to Pete's left, pointing through the gate and nodding animatedly. 'I'm pretending to be a tourist,' he told her when she frowned at him. 'Play along.'

Pete's comb was metal, apparently stainless steel, and he had broken two teeth off one end of it and bent kinks into them. Now he had tipped up the padlock on the gate and was carefully fitting the teeth into the keyhole.

Cochran stared between the bars of the gate at the house. Past a row of pink flowering bushes he could see the closest corner of the vast Victorian structure, a circular porch with a cone-roofed tower turret over it. Through the veils of rain beyond it he could see other railed balconies and steeply sloped shingle roofs, and dozens of windows. Lights were on behind many of the windows, and he hoped Pete's hands could work quickly.

'When I say *three*,' said Pete as he twiddled with the comb teeth in the lock mechanism, 'we'll all go through the gate and then walk fast to the corner of that box hedge by the porch. I can see a sign on a post, I think tourists are allowed to be there.'

'Yeah,' said Cochran, 'it's part of the garden tour – that's self-guided. But they may not have the gardens open, on a rainy day like this.'

'Great. Well, if anybody comes up to us,' Pete said grimly, 'smile at 'em and talk in a foreign language, like you wandered out here through the wrong door. And then—' He looked down at his busy, pacifist hands. 'Sid, you'll have to cold-cock 'em.'

Cochran thought of Kootie and Mavranos back at his house, ready to risk their lives, and of the Sullivans, who had reluctantly committed themselves to this, and of Plumtree, hoping to undo the murder of the ghost that was standing right behind them. He looked back at the bearded figure, and noticed without surprise that the king's ghost was now wearing a sort of tropical white business suit, though still barefoot. The ghost, as apparently solid as any of them, looked like a visiting emperor.

'I can see the necessity of that,' Cochran said to Pete. 'Let's hope nobody notices us.'

Pete nodded, and Cochran heard the snap of the lock. 'One, two, *three*.' Pete was lifting the gate as he swung it open, and the wet hinges didn't squeal; then Cochran took hold of the elbow of Plumtree's leather jacket again and they were hurrying across the cobblestone driveway to the sign. Behind him Cochran heard the gate clink closed again, and Pete's footsteps slapping up to where the rest of them now stood.

They halted there, rocking, and Cochran stared fixedly at the lettering on the waist-high sign while he tensed himself for any evidence of challenge; but the only sound was the timpani drumroll of the rain on the cobblestones and the smack of bigger drops falling from the high palm branches that waved overhead, and his peripheral vision showed him no movement on the shadowed porches or the walkways or hedged lawns.

Plumtree had actually read the sign. 'That iron cap in the ground is to the coal chute,' she told him. 'And those windows up on the second floor there to the left are where the old lady's bedroom was. The Daisy Bedroom – huh!'

'We're supposed to,' panted Pete, 'find the Winchester woman's ghost – and, I guess, a – container? – of the *pagadebiti* wine.' He turned to the ghost. 'You can do those things?'

The tall, bearded ghost was looking at Cochran when it echoed Pete's last sentence: 'You can do those things,' it said hollowly.

'I guess that'll do,' sighed Pete. 'Up onto the porch there, everybody, and I'll unlock us a door.'

They found a modern-looking glass door with an empty carpeted hall visible inside. A decal on the glass read PLEASE NO ADMITTANCE EMPLOYEES ONLY, but Pete was able to pop back the bolt with a contemptuous fiddle-and-twist of his kinked comb-teeth.

'We should hear a tour-party, if one's nearby,' whispered Cochran as he stepped inside. Angelica was leading the king's ghost by the hand, and Plumtree had sidled in ahead of them and was now carefully standing on the other side of Cochran from the ghost. 'We'll hear the guide talking, and the footsteps. Move the *other* way if we do, right?'

They hurried down the corridor toward the interior of the great house, and soon the corridor turned left and they were in a broad, empty Victorian entry hall lit by electric lights that mimicked gas lamps. Polished carved mahogany framed the windows and doors and the corners of the ceiling, and panelled the walls from the wainscot down; and the floors were a sort of interlocking-plaid pattern of inlaid maple and walnut. The panes in the two front doors were hundreds of carved quartz crystals arranged in fanciful flower and fleur-de-lis patterns, set in webs of silver and lead and bronze.

'How many rooms did the old lady build here?' asked Angelica in a whisper.

'I don't know,' said Cochran. 'Two hundred.'

'Can we – *call* her ghost, somehow? We can't search every damn room!'

'The goose of Winchester can't hear to hiss,' said the king's ghost. 'A bolt-hole, a hidey-hole, is where she is – hidden, escaped from Dionysus like a possum hidden in its own pouch.' He touched the glossy, deeply imprinted white wallpaper.

'Swell,' said Cody. 'Let's move on.'

They hurried down the hall, and found themselves in a vast, dark ballroom. Even in the shadowy dimness Cochran could see that the floor, and the framed and panelled and shelved walls, and the very ceiling way up above the silver chandelier, were of glossy inlaid wood. Far out across the floor on one side was a pipe organ like a cathedral altar, and in the long adjoining wall a fireplace was inset between the two tall, narrow windows that let in the ballroom's only light.

Cochran could faintly hear the muffled creak and knock of footsteps on the floor above, and he looked around helplessly at the huge, high-ceilinged room. He was aware of nearly inaudible creaks and rustles from the far, dark corners of the room, and realized that he'd been hearing these soft flexings ever since they had entered the house; and he had steadily felt attention being paid to him and his companions, but it felt childish and frightful, nothing like a tour-guide or a security guard. Could the ghost of Mrs. Winchester be looking at them now from some remote shelf or alcove, flitting along after them from room to room? He flexed his right hand – but got no sense of help from the god.

'Let's just goddamn keep going,' he whispered.

'Sid—!' gasped Plumtree. 'Look at the stained-glass windows!'

Cochran focussed his eyes on the panes of leaded glass that glowed with the gray daylight outside, and he noticed that they each portrayed a long banner curling around ivy-vine patterns. And there was stylized lettering, capitals, on each banner – WIDE UNCLASP THE TABLES OF THEIR THOUGHTS, read the one in the left-hand window, and on the banner in the right was spelled out THESE SAME THOUGHTS PEOPLE THIS LITTLE WORLD.

'The left one's the *Troilus and Cressida* quote,' said Angelica softly, 'though "table" isn't supposed to be plural. And the right one is from *Richard II*, when the king is alone in prison, and conjuring up company for himself out of his own head.' She shook her head. 'Why the hell would Winchester have put them up here? The *Troilus and Cressida* one is from a speech where Ulysses is saying what a promiscuous ghost-slut Cressida is!'

Plumtree's cold left hand clasped Cochran's, and was shaking.

'It'd get a raised eyebrow from any Shakespeare-savvy guest,' agreed Pete.

'Is that a *clue*, is she in *here*?' snapped Cochran, looking from the windows to the ghost in the white suit.

'Probably not in a room with a fireplace,' said Pete. 'Fireplaces would be the … portals for ghosts to get broken up in and sent to the god, like the ashtrays you see with palindromes lettered around the rims.'

'She was talking to *me*,' said Plumtree flatly. 'Those windows were put there as a message for … for the person who looks like is turning out to be me, all these years later. This little *head*. Shit, she must have been, voluntarily or involuntarily, a multiple-personality herself.'

'So what's the message?' asked Angelica.

'She – she didn't want to go smoking away up one of the chimneys,' said Plumtree.

'Sail on,' said Scott Crane's ghost, with a chopping wave toward the rest of the house.

They found a broader hall and tiptoed along it, instinctively crowding against one panelled wall after another, and darting quickly across the wide, gleaming patches of hardwood floor between. The electric lights were far apart, but the open rectangular spaces were all grayly lit by the dozens of interior windows and arches and skylights. In fact the layout of the rooms was so open and expansive that the sprawling scope of the house was evident at every turn, from every obtuse perspective; at no point could one fail to get the visceral impression that the house was infinite in every dimension, like a house in an Escher print – that one could walk forever down these broad, carpeted halls, up and down these dark-railed stairs from floor to ever-unfamiliar floor, without once re-crossing one's path. And Cochran remembered Mammy Pleasant saying that the place had been built to attract, and trap, and dispatch to the afterworld, wandering ghosts reluctant to go on to the god.

'It looks open,' whispered Angelica at one point, 'but she's made the geometry in here as complicated as the mazes in the Mandelbrot set; there are patches of empty air in here that might as well be steel bulkheads. You'd never know because you could never quite manage to *get* to 'em.'

Cochran found a stairway, but it ran uselessly right up against the ceiling, with not even a trap-door to justify it; then he led his party up another set of stairs that switch-backed seven times but only took them up one floor, for each step was only two inches tall; and he led them through galleries with railed-off squares to keep one from stepping into windows that were set in the floor, and through a broad hall or series of open-walled rooms in which four ornate fireplaces stood nearly side by side; and they shuffled past mercifully locked windowed doors that opened onto sheer drops into kitchens and corridors below.

'More a house for birds,' said Cody at one point, 'or monkeys, than for people.' 'Aerial manlike entities,' agreed Angelica with a glance at the dead king. 'Smoking away up the chimneys,' said the bearded figure, drawing a frown from Plumtree.

At last they found themselves in a room with an open railed balcony on the fourth floor, unable to climb higher. The room was unfinished, with bare lath along one wall; an exposed brick chimney, with no fireplace, rose from the floor to the ceiling in the left corner.

Pete stepped toward the balcony, crouching to peer out over the green lawns and red rooftop peaks without being seen from below.

'It's infinite,' he said hopelessly. 'I can't even see an end to the house, from here. You'd think I could see the freeway, or a gas-station sign, or something.'

'This place is still a supernatural maze,' said Angelica. 'It's got to be drawing ghosts like a candle draws moths, still. I swear, down in those endless galleries and halls I could feel all their half-wit attentions on us. Old lady Winchester "wide unclasped the table of her thoughts" – her patterns of thoughts, her accommodating masks – to every footloose ghost in the West, she was no virgin, psychically; and "these same thoughts people this little world." Except it doesn't look so little, from inside.' She shook her head violently and then startled Cochran by spitting on the floor. 'They're all around us right now, like spiderwebs. These fireplaces should be running full-blast, twenty-four hours a day.'

'She probably assumed they'd be used, in the winter at least,' said Cody. 'After her death.'

Cochran looked away from Angelica, toward the corner of the room.

'This chimney is like the first stairway we tried,' he said, 'look. There's no hole in the ceiling for it.'

Pete Sullivan walked over and reached up with both hands to hook his fingertips over the uneven row of bricks at the top edge of the chimney, which did end several inches short of the solid ceiling planks. 'My hands are twitchy,' Pete said, 'like they want to ... *participate* with it. Did Houdini ever do an escape from a chimney?'

The white-clad-ghost strode over and, taller than Pete, was able to slide its whole hand into the drafty space between the bricks and the ceiling planks.

'Clean, uncarboned brick,' the ghost said solemnly; 'and gold. I can smell gold on the draft.'

'Gold?' echoed Cochran, disappointed that they had apparently found some old treasure instead of the old woman's ghost.

'Well now, gold would damp out her wavelengths,' said Pete, lowering his hand and brushing brick dust off on his jeans. 'Ghosts are an electro-magnetic agitation she'd have to be locked up in something shielding, to be hidden. People used to make coffins out of lead, to keep the ghost in, contained and undetectable. Gold's not quite as dense as lead, but it'd certainly do.'

'And,' said Cochran, nodding, 'if chimneys generally destroy ghosts, if that's common knowledge, then you certainly wouldn't ever look for a ghost to be *hiding* in one.'

'Not unless you knew it was a dummy chimney,' agreed Angelica. 'And with a hundred *real* fireplaces and chimneys around the place, who'd notice that *one* was a fake?'

The ghost's white sleeve disappeared behind the top row of bricks ... and Cochran noticed that the figure was leaning braced against the chimney with one knee, for the other leg appeared now to be just a hanging, empty trouser leg, its cuff flapping over an empty white shoe.

'The chimney is like the hole Alice fell down,' said the ghost softly. 'Tiny shelves all the way down, with papers and locks of hair and rings and stones and dry leaves.' After another moment, the ghost said, 'Ah.'

Then the trouser leg filled out and the cuff lowered to cover the shoe, which shifted as weight visibly settled into it again.

A clunking, scraping noise at the top of the chimney made Cochran look up – and the ghost was trying to rock something out of the chimney, apparently struggling to angle it out through the narrow gap between the bricks and the ceiling planks.

The hard object was not coming out. 'Break away a brick or two,' suggested Cochran, looking nervously toward the stairs. He could hear voices now, and the knocking of footsteps. "I think a tour's coming.'

Pete reached his own hand in next to the ghost's, and then shook his head. 'It's not that it won't fit out,' he said through clenched teeth, 'it's just *stopping*, in mid-air, like the thin air turns rubbery, like we're trying to push two big magnets together at their positive ends.'

Cochran could definitely hear voices mounting from below now. 'What *is* it?' he asked anxiously. 'If it's just an old magnet or something, drop it and let's go!'

'It's rectangular,' gasped Pete, 'heavy.'

Plumtree stood by the chimney and jumped up, to peek into the gap. 'You've got a gold box,' she said when her sneaker soles had hit the floor again.

'Dead woman's gold,' said Angelica, 'she's probably got the geometry of the chimney-boundary magicked to not let it pass.'

'Let's see if the chimney can tell the difference between that and a dead *man's* gold,' said Plumtree. She dug the gold Dunhill lighter out of her pocket and tossed it up in a glittering arc toward the gap.

The lighter knocked against the wooden ceiling and disappeared behind the bricks, down inside the chimney, and then Pete jackknifed backward and sat down hard on the wooden floor, holding in his lap a metal box that gleamed gold under a veil of cobwebs.

Scott Crane's ghost had leaped back, or *flickered* back like an image in a jolted mirror; and when Cochran heard a scuffling flutter behind him he spun around to see a white-painted canvas banner settling onto the floor. The word GARLIC was painted on it in cursive blue letters, and the king's ghost was gone.

Cochran looked back at Angelica and Plumtree, who were staring wide-eyed, at the empty canvas. Cochran shrugged at Plumtree. 'You tossed his lighter,' he said.

'Good,' she said with a visible shiver.

'Is there somebody up there?' came a voice from the stairs at the back of the room.

Plumtree grabbed the dusty, cobwebby box from Pete and took a long step toward a doorway that led away from the stairs. She jerked her head for the others to follow.

Cochran helped Pete to his feet and followed Angelica and Plumtree down this unexplored hallway. Let the tour-guide explain the garlic banner, he thought: *Damn ghosts! – leaving their goofy shit around everywhere.*

They hurried on through a hastily glimpsed kaleidoscope of architecture, with skylights below them and stairways curling around them and interior balconies and windows receding away at every height in the patches of electric lamp-glow and lancing columns of gray daylight.

At the top of one white-painted stairway Cochran's right hand was suddenly tugged diagonally out and down. He crouched and made a *ch-ch!* sound, and then started hopping down the stairs before his hand could pull him off balance and send him tumbling down them. He could hear the others following behind him, but he didn't dare lift his eyes from the crowding-up stair-edges to look back.

The stairway continued down past the next floor, but was bevelled dark wood now, and the walls and doors and ceilings were framed in carved mahogany. Cochran's hand was pulled out horizontally away from the landing and down a hall, and he almost thought he could feel a warm, callused hand clasping his palm and knuckles, and a deeply jarring pulse like seismic tremors.

Helplessly Cochran led his companions through a wide doorway, and his first impression was that they had come to another unfinished section – but a closer look at the walls showed him that the wide patches of exposed lath were edged with broken plaster and torn wall fabric.

'This must be the earthquake-damaged section,' Cochran whispered to Plumtree, who was holding the gold box in both hands.

She stepped carefully over the uneven floor to the window's, which were panes of clear glass inset at the centers of stained-glass borders.

'We're in the, what was it, the Daisy bedroom,' Plumtree said breathlessly, peering out at the grounds, 'or near it. You can see the sign we reconnoitered at down there to the left. This here would be where she was sleeping on that night in 1906, when Dionysus knocked down the tower onto her.'

Cochran flexed his hand, then waved it experimentally in the still air; and it seemed to be free of any supernatural tether now.

'It must be here,' he said, 'whatever we're supposed to find.'

Two big, framed black-and-white photographs were hung on one raggedly half-plastered wall. Still hesitantly holding his hand out to the side, Cochran walked over to the pictures, and saw that they were views of the house as it had stood in the days before the top three stories had fallen; and the additional crenellations and pillars and balconies, and the peak-roofed tower above it all, ashen and fortress-like and stern in the old gray photographs, made the structure's present-day height and red-and-beige exterior seem modest by comparison.

'The House of Babel,' said Plumtree, who had walked up beside him with her hands in the pockets of the leather jacket. 'I guess that's how the god looked at it.'

'There was a fireplace over here,' called Pete softly from the other side of the room, 'at one time.'

He was standing beside a chest-high square gap in the wall, through which the exposed floor joists of another room were visible on the far side. Pete crouched and looked up at the underside of the gap. 'You can see the chimney going on upward.'

A piece of white-painted plywood had been neatly fitted in to cover the spot where the hearth would have been, and Cochran crossed to it and then knelt down on the floor beside Pete's knees to take hold of the edge of the board. Pete stepped back.

'I'm certain this must be bolted down,' Cochran said softly.

'Think of young King Arthur,' said Angelica behind him, 'with the sword in the stone. You're, the – the guy with the Dionysus mark on his hand.'

Cochran yanked upward on the board, and nearly fell over backward as it sprang up in his hands. He shuffled his feet to regain his balance, and leaned against the board and pushed it forward onto the floor joists of the next room; then for several seconds he just peered down into the rectangular brick-lined black hole he had exposed. He dug a penny out of his pocket and held it over the hole for a moment, then dropped it; and he waited, but no sound came back up.

At last he stood up and quickly stepped away from the hole. Instead of stepping over to look for themselves, Angelica and Pete and Plumtree stared at him.

'Well,' Cochran said, 'there's – it's very fucking dark down there, excuse me. But there's *rungs*, starting a yard or so down.'

'Rungs.' Angelica quickly crossed to one of the windows and stared out at the shaggy palm trees nodding out in the rain. 'Damn it, we were just going to get … *gas*, and *beer*, and *batteries*,' she said harshly. 'Kootie's ordering a *pizza*. I'm not – hell, I'm not even *dressed* for climbing down into some goddamn – unlit – spidery *catacombs* in a *haunted house*.' She turned around and glared at Plumtree. 'If *only*,' she cried out, 'you hadn't killed Scott Crane!'

Plumtree opened her mouth and blinked, then snarled, 'And who did *you* kill, lady? "*If only*"! Back in your shanty house in Long Beach, you told me that each of you was responsible for the death of somebody, and had guilty amends to make. You told me you can't get rid of the guilt and shame without help, that that'd be like thinking one hand could fix what it took two to break, remember? I've had stinking *beer cans* wired to my ankles, and I've been taped into a chair and then thrown onto a backyard faucet hard enough to crack my ribs, and, and I get the idea that it's a big honor for me to be allowed to *eat* with you all.' Her voice was shaking, and her lip was pulled back to expose her lower teeth as she went on, 'So tell me, bitch – who did *you* kill?'

Angelica stared at Plumtree blankly. Then she said, 'Fair enough. Okay. I was a psychiatrist in private practice, and I used to perform fake Wednesday-night seances to let my patients make peace with dead friends and relatives; and five Halloweens ago one of the seances, right in the middle of it, stopped being make-believe. A whole lot of real, angry ghosts showed up, and among other things the clinic caught fire. Three patients died, and five more are probably still in mental hospitals to this day.' She took a deep breath and let it out, though her face was still expressionless. 'One of the ones that died was in love with me; I wasn't in love with him, but I – didn't really discourage him. Frank Rocha. I killed Frank Rocha, through careless-ness in the expertise I was trained for, the expertise he had paid me to use. His ghost troubled me for two years, and the police have been looking for me ever since.' She smiled tiredly and held out her right hand. 'I do apolo-gize, Cody. Are we friends?'

Plumtree was shaking her head, but apparently more in bewilderment than denial. She took Angelica's hand and said, 'I never had a friend before.'

'It's a tricky flop,' said Cochran shortly. He could feel a jumpy restlessness in his right hand, and he knew it wanted to point toward the brick chim-ney hole in the floor. Climb down before it pulls you down, he thought. 'Somebody give me a ... a Bic lighter or something, since we don't have the Dunhill anymore.' He sighed and ran his hands through his hair, patted the gun under the windbreaker at the back of his belt, then walked over to the hole and sat down on the floor beside it, swinging his legs into the dark empty space.

Plumtree pulled a red Bic out of the leather jacket pocket. 'Here, Sid – and I'm right behind you.'

'So are we, so are we,' sighed Angelica.

Cochran slid himself forward, down into the hole, so that his toes and the seat of his jeans were braced against opposite brick surfaces and most of his weight was on his elbows. The angular bulk of the holstered .357 jabbed him over his right kidney. 'Just a bit lower than you'd like,' he said breathlessly through clenched teeth, 'there's a rung you can get a foot onto. Then I guess you just drag your back as you go down until you've gone far enough to get your hands onto the rungs.'

He heard several sighs behind and above him, and then Pete's voice said, 'I'll go last, and pull the plywood cover back over the hole.'

CHAPTER TWENTY NINE

Roma, tibi subito motibus ibit Amor ...
> —Sotades of Maroneia in Thrace, c. 276 B.C.

The shaft was wide for a chimney, but the rough brick sides kept snagging the elbows of Cochran's windbreaker no matter how carefully he kept them tucked in against his ribs, and after Pete pulled the board over the top of the shaft there was no light at all, and the close amplification of panting breath and the gritty scuff of feet on iron rungs emphasized the constriction; Cochran was terribly aware that even if he unhooked his gun holster and pressed his back flat against the wall behind him he would not have had room to bring his knee up to his chest.

Bits of mud dislodged from Plumtree's sneakers tapped his head and face and hands in the total blackness, and he thought about pausing to strike the lighter; but the strong clay-scented draft from below would probably have extinguished the flame instantly, and anyway he wasn't sure he wanted to *see* how close in front of his face the bricks were, and *see* the narrow space overhead blocked by the shoe-soles of only one of the three people whose bodies clogged the way back up to air and light and room to move. When his right elbow swung free in a side opening, Cochran's eyes had been in total darkness long enough for him to detect a faint gray glow from the side tunnel, which slanted downward at roughly a forty-five-degree angle. Faintly he could hear voices coming up through it.

'Side chute to one of the fireplaces,' he whispered upward. 'Don't take it – keep going – straight down.'

He heard Plumtree relaying the message up to Pete and Angelica as he resumed abrading himself down the angular stone esophagus.

After a dozen more rungs he knew he must be well below the level of the ground floor – and when he had hunched a few yards farther down he was sure that he heard far-distant music from the impenetrable darkness below his feet, and that the upwelling draft was elusively scented with hints of cypress and coarse red wine and crushed night-time grass.

He thought of whispering *Getting close how*, but told himself that the others would detect it too.

He didn't realize that he'd been nervously bouncing the heel of each shoe off the back wall between rung-steps until the moment he swung one foot back and it met no wall; and he almost lost his grip in surprise. But then he noticed that the scuff of his feet wasn't tightly amplified anymore, either, and soon he felt the bottom edge of the scratchy brick surface at his back scrape up across his shoulders and then ruffle the hair at the back of his head. He could stretch out away from the iron ladder in the darkness now, and the sound of his breathing scattered away behind him with no echoes.

And, though it was only the dimmest ashy diffraction, there was light – Cochran could see the backs of his hands as faint whitenesses bravely distinct from the background blackness.

Soon came a moment when his left foot reached down and instead of swinging through empty air struck a gritty, powdery ground, jolting his spine. He got his other foot down onto the ground too, but he whispered for the others to stop, and then spent several seconds pawing around with his shoe soles and flexing his knees before he dared to unclamp his hands from the last rung. He flicked the lighter then, and, looking away from the dazzling flame, saw that he was standing on a patch of soot that covered this corner of a broad dirt floor. Stone walls and a low stone ceiling receded away into shadows, but he could see an arched doorway at the far end of the room. The distantly musical and sylvan breeze was even more remote now, but seemed to be coming to him through the arch.

He cupped his free hand around the lighter flame until his three companions had climbed all the way down out of the chimney shaft and joined him on the sooty patch of dirt, and by that time he was able to look directly into the flame without squinting. When he let it snap off to cool his thumb the darkness seemed absolute again by contrast.

'There's an arch ahead of us,' he whispered.

'No ... presences,' whispered Angelica; 'I don't sense ghosts down here.'

At that moment Cochran jumped and gasped in pure panic, for he had the clear but visually unverifiable impression that a big, warm hand had clasped his right hand, and was gently tugging him forward out across the dirt floor. 'Follow me!' he choked urgently to the others as he stumbled forward.

By the echoes of his panting breath he knew when he was passing through the stone arch – and then the dim gray light was strong enough for him to see his empty hand stretched out in front of him. And as soon as he could see that no other hand held his, the sensation of it vanished. He lowered his arm, aware now that his heart was pounding rapidly, and as the sweat cooled on his face he blinked around at the racks and knobs that covered the closest wall.

The racks were wine racks, and the knobs were the foil-sheathed necks of bottles lying horizontally in them. 'We're in the wine cellar!' he whispered. He remembered Mammy Pleasant telling them yesterday that Mrs.

Winchester had walled up the wine cellar after seeing the black handprint of her dead husband on the wall.

He flicked the lighter again, and by the sudden yellow glare he walked over and lifted one of the dusty bottles out of the nearest rack, and wiped the label on his windbreaker – and when he had peered at it he shivered and glanced around in suspicious fright, for what he held was a bottle of the fabulous 1887 Inglenook Cabernet Sauvignon, the very same California vintage that Andre Simon had described in 1960 as 'every bit as fine as my favorite pre-phylloxera clarets.'

He heard a rattling knock from behind him, and Angelica yelped, 'Jesus, a skull! There's a goddamn *skull* on the floor here!'

Cochran turned around, still holding the bottle; Angelica was standing stiffly by the arch, her feet well back from what did appear to be a human skull lying on the dirt. Focussing on the dim corners around the room, he now saw pale curls and ribby clusters that might be other bones.

'At least one other skull,' whispered Pete through an audibly tight throat, 'over here. And – an antique revolver.'

'They're old,' Cochran said to Angelica. 'They may have been down here a hundred years.'

'I know, I know,' she said, obviously embarrassed at having been frightened. 'Sid,' called Plumtree softly from the opposite wall, 'bring your lighter over here a second.' She was standing beside a section of plain white plastered wall, pointing at a shadowed spot down by her knee.

Still holding the gas-release lever down, Cochran carefully carried the light over to where she was pointing, and crouched to illuminate the spot.

It was an old mark, in still faintly adhering soot, of a tiny hand.

Angelica had hurried up beside Cochran, and now she bent over to look at the handprint. 'Ah!' she exclaimed sharply, stepping back. 'The baby! It wasn't her dead *husband's* ghost that the god finally asked Mrs. Winchester to give over to him! Mammy Pleasant had that wrong. It was the ghost of Winchester's dead *baby daughter*!' And Cochran saw the *bruja* of Solville make the Catholic sign of the cross. 'She couldn't bring herself to do *that*, just as Agave couldn't disown the ghost of her killed son, in Arky's Euripides play!'

'And she entombed the wine,' said Pete Sullivan shakily, 'but she left a chimney air shaft to link this cellar with her bedroom. I'll bet she never permitted any fires in any of the fireplaces that connect with that chimney, after she walled up the cellar.'

Cochran let the lighter flame go out, and he handed the hot lighter to Plumtree while he walked back to the rack to reluctantly replace the legendary Inglenook. And after he had put the bottle back, his hand twitched to the side—

—and in his nose was the sagebrush-and-dry-stone smell of the Mojave Desert outside Las Vegas, and the acid perfume of Paris streets after rain, and the hallucinated mildewy staleness of the Victorian hall in which he had seen Mondard in a mirror—

—and his fingers were pressed firmly around another bottle. He lifted it out carefully and carried it over to Plumtree, who struck the lighter.

The label on the bottle was Buena Vista, Count Haraszthy's old Sonoma vineyard; and below the brand name and a statement of limited bottling was the date, 1860, and the single word PAGADEBITI.

'I've got the wine,' he whispered. 'Let's *esplitavo*.'

'God,' said Angelica, 'back up that chimney?'

The dirt floor shook then, and Cochran was so careful not to drop the bottle that he fell to his knees cradling it. Plumtree had let the lighter snap off, and when she flicked it on again there were vertical streaks of dust sifting in the air below the stone ceiling. And through the arch behind them came the echoing rattle of bricks and iron clattering down in the old chimney shaft.

'*No*,' said a new, deep voice.

Again Plumtree let the lighter go out – and when the flint-wheel had stutteringly lit the flame again, Cochran jumped in surprise to see a tall, broad-shouldered black man standing in the open arch. Even in the frail lighter glow, this newcomer seemed *solider* than Cochran and his companions – glossier because of reflecting the light more strongly, his feet more of a weight on the dirt floor, the very air seeming to rebound more helplessly from his unyielding surfaces.

The man, if it was a man and not some sort of elemental spirit, was wearing a spotted animal skin like a toga, and leafy vines were tangled in his long braids; in his hand was a staff wrapped with vines and capped with a pinecone.

'*I am the guardian of the god's blood*,' the figure said. The voice shook the streaks of dust that hung in the air, and his breath seemed to carry the faint music and the forest smells. '*Did you think there would be no guard? Nobody takes the god's blood out of the tabernacle past me*.' He shifted the staff to his right hand, and it gleamed in the frail light now, for it had become a long, curving sword, and muscles flexed in the strong black arm to hold the weapon's evident new weight.

'Well I say *goddamn*!' burst out Plumtree. The lighter was jiggling wildly in her hand, and Angelica took it from her and re-lit it.

'The,' said Pete Sullivan quickly, 'the god wants us to take the wine. He led us here, to get it!'

'*So these others claimed,*' said the black man, rolling his obsidian head around at the bones without looking away from the four intruders. '*Did you think there would be no guard? Nobody takes the god's blood out of the tabernacle past me,*' When he inhaled, Cochran yawned nervously, expecting his eardrums to pop.

Cochran held up the back of his right hand. 'This is the god's mark, given to me when I put out my hand to save the god's vine from being cut back!' He made a fist. 'The god led me into this room, *by* this hand, half a minute ago!'

'*So these others claimed,*' repeated the tall black man, again rocking his head.

Cochran realized that the figure was not listening to what they said; perhaps didn't even have the capacity to understand objections. It was some kind of idiot *genius loci*, an apparently unalterable part of the gods math, as implacable and unreasoning as an electrified fence. With his free hand Cochran reached around under the back of his windbreaker and, though hollowly aware that the 'antique revolver' had apparently been of no use to one long-ago intruder, nevertheless unsnapped his holster.

Beside him, Plumtree shivered.

'If I – put the wine back—' Cochran began hoarsely.

All at once the supernatural guard stamped far forward into the room, sweeping the sword in a fast horizontal arc – the blade whistled as it split the quivering air—

—Hopping back, Cochran snatched the Pachmayr grip and yanked the gun out of the holster, and despairingly pointed the muzzle into the center of the broad chest—

And in the same instant Plumtree stepped forward so that a backswing from the sword or a shot from the gun would hit her; and Mammy Pleasant's imperious voice said, 'Bacchus!'

The curved sword blade paused behind the black man's left shoulder like the rising crescent moon behind a mountain, and Cochran tipped the gun barrel upward.

'Don't you recognize me, Bacchus?' spoke the old woman's voice from Plumtree's mouth. 'I'm Mary Ellen Pleasant, the poor old woman you took *custody* of, in '99! You were there when I died, five years later – and you were there too when the god came breaking down Yerba Buena for my ghost, three Easters after that.'

'*I – do recognize you,*' said the solid black figure.

'Am I, like you, a totally surrendered servant of the god?'

'*You are.*'

'I am,' said Pleasant as Plumtree's blond head nodded. 'And I tell you that the god has sent me to fetch out this wine, and bring it to the king.'

Without looking away from the creature's eyes, she held out one hand toward Cochran. He carefully laid the bottle in her palm.

For several long seconds the tall black figure stood motionless. Cochran kept the gun pointed at the ceiling but didn't take his finger out of the trigger guard.

Then the apparition tossed the sword through the eddying air to its left hand, and the sword again became a vine-wrapped staff with a pinecone on it.

The figure waved it and said, '*Pass.*'

Again the ground shook, and this time the bottles on the walls clinked and clicked like castanets and temple bells, and didn't stop rattling; and Cochran didn't fall to his knees this time, but just crouched like a surfer to keep his balance on the gyrating floor.

While the floor was still shifting, Plumtree turned and began dancing like a tightrope-walker into the darkness at the far end of the cellar, away from the arch and the supernatural guard. Angelica let the lighter go out as she went hopping, and skipping after her, and Pete and Cochran were bounding along at her heels.

And, over the bass drumming of the earth, Cochran thought as he ran that he could hear distant pipes playing, unless that was just some whistling overtone of his panicky panting breath as he followed the sounds of Pete and Angelica through the rocking pitch blackness.

Soon they were able to see slanting gray light ahead of them and hear the crackle of rain, and when they had hurried to the muddy end of the tunnel, and climbed up over tumbled masonry out onto wet grass in a battering showery wind, they could see that they were in some kind of park. Cochran hastily shoved his revolver back into its holster, and pulled the back of his windbreaker down over it.

The rain quickly made runny black mud of the soot that smeared their backs and knees, and by unspoken agreement they didn't run for the shelter of the corrugated metal roof over some nearby picnic tables, but plodded through the cleansing shower straight across the grass toward the nearest visible road.

When Plumtree glanced at him, Cochran saw that she was Cody again. 'I guess I look as shitty as you do,' she said through chattering teeth.

'I guess you do,' he said stolidly.

She touched the angular bulge at the bottom of the zipped leather jacket, right over her belt, and Cochran realized that it must be the gold box from the chimney. 'I swear I can feel her kicking in there,' she said.

CHAPTER THIRTY

Hades and Dionysus, for whom they go mad and rage, are one and the same.

—Heraclitus

The road proved to be called Tisch Way, and they trudged a quarter of a mile west along its gravel shoulder through the downpour to the intersection of Winchester Boulevard, with the rushing lanes of the 280 visible now just past a chain-link fence on the other side of the road.

When they had wearily got back into the red truck and wedged the bottle of *pagadebiti* securely in the glove compartment, Pete started the engine and drove out of the Winchester Mystery House parking lot, but then just made a left turn onto Olsen Drive and an immediate right into the parking lot of a big new shopping center; he drove up to the empty Winchester Boulevard end of the rain-hazed lot and pulled into a parking space under a towering three-panel movie-theater sign and turned off the engine. The rain drummed on the truck roof, and every five seconds a drop collected on the rusty underside and fell soundlessly onto the soaked thigh of Plumtree's jeans.

She was sitting in the back seat beside Cochran, and she fumbled the gold box out from under the soaked leather jacket. It was no bigger than a couple of decks of cards stuck together back-to-back, and its lid appeared to be an unhinged plate held in place by six gold screws.

'Find me a screwdriver, Pete,' she said. 'A flat-tip one.'

'No,' said Cochran, 'don't open it. We're supposed to pitch it into the ocean.'

'Not still shut up tight, though, right? Or she might as well have stayed in the chimney – there'd be no difference between the box sitting there or sitting still-sealed at the bottom of the bay. She's gotta be broke open, like an egg into a fry pan.' Plumtree leaned back in her seat and closed her eyes. Her wet hair was plastered to her head and streaked with black. 'Is Mammy Pleasant going away voluntarily? Or are you just gonna be shoving her in?'

'Voluntarily,' Cochran said. 'She's going along, anyway. She appears to be resigned to it.' The interior of the truck felt warm and close after the gusty chill outside, and he wrinkled his nose against the remembered childhood smell of doused campfires.

'That's what I thought.' Plumtree fitted her thumbnail into one of the screw slots and twisted gently, but it didn't move.

'I don't know if ghosts really have a whole lot of capacity for voluntary action actual *volition*,' said Angelica from the front seat; and immediately she frowned, as if ashamed to have had the thought.

'These *are* dead people, Cody,' Pete said.

'Like Valorie,' Plumtree agreed, nodding expressionlessly. 'Where's that screwdriver?'

Pete sighed and bent forward to grope under the front seat.

'If you let her out;' said Angelica, clearly nettled but not quite ready to interfere, 'she'll be gone as quick as a puff of steam.'

Pete had dragged a black metal toolbox onto the seat, and unsnapped the catches and opened it. Wordlessly he passed a screwdriver over the back of the seat.

'I don't think she will,' said Plumtree. 'Obviously I wasn't busted out of the madhouse and made a part of this company just so you'd be able to question my father and hell, I've already hosted Mammy Pleasant.'

'... Oh,' said Angelica, humbly. 'I – I see. Cody, I do think you could get away with not doing it.'

Plumtree had already used the screwdriver to back one of the screws out of the box. 'Look at that,' she said, holding the screw up. 'All gold, not just the head.'

'I don't imagine she'd scrimp,' said Cochran bitterly, 'on what she thought would be her eternal resting place.' He knew he wouldn't be able to talk Cody out of hosting the old woman's ghost, if it was still viable in there, and he only hoped Winchester wouldn't set her into any trouble or hurt her ribs or her hand. 'I wonder when she decided to have this box and these screws made.'

'After 1899, I guess,' said Angelica, 'if that's when her daughter's hand-print showed up. The old lady was apparently a loyal servant of Dionysus before then.'

'Call her Mrs. *Winchester*,' said Plumtree. 'I've got three of the screws out, she may be able to hear you.' Plumtree was rocking slightly on the truck seat, and Cochran could just hear what she was humming: *Row, row, row your boat* ... She peered out the windows at the agitated puddles on the asphalt. 'Don't tell me, if it's too horrible, but how did we get away from the big black genie-guy?'

'Mammy Pleasant knew him,' said Pete. 'I think he was a bit of the god's remote attention, not able to make many decisions – like a horse's tail, swatting flies while the horse looks at something else. But he recognized her, and he let us get out with a bottle of the super-Zinfandel.' He stared out the window at the rain that was splashing up in waves of mist across the parking lot. 'Poor Johanna,' he said quietly. 'The roof in Solville must be leaking like six firehoses. '

Plumtree had unthreaded the last screw and lifted it out of the hole. Now she slid the cover off the gold box, and lifted from a nest of ribbon-tied locks of smoky-fine hair and folded strips of newsprint a corked but apparently empty glass test tube.

'Careful you don't just *eat* her, the way Sherman Oaks or your Dr. Armentrout would,' said Angelica nervously.

'I didn't *eat* old Pleasant, did I?' Plumtree lifted the tube and stared through it. 'I've got plenty of practice at just standing aside and making room for an incoming personality, like when the phone rings.'

She frowned slightly, and Cochran knew she must be thinking of Janis, whose job it always was to answer telephones.

'Wide unclasp,' she said then, perhaps speaking to the glass tube. 'I'm the one who got the message in the stained glass. Meet the ones that people *this* little head.' And with one motion she bit out the cork and inhaled strongly over the open tube.

The cork fell out of her lips and she sat back in the seat.

'Oh my Lord,' she said then, exhaling and staring wide-eyed at the three people in the truck with her, 'has found me, hasn't he?' The voice was strong but higher in pitch than Cody's or Pleasant's.

'No,' said Cochran, 'we're – well, yes, I suppose so. We're sort of contract labor for him, I guess.'

Tears gathered in Plumtree's eyes, and spilled down her sunburned cheeks.

'You don't have to go,' said Angelica suddenly, 'if you don't want to. We can ... I don't know. Damn it! Is there a way to ... hide you again, hide you better?'

Beside her, Pete looked as though he wanted to object, but he just pressed his lips together and rolled his eyes to the rusty ceiling.

Plumtree's eyebrows went up. 'No, there's not.' She raised Plumtree's hands and flexed them in front of her face. 'I'm ... out now! ... and bound for the god, bound for the sea; and I'll take my baby's ghost with me, at least, dry dust though she is. Lord, I did think we'd have to spend eternity in that box. I ran out of thoughts after only a few hours, I believe, and even my dreams were just of being in the box. The memories of her that I kept, defiantly kept, were just black dust after all. Nothing but soot. I should have known.' The eyebrows went up even further when she looked down at the soaked leather jacket and jeans she was wearing. 'I'm ... grateful to this person for a little interval time in which to breathe fresh air.'

Hardly very fresh, thought Cochran. He yawned from sheer nervousness, anxious to have Cody back on again.

'What,' asked Mrs. Winchester as Cody's body seemed to brace itself, 'is the date today?'

'Monday the thirtieth of January,' said Pete, 'uh, 1995.'

The news appeared to alarm Mrs. Winchester, and Cochran thought it was learning what day of the month it currently was, rather than that seventy-odd years had passed since her death, that had upset her. 'When is the Chinese New Year?' she asked quickly.

'Tomorrow,' Cochran told her. 'The Year of the Pig.'

'And today's already dark? How is it that you've dawdled so? We can't wait around through the passage of another year, before we get consumed! We're far past stale already, my poor shred of a daughter and I. Has the god chosen a king?'

'Yes,' said Pete and Cochran and Angelica simultaneously.

'Go to where he waits, then, and stop wasting time. Go quickly – this *is* some species of *automobile*, isn't it? Has one of you taken a drink of the wine?'

'No, ma'am,' said Pete in a harried tone, turning around to face the dashboard and twist the key in the ignition.

'Ah, one of you should have! – back in my house, if that's where you found me, if it's still standing. You *do have* the wine, don't you? The god will take some host for himself, for the ceremony, but first one of you must thus ... formally *invite* him. You've got to awaken him, and bring him.' She peered in bewilderment out the side window at the shopping-center parking lot. 'Find a grove, wooded groves are still implicitly sacred to him – or a cemetery, a quiet cemetery with trees.' Softly, perhaps to herself, she added, 'I can remain rational through this final event, if it happens soon.' Then she looked around quizzically at the three people in the old truck with her. 'I don't know you people, but I presume you know each other. It should be obvious who is to take the drink.'

'I guess,' Pete said through clenched teeth as he gunned the engine and then clanked it into gear, 'we could draw straws—'

'It's me,' said Cochran, 'it's me.' His heart was pounding, but like Mrs. Winchester he somehow didn't seem able to find the prospect of cooperating with the god totally repellent. 'Dionysus led me by the hand into the wine cellar, so I guess I should be the one to lead him by the hand to the Sutro ruins. And I do have to finish giving somebody over to him; I know which cemetery. It's right on the way, just off the' – the monstrous, he thought, the merciless – 'the 280.' I might as well have taken the drink of forgetfulness when Mondard first offered it to me, he thought defeatedly, in the courtyard of the Hotel de l'Abbaye in Paris.

He remembered what Nina's ghost had told him, in the kitchen of their house two weeks ago, when he had said he wanted to have the mark removed from his hand: *I would never have – I would not have your child, if its father were not marked by* him. *I was married to him, through you.*

'It's me,' he repeated. But he remembered too the vision he'd had in the Solville hallway, of the Mondard in the mirror, and he remembered his apprehension then that the fatally loving god would next ask him to give over his memories of a deceased Plumtree. 'But he will take only one woman from me.'

'He'll welcome into his kingdom whomever you love,' flatly said the old woman out of Plumtree's lips, 'unless he so loves you that he welcomes you first.'

As Pete steered the truck away from the tall theater sign. Cochran noticed the titles of the movies that were showing in the three theaters: *Legends of the Fall*, *Murder in the First*, and *Little Women*.

Cochran's South Daly City house was just on the other side of the 280 from Colma, but the little town was in the area he always thought of as 'north of south and south of north' – when he was travelling to or from Pace Vineyards or San Francisco he used the John Daly Boulevard exit north of the town, and when he had business in Redwood City or San Jose he used the Serramonte Boulevard exit south of it; and so, though he knew the rest of the peninsula cities well, the peculiar little town that he could see across the highway lanes from his back yard was almost totally unfamiliar to him.

The last time he had visited the place had been two years ago, when he and Nina had driven straight across the highway to pick out adjoining plots at the Woodlawn Cemetery. And now Nina and their unborn baby had been cremated, and he had acceded to her parents' wishes and taken the urn to France, where it would stand forever on the mantle in their house in Queyrac in the Bas Medoc; and the grass grew undisturbed on the plot in Colma.

Colma was the town to which all the graves of San Francisco had been transplanted; until 1938, nearly a third of the Richmond district of San Francisco, from Golden Gate Park north to Geary and from Park Presidio east to Masonic Avenue, was still occupied by cemeteries, as the whole of the district had been before 1900. Colma, six miles to the south, had taken the evicted dead, and on the day Cochran and Nina had gone to buy the plots, Nina had remarked that the town's dead residents outnumbered the living ones seven hundred to one.

Cochran had Pete steer the truck off the 280 at Serramonte Boulevard, but had him turn east, away from his house, to El Camino Real; and as they drove up the weaving, rain-hazy road, past roadside 'monument' shops and misty rolling green hills studded with white grave markers, Cochran tried not to remember the sunny, gaily mock-morbid drive he and Nina had taken along this same road.

Following Cochran's directions, Pete turned left up the sloping driveway of Woodlawn and parked at the curb, in front of the grim stone tower that stood between the two stone arches opening onto the grounds. The four dishevelled travellers pushed open the truck doors and climbed out, and walked through the south arch and then trudged uphill along the gravel lane that led to the graves.

Cochran was carrying the bottle of *pagadebiti*, and in his pocket he now had Mavranos's bulky key ring with its attached Swiss Army knife. The tall palm trees and twisted cypresses that stood at measured intervals across the green hills gave him no clues as to what spot he and Nina had chosen on that long-ago sunny day, and the gray roads curved around with no evident pattern.

He had kept glancing at Plumtree during the drive up from San Jose, but the woman who had looked apprehensively back at him each time had clearly been Mrs. Winchester, blinking and shivering in the unfamiliar body in the big leather jacket; and so he was glad when Plumtree took his hand now and he looked at the face under the wet blond bangs and recognized Cody.

'I see by our outfits that it's the same day-o,' she said quietly, glancing back at Pete and Angelica; 'but what are we doing in a cemetery?'

'I—' he began; but she had gasped and squeezed his hand.

She was staring at the grassy area to their left, and he followed her gaze.

They were next to what he recalled now was the children's section of the cemetery, and on a pebble-studded slab of concrete on the grass stood eight painted plaster statues, one of them two feet tall and the others half that. They were the Disney-images of Snow White and the Seven Dwarves; and behind them, on a truncated section of decoratively carved and pierced marble, stood a verdigrised brass plaque on which he could make out the raised letters,

SUFFER LITTLE CHILDREN
TO COME UNTO ME

'"Suffer, little children,"' Plumtree read aloud, in a panicky voice. 'Sid, *who are we here to bury?*'

'My dead wife,' he told her hastily, knowing that she was thinking of Janis. 'Or not *bury*, so much as *disown*. Give to the god.' He waved the bottle of antique wine, idiotically wondering if he was stirring up sentiment in it. 'I've got to drink some of the *pagadebiti*, to summon Dionysus.'

Her hand had relaxed only a little in his. 'Oh, Sid, don't – your wife – I'll do it, I'll drink it.'

'You—' he said, then paused. *You would probably lose Valorie*, he thought; *and we might need her.* 'You don't have to,' he finished. 'I can do it – she's dead, and her ghost is gone, and – actually, my wife was, was more married

383

to the god than to me, even when she was alive.' Only after he'd begun speaking had he decided to tell her that, and he was remotely surprised now at how difficult it had been to say.

Cody bared her teeth and nodded. 'And we *might* need *her.*'

Cochran knew she meant Valorie, and he wondered if she had actually read his mind or simply knew him well enough to guess his thoughts.

'My wife and I bought a pair of plots,' Cochran said, loudly enough for Pete and Angelica to hear too; 'further uphill somewhere, across this road. That would be the place where I should drink it.'

On the lawn to their left, isolated stone angels and Corinthian pillars stood on pedestals above clustered ranks of upright black marble slabs with gold Chinese ideographs and inset color photo-portraits on their faces, while the lawns stretching away to the right were dotted with rows of flat markers like, thought Cochran, keys on a vast green keyboard. The gray weight of the spilling sky seemed to be held back by the brave yellow and red spots of flower bouquets around many of the headstones, and in the children's section behind them, silver helium balloons and brightly colored pinwheels had made an agitated confetti glitter against the carpet of wet grass.

They stepped up to the curb, over cement water-valve covers that looked at first glance like particularly humble little graves, and plodded out across the grass.

Far up the hill they came upon a scene almost of ruin. To the right, the grass had been stripped away from a broad area, leaving puddles and hillocks of mud around the stranded stone markers; an iron sign on a pole indicated that the grounds were being renovated for installation of a new sprinkler system and would be reseeded, and warned passersby that WOODLAWN WATERS ITS LAWNS WITH NONPOTABLE WELL WATER. And to the left, farther away across the grass, a gigantic oak tree had fallen over in the direction away from them, probably during the storms that had ravaged the California coast on New Year's Day; where the base of the tree had erupted out of the ground, the uplifted knotty face of dirt-caked roots was a monument taller than any of the carved marble ones, an abrupt black section of natural wall whose bent topmost crown-spikes stiffly clawed the sky far higher up than a man could reach. As he and Plumtree walked hand-in-hand around the fallen giant, he saw a thick carpet of fresh green grass still flourishing on the once-horizontal surface far overhead, as if in defiance of the piles of orange sawdust and the vertical saw-cuts visible farther along the trunk, evidences of toiling attempts to dispose of the gigantic thing.

And sheets of rain-darkened plywood had been laid across the grass to form a wheelbarrow's road toward an open freshly dug grave; the mound of mud beside the hole was the same orange color as the sawdust. For a moment Cochran thought the grave had been dug in one of the plots he and

Nina had bought, and he quailed at the thought of standing on the grass verge and staring down into the hole; then he noted the position of two nearby palm trees relative to the road and realized that his plots were on the far side of the open grave.

'Over here,' he said, stepping up onto the plywood walk and striding along it. Plumtree was beside him, and he could hear the drumming of Pete's and Angelica's footsteps behind.

Nina's ghost was gone, exorcised over a coffee cup full of tap water in his kitchen two weeks ago. Today he was going to relinquish whatever might be left of his love for her, of his possession of her.

I caught you in a wine cellar, he thought bewilderedly as cold water ran down his heated face, and now I'm going to drop you out of my heart, beside an open grave, with a swallow of wine. I really only interrupted your fall, didn't I – delayed your impact by four-and-something years.

And, he thought, fathered a companion for you to take with you. Was that death a part of your plan, of the god's plan? How can I be giving to the god someone I was never allowed to know?

He didn't know or care if tears were mingling with the rain water on his face.

'This will do,' he said harshly, stepping around a winch-equipped trailer with a big rectangular concrete grave-liner sitting on the bed of it. There were of course no markers to indicate which patches of grass were his plots, so he just stood on the grass with the open grave at his back and clasped the bottle under his arm as he pulled Mavranos's key ring out of his pocket and pried out the corkscrew attachment.

Rain thumped on his scalp and ran in streams from his bent elbows as he twisted the corkscrew right through the frail old lead foil on the bottle; and when the corkscrew was firmly embedded in the cork, he paused and looked at Plumtree.

'I don't want to love her anymore,' he said breathlessly; 'and I was never permitted to love the child.'

Plumtree might not have heard him over the thrash of the rain; at any rate she nodded.

He tugged at the red plastic knife handle, and with no audible pop the cork came out all in one piece in spite of its age.

Abruptly the wind sighed to a halt, and the last drops of rain whispered to the grass, and even the drops of water hanging from the cypress branches seemed to cling for an extra moment to the wet leaves so as not to fall and make a sound. In that sudden enormous silence Cochran would have tapped the knife handle against the glass of the bottle to see if his ears could still hear, except that he knew he was not deaf, and except that he didn't dare violate the holy stasis of the air.

He tipped the bottle up, and took a mouthful of the *pagadebiti*.

At first it seemed to be cool water, so balanced were the tannins and the acids, the fruit so subtle as to be indistinguishable from the smells of grass and fresh-turned earth in his nostrils. Then he swallowed it, and like an organ note rising from total silence, that starts as a subsonic vibration too low even to feel and mounts mercilessly to a brazen chorus in which the very earth seems to take part, bringing tears to the listener's eyes and standing the hairs up on his arms, the wine filled his head with the surge of the spring bud-break on the burgeoning vines, the bursting slaughter of ripe grapes in the autumn crush, the hot turbulent fermentation in the oaken casks as the soul of the god awoke in the crucible of fructose and malic acid and multiplying yeast. And Cochran was able to see as if from a high promontory the track of the god's endlessly repeated deaths and resurrections, through the betrayed vineyards of the Gironde and Loire valleys, back to sacred Falernum on the very slopes of slumbering Vesuvius, and the trellised vine gardens at Nebesheh and below the White Wall of Memphis on the Nile, eastward through Arabia, Media, Phrygia and Lydia, and the terraced temple vineyards on the ziggurats of the Babylonians and Sumerians, dimly all the way back to the primeval *vitis vinifera sylvestris* vines of lost Nysa in the mountains above Nineveh at the source of the Tigris River.

And then he was looking out through a crudely cut earthen doorway at the gray sky; no, he was lying on his back, and the ringing in his head and the jolt throughout his frame was from having fallen backward into the opened grave. The breath had been knocked out of him, and until his lungs began to heave and snatch at the cold air it seemed that his identity had been knocked out of him too.

Now three faces appeared around the edges of the grave, peering down at him; Plumtree was standing closest, leaning over, and he could see that she was holding the bottle of *pagadebiti*, apparently having taken it from him in the first transported moments.

'He's killed,' said Angelica.

'No, he's not,' said Plumtree angrily. 'Sid, get out of there.' The voices of both of them were oddly muffled and ringing, as if the women were embedded in crystal.

'I'm … not killed,' Cochran said. He rolled over and got to his hands and knees, and then, hitchingly, straightened all the way up to a standing posture, bracing his hands on the back-hoed clay walls; and the color of the exposed dirt darkened from orange clay toward black topsoil as he painfully hiked himself erect. 'Pete,' he said, trying to pitch his voice so that it would carry in the changed air, 'give me a hand.' He tossed the Swiss Army knife up onto the grass by Plumtree's feet.

Pete and Plumtree both leaned over so that he could grasp their wrists, while their free hands extended back to Angelica, who clasped them firmly and braced herself. With a heave from above, Cochran was able to walk up the side of the grave and take two balance-catching steps out across the grass.

I don't feel any different, he thought cautiously. I swear I don't. If the god's riding on me now, he's riding lightly.

Pete had bent to pick up Mavranos's knife, and now he twisted the cork off the corkscrew and held the cork out to Plumtree, who shoved it into the open mouth of the bottle as if hoping to stifle some shrill sound.

But in fact it was the *silence* that Cochran wished would stop. The plywood sheets thumped underfoot as he followed Plumtree and the Sullivans to the gravel road and hurried down it toward the distant front gate, but the sound of their footsteps seemed to agitate the air only very close by. No rain fell, and Cochran couldn't shake the notion that all the raindrops were hanging suspended under the clouds, like rocks in a Magritte painting.

As he reeled past the Snow White and the Seven Dwarves statues, Cochran was nervously ransacking his memory. He had forgotten something here today – he had known the wine would make him forget it. But what had it been? Then he remembered saying to Cody, *My dead wife*; and, *my wife was more married to the god than to me.* Apparently he had been married, and the wife was dead. He had to concentrate to keep the idea from sliding out of his mind, like thoughts that occur late at night in bed when the light has been turned out. I was, he thought – what? Somebody was more married to the god than to me. When was anybody ever married to me ...? Married to the god – to Dionysus? I must have been thinking of the woman in that strange version of *A Tale of Two Cities*, Ariachne. Something about a Dickens novel ...? I can't remember.

Finally he was just aware that he had forgotten something; but the awareness carried no anxiety. It didn't have the mental flavor of importance. If it was important he thought, I'll no doubt be reminded of it.

He remembered vividly the climb down the chimney in the Winchester House and the supernatural black man in the wine cellar, and Mrs. Winchester's occupation of Plumtree's body, and her insistence that they perform the resurrection soon, today, now.

Twice – once as they passed under the stone gate, and once as Pete pulled open the driver's-side door of the red truck – Cochran got the impression that Mrs. Winchester had come on; both times Plumtree gasped, and blinked around in a terror that was not Cody's, and then only a moment later recognizably *was* Cody, catching her balance and gripping the bottle and counting her companions.

They had all got into the truck and pulled the doors closed, but Pete was still fumbling with the key ring, when the engine roared to life. Pete stared at the empty ignition keyhole, then stared at Angelica beside him. With a shrug he put the key into the ignition anyway, and turned the switch into the on position.

Slowly he clanked it into reverse gear, and then tugged at the wheel as he backed out of the parking space; the truck wobbled obediently. 'I was afraid it was going to drive itself again,' he muttered, 'like it did when Arky got shot.'

'Don't speak,' choked Angelica. 'Get us – out of here.'

Pete steered the truck in a back-and-fill star pattern to drive back down to El Camino Real. A white car going north squealed to a halt and honked twice as Pete turned south, and then brake lights flared redly at the back of the shiny new white car in front of the truck.

'What are these white Saturns,' said Pete.

Cochran was already frightened – the wine he had drunk was making him dizzy, and he had the crazy impression that the action and speech around him were subtly happening at the wrong speed, as if somebody had filmed cars and actors moving and speaking too rapidly, and then projected it at a slowed-down speed to make it all appear normal – but with the gaps between the frames subliminally perceptible now – and Pete's remark about Saturns seemed to carry huge portent.

'There's another,' said Angelica, her finger repeatedly bumping the windshield as she pointed toward the oncoming lane; and though her voice was if anything shriller than normal, Cochran thought he could hear every click and release of her vocal cords.

'This flop is all face-down,' said Plumtree hoarsely – her voice too was muffled and fragmented, and even though he was sitting right beside her in the back seat Cochran could hardly make out her words—

Abruptly a harsh animal roaring shattered the stale air inside the truck, and the physical shock of it peeled Cochran's lips back from his teeth and jerked his right hand to the small of his back, where his revolver was holstered. Squinting against the stunning noise, Angelica fumbled the stuffed toy pig up from the front seat – and Cochran realized that the bestial clamor was coming from the pig. But, he thought in real, angry protest, it hasn't even got a battery in it!

In the center of the cavernous roaring, Angelica was frenziedly bashing the toy against the dashboard, to no apparent effect – the toy pig was smoking, and Cochran could see bright dots of tiny burning coals in its pink nylon fur—

Out one of the windows – in the confusion Cochran somehow couldn't tell if it was through one of the side windows or through the windshield – Cochran glimpsed a glittering golden vehicle, and in it a carved wooden mask; and an instant later he was deafened by a tremendous metallic crash, and the truck was halted, rocking violently as its passengers rebounded from seat-back and dashboard.

Cochran had wrenched open the door and reeled out onto the pavement, and the smoking pig bounced past him, rolling toward the gutter. The rain was coming down again like a battering avalanche, and the car behind the truck – a white Saturn – had stopped, and a portly white-haired man had opened the passenger-side door and stepped out.

Cochran waved at him. *'Cet ivrogne m'est rentre dedans!'* he shouted over the roar of the rain. He stopped speaking, wanting desperately to run to the side of the road and throw himself down on the wet grass; what he had just said was French, meaning, *This drunkard crashed into me.* 'Do you,' he shouted, listening to his own words to be sure he was speaking English, 'have a cellular—'

The man standing by the other car was staring at him, in obvious surprised recognition. Cochran cuffed rain water from his eyes and peered at the man … and with a sudden cold hollowness in his chest recognized Dr. Armentrout.

Someone was tugging at Cochran's sleeve, and shouting; he turned and saw that it was Cody, and that she didn't seem to be injured. 'The truck started again!' she was yelling. 'It's not hurt, nobody's hurt, we didn't even hit anything – get back in!'

She hadn't noticed Armentrout. Cochran nodded at her and put one foot up on the truck floor as she climbed back inside – but he saw Armentrout getting back into the Saturn.

The truck was shaking as Pete gunned the engine; it did seem to be capable of driving.

But so was the Saturn. And all Cochran could remember now was Armentrout saying to him three weeks ago, *I will heal you, Sid. That's a promise.* Still perceiving all the motions and sounds as discrete fragments, Cochran fumbled under the back of his sopping windbreaker and pulled out his muddy revolver; and he aimed it at the white hood of the Saturn, between and just behind the headlights, and pulled the trigger.

The flare was dazzling, but the noise of the gunshot was just a thud against his abused eardrums. He fired again, and then Plumtree had leaned out of the truck and closed her fist in the fabric of his shirt. The truck was moving, slowly. Cochran flailingly pulled the trigger again, and one of the Saturn's headlights exploded; and then he threw the gun onto the truck floor and lunged inside.

Pete must have floored the accelerator then, for Cochran was tumbled into the seat half across Plumtree's lap, and the door slammed shut without his help. The interior of the truck was dark in the renewed rainstorm.

'—*the fuck were you doing*—!' Pete was shouting, and Cochran yelled back, overriding him, '*It was Dr. Armentrout.*' In the instant of silence this news caused, Cochran sat up and added, 'In that car. He would have followed us. He shot Kootie, remember?'

The roar of the engine rose and fell as Pete swerved from lane to lane to pass slower-moving cars. He had switched on the headlights, and the road ahead was only dimly visible behind a glittering curtain of rain.

'Good,' panted Angelica, 'that was good, you were right to shoot him.' She was glancing around wildly, wide-eyed. 'What the fuck *hit* us, Pete? How can the truck be running? We should be—'

'The god hit you,' said Mrs. Winchester from the shadows beside Cochran, in a quavering voice that seemed to carry a trace of satisfaction, 'a good deal less hard than he hit my house in 1906.'

'I didn't shoot *him*,' said Cochran loudly, 'I shot the *car*, the *radiator*.'

'We've got to cross the 280 and pick up Kootie and Arky,' said Pete.

'No,' said Angelica, 'there were other white Saturns driving around back there, and Armentrout's still fucking alive. We might lead them to Kootie – and this truck's a beacon, magically and plain-old visually. And turn off your headlights.'

'These are sorcerous bad guys, Angie,' said Pete, nevertheless reaching forward to switch off the lights. 'What do you think they were *doing* down here? Following *us*? I bet they were tracking the new king, which is Kootie. They might be zeroing in on Cochran's house right now.'

'Ah, you're right, you're right,' said Angelica desperately. 'Get on the freeway, get right over in the fast lane to draw any pursuit, and then cut off hard at the first off-ramp, hard enough to send 'em on past it, if they are following us. We'll call Kootie from a pay phone.'

'It's getting late, you must let this *Kootie* person fend for himself,' said Mrs. Winchester's voice. 'I *heard* that!' added Cody; 'they'd surely kill the boy, and anyway we need his help, and Arky's, to get this thing done.' And then Valorie's flat voice said, 'O, what form of prayer can serve my turn? "Forgive me my foul murder."'

'A pay phone at a gas station,' said Pete, his wet shoe sole squeaking from the gas pedal to the brake and back. 'We're gonna need gas.'

Pete followed Angelica's directions so exactly that Cochran thought they were all going to be killed. From the fast far left-hand lane of the northbound 280, while a scatter of anonymous headlight-pairs bobbed behind them at hard-to-judge distances, Pete cut the wheel sharply to the right, and the truck veered across the shiny black lanes like a banking surfboard, booming over the lane-divider dots in brief staccato bursts, finally half-missing the exit and throwing Cochran onto Plumtree again as the two left wheels slewed on the shoulder.

Then he had straightened the wheel, braked down to about twenty miles per hour without quite making the tires squeal, and pulled sedately into a Chevron gas station, steering the truck around to the back by the rest rooms and pay phones. The headlights were still switched off.

He pushed the gearshift lever over into neutral. 'No—' he began, but his voice was squeaky; 'nobody's followed us here,' he said in a deeper tone.

'Guess not,' said Angelica faintly. Then she stirred herself and pushed open the door. 'Let's call ...'

She froze with one leg extended out into the rain, and Cochran followed the direction of her gaze to the cone of light around the pay telephone.

At first glance he thought the light was full of moths; then he saw that the fluttering streaks of light were rain-gleams on transparent figures: the streak of a contorted jawline here, the squiggle of a flexed limb there, invisible wet lips working in imbecilic grimaces.

'Something's got all the ghosts worked up this evening,' Angelica said. 'They're drawn by the magnets in the phone, or they each want to call somebody and haven't got any quarters.' She gave Pete a stricken look over her shoulder. 'I'm not masked enough for this. Breathing, *talking on the phone*, in that stew? My voice – and Arky might say, my name! I couldn't hide my – my psychic locators, my name, my birthday – from all of them. At least a couple of them would be into my head like piranhas in five seconds.'

'"These same thoughts people this little world,"' said Mrs. Winchester confidently out of Plumtree's mouth; to which Cody added, 'All us kids on the bus got bogus birth-dates and somebody else's picture on our IDs,' and the flat voice of Valorie said, 'I shall play it in a mask, and you may speak as small as you will.'

'Oh, thank you—!' said Angelica to Plumtree, clearly at a loss as to what name to use. 'Give her a quarter, Pete,' she added as Cochran opened the truck's back door and stepped down into the rain. 'Speak this: tell Kootie and Arky to get out of there,' she told Plumtree urgently. 'Tell 'em don't take the Granada, we were driving that when I shot at the bikers out at the yacht club, they might remember it. Tell 'em to take the old Torino out back.'

'And bad guys might be out in front of the house, nervous about our guns and waiting for reinforcements,' added Pete. 'Tell Arky to drive right out *through* the greenhouse, like Cochran said this morning – there's apparently a mud road that leads down the backyard slope right to the 280.'

Cochran could see that Plumtree had to do this, but after she had stepped wearily down out of the truck he grabbed her unbandaged hand and said, 'Would it help to have another person beside you? I can concentrate on *you*, and not pay attention to the ghosts.'

The tired lines in her face lifted in a wan smile. 'I'd like that, Sid. Yeah, you'll be safe enough if you just don't speak a word, and look nowhere but at me.'

'That's my plan.' He was nervously pleased to be speaking coherently, after having drunk the *pagadebiti*; and he was reminded of a time an unidentified snake had bitten him on a hike, and how he had monitored himself for the rest of the day, watching for slurred speech or numbness or any other symptoms of poisoning.

Plumtree took a quarter from Pete, and then she and Cochran walked hand-in-hand across the pavement to the cone of rain-streaked and ghost-curdled light around the telephone.

The ghosts were whispering and giggling in Cochran's ears, and though he tried not to listen he heard faint, buzzing sexual propositions, pleas for rides to other states, demands for money, offers to wash his car windows for a dollar.

Cochran kept his eyes on Plumtree. Her face was shifting in response to it all, like a fencer parrying in different lines, and once Cochran got a broad wink that he thought must have been from Tiffany. She reached through the contorting forms as if through cobwebs to drop the quarter into the slot, and punched his home number into the keypad as if emphasizing points by poking someone repeatedly in the chest.

After a few moments she tensed and said, 'Hi. It's me, the girl-of-a-thousand-faces. Use the old king's eye as a scrambler to call me back at this number.' And she read off the number of the pay phone and hung up the receiver.

'Good thinking,' said Cochran through slitted lips.

'Don't talk! – they could get down your throat. They do but jest, poison in their jest; no offense i' the world.'

At last the telephone rang, and Plumtree snatched up the receiver. 'Hello? *Hello?*' She took the receiver from her ear and knocked it against the aluminum cowl around the phone. 'I'm deaf!' she said loudly. Into the phone she said, 'Kootie, Arky, I hope you can hear me. I'm deaf, so just listen!' Her voice softened. 'Arky, you've got the cutest butt. *Out!*' Cody yelled, apparently at Tiffany. 'Listen, you've both got to get *out* of there, right now – take the—'

She looked at Cochran in panic, and he knew that it had just occurred to her that *Janis was listening*, and could relay their plans to Omar Salvoy, in her mental Snow White cottage. 'The way Sid told Arky this morning, *exactly* that way, are you following me?'

She flipped the receiver around in her hand and bit the earpiece – and Cochran realized that she was hearing by bone conduction. She fumbled the receiver back to her ear. 'Good, don't say anything more, we're being overheard here in spite of your scrambler, it's enough that I know I'm not just talking to somebody who likes calling pay phones. Listen, we're going, *right now*, to – to George Washington's head.'

Cochran nodded. Janis hadn't been on when they had hiked through the tunnel at the Sutro Bath ruins and seen the boulder that he had said looked like Washington; and Cody wasn't saying that this was *the big event*, happening today instead of tomorrow as they had all expected. Janis could relate all of this to her father without his knowing where Kootie and Mavranos would be going.

'Tell me you understand,' Cody said, and again bit the receiver. Then she said into the mouthpiece, 'Good. Oh, and Kootie better bring that ... that little yellow blanket that the bald lady gave him, if he's still got it.' She sighed. 'Go,' she added, and she hung up the chewed and spitty receiver. Cochran faintly heard one of the ghosts say that the telephone was for calling room service to order food, that one didn't eat the telephone.

Plumtree took Cochran's elbow and led him out of the swarm of idiot ghosts, and neither of them inhaled until they had got back to the truck.

'That was Kootie,' Plumtree panted, 'and then Arky. They understood, and I didn't hear either of 'em say anything that would clue anybody. They'll meet us there.' She looked nervously at Cochran. 'I can hear the rain, now, but I don't know about voices. You say something.'

He smiled at her. '*Vous etes tres magnifique*,' he said, and he was sure that it had been his own deliberate decision to speak in French.

She laughed tiredly. 'Thank you very kindly, sir, now I hear you clearly.'

'Back in the truck' said Pete, 'everybody don't want Kootie to get there before we do. Sid, you got a ten for gas?'

CHAPTER THIRTY ONE

> Yes. Like the mariner in the old story, the winds and streams had driven him within the influence of the Loadstone Rock, and it was drawing him to itself, and he must go.
>
> —Charles Dickens, *A Tale of Two Cities*

The secret switchboards of the city logged dozens of calls in the ordinarily slow witchery-and-wonders categories, as reports of supernatural happenings were phoned in from Daly City south of town up to the Sunset area around Ocean Beach and the Richmond district north of Golden Gate Park – accounts of brake-drums singing in human voices, root beers and colas turning into red wine in the cans, and voices of dead people intruding on radio receptions in unwelcome, clumsy karaoke. In Chinatown, under the street-spanning banners and the red-neon-bordered balconies and the white-underlit pagoda roofs, hundreds of nests of firecrackers were set hopping on the puddled sidewalks, clattering like machine-gun fire and throwing clouds of smoke through the rain, and the lean young men noisily celebrating the new year frequently paused below the murals of dragons and stylized clouds to listen to the storefront radio speakers, out of which echoed an Asian woman's voice predicting earthquakes and inversions and a sudden high-pressure area locally.

Old Volkswagens and Chevrolets and Fords, painted gold and hung with wreaths at the front and back bumpers, roared with horns honking north through the hospital glare of the Stockton tunnel, to emerge in Chinatown at Sacramento Street still honking, the passengers firing handguns out the windows into the low sky. Police and paramedics' sirens added to the din, and under the gunpowder banging and the electric howls was the constant hiss of the night rain, and the unending echoing rattle of the cables snaking at their steady nine-miles-an-hour through the street-pavement slots.

On the Bay Bridge, from remote Danville in the hills over on the east side of the bay, three white Saturns passed over the Coast Guard Reservation on Yerba Buena Island on their way in to the China Basin area of the Soma district; and two more were moving west up Ocean Avenue toward the Great Highway and Ocean Beach.

Dr. Armentrout had had to insist, almost tearfully, that the driver of the lead car get off the 280 at Ocean instead of continuing toward Chinatown.

Armentrout was sitting in the back beside Long John Beach and the two-figure mannikin appliance, but the Lever Blank man in the front passenger seat shifted and said, 'It's the pomegranate.' He turned around. 'What does it do, point?' When Armentrout just gripped the dry gourd and stared belligerently, the man added, 'We won't take it from you, if you tell us where we can get another one.'

'I picked it from a bush in the meadow where Scott Crane was killed,' Armentrout muttered finally, 'at his compound in Leucadia.' He held the thing up and shook it, and dry seeds rattled inside. 'In daylight, even such daylight as you get up here, its shadow is perceptibly displaced toward the king, which is the Koot Hoomie boy, I think. I've been – *shadowing* him.' He choked back a frightened giggle, and sniffed; he was still shaking, and his shirt was more clammy from sweat than from rain. 'And,' he added, 'tonight it ... even *tugs* a little.' He nodded toward the windshield. 'That way.'

Armentrout had hysterically demanded that the two-figure mannikin appliance be brought along in this car too, and now it was sitting ludicrously in Long John Beach's lap beside him. Armentrout wondered if Long John Beach too found the two figures *heavier* lately than they used to be.

'The royal tree,' said Long John Beach from behind the two Styrofoam heads, in what Armentrout had come to think of as the Valerie-voice, 'hath left us royal fruit.'

'It led us to the red truck,' said the driver, 'back there in Colma where we had to switch cars. Was the boy in the truck?'

'I don't know,' said Armentrout. 'I don't think so.' *Sid Cochran and Janis Plumtree* were in the truck, he thought. And Sid Cochran, who I heedlessly let slip through my net back at Rosecrans Medical, shot a *gun* at me! 'I think they were all staying somewhere in the area, and we just ran across the truck before we found the boy. But they must have gone to him after they evaded you people, or else they called him.' He shook the pomegranate, again, and felt its inertial northward pull. 'The primary is certainly northwest of us now. I can't imagine why Salvoy didn't *call* me – we could have been waiting for the boy right now, at whatever place they're going to, instead of just chasing him this way.'

The radio on the dashboard clicked, and then an amplified voice said, 'I thought we were going to where the Macondray chapel used to be.'

The driver unhooked a microphone from the console. 'The—' He smiled at Armentrout in the rear-view mirror. '—*dousing rod* is apparently indicating the west coast,' he said. 'Tell the brothers coming in from Danville not to waste time circling the Washington and Stockton site. Straight west on Turk to Balboa, tell them, and link up with us probably somewhere below the Cliff House.'

'Aye aye,' said the man in the following car, and clicked off; and Armentrout thought *eye-eye,* and remembered the tiny pupils of Plumtree's eyes.

'The woman who pulled ... the gunman back into the truck,' Armentrout said, 'was Janis Plumtree, the one with your man Salvoy in her head. I'd like to ... *have* her, after Salvoy has moved on.' Moved on to his eternal reward, ideally, he thought.

'Everybody except the king has got to be retired, sorry,' said the man in the front passenger seat. 'But we do have to wait until we figure out who the king *is,* and what body he's in.' He reached out and unhooked the microphone. 'Andre,' he said, 'tell the field men not to go shooting anybody until the subjects are out of the vehicles, and even then no women or boys. Got it?'

The driver was shaking his head. 'Crisis of faith!' he said quietly.

'Nix,' came the voice from the radio. 'The field men understand that the true king can't be hit with a casual bullet.'

'But he might not be in his chosen body yet!' protested the man in the front seat. 'You can tell 'em that, can't you? It's nothing but the truth.'

'Better we don't introduce the complication,' insisted the voice from the radio, 'and hope for the best.'

The man replaced the microphone and fogged the window with a sigh. '*Field men*,' he said. 'Manson-family rejects.'

'Knuckleheads, panheads, and shovelheads,' agreed the driver. 'Look, the Koot Hoomie body *is* the *king*, and it'll deflect bullets. All we stand to lose is old Salvoy in the Plumtree, and that might not be altogether a bad thing.'

Armentrout touched the little lump in his jacket pocket that was the derringer. No casual bullet, he thought. But nothing fired from this gun is casual, and I've got a couple of very serious .410 shot-shells in it. That's the way this has got to work out – these Lever Blank boys kill the Plumtree body and everybody in it, and I kill the Parganas boy.

And then stay well clear of the zealot field men.

On the long straight stretch of the Great Highway with the black-iron sea to the west, a relayed spot of darkness moved up the coast as each of the sodium-vapor streetlights went out for a moment when the red truck sped past on the pavement below.

Pete Sullivan was driving, and beside him Angelica was irritably drying off the .45 carbine with a handful of paper towels. The knapsack with the spare magazines had been under the seat too, and was also soaked by the rain water that had puddled on the floorboards.

She laid the gun down on the seat, then snapped open the glove compartment; and when she shifted around to look back at Cochran and Plumtree, she was holding the *pagadebiti* in her hands. 'I never brought the ... the hardware into your house,' she said to Cochran. 'I think the Wild Turkey bottle that had Crane's blood in it is behind you, in the hub of Arky's spare tire.'

Cochran winced, for he'd been able to feel Plumtree shivering beside him, even through the soaked leather jacket she was wearing, ever since they'd stopped to call Mavranos and Kootie, and this reminder of the stressful failure two weeks ago wasn't likely to cheer her up. But he rocked his head back to peer into the truck bed. 'Voila,' he said. 'Still there,' he added shortly.

He had been mentally reciting the multiplication tables to monitor his own alertness, and now he had forgotten his place.

'Here,' said Angelica, handing the wine bottle over the back of the front seat 'Pour some of this *pagadebiti* wine into it, and swish it around and then pour it back.' When he just stared at her, she added, 'I say that in my capacity as the king's ad hoc *bruja primera*.'

Cochran took it from her. '*O-kay*.' He hiked one knee up onto the seat to be able to reach back with his free hand to the Wild Turkey bottle. Sitting back down again, he gripped the wine bottle and the pint bourbon bottle between his thighs, and pulled the corks out.

'When I close my eyes,' said Plumtree in a voice that was shaky but recognizably Cody, 'I'm in a bus seat, and the crazy smashed-up man is standing at the front and holding a gun on the driver. *Row, row, row your boat.*'

Cochran carefully lifted the wine bottle and tilted it over the pint bottle and poured a good four ounces of dark wine into it. He re-corked the little bottle and shook it up, then uncorked it and poured its foaming contents back into the bottle of *pagadebiti*.

'*So* far,' said Angelica to Plumtree judiciously, 'you're better off keeping your eyes open, then. But, any time now, that vision might be preferable to what's actually going on outside your eyelids.'

'Oh, *that's* helpful,' snapped Cochran as he shoved the corks back into the bottles and reached around to drop the Wild Turkey bottle onto the wet truck-bed floor behind his seat. He wiped his hands on his damp jeans, glad that he had taken his own sip of the wine before this adulteration.

The truck was moving up a grade now, and angling to the left. Cochran peered out through the rain-streaked window and saw concrete barriers on the right shoulder, with yellow earth-moving machines and black cliffs beyond it.

'Cliff House coming up on the left,' said Pete. 'I'll go on past and park in the Sutro Heights lot, up the hill. Rainy walk back down, but I guess we can't get any wetter than we are.'

'Sorry,' Angelica told Cochran. Then she said brightly to Plumtree, 'Of course nothing bad will happen to any of us. As soon as we're done with this, we could all take Scott Crane to dinner at the Cliff House Restaurant, even.' She snapped her fingers. 'Oh, except that we're drenched in black mud!'

Plumtree gave a hitching laugh. 'And Crane'll p-probably be wearing that garlic banner again,' she said. 'And some restaurants,' she added quietly, 'don't like you bringing your own wine.'

Pete turned in to the Sutro Heights Park driveway, and drove slowly up the hill with the headlights off and parked the truck against a dark grassy bank with overhanging elms. The nearest parking lot light dimmed but didn't go out – and Cochran was glad of it as he climbed out of the truck carrying the wine bottle, for the overcast sky was already winter-night-time dark. There were many other cars in the lot, and they all seemed to have wreaths hung on them, but Cochran didn't see any other people.

The wind sweeping up the cliffs from the sea was cold, and his wet clothing was no protection at all. He was glad that Plumtree at least had the leather jacket.

Angelica had stepped out onto the wet pavement, but now she leaned back in and tore the woven blue seat cover off the front seat, yanking on it to break the strings that tied it to the struts, and when she had dragged it out and shaken dust and cigarette butts out of it she wrapped up her short rifle in it; the stock was folded forward, and the bundle was no more than a yard long, with the ends flapping loose over the pistol grip. She laid it on the truck hood while she shouldered on the sopping knapsack.

'You've got what, three rounds left?' she asked Cochran as she picked up the bundled rifle.

Taking the question as a fresh test of his mental acuity, Cochran called up the details of his shooting at the Saturn. 'That's right,' he told her firmly.

'I've got seventy rounds of mixed hardball and hollowpoint, but the magazines have been sitting in greasy water for a couple of days. Oh well – I've heard .45s will even fire underwater.'

'I hope the *omiero* hasn't washed off of the hollow-points,' said Pete as he slammed the door on his side and walked around the back of the truck.

'I imagine the ghosts will all be gone, at least,' said Plumtree, 'after what's-his-name shows up, old Dickweed McStump.'

'What?' said Angelica. 'Who?'

'This famous Greek god. What's his name?'

'*Dionysus*,' said Cochran with an apprehensive glance at the bottle in his left hand. 'This isn't the night to be dissing him, Cody.'

'*Whatever*,' said Plumtree. 'It sounds like he takes ghosts away with him. The big trick,' she added, 'will be seeing to it that he doesn't wind up taking any of *us* along in that cnrwd.'

'Well, *that's* cleared it up,' said Cochran. 'You've put your finger on it, all right.'

'I'll put my finger in your *eye*, if you don't shut up,' she told him; but she linked her shivering arm through his as they began trudging down the park driveway Cochran was holding the *pagadebiti* bottle with both hands.

When they got to Point Lobos Avenue, they had to walk south along the shoulder for a couple of hundred feet, and almost didn't dare to cross at all, for cars with no headlights on were hurling their dark bulks around the corners from north and south, so fast that the tires yiped, and their passengers were leaning out of the windows and firing guns into the air as they swooped past. But finally there was a quiet gap, and Cochran and his companions sprinted wildly across the lanes and sprang over the far curb onto the sidewalk.

Leaning on the wet iron railing on the seaward side of the highway, they could see through the marching curtains of rain, patches of bright flame on the dark plain below them. Dots of yellow fire that must have been torches bobbed and whirled on the line between the vast rectangular pool of water and the open sea beyond, and Cochran realized that people must be out dancing along that narrow concrete wall. And even way up here on the highway ridge he could hear distant drumming over the roar of the rain.

'Damballa!' said Plumtree huskily; then, 'The sounds of hammering and sawing must not cease.'

'It's good, the drumming's good,' agreed Angelica nervously.

'Scott Crane is down there somewhere,' whispered Plumtree. 'Tonight I'll face *him*, not his ghost.'

The statement seemed to click a switch in her head, and at long last Valorie had no choice but to remember New Year's Day. After dawn, first:

Trucks and cars on the road behind the gas-station telephone booth had been drumming their tires over a step in the asphalt, and Plumtree had had to hold her free hand over her ear to hear the 911 operator. 'You killed him with a speargun?' the voice said.

'No,' said Plumtree in a harsh voice. Cody hod been the one who had taken this flop, this early-morning telephone call, and an emotion had been interfering with her speech. 'A spear from one. I stabbed him in the throat. He was stabbed with it before, in 1990?'

'You stabbed him in 1990?'

'No, this morning, an hour ago.'

'He was known as ... the Flying Nun?'

'I don't know. That's how I was thinking of him.'

Valorie had been aware of Cody's guess that the 911 operator was just keeping her talking, keeping her on the line ...

And a police car had soon come chirruping up behind her, and policemen with drawn guns had shouted at her: 'Drop the phone! Let us see your hands!' One had wanted to shoot her; then he'd wanted to mace her. 'Take it easy.' another had said, 'She's just a ding.'

They had handcuffed her with her hands in front. 'Let's go. Show us where you killed him.'

But when they had driven her to the slanting meadow above the beach, and got out of the car, the field was silvery bright with fresh vines and grasses and fruit; and since there had been only the cries of wild parrots in the meadow on that morning, Valorie's memory now had to make the birdcalls loud and harsh and poundingly rhythmic.

The policemen said it was obvious that no one had stepped across the grass in the last day, and so they had marched her back into the car, and driven here to the jail and put her into a cell with mattresses looped over the white-painted steel bars and steady clanging from one of the other cells. Lunch had been hot dogs and sauerkraut, and when they had offered to let her make a call, Cody had declined, but asked if she could have the twenty cents anyway, or a cigarette.

*

And then, finally, Valorie let herself remember the actual dawn:

In her father's voice, Plumtree's body had called to the bearded man who had stepped barefoot into the meadow: 'Get over here, Sonny Boy.'

But when the man had walked closer, her father had abruptly receded, and it had been Cody who found herself standing over the little boy who was lying on his back on the dirt. Plumtree was holding the spear with the points at the little boy's throat.

She looked up at the tall bearded king, and her vision was blurry with tears as she said, 'There's nothing in this flop for me.'

'Then pass,' said the king in a quiet voice. 'Let it pass by us.' After a moment he nodded at her, almost smiling, and said, 'In the midsummer of this year, you and I will be standing in happy sunlight on the hill in the lake.'

'I don't think so,' said the reintruded father, breathing in a choked way while the little boy shivered at his feet, 'I'll call – I called you this morning! – and I raise you the kid.' Plumtree's eyes darted down to the pale child under the spearpoints. 'That's a raise you don't dare call, right?' Tight laughter shook Plumtree's throat. 'This flop . . . finally! . . . gives me a king-high flush in spades. It's the first day of the new year, and you've got to face the Death card – the suicide king.'

The bearded man stepped back. 'I've – seen you before,' he said. 'Where?'

'I'm – I'm putting the clock on you, here, no more time – and I won't give you any psychic locators on me—'

'You're shaking,' said the living king. 'Throw the spear away. Don't tell me anything, I'll let you take back your bet.'

'You think I'm afraid of you? Now? It was in a poker game on Lake Mead, almost five years ago. You were disguised as a woman, and the other players called you "the Flying Nun."'

The king was frowning. 'And you failed then, didn't you? You failed to assume the hand, assume the Flamingo, take the throne. You'll fail this time, too, I swear to you, even if you ruin everyone in trying. You flinched away just now, when I approached you. Let it pass.' He raised one hand toward the road. 'Go away now, in peace.'

'Lest you dash your foot against a stone. Don't patronize me, you, you kings.' Plumtree's hands gripped the spear shaft more tightly. 'Do you call?'

Through clenched teeth, the king said, 'No, I do not.'

'Then step closer,' hissed the father in Plumtree. And when the king had walked up beside them, her father said, 'See you in the funny papers,' and snatched the spear away from the child and drove it into the king's throat.

Plumtree let go of the iron railing as if it might collapse, and clung to Cochran's arm so tightly that he nearly dropped the bottle. Cochran thought it must have been Janis, or even Tiffany, but the sharp profile was clearly Cody, and she was staring down at the fires on the plain.

'What?' he snapped, his knees shaking at the thought of dropping the *pagadehiti* now.

'Nothing,' she said, shaking her head. 'Just remembering why I'm here. Let's get it over with.'

Angelica seemed to agree. 'Let's get down there before Kootie does,' she said.

They found the gate in the chain-link fence and started down the path that led between high dark hedges and ivy-covered mounds, and after the first few steps Cochran felt as if they had left the highway and all of San Francisco, even the twentieth century, far behind. The night wind in the bending cypresses, the monotonous distant drumming weaving in and out of the boom of the surf, the bonfires and waving torches, and the smells of ocean and wet leaves on the cold wind, all made him think of some pre-Christian Mediterranean island, with mad, half-human gods demanding worship and sacrifice.

He was looking to the left, out across the broad dark slope of the basin, when the whole quarter-mile from the Cliff House to remote Point Lobos was lit in glaring white, halting raindrops as shotgun patterns of dark stippling against the marble undersides of the clouds; and when the instant explosion of thunder threw the raindrops against his face and extinguished the light, he carried on his retinas a vision of the slope as a ruined amphitheater, the collapsed walls and sagging foundations undisguised beneath the froth of wild vegetation.

By the yellow glitter of flame reflected in the lake-like puddles, he could see that the path levelled and broadened out ahead of them, and he could make out the low stone building in which he and Plumtree had first met up with Mavranos and Kootie again after fleeing Solvilie. The uneven windows and the top of the roofless wall were silhouetted by fires on the sand floor within, and he could see apparently naked figures dancing on the wall rim.

Half a dozen torch flames were bobbing toward Cochran and his party now across the mud-flats, and he reached around with his right hand to touch the grip of his revolver as he squinted at the approaching forms.

He was able to see that they were people by the bronze glare of the torches many of them were waving, but their bodies and staring-eyed faces were plastered with wet pale mud, so that they seemed to be figures of animated earth, naked and sexless. There were more of them than there were torches, and many carried fist-sized stones. Two or three even had pistols.

Angelica had raised her seat-cover bundle, and Cochran drew his revolver and held it out away from him, pointed at the ground for now. His ears were ringing and his breath was short with the thought of raising the gun, of firing it at these people.

He opened his mouth to speak, but the mud-figures had halted a dozen feet away; and now the torches dipped as they all got down on their bare knees in the mud.

A hot wave of relief rippled up from Cochran's abdomen – but when he glanced at his right hand he saw that it wasn't the gun, or even the bottle of wine in his left hand, that had cowed them.

The night seemed suddenly less dark – variations of grays – in contrast to the ivy-leaf mark on the back of his right hand; it shone with such an intense, absolute blackness that his first, spinal impulse was to somehow instantly cut it off.

Far out in the rainy basin, out among the ruined buildings and crumbled pool copings and the ledge where the tunnel mouth gaped against the fire-light, the drumming became louder, and faster.

'We knew you'd come,' called one of the figures hoarsely.

'From Phrygia,' wailed one of them in a woman's voice, 'from Lydia, from *India!*'

To his horror, Cochran's right hand twitched and clenched and *raised*; he was able to push it up still further in the instant before it fired the gun, so that the bullet flew away over the top crags of Point Lobos, but the sound and flash of the shot were lost in another simultaneous blast of white light and ground-jolting thunder, and as the echoes rolled away to shake the trees on the slopes he hastily fumbled the gun back into its holster.

The mud-people might not even have been aware of the gunshot; or they might have *expected* their god to greet his worshippers by trying to murder one of them out of sheer love; they bowed their heads, and began doing a fast, counterpoint hand-clapping that jangled Cochran's thoughts the way drumming was supposed to confuse ghosts.

'And here is your king!' shouted one of the sexless clay people, pointing behind Cochran and his companions.

Cochran turned, half expecting to see Scott Crane restored already – but what he saw through the driving rain was a tall figure and a shorter one reel-ing down the path from the highway; they were hardly a dozen yards away, and after a moment he recognized Mavranos and Kootie.

The recognition was soon mutual: Kootie's eyes widened and he hurried forward toward Pete and Angelica, and Mavranos trudged up and called, with forced and haggard panache, 'What *seeems* to be the problem?'

'What's going on?' yelled Kootie over the noise of the storm. 'We drove the car right through the greenhouse in low gear, right over Scott Crane's skeleton!'

'This is it,' Plumtree told him shrilly. 'We picked up Scott Crane's ghost hitch-hiking, and he led us to the devil's wine!' The boy had stumbled closer across the splashing mud now, and she was able to speak in an almost conversational tone when she added, 'And we picked up the other old lady ghost, too.' She tapped the side of her head. 'It looks like we're doing it right this time!'

Kootie and Mavranos were bundled up in raincoats, and Mavranos was wearing his Greek fisherman's cap while Kootie had on an old felt fedora of Cochran's.

'But Chinese New Year isn't until tomorrow!' protested Mavranos, staring at the blackly blazing mark on Cochran's right hand. 'Not until midnight, at the soonest! They can't just change it this way! I haven't had time to think—'

'Midnight?' said Pete. 'Is that standard time or daylight savings?' He waved at the rain-swept dark sky. 'This day is over.'

Kootie was blinking at the bottle of wine in Cochran's left hand. 'Yeah,' he said bleakly, 'the sun's down. I guess there's debts you don't carry into the new year.'

Mavranos scowled around at the kneeling clay people in the guttering torchlight. 'Are you people *volunteers*?' Mavranos roared at them, and Cochran thought there was a note of desperate hope in the man's voice. 'Do you *mean* to put yourselves in the way of what's happening here?'

'We're here of our own will, which is the god's will,' called one of the figures.

Mavranos nodded, though he was still frowning and squinting as if against the glare of the vanished lightning. 'If this cup may pass away,' he muttered. Then, more loudly, he said, 'Let's get to the cave.'

Plumtree took Cochran's right hand, and the two of them set off across the marshy plain, with the others following; the mud-people did appear to be allies, but when Cochran glanced back he saw that Angelica with her bundle of soaked fabric, and Mavranos with his hand in the pocket of his raincoat, were hanging back a few paces to watch the roofless building and the landward slopes and the path behind.

Cochran was suddenly, viscerally sure that not all of the king's company would survive this night; and he was still dizzy from his mouthful of the forgiveness wine, and wondering what memories and loves it had taken from him and if it might soon take more.

'This is like in a chess game,' he said to Plumtree through clenched teeth, 'when all the castles and bishops and knights are focussed on one square, and there's like a *pause*, before they all start charging in and knocking each other off the board.' He walked faster, pulling her along the slope up toward the cave mouth, so that several yards of thrashing rain separated them from Pete and Kootie.

'I don't care what—' he said to her, 'well, I do, I care a lot – but *whatever* you think, whatever your feelings are, I've got to tell you—' He shook his head bewilderedly. 'I love you, Cody.'

She would have stopped, but he pulled her on.

'*Me?*' she said, hurrying along now. 'I'm not worth it, Sid! Even if I love you—'

He glanced at her sharply. 'Do you?' he asked, leaning his head toward hers to be heard, for his heart was thudding in his chest and he couldn't make himself speak loudly. '*Do* you love me?'

She laughed, but it was a warm, anxious laugh. 'How do I love thee?' she said. With her free hand she pulled her soggy waitress pad out of her jeans pocket. 'Let me read the minutes.'

From far away behind them, somewhere on the overgrown terrace paths above this plain but below the highway, came two hard pops that were louder than the drumming; and Cochran was still wondering if they had been gunshots when several more echoing knocks shivered the rain, and then the dark basin behind them was a hammering din of gunfire.

He looked back, crouching and stepping in front of Plumtree. Mavranos had his revolver out as he backed fast across the mud, and Angelica had thrown away the bundle of cloth and was holding the pistol-grip .45 carbine in both hands. Cochran could see winking flashes now on the distant ruined buildings and along the seawall; most of the shooters seemed to be firing into the air, and perhaps this whole barrage was just a live-ammunition variation on the Chinatown firecrackers.

But Cochran drew his own revolver again, hollowly reflecting that he now had only two rounds left in the cylinder.

'I'm still here,' said Cody wonderingly as the two of them scrambled on up the muddy slope. '*Gunfire*, a *lot* of it, and I haven't passed the hand.'

CHAPTER THIRTY TWO

> False eyebrows and false moustaches were stuck upon them, and their hideous countenances were all bloody and sweaty, and all awry with howling, and all staring and glaring with beastly excitement and want of sleep.
>
> —Charles Dickens, *A Tale of Two Cities*

Dr. Armentrout and Long John Beach had jumped off the muddy path to the left after his first reflexively answering shot had provoked so much return fire, and the two of them had tumbled over an old ivy-covered stone wall, with the two-mannikin appliance flailing wildly on Armentrout's shoulders, and then they tumbled and spun down a mud slope in darkness, away from the torches up on the path. He believed at least one of the Lever Blank men had been shot.

When they had still been in the car the pomegranate had been pulling hard enough to jump away from his hands when he had let go of it, and so he had made sure to grip it tightly as they had climbed out of the Saturn in the parking lot up the hill – he could imagine the thing getting away from him and rolling off into the night to find the king by itself. He had ordered Long John Beach to strap the heavy two-man appliance onto him, and he had held the pomegranate tightly in each hand while sliding the other through the arm loops – even when the left-hand-side Styrofoam head had nuzzled his cheek in an eerie similitude of affection or attack.

With the mannikins flanking him, the leisure-suited aluminum-pole arms around his shoulders, there had seemed to be six people who ran across the drag-strip highway and started down the path toward the Sutro Baths ruins, and they must have been conspicuous; before Armentrout and Long John Beach and the two Lever Blank men had walked ten yards, their way had been blocked by torch-bearing figures of a sort Armentrout had seen before, on the Leucadia beach.

And tonight again he had stared at the human eyes in the clay faces, and again he had used his most authoritative doctor's voice as he'd said, 'What, precisely, is your business here? Get out of our way, please.'

An earthen hand pointed at the pomegranate he held, and a red mouth opened on teeth that glittered in the close orange torchlight: '*That's* what you took,' said an adolescent voice, 'from up the stairs at the Leucadia Camelot.'

With his free hand Armentrout pulled the little derringer out of his inside jacket pocket. He levered the hammer back, and then confidently raised the gun and pointed it at the center of the breastless, clay-smeared chest. 'Get out of our way, please,' he said again.

And then a ringing explosion flared in the ivy to the right, and Armentrout was tugged around in that direction by a punch to his right-side mannikin.

His instant twitch of astonishment clenched his fists – the hollow pomegranate crumpled in his left hand, and his right hand clutched the little gun—

—and then his wrist was hammered by the impact of the wooden ball-grip being slammed into his palm, and the muzzle-flash burned his retinas – but not so dazzlingly that he wasn't able to see the clay-smeared figure step back and then sit down abruptly in the mud, with a ragged golf-ball-sized hole in its chest.

The shrubbery had seemed to erupt in glaring flashes and deafening bangs then, and Armentrout and Long John Beach had vaulted over the ivy on the downhill side of the path. In the ensuing tumbling slide, Armentrout just tried to let the aluminum bodies and the grunting mannikin heads take the abrasions and knocks, while he kept his hands clamped on the gun and the broken pomegranate.

When they had rolled to a halt in a rainy pool down on the plain, Armentrout sat up in the water and squinted sideways at the Styrofoam head on his right shoulder. A great red flare of afterimage hung in the center of Armentrout's vision, but he could see that the Styrofoam man had been shot squarely through the forehead – and then he looked away again quickly, because for just an instant the blank white features had been the face of Philip Muir, pop-eyed and gaping as it had been after Armentrout had put a point-blank load of .410 shot between Muir's eyes.

All he could hear down here, through the ringing in his ears, was a rapid drumming – and then he became aware of a whole siege of popping, spattering gunfire, none of it very close. Peering out through the curtains of cold rain, he saw blinks and flashes of light all along the walls and paths on the plain.

The Maruts, he thought almost in awe; the militant youths described in the Rig-Veda, springing up spontaneously on this western American shore, armed with guns now instead of swords and spears, and wearing earthen rather than golden armor. And they're embodying the Cretan Kouretes, too, protecting the new king by making a distracting racket with their weapons.

The pomegranate was still pulling in his hand, though it was cracked now and bright little seeds were popping out of it and flying away toward the dark cliffs of Point Lobos on the far side of the lagoons and the low stone buildings. 'We have to find the king,' he gasped to Long John Beach as he struggled painfully to his feet and thrust the leaking pomegranate into his pocket. 'Come on!'

Long John Beach pushed himself up with his one arm – and then, without falling back, impossibly lifted the arm from the water to push his sopping white hair back out of his face while he was still propped up at an angle out of the pool.

Then he had got his feet under himself and stood up, and the tiny miracle was over. 'I do stand engaged to many Greeks,' the old man said in the dead Valerie-voice, 'even in the faith of Valerie, to appear this morning to them.' Then he blinked at the three heads on Armentrout's shoulders as if all of them were alive; and after staring attentively at the one beside Armentrout's left shoulder, he looked the doctor in the eye and said, 'Your mother, in most great affliction of spirit, hath sent me to you.'

In the moment it took Armentrout to remember that he now had only one .410 shell left unfired in the magical gun, he was ready to shoot Long John Beach; then he tried to speak, but all that came out of his mouth was a hoarse stuttering wail like a goat's. Frightened and angry, and desperate to be once again free of all the demanding dead people, Armentrout just tucked the gun too into his pocket and shoved Long John Beach forward toward the cliffs.

Cochran and Plumtree had scrambled up to the ledge road, and the cave was only a dozen feet to their left.

Cochran wasn't aware that he had been hearing idling engines until the headlights came on, up the slope to the right – single headlights, motorcycles – and at the same moment he heard the whirring clatter of Harley-Davidson engines throttling, Cochran clutched the wine bottle to his ribs with his left hand and cocked the hammer of his revolver with his right. Because he had been half thinking in French all evening, he was able to recognize the chorus of yells from the riders: *Vive le Roi! Vive le Roi!*

The flashes of the first cracking gunshots were aimed toward Pete and Kootie, in the middle of the group. Cochran raised his revolver and saw, in razory tunnel-vision over the gun sights, a bearded and wild-haired rider swinging a pistol left-handed toward Angelica and Mavranos.

And Cochran touched the trigger. Blue flames jetted out in an X from the gap where the cylinder met the barrel, and the hammer-blow of sound rocked him as much as the recoil did, but he glimpsed the rider rolling over backward as a booted leg kicked out and the motorcycle's wheels came up and the bike went down in a plowing slide.

A second motorcycle rode down into the fallen one and then stood up on end and somersaulted forward, tossing its rider tumbling across the mud to within a yard of Cochran's feet as the heavy bike clanged away downhill through the curtains of rain; Cochran was aiming now at two more riders who had banked down toward Pete and Kootie.

But Angelica's carbine and Mavranos's .38 were a sudden jack-hammer barrage, flaring like a cluster of chain-lightning, and then the motorcycles wobbled past as Kootie dived one way and Angelica leaped in the other direction – one of the machines crashed over sideways, throwing its rag-doll rider to the ground, while the other bounded straight over a low wall into the big rectangular lagoon with an explosive hissing splash.

Cochran spun to the man who had fallen at his feet – and saw Plumtree straightening up from the man's bloody, sightless face and tossing away a wet rock; raindrops splashed on a stainless-steel automatic that lay in the man's limp hand. Plumtree's eyes were bright, and she cried, 'It's still me, Sid!'

And not Salvoy, he thought, remembering the story of the would-be rapist in Oakland in '89. Cochran's right hand was twitching, re-experiencing the hard recoil of the gun, as if his very nerves wished the action could still be cancelled; and he cringed for Cody's sake, at the thought that she had now been permitted to commit homicide for herself.

A fresh volley of gunfire erupted from down the slope, and stone splinters whistled through the air as bullets hammered into the cliff face to his left and behind him and ricochets twanged through the rain. Then someone had grabbed Cochran's arm and yelled into his ear, 'Back – Arky's been shot, and there's bikers in the cave.'

Cochran threw his arm around Plumtree's shoulders and pulled her away from the dust-spitting cliff face, back down the mud slope toward the fires. He realized that it was Pete who had seized him, and he glimpsed more moving headlights up the slope on the right. The cold rainy air was fouled now with the smells of motor oil and cordite.

'This isn't aimed at us!' yelled Pete over the banging din.

'*Gooood!*' wailed Cochran, gritting his teeth and trying to block Plumtree from at least one quarter of the banging, flashing night. The two of them stumbled and slid back down the slope after Pete; squinting against the battering rain, Cochran could see Mavranos being half-carried back toward the roofless stone building by one of the naked-looking clay-people, with Angelica and Kootie hunching along after. The flames that boiled up from within the stone walls were huge now, throwing shadows across the mudflats and clawing the night sky, seeming even to redly light the undersides of the clouds.

'The men on m-motorcycles,' said Pete, speaking loudly to be heard, 'think-kuh Kootie is the khing, but they want him to be-be *their* king. They'll – kill – everyone else, if they *cannn.*'

Sound was becoming jerky and segmented again, and Cochran again felt that he was experiencing time in fast but discrete frames – the unceasing rattle and pop of gunfire near and far began to be *paced*, in a fast, complicated counterpoint tempo like the hand-clapping of the clay people—

—Cochran was stumbling, suddenly feeling very drunk, with the taste of the *pagadebiti* wine blooming back into his throat and expanding his head—

—Clumsily he pushed the revolver back into the holster at the back of his belt so that he could hold the bottle with the black-stained hand too—

—And then in an instant all the noise *stopped*, with one last distant rebounding echo to deprive him of the consolation of believing that he had gone deaf; and as if the stunning racket had been a headwind he'd been leaning against, the abrupt cessation of it pitched him forward onto his knees in the mud.

The cork popped out of the bottle's neck, and Cochran thought he could hear the *smack* of it hitting the mud a moment later.

Even the rain had stopped – the air was clear and cold, with no slightest breeze, and the fire in the stone building convulsed overhead for another moment and then stood up straight, a towering yards-wide brushstroke of golden glare against the black night.

Cody Plumtree was on her hands and knees beside him, panting. 'When the shooting started,' she whispered, 'the other girls fell back, and I was on the bus alone, in the driver's seat, driving away from them.' Her voice was faint, but in the silence Cochran could hear every sound her teeth and lips and breath made. 'But the man standing beside me in the vision wasn't the broken lunatic anymore – it was Scott Crane, all strong and excellent and wise, guiding me; and we sped up and leaped the bus right over the gap in the freeway, and landed whole on the other side.'

From *Dirty Harry* to *Speed*, thought Cochran. That's good, I guess. 'Kootie did say,' he whispered cautiously, 'when we were here two or three weeks ago, that you're probably carrying Crane's ghost on you.'

'Tonight he gets washed off.'

Cochran remembered the motorcyclist she had killed and the automatic in the man's limp hand. 'Cody,' he said, 'you saved my life.'

'Old Chinese proverb,' said Plumtree hoarsely. '"Whoever saves another person's life should dig two graves."'

Kootie came plodding up to where Cochran and Plumtree knelt. And the boy's splashing footsteps in the mud awoke a wind from over the eastern slopes – the gusty breeze swept down the bowl of the vast amphitheater, bending trees and rippling the ponds, and twitched at Cochran's wet hair as it stepped over him and his companions and moved out over the dark ocean. The air smelled of dry wine and fresh tree sap.

'Give me the wine,' said Kootie, his raincoat flapping in the breeze. He had lost Cochran's hat at some point.

Cochran looked past Kootie. The tall flame was curling and snapping again, and by its yellow glow he could see Angelica standing close behind Kootie, and next to her Mavranos with his left arm around Pete's shoulders and his right hand pressed to his side. Cochran lifted the bottle over his head with both hands and the boy took it.

'Now I think Dionysus … *set me up* to kill that woman, meant me to do it, in his boarding house,' the boy said quietly. The firelight made deep shadows of his cheeks and his eye sockets. 'But I did kill her – I do still have to offer my neck to the Green Knight's blade.' Angelica would have said something, but Kootie raised his hand 'We won't be able to get into the cave, until I do – and I know the god will kill us all here tonight if I don't. Remember the end of that play Arky told us about, the one where the people refused to drink the god's wine.'

'*The Bacchae*,' said Mavranos through clenched teeth.

A deep, hollow drumbeat rolled down the strengthening breeze; then after a few seconds came another. Like two very slow steps.

'Get up,' Kootie told Cochran and Plumtree. 'Let's go over by the water—'

Cochran struggled to his feet and helped Plumtree up, and with Angelica and Pete and Mavranos they followed the boy down the slope toward the black water beside the stone building. The heat from the flames was a sting on the right side of Cochran's face.

They passed half a dozen of the mud-smeared youths, all of them kneeling; several of them, and many others on the plain, were facing away, toward the Point Lobos cliff, and holding pistols and even rifles at the ready. *Bikers in the cave*, Cochran remembered. Four ragged figures were trudging at a labored pace down from the highway-side slope into the light; one was limping, evidently supported by two of his companions.

The drumbeat had continued as the wind strengthened, and was now thumping a little faster. At least two other drums, at other points across the dark basin, had joined the first one in the same rhythm. White patches showed in the eastern sky, where the moon was breaking through the wind-riven clouds.

But it can't be the moon, thought Cochran. The moon has been waning for a week, it was full on the first of the month, it should be totally dark tonight.

The ground sloped right down into the water here, any original wall long gone, and Kootie halted with his boots a yard from the water. He dug a fluttering paper out of his raincoat pocket and passed it carefully to Cochran. It was a car-registration slip.

'Arky wrote the palindrome on that,' Kootie told him. 'When I give you a nod, read the last line aloud.'

'Right,' Cochran said, in a rusty voice. When I read each of the two previous lines aloud, he thought, Crane's ghost showed up; first as our taxi driver after I read the Latin on the ashtray at the Mount Sabu bar, and then as a naked flickering image right here, after I read the next line from Valorie's matchbook.

'When are you going to drink the wine?' asked Angelica with badly concealed urgency. Her wet black hair was blowing in tangles across her lean lace.

'When we get back up to the cave,' Kootie told her firmly.

The drumbeat was pounding exactly in time with Cochran's pulse now, and he intuitively knew that his companions were experiencing the same synchronization.

Quickly, before Angelica or Pete could react, Kootie raised the wine bottle and tipped it up to his lips; and when he lowered it, Mavranos quickly reached out and took it out of his hands.

'*Aaah!*' Angelica's wail was snatched away over the sea by the wind, and Cochran knew that she had intended to stop the boy, and that Kootie had known it too.

The boy reeled back across the mud, away from the water, but he didn't fall; well, thought Cochran, *he* wasn't standing next to an open *grave*.

Kootie reached jerkily into an inside pocket of the raincoat and yanked out the dirty little yellow blanket that he had been given by the Diana woman, Scott Crane's widow. For a moment Cochran thought he was going to throw it away. Then the boy pulled it around his shoulders, and he was suddenly closer, or taller, and the blanket seemed to be a spotted yellow fur. Cochran was having trouble focussing on him in the light of the gusting fire.

Cochran shoved the wet car registration into his pocket. His right hand was still flexing, and he was trying to focus his eyes clearly on anything – the low stone walls that stretched away in the darkness, Plumtree's face, his own hands – and he found that he couldn't make out the exact shape of the black hole in the back of his twitching right hand, no matter how he blinked and narrowed his eyes—

The drumbeats were coming more rapidly – the mud-smeared people had got to their feet and were milling around uneasily, swinging their rifles and pistols – and now fast-thudding footsteps from behind were matching the drum's strokes.

Cochran turned, and flinched even as his right hand sprang once again toward the holster at the back of his belt.

The fire-lit figure rushing straight at them across the mud looked at first like some hallucinatory three-headed Kali with four waving arms, and Cochran's abdomen momentarily turned to ice water; then he saw that it was a portly white-haired man, with a pair of life-size gesticulating mannikins attached to his shoulders; and as Cochran fumbled the gun out of the holster he recognized the muddied, grimacing face – it was Dr. Armentrout, and one of the doctor's hands clutched a tiny silver pistol.

But another man was running up behind Armentrout, and now caught the doctor; and he must have punched him between the shoulder blades, for Armentrout's head rocked back sharply and he plunged forward face-down into the mud. The little pistol flew out of his hand and bounced once off the mud and splashed into the dark water.

Before the doctor's encumbered form had even stopped sliding, his pursuer had leaped onto his shoulders, and Cochran saw that it was Long John Beach. The one-armed old man was gripping the back of Armentrout's neck – the two artificial white heads were splayed out to the sides in the mud, their aluminum neck-poles bent, and between them the doctor's head was jerked violently to the side each time Long John Beach's shoulder stump flexed over him.

Cochran was pointing his revolver at the pair, into the middle of the spider-cluster of mismatched arms and heads, but the muzzle wavered. He was aware of Plumtree standing beside him, breathing fast.

Without halting his invisible beating of the doctor, Long John Beach raised his round white-whiskered face, and his little eyes seemed to be squinting fearfully up at Kootie. 'A three-headed dog – on your altar,' he said, panting as his shoulder spasmed metronomically and blood began to blot through the doctor's snapping white hair. 'Your way,' he gasped, 'is – clear.' Then he leaned down over the doctor's limp, jerking form, and a woman's voice cawed, *'Can you breathe, Richie dear? Say something if you can't breathe.'* The voice must have come from Long John Beach's throat, but Cochran thought the left-side mannikin head had been jerking in time to the words.

A dozen drums were pounding in rapid unison now, and though it was no longer synchronized with even his presently very fast heartbeat, Cochran thought the drums were matching some other rhythm inside him – an ancient, savage brain-frequency that made thought impossible. His open mouth was fluttered by the wind, and his nose was full of the wine and sap smells.

A warm, strong hand gripped Cochran's shoulder – and he found himself helplessly pointing his revolver at the two jolting figures on the mud in front of him, and then he pulled the trigger – but he must have miscounted his previous shots, for the gun didn't fire.

He was dizzily ready to crouch beside Armentrout and begin pounding on all three of the twitching heads with the pistol grip; but the hand on his shoulder pulled him back and gave him a shockingly hard shove that spun him around twice before he was able to flailingly catch his balance. In the fire-lit wheeling blur he had glimpsed a wooden mask on broad, fur-caped shoulders, but the urgency was now somewhere else; Cochran was still off-balance, somehow.

The clay-smeared people had all stood up at once from the mud around him, and were walking, then striding, toward the Point Lobos cliff. And in a moment they had opened their mouths in a shrill, ululating chorus, and they were running. Cochran let himself start to fall in the same direction.

And then Cochran and Plumtree were running too, right with them, and Cochran didn't even know if he was joining in the predatory yelling as his feet thudded in the mud and flames whirled around him and Plumtree. No particular sound in the shaking din told him that the struck bullet in the gun he was carrying had belatedly fired into the ground, just the jolt in his hand and the flare at his thigh; he didn't even look down, just flipped the gun around in his hand so that it would be a better club.

He did hear shots from up the slope ahead – a rapid-fire stutter that conveyed desperation and panic – and over the close tossing clay dreadlocks

Cochran could see muzzle-flashes from the mouth of the cave. None of the sprinting youths appeared to be shooting back – like Cochran they were waving their firearms overhead like clubs, or just tossing them away.

Cochran and Plumtree leaped over wall sections and fallen naked bodies, and then he had lost the gun and they were scrambling up the mud slope toward the cave, imitating the naked earth-people around them in hunching forward to pull themselves up with their hands as well as push themselves along with their feet. All the torches and even the guns had been dropped and left behind, and it seemed to be a pack of four-legged beasts rushing up the path to the cave.

The gunshots were just sporadic punctuation to shrill screams now, and the cave was packed with straining, clawing forms streaked only with re-flected moonlight. Cochran was breathing fast through his clenched teeth as he fought to get through the press of bodies to the prey; until a heavy, hairy ball rolled over the shoulders in front of him and fell into his empty hands.

He stared at it. For one transfigured moment it was the head of a lion, shining gold – then it was a human head in the silver moonlight, bearded and gap-toothed and wide-eyed, leaking slick hot blood onto his hands. The nose and ears were torn and bent and tangled in the bloody hair, and an actual thought appeared in Cochran's fevered mind: This was *twisted off* of its body.

He stumbled back and shook the thing free of his hands, and it fell into a tangle of vines at his feet.

Looking up, he saw Plumtree backing away, dragging her right shoulder across the clustered fluttering leaves that covered the cliff face, while her left shoulder was jostled by the muddy, sexless figures. She was biting her knuckles and staring toward where Cochran had dropped the severed head; and her face was bone white in the moonlight, but when she looked up at him she was recognizably still Cody.

Cochran dodged his way over to where she stood, and he started to hold out his hand to her; then he saw that it was gleaming black with blood.

But she clasped it anyway, and he leaned beside her against the leaf-covered unevenness of the cliff.

The clay-smeared youths were dancing away from the cave now, whirl-ing and leaping out of the tunnel and waving over their dreadlocked heads pieces of human bodies as they whirled away back down the slope to the wild beat of the drumming.

And the bounding dancers didn't pause, but the crowd of them split widely around a figure that was striding up the slope now.

Angelica and Pete, supporting the limping Mavranos, were following it.

It wore no mask, and of course it was Kootie – but the boy was taller, and the skirted raincoat and the blanket around his shoulders flapped like robes in the driving wind, and his stern face was dark and Asian in the moonlight. Cochran remembered that the boy's last name was something from India.

The clay-smeared youths were dancing and running around the fire in the roofless structure now; but other figures, clothed and wet and-limping, were toiling across the mud-flats toward the cliff; one was as short as a child, and poling itself forward on crutches.

The impossibly full moon was a white disk hanging over the waving trees at the top of Sutro Park above the highway, and by its light Cochran could see that the whole Point Lobos cliff behind himself and Plumtree was covered with vines; and bunches of grapes swung heavily in the wine-reeking wind.

Cochran and Plumtree stepped back and lowered their eyes as the tall figure that was at least partly Koot Hoomie Parganas stepped up to the broad ledge; tracks of motorcycle tires, and swirling gouges left by motorcycle footpegs and handlebars, stood out in starkly shadowed relief in the mud, but Kootie's boots sank deeper, and the holes of his bootprints quickly filled with dark liquid.

The god just walked past you, Cochran told himself; Dionysus, walking the Point Lobos cliffs on this broken night.

But the thought was too big to grasp, and slid off his mind, and he could only look away, down the slope.

CHAPTER THIRTY THREE

Soon wild commotions shook him and made flush
All the immortal fairness of his limbs;
Most like the struggle at the gate of death;
Or liker still to one who should take leave
Of pale immortal death, and with a pang
As hot as death's is chill, with fierce convulse
Die into life ...

—John Keats, *Hyperion*

Mavranos's head was lowered, but he was thrusting himself up the slope strongly with his good left leg; the right leg of his jeans was dark with blood. The faces of Pete and Angelica on either side of him were strained and expressionless with the work of supporting his weight as they climbed the slope. Angelica had apparently lost her carbine, but she was gripping the bottle of *pagadebiti* in her free hand.

When the path levelled out, Mavranos lifted his head, and his stony gaze swept down across the vine-covered cliff to Cochran. 'Are there any of the,' Mavranos said through clenched teeth, 'mud-kids still in the tunnel?'

Kootie had already disappeared into the tunnel, and Cochran plodded carefully to the cave mouth, stepping out wide of it and peering. The tunnel was nearly as dark as the mark on his hand, but beyond the tall, slowly receding silhouette that was Kootie he could see moonlit rock surfaces beyond the arch of the far opening, and no other people.

He shambled back to where Pete and Angelica and Mavranos stood swaying before he answered, for he didn't want to seem to be calling down the tunnel.

'Nobody at all, but Kootie,' he said. 'They all ran back to the fires, after they – when they—'

Angelica nodded. 'We saw what they were carrying.'

'Then,' said Mavranos in an anguished voice, '*who?*'

'Sid,' said Angelica, 'help Pete carry Arky.'

Cochran stepped up beside Mavranos, and Angelica got out from under Mavranos's left arm and draped its weight around Cochran's shoulders. And then Angelica went sprinting to the cave mouth and disappeared inside, still carrying the bottle. Drops of the wine splashed out onto the mud, and fresh leafy vines curled violently up out of the ground where they had struck, like convulsing snakes.

'I'll watch her,' said Plumtree to Pete, and she hurried into the cave after Angelica. Cochran gritted his teeth, remembering that Cody hated caves.

'Come on,' said Pete, starting forward strongly; Cochran braced his right arm around Mavranos's ribs and followed, and the two of them were in effect *carrying* Mavranos into the gravel-floored cave, in spite of occasional help from Mavranos's one good leg.

Cochran could feel the short hairs standing up at the base of his neck at the sharp metallic smell that filled the tunnel, and when he realized that it was the smell of fresh blood he made sure to breathe only through his mouth.

Their footsteps crunched and sloshed along the puddled gravel floor, and over the hooting whistle of the wind Cochran could hear sea water crashing and guttering on rocks in the holes below the remembered iron railing that was invisible in this darkness.

'Crowd your wall,' he gasped to Pete, for the railing had been on the left.

Then he could see the iron railing below Mavranos's dangling left hand, silhouetted against the luminous foam of the waves outside, beyond the rock wall. *A seething bath*, he recalled Valorie saying here, *which yet may prove against strange maladies a sovereign cure.*

As his shoes deeply furrowed the unseen wet gravel, he twice felt the brief entanglement of strips of cloth, and once he kicked a boot that rolled away too loosely to still have a foot in it – his feet didn't bump anything that felt like flesh and bone, but he was still breathing through his mouth.

When Kootie had stepped out into the diffuse moonlight on the ledge over the water, and the hurrying silhouettes of Angelica and Plumtree had brightened with detail as they shuffled outside too, Cochran could hear footsteps rattling the gravel some distance behind him; but he couldn't free his head to look around. Pete must have heard the steps as well, for he joined Cochran in striding along at a quicker pace.

At last the three of them stumbled out into the relative brightness of the moonlit cloudy sky. Kootie was standing at the seaward lip of the ledge, staring out at the dark Pacific Ocean. He was clearly taller than Plumtree now, who was braced against the seaward rock face beside Angelica, and he even seemed through some trick of moonlight and perspective to be bigger than the great stone profile, across the splashing gap to the right, which was itself staring out to sea in the same direction.

Cochran had to look away; an aura played about Kootie's fur-draped shoulders, and Cochran's eyes hurt when he tried to focus on the boy. He was aware of heat radiating from that side of the ledge, and he wondered helplessly if apotheosis might cause Kootie to spontaneously combust.

Mavranos pushed himself away from Cochran and Pete and stood swaying by himself, blinking around at the stone head and the other huge boulders and tumbled stones piled against this side of the Point Lobos cliffs.

Free of the heavy arm on his shoulders; Cochran quickly turned to look back down the tunnel. At least two silhouettes were trudging this way up the wet stone windpipe; and he was sure that the one struggling along on crutches could be no one but Thutmose the Utmos', the dwarf junkie he had met at the Seafood Bohemia bar, apparently still desperate for a sip of the forgiving wine.

Cochran hurried across to stand beside Plumtree. 'We got,' he gasped, 'company.'

The figure in the aura at the seaward side of the ledge turned ponderously, rippling the gusty air, and through the optical distortions the inhumanly calm wooden mask nodded at Cochran. There was respectful greeting in the gesture, possibly even a blessedly remote affection, but there was also command.

Pete was braced against the wall beside Angelica, and now appeared to be holding her back from rushing at the god.

Cochran dug his cold-numbed fingers into his pocket and pulled out the soggy car-registration form.

The light was far too dim for him to read any words off the water-darkened paper; and in sudden abysmal panic he realized that he couldn't remember one word of the Latin.

He lifted his right hand toward his face to rub uselessly at his eyes – and then noticed that the black mark on his knuckles seemed to radiate darkness, so that the letters on the paper shone clearly with the same intense, reflected blackness.

He took a deep breath of the cold wine-and-blood-scented sea air.

'*Sole*,' he read, calling loudly to be heard over the wind whistling in the tunnel at his back, '*medere pede: ede, perede melos.*' And now he remembered the translation the woman had given them: *O Sun, remedy the louse: give forth from yourself, and give forth from yourself again, your devoured limb.*

The masked figure that was no longer recognizable as Kootie was shaking, and Cochran could feel heat on his eyes. He stepped back, raising his hand to throw a cool shadow across his face, and saw Long John Beach shamble out onto the ledge.

Cochran tensed and stepped around in front of the man to grab Plumtree's arm; but the old man was cowering, and his single arm was shaking as he pointed behind and above Cochran.

The waves of the sea glittered silver as a wash of bright moonlight swept in from the horizon toward the shore with eerie speed, and then the full moon was suddenly above the cliffs, shining down onto the rocks, and Cochran could see a naked, bearded man, seeming to stand as tall as Michelangelo's *David*, on the top of the George Washington boulder.

Cochran shivered, flinching in the moonlight. Dionysus *and* the Moon Goddess, for this, he thought. It must have been Diana's baby blanket that called *her.*

The tall figure in the wooden mask shifted ponderously around to face the boulder, and Cochran's eyes narrowed against the radiant heat.

'No!' shouted Long John Beach into the eddying wind. 'Wait, listen to this person!' Still cowering before the mask and the moon, he nevertheless shambled out across the ledge toward the masked god. 'Look who thinks he's nothing,' he said in a whimper; 'but the voice from the sky said, "Let go of the tree."' More loudly, he called to the expressionless mask, 'Now *you're* killing the boy! Take – take *this* body – it's presumed to do a lot of your proper work, in its time – and it's … pruned.'

Long John Beach hunched forward across the slanted ledge in the stark moonlight – against evident resistance, as if he were weighed down and struggling uphill; Angelica started to push herself away from the cliff to stop him, but Plumtree and Pete both caught her and pulled her back out of the wind.

Cochran was sure that the wind or magnetic repulsion or tilted gravity was going to topple Long John Beach impotently over backward—

—the one-armed man slid back a yard, away from the god—

'*Okay!*' howled the one-armed old man to the sky, and the wetness on his haggard face had to be tears, 'I do it, I let go, I – I surrender everything!'

All at once the old man was laughing, and just for an instant another figure seemed to be superimposed on him, out of scale and suspended as if in mid-dance-step above the stone ledge – a young man in patchwork clothing, with two arms, and a pack over his shoulder and a dog snapping at his heels – and then he was just lone, haggard old Long John Beach again, but standing now right in front of the Dionysus figure.

The lone arm stretched out, and one of the old man's fingers reached through the rippling aura and touched the mask.

And then Long John Beach spun around to face the naked figure up on the top of the boulder, and he seemed to Cochran's aching eyes to have spun a number of times, just too fast to catch. And now he was taller, broader-shouldered, and draped in a flapping silver leopard-skin, and it was his face that was hidden by the mask.

Kootie collapsed off to the side in his floppy raincoat, and Angelica and Plumtree both caught him and fell to their knees to lower him gently to the puddled stone surface; Angelica had dropped the bottle, and it had bounced off her foot and was rolling on the ledge, spurting dark wine onto the wet rocks. For a moment Kootie was struggling weakly in the arms of both women, the raincoat collar half hiding his face, and then Plumtree disengaged herself and snatched up the bottle.

Scott Crane's ghost was flickering up on top of the boulder, like a figure badly projected on a drive-in movie screen – and now Kootie was shaking violently in Angelica's arms, in the same rhythm.

Mavranos took a step forward, and his right leg folded under him and he fell to his knees in front of Plumtree. 'Oh, it *will* be Kootie,' he gasped, 'if *I* don't do it. I hoped one of the killer clay-kids would volunteer to do it, that this cup wouldn't be for me, but – ahh God.'

He reached up and grabbed the bottle from Plumtree – and then he tilted it to his mouth, and Cochran could see his throat working as he swallowed gulp after gulp of the bloody wine. Cochran winced in sympathy, remembering what Mavranos had said at their first attempt, out on the yacht-harbor peninsula: *What your girlfriend is ready to do ... I don't think I could do.*

A wail echoed from the mouth of the tunnel behind them, and Thutmose the Utmos' came skittering and thrashing out onto the ledge in a tangle of aluminum crutch-poles. 'For me! The holy blood – I've worked harder—'

Mavranos lowered the bottle and scowled, and the dwarf subsided into silence. 'I was – dying of cancer!' shouted Mavranos through the rain, staring at his empty left hand, 'when I met Scott Crane! And what he did cured me!' He made a fist, and when he went on it was in a voice almost too low for Cochran to hear: 'This five years has been gravy. Tell Wendy and the girls that I ... paid my debts. Tell them they had a husband and father they could be proud of.'

He stood up, not wincing as he put weight on his right leg, and he walked across to stand balanced on the seaward rim of the ledge, nearly eclipsed by the tall masked god whose outlines roiled beside him. Mavranos squinted the other way, up at the towering naked bearded figure on the rock, and he called out strongly, '*Scott! Pogo, do you hear me? Jump this way, old friend, I'll – catch you!*'

And Cochran raised his marked right hand against the wind.

Cochran made himself stare across the ledge into the carved, placid features of the wooden mask that he had seen on Vignes Street in Los Angeles and in the mental hospital in Bellflower; and to it he called, '*I'm Scant Cochran – extend to Scott Crane the favor you owe me.*'

Dionysus swept down one muscular arm and punched Mavranos off the ledge – Mavranos threw his arms out to the sides as he fell away toward the sea, and then he was gone, the bottle spinning away with him.

Thutmose the Utmos' sprang howling away from the wall and covered the length of the ledge in three slithering hops, and then he had dived off the rocky rim and disappeared after Mavranos.

A crash of thunder like a basso-profundo shout from the cliffs themselves shook the air, and in the same instant a blast of white buckshot abraded the cliff face and punched Cochran solidly into Plumtree, and his first thought was that the rushing moon had exploded; but when the blast struck again, and then was followed by sheets of battering rain, Cochran looked down at the white pellets rolling on the stone surface by his shoes and saw that the white buckshot had been BB-sized hailstones.

Cochran forced his head around against the whipping onshore wind, and through tearing, narrowed eyes saw that there was no figure up on the George Washington head now; and the corner of the ledge was empty where Long John Beach or Dionysus had stood.

We failed at it again, he thought incredulously. He clung to Plumtree as tears were blown out of the corners of his eyes and his shoulders heaved. All of us have about killed ourselves, and Arky *has* killed himself, and we've failed. Suddenly Plumtree gripped his upper arms hard.

Over the racket of the storm, someone was roaring, or screaming, out in the ocean; and through the rain the cliffs echoed with the baying of a hound. And the ledge was shaking.

Cochran crouched and pulled Plumtree down, and then he reached past her and tugged hard at Kootie's raincoat, trying to help Pete Sullivan to drag both the boy and Angelica toward the tunnel. Boulders were moving out in the curtains of rain, and rocks were toppling from the crests of the cliffs and spinning down through the air to crack and rumble in pieces into the churning sea; and some kind of water main must have broken in the core of Point Lobos, for solid arching streams were shooting out far above the boulders and being torn to spray by the wind.

'Get inside!' Cochran yelled at Angelica. 'Rock fall!'

'Wait for him!' she screamed back.

Cochran was panting in pure fright as he clung to the heaving ledge over the boiling sea; his tears were flying away past his ears, and the spray in his open mouth was fresh water. He turned around with his hands splayed flat on the wet shifting stone, and shouted to Plumtree, 'Get in the tunnel!'

A falling rock impacted so hard with the ledge rim in the moment of shattering like a bomb that the very concussion of the air stunned him and he thought his wrists were broken just from the jolt through the stone.

Two weeks ago the shooting at the ruins on the yacht-club peninsula had shocked him with the facts of velocity and human mercilessness; now his mind was seized-up with a cellular comprehension of force and physical mass and Nature's mercilessness. Hail and gravel and rain lashed like chains at his back, and he tried to block Plumtree from it as he pulled her toward the tunnel. The ledge had shifted under his knees, and he was sure it was within moments of breaking away and falling into the sea.

But Plumtree grabbed his chin in her cold hand and yelled, 'Look!' – and she stared past him, toward Pete and Angelica and Kootie.

Feeling as though he were turning himself inside-out, Cochran tore his eyes from the close darkness of the stone tunnel and twisted his head around to look toward the open sea.

A man was climbing up out of the waves onto the shaking ledge, clutching each new, bucking handhold with bunched muscles and straining tendons. He was shirtless, and a thick dark beard, sopping wet, was matted across his broad chest. When he had hauled himself up and got one knee onto the shelf, Cochran saw that he was naked, and that a wound in his right side was bleeding; Kootie pushed himself away from Angelica and began unbuttoning his raincoat.

A big black dog, wet as a seal, was scrambling up the rocks on the side of the ledge closer to the George Washington boulder, and Kootie paused to scream 'Fred!' over the howling of the storm.

The dog clawed the stone and got its legs under itself and then bounded to the boy, water flying from its weakly wagging tail.

Cochran met the dark eyes of the bearded man—

And with a sudden hollowness in his chest he recognized Scott Crane, alive in a living body at last.

Blood was streaming away in the rain from the man's nose and mouth and ears, but he smiled through evident pain; and then he braced himself and straightened his legs and stood up. Blood ran down his right leg from the gash below his ribs.

Cochran was sure the man would just be blown right back off the ledge and broken to pieces on the rocks – but the wind rocked to a halt as if Scott Crane had put his aching shoulders under it, and the cliffs stopped shaking under the weight of his bloody bare feet.

In spite of the glad leaping of the dog, Kootie had managed to shrug out of the raincoat, and he knelt forward to hold it up toward Crane. The bearded man took it and slowly pulled it on and belted the yellow sash, and at once he no longer appeared to Cochran to be some sea god risen from the waves just a robed king, barefoot and wounded.

The rain was falling vertically out of the sky onto the surfaces of stone now, and the arching streams of water had stopped gushing from the cliff. Scott Crane's gaze travelled from Pete and Angelica and Kootie and the dog to Cochran and, finally, to Plumtree. Cochran wasn't touching her, but could feel her flexed tension, and he thought he heard a high, keening wail.

Crane smiled at her, and nodded in recognition.

Then Crane's great bearded head turned as he looked around at the surrounding boulders and the tunnel opening. 'Where is Arky?' he said, and his low voice cut effortlessly through the hiss and spatter of the rain. 'He called me, all the way from Persephone's shore, beyond India.'

Plumtree was on her hands and knees, but now she cautiously stood up, bracing herself with one hand against the rock wall. 'The gunshot wound in your side,' she wailed, 'is all that's left of him. He gave you his body – and you've transformed it into your own.' She was shaking against the stone, and Cochran realized that she was sobbing. 'He restored you to life.'

The bearded king was visibly shaken by this. 'Is this true?' he asked hollowly.

Cochran realized that it must be, and he nodded even as Kootie said, 'Yes.'

Crane raised his bearded head and stretched his arms out to the sides – as Mavranos had when he had fallen into the sea – and he roared a wordless yell that echoed back from the cliffs, and fell to his knees.

'How can I take this?' he said loudly. 'Is this how Dionysus gives his favors?'

'Yes,' said Cochran, and he was aware that he and Plumtree had spoken the word in unison.

'Yes,' echoed Kootie.

'*Medere pede*,' said Crane, quietly but clearly; '*ede, perede, melos*. I heard that and assented to it – I came back, on those terms. And there's more blood owed on the account, shamefully proxy blood, still. But after this dawn I can make sure it's only *me* that pays, every winter.' He exhaled a long, harsh *aah*. 'But what can my kingdom be, without ... loyal, old, Archimedes Mavranos?' Still kneeling, Scott Crane looked across the ledge at Kootie. 'You're the ... young man who held the crown.'

'Fumbled it,' called Kootie miserably over the rain. He was hugging the big black dog. 'I ran away, on the morning of Dionysus's day. And I ... can't remember what I did then, but ...'

'My family,' said Crane. 'My son Benjamin, my wife – do you know if they're all right?'

'They're fine,' said Plumtree. Cochran believed that she needed to talk to Crane now, in spite of her guilt – that she needed to keep on establishing that the man really had returned to life. 'According to a woman called Nardie Dinh,' Plumtree went on, 'who's taking care of your place.'

'Nardie,' said Crane hoarsely. 'That's good.'

Again Crane got to his feet, smoothly but with pain evident in the stiffening and sudden pallor of his face. 'Stand up,' he said. 'You five constitute my army and my field marshals.' Bloody teeth showed through the soaked curls of his beard as he gave them a clenched but resolute smile. 'Have you got a car?'

'A Torino.' said Koorip planning at Cochran and Plumtree.

'Which is stolen,' said Plumtree. 'We've got Arky's truck.'

Crane winced, either at the evident pains of his transfiguration or at the mention of Mavranos's old Suburban. 'Take me to it, and one of you drive,' he said. He stared into Plumtree's eyes then, making her flinch. 'We've got two poor bankrupt old women to see off at the cemetery dock.'

'Im – immediately?' asked Cochran, trying to make his voice neutral. All of them had been soaked with cold rain in cold wind for hours, and he had been passionately looking forward to a car heater and a hot shower and then enough to drink so that he could drive out of his mind the image of a severed head in his hands.

Then he glanced at Crane, naked under the raincoat and drenched in sea water and wounded, too, and he was ashamed of having asked. 'Not that I—'

'I reckon it'll be immediate by the time we get there,' said Crane, 'yep. We've got to go to the cemetery marble temple, out at the end of the peninsula. I think you've been there before.'

And been shot at, thought Cochran. 'Yes,' he said.

There appeared to be nothing more to say. Plumtree and Cochran led the way-back down the tunnel to the slope that descended to the amphitheater plain. The lull moon had disappeared behind the clouds, and the fire in the roofless stone structure had died down to a height hardly above the ragged walltops, and the dancers were moving in rings now, waving their torches in unison to the quieter drumming.

It was just a Bacchanalian revel now, no longer a Dionysian hunt. The gods were no longer present.

CHAPTER THIRTY FOUR

Ghosts all! The ghost of beauty, the ghost of stateliness, the ghost of elegance, the ghost of pride, the ghost of frivolity, the ghost of wit, the ghost of youth, the ghost of age, all waiting their dismissal from the desolate shore, all turning on him eyes that were changed by the death they had died in coming here.

—Charles Dickens, *A Tale of Two Cities*

'Like a bruise all over,' said Plumtree intently as Scott Crane labored up the steep driveway toward the Sutro Heights parking lot, 'isn't it? Like you've been hammered with a meat tenderizer, especially on the insides.'

'It is – like that,' panted Crane. 'Who – *are* you?'

'Cody. Cody Plumtree.'

They were skirting the illuminated patch of asphalt under one of the park light poles, and Cochran looked back at the king. The man had refused any help from him or Pete, and he was striding along steadily, but the moisture on his bearded face was clearly as much sweat, and perhaps tears, as cold rain. Kootie and the black dog were running on ahead and then running back, staying in sight.

'Ch-ch-changes,' said Plumtree. 'At least you're not changing your sex.'

'I can imagine,' Crane said, nodding stiffly, 'that that would be rough.'

Cochran could see the red truck under the overhanging elms ahead, still parked among the nondescript but gold-painted old sedans and station wagons. 'Don't be bothering him, Cody,' he whispered.

'I'm not bothering him. Am I bothering you?'

'The climb up the rocks,' said Crane, 'took a lot out of me. I made hard use of a lot of – rearranged muscles that were still too shocked to register their initial pain yet.'

Pete had fumbled out Mavranos's key ring with the Swiss Army knife on it, and was trying to find the key. Kootie and the black dog were already standing by the front bumper.

'Could you open the tailgate?' asked Crane. 'I'd be more comfortable lying down in the back. I've travelled back there before, when the winter was a bad one.'

More recently than you know, thought Cochran, feeling his face stiffen at the idea of the living man riding back there where his corpse, and then his wrecked skeleton, had been carried around for a week. 'Sure,' said Pete.

'Jeez, we should sweep it out,' said Plumtree in an awed voice. 'There might still be bits—'

Cochran silenced her with a wide-eyed look behind Crane's back. After Crane had sweatingly but without help climbed up into the truck bed and stretched out, Pete closed the tailgate and then got in behind the wheel next to Kootie and Angelica, while Cochran and Plumtree got into the back seat, with the dog sitting up panting on the seat between them. When the doors had all been chunked shut, Pete started the engine and backed the track around, then drove slowly down to the coast highway with the windshield wipers slapping aside the steady streams of rain, and turned right. Everyone seemed to be on the point of saying something, chin and eyebrows raised, but no one spoke as the truck swayed and grumbled through the landscape of gray woods and rock outcrops, looping around the curves of Point Lobos Avenue to the north and then straightening out onto Geary Boulevard, heading east.

The little restaurants and stucco houses on Geary were all dark behind the rain-veiled streetlights, and Cochran wondered what time it could be. If the impossibly full moon had been moving in real time, it might be nearly dawn now. At least the truck's heater was on full, blowing out hot air that smelled of tobacco and stale beer and dispelled the dog's odor of sea water and wet fur.

Plumtree had dozed off against the left side window, and though she whimpered and twitched in her uneasy sleep, Cochran had thought it kinder not to wake her; but as the truck was passing a gold-domed cathedral she abruptly hunched forward and spat. Cochran shifted to peer at her past the wakeful, whining dog.

'Just let me talk,' Plumtree whispered. 'A condemned ... person should get to make a last statement, especially when there's gonna be no trial before the execution.'

'Cody!' said Cochran sharply, thinking she was still in the middle of a dream. 'We're in the truck, and the restoration-to-life worked this time, remember?'

Plumtree looked up at Kootie, who was peering back from the front seat; he looked startled, and might have been asleep a moment ago himself. 'Then you're not the king anymore,' she whispered, 'but will you give me permission to talk, to be heard?'

'Uh,' said Kootie, clearly mystified, 'sure.'

'Okay,' came the whisper; then Omar Salvoy's voice said, 'Plumtree is gonna have to die. A death is still owed in this math, and blood and shattered bone. Your Mavranos just died to provide the *body*. Somebody's still gotta pay Dionysus for return of the king's *soul*.' Salvoy smiled, and the face wasn't Cody's anymore. '"For me, the ransom of my bold attempt shall be this cold corpse on the earth's cold face," as the Valorie one would say. Ask *the king* if I'm making this up.' Plumtree's body shifted over against the far window, as if Salvoy didn't like contact with the dog.

I thought you were deaf, thought Cochran helplessly; then he remembered that Janis had taken on the deafness.

After a moment of silence except for the roaring of the engine and the rippling hiss of the tires on the pavement outside, Scott Crane said, wearily, 'He's right.' Behind them he sat up and shifted around in the bed of the truck. 'Even if I – were to kill myself, Dionysus will demand a payment for the fact of this night's resurrection.' He sighed. 'I get the idea you people – didn't *know* this? – before you undertook to call me back from Erebus.'

'It'll be poor gallant Plumtree,' said Salvoy, shaking Plumtree's head, 'if nobody else volunteers.' Plumtree's eyes darted warily to Angelica, who had opened her mouth. 'The boy said I could talk!'

'I'll volunteer,' Cochran found himself saying.

'Of course,' Salvoy went on, ignoring him, 'I wonder if it really shouldn't be somebody with a cold-blooded murder to atone for, somebody who is already owed a stroke from the Green Knight's axe. Kootie? What *did* you do, that morning at Mammy Pleasant's boardinghouse?'

'I – can't remember,' said Kootie. 'But I do remember saying – something? – about the Green—'

'It'll be "poor gallant Plumtree,"' interrupted Angelica loudly, 'and *you*, mister. I like Cody, but all of you in there committed or abetted the murder of—' She waved at the bearded man sitting up in the back of the truck. '—of *him*, and if somebody's got to die for it, take the fall for it, it's the Plumtree crowd.'

'Dionysus will decide,' said Scott Crane. 'It's his show.'

'Scant here volunteered,' said Salvoy, speaking faster. 'Let me talk, Kootie's not a child! You could kill him, Kootie, just assist in his voluntary suicide, and become the king yourself – Crane is old, and doesn't have his strength back yet – let *him* go home and tend to his rosebushes – and then you could forget that killing, and *all* your sins! – with the *pagadebiti*. The king can always score a bottle of that. Don't talk, listen! Think of it – you must have experienced a taste of it while Crane was dead – the sensory-neural awareness of the whole American West: cracking your joints and stretching with the sun-warmed mountains and freeway bridges at dawn, drinking the snow-melt from the granite keeps in the Sierra Nevada through the Oroville dam, inhaling and exhaling all the millions of suffering births and deaths!' Salvoy's voice was strained. 'Work with me, boy!'

Cochran could see Kootie's lower lip pulled away from the teeth, and could see the glitter of tears in the boy's eyes; and he was suddenly afraid that Salvoy would abandon this dangerous gambit of dialogue and switch deaf Janis on at any moment.

Cochran silently drew a deep breath, but before he could speak, Kootie looked away from Plumtree to the dog and said, clearly, '*Mom!*'

The dog licked his face, and Angelica hugged him.

Plumtree's face had started to kink into Janis's puzzled frown even as the boy had spoken, and for several moments her face twitched with conflicting personalities; then it was recognizably the mother's voice that said, triumphantly, 'Hah! I am out in the world!' The eyes that seemed closer-set blinked at Cochran. 'Are we going to the sea? Are you going to send her past India at last?'

'Oh, *Cody*,' Cochran groaned.

Plumtree cringed back in the seat, but the Follow-the-Queen trick had worked – it was Cody's voice that said, 'God, it was *him*, wasn't it?' She spat again. 'Don't let me sleep any more. Get to the goddamn temple on the peninsula and let's get this *paid off.*'

Cochran realized as he put his arm around her stiff shoulders that she had known all along that a death would be owed in payment.

But he was resolved that it would be his own.

The dark clouds were breaking up, and the sky was clear and molten red over the long piers of Fort Mason nearly a mile away to the east when Pete drove the truck slowly down the service road behind the yacht club; when they had passed the end of the asphalt and the tires were grinding in sandy mud, Cochran saw that the chain with the NO ADMITTANCE sign hanging from it had been hung across the path again.

'What's another dent,' said Angelica hollowly.

'We won't be getting shot at, this time,' said Pete.

'Ideally,' put in Cochran.

'Sometime,' came Scott Crane's hoarse voice from the back of the truck 'I will need to hear about all this.' He spoke absently, blinking and squinting as he tried to look at the red sky ahead. 'My first dawn,' he said. 'It's very bright.' Tears were rolling down over his prominent cheekbones now, possibly from trying to stare at the dawn.

Pete clanked the engine into low gear, and Cochran heard the groan and snap of the chain breaking, and then the rustle as the broken ends sprang away into the shrubbery.

Cochran had rolled down the window, and in spite of the dawn chill he was taking deep breaths of the sea air. He could smell flowers and fresh-turned loam on it too, and he saw that the roadside anise bushes that had been brown and dry when they had been out here two weeks ago were now brightly green and bursting with tiny white flowers.

Pete brought the truck to a slow, squeaking halt a few yards short of the descending stone stairway, up which Angelica had carried Crane's skeleton in the rain two weeks ago, when dead birds had been falling out of the sky. And Cochran thought he could see a slowly rocking shimmer beyond the stone walls.

Cochran's face was wet and his mouth was dry, and he was breathing shallowly; and his thoughts were chasing each other around in his head without becoming complete sentences: *We'll all step down there, but not all of us will – me, rather than her, but I hope – think, will you, there must he some way to – but me rather than her, me rather than her—*

He didn't fumble in levering open the door, and when he stepped down onto the gravelly sand he was steady enough not to be knocked over when the big black dog bounded out and collided with his legs. He reached up and took Plumtree's hand as she hopped out of the truck, and they could hear the rusty squeal as Pete swung the tailgate down.

Plumtree was staring south across the narrow inlet at the white house-fronts of the Marina district – the windows were dark, but a few bicyclists were distantly visible on the sidewalks of the Marina Green.

'My male parent probably told you I'll die here,' Plumtree said quietly, 'and that may be true. I think I wouldn't mind that – I knew that might be part of the price of undoing our murder – if I hadn't met you, Sid.'

Cochran opened his mouth, but couldn't think of anything to say. If he did manage to pay for the murder himself, he and Cody would still not be together.

'I – feel the same way,' was all he could come up with.

There was faint music on the gentle breeze from over the water, distant bells and strings tracing a melody he knew he had loved long ago: bright and almost sprightly, wafting with forlorn insouciance around a core of nostalgic despair. At each moment he could almost anticipate the next note – could almost have hummed along, if his throat had not been choked with grief – and he knew this was only the bridge, that the melody would soon be returning to the valiantly, uselessly brave tragedy of the main theme.

Scott Crane had walked to the head of the white marble stairs, and stood for a moment looking down toward the cobblestone-paved dock. Then he sat down on a broken Corinthian pillar and lowered his head into his hands. Blood was still running from his ears, and his bare right foot shone red in the strengthening light.

Cochran took Plumtree's hand and walked across the crunching sand to the head of the stairs. He could hear the others following him, and the pad and panting of the dog.

At the top of the stairs he stopped, staring down at the dock-like pavement below.

At first he thought a stray patch of fog had clung to this corner of the choppy bay water; then his eyes shifted their perspective in some way ...

And a crystal boat rocked in the gray water under a glassy mast, and smoky transparent forms sat at the thwarts; they became fleetingly clear when he looked squarely at them, then flickered away in a kaleidoscope tumble of diaphanous faces and hands, and he saw that they were frail shells of people, ghosts, blinking around in the dawn. He recognized old blind Spider Joe, who still wore the daddy-longlegs filaments around his waist, and thought he saw Thutmose the Utmos', though without crutches now; and then he saw, clearly, Archimedes Mavranos standing up by the bow. Mavranos was looking back at the people on the dirt above the dock stairs, and Cochran thought he was smiling and waving.

The faint distant music paused for a full second, like a dancer on tiptoe; then it swept back, stronger – gracious and smiling and evoking sun-dappled streets and old walled gardens even as it bade farewell to all things and bowed to oblivion.

Plumtree pulled her hand free of his; there was a finality to the gesture that chilled him, and he spun toward her.

And as if she stood in the center of a ring of mirrors, he saw more than a dozen of her, opaque enough so that where several overlapped he couldn't see the red of the truck through them.

Then he saw that two were still solid – no, it was only one, but it was alternately Cody and then Janis, and Plumtree appeared to shift her position against the distant buildings as she changed from one to the other, as if he were helplessly looking at her first through one eye and then through the other. Her ragged blond hair gleamed or was backlit in the dawn's glow.

'I'll take this flop,' said Cochran hastily. 'I'll pay the life.'

'You didn't kill him, Sid,' said Cody. 'I'll go. I've loved you, Sid, and that's a real magic trick – that was never a part of me—'

She shifted, backlit against the brightening sky, and 'No,' came one voice that was both Janis and Valorie speaking; '"madame has forgotten that we agreed to play in partnership this morning."' It was clearly Janis who went on, 'That's James Bond to Tracy di Vicenzo, in *On Her Majesty's Secret Service*, when he volunteers to cover her gambling losses. You wouldn't remember it, Cody – you set the book on fire.' The Janis figure clenched her fists, as if against an internal struggle. 'I'll never ditch you. Daddy – where I go, you go, I swear on my life!' Then she sagged, and it was a lifeless face that swung from the boat to the brightening dawn behind the distant piers, and back. 'See how the morning opes her golden gates, and takes her farewell of the glorious sun!'

There were two Plumtree bodies now; Cody was clearly standing away from the figure that was Janis and Valorie; and that figure was fading.

Janis's bright eyes in Valorie's dead face turned on Cochran as the face became transparent. 'And so farewell,' said the figure that was now just one more ghost, 'and fair be all thy hopes, and prosperous be thy life!'

The ghost spun in a casual pirouette, and gathered into its insubstantial self all the other Plumtree ghosts; and Cody was left standing solidly on the sand beside Cochran. He seized her hand, both to be sure she was a living human being and to prevent her from following the ghost, which was now gliding down the marble stairs and across the cobblestone dock toward the boat; and for a moment now the faint music seemed to be the strains of 'I'll Take You Home Again, Kathleen.'

'But I'll be alone!' wailed Cody, in a voice that shook with absolute loss.

'No, you won't,' said Cochran strongly. He gripped her shoulders and said again looking into her face, 'No – you won't.'

'No,' she agreed brokenly, 'I won't.' She fell forward against him, and he hugged her tightly.

Omar Salvoy's words were echoing in his head: *A death is still owed in this math.* But that was it, Cochran thought shrilly; poor Janis just died, along with Omar Salvoy at last, and Tiffany and the rest of them. Wasn't that death enough for the god?

And the rest of what Salvoy had said …

Then Plumtree stiffened in his arms, and he felt her ribs clench as she screamed. A moment later Pete and Angelica yelled in alarm, and the dog was barking.

Cochran wheeled around, crouching and dizzied.

If he had not seen Dr. Armentrout running at them last night like a spidery Vedic demon, he would not have recognized the battered monster that had clambered out of the bay to his right and was now rushing at Scott Crane; and even so his chest emptied for a moment in cold horror.

The two figures that were attached to Armentrout's shoulders were twisted and draped with seaweed, and their grimacing fleshy heads were canted outward like the leaves on a fleur-de-lis; but Armentrout's right hand held the muddy derringer that had bounced into the lagoon last night, and the bloodshot eyes in Armentrout's swollen purple face were fixed on Scott Crane.

Cochran leaned into the monster's path, stretching out his right leg and hand. The mannikin heads were yelling suddenly – '*Feel good about yourself!*' one was cawing, and the other was shrilling, '*Pull the plug, let me up!*'

The little gun was coming up in the pudgy hand as Armentrout took another running step – Scott Crane had lifted his head and turned on the pillar, but he would not be able to dive out of the way – Pete and Kootie had started forward, and the black dog's forelegs were raised in a leap – and Angelica had drawn the .45 automatic clear of her belt, but Armentrout would have time to fire the derringer before she would be able to swing the heavy gun into line.

In Cochran's memory the silvery edges of the pruning shears plunged toward the old king's face, and Cochran instinctively blocked the thrust with his right hand.

The flat, hollow *pop* of the .410 shell deafened him, and he lost his footing as his right hand was punched away upward. The marble-and-brick-peppered sand plunged up at him and he twisted his left shoulder around to take the jarring impact as he slammed against the ground. With a ringing crystalline clarity Cochran saw drops of his own blood spattering down onto the wet sand around the truck's front tires.

Then he rolled his head down to look at his right hand, and his vision narrowed and lost all depth – for above his wrist was just a glistening red wreckage of torn skin and splintered white bone, and blood was jetting out into the air.

The rest of what Salvoy had said flickered through his stunned consciousness – *Blood and shattered bone—*

Later Cochran learned that Fred the dog had hit Armentrout and knocked him over backward, so that Armentrout had dropped a broken dry pomegranate that he had been carrying in his left hand – it had rolled uphill to Scott Crane's foot, onto which it had spilled clinging red seeds like blood drops – and that after trying to shoot the emptied gun at the dog that was tearing at his four arms Armentrout and his two attached figures had gone stumbling back down over the wet tumbled rocks into the sea to get away.

But all Cochran saw when he swivelled his shock-stiffened face away from his ruined hand, toward the yelling that was so loud that he was able to hear it even through the ringing in his ears, was Armentrout standing thigh-deep in the shallow sea and doing something strenuous with two people: one was a heavy-set old woman in a sopping housedress, and the other was a slim young man with protuberant eyes and a blackened ragged wound in his forehead.

The dog kept running back and forth between Cochran and the water, and everyone behind him was shouting too. Somehow it didn't occur to the stunned Cochran that the three figures out in the water were *fighting* – Armentrout's companions appeared instead to be forcibly giving him something like a full-immersion baptism, dunking him under the water and then hauling him up to shout at him, and then doing it again, and the white-haired doctor did seem to be responding with denials and oaths and genuflections. It was violent, certainly, but to Cochran it seemed that all three were trying to get an important job done.

Angelica was kneeling beside him on the wet sand, urgently saying things he couldn't hear and tightly tying a leather belt around his right wrist. But finally a moment came in which it dawned on Cochran that the woman and the pop-eyed young man had held Armentrout under the waves one last time and would not ever be letting him up at all.

'They've killed him!' Cochran yelled, struggling to get up.

Behind and above him he heard Angelica say, 'Is that a bad thing, Sid?'

Out in the water the old woman and the young man with the holed face seemed to merge, and then become a shape *superimposed* on the seascape instead of *in* it: the stylized black silhouette of a fat man with stubby limbs and a warty round head. And as it shrank, or receded in some nonspatial sense so that it didn't disappear into the water, it flickeringly seemed to be a very fat naked white man with tattoos all over him, and a middle-aged Mexican man, and a pretty Asian woman, and others ...

Then it had faded to nothing like a retinal glare-spot, and the sea was an unfeatured expanse of rippled silver all the way across to the Marina.

'No,' Cochran said. A death *was* still owed in the math, he thought. A physical heart had to literally stop. 'No,' he said again.

Cochran was lying on his back. He twisted his head to look up at Angelica, and then he focussed past her. Two transparent old women stood above and behind her and their milk-in-water eyes were fixed on the puddle of blood on the dirt below Cochran's tourniquetted wrist. Their hands were reaching toward the blood, and their fingers were stretching like old cobwebs disturbed by a solid person's passage.

Up the slope by the stairs, Scott Crane had at some point got to his feet. His beard had dried enough to be lustrous and full, so that seen from below this way he looked like a schoolbook picture of Solomon or Charlemagne; and in a voice so deep and resonant that it cut through the shrilling in Cochran's impacted eardrums, Crane said, 'Hot blood is what you're leaving behind forever now, ladies. Get aboard the boat now; the tide is about to ebb, and you have to go.'

The ghosts of Mrs. Winchester and Mammy Pleasant swirled away to the steps and down toward the insubstantial boat, and then the first rays of the rising sun touched the iron lamp-post at the end of the peninsula. Cochran thought he could hear distant voices singing.

He was sagging with fatigue, and he wondered that he was able to hold his head up; and then he realized that Cody Plumtree was sitting on the sand behind him and cradling his head in her lap. Kootie was kneeling white-faced behind Plumtree, with his arms around the black dog's neck. Blood was trickling down Kootie's own neck from a long, shallow cut below his ear, where a stray shot-pellet had evidently nicked him.

Cochran rolled his eyes to look back out at the water of the bay, but it was still empty – the blobby black figure had certainly gone.

The Green Knight gave the boy just a token cut, Cochran thought; and he settled his head more firmly against Cody's warm, solid legs. The retribution-aspect of Dionysus was merciful, this morning.

Pete was behind the wheel of the truck, and now started up the rackety old engine; and just because of the new noise Cochran became aware that at some point violin-pure voices had begun singing out of the pipes that stood up from the masonry, a high solemn wordless chorus that now coaxed Cochran's sluggish pulse to meet the vibrant cadences implicit in the new dawn.

'Get up, Sid,' said Plumtree, and Angelica added, 'On this morning you can go to a hospital, with no fear of ghosts.'

Cochran got dizzily to his feet, leaning heavily on the two women as he shambled up the slope toward the shaking truck.

White seagulls, luminous in the new daylight, were circling high over-head against the blue of the clean sky, whistling and piping in the open, unechoing air as if calling out the news of the soon-returning spring.

EPILOGUE

'In the Midsummer of this Year ...'

All, all is yours,
The love I owed my father, who is dead,
The love I might have given to my mother,
And my poor sister, cruelly doomed to die.
All yours now, only yours.

—Aeschylus, *The Libation Bearers*

Cupped at the very top of the steep green hill, above the lake that encircled the island and above the fenced-in reservoir that fed the waterfall, was a little lake surrounded by cherry laurel trees and standing green and orange stones. The lake water was so still that every tree branch against the blue sky was reflected motionless in the water.

Cody Plumtree had run up the steps of half-buried railway ties ahead of the others, and now she carefully lifted the hem of her white linen skirt and stepped up onto the altar-like rock at the east end of the little lake. This rock looked as if it were once a source for a waterfall into this lake, and it also looked as if it had been the site of fires in remote times. She remembered Sid saying that these moss-green stones were druid stones, magically counterweighted by the monastery stones around the lake below. Sid might not remember that now, but he would know it if she told him about it and then made sure to tell him about it again a few times.

It was a topic that was connected to his memories of his dead wife, and all those memories really had disappeared. He knew these days that he had been married, and he could even recognize photographs of the Nina woman, but he was like an amnesia victim – except that an amnesia victim would probably want to learn about the lost past. Along with the memories, Sid had lost any interest in what they had been of.

Cody didn't mind, and she would probably not remind him of the history of the stones.

The two of them had been living in Sid's South Daly City house for five months now, but somehow – like, she thought helplessly, the Solville piece of string that couldn't ever quite be cut – it had consistently been a

433

celibate relationship. That would change after this ceremony today, she was certain.

Cody had not lost any memories at all, and she still dreamed of the other girls that had occupied her head with her. On some nights she even dreamed of the day the sun fell on her, the day – twenty-six years ago now to the day, perhaps to the hour – when her father was thrown off the building in Soma; it was a harrowing dream, but she was glad to experience it, especially since she saw it in *color* – it indicated that she had absorbed, taken as her own, those earliest memories that had been in the sole custody of dead Valorie.

And last night she had dreamed of driving the bus, speeding up and jumping across the wide empty gap in the freeway to land safe on the other side, and the man standing beside her had been Sid Cochran.

Two miles away to the southeast she could see the tall X-shaped TV tower on Mount Sutro; and when she shifted around, she could see the two distant piers of the Golden Gate Bridge, appearing in foreshortening to be standing next to each other on the horizon.

The other people were scuffing up the steps now – and she saw Scott Crane come striding lightly across the grass first, tall and brown and smiling through his lustrous coppery beard; he was fifty-two years old now, but hardly looked thirty-five, and on this midsummer's day his wound didn't make him limp at all. He wasn't dressed as any kind of priest, though that was the function he would be serving here today; he wore a navy blue suit with a white shirt, and his long hair was tied back in a ponytail secured, she had noticed on the walk over the bridge, with a gold Merovingian bee.

The others from the Leucadia compound were right behind him, led by lithe Nardie Dinh and Diana with her three-inch thatch of radiant blond hair. Arky's widow, Wendy, was leading their two teenage daughters; Plumtree had been afraid to meet them at first, and then had been surprised by their unaffected friendliness and their eagerness to hear stories about Arky's last month. Diana's boys Scat and Oliver appeared next, herding the children up into the clearing. Behind them she could hear a barking dog, which meant that the Solville contingent was coming right up.

With the Valorie-memories which were now her own, Cody called across the hilltop glade to Crane, 'Standing in happy sunlight on the hill in the lake!'

Crane laughed quietly, and the sound seemed to shake the green leaves and send ripples across the little lake.

Through the green branches overhead, the sky was a cloudless, deep blue. It was a good day for a wedding.

Sid Cochran was glad now that he hadn't acceded to the advice of the other sales representatives at Pace and worn some kind of tuxedo. His suit was formal enough, and in these wooded sunlit groves the affected pretension of a tuxedo would have been ludicrous. In the same spirit, he had left his prosthetic hand in the car's glove compartment, and was just wearing a white sock over the stump of his right wrist.

Behind him Fred was bounding along the cinder path on a leash, for Angelica hadn't wanted him jumping up on people's nice clothes, and Kootie was kept as busy as a fishing boat trying to stay over a powerful marlin, with the dog wanting to sniff at the mossy stones along the path and go loping and barking across the grass. Kootie had left his sport coat in the Solville van, and Cochran could see that there was no bandage anymore under the boy's white shirt. Angelica had told him that Kootie's two-year-old wound had finally healed up within a week of their return to Long Beach.

'And the cement *Eleggua* figure was back in its cabinet, when we got back home,' said Angelica now, striding along between Cochran and Pete Sullivan.

'With a bunch of snapshots in the cabinet with him,' added Pete. 'Pictures of the Eleggua statue in front of Stonehenge, and at the Great Pyramid, and at Notre Dame cathedral ...'

Cochran glanced sharply at him, but Pete's face was resolutely deadpan and Cochran couldn't quite decide if he was kidding or not.

Cody had kept in touch with Angelica during these five months, and the two of them had cautiously agreed that there appeared to have been, so far, no legal or psychic or underworld repercussions from their arduous January. Cochran and Plumtree had heard nothing from Rosecrans Medical – possibly because, according to the newspapers, Dr. Armentrout had run off with a number of patient files before allegedly murdering intern Philip Muir at the borrowed house of an absent neurologist, and then disappearing for parts unknown – and Cody had anonymously, and grumblingly, sent money to the people whose purse and car she had stolen, as well as twenty dollars to the Frost Giant ice-cream shop and a hundred to Strubie the Clown; and Angelica was still safely doing underground-occult consulting work among the Long Beach poor, though she no longer corralled ghosts for clients, and nobody had come looking for Spider Joe, who would ideally rest in peace forever beneath the Solville back parking lot.

The newspapers had reported that Richard Paul Armentrout had apparently been a victim of childhood incest at the hands of his alcoholic single mother, and that he had been committed to a men's psychiatric hospital and had undergone electroconvulsive therapy at the age of seventeen, after killing her.

That bit of news had obscurely upset Cody, and she had spent a good part of the afternoon sitting in the bone-strewn ruins of the backyard greenhouse, uncommunicatively drinking vodka; Cochran had eventually got her to come inside, and they had got stoically drunk together.

With the loss of his hand, Cochran had become unfitted for his cellar-and-vine-yard work, and now was working out of the office as a sales representative; the change had-been disorienting at first, but he had really had no choice, for along with his hand he had lost too his instinctive understanding of the soil and the vines and the slow pulse of the wines maturing in the casks.

Above him the path levelled out between the descending green slopes, and the trees were farther apart.

They had reached the clearing at the top of the hill, and Cochran could see his bride-to-be standing with Scott and Diana Crane on the far side of the little lake, talking with them and the Nardie Dinh woman and Mavranos's widow, while a gang of children climbed around on the rocks. Cochran had seen Cody's white skirted suit when she had got into the blue truck from Leucadia, but when he looked at her now, standing over there straight and slim and softly laughing, her blond hair in a long pageboy cut, he thought she looked even more beautiful than Diana Crane.

Scott Crane had seen the newcomers step up onto the level grass, and he held up one hand – and then walked down the shallow slope and waded several steps out into the lake, until the water was above his ankles. Fred barked at the spectacle, until Kootie shushed him.

With his beard and broad shoulders, Crane still seemed taller than everyone else. 'This is a balanced place,' he said in his deep, rolling voice, 'and we want to maintain that and not be showing up as a spike in anyone's charts.' Diana and Mavranos's widow seemed to be the only ones who knew what he was doing – Diana was looking away, down the grassy slope toward the surrounding lake, and Wendy was staring thoughtfully at Crane.

Crane went on, slowly, 'When I came back, five months ago – through the self-sacrifice of my best friend – I accepted certain terms, the terms stated in that palindrome. I expect now to spend the January of every year in Erebus, as I did this winter – but with my lifeless body in Leucadia, and not requiring strenuous help to come *back* to life, each time. Three representatives of Death, two ghosts and one murderer who was shortly to die, brought me the requisite sacrament.'

He held up a lumpy little brown ball that seemed from this distance to be cracked. 'A pomegranate,' he said, 'which Nardie tells me was brought all the way from my own back garden ... appropriately.' He broke it and let most of it fall into the water, but held up something tiny between a thumb and forefinger. 'One seed,' he said. 'Like what Persephone ate.' And he put it into his mouth, and swallowed.

The children had paid attention when he had walked out into the water, but had lost interest when he had paused to talk; Kootie had dropped Fred's leash, and now the children and the dog were happily climbing around on the rocks in the dappled sunlight.

Scott Crane had seemed to go pale for a moment, but he inhaled deeply in the flower-scented air, and smiled toward the oblivious children. 'This *is* a happy day,' he said, 'all of us obedient to our proper places in the seasons. And,' he went on, looking into Cochran's eyes for a moment, 'summer is the season for weddings.'

He turned and walked back out of the lake, the cuffs of his pants flinging bright drops of water out onto the grass.

'Cody Plumtree,' said the king, holding out his left hand to her, 'who wide unclasped the table of your thoughts, so that intercessors of one sort and another could help me through all the houses of the year.'

Cody stepped up to where he stood and took his hand with her right hand.

'And,' called the king, now holding out his right hand and looking across the lake, 'Sid Cochran, who reached out your hand twice to save the old king, and selflessly held the god's favor to give to me.'

Everyone, even the children and the dog, was looking at Cochran; and he was sweating and awkward and he wanted to put the stump of his right wrist into his pocket. This hilltop clearing and lake, with the ring of leaning old laurels and redwoods around the perimeter, looked oddly familiar to him. He thought he might have been here once before, a very long time ago ... happily ... ?

'Go to your bride,' muttered Pete Sullivan, nudging him in the back.

And Cochran met Cody's blue eyes across the lake, and she was smiling at him – and he smiled back at her, and walked straight toward her, down the bank and into the lake and striding through the clear, cleansing water all the way across while the children laughed delightedly and the dog barked, though the water rose to his waist in the middle of the lake and was cold down around his toes and ankles, striding finally up the far bank and stepping up onto the sunlit grass beside her and the king to take his vows, profoundly glad.

Tim Powers was born in Buffalo, New York, and educated at California State University, gaining a degree in English. It was at University that he met K.W. Jeter and James Blaylock, who became friends and occasional collaborators, and the three of them are regarded as the founding fathers of the steampunk literary movement. He was also a friend of noted SF writer Philip K. Dick. Among his many honours are two Philip K. Dick Awards (for the *Anubis Gates* and *Dinner at Deviant's Palace*) and two World Fantasy Awards (for *Last Call* and *Declare*). The fourth *Pirates of the Caribbean* film is based on his 1987 novel *On Stranger Tides*. He lives in California.

A full list of Fantasy Masterworks can be found at www.gollancz.co.uk